Books by ~~Aung~~

HUNTERS
UNLUCKY

ABIGAIL HILTON

Pavonine
Books

© 2013 Abigail Hilton
Second Edition 2024
Cover art by Iben Krutt
Size chart and interior sketchs by Sarah Cloutier.
Maps, silhouettes, and cover sesign by Jeff McDowall.
A product of Pavonine Books.

For my brother, Hughes,
who read the first draft when it was still warm from the dot
matrix printer.

Special thanks to other people who helped with this book,
including:

Jeff McDowall
Amy Watkins
Mistie Watkins
Sarah Cloutier
Rose Spinoza
Lucie Le Blanc
Bess Gutenstein
Blue Thiele

.

Table of Contents

THE ISLAND OF LIDIAN

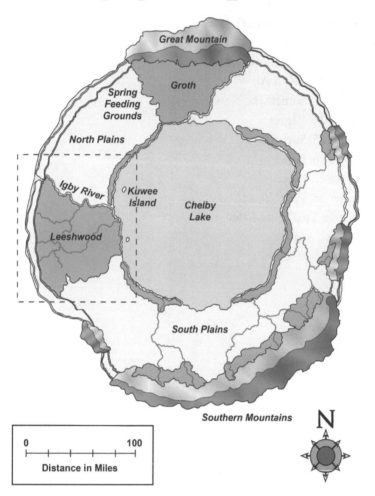

Great Mountain

Groth

Spring
Feeding
Grounds

North Plains

Igby River

Kuwee
Island

Cheiby
Lake

Leeshwood

South Plains

Southern Mountains

N

0   100
Distance in Miles

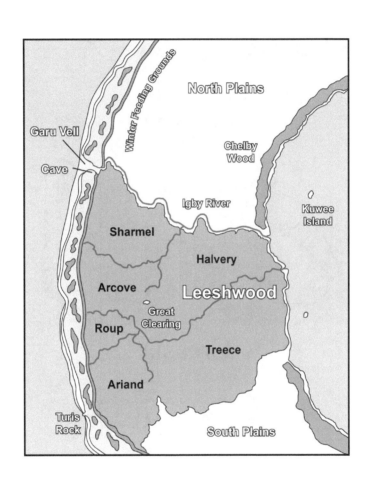

Ferryshaft

Creasia

Curb

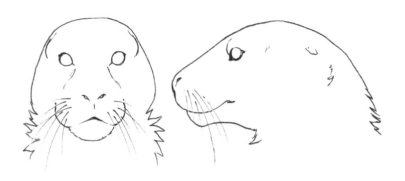

Telshee

Ely-Ary

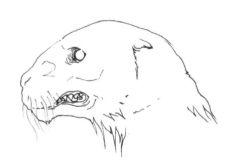

Lishty

Part I

Storm

1

Hunter's Moon

On the worst night of his life, Charder Ela-ferry stood on the blood-red rock of a steep cliff trail and argued with an insane child. "There are ghosts up ahead," she whimpered, tucking her tail and crouching against the path. "I can smell them. Please, Charder, don't make me go! Please!"

"Lirsy, stop it!" Charder planted all four hooves and used his teeth to drag her up by the back of the neck. They were both ferryshaft, but Charder was an adult, and Lirsy was not yet a year old. He tried to be gentle, but he was shaking, and her skin felt as fragile as a bird's. He saw the outline of her ribs through thin fur as he released her, and he felt ashamed. *When did she stop eating? Two days ago? Four? Why didn't I notice?*

Charder himself had not eaten in three days, but he'd thought the foals were getting something. Between all the fighting, it was hard to remember to check. *But I should have remembered.* Coden had asked only two things when he'd left Charder in charge of the ferryshaft herd. "Hold these caves and protect my daughter."

I'm not doing so well on either count.

Lirsy was rocking back and forth, staring upward. "There's a jellyfish in the sky," she breathed.

"That's the moon," said Charder wearily. *A bright, full hunter's moon, and this night belongs to hunters.*

"Lirsy, please get up." He decided to risk the truth—a little of it, at least. "One of your father's friends came back to the caves this evening." *He was dying.* "He told us that your father…"

Lirsy was staring at him so intently now with her sea-gray eyes—Coden's eyes—that Charder had to look away. "He's dead, isn't he?" she whispered.

Probably. "No," said Charder. "I mean, he may have hidden somewhere. He's good at hiding—your father. But I don't know how much longer we can hold the caves, and I think the creasia will hurt you if they overrun us." *I think Arcove wants a surrender, not an extinction. But you're the last of Coden's foals, and he'll see you as a focal point for future rebellion. He'll kill you.*

Lirsy's eyes searched his face.

"So I am taking you to Keesha," continued Charder. "You remember Keesha, don't you?"

Lirsy cocked her head. "The big white snake that sings?"

"Yes." Charder felt a measure of relief. She was making more sense than she had at any previous point in the evening. "And the closest entrance to Syriot is on the beach on the other side of the cliffs. We just have to get there. You can do that, can't you?"

Lirsy considered. "Will Mother be there?"

Charder could have howled in frustration. *Will she never stop asking that?* "No." *You saw her die; don't you remember?* "Your mother cannot be there. Now come on."

He was immensely relieved when she trotted after him again, though her moment of lucidity seemed to have evaporated. "The jellyfish is singing," she told him.

"Of course," mumbled Charder as he tried to make her move faster.

"It's singing to the ghosts," said Lirsy.

"Whose ghosts?" asked Charder. *Not your mother's, obviously; I can't get you to remember that she's dead.*

Lirsy made a show of squinting at the top of the cliff. "They look like us," she said at last, and Charder felt a chill. "I think they're our ghosts, Charder."

The hunter's moon was sinking down the western sky, throwing the trail into shadow, by the time Charder and Lirsy reached the cliff top. Lirsy was crowding closely against him, wide-eyed. Charder did not dare ask what she thought she saw.

He hesitated for a moment, blinking in the brilliant moonlight. The cliff's edge stretched to their right and left as far as Charder could see. Beyond the bare rock, the trees began. Charder strained his nose and ears, but caught only the usual scent of pine and the distant salt tang of the sea. *I have done the right thing,* he thought, *and I have done it in time.*

Charder moved forward, into the wood, and Lirsy followed, ducking and weaving, as though to avoid an invisible crowd. It seemed very dark under the trees. Charder reminded himself that the wood, though dense, was not wide. *The creasia are far away,* he told himself, *chasing Coden...or killing him...or celebrating his death. This is the only thing I can do for him.*

Then Charder heard a soft rustle in the quiet of the wood, like wind among leaves. Except there was no wind. Without stopping to look around, Charder bolted forward with a cry of, "Run, Lirsy!" The shout startled her, and she leapt after him. For a few moments, Lirsy and Charder raced side by side.

He heard a muffled thump behind them, nothing else. *Creasia run so softly...* Charder resisted the temptation to look back. He galloped with Lirsy through light and shadow, over logs and under branches, always with a silent terror at their heels. Charder's heart gave a bound as a brighter patch appeared through the trees ahead: moonlight glistening on water.

Then a shadow appeared before the trees in front of them—a shade blacker than all the rest. Charder knew that shape. He'd seen it in battle...and in his nightmares.

Stung with fear, Charder veered away, and for one moment he forgot about Lirsy. Before he could turn back for her, three enormous cats flashed out of the darkness ahead. Charder reared and spun, lashing out with powerful back hooves, snapping with his teeth. He felt one blow connect with a creasia's ribs and the unmistakable give as something broke. He danced out of the path of a charging cat, caught a mouthful of the animal's shoulder and flipped it with its own momentum. He tore at its belly with his teeth and would have had its guts out on the ground if its companions had not already been on top of him.

At his peak, Charder might have handled the lot of them, but hunger and exhaustion made him slow. A cat caught him across the shoulders as he ducked away, and the pain reverberated through his body like the echo of a scream.

Lirsy galloped past him, running unevenly now, and Charder guessed that she had been injured. The three creasia abandoned Charder to race after her along the cliff. Charder tried to follow, but the muscles of his wounded shoulders pulled painfully.

To his right, the Sea Cliffs made a dizzy drop to the beach. He did not think he would ever reach it now. Lirsy was still slightly ahead of her pursuers when she turned inland, back towards the wood. Charder decided that she must have encountered a fissure in the cliff. Although she appeared to have gone into the trees, she must really be behind them.

Just before the first cat disappeared behind the blind, Charder heard a shriek and the rattle of loose stones. Charder's heart sank as he put on one final burst of speed, reaching the edge of the fissure a short distance behind the last of the creasia.

The cliff looked just as he had imagined—a long, jagged arm of the sea, cutting sharply inland and leaving a narrower space between the edge of the forest and the lip of the crag. The edge looked crumbly at one particular spot. The creasia were nosing about without much interest, for it was obvious what had become of their victim. Charder remained rigid, staring at the cliff. He was still standing there when a shadow fell across his head and obscured the moonlight.

Charder spun to face his enemy. *Arcove. You were supposed to be chasing Coden.* Arcove Ela-creasia was the undisputed champion of his violent and aggressive race. He was the largest creasia that Charder had ever met—a massive, night-black cat in his prime, who outweighed Charder by at least four to one. Charder's head did not come much past Arcove's shoulder, and even without these obvious advantages, Arcove had a reputation for skill and ferocity in battle that made Charder dizzy with fear.

Arcove stood close enough to pounce, but he didn't.

Charder felt numb with his injuries and the loss of the foal he had sworn to protect. *It's over.* He stood his ground and steeled himself for death.

Arcove sat down. He was so close that Charder could see the individual black whiskers.

"Charder Ela-ferry. I had hoped to have a word with you this evening."

Charder glared. *He's playing. Begin the fight yourself.* But he could not move. He was afraid to die, and hated himself for it.

"The ferryshaft herd is crumbling," said Arcove, his deep voice so quiet it was almost a whisper. "Soon they will need a new leader."

Charder should have seen it coming, but he hadn't. "No," he said weakly.

"No, what?"

"No, I wouldn't—" He couldn't say it. "They haven't chosen me." *Attack him! Just attack him!*

"They will. You know they will. You're the only officer left."

"The only one you haven't killed?"

Arcove's voice dropped to a growl. "The only one I haven't chosen to kill."

Charder trembled.

"Would you like to start by improving their lives or by torturing them?" asked Arcove. "You would like to feed them, yes? You would like to tell them that their foals will see adulthood, knowing that they can wake up in the morning and find water to drink?"

I can't believe I'm having this conversation. "I can't surrender the ferryshaft." Charder almost choked. "They're not mine to give! Go to Coden with your vile proposals. You won't wait long for an answer!"

"That's true," said Arcove, "but it won't be true by tomorrow. The ferryshaft will need a new leader, soon, and they will choose you...if you are there to be chosen."

Charder despised the trembling in his hooves, yet he could not still them.

"Your choices," said Arcove, "are few. I have the power at this moment to exterminate every ferryshaft on Lidian. However, digging you out of those caves will be difficult and bloody. It will cost many creasia lives. I prefer peace. If you seize the opportunity I am offering, you and yours will live. If not, I am sure others will pounce on the chance."

Charder said nothing. His thoughts raced like rabbits pursued by a hawk.

Arcove flicked his tail. "The choice is yours. The effects upon your herd will be the same. If you do not surrender, someone else will." He leaned forward until his whiskers tickled Charder's ear. "If you refuse me, you will die here and now." Charder could feel the cat's hot breath on his neck. He could smell his own fear. He was aware of the other three cats, standing a respectful distance away, but watching closely. "Lirsy came to a swift end. You will not be so fortunate. We have all night. Need I go further?"

He certainly need not. Charder tucked his tail against his belly and crouched down to get away from Arcove's mouth. He felt sick. "Alright," he heard himself whisper. "As long as you stop killing the ferryshaft, you can have your surrender."

"You are in no position to make conditions," rejoined the cat. He took a step back. "We'll call this war over for the moment and discuss your terms of surrender in the morning."

Charder raised his head, eyes burning. "Your methods," he hissed, "are not those of a warrior, but of a vulture!"

Arcove watched him without emotion. "If the methods of vultures win battles, then I will study them. I could hardly expect you to praise me. Nevertheless, you will submit. If you betray me, I promise that you will regret it every bit as much as you hate me."

"I keep my promises," snarled Charder.

Arcove sniffed. "A debatable contention. You'd best keep those you make to me, at least."

The words stung like saltwater in a bleeding wound. Charder's gaze dropped. *He's won. In every way.*

Charder remained on the cliff for some time after Arcove had gone. He could have returned to the ferryshaft herd, but the thought of trying to look them in the eyes repulsed him. He was trying to work out how he would give them the news when he heard the first sounds of commotion from the north—snarls and hisses of cats, and their voices shouting orders.

Not so far away, Turis Rock jutted against the yellow moon. It was the highest part of the cliff, and it hung, not over the beach, but over the sea itself. Charder watched as two animals shot out of the wood into the open ground at the base of the rock. At first, he could not tell who or even what they were. Not until three more creasia came out of the woods and forced them apart did Charder realize that one was a ferryshaft.

Charder's breath caught. Then he was running. *I have to help him! I can't...can't...* He stopped. His wounds were already beginning to pain him, and Turis Rock was farther away than it looked under the brilliant hunter's moon. *But I could reach it. Coden will hold them that long. Better to die fighting beside my king than to...*

He could almost hear Arcove's voice. *You'd save no one and kill yourself.*

So... I will leave a friend to die alone?

Charder paced, but he could already see the terrible shape of his choice. *You've sold your honor. It's done. You're afraid of Arcove, and he knows it. He's kept you alive for this.*

Nevertheless, Charder kept walking. He did not run, but he continued towards Turis, sometimes stumbling, never taking his eyes off the fight. The four creasia were holding Coden at bay, but he was making them pay for it. Charder thought he saw a creasia body on the edge of the trees. Two of those on their feet were limping badly.

As Charder watched, Coden whipped around an attacker and chomped off most of his tail. The creasia roared in pain and fury. Charder squinted. *Halvery?* He was Arcove's third in command and probably the one in charge of this clutter. *He'll be seeing red after that.* Loss of a tail was a particularly insulting injury, thought to signify cowardice and retreat, and Halvery was an arrogant creature.

Is Coden trying *to make them kill him?*

Charder was just close enough now to hear some of the shouted insults. "What's the matter, Halvery?" Coden snarled. "Are the rocks too sharp for your tender paws? Are your claws trapped inside your feet?" The ferryshaft slashed at a cat with his teeth, while deftly sending a small stone in Halvery's direction with a back hoof. "Or are you infested with ticks? Are they sucking all the courage out of you, Halvery?"

They're not supposed to kill him, thought Charder. *They're supposed to wait for Arcove.* Charder felt a moment of sick vertigo as his surrender replayed in his head. *Arcove knew this was about to happen. He was warning me not to interfere.*

Halvery roared. Soon he was slashing as savagely as his subordinates, but they made little progress. Coden was too quick, and they were getting in each other's way. Gradually, they all slowed and then paused to pant and glare.

Coden was lean and ragged. It was obvious that he'd been running from the creasia for days. But he was not badly injured. Not yet. His pale gray fur, so unusual in a ferryshaft, looked almost luminous in the moonlight. He still carried his bushy tail high, and his chin had that defiant tilt that Charder remembered.

You were always an excellent fighter, thought Charder, *but you're a trickster at heart. Run away, Coden. Please. Look up and see me and run.*

Lirsy is dead, Charder remembered. *Will I have to tell you that?* Charder could not decide, for an instant, whether he wanted Coden to see him.

It did not matter, as Coden's attention was wholly focused on the cats. Halvery was saying something, but Charder was too far away to hear their quieter voices. Coden sneered a reply.

Charder's thoughts stumbled on. *Would Arcove really have killed Lirsy if I hadn't tried to run with her? Would she have survived a surrender if I had just waited? What if Coden survives this fight?*

His mate is dead, most of his friends, and now the last of his foals. He was already half-mad with grief and now...

Halvery and Coden looked like they were escalating to another engagement. Charder could tell from Halvery's posture that Coden was baiting him, and it was working. *Do you want to die, Coden?* And then, in a moment of brutal honesty, Charder asked himself, *Do I want you to die?*

Charder caught a ripple of movement on the edge of the trees beyond the combatants. He blinked. The moonlight caught the glint of eyes, and he could see a roiling of twitching, pacing movement in the shadows. The rest of the creasia had arrived. *Too late to run.*

But not too late for me to redeem myself. Coden shouldn't have to die alone. Charder started walking again, more slowly this time. He felt as though he were struggling through deep mud. He could not quite catch his breath.

Arcove emerged from the trees. He looked like a piece of the midnight sky against the red rock. He said something to Halvery, who hung his head and stepped back. Coden stood his ground, bristling. They spoke to each other. Charder heard the bass rumble of Arcove's implacable growl and the crackle of Coden's contempt, but he could not catch the words. He didn't really need to.

Arcove is going to fight him one-on-one, thought Charder, with a degree of admiration. He'd never heard of a creasia hunt ending this way. Single combat was a courtesy cats reserved for each other, not for ferryshaft. *And with all the other creasia watching... This is how they choose kings.* It was probably the greatest compliment Arcove could pay to a rival, but it only felt like torture to Charder.

Why am I still standing here? I should be there. I should be beside Coden. I should.

Arcove and Coden leapt at each other. The fight was not long, but it *was* impressive. Charder had known that Coden was quick and that he could be clever when tackling larger enemies. But, exhausted as he must be, Charder would never have expected Coden to hold his own in a fight against Arcove. There was a moment when they came together in the air, and Coden landed such a solid blow to Arcove's chest that Charder thought it might stun the cat long enough for Coden to open a vital vein.

Arcove did stagger when he hit the ground, and Coden did kick him in the face hard enough to bloody his nose. But then that enormous mouth opened, Arcove's white teeth flashed, and the cat was up again. This fight could have only one outcome.

A time came when Coden did not leap away quickly enough. Arcove's claws caught him under the belly and flipped him. Crimson stains began to soak through his pale fur. A moment later, Coden slipped in his own blood. Arcove's teeth locked in the elbow of his left foreleg, ripped the tendon, and crippled the leg. Coden fought on. He limped, but he never whimpered.

Charder was close enough now that he could easily have called to Coden. He both wanted and feared that Coden would see him. *You are my king. Tell me what to do. Please, please.*

My king, but also, my friend, thought Charder. *My king, but also...*

He remembered the day Coden had been born to one of his brightest councilors. He remembered watching Coden grow up, always a step ahead of the other foals, always with grander ideas. Coden had made friends with telshees and curbs and ely-ary. He'd wanted to explore the island to its heights and depths. He'd wanted to wander the seas and learn the secrets of the humans. He'd wanted... *So much more than ruling the ferryshaft.*

But I talked him into it, thought Charder, *because I thought he could win this war—so young and so full of ideas. And he almost did win. Almost. But instead, the war just broke his heart, and now Arcove is going to break the rest of him.*

Charder realized that he must have made a noise, because Halvery turned suddenly and looked directly at him. Charder froze and waited. He felt terror and immense relief. *This is the right place for me to die.*

But then Halvery turned away and looked back towards the fight. Charder felt as though someone had kicked him in the belly. *They've got orders not to kill me. Arcove is* that *certain of my cooperation.*

For just a moment, fury overcame Charder's terror and iner-tia, and he picked up his pace. He did not, however, walk closer to the crowd of creasia. Instead, he angled along the edge of the cliff, into the long shadow cast by Turis Rock. He could not see as much of the fight from this angle, but he was physically closer to the combatants. He could hear them better, and he had an insane idea of calling to Coden, begging him to run. *He might still get away. If he really wanted to. I could help him reach Syriot...save him instead of Lirsy.*

The pair was coming closer as, step by step, Arcove pushed Coden up Turis Rock. Charder could hear them panting and their grunts and growls as they struck at each other. Coden's fur had looked more red than gray last Charder had gotten a good look at it, but he caught only glimpses of their legs now.

There was a pause. Charder was surprised to hear Arcove's voice, pitched so low that Charder doubted the watching cats could hear. "Coden," Arcove panted. "I'll end this cleanly if you'll stand still a moment. There are those watching who do not wish to see you die in pieces, and this is the only gift I can give."

"You'd like that," spat Coden. "My tail to wave under the noses of the other ferryshaft? A trophy for your den?"

"You know that's not true. It doesn't have to end this way."

Charder drew in his breath to shout, but hesitated. Arcove's words surprised him, but more than that, the timbre of Arcove's voice had completely changed. Even Coden sounded different—less defiant, more tired and more bitter.

"I will *never* surrender the ferryshaft," said Coden. "They will fight again, and they will do it quicker if they do not see me roll over for you." He was talking so quietly that Charder had to strain to hear. He wished he could see their faces.

"I don't want this," said Arcove.

Charder could hear the smile in Coden's voice when he answered. "Arcove...for just this moment...it's not about what you want." Then, to Charder's horror, Coden turned and jumped. He sailed from the pinnacle of Turis Rock in a smooth arc, still graceful, and then dropped into the coral sea far below.

Charder's heart dropped with him. He stared at the water, then back up at Turis. Arcove had come to the edge and was looking down. Charder had no idea whether Arcove noticed him in the shadow of the rock on the cliff below. Charder didn't think so. Arcove was staring down at the white-capped waves and the reflection of the yellow moon farther out to sea. His face had an expression that Charder had not expected and could not interpret. Arcove shut his eyes, and the expression vanished. He seemed to compose himself and then turned back to the waiting creasia. As he descended the pinnacle of rock, Charder heard him say, "The war is over. We have won."

Something inside Charder broke. He threw back his head and howled his grief and self-reproach to the cold stars. No one came to join him or to stop him. No one paid any attention to him at all.

This is how the creasia remembered the final fight between Coden Ela-ferry and Arcove Ela-creasia. They said that Arcove and Coden were quicker than thought and lighter than shadows, that they circled and struck and ducked and leapt too fast for the eye to follow. They said that Arcove was as black as midnight with a blow like lightning, and that Coden was as gray as the sea and agile as water. They said that their fighting was like a dance of ash and moonbeams. No one who watched the fight ever forgot it, and they told the story to their cubs and grandcubs. That is how the creasia remembered it.

That is not how Charder remembered the fight. Charder remembered it as the night he watched a hero die…and did nothing.

2

Twelve Years Later

So-fet's mate was not quite dead when she arrived, though the vultures were already picking at his entrails. She laid her head beside him as his eyes glazed.

Voices and faces whirled around her.

"Poor thing—"

"Her first mate—"

"—the last raid of the season—"

"The spring grass is already showing! They hardly ever come so late."

"—and they only killed three."

"Poor luck for her...to lose him now, so close to the end of the raiding season."

"Unlucky."

"Yes, unlucky."

"So-fet, come away. There's a storm blowing in."

So-fet stood and slipped in her mate's blood. Something stirred inside her, as though in sympathy with her pain. She vomited and gagged. Blood and water coursed down her thighs.

Her friends sniffed in alarm. "She's foaling! Get her into a cave!"

They pushed her, nipped at her flanks, and pulled at her shoulders. Somehow they got her up a path into a cave at the foot of the cliffs. Just as the first fury of the storm broke over Lidian, So-fet heaved her firstborn onto the rock floor, his birth-blood mingling with the blood of his dead father. He was tiny, born too soon.

He lay shivering there amid the strobe lightning, and tried to suck milk from a dry udder. His mother did not stop him. She did not seem to see him. In desperation, he licked up the blood in her fur.

Finally, towards morning, So-fet stirred. She looked at her foal and noticed that he was not only tiny, but dark—much darker than the light brown coats of most foals. She looked at the driving rain and at her infant son—forced from her body too early and orphaned in a single stroke—and she named him Storm.

Her milk came two days later. Everyone said he would die.

He didn't, but he was too weak to stand when she nursed him for the first time. The storm had blown itself out by then, and the numbness of So-fet's grief had passed. She did not think about the sodden, half-eaten body on the edge of the plain. She gave all her thoughts and all her love to the wobbly, undersized foal who had no father.

Half-orphan, full orphan—it was nearly the same thing in the ferryshaft herd. Little Storm would have to fight to survive. He would need to be strong, and, for this, he must have good milk. His mother ate for his sake. She had lost her status as a mated female, but she fought the higher ranking females for the good grass.

Storm did not starve, though he did not thrive. By the end of spring, he was still the smallest foal in the herd. When the scarcity of water drove the ferryshaft on their annual migration across the plain to Chelby Lake, he could not keep up with the rest, and So-fet had to spend a night on the plain alone with him.

This frightened her. Sometimes the creasia ranged far afield, and there were other hunters who would scruple even less to take a runty foal and his mother caught away from the herd by night. Dawn, however, found them still alive, huddled together in the dewy grass. By the next evening, they had rejoined the herd near Chelby Lake.

The abundance of the season made life easier for them. The ferryshaft settled into a comfortable routine—feeding on the plain in the morning and drinking by the lake in the evening.

So-fet hoped that Storm would forget that fearful spring. She wanted his first memories to be happy ones. As he grew and became more self-aware, he did seem happy, though his isolation puzzled him. He did not understand why the other foals snickered when he approached, why they melted away when he wandered towards their games.

So-fet pretended not to understand when he questioned her. The reason was simple: he was still too small. Even the females out-measured him. So-fet played with Storm alone, fretting to herself.

During their first summer, most foals joined small social groups. They played, practicing skills they would need in the coming winter. Hierarchies arose first within these groups, often based on the status of parents. A foal with two parents might get help from them finding food during the winter, but a half-orphan without a clique would never see his second spring. Storm met nothing but rejection when attempting to join even orphan cliques. The prominent did not want him because he was insignificant, and the insignificant did not want him because he was not strong.

Yet So-fet remained hopeful. She said little, loved much, and waited.

3

The Grass Plains

One day in early fall, Storm was resting beneath a scrub tree, admiring the new colors in the leaves, when he caught sight of an animal on the distant plain. It looked brownish and large, and it was moving in a straight line at a steady pace. He could tell that it was not a ferryshaft, but that was all. Storm was instantly curious.

He was about to go ask his mother to identify the new animal, when it vanished.

Storm forgot completely about what the animal had been in his wonder at where it had gone. On an impulse, he got up and started running. The sun was sinking down the western sky by the time Storm reached the spot where he thought he had seen the animal disappear. He snuffled about in the tall grass, but found nothing to explain what he'd seen.

Storm knew he should return to the herd. His mother had forbidden him to wander at night. He turned back towards the lake… and froze. He was alone upon the plain! The entire ferryshaft herd had vanished. In a panic, Storm galloped in the direction of the lake. *What if I'm lost? What if I can't get back by nightfall? What if I am alone on the plain after dark? What if…?*

The herd reappeared. Storm stared. Suddenly he understood. *The plain isn't flat.* Now he knew how the animal had disappeared. *Just a few steps in the right direction could put me out of sight of the herd…of the lake…of another animal.* Beaming with his discovery, Storm galloped back to tell his mother.

However, So-fet did not share his enthusiasm. "What were you *thinking*, Storm? Leaving the herd at dusk?" She snuffled all over him to make sure he wasn't hurt, then nipped hard at his ear. "Never do that again! Do you understand? Never!"

Storm understood only that he'd made his mother angry and somehow frightened, but he said nothing else until the next day, when he thought to ask about the strange animal.

So-fet stared at him. "You went *looking* for a strange animal on the plain?"

"Well, not exactly," began Storm. "It disappeared, and—"

"Storm, you must *never* go chasing after strange animals again."

"Why? What are they?"

"I don't know what you saw," said So-fet, "but—" Her mouth snapped shut. "Just do as I say, Storm. I love you, and I want you to live a long life."

Storm snuggled against her, although he was not satisfied. If he'd had anyone else to ask about the animal, he would have asked, but Storm had no one. He spent more time than ever on the plains after his discovery. He found troughs that ran for great distances. They could hide an animal from view. He learned to lie still in a dip amid the tall grass. He learned, in his loneliness, how to spy.

"Storm," he overheard one female snort. "Raindrop would have been a better name. I've seen foals like him come and go."

"Perhaps," whispered another, "but not with his color—"

"Oh, the fur, yes. It will probably attract attention from predators, but not before he kills his foolish mother."

Several listeners gasped.

"So-fet is stubborn. When winter comes, she will try to feed that runt and eventually starve herself. I've seen it happen before. One ferryshaft cannot provide for herself and a growing foal in winter."

"I heard she foaled early when she saw his father dead," whispered one. "That's why he's so small and ugly. She should have named him Vearil—bad luck."

They kept talking, but Storm stopped listening. He didn't eavesdrop anymore after that. He didn't listen to the other ferryshaft much at all.

4

Pathar

Near evening of each day, the herd traveled to Chelby Lake to drink. The ferryshaft were in their best spirits, then. They told stories, gossiped, and played. Storm watched the other foals, hoping someone would invite him to join in. One day, he started to practice the game sholo, in which one tried to balance a stick on one's nose for as long as possible. Normally, other foals tried to distract the player without actually touching him. Storm didn't have anyone to distract him, so he walked along the muddy bank of the lake, balancing his stick. He hoped the others would see and be impressed, but they ignored him.

A few days later, he slipped while engaged in his solitary pastime, and toppled into the water. It was deeper than he'd expected, and for one panicked moment, he didn't know which way was up. Then something grasped him by the back of the neck and hauled him to the bank. Storm looked up, dripping and trembling. He saw a male named Pathar—the most ancient ferryshaft in the herd, with fur more white than brown. Storm had often sat where he thought no one noticed him, listening to Pathar's stories.

"Your instincts are fine, but your stroke is all wrong," said Pathar. "Keep your head up. Move your legs like you're walking. Don't panic. Go on, let's see you do it."

"B-but," Storm stammered, "I—I've never—swum—"

"And you never will unless you get back in the water. Go on."

He did. By the end of the afternoon, he was swimming to Pathar's satisfaction. That evening, he sat and listened to Pathar talk about edible roots to an attentive group of foals. None of them looked at Storm, but Pathar acknowledged him and even quizzed him afterwards.

Storm had no idea why a prominent elder had taken an interest in him, but he was determined not to lose Pathar's attention. So-fet seemed just as confused, but pleased. "Be polite to him, Storm. Do everything he says. He can teach you things that I can't."

Storm was delighted to have someone else to talk to, even if Pathar did snap at him and occasionally ignored him for days. Storm learned about weather patterns, poisonous plants, and the habits of other animals. He learned about parts of the island he'd never visited—dense forests to the south, cliffs and ocean to the west. Pathar answered all of Storm's questions until one day when Storm asked about Kuwee Island.

Kuwee was a hump of wooded land in Chelby Lake. Most of the tiny islands scattered near shore had no actual soil, just trees, but Kuwee Island had a narrow beach. What was more, it rose up to a hill that would have given a good view of the lakeshore for quite a distance. The island lay just far enough away to discourage a swim, but close enough to make a curious foal think about trying. As soon as So-fet heard that Storm had learned to swim, she told him that he must not go near Kuwee. She said it was forbidden, although she did not know why.

Pathar snorted when Storm mentioned the island. "There's nothing over there," he said. "Nothing but trees and dirt and a few caves."

"Then why is it forbidden?" asked Storm. "What is everyone afraid of?"

Pathar hesitated. "They're afraid of the past."

The next day, Pathar approached Storm and So-fet shortly after they woke. Storm greeted him happily, but Pathar brushed him aside. "I have come to talk with your mother." So-fet seemed startled, but she followed Pathar some distance away, where the two spoke in low voices. Storm felt he would die of curiosity before they returned.

"Your mother is willing for you to spend the day with me away from the herd," Pathar told him. "Come." Storm followed Pathar, glancing over his shoulder at his mother. She smiled, but he thought she looked unhappy.

"Pathar, where are we going?"

"To Groth."

"What is Groth?"

Pathar didn't answer.

Storm felt pleased to be on an adventure, even a mysterious one. Morning sunlight streamed over the plain as the two ferryshaft moved north along the edge of Chelby Wood. The breeze smelled of dew-soaked earth and grass. They saw groups of ferryshaft at first, some still sleeping, but soon they left the herd behind. Twice, they startled deer as large as themselves. They bounded away through the long grasses, putting birds and insects to flight.

The day was clear, and Storm could see far away across the plain. He even saw the outline of the Red Cliffs off to their left. So-fet had told him that the herd would move there for winter. In the misty distance ahead, a mountain stood up against the sky. Between themselves and the mountain, Storm saw a dark border that might have been woodland.

They stopped often to rest. Storm had never traveled all day, and he grew tired. Pathar grumbled under his breath, "A fine pair we make—too old and too young—but maybe not too stupid."

"What are you talking about?" asked Storm.

"Do you smell anything?" asked Pathar in his abrupt way.

"No—" Storm stopped. "Yes." He *did* smell something. Sweet… alluring, yet a deep, instinctive fear stirred in his gut. "What is it?" he whispered.

"It is Groth," said Pathar in a low voice.

The two ferryshaft had drifted into the wood beside the lake as they walked, and they emerged suddenly from the trees, blinking in the brighter light of an unexpected clearing. Storm looked into the strangest forest he'd ever seen. The plants looked like enormous, deep-throated flowers. Some were as tall as trees, hollow and heavy with collected rainwater. Others grew nearer the ground, forming bowls full of clear liquid. Their glossy stalks were dark green at the base, morphing to vivid pink around their speckled, lacy rims. Some looked very old, with thick, woody bases, while others were delicate and young with more vivid colors. Storm could see no other types of plants in the strange woodland. The ground was thick with the decaying remains of their bowls.

Pathar strolled, unperturbed, along the edge of the forest. "Groth eats things."

Storm trotted beside him. "Things?"

"Mostly birds and small animals. They crawl into the bowls, drown, decay, and are absorbed."

Storm shuddered. "Why don't the birds and animals climb out before they drown?"

"Because," said Pathar, "the water in their bowls is sweet with sap. Some say the sap is poison, that it causes insanity or sleep." Pathar examined one of the bowls critically. "It is also said that those who drink will dream the future." Pathar bent and drank.

5

Dream the Future

Storm spent a sleepless night beside Pathar in Chelby Wood. "If I die," Pathar whispered, "you must follow the edge of the lake back to the herd."

"Why did you do it?" whispered Storm. "Why?"

Pathar didn't answer. He trembled so violently that his worn teeth knocked together. Sometimes his breathing grew so shallow that Storm feared it would stop. He twitched and whimpered. Once he got up and wandered with sightless, staring eyes through the trees. Storm had to keep him from walking into the lake or back towards Groth.

"Coden?" whispered Pathar. "Is that you?"

Storm had never felt so wretched or so frightened. Towards dawn, Pathar lay down and grew still. Storm lay down beside him and slept.

"Well, get up."

Storm opened his eyes. Pathar was looking down at him. It was near noon. "Pathar!" Storm wobbled to his feet. "I thought— Why did you—?"

"We'll need to hurry if we want to get back to the herd before dark." He was already starting away, and Storm had to trot to keep up. He didn't know what to say.

"Pathar, why did you do that?"

"Do what?" Pathar didn't look at him, but he had an odd little smile on his face.

"I thought you were going to die," said Storm.

"That bad?"

Storm stopped moving. "I don't understand why you did that. I don't understand anything about you. Why do you talk to me? Why do you teach me things? Everyone else thinks I'm bad luck, that I'm going to die this winter, that I'm going to get my mother killed." He stopped. He hadn't meant to say those things.

Pathar turned. "But you don't believe them."

"No," hissed Storm between clenched teeth. He could feel the unfamiliar sensation of his fur bristling and his ears settling against his head.

"You're young to be so angry," said Pathar.

"I'm not angry!" shouted Storm. *I'm lonely, and you're not my friend. I don't know what you are.*

"You're not going to die this winter."

Storm stared at him. "Did you really see the future?"

"Maybe."

Storm brought his ears up and his tail down. He came forward meekly, curious, the tightness gone from his chest and head.

"I dreamed many things," said Pathar, "the past, perhaps the future. My own death, I think. I don't understand most of what I saw, but I understand enough."

"Enough for what?"

"Enough for hope." Pathar nipped at him like a foal, surprising him so much that Storm nearly fell over. In the end, they played tag through the woods and raced each other through the grass until dusk, when they rejoined the ferryshaft herd.

6

Snow and Mushrooms

Two days later, the first frost killed much of the grass, and the herd started south. They were restless and excited. Fights broke out more frequently, occasionally with biting and kicking. Everyone's fur had grown thicker, so they were well-padded.

One evening, they arrived on the banks of the largest river Storm had ever seen. "This is the Igby River," So-fet told him. "The herd will follow it to the winter feeding grounds." Tall trees grew along the edge. On the far shore, Storm glimpsed the Southern Forests, of which Pathar had spoken. The dense trees looked dark and mysterious. The herd traveled along the bank all day, throwing up dust and trampling the dry, brown grass.

Storm woke a little before dawn in unfamiliar surroundings. He felt the boulder at his back and remembered. *The winter feeding grounds.* He'd gone to sleep beside So-fet at the foot of the cliffs—a sheltered area that the ferryshaft called the Boulder Mazes. When they'd arrived last night, Storm had been too exhausted to do more than glance around before lying down to sleep.

So-fet was not with him this morning. Storm heard the sounds of the herd and started picking his way towards them through the boulders. He found the other ferryshaft on the edge of the plain beside the belt of trees that bordered the river. Their behavior puzzled him. They were not sleeping or eating. None of the youngsters fought or played. A few adults paced. Others talked in low voices.

"Storm!" He turned to see So-fet coming towards him with a relieved expression.

"What's happening, Mother?" he asked when she stood beside him.

"Oh, Storm." So-fet glanced toward the river. "Come away from here. I'll show you some good grass." Still wondering, Storm followed her away from the herd and back into the boulders. The Red Cliffs rose above them—majestic and intimidating. A strange group of animals fled as the ferryshaft approached—white, fluffy creatures about two-thirds the size of a grown ferryshaft.

"Those are sheep," So-fet told him. "Some ferryshaft eat them in winter, but they are hard to catch."

The pair sighted a narrow vale in the cliff, and So-fet moved towards it, threading her way among the boulders. They found a grassy space, sheltered from frost and fed by a tiny spring. Storm and So-fet fed for a time without speaking. Finally Storm said, "Mother, what's happening back there?"

"A conference. It happens every year."

"Who—?"

"Storm, do you remember when you were little how I used to find mushrooms for you? You wanted to find them yourself, but you were too young. You would have eaten the poisonous ones. Eventually, I taught you which ones were right to eat. Then I wouldn't find mushrooms for you anymore, and you had to find them yourself. It was nicer when I did all the work for you, but once you knew, you could never go back. This conference and what it represents—it's like the mushrooms. Do you understand?"

Storm understood only that his mother would answer no more questions. He meant to ask Pathar about the conference, but did not see him that day. In the meantime, the winter feeding grounds were an interesting place. So-fet forbade Storm to climb the cliffs or to cross the river, but otherwise he had more freedom than ever before. He was particularly fascinated by the caves. Some had large, open mouths, and ferryshaft used them for shelter. Others had small, black openings that connected to winding tunnels. During the first few days at the cliffs, Storm could not muster enough courage to do more than stare timidly into their depths.

The first snow delighted Storm, even though So-fet warned him that it meant the beginning of hunger. They slept in the caves and emerged each morning to heavier layers of white. Then one night the river froze, and a nightmare began.

7

Horror

Storm woke to a world of glistening ice. The snow had transformed boulders into giant mushrooms, trees into knobby skeletons, and the plain into a white desert of silver sand. As he emerged from his cave, he saw a group of foals heading towards the river. They seemed excited, and Storm followed them.

The river was solid! Ice had choked the banks for days, but now the river was hard enough to walk on. One two-year-old foal gave a whoop of glee and called to his friends. "Look everyone! The river's frozen! Come out and play!" Storm watched in amazement as the foal floundered for a moment, but finally got his balance. He was soon joined by his companions, who slid and capered on the ice.

The sun was well up now, and most of the ferryshaft had gathered along the northern shore. The adults were heavier and less resilient than their offspring, and most preferred to watch from the bank. The bravest foals had found a hill from which they could slide down onto the ice. Storm joined in the fun. In their excitement, several of the other foals even spoke to him or laughed with him when they bumped into each other.

The oldest foals played games of skating tag farther out from the bank. They flew back and forth as though on wings. Storm watched, enchanted. He tried to imitate their movements, but his legs kept coasting out from under him. He watched the games of ice tag, and laughed and pranced and called encouragement to the fastest foals. He forgot everything else. He even forgot to be angry for all the times they'd made him feel like an outcast. Storm thought this was the most fun he'd ever had, perhaps the best day of his life.

Then someone screamed—not a laughing scream, but a strangled cry of fear. Storm heard someone whisper, "creasia." He turned to see a number of large animals emerging from the trees on the opposite side of the river. They were about the height of a ferry-shaft, but heavier and longer. They looked like a larger version of the oories he'd seen in Chelby Wood—small, shy cats that hunted rodents and birds. These new animals resembled the oory only in form. They were neither small nor shy.

For a moment, both creasia and ferryshaft seemed as frozen as the ice on which they stood. Then every ferryshaft on the river made a dash for the northern bank. Storm ran with them, spurred by the smell of their fear.

The cats soon reached the stragglers and wove a line through the terrified animals, separating a few from the herd. They chased the whole group to the northern bank, where they picked up several adults. The cats then herded their selections back onto the river. By sheer luck, Storm happened to be toward the center of the fleeing ferryshaft, and he was not chosen.

The cats showed no further interest in the rest of the herd. They paced around their victims for a moment, their movements light and quick. Storm saw eight cats, and at least twenty ferryshaft on the ice. The ferryshaft stood trembling, eyes dark with terror. Finally one foal sprang towards the bank, crying, "Mother!"

A creasia pursued her. His long legs covered the distance easily, and for a moment he loped alongside her. Just before she reached the bank, he snapped her up in his jaws, and her scream ended abruptly in a flail of legs and bushy tail as the cat shook her and then tossed her into the air.

They were so close that Storm heard the crunch as her spine snapped, and the leaden *thump* as her body hit the ice. The ugly sight seared into his brain—the unnatural sprawl of legs, her tiny body—so recently in motion—now so terribly still.

Storm thought that he should run—fast and far and never stop. Yet he could not tear his eyes from the river. Not until the last ferryshaft on the ice lay dead did Storm remember the rest of the herd. He glanced around in a panic, fearing that they had fled, leaving him alone with these monsters. Storm was relieved to see the herd still scattered throughout the belt of trees.

Then he blinked. Some of the adults were *feeding* along the forest's edge. Their indifference shocked and sickened him. *Can no one else hear what I hear and see what I see?*

But, no. Looking more closely, he saw foals like himself, transfixed with horror. He watched an adult male tear a mouthful of frozen grass from the earth, root and all. He did not bother to shake the dirt out before he chewed. Storm could hear the grains of sand grinding between the adult's teeth. He chewed until blood trickled down his chin, eyes staring straight ahead.

When the creasia had finished, they ate a little, made noises that meant nothing to Storm, and finally trooped back into the forest. They did not consume more than a tenth of the creatures they had slaughtered, and soon large, black birds began to sail from the sky to pick at the dead.

As the vultures gathered, the ferryshaft finally drifted away. At the edge of the trees, Storm found his mother. They said nothing, but met each other's eyes evenly, sharing at last the wretched knowledge of an ugly secret. Then So-fet gently embraced Storm with her neck, and he buried his trembling head in her soft fur.

That evening, the sun went down in a sea of crimson and gold, and the sight should have been beautiful. But, to Storm, it seemed that all the world melted in shades of red, and that the dusky rocks were bathed in blood.

8

Why?

Three days later, Storm found Pathar by a stream among the boulders. He was sure that the old ferryshaft had been avoiding him. "Why?!" Storm demanded without even a greeting. He'd never been so rude to his teacher.

He half expected Pathar to walk away without speaking, but Pathar answered mildly. "Why is such a big question."

"You know what I'm talking about. Why did it happen? Why did no one tell me it would happen? Why will no one talk to me about it?" He'd been trying to talk to So-fet, but she only shushed him, and he'd noticed that his attempts drew uneasy looks from any ferryshaft within earshot. In vain, he hid near gossipy groups, hoping for some insight, but they continued their usual round of speculation about mating, the progress of various foals, and likely locations of the best grass in winter. To his astonishment, no one seemed to be talking about the killings.

Pathar sighed. "We don't talk about that. What good would it do?"

"The cats—"

"They're called creasia."

"The *creasia*," Storm rolled the word around on his tongue. "Do they come every winter?"

"Every 10 or 20 days, yes."

Storm was horrified. "They'll be back?"

"Yes. You should try to stay near the center of the herd if you see them coming. They never cut out large groups, just small ones, random ones. They're not particular. They don't kill young more than old or females more than males, just whoever happens to be nearest when they're doing their cull."

"Why?" whispered Storm.

Pathar looked off into the distance. Storm thought that he wouldn't answer, and then he said, "So that we will not become too many for them to control. So that we will be afraid...and ashamed."

"Why don't we fight?" demanded Storm. "There are more of us than of them."

Pathar watched him and said nothing.

"Even the parents of those foals on the ice...they just... *watched!*"

"You think they should have died with their offspring?"

"No! I think we should have all run out there and...and done something!"

"We've agreed not to."

Storm was dumbfounded. "We've...*agreed*?" Storm remembered suddenly the tension in the herd when they'd first arrived at the cliffs.

"A conference," his mother had said. *"It happens every year."*

"What— Who—?"

"If I tell you more and others learn of it, I could be killed." Pathar spoke with appalling mildness. "Watch and listen, Storm, until you're older, until you understand better what you're asking."

Before Storm could respond, Pathar continued. "Creasia and ferryshaft are not the only intelligent animals on Lidian."

Storm was surprised. "What do you mean by 'intelligent?'"

"Animals who can talk to each other," said Pathar. "Who could...tell you things."

Storm was instantly curious. "I didn't know the creasia could talk. I couldn't understand any of the sounds they made."

Pathar laughed. "They sound a little different. They use a few words that we don't have, and we use a few words that they don't have. But it's the same language. All the intelligent species on Lidian speak the same language, except the ely-ary."

"How many intelligent species are there?"

"Seven. They are the ferryshaft, the creasia, the ely-ary, two species of curbs, and two species of sea snakes."

"Why don't I ever see them? What do they look like?"

"You don't see them because, mostly, we don't share territory. Curbs do cross our paths sometimes, especially the smaller lowland variety. The bigger, highland curbs are rarer. Their home range is far away in the southern mountains, but their queens like to know what goes on all over the island. They send patrols that live out here and report back. Highland and lowland packs fight with each other in the mountains, and they'll fight out here, too. They look a little like foxes, but are about the size of the cliff sheep. That's mostly what they eat. Curbs are not dangerous to ferryshaft in groups, but they will attack lone individuals, the injured, or the young. That's one reason you should not travel far from the herd alone.

"As for the other intelligent species—the ely-ary are huge eagles that live on the Great Mountain in the north. And, of course, you've seen the creasia. They live in the Southern Forests, which they call Leeshwood."

"What about sea snakes?"

Pathar hesitated. "They live in the ocean and on the beach, as well as in some of the caves. The two species are called telshees and lishties." Pathar stopped suddenly. Storm followed his gaze across the stream to a large, dark red ferryshaft, who sat watching them in the shadow of a boulder. Storm wondered how long he'd been sitting there.

When Storm glanced back to Pathar, he could have sworn that the old ferryshaft looked guilty. The stranger gave a twitch of his head, and Pathar rose.

"Who's that?" whispered Storm.

Pathar spoke without expression. "Charder, our herd leader." He gave a quick, irritated flick of his ears. "Does your mother teach you nothing?"

Storm felt embarrassed and looked at the ground. When he looked up again, Pathar had crossed the stream and stood talking to Charder, who never took his eyes off Storm. Storm felt simultaneously uncomfortable and annoyed. He stared insolently back.

At last, Pathar returned. Storm thought he'd never looked older or more tired. "I have to go. I apologize if anything I've said has upset you, Storm. Sometimes age doesn't make us wise."

Before Storm could think of anything to say, Pathar turned, splashed through the shallow stream, and rejoined Charder. They walked away, talking softly and not looking back.

9

To Bend and Not Break

Storm tried to get Pathar to return to the subject of intelligent species on several occasions. Which ones might talk to him about the creasia? None of the species Pathar had listed sounded safe or friendly. Pathar, however, had become evasive. He would talk only of survival skills—a subject that concerned Storm more and more as winter deepened.

Grass became scarce. Storm had to paw through snow drifts to get at the frozen stems. Sometimes, he dug laboriously though the frozen surface, only to find the ground scraped bare beneath.

Hunger became a constant specter. Storm ate tree bark, evergreen leaves, roots, anything within reach. He learned to hunt rock rats and rabbits. He learned how to find frogs and turtles in their winter burrows and to stalk mice in their snowy runways. Meanwhile, the ferryshaft ranged back and forth along the foot of the Red Cliffs, eating as they went and traveling on when there was nothing left.

As Pathar had predicted, the cats returned at regular intervals. They never killed more than a few animals, but the brutality of the killings made these deaths seem worse than those of the ferryshaft who died of cold or hunger. However, knowing the pattern of the killings gave Storm a degree of security. *Creasia like to kill us in groups,* he reasoned. *They don't kill for food, so why should they attack a small, lone ferryshaft?*

Storm had reason to hope he was right, because he was wandering farther on his own, both for food and for sport. So-fet did not try to stop him. She had joined a group of other adult females. They were not entirely friendly to Storm, although So-fet tried to cover for their rudeness. Whenever Storm spent more than a day with So-fet, she tried to give him food, which he knew she could not afford. So he kept away.

Storm still enjoyed playing on the ice. The Igby provided the best sport because of its size and smoothness, and Storm occasionally made all-day excursions to the river, following groups of foals whenever possible. He would have liked to play with them, but he was never invited.

The river helped Storm forget his troubles. The wind hit his face, the ice fled beneath his hooves, and he flew like a leaf before the wind. He was particularly fond of his ability to change directions quickly—a skill which Pathar had assured him was more valuable than speed. "Rabbits don't escape hawks by being faster," Pathar told him. "They don't outrun. They outmaneuver."

As the grass grew more difficult to find, Storm turned ever more to small animals as his mainstay. He hunted at a disadvantage because he did not belong to a clique. Cliques of foals hunted together and shared food. Lone hunters had to work harder.

In spite of everything, Storm could have managed, had he not encountered an unexpected problem. It began the first time he caught a rabbit. Storm had stalked the creature for some time. After losing it in the initial rush, he had crouched outside its hiding place for a quarter of the day until it emerged. One piercing shriek, and the chase was over.

Storm felt a surge of pride and pleasure. He was cold and stiff from sitting so still, but the reward would be warm and satisfying. His saliva had already begun to seep into the rabbit's fur.

However, the animal's dying cry had attracted the attention of another group of foals. They approached Storm, eyeing him with hungry interest. Storm's nostrils twitched. *An important clique,* he thought, *all high-noses from prominent families. What's their leader's name? Kelsy. A big two-year-old, and he can fight. Even the three and four-year-olds get out of his way.*

Storm recognized the foal almost as soon as he remembered his name. No mistaking Kelsy—fine nut-brown coat, deep hazel eyes, intelligent and proud. "Hey, runt, is that your rabbit?"

"Yes," said Storm, muffled around the rabbit.

Kelsy advanced until only a pace separated them. Storm had to tilt his head up to look Kelsy in the eyes. "I don't think you understood me. I said, is that your rabbit?"

"And I said that it is," replied Storm with his mouth full.

"Wrong!" In one movement Kelsy snatched the rabbit and left a clean slash in Storm's cheek. "It's my rabbit!"

Storm's eyes opened wide, and so did his mouth. Blood began to trickle from the cut, and the watching ferryshaft exploded into laughter. "Did the little orphan lose his favorite toy?" they cooed. "Well, you don't deserve a rabbit if you can't keep it. Isn't that right, chief?" Kelsy grinned, the rabbit dangling from his jaws. Then they turned and trooped off without a backward glance.

Storm sat on the cold stone and stared after them. His belly rumbled. As he turned away, he could not suppress a whimper of frustration and pain.

In the days that followed Kelsy's clique continued to persecute Storm, relieving him of his prey every time he caught anything of significance. Storm's search for a solution intensified as he grew thinner. So-fet watched with concern, but she could offer little assistance, as the attacks always came when Storm hunted alone. She tried to find extra food and often went hungry for him, but she could not support him entirely.

Storm was not the only youngster who suffered thievery. Older and bigger foals often stole from the younger and weaker, but it only happened to the same foal *occasionally*.

Kelsy's clique had chosen to heckle Storm on a more personal level. "Is it a ferryshaft?" asked one with mock uncertainty.

"I don't know. It looks like a rat to me."

"Yes, with all that ugly fur. No ferryshaft has fur *that* color. It must be a rat."

"Poor, scrawny rat. I wonder if it's hungry?"

"Are you hungry, rat?"

"Where's your father, rat? Don't you have a father? My father says the herd is stronger when the weak don't live to breed."

"Why are you doing this?" Storm almost screamed. "What did I ever do to you?"

"It's not what you did," returned Kelsy, his eyes half closed. "It's what you *can't* do."

Perhaps Kelsy's clique did not know they were killing Storm. Storm got the idea that they taunted him more for entertainment than out of malice. Of course, they also enjoyed the extra meat. They were hungry just like everybody else, but they could have survived without the food, and Storm could not.

After one particularly demeaning episode, he ran whimpering to Pathar. Blood trickled from his nose, and his gray eyes looked unnaturally large in his thin face. "Pathar," he wailed, "they're awful! They won't let me keep anything I kill. I can't find enough grass to survive. What will I do?"

"Kelsy's clique?" asked Pathar as if he didn't already know.

"Yes! Just Kelsy, really. If *he* didn't harass me, the others would leave me alone. I'll starve if they don't stop, Pathar. Please tell me what to do!"

Pathar watched him. "Storm, do you know why I chose to teach you?"

"No," said Storm miserably. *I don't know why you do anything.*

Pathar smiled. "I chose you because you don't give up." Half to himself, he added, "And neither did your mother."

"But, Pathar, it's not fair—"

Pathar's voice grew harsh. "Storm, nothing in your life will ever be fair! You should have died when you were a baby, and everyone knew it. You remember being angry last summer because adults predicted your death this winter? This is exactly what they were talking about."

Storm flinched.

Pathar's eyes softened. "Storm, do you see those trees up there?"

Storm followed his gaze to a few gaunt trees, hardly more than bushes, that grew, spider-like, from crevices on the cliffs. "Those scrawny things are the only kind of tree that grows on the cliffs. You would expect a sturdier tree in such harsh conditions. But those tall, proud trees by Chelby Lake could never survive up there. Do you know why?"

"No."

"Because, at Chelby Lake, trees grow close together to shield each other from the wind. Soil is scarce on the cliffs, and the trees must stand alone. They survive up there, all alone, in winds that would snap those tall, straight trunks by Chelby Lake. Do you know how they do it, Storm?"

Storm squinted. "They bend?"

"Yes. They don't fight the wind. They bend, but they don't break."

Storm felt tired. His belly rumbled. "So you don't have any *real* help?" He'd been half hoping that Pathar would give him something to eat. Many ferryshaft brought gifts of food to Pathar when they asked his advice.

Pathar sighed. "I see only two options. You can fight, or you can run."

"But, Pathar, I can't fight Kelsy! He would kill me! Run? Their legs are so much longer than mine—!"

"Storm!" Pathar almost barked. "I have given you my thoughts and my council. I have nothing else to offer. You will solve this problem yourself, or you will not see another spring."

10

Pursuit and Evasion

Storm thought. He went to sleep thinking, and he dreamed about rabbits and hawks and things that fight and things that flee.

Next day, he hunted deliberately, choosing rabbits, since they had been the beginning of his troubles.

His tormentors appeared predictably. "I think you have something for me," said Kelsy when Storm did not respond at once. "Drop it, rat."

Storm did drop it, but he didn't back away. "My name is Storm, and if you want it, come and get it." He snatched up the rabbit and ran.

"Haven't you grown suddenly bold!" exclaimed Kelsy behind him. "Or should I say stupid?"

As Storm listened to the voice growing fainter, he felt a prickle of fear, as well as a surge of pleasure. *Whatever happens, the expression on his face was worth it.* The rabbit waggled in Storm's mouth as he ran over the snow-dusted rocks. He could hear his pursuers, their hoofbeats clattering. They were not far behind him, but they *were* behind and out of sight. Storm assumed he was getting away.

Not until he raced around a rock and came face to face with Kelsy, did Storm realize his mistake. He made a dodge that would have certainly been unsuccessful. Fortunately for him, the rest of Kelsy's clique galloped around the rock at that precise moment, and collided with their leader. The group took only an instant to disentangle themselves, but Storm was running again, now just a few lengths ahead of them.

Kelsy ran to the unbroken ground on the edge of the boulders, Storm realized, *where he could move faster and more quietly. I ran in a straight line. He guessed which way I'd go and got in front of me. I can't be so predictable.*

Storm heard a crunch and realized that he was gripping the rabbit tightly enough to break bones. His legs felt wobbly. *If this doesn't end soon, I'm done.*

Meanwhile, Kelsy was berating himself for not being quicker. He thought of how foolish he would feel if stories went round that he'd been outrun by a lone runt with no fighting experience.

Then Storm disappeared behind a boulder that Kelsy recognized. "Len, you and those others go around, and I'll take these five straight through." Storm had entered a short slot canyon. Kelsy planned to send one group of foals to the opposite end of the passage and another through the front, trapping their prey in the middle.

Kelsy's eyes widened in surprise when he charged the length of the slot and slid to a stop. His friends swore that Storm had not left from their end, and no ferryshaft foal could have jumped over the high walls.

Arguments erupted, and everyone accused everyone else so fiercely that Kelsy thought they might fight. "Listen to me!" he barked. "No one made a mistake! If that foal did not leave by either end of the canyon, then he must still be inside. How many places can he hide?"

So the clique stopped fighting and spread out to search. Before long, they were scouring the thorn bushes that grew thick along one wall of the passage. "He must be in there, Kelsy. Like you said, how many places could he go?"

"But I went through that whole section already," argued another. "It's not deep."

"Here's the answer to your riddle," called Kelsy, who had left them and begun poking among the thorns. The foals gathered around him. Kelsy stood in front of a hole in the rock, hardly bigger than a fox's den. The thorns had overgrown it, but a faint trail of beaten branches revealed that some animal had been coming and going recently, prying back the thorns to get inside. Kelsy stared into the darkness.

"Well," he said, after a moment's dismal silence, "I suppose we weren't so far off when we called him a rat. He certainly goes to ground like one."

His clique gave a few half-hearted chuckles.

"Don't worry, friends. We'll have other days. I don't know how far back that tunnel goes but...Storm! If you can hear me, I hope you realize that this isn't over! We're not playing games anymore!" He turned, tail still high, and the group trotted away.

"It was never a game to *me*," muttered Storm. He crouched only two lengths away and breathed a sigh of relief when they had gone. For a moment, he remained perfectly still, savoring the silence and safety. Then, as the tension left his body, he began to laugh, softly at first, then louder. "I *am* going to survive this winter, Pathar." And he settled down to enjoy his meal.

Kelsy did not catch Storm the next time he chased him, nor the next. Soon the clique chased Storm every time they saw him, whether he had food in his possession or not, and still they could not catch him. Storm had a new hiding place every other day. He was so small that he could fit almost anywhere. Other foals laughed at Kelsy because of Storm, but not too loudly. *They* were not so clever at hiding.

11

A Race and a Corpse

Kelsy, as it turned out, had the sense to know when to quit. His efforts to catch Storm were only calling attention to his failure. Within a month, the chases ceased. No one tried to steal Storm's food, and he received no more ripped ears or torn shoulders. But in solving one problem, Storm had created another. At least while the foals chased him, they acknowledged his existence. Now they completely ignored him.

Storm discovered, even as he enjoyed his meals, that he missed the chases. He still explored the rocks and caves, but no crisis arose to give meaning to his actions. As the days passed, he grew bored and lonely.

One bleak day in midwinter, Storm followed a group of foals to the Igby to skate. The sky was a dismal gray, and it fit his mood as he drifted back and forth some distance from the others. He practiced by running as fast as he could and then stopping as quickly as possible.

He became so preoccupied with his efforts that he did not notice a light brown male of about his own age, who glided by with increasing frequency and finally stopped to watch him. The newcomer laughed.

Storm looked around.

"What are you doing?" asked the stranger.

"Practicing stopping."

"What's the point of that?"

"So that I can turn faster."

"I don't see how stopping can help you turn," observed the newcomer, "or what good turning is for that matter." There was an uncomfortable pause, during which Storm fervently hoped that the foal would leave. "Do you want to race?"

That question caught Storm by surprise. He did not care to inform this person that he had never raced another foal before. "Alright."

"We'll race to that big tree across the river. Do you see the bird sitting on the closest branch? We start when it flies." The two foals crouched in tense silence. At last the bird ruffled its feathers, flapped into the air...and they were off!

It didn't take Storm long to relax and enjoy the race. Although he wanted to be annoyed by the stranger's remarks, something inside him glowed under the unexpected attention. The pair was evenly matched, and they flew side by side over the frozen surface, laughing at times when they hit a rough place and skidded.

However, when they finally reached the tree, the stranger was ahead by a body length. Storm found that he didn't mind. The two stood together for a moment, catching their breaths. "You're not a bad runner," said the newcomer. "I didn't win by much, and my legs are longer."

Storm smiled. "Yes. But I've played your game, and now it's only fair that you play mine."

"Oh?" The foal looked surprised. "And what is that?"

Storm shoved off, putting several lengths between them. "Catch me if you can."

Some time later, the stranger stood panting on the ice. Storm watched from several lengths away, winded, but laughing. "Do you give up?"

The other foal smiled. "Yes. I've never seen anyone run like that. You double like a squirrel under a hawk! What do they call you?"

"Storm."

"My name is Tracer, and I know some friends who might like to meet you. If you come with me, I'll introduce them."

Storm knew what he was being offered. He knew he should pounce on it, yet he hesitated. "Why would they want me?"

"Because I say you can run." Tracer was smiling, but there was something desperate and brittle behind his eyes. "We're orphans," he added, after a moment. "Our best runner died yesterday. Are you coming or not?"

Storm followed Tracer back across the river, but he almost turned back when he saw the group, tearing at a sheep they'd managed to bring down in the deep snow beneath the trees. No clique would allow a stranger to approach a fresh kill, and these foals looked rough—scruffy and half starved, with a few open sores.

The two largest bared their teeth at Storm. He was instantly aware of Tracer at his back. He was aware of something else, too. The sheep was not a sheep.

Storm swallowed. Suddenly, the air felt too thick to breathe.

"She was already dead," said Tracer behind him. "She slipped and broke her leg a few days ago."

Storm hardly heard him through the hammering of blood in his ears. There were five other foals, counting Tracer, and they'd already surrounded him. *Did he do all that running to tire me out?*

"What is *this*?!" snarled the largest foal. Storm judged him to be at least two years old—dirty brown with a ripped ear and a broken front tooth.

"He can run," said Tracer calmly. "We need a new runner."

"You could have brought him later! If he goes to the elders, they'll kill us."

"He won't do that," said Tracer. "He's alone, Mylo."

"He looks awfully well-fed to be alone." Mylo came forward, bristling, and sniffed.

Storm cowered to the ground. It was too late to run. They were all around him. His fear that they'd brought him here to eat him gave way to fear that they would kill him to keep their secret. Elders *did* kill ferryshaft who were discovered feeding on the bodies of their own dead. Behind the others, a single foal continued to methodically devour the corpse.

Another foal, almost as big as Mylo, gave Storm a shove with his scarred muzzle. "He's a runt. He probably lives on roots. He won't starve until next winter when he's bigger. In the meantime, he's useless."

Tracer seemed unperturbed. "He—can—run. He can get into small spaces, Callaris. *We* will starve without someone like him to flush the prey."

"Ally can get into small spaces," countered Callaris with a jerk of his head and a sneer in his voice that told Storm exactly what he thought of Ally.

A tiny foal, even smaller than Storm, limped out from behind a tree. Something was wrong with one of his back legs. It was small and twisted—a birth defect that should have been a death sentence. His large eyes met Storm's and then jerked away. *So, six of them,* he thought. *But this one won't kill me. He'll just eat my liver after I'm dead.*

"Ally can't run," persisted Tracer.

"Who are your parents, runt?" asked Mylo.

Storm swallowed. "My father died before I was born. My mother is So-fet."

"Only *half* orphan," spat a medium-sized foal who'd not yet spoken. "I've seen him with that high-nose, Pathar, back at Chelby Lake. He gets special favors."

Storm scowled. *I'm dead anyway. Might as well be honest.* "No, I don't. I have to hunt for my food just like you do."

One of the foals who'd circled round behind him drew in a sharp breath. "I thought he looked familiar!" He trotted back into Storm's line of sight—a leggy yearling with fur even blacker than Storm's. He turned to Tracer. "He's the one they call The Rat! The one that Kelsy nearly bit his own balls trying to catch! He *can* run."

Mylo's scowl slipped a little. Several of the others started talking behind him. Tracer gave Storm a shove. "Stand up," he hissed.

Storm obeyed.

Tracer glanced at him sidelong and grinned. "I didn't realize I'd found someone famous."

Storm looked at the ground. "I'm not famous. But I did keep my kills from Kelsy and his clique. I ran from them until they stopped chasing me."

Silence greeted this remark, interrupted only by the crunch of a bone from the foal who was still eating.

Storm raised his head. Mylo was staring at him. "You ran until…they stopped chasing you?"

The black foal piped up again. "Yes, it was the height of gossip for a few days. Kelsy couldn't catch him. When he got tired of looking silly, he stopped trying."

The foal with the scarred muzzle—Callaris—harrumphed. Storm realized a moment later that he was laughing. Several of the others joined in. Mylo's face relaxed a fraction. He didn't laugh, but he did smile. "Do you have a name, or do you go by Rat?"

Storm returned the smile hesitantly. "My mother calls me Storm."

"And what do your friends call you?"

"I guess I'll find out."

Mylo did laugh, then. "Well, *friend,* have a share of our meal here, and you can stay."

Storm swallowed. "You want me to…"

"You're either part of our clique or you're not," said Mylo coldly.

They'll kill me if I don't, thought Storm. *They'll think I plan to tattle to the elders.* He took a deep breath and sidled up to the carcass. It really didn't look much like a ferryshaft anymore. It could have been a fawn for all that remained of it. Except for the face. *Don't look. Don't look.*

Storm avoided eye contact with the foal who was still munching on a femur. He bent his head, shut his eyes, and pulled lose a rib. He took it with him, back to the center of the group, where he sat down and began cracking it open to get at the marrow. Storm was ashamed at the way his mouth watered. *I'm not really that hungry. I've never been* that *hungry.* But it tasted like any other marrow—rich and warm.

He sensed, more than saw, that the biggest foals were drifting away—satisfied that he had passed the test. Storm finished extracting the pitiful amount of marrow from the rib. He dared an upward glance and saw the black foal. He felt like he should thank him for something.

Tracer was all smiles beside him. "Storm, this is Leep—expert on herd gossip and, apparently, on your exploits."

Storm laughed. "I don't think I have many exploits."

"Oh, but you do!" said Leep. "Did you know that Kelsy nearly lost his clique over you? Three foals challenged him. He was probably too busy fighting them to keep chasing you."

Tracer was talking quietly. "Mylo is our leader. He's not as mean as he seems. Not mean at all, actually; he let Ally stay."

"Ally is Ishy's twin brother," said Leep. "Ish tries to take care of him, but... Well, it's hard for them."

"Callaris is our muscle," said Tracer. "He's pretty affable as long as you let him have first turn at the food. It's hard to get enough to eat when you're that big. He's only a yearling; he just looks older."

"Speaking of food," began Leep, "do you want any more…?"

"No," said Storm quickly.

He followed grudgingly as the two walked over to the corpse. For the first time, he actually looked at the foal who was stripping meat from a hind limb. It was a female. She was painfully thin, worse than the rest. Her movements had a feral quality. "And this," said Leep, "is Tollee. She came to us about five days ago. She was pretty hungry."

Tollee looked up, the blood hardly noticeable on her brindled muzzle.

Storm thought he could understand her preoccupation with food. Still… "How can you do that?" he blurted. "Didn't you know her?" *At least* I *didn't know her!*

Tollee stood up and licked her jaws. "Not very well. But it wouldn't matter if I had. She's just meat now. Like you, like me, like all of us." She rose and stalked away, a little wobbly.

"I think she's improving," said Tracer with mad cheer.

"Absolutely!" said Leep. "We should start sending her to greet new arrivals."

Storm looked between them. "You're both insane."

"But extremely good-looking," said Leep, whom Storm suspected would be popular with the females if he ever reached breeding age.

"And intelligent," said Tracer.

"And even edible!" quipped Leep.

Storm laughed. "Thank you." He swallowed. "I've never— No one has ever— Thank you."

12

At the Top of the Cliffs

Storm could tell that his new clique was still watching him for signs of treachery. After six days had passed without any sign of an elder, after the bones of the unfortunate foal had been covered in a fresh layer of snow, after Storm had helped to catch several doves and rabbits—the clique began to relax.

Then one day, they took him up the cliffs. It was a dangerous thing to do, though perhaps not so dangerous as eating fallen fer-ryshaft. Hunting and foraging was said to be better in the woods at the top, and Tracer and Leep assured Storm that the view of the ocean was spectacular. Storm had never seen the ocean and was skeptical. He imagined something like Chelby Lake from a great height.

"Stay on the paths we show you," warned Tracer. "If you stay on the good paths, you'll be fine."

Mylo led the way as they started up the trail, picking the best places to walk. Storm felt a growing sense of excitement as the ground fell away beneath them. He could see the boulder mazes much better, and tiny ferryshaft dotting the landscape. The path narrowed, so that they sometimes went single file. The wind became fierce and whipped sand and red dust into their faces as they climbed.

At one point, the foals encountered a boulder blocking their way. There was a little room on the outer side, but no one wanted to inch across that narrow ledge with the dizzy drop only a hoof's slip away. In the end, they all jumped onto the rock and down the other side, staying as close to the cliff wall as possible.

Storm went first since he was small and less likely to start the boulder rolling. As he scrambled over the rock, he startled some sheep on the far side. For an instant, the animals just looked at Storm. Then Leep clambered over the boulder, and the wooly creatures fled with their tails in the air. They left the path almost immediately and bounded away over a slender thread of rock that sometimes vanished altogether on the sheer cliff face. Storm stared after them. *If only I could have done* that *when Kelsy chased me.*

"That is a sheep trail," said Leep behind him, "Callaris's parents died trying to catch game on a trail like that."

Storm turned away.

Much later, after his eyes had begun to sting with the force of the wind, the group struggled over the lip of the crag. They rested for a moment, looking down out over the island. Storm could see all the way across the plain to Chelby Lake, sparkling like the blue eye of a flower. Beyond the plain to his left, he saw Groth—a denser line of green—and the Great Mountain rising behind it like the head of a snake. To his right, he saw the thick foliage of the southern forests—creasia territory—and beyond that, more fields like those of his birth, racing away toward the mountain ranges in the south.

"Pretty, isn't it?" said Leep.

"It makes me wish I were a bird," said Storm.

"Wait until you see the ocean," grinned Tracer.

Storm turned to follow the others away from the Red Cliffs. "There's a strip of wood here," said Tracer. "It isn't wide. Listen..."

"What is it?" asked Storm after a pause.

"The sea. It never stands still."

"I don't understand."

Tracer just shook his head. He led Storm through the wood toward the Sea Cliffs. "Have a look," he said, "and then we can forage."

As they emerged from the shadow of the trees, Storm froze. He blinked hard and stared.

Tracer laughed. "See! What did I tell you? Look at it! Smell it! Listen to it!"

Storm didn't answer for a moment. Water as blue as a summer sky stretched as far as his eyes could see. The restless waves ran up to the sand far below and away again in an endless dance that filled the air with strange music. The salt smell made his nostrils twitch.

"Well?" Tracer prodded.

"There's so much of it," whispered Storm. "It's nothing at all like Chelby Lake." He smiled. "It's like something in my dreams."

Tracer kicked him playfully. "If you dream of something besides food, you're doing better than most of us."

They went back into the trees where they found Leep stripping needles from an evergreen. The needles had a harsh, unpleasant taste, but they filled one's belly. Unfortunately, the sheep had already gleaned most of the material that Storm could reach. However, Leep and Tracer occasionally dropped greens onto the ground and pretended not to notice when Storm picked them up. When Storm caught a squirrel later in the day, he shared it with them.

The group browsed until evening, then went to the Sea Cliffs and watched the sun sink into a haze of brilliant pink. Everyone had found enough food to feel satisfied, and they lay companionably close, sharing each other's warmth as the last hints of evening faded and a full moon rose over the trees. The cliffs were too dangerous to navigate in the dark. They would go back to the plain in the morning. It was the sort of expedition Storm would never have attempted without a clique, and he basked in this new sense of freedom.

"Why don't we tell stories?" suggested Leep. "Storm, you're new. We've never heard any of your stories, so you can go first."

"I don't know any stories," he protested, suddenly shy.

"Make it scary," murmured Leep. "I know! Tell us about the telshees, Tracer."

Ally startled Storm with an enthusiastic squeak. "Yes, Tracer! Tell us about the telshees!"

Tracer grinned. "Have you heard any telshee stories, Storm?"

"No," said Storm. "I haven't heard much about telshees at all."

Tracer's eyes glinted in the moonlight. "We'll fix that."

13

Tales in the Dark

"Telshees," whispered Tracer, "live in the sea. They look like snakes with fur, and they're bigger than any other creature alive."

"Bigger than the creasia?" asked Storm.

"Bigger than the creasia! They have white fur and a face like a seal."

"What's a seal?" interrupted Storm.

"They're animals that live in the ocean and on the beach," said Tracer impatiently. "You'll see them when we forage down there. They're a little like…big otters. You've seen otters by the lake, right?"

"Yes."

"Alright, like an otter. Telshees have big, green eyes, and they can hypnotize you."

"What is hypnotize?" asked Storm. From the way Tracer said it, he knew it must be something terrible.

"Hypnosis is when they control your *mind*," breathed Tracer. "They sing at night on the beach, and if they find you, they eat you! Their singing makes your legs stiff and your brain fuzzy, so that they can catch you in their crushing coils. You know what's happening, but you can't move."

A chill ran down Storm's spine—a sensation somewhere between fright and pleasure. He watched the others, and from their rapt attention, half smiles, and shining eyes, he knew they felt it too. *Tracer is making this up,* thought Storm, and he sighed with relief.

Tracer's eyes narrowed to gleaming slits as he continued. "I've even heard that some telshees are poisonous, so that one bite will kill you in the count of three breaths. They have slanted eyes that glow in the dark, and they can see at night. They can see you. But you can't see them. They live mainly in the rocks along the beach, and they only come out at night. Most of them stay in the Garu Vell."

"Where is that?" asked Storm.

"The Vell is the only place on the island where a rift cuts all the way through the cliffs to the beach. Actually, it borders on creasia territory, but there's no need to worry about cats in the Garu Vell. They don't like to go there anymore than we do. Some say that telshees keep their young in vast caverns under the Vell. Some say that they come out at night and wage wars with the creasia. Sometimes they wander into our territory, and if they find you sleeping..." *Snap!* Tracer brought his jaws together.

Ally jumped. "Tracer," growled Ishy, "either tell your story or let somebody else go before you give us all nightmares."

Tracer laughed. "I was just trying to explain telshees to Storm. Now, there once lived a foal named Nithl. He had heard stories about telshees all his life, but he didn't believe them. His clique argued about it all the time. Finally, Nithl thought of a plan to prove his point. He would take a group of his friends all the way through the Garu Vell at night. The Vell is no wider than the cliff top, so it can be crossed in a short time. 'We will come out on the other side, and you will see that nothing has harmed us,' Nithl said.

"His friends begged him not to do it, but he wouldn't listen. The next night, he and four friends set out across the Garu Vell. The rest of the clique waited on the other side. They had agreed that if Nithl and company got safely through the Vell, the others would accept their opinion that telshees did not exist.

"Time passed, but Nithl's group did not emerge. 'Maybe they're hiding,' said one of the waiting foals, 'trying to frighten us.' Others predicted a cry for help from the Vell, but the night remained quiet. Hours passed, and finally the foals dozed.

"They woke at dawn and looked at each other, knowing that something terrible must have happened. The clique called for their friends, but no one answered.

"Finally, they decided to go back over the cliffs and follow Nithl's path into the Vell. Perhaps a tide pool had trapped their friends. Perhaps they had gotten lost. 'Telshees don't come out in daylight,' they reasoned.

"The clique did not have to go far into the Vell. The trail stopped thirty paces into the rocks in a clearing of white sand. What they saw in the center made them shake with fear!"

Tracer paused and looked around at his audience. "What, Tracer?" exclaimed Ally at last. "What did they see?"

"They saw Nithl. He stood with his back to them, staring straight ahead. They called to him, but he neither turned nor spoke. When they moved in front of him, they saw that his eyes were fixed and glassy.

"They also saw four long brownish objects lying around him on the ground. They were ferryshaft tails—all that remained of Nithl's companions. The sand was perfectly smooth, with no trace of blood or a struggle.

"One of the bravest foals ventured to approach Nithl and touch noses with him, but he was dead, stone cold, standing on his feet. Eventually, they all stole away with their tails between their legs. And that is why whenever a telshee kills a ferryshaft, he leaves behind the tail as a warning to those who doubt his existence!"

A dramatic hush followed, and several foals shivered. Tracer opened his mouth again, but Mylo interrupted. "Who wants to go next?"

The foals shifted their hooves. They cleared their throats and shook their heads. Finally, Leep spoke, "Something funny happened to me last spring when—"

"I have a scary story." Everyone looked at Tollee. It was the first time Storm had heard her speak since the day he arrived.

"Oh, well—" began Leep.

"You wanted a scary story, right?" Tollee was glaring at Tracer, who sunk down a little against Storm. "Once upon a time, there was a foal who lived with her mother and father by Chelby Lake, but then the winter came. During the first blizzard of the season, her father slipped on the ice while trying to get to a cave for shelter. He broke his leg, so he couldn't forage properly, but his mate and his daughter kept trying to feed him.

"Then one day, while they were foraging on the edge of the plains, a pack of curbs found them, and they attacked her father, because he was weak and injured. Her mother tried to defend him, and the curbs pulled them both down. They started eating before her mother was even dead. The foal crawled into a crevice in the rocks where the curbs couldn't reach her. She was trapped there for two days because they kept returning to the bodies to feed."

"That's enough!" snarled Ishy. Ally had buried his face in his brother's fur. He was moaning softly.

Tollee looked around at them with disdain. "I thought you all wanted a scary story—"

"Not a *true* story," barked Leep. He actually looked angry.

"My stories are true," said Tracer, but without much conviction.

Storm heard himself say, "I'll tell you a true story." He was on his feet without quite knowing how he got there, standing between Tollee and Leep. *Please don't fight. We all know too many scary stories.* "I'll tell you a true story that's only a little scary. It involves Kelsy and a dead rabbit. Does anyone want to hear it?"

He was extremely relieved when they did.

14

Various Kinds of Traps

The foals rose at dawn and spent the morning foraging, intending to start down the cliffs in the afternoon. Storm had more than a few questions from the night before, but he waited until he and Tracer and Leep had wandered a little away from the others. Finally, he said, "If Tollee's parents died near the beginning of winter, what has she been doing between then and joining your clique?"

"Same thing you've been doing, I expect," said Leep without turning from the tree he was stripping.

"But, I've never…" Storm thought about it. "I've never seen a female without a clique."

Tracer snorted. "She didn't want a rogan, but they wore her down."

"A what?"

"A promised mate," said Leep. He looked around at Storm. "You really have been living on the outside, haven't you?"

Storm thought, *I know all about intelligent species, and I've been to Groth!* But he kept quiet. Pathar had obviously neglected some aspects of his education.

"Females can always find a clique," said Tracer, "but if they're young, it comes at a price. The dominant male, or sometimes another high-ranking male, becomes her rogan—her promised mate. She becomes his ru. In exchange, he protects her from other males and shares food."

"If she's an adult," put in Leep, "she may be able to join an all-female clique. The others will help her fight off unwanted males, and they'll choose their own mates. But, if she's orphaned young, well…you know how hard it is to survive without a clique."

Storm frowned. "So Mylo is Tollee's rogan?"

"Yes," said Tracer in a low voice. "We all witnessed the agreement, although she didn't like it much. The younger a female is when she's orphaned, the lower-ranking her rogan is likely to be. A foal less than a year old is a big risk. It'll be three or four years before she reaches breeding age. A male could expend a lot of energy on her, only to have her die at some point during that time."

"Then why did Mylo take her?" asked Storm.

Tracer guffawed. "In case you haven't noticed, we're pretty low in the herd hierarchy. Where else is Mylo likely to find a mate? He could wait and hope that one of the adult females chooses him, but he's not exactly a beautiful specimen. Sometimes, the females will agree to mate with the winner of a fight, but those fights get nasty. This way is more certain if he can keep her alive. He could end up with three or four mates this way."

"What if Tollee doesn't want to mate with him in three or four years?" asked Storm.

Tracer looked uneasy. "Well…he'd be within his rights to kill her. He wouldn't necessarily, but it does happen. The herd wouldn't punish him, not if he was her rogan."

Storm didn't like the sound of that. "Why don't the orphaned females form cliques like the males?"

Leep sighed. "They try, sometimes, but all it takes is two or three big males attacking them and taking their food until they agree to make the attackers their rogans or find other males to protect them. The harassing males are often adults or four-year-olds. The orphan females are young. They give up."

"I heard of one female clique of orphaned foals who made it all the way to adulthood without rogans," said Tracer. "Maybe it's just a story, or maybe it really happened. It's a good story, though. I'll tell it some evening."

Storm thought of his mother joining the female clique that winter.

Leep grinned and nudged him. "Nobody fights over us males. We may never breed, but at least we're free to die wherever we like."

"'We may never breed,'" scoffed Tracer. "If Leep isn't very careful, one of those female cliques will make him *their* ru."

Leep looked almost embarrassed. He opened his mouth to say something, and then stopped. "What's that?" His voice sounded so taut that Storm looked around in alarm.

"What's what?"

Leep bent down and nosed at something on the ground. Storm thought at first that it was snow or ice, but then saw that it was white fur. There was more—wispy hanks scattered along the ground.

Leep started backing away as though from a snake.

"Leep, it isn't—" began Tracer. "It can't be; we're on the cliffs."

"How do you know?" hissed Leep. "Do we really know anything about them?"

Storm wasn't sure what they were talking about. He saw another clump of fur drifting down and retraced its path upwards. He squinted. "Is that a sheep?"

Leep and Tracer stopped arguing. They followed Storm's gaze upwards.

"Oh," said Leep. He sounded relieved.

"See," said Tracer, "just a curb trap."

"So, we'll be killed by curbs and not telshees," said Leep. "That's a relief."

"It's a sheep!" said Storm stubbornly. "Are you blind? That's a sheep hanging from a—a—"

"A curb trap," finished Leep. "Come on, let's get the others."

Within moments, the entire clique was standing beneath the body of a young sheep, hanging several lengths from the ground by what appeared to be a tangle of vines around its neck. "Do you think the curb pack is nearby?" muttered Ishy.

"Doesn't matter," said Callaris. "There's enough of us to drive them off."

"A big pack might not find us intimidating."

"Chief?" asked Callaris.

Mylo was examining the sheep from all angles. The meat would make their trip up the cliffs more than worth the effort. "We take it," he said at last.

"What's a curb trap?" whispered Storm to Tracer.

Tracer tried to explain. "Curbs make traps for sheep and young deer. Adult ferryshaft are usually too big, but foals get caught sometimes. You choke if someone isn't around to chew you lose. Sometimes, the curbs use poison on the vines. It's dangerous to rob the traps, even if the pack isn't nearby."

"But how does it work?" persisted Storm.

Tracer just shook his head.

Mylo and Callaris had jumped up and each grabbed a leg of the dead sheep. Their combined weight brought the animal low enough for them to touch the ground with their back hooves, but the vines holding the sheep did not break. Ishy and Leep each grabbed a leg as well, and they worried the animal this way and that, trying to break the trap.

Storm was suddenly aware of Tollee sitting beside him. "Cowards," she muttered. Then, more loudly, "I'll get it."

"No—!" said Tracer, but she'd already run forward.

Tollee leapt into the air and, with a tremendous chomp, severed the viney trap. The four males who had hold of the sheep stumbled back in all directions.

Mylo rose, sputtering, and turned on Tollee, but she faced him levelly, ears flat, tail bristling. "I won't eat my portion until you're sure I'm not poisoned. That way, the meat won't be wasted if I die. Happy?"

Mylo deflated a little. He inclined his head.

Storm had gone over to sniff at the vines that had been used in the construction of the trap. He thought he recognized them and their faintly sweet aroma. He'd seen vines like that before among woody bowls of clear, sweet-smelling fluid, standing with Pathar on the edge of Groth. Storm did not think Tollee would be poisoned, but he wondered what she would dream that night. Behind him, the foals began to divide the meat. He heard Tracer say, "Don't leave Storm out; he's the one who spotted it" and smiled.

He stood up and turned, but almost tripped when he took a step. Looking down, Storm saw a tendril of vine wound around his foot. He shook it loose as though stung and then stood staring at it. He tried to convince himself that he'd snagged it with his own clumsiness, but he knew that wasn't true. The fur on his neck prickled, and Storm looked up to see Tollee some distance away, watching him.

15

Ally

Later that day, as they were trudging down the cliffs, Storm said, "Leep, did you really think that white fur came from a telshee?"

Leep looked embarrassed and didn't answer.

Tracer said, "We saw one."

Storm was impressed. "Really?"

"Last year about this time. We were..." He trailed off and glanced at Leep.

Leep twitched his tail and tried to look indifferent. "You can tell him."

"We were foraging in the Southern Wood."

Storm was astonished. "In creasia territory?"

"They're not everywhere," said Leep. "I've never seen them except when they're attacking the herd."

"We were orphaned in the same raid," Tracer tried to explain. "So we stuck together. We hadn't found a clique then, so we were desperate, and there's good foraging across the river if you're brave..."

"But you don't go over there anymore," said Storm.

Leep shook his head. "We passed the Garu Vell one evening. It's less than a day's journey from the river. And we heard... singing."

"It's not really singing," said Tracer. "It's a sort of rising and falling hum. It *sounded* very close." He shuddered.

"You can't tell what direction it's coming from," said Leep. "I think that's why they do it—to panic their prey."

"Well, *we* panicked anyway," said Tracer. "We ran among the rocks, but instead of getting away from it, we ran right into it. Only, it wasn't singing for us."

"It had caught a creasia," said Leep in a low voice. "It hadn't seen us, and we were too scared to move. The cat was fighting, but the telshee had it mostly wrapped up in its coils. Then it started to *squeeze*."

Tracer made a face. "I almost felt sorry for the cat. I vomited, and that was noisy. The telshee looked around and *saw* us."

"It had blue eyes," said Leep. "Very big blue eyes—not green like in your stories."

Tracer shuddered. "Who cares what color eyes it had? We didn't stop running until we crossed the river. We found Mylo and Callaris not long after that. We never went back into the forest."

Storm considered this. "Why didn't you tell *that* story to the others up on the cliff? It's a lot scarier."

Leep scowled. "Why don't we tell stories about creasia raids? Why don't we tell stories about losing our parents? Storm, if you don't understand that, then you don't understand anything." He trotted on ahead and Storm felt small and foolish.

"Don't let him bother you," said Tracer. "The beginning of last winter was a bad time. He doesn't like thinking about it."

Storm looked out over the island. "No, he's right. I don't understand anything."

Storm half-hoped to see a telshee that winter, but he didn't. He did journey up the cliffs half a dozen times with his clique and even descended twice to the beach, where they spotted a few seals and devoured strange, crunchy animals from the tide pools. It was an odd period for Storm—a period of cold and hunger, but also of friendship and belonging. He had a place in the world, and he was content. His mother seemed proud of him, though he visited her rarely so that she did not feel compelled to give him food. He did not visit Pathar at all for the rest of the winter, as he did not wish to be suspected of betraying his friends for their brief act of cannibalism.

Towards the end of winter, they did find and eat one more dead foal. Storm could not see the harm. They'd caught no game for three days and were very hungry. The foal had obviously died of starvation. Storm chewed on a piece of the ropy meat, but it was sour on his tongue. He swallowed it almost whole and let the others finish. He needed less food than most of them—one advantage of being small.

Everyone said that this was the hardest time of year—right after everything had been eaten and right before the grass started to grow. The ferryshaft herd had traversed the length of the cliffs twice, and now they were going over the ground a third time, heading away from the river. The snow was already beginning to melt, and the ice had become unsafe to play on. Everyone said the grass would come soon.

One ill-fated day, Mylo's clique made the dangerous trek to the top of the Red Cliffs to search for food. Even this area had been well picked over, and the foals spread out among the trees, consuming everything within reach. Storm was stripping bark from a low branch when he heard someone shouting from the direction of the Sea Cliffs. He moved toward the sound and soon emerged from the trees.

Grass! Little Ally had found some of the first tender blades in a tiny patch of dirt between the woods and the rocks. Storm was impressed that he'd called the others to share his prize, rather than eating it quietly by himself. None of them had eaten fresh grass since summer, and they came running. The patch was not large, but there was enough for all to have half a dozen mouthfuls of the sweet, tender stems.

However, the youngsters had not eaten a quarter of the patch before Ishy glanced up and went rigid. He snorted, and all the foals followed his gaze to the edge of the trees, where another group of young ferryshaft had appeared. Storm recognized Kelsy at once.

He had not seen his old opponent since he'd joined Mylo's clique. Seeing him now made Storm feel a little queasy. He couldn't help eyeing all available escape routes.

If Kelsy recognized Storm, he gave no sign. The other clique's wishes were obvious, and Storm knew what Kelsy would say before he even opened his mouth. "I believe that you're eating our grass."

"Grass belongs to anyone who finds it." Mylo spoke without conviction, and Storm could tell from his stance that he did not intend to fight.

"Yes, and we just found it. We outrank you and outnumber you, and we can outfight you. Don't make this ugly, orphan."

For an instant, Mylo hesitated, and Storm could see that he would very much like to fight Kelsy. *But Mylo is no fool.*

He tossed his ragged ears and turned away. "Come, friends. There will be other grass."

Most of the clique followed Mylo as he started into the wood, but Ally lingered. "We warned you, foal!" snarled one of Kelsy's party. "Leave. We don't want to eat grass soiled by orphans."

"Then don't." The words were soft but audible, and Mylo's clique turned in surprise.

"What does Ally think he's doing?" whispered Leep.

Kelsy cocked his head. "You're brave for someone on three legs. Get out of here before I break one of them."

Behind him, a foal snickered, "Don't make him piss himself, Kelsy; he's still standing in the food!"

Ally didn't move. The crippled foal was foraging very poorly at this point in the year, and he looked like skin stretched over a collection of sticks. Nevertheless, he trembled with every appearance of rage. "Mylo is right: grass belongs to whoever finds it. We found it first. Go find your own!" He took a step forward, and his scraggly coat bristled. Meanwhile, his companions had started to walk back toward the cliff. Storm could tell that Mylo was embarrassed and a little angry. If Ally's actions resulted in a fight with injuries, Ally would pay for it later.

Kelsy looked a little flustered. There was no glory to be gained in hurting a crippled runt, and if Ally put so much as a scratch on Kelsy, it would be humiliating. "You stupid foal," he said quietly, "my clique will eat this grass one way or another. Getting yourself killed will not help anyone. If you walk away now, I'll forget what you just said."

Ally didn't say anything, but he moved back a pace, and Kelsy took that for acceptance. "A wise decision." He turned away, giving the orphans an opportunity to remove themselves from what had become a dangerous situation.

Kelsy, however, had misread the signs. No sooner had he turned his back than the sullen Ally flew at him. He sank his teeth into Kelsy's back leg in an attempt to hamstring the larger foal.

Kelsy's reflexes were instantaneous. He whirled to snap at his attacker, lashing his body violently in an effort to dislodge him. Kelsy's teeth raked Ally's spine, but the whipping motion did the most harm. The tiny foal was so light that he lost his hold and went sailing through the air. He landed on the very lip of the crag. Storm watched in horror as Ally, disoriented, tried to stand, failed, and, with a scream of terror, vanished over the edge.

For an instant, they were all too stunned to move. After a ghastly pause, Kelsy turned to Mylo's clique. He looked shaken. "I…did not mean for that to happen."

Storm heard Ishy moan.

"I gave him every chance," persisted Kelsy.

Storm thought Ishy might attack Kelsy, but instead he just ran away into the trees, keening softly.

It was then that Kelsy noticed Storm. Their eyes met, and a look of recognition shot across Kelsy's face. *Is that guilt?* wondered Storm. *Because of me or because of Ally?*

"I did all I could," said Kelsy again, as if trying to convince himself. The orphans bowed their heads and slunk into the trees.

Two days later, the grass came.

16

Spring

Grass grew in every hollow and under every leafing and budding tree. The ferryshaft lost their winter coats in ragged chunks. The ground around their sleeping areas grew matted with fur, and Storm saw the birds plucking it up to line their nests.

Storm's short summer coat was a much paler gray with only smudges of dark smoke. "It's a good thing we don't have to hunt much in summer," Leep told him. "You'd scare the game. In dirty snow, though, you'll blend right in."

Storm butted Leep with his head. "As though you blend any better!"

Leep's summer coat was sleek and black, with just a trace of white around his muzzle and ears. They'd all been eating better, and it showed. Storm couldn't help noticing how the females watched Leep whenever they passed.

"He's only a two-year-old," Tracer would shout, "but we'll loan him to you if we can hunt with you next winter!"

"Tracer, shut up!" Leep would hiss.

The herd now occupied the spring feeding grounds—an area farther north than Storm had ever been in his winter explorations. As the snow melted from the plain, many of the ferryshaft moved out of the rocks in favor of the green fields. The expectant mothers, however, stayed close to the cliffs. The region had an uncommonly large number of dry caves, and these became birthing chambers for the ferryshaft.

So-fet was not among them. Storm was old enough now to realize that his mother's friends—including the ones he disliked—had helped her to fight off unwanted male attention last fall. She had avoided having another foal so soon in order to better care for him. As the abundance of the season provided delicacies, he sometimes brought her mushrooms, clover, or bird's eggs. He found he enjoyed spending time with her again, now that he knew he was not a burden.

Life became happier for another reason as well: the creasia stopped coming. Storm gathered from the conversations of adults that they never raided in the spring and rarely in the summer. *They're giving us a chance to grow,* he thought bitterly, *so that they'll have more to kill in the winter.* Nevertheless, the release from fear was blissful.

The close bonds of cliques, so vital during winter, loosened as the weather grew warm. They had been essential allies. Now they were only occasional playmates. Storm still spent time with Leep and Tracer, but he hardly saw Mylo, Callaris, Tollee, or Ishy.

Storm even risked a visit to Pathar. The old ferryshaft seemed pleased to see him and did not seem to regard Storm's winter absence as a betrayal.

Storm spent long, pleasant days playing sholo and hide-and-hunt among the rocks and up and down the cliffs with Tracer and Leep. Sometimes, they hunted lambs, for the sheep were giving birth as well, and newborn lambs were clumsy.

More often than not, their quarry escaped over the slender sheep trails, where no one dared to follow. Storm was fascinated by these precarious paths. He began, slowly and in private, to explore a few of them. They were *very* dangerous, but he took his time and always turned back if he could no longer see a path. Storm could not help remembering those early days in winter when hide-and-hunt had not been a game to him. *I'm getting too big to fit in my old hiding places, but something like this might work if I ever have to flee for my food again.*

Rarely, the sheep trails led to caves in the cliff. Storm considered these the ultimate find—places where he could rest and eat a meal without fear of falling or of being caught. It was in one such cave that he first noticed strange markings—lines scratched in the stone, with shapes and circles scratched over them. The markings looked purposeful—like something a ferryshaft could have done with a sharp rock. He couldn't imagine why anyone would do such a thing, but the sight made him uneasy. Something other than sheep had been in these caves.

He thought of asking Tracer or Leep about it, but he was sure they would only tell him he was a fool for traipsing about on sheep trails. His mother certainly didn't want to hear that he'd been exploring such dangerous places. In the end, he asked only Pathar about the markings.

Pathar smiled in an odd way. "I have no idea what those could be, Storm."

Storm stared at him. He knew, beyond a doubt, that his teacher was lying. Before he could formulate a response, Pathar continued. "You might find more of these markings—of which I know nothing—in other caves on the ground, especially near water."

After that, Storm looked for the markings everywhere. He found them, as Pathar had said, most often in caves where he could hear the distant murmur of an underground stream. Sometimes, he almost imagined that he could discern a pattern. Perhaps the markings meant "drinkable water" or "safe birthing cave" or even "danger of rockslide." But nothing that he could think of applied to all the places where he found the markings.

And then the season ended. All too soon, the last of the foals were born, the weather grew hot, and the streams dried up. Water became scarce, and finally word trickled through the herd that Charder, their leader, had judged the time was right to move to Chelby Lake.

17

A Narrow Escape

One hot summer day around noon, Storm went for a dip alone in the lake. Last year he would not have dared to do this, for the rest of the herd was still on the plain. But he was a yearling, and age brought freedom. He stood blinking in the belly-deep water, his hooves half-sunk in mud, thinking about nothing in particular.

A voice startled him. "Storm, do you know what the curb trap was made of?"

Storm turned towards the bank. He was further surprised to see Tollee.

"I've never seen vines like that before," she continued, not quite looking at him. "I thought I might see them at the spring feeding grounds. I was too young to remember that sort of thing last year. But they weren't there, and there's nothing like them here. You—" She faltered. "You sniffed them afterwards like…like you knew."

Storm cocked his head. *You've been wondering about that all this time?* He slogged up the bank and shook himself. Tollee backed away from the spray of water. "They're from Groth," he said.

She looked at him blankly.

"The forest on the edge of the plain to the north. The herd never goes near it, but Pathar took me once. It…it eats things."

He could tell that she did not understand.

"The plants…they don't look like anything you've ever seen. They—" A thought occurred to him. "You were watching me when I sniffed the curb trap that day on the cliffs?"

"Yes."

Storm took a deep breath. "Did it…move?"

Tollee hesitated. "Yes."

Storm sat back. "It wrapped around my hoof, didn't it?"

"Yes. It looked reflexive…like a branch springing back when you press it to the ground. It didn't look…alive."

Storm thought about that.

Tollee turned away.

Storm called after her. "Tollee… You're not going, are you?"

She looked back at him. "Going where?"

Storm thought she sounded too casual. "You are, aren't you? You're going to have a look at Groth."

Tollee didn't say anything.

It'll be my fault when she doesn't come back.

"Let me go with you."

Her ears flattened, but he kept talking. "It's a day's journey, and I've been there before." He thought of Pathar, stumbling through the wood, calling to ghosts that only he could see. "Please don't go alone."

Tollee looked noncommittal.

"Tomorrow morning," said Storm desperately. "You're sleeping near Mylo and Callaris, right? I'll come and get you. We'll be gone for two days. Will Mylo care?"

"No," said Tollee.

"Well, then, we'll go." *And if you change your mind by tomorrow, all the better.*

66

She did not change her mind. In fact, she was gone when Storm arrived in the misty dawn of the next day. He found the flattened grass where she'd been sleeping and didn't bother to wake Mylo or Callaris. The scent was fresh enough to imply that she'd lain down that night, but the spot was cold. She'd been gone for some time.

Storm used a few of the curse words he'd learned from Tracer as he hurried away along her trail. He'd gotten much better at tracking since he'd been running with Mylo's clique. Ishy and Tracer were both better than Storm, but he *could* follow a fresh trail.

He lost her briefly amid the scents of so many other ferryshaft and had to spend precious time combing the edges of the herd's sleeping area until he found her scent again, heading north along the edge of Chelby Wood. She crossed a stream and Storm lost her again. It took a while for him to realize that she'd walked in the stream all the way to the lake and then swum for a brief distance before climbing out again.

She is trying to make sure that no one follows her. "Well, I know where you're going," he said aloud. "Muddy the trail all you like, I'll still find you." *Why does she want to go to Groth? Why alone?* He thought of the way she'd bitten the curb trap when she knew it might be poisoned. He shivered.

The sun rose and made the grass glow golden. Storm was reminded of coming this way with Pathar. What an adventure it had seemed! Now he just felt worried. His mood did not improve when, about midmorning, he looked back and saw a collection of black dots on the distant plain behind him. He thought he knew what they were—curbs. He'd seen one last year, probably. Only then he was too young to know his danger.

Storm abandoned Tollee's trail through the grass and moved into Chelby Wood. The going was slower beneath the trees, among roots and through underbrush, but he thought it possible that the curbs had not seen him, and he wanted to keep it that way.

He regretted his decision when he emerged from the wood around noon. The shapes were much closer. He could count six of them, and he could even make out individual legs and bushy tails. *Only a small pack,* Storm told himself.

They had clearly elected to stay with Tollee's scent trail, rather than following Storm's trail into the trees. This had allowed them to close much of the distance while he was moving more slowly through the wood. *I am doing everything wrong today.*

There seemed to be no point in going back into the trees. If he could see them clearly, they could see him. Storm knew that curbs preferred to attack animals that were young, sick, injured, or alone. However... *I do seem to be alone. Tollee has probably already gotten herself eaten.* By size and at a distance, Storm might even be mistaken for a young foal—one of those born that year by the cliffs. *They are hunting me,* he realized and felt a stab of panic.

Storm started to run. He ran and did not look back as the sun passed its zenith. He had no idea whether he was still following Tollee's trail. In the hottest part of the day, as the sun was starting down the sky, he pulled up, panting, and allowed himself a backwards glance.

To his horror, the curbs were closer. *Much* closer. They would be on him in moments if he did not move.

Storm started away again, and then...hesitated. *This isn't working.* He remembered Pathar teaching him to turn on the ice instead of running in a straight line. *"Not outrun. Outmaneuver."*

Storm felt like a fool. He'd been doing just that—panicking, trying to outdistance his pursuers in plain sight without a plan. *Dare I go back into the trees?* The trees had slowed him before and allowed the curbs to catch up. *What about the lake? Would they follow me if I tried to swim away?* Storm wasn't sure, but it was a better plan than letting them catch him in the open. However, he didn't think he had enough of a lead to reach the water.

He'd been afraid to leave the edge of the trees because they offered some cover, but... Storm veered straight away onto the open plain. He did not know this area at all, but he *did* know something about the plain. *I saw a curb disappear out here last year. Let's see if I can make it happen again.* The grass was tall farther away from the trees—tall enough to crouch down and hide, but that wouldn't help with the curbs on his scent trail.

However… *They're hunting by sight,* Storm realized. *They can run faster when they don't have to follow a scent. I've been providing them with quarry that they can see.*

The ground began to slope gently down, and he felt a thrill. When he looked back, he could no longer see the curbs. *I'm in a trough. They're still very close. I just can't see them…and they can't see me.*

Storm changed directions, angling back south towards the herd…and possibly towards the curbs. He'd never once run in that direction all day, and he didn't think the curbs would expect it. He ran as hard as he could, using precious energy, but this time it would not be wasted. *They will be slower, following the scent, and I will be faster. I will get a better lead.*

Storm made a broad loop, hoping that they wouldn't guess he was headed back towards the lake. He was sure his lead had improved—or at least not worsened—otherwise, they would have been on him by now. At last, he came thundering out of the grass, headed straight for the trees. Subterfuge was over. Now, he needed to reach the water before he was caught.

Storm heard a yip behind him and felt a new stab of fear. He bounded through the trees, branches slapping his face, thorns and bushes clawing at him. He nearly stumbled on a root. He was sure that, if he fell, he would never get up.

Through the trees ahead, he saw a blue glimmer. Then hot pain stabbed his flank, and Storm screamed. His body lashed instinctively, and the pain fell away, but they were all around him now, running with him, jumping at him, snapping, and then he was skidding and stumbling down the muddy, root-tangled bank of the lake. He landed heavily in shallow water with a curb beside him, leaping at his throat. It clamped down with horrible force, and its weight forced his head underwater. He couldn't breathe.

And then he could.

Storm's head shot out of the water. Dimly, through his fear and pain, he heard a piercing yelp—snarls, a whimper. Someone was shouting his name. "Storm! Get up! Get up, you lizard turd! If your leg is broken, I swear I'll gut you myself! Get up!"

Storm was already on his feet, staggering through hock-deep water. Tollee stood on the edge of the muddy bank, head low, hackles high, teeth bare to the gums. She was snapping and darting at three curbs. The body of a fourth lay sprawled at the base of the bank.

Another curb leapt at Storm. This time, he reared back and his lashing hoof caught it a glancing blow. The animal yelped. Before it could get its balance, Storm brought both front hooves down on its head and back, driving it deep into the muddy water. He felt the animal struggling and applied all his weight. A moment later, it was still.

When Storm looked back to the top of the bank, Tollee was standing there alone, panting.

"Are they gone?" Storm managed between gasps.

"Think...so..." she said.

After a moment, Tollee skidded down the bank, nearly tripping over the body of the curb she'd killed. She buried her muzzle in the water and drank. Storm watched the trees, but nothing moved. He looked back at Tollee.

"I thought I came out here to save your life. Seems to be the other way around."

Tollee smiled. Storm didn't think he'd ever seen her smile. "They probably would have killed either one of us alone. Two of us aren't worth it. Why did you run from them? Better to put your back against something and fight."

Storm shook his ears. "Running is what I'm good at."

Tollee smiled again. This time it was more of a smirk.

"And, yes, I know that it wasn't working very well," said Storm.

"You're bleeding," she said.

Storm twisted around to inspect the bite wound on his flank.

"Looks like more of a large bruise than a deep bite," said Tollee. "You get that when they're trying to latch on and drag you down. Your neck will probably be bruised, too."

Storm nodded. He felt sore, but not badly injured. The curb that he had drowned had floated to the surface. Storm examined it curiously. The animal did look superficially like a fox, but it was much bigger—almost as tall as Storm—and it had stripes along its lower back. Its short, tan and black fur covered lean muscles. It looked rugged and fierce, even floating dead in the water.

Tollee nosed around her own kill, then clambered up the bank. Storm saw that she'd hamstrung the curb. From the way it was lying, he guessed that she'd then broken its back. It had no other wounds—a very neat kill. Storm was impressed.

They moved through the wood until they found a patch of nut-bearing trees. They proceeded to comb over the ground for the rich, flavorful nuts. "Did you see Groth?" asked Storm as they ate.

"Yes."

He felt relieved. "I thought maybe you wanted to—"

"To walk away in there?" She twitched her tail. "I thought about it."

"Why?"

"You wouldn't understand."

Storm frowned. "Is Mylo…unkind?"

Tollee laughed. "No. No, I chose Mylo because he *wasn't* asking." She glanced at Storm sidelong. "But you didn't have to join a clique at all. You were doing fine on your own."

Storm shook his ears. "Because I'm good at running away." He had a flash of insight. "But you never ran, did you? You fought."

Tollee said nothing.

Storm remembered how ragged she'd looked the first time he'd seen her. He'd thought it was just malnutrition, but maybe not. Maybe she had a lot of scars under that glossy summer coat. "You can run from a whole clique," said Storm, "but it's pretty hard to fight all of them, even if you are good at it."

Storm remembered what Tollee had said on the cliff before she'd bitten through the curb trap, the contempt in her voice as she'd said, "Cowards."

"The ones who harassed you before you joined Mylo's clique," said Storm slowly, "they were attacking you for different reasons than they were attacking me. I made myself inconvenient, so they stopped. They would *never* have stopped with you. You did the right thing—joining a clique, asking Mylo to be your rogan."

"It wasn't just foals," said Tollee quietly. "Adult males, too—the ones who didn't feel they could attract a willing mate."

Storm didn't know what to say, so he chewed on a nut. Finally, he said, "I'm glad you didn't walk off into Groth. You didn't drink the water in the bowls, did you?"

Tollee looked at him curiously. "No. I wanted to. It smelled so nice. But I thought it might be poison."

"It is...sort of."

"What is that supposed to mean?"

Storm squirmed. "Pathar said that animals drink the water and crawl into the bowls and drown, but he also said that if you drink, you dream the future." Storm didn't feel the need to explain that Pathar had given a demonstration.

Tollee stopped eating. She was very still for a moment. "After the curb trap, for a few days, I had strange dreams."

"Oh?"

"Yes. The forest...Groth...it was in my dreams...even though no one had ever told me about it or what it was called."

Storm waited.

Tollee shook her head. "There was a blue stone...a black creasia with glowing green eyes...a telshee...and you."

"Me?" Storm was surprised.

"Yes." Tollee did not meet his eyes. "In the dream, you were running away into Groth. Only I didn't know what it was called until now."

Storm felt a chill. "I don't believe in dreams." He spoke without much conviction.

Tollee smiled. "Me neither."

Storm laughed shakily. "How can you say that? You saw Groth before you saw it!"

Tollee shook her ears. "Maybe it's only what *might* happen."

Storm liked that better.

They spent the rest of the evening making themselves comfortable in a dense thicket, where they would hear the crackle of anything trying to approach. They slept in turns, huddled together, listening for curbs, but nothing disturbed them. By the next day, they had rejoined the ferryshaft herd.

18

A Thousand Faces

Storm saw no more curbs that summer, nor did he travel to Groth again. He did not tell Leep and Tracer about his experience, nor, he suspected, did Tollee tell Mylo and Callaris. However, he did speak more frequently to Tollee. As the summer wound down, they developed a genuine friendship.

This provoked a certain amount of teasing from Tracer and Leep, especially as the fall season brought mating to the front of everyone's minds. "Better watch out," said Tracer. "You'll be fighting Mylo for her."

Mylo did, indeed, fight off three male foals who challenged him over Tollee's status, and the entire clique helped fight off two adults. Storm knew that, had she been alone, she would have dealt with constant harassment. Mylo's status as clique leader entitled her not only to his protection, but to the protection of his entire clique. The others did stand to gain from Tollee's presence as a hunting partner that winter, so they defended her readily enough. She was a good hunter, and no one wanted her to be spirited away by another clique.

"I couldn't be Tollee's rogan," Storm told Tracer. *And she wouldn't like me if I was.* "I can't fight like Mylo."

This was true. Mylo did not seem to regard the diminutive Storm as a rival and showed no sign of jealousy over his friendship with Tollee. They were both yearlings, after all. The other members of the clique were at least two years old, while Mylo was three.

Meanwhile, So-fet selected a new mate, Dover, from the comfort of her female clique. Storm did not like him much, and the feeling was mutual. So-fet, however, seemed content, and that was all that mattered.

Soon the trees began to shed their leaves. Storm's fur thickened, and the winds blew colder off Chelby Lake. One cloudy day with a stiff breeze sighing over the plain, Storm found himself again on the long march to the cliffs.

As he jogged along with his friends, he watched the new foals—all of them with at least one parent, and most with two. They were wide-eyed with wonder, looking at everything—the broad Igby River, the Southern Wood beyond, the distant cliffs. Some of them capered, pulling the tails of adults and then racing away.

They don't know what's coming, thought Storm. For the first time since spring, he thought of the creasia. *There's nothing to do about that. Better to think on things I can do something about.*

As much as he dreaded the hardships of winter, Storm felt he had a firm grasp on what to expect this year—the dangers he might face and how to avoid those that were avoidable. In this, he was entirely mistaken.

The first hint came with the weather, which seemed increasingly oppressive. By noon, thick clouds had gathered, with the sun only a faintly brighter spot above the haze, drenching the plain in eerie half-light. The wind—which usually came off the lake during the day—was blowing from the west. It gusted and tore at the grass, whipping the Igby into choppy waves.

The herd seemed depressed. The new foals stopped playing and hung close about their parents. Storm was surprised when his own mother sought him out. "Storm, come and walk with me." She'd not been so direct since last winter.

He came to her, though he felt awkward with her new mate walking nearby. "Mother, why is the sky so dark?"

"A storm." She seemed distracted.

"I don't remember the winter storms looking like this."

So-fet didn't answer.

Storm was pleased to see Pathar up ahead. He was about to go to him and ask about the weather, when So-fet put her head out and stopped him. "Not now, Storm."

Storm saw that Pathar was talking to two other elders as they walked. They kept looking up at the clouds. As he watched, Charder—the big, dark red ferryshaft who led the herd—approached them and joined in the conversation. They all looked quite serious.

At last, the four of them split up and hurried off in different directions. Moments later, the word came trickling down through the ranks of ferryshaft: they needed to reach the shelter of the cliffs as soon as possible. They needed to run.

"What are we doing, Mother?"

"Just eat, Storm."

"But I'm not hungry."

"I said, *eat!*" Her tone brooked no argument.

Feeling like an infant, Storm bent his head and obeyed. A moment later, So-fet turned her back, and he looked up rebelliously. It was evening, nearly dark. The exhausted herd should have been nestled among the warm rocks and in the caves below the cliffs, resting after their long journey and sheltering from the coming storm. Instead, they were scattered over the plain, eating as if they had not tasted grass in a season. A few stragglers were still trailing in along the edge of the river, and these, too, fell upon the grass as soon as they'd caught their breaths.

We should be taking shelter, thought Storm. The wind had become fierce, peppered with stinging rain. Storm stared at the roiling clouds now filling the western sky. Not a star showed, and the moon peeked down only occasionally.

Yet all the oddities of nature paled in comparison to the latest mystery. When Storm went to the river to drink, he had seen several creasia across the Igby and on his own side as well. Normally the ferryshaft ran when they saw a creasia, at least until the killing began. But tonight neither species paid any attention to the other. The cats paced or lay on the bank, eyes closed, breathing quickly.

Storm struggled to recall exactly what had happened this time last year. He remembered that the herd had been nervous, had appeared to wait for something. *Mother said it was a conference, and Pathar said it had something to do with the cats. But it was nothing like this.*

He wondered where his friends were and what they thought. He'd lost track of them after the herd began to run. He kept hoping to see someone he recognized, even Pathar, but in the deepening twilight, with everyone milling, heads down to feed, it was difficult.

"Storm!" So-fet's voice made him jump. With a sheepish expression, he lowered his head to the grass again.

At last, Storm did recognize someone. Charder came trotting out from among the boulder mazes, Pathar at his heels. A dozen other elders and high-ranking adults came forward to talk. Storm tried to observe from a distance, but shifting animals kept blocking his view. Then Charder said something that Storm did not hear, but the order passed through the ranks, echoed and repeated by hundreds of voices. They were to move...somewhere.

He looked to So-fet and found her whispering with Dover. "What is happening?" he demanded. "Where are we going?"

So-fet turned to her foal. "Listen closely, Storm. Soon there will be a lot of confusion, and everyone will run forward at once.

Stay near me if you can, and don't fall no matter what. Do you understand?"

"Yes. But what—?"

"A monstrous storm is coming. We call it the Volontaro. We would not be safe in the caves where we usually stay during the blizzards. There is only one cave in this part of Lidian that is safe and big enough for all of us. We are going there soon."

"Are the creasia coming too?"

"Yes, but don't be afraid. We have a treaty agreement during the Volontaro."

"Then…this happens often?"

"There is a chance of a Volontaro every year."

At that moment, the ferryshaft herd surged towards the cliff. Storm understood his mother's warning immediately. The animals ran fast and close together. A small ferryshaft might easily have been trampled.

The situation did not improve as they entered the rocks. The herd's anxiety seemed to escalate into a near-stampede. Storm had to concentrate to stay on his feet, and he wondered again how the rest of his clique was faring.

When they reached the foot of the cliffs, the herd went straight up a trail. Storm had never used this path himself, although he had seen it. Tracer had told him that the path led to a stone bridge that spanned the Garu Vell, and the clique avoided anything to do with the Vell.

The path was broader than he had imagined, with room for at least six ferryshaft to walk abreast. Up the cliffs they galloped, rising higher and higher, and all the while moving steadily south towards the Igby. They passed over the river, where it spilled out of the cliff below. The banks seemed deserted, the surrounding plain very dark. The wind was making an appalling shriek among the rocks.

Soon, Storm noticed that the animals ahead were muttering and snapping at each other, crowding more closely together. Storm turned all his attention to the twin tasks of staying on his feet and keeping near So-fet. Even Dover was no longer with them.

Presently, Storm noticed that the animals ahead were thinning and forming a line. Finally he could breathe. Then the animal in front of Storm stepped forward, and Storm found himself on the verge of an abyss. He reared and tried to back up, but the ferryshaft behind pushed impatiently. For one awful moment, Storm thought they would send him over the edge.

Then he saw it—a narrow thread of rock, only about half a length across, spanning the entire Vell. A line of ferryshaft were laboring over it, nose to tail on the slender bridge, heads down, eyes fixed on their feet.

Storm felt another shove behind him and heard a muffled curse. "Move!"

He gulped, heart racing, and skidded down the last few lengths onto the bridge. The wind hit him full force, and Storm struggled to keep his balance. One brief glance into the yawning emptiness told him that he should not look down. "Just keep your eyes on the path, Storm," came his mother's voice a couple of animals behind him. "Just look at your hooves."

For what seemed an eternity, Storm struggled over the bridge. His heart pounded in his throat, and his legs wobbled as though they were made of mud.

At last, Storm felt the force of the wind decrease, saw other animals around him, and realized that he had stepped off the bridge. The cave beyond was dim. He sensed, however, that it was vast, with a high ceiling and a great many animals jostling around him. Then a ferryshaft to his rear kicked him, and he realized that he was obstructing traffic. Disoriented, Storm stumbled forward.

In the confusion, he realized that what he had feared had happened—he could not see So-fet. Storm raised a tentative voice, calling her name through the crowd, but he was one of many doing the same thing. Still, she'd been only a few animals behind him, and he was almost certain that she'd made it off the bridge. Trying to reassure himself, Storm pushed his way deeper in the cave, away from the chaos around the entry point.

He found the back of the cavern moderately calm, with many ferryshaft lying down to sleep. He noted the distracting smell of creasia, though he could not see them. No one seemed concerned, so he tried to ignore the unnerving smell. The floor of the cave was soft with sand, probably blown in through the large mouth, which was almost as wide as the cavern itself.

Storm worked his way to a wall and lay down, damp, cold, and exhausted. Now he understood why his mother had commanded him to eat. *Who knows how long it will be before we see grass again.*

For the moment, however, Storm felt safe. Not far away, a clique of older foals was quietly telling stories. Storm couldn't understand the words, but he felt comforted by their cheerful tone. Lulled by the patter of rain and the soft breathing of resting animals, Storm began to doze.

Somewhere nearby, a mother ferryshaft sang softly to her foal:
Chase me if you must
Catch me if you can
But never, never think that you can kill me
I have a thousand faces.

It was an old lullaby that Storm had heard times beyond counting. The tune was so familiar that he hardly thought about the words. They ran round and round in his head as he drifted off to sleep.

"A thousand faces…a thousand faces…we have a thousand faces."

19

A Line in Stone

In his dream, he saw her running—that foal who had not yet seen the end of her first winter...and never would. The creasia pursued her, muscles bunching and stretching beneath sleek, dark fur. As Storm watched, the foal spun on the ice to confront her pursuer. Storm saw her face—Tollee's face.

"No!" he shouted. "Run! Don't fight! You can't win! Run!"

But she jumped at the cat, snarling, and there was a slash of claws and a scream and entrails steaming on the ice. The cat turned to Storm and roared. The noise was horrible, so loud that it didn't even sound like an animal. Storm ran, but he knew he couldn't escape. The roaring grew louder.

Then someone kicked him.

Storm opened his eyes and looked up at a glaring adult ferryshaft. "Stop kicking," she hissed.

Storm realized that he'd been running in his sleep. "S-sorry," he stammered. "It's the smell...the cats."

She huffed and lay back down. Storm had to raise his voice to be heard, and he realized that the roaring in his dream was real. The wind was screaming among the rocks outside, but apart from that came a howling, rumbling noise that grew louder by the moment.

The Volontaro.

It came out of the west and raced screaming up the Vell from the sea. Then it was outside, obscuring the mouth of the cave in a blinding sheet of rain. Storm heard boulders crashing down the cliffs. *That's why the other caves are unsafe,* he thought.

After a while, Storm's fear diminished, although the wind and rain continued to batter the cliff. He no longer felt at all sleepy, and he was seized by a desire for a closer look at this greatest-of-all storms. So he rose, picking his way carefully between resting ferryshaft, and approached the mouth of the cave. He passed the last of the ferryshaft long before reaching the edge.

Storm crept cautiously over the wet rock. Wind-driven rain tore at his fur, but he pressed on until he could peer down into the tempest. It took him a moment to understand what he heard, what he could glimpse through the rain. The Garu Vell was underwater! The surf, which normally lapped on the beach, was pounding in the rock mazes. Boulders, he guessed, must be shifting like pebbles underfoot. Even from this height, Storm could hear a distant grinding and see the flash of whitewater.

He jumped as something grabbed him from behind. Storm tried to turn, but was swept off his feet as the intruder gripped him behind the head and dragged him back into the cave. Storm pulled free and spun around to find his mother glaring at him. He was relieved to see her, although he gathered from her expression that she disapproved of forays to the lip of the cliff. The noise of the storm made conversation impossible, so he merely turned and followed her back into the cave.

Storm woke to weak morning sunlight. He felt warm and comfortable, lying against his mother among other sleeping ferryshaft. His stomach growled, but he ignored it. The wind was still blowing outside, but with less violence, and the rain had stopped.

Storm wondered what the rest of the cave looked like. His impressions from last night had been muddled by the dark and by crowds of pushing, half-panicked animals. Curious, Storm rose and looked around. He appeared to be toward the western end of a vast, wide-mouthed cavern. Rock formations partially obscured his view. Resting ferryshaft covered the floor for as far as he could see, which was, admittedly, not very far. Storm thought he heard water near the pile of rocks towards the center of the cave.

Stepping carefully to avoid waking anyone, Storm made his way east. When he reached a rock formation, he clamored up and finally got a decent view of the cave. The creasia were at the eastern end. He could see the brindled brown and black and gold of their coats covering the cave floor in that direction. Very near the center of the cave mouth, he could see the bridge. Towards the ferryshaft side of the bridge, a shallow stream crossed the cave floor. He must have splashed through it last night, but probably hadn't noticed, as wet as he'd already been.

He did not see any ferryshaft beyond the stream now. However, he also saw no sign of violence, nor did he smell any blood. As he watched, a ferryshaft approached the stream and drank before moving away. *It must be safe.*

Still moving cautiously, Storm climbed to the ground and picked his way through the ferryshaft herd until he reached the stream. The cave floor was uneven, and he couldn't actually see any of the resting creasia from the spot where he chose to drink. He found that he was quite thirsty after the previous day's exertions. The stream was little more than a shallow sheet of water running over stone, and Storm had to lap at it for some moments to get an adequate drink.

When he raised his head, he was surprised to see movement about twenty paces away on the far side of the stream. A small animal seemed to be staggering around on the ground. Storm reared up on his hind legs to get a better view. It looked like a rock rat—possibly sick or injured.

Storm's stomach rumbled, and he had to swallow his saliva. He hadn't expected to find any food in the cave. He put a foot in the stream.

"Don't go over there." Storm turned to see an adult ferryshaft—a stranger to him—bending to drink. "They're just trying to trick you," said the stranger without looking at him. "This is our side. Stay here."

Storm sat down in surprise.

After a moment, a small creasia slunk out of the rocks. Storm was even more surprised. It was a cub, standing no higher than Storm's own shoulder. Still, it could easily have killed him. The cub scooped up its prey and sat watching the two ferryshaft, the injured rat still squirming in its jaws.

"See," said the adult. "They play this game with new foals or young adults who've never been through a Volontaro before."

Storm stared at the adult. "That cub would have killed me if I'd gone for the rat?"

The adult just looked at him as though he were an infant.

"But why won't they come after us over here?" persisted Storm.

"That's the treaty," said the adult simply. "This is our side. That is the agreement." He turned and walked back toward the herd. Storm remained by the stream a little longer, but the cub was leering at him in a way that made his skin prickle. To his consternation, the cub started down towards the stream as if to drink. Storm backed off and made to leave.

However, just as he was turning away, something caught his attention. On the lip of the rise behind the stream, just on the edge of his line of sight, he saw a tall stone with a relatively flat face. On this surface, someone had scratched an enormous stick shape. Storm blinked hard. It was exactly the sort of shape that he'd been finding in the caves by the spring feeding grounds. He'd never seen such a large one in such an open place.

Storm glanced at the cub. He was almost certain now that she was female. She'd set the rat on the ground, still half-alive, and was lapping water as though Storm were not present. Feeling suddenly bold, he said, "Do you know what that marking is on the rock in the center of the cave?"

She glanced up with a look of surprise. There was a long pause. Finally, her mouth twitched. "Come over here, and I'll tell you." Her speech was slow and heavily accented, but Storm could understand. It was the first time he'd ever understood something a creasia had said.

Storm bristled. "You already have enough to eat."

The cat yawned, showing all her teeth. "Does one ever really have enough?"

"You don't kill us because you need to eat."

The cub watched him. "Maybe not. Not always."

"Why, then?"

She licked her lips and looked away. "You'd better stay on your side of the stream, little ferryshaft. My father is hungry, and a rat won't satisfy him." She turned and stalked off.

Storm went looking for Pathar. He wanted to know about the large marking. Instead, he found Tracer and Leep, looking exhausted and hungry where they huddled with a number of other low-ranking ferryshaft. Storm felt guilty. He sometimes forgot that his mother, though not prominent, still gave him resources and a degree of protection unavailable to his friends.

"We can't find Ishy," Tracer said at once. "We've been all through the herd. Mylo thinks he fell or got trampled."

Storm felt a sudden heaviness. He'd not known Ishy well. The foal had been withdrawn and quiet since the death of his brother. Still, Storm had assumed that he would recover with time.

"We may be replacing him," said Leep dully, "with a female Callaris found. Her father died last winter before she was born, and she hasn't found her mother since the initial rush to the cave. She asked Callaris to be her rogan. He's already fought off two other males and is about to engage a third. Mylo is helping him." Leep made a vague gesture towards the distant cave wall. "What have you been up to?"

Storm told them about the boundary stream and the cub's deadly trick with the rat. He did not try to explain the strange marking and how it reminded him of others he'd seen last spring.

Tracer's eyes widened. "Well, that's good to know. I was about to get a drink." He shuddered. "Maybe I'll just wait. I heard an elder saying that we may leave soon—if they decide that the storm is really over."

The creasia left the cave that evening, filing out in a long line into the fading light. Most of the ferryshaft had moved to the back of the cave to be well out of the way. Storm, however, felt that this was likely his only chance to get a close look at a creasia without danger, and so he edged to the front of the crowd. He soon found himself surrounded by elders and prominent adults—the only other ferryshaft who seemed to have no fear of cats. They cast sidelong glances and frowns in Storm's direction, and one (Storm was pretty sure it was Kelsy's father) aimed a kick at him, which he dodged.

Storm watched the creasia file past with their cubs. He suspected that they birthed in the spring, like ferryshaft. The males were considerably larger than the females, and their coats were an array of brown and tan and gold. They completely ignored the ferryshaft, but occasionally scuffled among themselves. Storm thought he saw little groups within the larger group, and he wondered if creasia also had cliques. *What happens to their orphans? Are female cubs forced to choose a mate in order to survive?*

Gradually the stream of cats diminished. Storm felt the animal beside him grow tense. Looking toward the end of the line, he saw a cat, larger than all the rest and as black as starless night. He came last, his pace unhurried, watching the ferryshaft and the progress of the other creasia. Storm noticed that the adult ferryshaft around him—the wisest and strongest in the herd—all lowered their heads and averted their eyes.

When the black creasia reached the mouth of the cave, he turned and looked back—casually, as though to make sure he hadn't forgotten anything. Storm fancied that the green eyes focused on him, and he thought—although he was never quite sure—that the cat hesitated. Then something jerked Storm's tail so hard that he sat down. The legs and bodies of taller ferryshaft obscured his view of the creasia. The adult who'd already tried to kick him once landed a successful blow to his shoulder that sent him sprawling. Clearly, he was not welcome among the elite.

Storm turned to scramble away and caught sight of Pathar. To Storm's surprise, he looked quite angry. "Were you the one who jerked my tail?" asked Storm.

Pathar didn't answer. Instead, he bent his head and hissed in Storm's ear. "Do not make me sorry for spending so much time on you, Storm! What were you thinking, drawing attention to yourself like that? By all the ghosts of all our ancestors, we'll be lucky if he doesn't ask about you!"

Storm was bewildered and humiliated. Nearby ferryshaft were giving them a wide berth. Storm knew that they thought he was being berated for inserting himself among the herd leaders. But that wasn't what Pathar was saying.

"That black creasia...?"

"His name is Arcove. He's their king. You do not want him taking an interest in you."

"But why would he...?"

"Because of your color." Still talking softly, but with a furious expression, Pathar said, "Now, we are going to pretend that this fight ended our friendship. Ferryshaft know that I taught you. They link us, and that is unhealthy. We will not be seen together in public on friendly terms again. However, you may come to me at night or alone, and I will try to help. I am doing this to protect you, Storm."

Storm did not have to pretend to be hurt. Pathar snarled loudly, probably for the benefit of those watching, and turned away. Storm resisted the urge to call after him, to denounce him as a hypocrite and a coward. *You probably go to those "conferences" every year. Where else would Arcove ask about me? What do you talk to him about, Pathar? Do you decide how many of us will get slaughtered?*

But he kept quiet. He wanted to believe that his old teacher cared about him and really was trying to protect him.

To get his mind off it, Storm went to get a better look at the stone with the strange marking, now that the eastern end of the cave was free of creasia. He soon realized that the creasia side was substantially larger. It also included an area where bats nested, and a colony of rock rats that appeared to live on the insects attracted by the bats' dung. These things constituted a food source, which was absent from the ferryshaft side of the cave.

However, Storm did not think this had always been the case. From either side of the marked stone, he found a deep line gauged in the cave floor from front to back. It disappeared over places that were too rocky or uneven, but picked up again on the far side. The line ran through the bat colony.

This is the true boundary, thought Storm. *This line splits the cave evenly—fairly.* He was still thinking about the implications the next morning, when the ferryshaft herd finally left the cave.

20

Ambition

Callaris's new ru was called Valla—a dainty, cream-colored foal, small for her age, and timid. By the time the river froze, the clique had added another new member, as well—a big yearling male named Tarsis—orphaned in the first creasia raid. The clique actually turned away another, smaller male, who tried to join about the same time. *Mylo thinks he can afford to be picky,* thought Storm.

Maybe he did, or maybe he just didn't think they could support another light-weight. Two rues were a lot for an orphan clique to defend, and Valla did not bring down her share of prey.

Storm thought that Tarsis might be scheming to take over the clique after Mylo moved on. He was smart enough, and he could fight. However, he wasn't too ambitious to be patient. Mylo would be four years old in spring. Some ferryshaft took a mate at four, but

Mylo did not have the looks to attract an independent mate, and Tollee was not old enough. More likely, Mylo would stay with the clique until he was five and better able to defend a ru on his own. At that point, Tarsis might be big enough to consider fighting Callaris for control of the clique.

At least, that was what Storm, Tracer, and Leep thought would happen. "And then there's us," said Leep with a thump of tail, "the solid middle. Big enough to matter, not big enough to rule. Or probably to mate, either."

Tracer snorted. "You could have a mate this spring if you wanted."

Leep had been spending excessive amounts of time flirting with various female cliques. He was getting less embarrassed about it. "You think so? At three? I couldn't father a foal...could I?"

"I think there are a few who'd let you try," snickered Tracer.

"Oh, well, you're one to talk—you and that butterfly-eyed... what's her name?"

"I don't know what you're talking about," said Tracer sweetly. He had, indeed, been making eyes at a young adult female who'd lost her mate last year. She was not high-ranking or particularly pretty, but she laughed whenever Tracer tried to be funny, and she just happened to be on the edges of her clique whenever he came around.

"Well, alright, her name is Mia," said Tracer. He glanced at Storm. "And if *I* can find an interested female, anyone can."

Storm did not rise to the bait. He was looking up at the cliff from where they lay in the lee of a boulder.

Tracer nudged him. "Oh, come on, you don't even try."

Storm smiled. "I'm only a yearling."

"You'll be two this spring. Foals like us have to start early—"

"I'm not like you," said Storm. "I'm a runt." He still stood a head shorter than any ferryshaft his own age.

Tracer squirmed. "That doesn't mean—"

"They talk about your fur," put in Leep. "They notice you, believe me."

Storm snorted. "They notice me. That doesn't mean they want to mate with me."

"They're curious," persisted Leep. "Rumors still go around about how Kelsy couldn't catch you. All you'd have to do—"

"I'm not going to flirt with the female cliques until someone deigns to notice me," said Storm. "I'm going to fight Mylo for Tollee."

A moment of perfect silence greeted this announcement. Then Tracer and Leep both spoke at once.

"Oh, Storm, no!"

"Bad idea!"

"What did you just say about being a runt?"

"If you win a ru in a fight, she has to *choose* you afterward," said Tracer. "You don't have the right to claim her the way a rogan does who has supported her all winter. Even if you manage to beat Mylo…she could just walk away!"

"Then she'll walk away," said Storm, still staring at the cliff.

"You *won't* beat Mylo," said Leep. "Storm, tell me you're not about to do this tomorrow."

Storm finally looked at him. "Of course not. Next year, maybe."

"Good. Then there's time to talk you out of it."

"Yes," said Storm, "but you won't. Instead, maybe you should help me learn to fight." He'd been working on his plan since the start of winter. Storm could tell he was filling out, putting on muscle, gaining better coordination. When he skated this year, he rivaled the three and four-year-olds for agility. He took long runs in the winter twilight, pushing himself for speed, building muscle that would put power behind his kicks.

He'd found the sheep trails again, too. Slowly and methodically, he'd begun to learn some of the ones near the winter feeding grounds. He chose his favorites and memorized every leaf-thin ledge, every drop and gap. Out on the windy cliff face, Storm's small size and light weight were an asset. He was becoming bolder. He searched for the trails that led to caves. Sometimes he left prey there. He would return for it days later and find it frozen, still fresh and undisturbed. *I can help feed a foal, and I can protect a mate. I might do it differently than others, but I am capable.*

Except the mate he wanted was Tollee, and to win her, he would have to fight—and probably kill—his clique leader. Storm did not dislike Mylo. He didn't think Tollee disliked him, either. *But she doesn't want to be his mate. She feels trapped.* He saw it in her eyes every time someone mentioned the coming spring—one season closer to fulfilling the bargain she'd made for protection.

"Just wait for her," Leep told him reasonably. "She's only obligated to stay with Mylo for the number of years he was her rogan. That would be…"

"Four," said Storm flatly. Ordinarily, mating relationships were renegotiated on a yearly basis. They usually lasted for several years, occasionally a lifetime. However, the rules for rogans and rues were different.

"So four," said Leep, as though that were not longer than any of them had been alive. "And probably less. Sometimes the rogans break up those long partnerships after a couple of years. If Mylo sires big, healthy foals or fights his way up the hierarchy, the other females will take an interest. Anything could happen in four years!"

Storm shook his head. "You don't understand." *Tollee saved my life from those curbs. Now I'm going to save hers. I'm going to give her back her freedom. She can do whatever she wants with it.* He was by no means certain that she would want *him*, although he tried not to think about that. To Leep and Tracer, he said, "Why don't you just show me how to fight?"

They tried. To their credit, they tried hard, but Storm soon realized that neither of them were very good at it. There was a reason that Tracer and Leep were not contending for the top positions in their clique.

In desperation, Storm finally went to Tollee and explained, awkwardly, that he'd like to learn to fight. She gave him a strange look, but she didn't ask why. As the winter wound down, he spent long afternoons with her, ducking and dodging, and trying to flip her over.

"You're quick," Tollee told him. "So very quick, Storm, but you'll lose in the real thing unless you fight dirty. You don't have any weight behind your attacks."

"What do you mean by dirty?" Storm asked.

Tollee shrugged. "Hamstring your opponent. Open an artery and just keep dancing away until he bleeds out. Slash at the forehead so that he has blood in his eyes and can't see what he's doing. Or…you know…back him off a cliff…or over weak ice."

Storm frowned. Ferryshaft didn't usually fight like that. They did not fight to kill. There was always the chance that an opponent would simply surrender. "Did you do that to any of the males who harassed you?" He'd wanted to ask before, but never dared. *She would have been less than a year old. Could she have managed to kill another ferryshaft?*

Tollee looked away.

"You don't have to answer," said Storm quickly, but she interrupted him.

"One. I thought about a lot of ways to do it, but I only killed one."

Storm wanted to go to her and nuzzle her cheek, but he didn't think she'd like that.

Tollee kicked at a rock. "I went to Mylo right afterward. I didn't think I could do it again."

Her eyes met Storm's and he stared back wordlessly. He wondered whether she'd guessed what he was practicing for. He wondered whether she would tell him not to do it. *She could fight Mylo better than I could,* thought Storm. *But she won't.*

The herd might punish a ru who attacked her rogan, but Storm wasn't sure that was why Tollee wouldn't do it.

Maybe Mylo will yield. Maybe he doesn't really want Tollee. Maybe I won't have to kill him.

"Storm," said Tollee, "don't do anything stupid."

"I won't."

21

Riddle of an Island

So-fet foaled that spring. Dover would not let Storm enter the cave at first—behavior that Storm found infuriating. Storm believed that Dover still harbored a secret suspicion that he took food from So-fet when Dover was not looking.

So-fet called, "Storm, is that you?" and he brushed past Dover into the cave. She was standing at the back. A tiny head peered from around her legs. So-fet gave a tired smile. "Meet your sister, Storm."

Storm sidled nearer and lowered his head to sniff. The newborn foal looked up with big, inquiring eyes and chirped at him. Storm loved her at once. "She's so small…" he whispered.

So-fet laughed. "You were smaller."

Storm gave the baby a playful lick on the nose. "What's her name?"

"Sauny."

"It's a good name." The foal was mouse-brown—not an unusual color. But as Storm gazed into her bright eyes, he noticed that they were as gray as his own.

Sauny grew quickly. Soon she was sniffing among the rocks, never venturing more than a few lengths from her mother. Storm visited them often. He renewed his habit of bringing small gifts of rare food, which seemed to appease Dover. Sauny adored her brother. One of her first half-pronounced words was "Sorm."

Storm's summer coat came in even paler than last year's. He was the color of smudged snow, almost white in places. *What must you think of my fur now, Pathar?* He thought of Pathar's ancient, graying muzzle. *We're almost the same color!* Storm had not spoken to his old teacher since the scene in the cave. He knew he might have sought him out at night among the rocks, but he didn't. He was tempted, as he tried to learn to fight, but something held him back—a bitterness that lodged in his throat and made it hard to talk. *If Pathar is ashamed to be seen speaking to me, perhaps it's better that we not speak.*

When they crossed the fields to Chelby Lake, Storm slowed his pace to match Sauny's. He was prepared to join So-fet and Dover in protecting her if they needed to spend a dangerous night alone upon the open plain. However, Sauny made the walk a little ahead of most of the other newborns. She was bright and alert early the next morning. "Look, Storm, look! Big trees!"

Dover groaned, and So-fet yawned. Storm got up. "Can I take her for a walk in Chelby Wood? We won't go far."

"Please," muttered Dover.

When the foal entered the trees, she was speechless with wonder. Seeing her here for the first time reminded Storm of his own first visit to Chelby Wood—one of his earliest memories. The scent of loamy earth, the play of dappled shadows, the sounds of birds, and the noises of squirrels among the leaves—it was all new again.

Finally, they reached the lake—cool and still in the late morning sunlight. Sauny let out a gasp of pleasure. "Storm! What is it?"

"That's Chelby Lake, Sauny. Soon I'll teach you to swim in it."

The baby gave an unintelligible reply and ambled down to the water, where she amused herself by wading on the edges and watching the minnows dart away. "What are they?! What are they?!" She squealed in excitement as she chased the flitting forms, trying to catch them in her mouth.

Storm laughed. "They're fish. Sometimes, if you sit very still, you can catch one of the big ones."

Sauny vowed to try, but she couldn't achieve more than an instant of stillness before leaping after the minnows again, squealing and splashing. At last, she grew tired and came over to sit with Storm on the bank. "What's that?"

Storm followed her gaze over the water. "Oh. That's Kuwee Island."

Sauny tottered up again. "Let's go there!"

"No, little one," smiled Storm. "No one goes there. You wouldn't like it—just a lot of vines and trees..."

He stopped. *What am I saying? I have no idea what's on Kuwee. I'm just repeating the sort of things Pathar said.* Storm felt disgusted with himself. "Sauny, someday I'll take you to the island...when you're big enough to swim that far." Sauny cocked her head at Storm's serious tone. Then a dragonfly caught her attention, and she dashed, snapping, after it.

Summer melted away, but Storm could not forget that conversation by the lake. Sauny's speech improved, and she began to play with other foals. Storm doubted that she even remembered what he had said about Kuwee Island, but his own words gnawed at him. Was he starting to think like an adult, keeping secrets that he didn't even understand?

Storm realized that he knew less about Kuwee Island than about Groth—surely a much more dangerous place. *Even Pathar said the island wasn't dangerous. What did he say...that we are afraid of the past?*

Storm had explored most of the plain and wood in the vicinity of Chelby Lake, and Kuwee Island became more enticing by the day. He could not have said for sure when he decided to swim over, but he knew when he woke that morning that he was going. It was early fall, and if he waited any longer, the water would be too cold. He debated on whether he should take anyone with him. Certainly he would not take Sauny, not until he knew what was over there. She wasn't a strong enough swimmer yet in any case. He thought about asking Leep or Tracer to accompany him. He wanted to ask Tollee. But he was afraid that one of them might try to stop him. In the end, he asked none of them and told no one.

Storm arrived at the edge of Chelby Lake just after sunup. A light mist hung over the water. He measured the distance with his eyes. It would be a long swim, but he had been swimming a lot lately—trying to strengthen his legs for the fight with Mylo.

Storm's fur had already started to thicken for winter, and the cold water took several moments to penetrate to his skin as he waded out. Soon he was paddling. The mist swirled around his head, making him uneasy. On land, he could see above the haze, but at eye-level with the water, the mist blocked his view of the island and all but obscured the shore.

Storm swam steadily on, the fog growing ever worse. He began to imagine shapes in the gray streamers—a shore that never materialized, phantom trees that retreated from him. He glanced back and found that he could no longer see the shore of the lake. *Storm, you fool, couldn't you have waited until the fog burned off? You had all summer to do this! Why choose today?* For a few sickening moments, Storm thought that he might have passed the island, that he might be swimming beyond Kuwee into the vastness of Chelby Lake. He wondered if he should try to go back. He wondered if he would just swim in circles until he drowned.

The sight of trees rising out of the mist came as a great relief. Moments later, Storm struggled out of the water onto a strip of sand and rock. The beach was not wide—three lengths at the most—and beyond rose a dense forest. Storm grinned and shook himself. He was standing on forbidden ground.

After a few moments' rest, he began to investigate the forest's edge. He found little in the way of trails—none of the usual beaten tracks that ferryshaft had wound through Chelby Wood. At last, he found what he took to be a deer trail—faint and rarely used—but it gave him a starting point to penetrate the underbrush.

Dim light filtered through the canopy as he started up the trail, and the fog was as bad as it had been over the water. Storm noticed that many of the trees were blackened and gave off a strange odor. He recalled that Pathar had once pointed out a tree struck by lightning with a similar smell and appearance. Storm struggled to remember the word for what had happened to the tree. *Fire. Fire is extremely hot and bright. It spreads and kills things, and often comes from lightning.*

Is that why the adults don't come here? But the fire had clearly not been recent, as underbrush had grown since. Storm could not smell anything that made him think of predators.

He wandered on along the faint line of the deer track, angling slightly uphill. He was beginning to feel vaguely disappointed. *What am I looking for? What did I expect to find? A creasia den? A nest of curbs? A whole cave full of strange symbols? A monster?*

He began to wonder if there was anything at all on the little island. The air was stuffy beneath the trees and quiet. At last, he stumbled over something lying beneath ferns. Curious, Storm reached down and, after a little digging, pulled the object free.

It was a skull. A brief examination assured him that it had not belonged to a deer. It was a ferryshaft skull. However, it was obviously many years old—brittle and decaying. Storm considered it thoughtfully. How had it come to be in this forbidden place?

As he continued, he found more bones. In fact, he soon realized that the island was covered with them. Some were ferryshaft, and some were another creature that Storm could not identify. Once he found a massive creasia jaw bone. *What killed them?*

Storm left the deer track and began to struggle directly uphill. He wanted to see what was at the island's crest. He was soon above the mist and walking through streamers of sunlight as the trees thinned. He saw bones everywhere now that he was looking for them. Many were half-buried, and all seemed to be about the same age.

At last, he came out of the trees into a clearing, where sunlight shone on warm grass. Here, the island's hilltop rose sharply to a crest of bare, blackened rock. *Lightning,* thought Storm. *This place has been struck by lightning, probably many times.* It explained the clearing and the signs of fire on the trees.

More bones poked through the grass around the hill. Storm identified two more ferryshaft skulls, along with parts of many skeletons. He found more of the strange creatures' bones, too—ribs that looked impossibly large and huge vertebrae. Again, all the bones seemed to be of about the same age.

He crossed the clearing and circled the rocky outcrop at its center. He had a mind to climb to the top and see whether he could get a view of the mainland over the trees. As he searched for the best way up, he rounded the hill and found a wide-mouthed cave angling down into it. The cave was not as large as the Volontaro cave, but it was still one of the largest he'd ever seen.

Storm ventured inside hesitantly. Some irrational part of his mind kept insisting that this was a monster's lair, but he fought it down. Any predator must feed regularly, and all of the bones were old. Whatever had killed them was long gone.

The black stone of Kuwee Island looked very different from the red rock of the cliff-side caves or the white, porous rock of the Sea Cliffs. Storm found translucent blue crystals growing on the walls. He grew bolder as his eyes adjusted to the gloom. He took a drink from a hollow in the rock and promptly spat it out because of the unpleasant mineral taste. Near the back of the cave, he found an enormous skull. The jaw was missing, but he still had a clear sense of the size of the beast. At first, he thought it was a creasia, but surely it was too large, even for that. This animal could have swallowed Storm without chewing.

A drop of water pattered on his shoulders, and Storm looked up. There was something wrong with the ceiling of the cave. The colors did not make sense—lines of white, a splash of pink. Storm backed in a slow circle, trying to understand. He kept feeling as though he'd almost grasped something important, only to lose the thread.

The enormous skull, the huge vertebrae, the lines on the ceiling... "It's a telshee," he breathed. He knew it an instant before he made sense of what he was looking at.

An image had been created on the ceiling. Storm could not guess how it had been done. A thick, white line delineated the long, coiling body of a telshee. The creature's face looked down on the center of the cave. It had one huge eye, made of a polished lump of blue crystal. Where the other eye should have been, Storm saw only a rounded indention in the stone, as though someone had scooped it out. The telshee's mouth was open, and Storm could see its pink tongue and long, white teeth. However, it looked more as though it were trying to say something than as though it were about to attack.

Storm stared at it for a long time. "What happened here?" he whispered. "Did ferryshaft and telshees fight? Or did something else kill both of us? What about the creasia jawbone? Who made this image? How? Why?"

Only the wind replied.

22

The Rules

As fall drew to a close, Storm found himself in a state of unexpected hostility with his mother and Dover over Sauny's education. She had progressed wonderfully that summer—learning to swim and fish and identify edible plants. She could play sholo as well as any yearling, and she'd acquired a group of well-placed friends, all foals with two parents and good social standing in the herd.

Sauny will never be a ru, thought Storm with pride. He had supervised many of her lessons, pushing her beyond what was usually expected of a female foal who had yet to see her first winter. Indeed, Dover clearly believed that Storm was overly-aggressive with Sauny's education, pointing out that she would never need to live by her own wits alone. So-fet did not like the long runs away from the herd on which Storm sometimes took his sister, and both parents objected when Storm and Sauny brought down a young deer late in the fall. Ferryshaft did not eat much meat in summer; there was no need, and deer could be dangerous game.

"All it would take is one kick!" thundered Dover, after Sauny had gone off with her friends. "One broken rib, Storm, and she'd start her first winter crippled! Is that what you want?"

"And how much easier will it be when she's faint with hunger and chasing a sheep through the boulder mazes?" snapped Storm. "At least now she knows how to bring down large game."

"It will be a year or more before that's expected!" snarled Dover. "I am her father, and I will provide her with assistance, as will her mother and her clique." Storm noted that the need for his own assistance was distinctly absent.

"Please let us raise her, Storm," said So-fet.

Storm could tell that she was tired of arguing, but Dover's sullen expression drew his ire. "What if you're killed in the first creasia raid," he shot. "What will she do then?"

Storm thought that his stepfather might strike him. Dover's ears settled flat back, and he raised a front hoof. "You will not speak that way to me, runt."

So-fet's head shot up. "Dover!"

"You haven't told her, have you?" said Storm, giving no ground. "You haven't told her about the creasia?" He was looking at his mother now.

"We will not speak of such things—!" began Dover, but So-fet cut in.

"How would that help, Storm?"

"It would prepare her!" exclaimed Storm. "She wouldn't be so shocked, and she'd know what to do."

"What she'll do is run," said Dover tightly, "just like everyone else. There's no technique, nothing to learn. Now, you will not speak of such things again in the presence of my mate or my foal. If I find that you have done so, you and I will have a serious altercation. Do you understand?"

"Dover, please," murmured So-fet.

Dover's blazing eyes never left Storm's face. "I understand," grated Storm. He walked away, but Dover surprised him by catching up a few paces distant. He trotted around Storm, and stopped in front of him, legs stiff, tail bristling. "Vearil," he spat in a voice too low to carry to So-fet.

Storm flinched without meaning to. It was what the adults had called him when he was no older than Sauny—unlucky, an ill omen, unfit to live.

"You're not of my blood," hissed Dover. "I have let my mate's compassion affect my opinion of you, but no more. You are the ill-favored child of a hapless, short-lived father—weak stock. You try to claim my foal because you will never make one of your own. If Sauny and So-fet did not dote on you, I would send you from here bleeding. Do not presume to challenge my authority over my family again, Storm Ela-ferry."

Out of the corners of his eyes, Storm saw other ferryshaft watching. *He's putting on a show,* thought Storm. *Why? Because others have been talking?*

Storm had been feeling very grown-up that summer. Now, he suddenly felt very young again, acutely aware that he was a small foal, only two years old, facing a full-grown, angry adult. He thought, *This is what the fight with Mylo will be like...except I'll have done something to really make him angry, and I haven't done anything to Dover.*

Storm turned and walked away. He half expected Dover to pursue or even to strike at him, but his stepfather seemed satisfied. *You've re-established your place in the herd,* he thought bitterly. *By making sure that everyone knows the runt isn't telling you what to do.*

Later, as Storm jogged beside the river with Sauny on the herd's annual migration, he wrestled with the problem of whether to defy her parents and tell her about the cats. "Sauny, there are certain problems in winter."

She smiled at him. "I know. Mother told me that last year there was a big wind, but this year, there won't be…because the herd elders said so."

Storm took a deep breath. "Last year, there was a Volontaro. They don't happen very often. But…many ferryshaft still die in winter—"

"Oh, I know we'll be hungry. Mother told me, but you taught me to hunt!" She gave a little skip—somewhat muted, because the long walk was wearing on her.

Storm didn't know what to say. Dover and So-fet were walking a few lengths away. They probably couldn't hear everything he said, because of the trampling of thousands of ferryshaft feet and their chatter as they walked. Still, he caught Dover glancing at him from time to time. Storm had half-expected another altercation, but Dover seemed confident in his authority.

Why shouldn't he be? thought Storm. *Sauny is not my foal, only my half-sister. And maybe he's right. Maybe she doesn't need to know about the creasia yet.*

Storm glanced sidelong at Sauny—her coat a glossy red-gold, her legs already longer than his had been at the same age. Sauny had never been mocked by the other foals as far as he could tell. She had two parents and a brother watching over her. He did not feel jealous, but he did feel a little distant. *Her life will be so different from mine… Maybe I have nothing to teach that's worth learning. Maybe I should just follow the rules.*

The next morning, at the foot of the cliffs, Storm felt the tension in the herd which told him that the "conference" was in session. The weather remained clear, however, and soon the ferryshaft were behaving normally again.

The winter snows came. Storm spent more time with his clique and less time around Sauny. However, he sought her out on the day that the Igby froze hard enough for skating. As he'd expected, she was excited.

"Oh, Storm, it looks like so much fun! But I don't want to break a leg! Storm, show me how to do it!"

Storm was laughing. "Alright, but you have to hold still. Come down to the ice…carefully! That's right. Now, lock your legs like this. I'll push you, and you can see what it feels like."

He'd seen siblings and even parents teach foals to skate this way. No one had done it for him, and he was curious to see how well Sauny would manage. Quite well, as it turned out. She squealed when he got them going fast, but as soon as she slowed down, she begged him to do it again. Sauny had begun to make tentative steps and pushing motions of her own, when Storm noticed a disturbance among the foals in his clique. They'd been playing older games out towards the middle of the river. Now, Callaris seemed to be having a standoff with another foal that Storm didn't recognize.

"Sauny," he said, "why don't you see if you can skate back to the bank? Carefully now! See where those foals are sliding down? It's a fun game, and they look about your age."

When she'd gone, Storm moved rapidly towards the center of the river, occasionally rearing up for a better look. The group of foals around his clique seemed vaguely familiar. He caught sight of Valla, standing uncertainly behind Callaris, and he understood. *Someone has challenged Callaris for his ru. Again.* Valla was much too pretty for her own good. She had a particularly pleasant scent, and a season's growth had only added to her appeal.

There's going to be a fight. While clique members were all-but-required to assist their leader in a fight for *his* ru, no such imperative drove them to assist lesser males. Friends often did help each other, and Mylo had helped Callaris drive off several other suitors. However, the rest of the clique had not gotten involved in previous fights over Valla. She did not hunt as effectively as Tollee, and it was the generally—though quietly—held opinion that her loss would be an improvement.

So why are they all excited now? Storm could see Leep's dark shape beyond Callaris, bristling hugely. Tracer was snarling, and even Tollee looked ruffled. Then he caught sight of the foal opposite Mylo, and at last the pieces fell into place.

Kelsy. Someone in Kelsy's clique had challenged Callaris. Not Kelsy himself, by the look of it, but one of his high-ranking subordinates. *And the whole clique may fight,* he thought, *because we've got a score to settle.*

Storm knew that Mylo had been itching to have a go at Kelsy ever since the incident with Ally. It wasn't so much that Mylo cared about Ally. The runt had been strange and simple-minded, but he didn't eat much, and he had a good nose. His brother, Ishy, had been the best tracker in the clique and one of Mylo's friends. Storm knew that Mylo credited Kelsy with Ishy's decline and death because of what had happened to Ally. *Mylo will fight, and he'll make it personal.*

Storm's heart was beginning to pound as he skidded to a stop among the onlookers. Callaris and Kelsy's subordinate had begun to make feints at each other, but Mylo and Kelsy were the real attraction. Storm didn't know what had been said before his arrival, but their blood was clearly up as they circled each other with hackles raised to their ears. They were both the same age—four years old, almost adults. Mylo had filled out in the last year and looked formidable with his torn ears and scarred muzzle. Kelsy was just as tall, but less massive and, Storm suspected, quicker.

A strange, half-formed idea twisted unpleasantly in the back of Storm's mind. *Can Mylo beat Kelsy?* Mylo looked fiercer, but nobody achieved Kelsy's status without being able to fight. He demonstrated the fact an instant later by making a feint, catching Mylo off balance, and sending him heavily to the ice with a cracking hoof blow. Mylo was up again in an instant and managed a shove that almost knocked Kelsy off balance and tore out a mouthful of fur. But it was only fur and no blood.

Behind them, Storm could see Callaris and his challenger snapping at each other—awkward because of the ice. The rest of the two cliques were bristling and growling, but not attacking, not yet. It looked to Storm as though Kelsy's clique had shrunk over the last year. *Probably because a lot of four and five year olds have found mates and gone off on their own.* Still, he hoped they didn't all fight. It might go ill for his friends if they did.

Storm saw a speckling of blood on the ice. Kelsy had caught one of Mylo's ragged ears and made it even more ragged. "Maybe *you* should have run away," Kelsy spat.

Storm felt a jolt. *Was Mylo taunting him about me earlier?*

The terrible thought squirmed again. *What if Kelsy kills him? Or wounds him badly enough that…that he can't defend a ru?* It was an unworthy thought, but Storm's mind raced on. *I can't beat Mylo. I know I can't. I've known all summer. But what if Kelsy does it for me?*

Stop! Storm ordered himself. *Mylo let me join his clique when no one else would have me—even though I'm small and a strange color. I can't wish this on him. He doesn't deserve it.*

You're not doing anything to him, answered the horrible, reasonable part of his mind. *You're just watching.*

"You're a bully and a thief," panted Mylo, "and so is your father." He managed to land a solid kick to Kelsy's shoulder, but Kelsy spun away as though he didn't feel it.

"At least he's alive," said Kelsy cheerfully. Storm could tell that Kelsy was winning, and he intended to win *hard*. Maybe he wouldn't kill Mylo, but he was going to hurt him.

In Storm's mind, possibilities blossomed—Tollee, easily won from a crippled rogan, her rare smiles growing more frequent, days and nights together, a foal in spring to play with Leep and Tracer's foals. He would bring up his own foal the way he wanted to bring up Sauny—with no secrets, and all the answers and all the skills he could provide. As Mylo staggered and Kelsy's teeth drew more blood, Storm's daydreams took wing. He hated himself, but he couldn't help it. He was watching the birth of his own freedom. He was watching…alone.

Storm felt a moment of vertigo. He'd been standing with a crowd of other foals. Now, he was inexplicably alone. Out of the corners of his eyes, he saw running ferryshaft—not playing tag, but running hard for the bank. He realized that the screams ringing in his ears were not insults shouted between the two cliques, but cries of fear.

Then Storm was running, too, because ferryshaft only ran like that for one reason. And then the reason was in front of him. Storm veered to keep from sliding into a cat, but another was looming over him, and then he was backing away into a frantic companion. The knot of ferryshaft around him were shoving and struggling, and everywhere he looked, he saw another cat.

It's happened, he thought, numbly. *Just like it happened the first time I skated three winters ago…only this time, it's happening to me.*

He looked over his shoulder and had to stifle a hysterical laugh. The creasia had scooped up nearly every foal from Mylo and Kelsy's cliques. *We were the ones not paying attention—the ones who ran too late.*

Kelsy looked truly frightened for the first time that Storm had ever seen. In a great stroke of irony, Mylo was leaning against him, gasping and bleeding, his eyes screwed shut. Leep had ended up on one side of Storm, Tollee on the other, and Tracer was behind him. They looked at each other wordlessly, breathless from flight and terror.

Then Tollee's eyes seemed to glaze. She turned her full attention to the creasia and bared her teeth. *She wants to die fighting,* thought Storm, *die with some dignity.*

But there would be no dignity. There never was in the brutal moments after the creasia selected their victims. Those who fought hardest usually died worst. *No one ever escapes. That's the rule.*

Storm looked at the creasia pacing around them. The animals had never seemed so huge or so terrifying. *So this is how it ends.*

No mates, no foals for any of them, no more playful springs or lazy summers. All the pain and struggle of winters past... It all came down to this—an ugly, meaningless death with his little sister watching. *No one ever escapes. That's the rule.*

One of so many rules.

Storm felt as though the world had gone silent. He glanced at his friends again. He wanted a last look at them. As he did so, Storm's eyes met Kelsy's, and he thought Kelsy said something, although he couldn't be certain. Then Storm looked at the creasia. Their pacing had slowed, as it always did just before they attacked.

How important are the rules to you? Very important...I hope.

23

A Problem

Sharmel counted again. Seventeen. "I thought I said ten."

An officer at his side squirmed. "The clutter got excited, sir."

"They always get excited."

"It's not my fault," said the other creasia. "The subordinates do the killing. Why don't you talk to them instead of lashing at the officers?" He walked away stiff-legged.

Sharmel sighed. *Well, we can't very well put them back. Easier to just cancel the next raid.* He raised his head to give the attack signal, but it seemed unnecessary.

One small, pale-colored foal had darted out of the knot of doomed ferryshaft, straight past Tharia. When this sort of thing happened, the subordinate creasia generally let their instincts take over. Tharia paced the foal for a moment before pouncing. However, to everyone's surprise, the foal changed direction at the last moment, so that she missed by a paw's breadth. She gave a small, frustrated growl and pounced again. This time, the foal changed directions so violently that Tharia's back legs went out from under her as she tried to follow.

Her companions, still pacing around the selected ferryshaft, snickered. Even Sharmel smiled. It was a comical sight, and Tharia did not often inspire comedy.

She roared and charged after the fleeing foal. Sharmel couldn't help thinking of a rabbit zigzagging under a hawk. *Where did it learn to do that?*

And then it disappeared into the trees.

Sharmel blinked. *What just happened?*

Every creasia on the ice stood still for a moment, and then they were all roaring and snarling and calling after Tharia as she disappeared in pursuit of the rogue foal. The pacing ring around the trapped group of ferryshaft broke up as the clutter wavered in the face of this unexpected event. Sharmel knew he should tell them what to do, but he wasn't sure himself.

When was the last time a selected ferryshaft had managed to get out of sight of the clutter? *Not in years!* Humiliation replaced astonishment. They were like cubs, playing with a mouse in their own den. They were so certain that it could not escape that they'd been careless, and somehow it had walked right out from under their noses.

We have to catch it.

The whole clutter seemed to realize this at once as Tharia did not emerge from the trees. With a collective snarl, they charged after her, Sharmel on their heels.

Storm ran. He did not think. He let his body do what it had done a hundred times before, and oddly, even as the creasia's deadly paws dropped down beside him…and missed…and missed again—even as the cat roared behind him—he felt himself relax. Sound came back into the world.

And then he hit a snow drift on the edge of the river. It was not high yet, for winter was still young, and Storm cleared it with a leap. He landed belly-deep and struggling. The cat jumped, too, and landed almost on top of him, but then Storm found the top of frozen crust. He was light, and he did not break through. The cat did, and he heard it crashing along furiously behind him.

He could hear the rest of the cats calling from out on the river. Were they coming closer? He hoped so. *Chase me. I'm the one who broke the rules. I'm the one you have to catch. Leave the others. Please.*

Storm was on a beaten path now, almost into the boulders. The running was easier, but it would be easier for the creasia, too. He thought the snow had given him enough of a lead to get beyond their sight among the rocks. *Make them run by scent. The curbs taught me that.*

He resisted the urge to look back.

Sharmel's embarrassment was solidifying into anger. His clutter was not listening to him. These cats hadn't chased a ferryshaft in so long that they had forgotten how, and their anger produced stupid mistakes. He'd shouted at them as they entered the trees to swing wide beneath the dense pines where the snow was shallow. If they'd done so, they could have easily flanked the foal, who'd bounded into a deep drift. Instead, they followed the ferryshaft and wasted precious time floundering through deep snow. Tharia broke the trail, and they'd all caught up with her by the time they emerged near the boulders.

Sharmel had taken his own advice and was well ahead of his clutter as he followed the foal into the mazes. The animal changed direction immediately, laying a weaving path through the rocks.

Sharmel barely managed to keep him in sight, even though he was right behind.

I'll catch him myself, thought Sharmel. *I'll make an example of him…and then I may have to make an example of this clutter!*

He could almost hear Ariand laughing: *"Sharmel's raiding party spent half the morning tramping around the boulder mazes chasing some foal!"*

Sharmel gritted his teeth. If the foal would just stop weaving and give him a clear pounce… He'd gotten a better look at it now. The foal was male, small but not as young as he'd first thought… and an odd color.

Then, to Sharmel's delight and relief, the foal started up a cliff path. The animal must not know that this path dead-ended a short way up. *He's just a panicked youngster,* thought Sharmel, *and now this little exercise is about to end.*

Sharmel slowed, secure in his confidence, as he followed the foal up the trail. *Will he beg for his life when he realizes he can't escape? Is it possible that some other ferryshaft trained him to do this? Could he be coerced into giving names?* Sharmel slowed a little more, wanting to give his subordinates time to catch up. *Perhaps,* he reflected, *I should let them do the killing after all.* They were so excited that only the sight of blood was likely to cool them.

Sharmel caught sight of the end of the path. Oddly, the foal wasn't slowing down. *Does he plan to make an end of himself before we can?* Sharmel bounded forward.

However, they were approaching the end of the trail faster than the cat had judged, and with one final leap Storm cleared the path and hit the sheep trail. He gave a triumphant whoop and sped away, bounding as effortlessly as a wild ram over the narrow thread of rock.

Sharmel skidded to a stop, panting and blinking. The idea that the foal might escape had never occurred to him. He had expected ridicule for even allowing such a thing to trouble him. But *this*… There was absolutely no excuse for *this*!

As he stared after the ferryshaft, he noticed the color again—*really* noticed it for the first time. He watched until the foal disappeared, probably into a cave, and then turned with a grimace to deal with his oncoming clutter. A moment later, a long, wavering howl made Sharmel bristle to his tail-tip. He knew then that he would be running all night, pushing for Leeshwood and home. He needed to report this. *Arcove, I think we have a problem.*

Part II

Arcove

1

Daydreams and Nightmares

He walked in darkness. How long he'd been there, he could not say. Occasionally, he distinguished the silhouettes of rocks or faint light reflecting off pools of water. He stayed well away from the water. Sometimes he heard noises—rustling, the rattle of pebbles, a soft sigh like fur over stone.

I will not run.

But he walked faster. He was looking for something…something he did not think he would find. He heard dripping, and that was normal, but then he heard a sharp patter, like an animal shaking water from its fur. Another swish, closer this time.

I will not break. I will not run.

Somewhere in the darkness, something began to laugh. "Hello, Arcove."

Then he ran.

Arcove woke with a start. It was late afternoon. Nadine stood over him, her eyes worried. Roup grimaced from a couple of lengths away. "You scratched me, Arcove."

The black cat sat up slowly, shaking his head to clear the afterimages. "How bad?"

"You mostly missed."

"Well, if you ever challenge me, I suppose you should do it while I'm asleep." Arcove avoided their eyes. "Did I startle anyone else?"

"Only Nadine. She didn't want to wake you."

"A wise mate." He did not add, *And a foolish friend.*

"Hunt?" offered Roup.

Arcove glanced at the sky. Evening was still hours away, and Leeshwood slept. Nadine nudged him. "Go on. If you sleep, you'll only dream again."

Arcove's tail lashed, but he didn't argue. Instead, he stepped lightly around three sleeping cubs, circled the hot spring that made this cave so comfortable, and started through the winter ferns towards the stream. Roup followed without a word. When he reached the stream, Arcove kept going. He trotted along the bank past three likely fishing spots.

Roup kept quiet and let him think.

"I haven't done that in years," said Arcove at last.

Roup almost said, *A gray ferryshaft hasn't outwitted a hunting party in years,* but he didn't. "What is it you dream about?"

Arcove slowed and waded into the shallows. The stream was called Smoky Branch on account of the hot springs that fed it. In winter, a hazy cloud of steam always hung over the water. It rarely froze. "Someone who's probably dead."

Roup splashed after him. "You really think so?"

"No." Arcove's paw flashed at a fish and missed. He was moving too much, tail twitching. Many fish wintered here, but they weren't torpid this early in the year.

Roup sat still and watched the silver bodies dart. "You think he could have something to do with that foal?"

Arcove considered. "If you wanted to cause trouble by training a ferryshaft to attack creasia, wouldn't you choose a gray one? And Sharmel said he howled."

"The howl was probably instinct," said Roup, "I don't think they're even teaching the foals not to howl anymore. The adults never do it, and the foals don't even know that they're not supposed to."

Arcove grunted. He struck half-heartedly at another fish.

Roup had a momentary flashback of a similar conversation in this very stream when they were little older than cubs. Arcove had been leading a clutter, then, and not all of Leeshwood. Roup, however, had done the same thing he was doing now.

"I think if Keesha wanted to get your attention, he'd do it more directly," said Roup.

Arcove laughed—a short, deep chuckle that temporarily dispersed all fish.

"I think this foal is just a foal," continued Roup. "Although he sounds bright. He didn't actually attack Sharmel's clutter. He just led them a chase. They were over-confident, and he went somewhere that they couldn't follow."

"Is that what you're going to say at council this evening?"

"Yes."

"And how do you think we should respond?"

Roup hesitated. "Halvery will tell you that we should find the foal and dismember him in front of the entire herd as an example. Treace will want to kill a hundred ferryshaft in retribution...but not the foal. He'll make the herd kill the foal themselves. Sharmel will try to agree with everyone, because he's embarrassed about what happened. Ariand will volunteer to go track down the foal himself because he'd rather deal with problems as he finds them."

Arcove smiled. "You've answered everything but my question."

Roup watched the fish. "You know what I think."

"I haven't heard you say it in a while."

"Because nobody listens."

"I always listen."

"Stop the raids," said Roup. "I know you're afraid of what will happen if they outnumber us, but every raid gives them a reason to fight. Don't make a martyr out of this foal, Arcove. Go talk to him yourself. Ask him why he did it."

Arcove laughed again, this time a little wistfully. "You think all the clutters will respect that...course of action?"

"Probably not. Treace will probably challenge you, backed by a quarter of Leeshwood. You'll kill him, they'll settle down, and the wood will be a better place."

"I don't know why you so dislike Treace. He's young. He's intelligent."

"Young, yes," said Roup. "Born in peacetime. He wants war, and he doesn't even know what it is."

"I don't think he wants war."

"He wants something. He's too quiet and too involved with all the discontents in every clutter. He'll challenge you one of these days."

"And, as you say, I'll kill him," said Arcove.

"If he doesn't cheat."

"That's a serious accusation, Roup."

"And I mean it seriously, Arcove." Roup dipped his head and caught a fish. It was the first time he'd struck since they'd started.

"Show-off."

"You weren't even trying," said Roup around a mouthful of squirming fish. He let the fish's furiously slapping tail touch the water, spraying Arcove in the face.

Arcove growled, but it was all play. "Oh, I'm trying now. I think I see a fish I can catch."

"That would be cheating."

"No, that would be winning."

And then they were splashing each other and chasing around the sun-dappled shallows. *There's your real laugh,* thought Roup. *Let's be cubs again…for just a little while.*

By evening, Arcove's officers had assembled on the warm rocks at the foot of the cliff for council. Sharmel had arrived late that morning. Arcove had let his news circulate throughout the wood, but had not asked his officers to report until nightfall. No sense in waking everyone for something that did not appear to be an emergency.

Roup let Arcove arrive first. It would only make Halvery more jealous if Arcove appeared to be discussing the problem with Roup before addressing the council. As Roup approached the meeting place, he heard voices already raised in argument.

"I can't agree with you," came Sharmel's smooth drawl. "That was a prearranged performance. No ferryshaft foal could rush onto a sheep trail and survive without knowing exactly what he was doing."

So much for agreeing with everyone, thought Roup. He'd rarely heard Sharmel so adamant.

"Well, you must admit that it sounds fantastic!" sneered Halvery. "A foal learns to run on the cliffs, then decides to try the trick on a bunch of creasia. He casually attacks them, then—"

"I didn't say that he *casually* attacked us, but I know that he didn't reach the end of the trail and go off on impulse. That foal knew what he was doing from the moment he set foot on that path—possibly from the moment he ran."

Halvery snorted. "I think it far more likely that he ran in blind panic and got lucky. He probably fell trying to get back to the path. He's probably lying dead at the foot of the cliffs as we speak."

"Luck had nothing to do with it," growled Sharmel. "I doubt very much that he's dead."

"I think we're missing the point." Ariand tried to step between Halvery and Sharmel. He was smaller than either of them, the lowest ranking of Arcove's officers. "The question is not what this foal did or how he did it. The question is: will he do it again?"

"And that," said Sharmel, "comes back to what I was saying. If he ran out of fear, he won't try again—not unless he's unlucky enough to get selected twice for the cull. But if he planned the whole thing..."

"He will try again." Everyone looked at Arcove—a darker shadow beneath the rock overhang. "If a ferryshaft succeeds once, he will continue to try until he is stopped. We have to decide how we're going to deal with that."

Treace spoke. He was the youngest of the officers, although he already outranked Ariand. "The herd must be punished. If we kill enough of them, they will see the futility in revolt."

Arcove flicked his tail. "Killing too many only makes them more determined."

Treace frowned.

"I think we should invite the foal to council," said Roup.

Halvery started to laugh.

Roup ignored him and continued. "They're three generations removed from the war. What do the youngsters think about us? Do they have any idea why we kill them? Maybe it's time for a new treaty."

Halvery's laugh turned nasty. "Now *that* is the most ridiculous thing anyone has said."

Roup kept talking. "Charder is tired and beaten. I don't think he even knows which way the wind is blowing. Pick one of the young ferryshaft who's clever and wants change. Put him in charge. Renegotiate the treaty. We might be able to stop the raids without risking reprisal."

Halvery snarled. "Stop the raids, and they will outnumber us three-to-one in five years or less. They'll come to Leeshwood some year and boil us in our own hot springs."

"You think that won't happen if we keep antagonizing them?"

"I think if you had your way, we'd hunt for them and babysit their foals!"

It was an old argument between the two highest-ranking officers. Sharmel and Ariand shifted uncomfortably. Treace uncurled with a yawn. "Why would we ever stop the raids?" he murmured, his sharp eyes on Roup. "It gives the subordinates something to look forward to."

Arcove spoke before Roup could. "I thank you all for your opinions in this matter. The episode with Sharmel's raiding party may mean much or little. We'll know soon.

"Sharmel, you will discipline your clutter on the proper hunting of ferryshaft. These animals are intelligent. They are not deer. They cannot be hunted like deer. Your clutter gave a sloppy performance in front of the entire ferryshaft herd. I trust I will not have to revisit this subject."

Sharmel's ears drooped. Roup could see he wanted to tuck his tail, but refrained with a modicum of remaining dignity. "No, sir, you will not."

"Good. Treace, go learn everything you can about this foal. Learn his name, his parents, his friends, his background, everything. Even if he's dead, I want to know."

"And then kill these animals?" asked Treace.

"Not yet." Arcove left the overhang and strolled into the deepening twilight. "We also need someone to go on another raid immediately. I think the foal will attack again, but I may be wrong. At any rate, I want to know how this affected the rest of the herd. Have they been inspired to open revolt, or is this individual still acting alone?"

"I'll go," said Ariand.

Arcove inclined his head, and the group broke up. "Well, that happened almost the way you predicted," muttered Arcove to Roup.

Roup flicked his tail. "The foal left quite an impression on Sharmel."

"I think he left quite an impression on *me*," said Arcove.

Roup looked at him quizzically.

"I think I saw him," continued Arcove, "in the Great Cave after the last Volontaro. As we were leaving, there was a gray foal standing among the herd elders. I remember turning for a second look."

Roup cocked his head. "Because...he resembled someone we once knew?"

"Mmm."

"That's not an answer."

"It wasn't supposed to be."

2

Repercussions

Storm felt a consuming elation as he bounded over the sheep trail. He could hardly believe that he'd gotten away with it. At last, he reached the isolated cave where he had often left rabbits to freeze on the stone floor. He whirled in the cave's mouth, panting, legs beginning to quiver. He half expected a creasia to charge in after him, but he heard nothing except his own labored breathing. At last, he crept to the entrance and looked back the way he'd come.

They were leaving! He could see the entire group heading back down the trail. The howl that broke from his lips surprised even Storm, but it felt right. He threw back his head and sang his triumph.

Then he collapsed on the cave floor. He started to shake all over. It occurred to him that the creasia might return to the herd and kill a different set of ferryshaft. *But not the same group as before.*

Storm remained in the cave all day, licking up snow to sate his thirst. He saw no creasia in the rocks below or on the trail. Still, he waited. As darkness approached, he realized that he would have to either leave the cave or spend the night, since he dared not risk a sheep trail in the dark. Hunger persuaded him, and he made his way tentatively back to the main path.

The night was fully dark by the time Storm reached the foot of the cliffs. His senses had remained taut all day in the cave, and now he felt suddenly exhausted. Storm picked his way through the rocks to the place where his clique had been sleeping. He wondered if his friends had any food they would be willing to share.

On his way to their sleeping place, he saw two other ferryshaft foals. He did not know either of them by name. Both took one look at him, stared, and then scampered off without a word. Storm wondered what they must be thinking.

He did not have to wonder long. Leep met him in the boulders before he'd reached the sleeping place. "Storm," he breathed. "It really is you."

"It's me," said Storm. "Do you have anything to eat?"

Leep didn't seem to hear him. "I can't believe you're alive. What happened?"

"I ran onto a sheep trail," said Storm. The story didn't sound nearly as exciting as it had felt.

"A sheep trail?"

"Yes, that one with the cave where I sometimes leave game. I'm sure I've mentioned it."

Leep just stared at him.

A moment later, Tracer trotted into view. "I heard—" he began, and then saw Storm. "You are some kind of crazy, Storm Ela-ferry."

"I saved your life," said Storm with a hint of irritation.

"You saved all of our lives. You should go talk to Tollee. She hasn't said a word since you ran off. Not a single word to anyone. But everyone else is talking. What you did...I don't think anything like that has happened before. Ever."

Storm frowned. "That can't be true. It... It really wasn't that hard. I just ran onto a sheep trail, and the creasia couldn't follow me. Did they come back and kill more ferryshaft?"

"Not yet," said Leep. "No one has seen the creasia since they took off after you, but a lot of the adults seem to think they'll punish us. You might want to keep out of sight for a while."

Storm felt mystified. "They're angry?"

"No, they're afraid," said Tracer, "but sometimes afraid looks a lot like angry."

Storm found Tollee curled up in the lee of a rock formation where the clique usually slept. She did not raise her head until he nudged her. "Tollee?"

Her head came up slowly, and she turned to stare at him. She'd never looked so young.

Storm smiled. "Hey."

She tried to say something, but no words came.

"I'm sorry I didn't make use of your fighting lessons," he continued. "Like I said, running is what I'm good at."

"Storm," she said at last. "How are you alive?"

"I just ran onto a sheep trail." He had a feeling that he was going to get tired of repeating this.

Tracer and Leep had come up behind him. "You *just* ran onto a sheep trail," snorted Tracer. "No, Storm, you just outmaneuvered a creasia on the ice in front of the entire herd."

Storm had almost forgotten that part. He smiled, and his tail thumped the ground. "It's all in the turns, Tracer."

Mylo, Callaris, Valla, and Tarsis had arrived. Mylo dropped a rabbit at Storm's feet without a word. He was limping a little. Storm remembered the fight with Kelsy and felt instantly guilty. "Thank you," he said as he tore into the rabbit.

Mylo gave a ragged laugh. "*You're* thanking *me*?"

Valla came up to him and began licking his face in a way that made him feel strangely warm and very awkward. He stepped away. "I was in that group, too. It's not like I didn't save my own life along with yours."

"What can we do to help?" asked Callaris.

Storm was confused. "Help?"

"The herd is talking," said Tarsis. "They seem to feel that the creasia will punish us severely if you're allowed to live."

Storm felt dizzy. He had never imagined such a repercussion.

"We can say we never saw you," continued Tarsis. "If you're gone by first light—"

"I'm not going anywhere!" exclaimed Storm. *As though I'd live long as an outcast from the herd.*

"Then hide for a while," said Tracer, his voice reasonable. "If nothing serious happens, they'll forget about it. They're just shocked. Nothing like this has happened before. They don't know what it will mean."

Storm wanted to go find his mother and Sauny to let them know that he was alive, but word seemed to be circulating, and he was *so* tired. He lay down next to Tollee, who draped her head over his shoulders, and was instantly asleep.

Storm woke with someone nudging him. "Storm," whispered Tollee. "Storm, get up." He opened his eyes. Tollee was standing beside him. He could sense her nervousness. Three adults he didn't recognize stood a few paces away. They were whispering among themselves.

Storm looked around for the rest of his clique, but didn't see them. He turned towards the adults, but they backed away and departed without speaking.

"They just keep coming to stare," muttered Tollee. "I don't like it."

"Where are Leep and Tracer and the rest?" asked Storm. He felt disoriented. He could tell by the slant of the light that it was midmorning.

"Foraging," said Tollee, "but we felt that someone should stay with you."

"I need to go find Sauny and tell her I'm alright."

"You *need* to stay out of sight," growled Tollee. "Some of those adults look hostile."

"Then I'll run away," said Storm with growing annoyance. "If the creasia couldn't catch me, I'm sure a bunch of ferryshaft can't."

He stood and started away before she could respond. *Mother and Sauny will be with the herd at this time of day,* he thought, *and they'll be on the edge of the plain.* There was still a great deal of grass beneath the snow at this time of year.

As they neared the herd, they encountered more ferryshaft. Most took one look and shied away. Storm felt as though he had a disease. They whispered as he passed. He caught one word over and over. "Vearil," they whispered. "Vearil, Vearil, Vearil…"

Tollee was bristling beside him. "Storm, please."

Then two adult males blocked their path. Storm blinked. One of them was Dover. "Do you have any idea what you've done?" he hissed. "Do you think they won't come looking for you and everyone related to you?"

Storm took a step back and bumped into Tollee. A brief glance over his shoulder told him that two more adults were standing behind. He felt like an idiot. *Why did I let Tollee follow me?* If he ran, she would be left alone.

"We are doing what is best for the herd," said one of the other adults. Storm didn't remember his name, but knew he was an elder. The circle was closing. Tollee's lips peeled back in a snarl. Storm's heart began to pound. He tried to remember what she had taught him about fighting.

And then there was a rush and a flash of red-gold fur, snarling everywhere and the sound of hooves connecting with bodies. Storm took a moment to recognize Kelsy in the act of knocking down Dover. Kelsy's clique swarmed around them, striking and snapping at the adults. "Go!" one of them shouted. "Run!"

Storm ran. The moment they were out of sight of the adults, he pushed Tollee away from him. "I'll hide for a few days," he panted. "You go back to Mylo. Keep your head down."

He could tell she wanted to argue, but he just turned and raced away, his mind spinning with the unfairness of it all. He wasn't sure where to go, but his feet carried him automatically back to the sheep trail.

Storm returned to the cave and lay down. *Do they really think that killing me will make the creasia happy? Will it? And what do they gain by making the creasia happy?*

Tracer's words bothered him. *How can nothing like this have happened before?* For the first time since his first winter, Storm wondered when the cats had started to kill ferryshaft and why. He wished he had asked Pathar about it more often. He wondered whether he would ever get the chance to ask Pathar anything again.

Towards evening, a ferryshaft came up the trail from the boulder mazes and stopped where the real path ended. Storm squinted at him from the cave entrance. The ferryshaft dropped something and started to turn away.

"Wait!"

Storm emerged from the cave, hopping and inching his way over the sheep trail to the main path. Kelsy waited for him. Storm saw that he'd brought the leg of a sheep, freshly killed. "Thank you," said Storm, "and thank you for what you did earlier."

Kelsy glanced around as though he were afraid someone might be watching, but they were completely alone. He sat down a few paces away. "I got a long lecture on misplaced gratitude from elder Sinithin."

Storm cocked his head. "Do you think killing me will help appease the creasia?"

"I don't know," said Kelsy. "I know I'm not going to help kill you."

Storm smiled. "You told me to run, didn't you? Out on the ice. You said, 'Run, Storm.'" Playing it back in his head, Storm could hear it clearly.

Kelsy grinned.

"Did you think I could get away?"

"I thought you could if anyone could." Kelsy hesitated. "How's Mylo?"

"Limping," said Storm, "but I think he'll be alright."

"My father killed his father in a fight years ago," said Kelsy. "He's never liked me...not that I've given him much reason to. I suspect that's why he invited you to join his clique—because you made a fool of me."

Storm looked at the ground. "That makes sense." *It surely wasn't because he thought I'd be useful. No one ever thinks that.*

"*I* almost invited you," said Kelsy.

Storm looked up in surprise.

"After you had us chasing in circles a few times," continued Kelsy. "I wanted to ask you to join, but I was afraid of what the others might say. *That* was the most foolish thing of all."

Storm smiled. "Well, at least you're bringing me food now."

The irony of this hit them both at once, and they laughed together for a moment. "You'll be a herd elder someday," said Storm.

Kelsy snorted. "Probably. But you, Storm Ela-ferry…you will be a legend."

3

Round One: Ariand

Storm remained in the cave all that day and all night. He had a full belly, thanks to Kelsy, but he missed the warmth of his companions as he curled against cold stone in the darkness. By morning, he felt stiff and restless. He wondered whether it was safe to come down. *Tracer said a few days. Could I really stay here for days?*

He watched the herd from his vantage point, foraging on the edge of the plain. *What do you think of all this, Pathar? Did you speak up for me? Or do you want me dead, too?*

And then he saw something else—darker shapes drifting through the boulders. Storm reared up and craned his neck. He wasn't high enough to see everything clearly, but he saw enough—panic rippling through the herd, the animals on one corner starting to run, and then all of them running. He would have laughed if the situation hadn't been so sad. *The herd wanted to kill me. And now, because they drove me away, I'm safe up here, while they're in danger.*

Storm wondered if the cats really were going to punish the herd by killing a large number of ferryshaft. Whatever they might do, they had certainly returned because of him. Creasia attacks never came so close together. *They're here to make up for last time.*

Ariand made a quick count of the selected ferryshaft. Ten. Exactly the number that Sharmel had intended to take before his clutter got out of order. Ariand had no intention of doing a punitive cull. His mission, as he saw it, was to find out whether anything had changed. He would conduct his raid exactly as usual, demonstrating to both the cats and the ferryshaft that the events of two days ago had been an anomaly, never to be repeated.

Ariand did not look too closely at the chosen ferryshaft as his subordinates herded them together. Ferryshaft were not deer, it was true, and it didn't do to look too closely. He adhered strictly to the rules. There was nothing exceptional about those who'd been chosen. They were random selections, unlucky enough to be in the wrong place at the wrong time.

A long ululating howl brought him bolt upright, bristling in spite of himself. It had been so long since he'd heard a ferryshaft howl. Ariand whipped around, along with every cat in his clutter, and saw the foal, perched atop a boulder on the edge of the plain. He *was* a familiar color—like dirty snow or a troubled sky.

The foal howled again, and the clutter reacted. Ariand didn't try to stop them. The foal might not be attacking, but his behavior was clear defiance and in violation of treaty law.

Ariand began calling instructions to his clutter as the foal leapt from the rock and vanished into the boulder mazes. They bounded forward—not frantic or careless with rage, but swift and eager.

I will succeed where Sharmel failed, thought Ariand. *He's getting old. Perhaps I should challenge him. At any rate, we will solve this problem before sunset.*

Storm knew his opponents would be more organized this time. They would expect him to head for the sheep trail, and he wasn't sure he could outrun them if they knew where he was going. So, instead, he struck out north through the boulder mazes.

He could hear the cats calling to each other in wailing, wordless voices. Their calls confirmed his suspicions. Several had gone straight towards the cliff, making no effort to adhere to his trail. However, the rest were right behind him, and they were signaling to the others to close in from his left flank.

Storm felt a stab of fear. In the past, hunters had followed him either by sight or by scent. He had always felt confident that a pursuer must do one or the other. However, the cats to his left were simply listening to their companions. They were outrunning him. Soon, they would be in front. Those behind would close the gap and surround him.

Storm moved in the only direction available—east, away from the cliffs and towards the plain. He realized his mistake an instant later as he caught a glimpse of the plain between the boulders. The snow out there was new and powdery, untrampled by the herd. It might be only knee deep to an adult, but it would be belly-deep for Storm, and there was no frozen crust on which to run. The creasia closed their trap from three sides, and he was pushed relentlessly towards the snow that would leave him helpless.

Storm could feel himself spiraling towards panic. The instinct to simply run flat-out became all but overpowering. Storm fought it down. *What's around here?* He'd had hiding places everywhere when he'd been running from Kelsy's clique.

Storm heard the cats behind him call again. They were *very* close, running by sight now, probably only lengths away. *They're waiting for the others,* he realized, *waiting for those who are flanking me to get completely around in front.* He had mere heartbeats to do something before that happened.

Storm stopped. He stopped so suddenly, that he actually spun on the dusting of snow and half-iced rock. He caught a glimpse of a surprised creasia's face as it tried to pounce at the last moment, misjudged the distance, and went sailing over his head. Storm came out of his dizzy spin, running in the opposite direction, all his energy unleashed in a sprint that would either save him or be his last. For an instant, scrambling cats were all around him, slapping and missing, off balance. And then he was past them, running south with the entire hunting party behind him.

Storm knew that he didn't have enough of a lead to reach the cliffs. He could think of only one hiding place nearby. It was not ideal, but it would serve. A moment later, he reached a crevice in the rocks—a tiny cave with a slit of a mouth so small that even Storm had to squirm to get in. He doubted he would be able to use this hiding place by next year, and he was certain that no creasia could follow.

The interior seemed even smaller than Storm remembered, and he crouched against the far wall, panting and feeling vulnerable. In a moment, cats swarmed around the entrance. One stuck a paw into the cave and slapped at Storm. Storm stared wide-eyed at the curved claws as they lashed less than a quarter length from his face. However, the cat could not reach him, and it finally withdrew with a snarl.

At last, a creasia face appeared at the entrance—a tan and black animal with pale yellow eyes that stared moodily at Storm. "What do they call you, foal?" It spoke with the strange creasia accent that Storm remembered from the cub in the cave, but Storm managed to parse the words.

"Vearil." He did not know why he said it. The word just slipped out.

Something about the cat's face grew still. Before he could speak again, Storm continued, "I'm *your* ill-omen."

The cat blinked. "Well, I'm Ariand."

"Why should I care?" snapped Storm.

"I just thought you might like to know the name of the animal who's going to kill you."

4

Trapped

Storm had a suspicion that hiding in a cave from creasia would not be as effective as hiding in a cave from ferryshaft. He was right. The creasia were more patient.

As the day wore on, and they did not leave, Storm became exceedingly sorry that he had not better planned his escape. *What was I thinking?*

He had been thinking, of course, that he would save more ferryshaft, who would then be grateful and less inclined to kill him. He was already an outcast with little to lose...or so he'd thought. Now, watching the creasia pace while his thirst mounted, he began to appreciate the advantages of being merely an outcast. The little cave on the sheep trail began to seem luxurious.

His current accommodation was no more than four lengths from front to back, with an uneven floor and walls. The ceiling was so low that Storm could not fully stand. Hardly any snow had blown into the narrow mouth, and no ice had formed on the walls, so there was nothing to drink. Storm did notice that the back wall was marked with one of the odd symbols that he had seen in the Great Cave and throughout the boulder mazes. He wished he knew what it meant.

Ariand came to the entrance near noon, his muzzle dripping with snow melt. "Thirsty yet, foal?"

Storm shut his eyes. After the morning's frantic run, his mouth felt as dry as sand. He was hungry as well, though he knew he could go several days without food if necessary. *Surely they will eventually get hungry, too, and leave.* Storm had never heard of creasia hanging around ferryshaft territory for longer than it took to raid. With an effort, he mastered his misery and escaped into sleep.

When Storm woke, he raised his head and listened. Not a sound. The fading evening light barely illuminated his cave. Storm sniffed the air. He could detect no scent of cats. His thirst returned, biting.

Storm came cautiously to the entrance of the cave and looked out. Silence. Evening shadows. Delightful drifts of snow mere lengths away. Storm repressed the urge to scramble out and start gulping up mouthfuls. He thrust his head out and one leg, then hesitated.

Silence. Not a bird trilled. Not a rat scampered among the rocks. He could not catch even a distant murmur of ferryshaft voices. Storm began to recoil.

He caught a quick movement out of the corner of his eye, jabbed his hind legs into the lip of rock, and shot backwards just in time. The cat jabbed its paw into the cave and swatted, but Storm was safe for the moment.

In front of the cave, the creasia were congregating again. They seemed relaxed and confident. One cat caught a rabbit and ate it where Storm could see. "Hungry, foal?"

Storm watched with growing despair. His head had begun to pound. With no other options, he relieved himself in the corner of the cave. The strong odor of his own concentrated urine made him feel ill. Finally, Storm escaped into sleep once more.

This time when he awoke the thirst was instant, acute. He struggled to his feet and felt a wave of dizziness. Not even moonlight broke the darkness outside. The moon must have already set. Storm could not hear any noises, but he knew the cats had not left.

This is hopeless. All they have to do is watch the hole until I starve or go mad with thirst. Did I really think I could outwit them? I only escaped the first time because I was lucky.

That thought made him laugh. *I have never been lucky.*

Storm buried his aching head between his hooves. *I should just make a run for it. I'm only getting weaker. Maybe I can outmaneuver them and get to the cliffs.*

This seemed unlikely. He couldn't even escape the cave's mouth without wriggling. *They'll rip me in half before I'm even out of the hole.*

Storm heard a grinding sound, and then he felt the wall behind him *move.* He leapt forward with a stifled yelp. Then, because he had nowhere to flee, he turned around. A section of the cave wall had vanished, leaving a dark, ragged hole. Storm held his breath, half expecting something terrible to emerge. After a few moments of perfect silence, Storm took a cautious step forward.

He saw no hint of movement in the blackness. A current of cool air wafted gently from the opening, showing that it connected somewhere to the outside. Storm ventured closer and tried to peer in, but he could see nothing.

He sniffed the incoming breeze. The air in the new chamber was fresh and damp, unlike the fetid stench of the cave. He could see now that it was a natural extension of his current cave—a tunnel. However, a large rock had created a false back wall. He noticed that the odd symbol was located on the rock. *Could I have leaned against it? Is that why it moved?*

Storm had to stifle a hysterical laugh. *Did I have a way out all the time?*

His ears pricked. Somewhere in the tunnel, he heard water. He took a step forward, but stopped. A strange scent drifted to him on the breeze. He did not remember having smelled it before, yet his fur stood on end.

Storm glanced at the large rock again. *Could I really have moved that by accident? And if I didn't move it, what did?*

His head throbbed. It was difficult to think. *What choice do I have? A moment ago, I was considering running from the cave, knowing full well the cats would kill me. This is a better gamble... isn't it?*

Storm hesitated between the two openings. *I have to decide soon.* Outside, he could see the boulder mazes a little more clearly. Dawn was coming. If he escaped from another exit or tried a run from the entrance, he would need the darkness for cover.

Ariand uncurled from a hollow in the lee of a boulder. He groomed himself, took a few mouthfuls of snow, and then trotted to the place where a sentry waited behind a rock. "Has he done anything?"

"No, sir. He hasn't stirred."

Ariand waved his tail. "He'll stir soon or I'm much mistaken." *If he was smarter, he'd have made a break before now. We would still have killed him, but he might have put up a fight. At this rate, he'll be too weak to even scramble out of the cave.*

If the foal actually died in the cave, Ariand would be disappointed, and his temporary escape was bothering Ariand more than he wanted to admit. *Vearil. That can't be his real name.*

Ariand started away and then changed his mind. "Perhaps I'll have a peek before I hunt." *I wonder if I can get him talking this morning. I should have tried harder yesterday.* Ariand approached the cave slowly. The foal's extreme silence bothered him. He slunk to the entrance and raised his head over the lip.

Ariand's mouth dropped open. He tried to push his head all the way inside, although he could already see every corner of the tiny cave. The foal was gone.

"He vanished. I have no idea how."

Roup noticed that Ariand did not quite meet anyone's eyes in the council. His posture was defensive. No one spoke for a moment after he'd finished his story.

"Are you sure you watched the cave *all* night?" asked Halvery. "The clutter had been awake all day. Perhaps a sentry dozed."

"I took sentry duty myself the first half of the night," said Ariand, "and then left a rotation of four creasia. They had such short shifts, I don't believe anyone could have fallen asleep."

"Well, he had to have gone somewhere," said Sharmel. "You're sure that there wasn't another exit from the cave?"

"Not that I could see. Of course I couldn't get all the way inside… But the foal looked miserable all afternoon. I think that if he knew another way out, he would have used it."

"Not if he was smart," murmured Roup. "Smart would pretend that he had no escape, wait until the clutter was complacent and mostly asleep, and then slip out the alternate exit. He'd be long gone by the time you started looking."

Ariand drooped. He said nothing.

Halvery snorted. "It's a *foal*, Roup, not a fox. And not a cunning ferryshaft with years of experience, either. Ariand, you had the longest shift. *You* probably went to sleep!"

Ariand raised his head. He didn't look at Halvery. He looked at Arcove.

He thinks he might lose his clutter over this, thought Roup. *After losing that fight with Treace...he's wondering whether Arcove really wants five officers.* Roup glanced at Arcove.

Ariand had been the last officer added during the war. He hadn't fought for the position. *He came to us and said that he could drain the lake.* Roup could still remember the gleam in Ariand's eyes then—little bigger than a half-grown cub. *Arcove gave him the cats to try. Afterward, they were his.*

Arcove stretched—a disarming gesture. Ariand relaxed a fraction. "Well, this raid has at least provided us with useful information," said Arcove. "I wanted to know whether the entire herd is in revolt. From what you say, they are not."

"I disagree," said Treace. "They have broken faith by not killing the foal. This must be punished."

Arcove's tail twitched. "Perhaps, but that is not the same as revolt." Treace opened his mouth again, but Arcove spoke first. "If they were in revolt, they would have torn Ariand's hunting party to pieces. Do you really think that ten cats could defend themselves against the entire ferryshaft herd? They allow our culls because they have submitted to our rules. They fear us. Beware the day they don't."

Treace grumbled something about cowards.

Arcove continued. "As I suspected, the foal was inspired by his success to try again. On the first occasion, he may have been merely running for his life. There is no rule against doing such a thing. However, no such excuse can be made for this second occasion. He is now in clear defiance of the treaty. However…"

"However," said Halvery with a grunt, "he's our problem not theirs."

"Correct," said Arcove. "As long as Charder and the herd elders aren't helping him, they're under no obligation to assist us. The day we can't take care of a problem like this is the day we are no longer frightening enough to rule them. Do I make myself clear?"

There was a murmur of assent.

Treace looked thoughtful. "You're not even going to talk to Charder?"

Arcove smiled. "Oh, I'll talk to him. If he's involved, I'll know, but I suspect he isn't. Did you get the information I requested?"

Treace stood up a little straighter. He was an exceedingly graceful animal with pale brown fur and sharp green eyes. "The foal's name is Storm." He paused. "I don't know why he called himself Vearil."

"I could hazard a guess," said Roup. "It's probably what the herd has been calling him. The ferryshaft put a lot of store by luck these days. Makes sense, when our culls are so random."

"Yes, but why would he call *himself* that?" asked Treace.

No one answered.

"He'll be three years old in spring," continued Treace.

Ariand looked surprised. "I would have guessed two."

"Lovely," grumbled Halvery. "Not only are we being bested by a foal; he's also a runt."

"His father was killed by a raiding party before Storm was born," continued Treace. "His mother's name is So-fet. She mated with another male, Dover, and had another foal, a female called Sauny. Storm has been on his own since his first winter. He made a bit of a name for himself by escaping from bigger ferryshaft foals who tried to take his kills. His friends are all low-ranking orphans."

Treace paused. "From what I gathered, none of the ferryshaft regard Storm and his family as very remarkable. The herd seems to hold him in disdain. He does not seem likely to attract followers."

A murmur of conversation went round the council circle. Roup turned to Treace. "How did you discover all that?"

"I caught a ferryshaft and told him that I would release him if he talked to me."

"And what did you do with him when you were finished?"

"Killed him, of course."

Arcove spoke over the babble. "I think you all realize that we must make an example of this foal while the herd still 'holds him in disdain.' If we kill him soon, he will be merely a cautionary tale. Who wants the next bite at this animal?"

"I do," purred Treace.

Almost as soon as Storm entered the tunnel, he smelled the water. He found it difficult to think of anything else, yet he forced himself to go slowly. The passage widened and sloped steeply downward. Storm could hear the clip-clop echo of his own hooves. The echoes seemed terribly loud, and he wondered if the cats could hear them outside.

He could hear the water now, too. His mouth was so dry... Storm's eyes were beginning to adjust to the extreme gloom, and he could faintly see the outline of another opening to his right. He followed the sound of the water and peered inside. Somewhere below, an underground stream rushed by in the blackness.

Storm licked his lips. The stream sounded only a short distance away. The air in the new tunnel felt cool, but no breeze stirred his fur. This was not the way out.

But when will I get another chance to drink in peace? A whole day had passed since he had had a drink, and he felt weak with thirst. Storm eased into the new passage. It was narrower and angled sharply downhill. He stifled a surge of claustrophobia and continued.

Finally the tunnel opened up, and Storm found himself on the edge of what sounded like a large river. It rushed by in front of him, cutting its dark path through the stone to either side. Storm buried his face in the stream and gulped. Water had never tasted so sweet.

As he drank, he became conscious of a faint greenish glow somewhere deep in the stream. It gave just enough light for his adjusted eyes to discern the outlines of his surroundings. Storm was beginning to puzzle over this, when there was a splash directly in front of him and a head popped out of the water.

Storm gasped. Pale fur, huge blue eyes, something like a seal, but longer, uncoiling out of the water.

Storm jumped back as the telshee darted forward. In a panic, he turned and raced up the passage. He heard a splash as the creature emerged from the water and the swish of its fur over stone.

Storm pounded out of the tunnel and started back the way he had come. *I'll take my chances with the creasia.* But he stopped before he had gone three steps. Storm blinked and stared in vain for the outline of the hole that led back to his rank little cave. He saw only a faintly glowing green mass strewn along the ground. He caught a glimmer of movement near the place where the hole should have been—white fur, gleaming eyes. *They covered my entrance!* Storm knew now what the strange scent must be. It was the scent of a telshee.

Storm ran in the only direction left to him—down the unknown passage in the direction of the incoming breeze. All of the telshee stories that he had ever heard flooded his mind. He wondered how many telshees were in the tunnel. He wondered whether he would run headlong into smothering coils. He wondered whether death under creasia claws would have been quicker.

Then, suddenly, the tunnel curved sharply upward, and Storm burst out onto open ground. He did not stop running until he had reached a cliff trail—not a sheep trail, but it would have to do. He climbed until dawn, whereupon he lay down on the rocky path, exhausted. He shut his eyes to rest…just for a moment.

5

Round 2: Treace

When Storm opened his eyes again, it was midmorning—bright and cold and clear. He started to stand up, thought better of it, and lay back down. He didn't think he'd actually climbed very high last night. His whole body ached, and his head was pounding. He licked up the snow around him on the ground.

Cautiously, Storm crept to the edge of the path and peered over. As he'd suspected, he was low enough for a clear view of the mazes and the cave that had been his prison. To his delight, the cats were still guarding it. His amusement when they discovered his absence could only be matched by his satisfaction when they left, going south in great haste. "Run home," he murmured, "and tell everyone that you've lost again."

When they were gone, Storm made his way quickly down the trail. He caught a rat in its snowy runway among the rocks, and felt much better. He wondered what he should do next. Return to the herd? Find his clique? Try again to find his mother and Sauny?

As he was debating, he ran into the last person he expected to see—Pathar, foraging alone among the boulders. Storm stopped when he saw him. He almost ran away, but hesitated. Pathar raised his head, saw Storm, and smiled. "So that's why they left. I didn't think they looked happy."

Storm swallowed. He felt a ridiculous urge to run to Pathar and put his head against his teacher's shoulder, as he had when he was small. However, caution and dignity prevailed. "Do you want to kill me, Pathar?"

Pathar cocked his head. "Why would I want that?"

"Some of the other elders do."

Pathar gave a shake of his head. "You've survived twice. You're the creasia's problem now. I think the elders will leave you alone."

"You didn't answer my question."

"No, Storm, I don't want to kill you."

"But you won't help me, either."

"What do you mean?"

"Has anyone ever escaped before, Pathar?" *I need to know. I need to understand what I've gotten myself into.*

Pathar took a deep breath. "Not in the last fourteen years."

"And before that?"

"Before that," said Pathar carefully, "we were not under creasia law. We were at war. We lost."

Storm grew very still. Pathar was actually telling him something new, probably something forbidden. "How long?" he blurted. "How long were we at war? Why did we lose?"

Pathar looked up at the blue sky. "I don't know how long, Storm. Maybe as long as there have been ferryshaft and creasia. When I was your age, we were winning. *We* used to cull *them.* Creasia are difficult to kill as adults, but as cubs, they are vulnerable. We would go into the forest every spring and kill as many cubs as we could find. We breed faster than they do, and we can eat almost anything, whereas they require meat. We should never have lost the advantage, but…Arcove is a clever leader. Now, he lets us survive, and that is the best we can hope for."

Storm felt as though a ray of light had fallen into a dark cave. For the first time, he glimpsed a past that affected him daily. "Why don't they just kill us all?" he whispered.

Pathar waved his tail. "The treaty was negotiated so that the ferryshaft would stop fighting. We were a desperate, starving lot, holed up in caves, but still dangerous. Annihilating us would have cost creasia lives that Arcove probably wanted to save. Now…well, he's always been one for keeping his promises. Arcove has not broken the treaty…yet."

Storm shook his head. "Why didn't you tell me everything before?"

Pathar surprised him with a full-bellied laugh. "Oh, I'm still not telling you everything, Storm. I've already told you enough to get myself killed or exiled if you repeat it. If you do repeat it… say that Ariand told you." He laughed again, more to himself, and trotted away.

He was already gone, when Storm thought, *You know Ariand's name…*

Feeling marginally safer because of Pathar's assessment, Storm started in the direction of the herd. He was not surprised to find Tollee and Tracer at the clique's sleeping spot. Tracer laughed out loud when he saw Storm. "Callaris owes me a rabbit."

Storm made a face. "You're *betting* on my survival?"

"Well, it's better than betting against it!"

Tollee looked almost angry. "Storm, why didn't you stay on the cliffs? You could have stayed on the cliffs!"

"And be an outcast from the herd? What kind of a life is that?"

"A longer life," she growled.

"How did you escape from the cave?" interrupted Tracer.

"You knew I was trapped in a cave?" asked Storm.

Tracer harrumphed. "Storm, everyone knew. It's not that far away. How did you get out?"

"I…" Storm hesitated. "I'd rather not say."

Tracer whined in protest, but Tollee was already talking again. "Kelsy offered to let all of us join his clique."

"Sort of," said Tracer.

"No 'sort of' about it," snapped Tollee. "He said that half of his clique members had gone off to be with mates last fall. He said there are only ten left—"

"*Only*," interrupted Tracer, "like that's a small number—"

"And we were welcome to hunt with them this winter," finished Tollee.

"Saying it that way didn't make it sound like joining, though," said Tracer. "It wasn't like he was trying to take the clique from Mylo, just...collaborate. You should have seen the look on Mylo's face, Storm. He had no idea what to say."

"I hope he said yes," said Storm.

"He's still thinking about it," said Tollee. "Storm, the creasia will be back."

"I know." He took a deep breath. "And before you say it, no, I wasn't thinking very clearly when I trapped myself in that cave. I'll plan better next time."

"I hope so," she said, "because I'm sure *they* will."

Storm did plan. He spent the next couple of days reviewing every cave and cliff trail in the area and especially the few sheep trails that he'd mastered. He left a rabbit in each of the two isolated cliff caves that he knew how to reach, and he made sure that snow was piled in the back for drinking.

As Pathar had predicted, no one bothered him. Most of the ferryshaft gave him a wide berth. They treated him as though creasia disfavor might be catching, but no one accosted him or attempted to harm him. Storm did not test their attitude by walking into the center of the herd during the day, but on the second night, he did creep over to the place where he thought Sauny and So-fet were sleeping. So-fet was lying beside Dover, and Storm was afraid of waking his stepfather. Sauny, however, woke at his approach. She jumped up and might have squealed if Storm hadn't shushed her.

They moved away from the others a little, and Sauny whispered. "Storm, you're amazing! Everyone is talking about you!"

"Are they?" he asked uneasily.

"Yes, two of the females in my clique want to be your mates," she announced.

Storm had to stifle his laughter. Sauny's "clique" was composed of females less than one year old who had parents and were more friends than hunting partners.

"Maybe they should wait and see whether I'm around in four years." He tried to say it jokingly, but Sauny's eyes grew instantly worried.

"Please be careful, brother."

"I will. I just wanted you and mother to know that I'm alright."

"We know," said Sauny. "It's what everyone talks about."

"They don't talk to me," said Storm. *No one talks to me except the ones I've saved.*

"They're just scared," said Sauny. "They'll see. When the creasia can't kill you, they'll see. You're the smartest, fastest, bravest ferryshaft there ever was, Storm."

Storm laid his head briefly across her shoulders. "Go on back now, little sister. I'll come again. Tell Mother I was here, but don't tell Dover."

The cats arrived three days later. They came around noon, but their behavior was unprecedented. They trotted around the edges of the herd, pushing the entire mass of animals together on the edge of the plain. They did not cut out a single group, nor did they charge. They circled, eyes scanning every ferryshaft.

The frightened, confused animals pressed together, those on the edges struggling to reach the center. Storm was not among them, as he'd been staying away from the herd. However, he did not wish to miss the creasia's next appearance, and so he was close enough to hear the screams, the pounding of running hooves, and the confused shouting when the raid began.

Storm approached cautiously, peered from behind a rock on the edge of the mazes. The creasia were behaving oddly. He wondered what it meant, and at the same time, he began to plan the chase that must follow. His heartbeat quickened, and he took slow, measured breaths. Any moment, he would leap out and draw them. Any moment...

A pale brown cat sprang lightly onto a rock, the others still pacing around the edges of the herd. "Where is he?" demanded the cat. Storm could tell that he was deliberately altering his speech so that ferryshaft could more easily understand. The cat spoke again, this time in a roar, "Where is he?!"

The herd had gone still. No one moved. No one said a word. The lead creasia leapt from the boulder and stalked *into* the clustered ferryshaft. They parted before him like water around a rock in a swift stream. Storm found himself thinking how easily they could have killed him if they had stampeded at that moment.

"Don't pretend you don't know who I'm talking about!" shouted the glaring cat. "If you bring the law-breaker to me, I will kill him, and you can all leave this place unharmed. If you do not bring him to me, thirty of your yearling foals will die!"

"The terms of the treaty prohibit hunting and killing of selected individuals, Treace."

Everyone looked in the direction of the speaker. Charder stood alone. He'd walked away from the rest of the herd, ignoring the pacing cats.

Storm was shocked and fascinated. This was not at all how he'd imagined the next raid.

For a moment, the cat, Treace, seemed startled, but his answer came readily enough. "The individual we speak of has violated the treaty and is therefore no longer under its protection. If you fail to produce him, neither are you."

Charder sniffed. "Such a thing has never been part of treaty law. The violation itself is questionable. The animal we speak of has run from you—hardly a violation."

"He howled!" snarled Treace.

"A minor offense," said Charder coolly. "He does not seem to be howling now."

The cat advanced, stiff-legged and bristling towards Charder, but the herd leader held his ground. Storm was impressed. He'd always imagined Charder to be a beaten coward where cats were concerned.

"You have no right to demand anything of us until agreed upon in formal conference," continued Charder as though Treace didn't look ready to kill him, "nor do you have the right to violate the treaty until formal exception is made. If you intend to cull, please do so. You are confusing my herd."

Storm held his breath as he watched the strange stand-off. Then Treace turned away. Storm thought that Charder had won until he saw the murderous expression on the cat's face. "Oh, we'll cull," he growled.

Treace leapt forward, caught a surprised adult by the back of the head, and crunched into its skull. Ferryshaft screamed and fled in all directions. The cats ran among them, maiming and killing. They made no attempt to encircle a group, but attacked every animal they could reach.

Storm gaped. *This is my fault.* He took a running leap and topped the boulder. "Here I am! Come and get me, you cowards!" He thought about howling, but saved his breath. He was shaken by what he'd just seen and wanted as much distance between himself and Treace as he could manage.

Unlike the chase with Ariand, Storm had no sense of what the cats might be doing behind him. They called to each other only rarely. Storm laid a twisted trail that he'd planned in advance— along a frozen stream that confused his scent, through narrow places in the rocks, and into one tunnel where the cats could not follow and would be forced to search for the exit without the aid of his scent to guide them.

Storm did all this, even though he already knew where he was going. He wanted to lead the creasia away from the ferryshaft herd first. He couldn't prevent them from returning to kill, but he could at least make it less convenient.

At no point in the chase did he feel truly pressured. *My practice has made a difference,* he thought, but a mental image of the leader's furious eyes made him feel cold.

Storm decided that he was done leading them about. He reached the cliffs and started up a trail he'd selected days ago. It wound steeply up and over jagged red rock, and he was soon panting hard. He was tempted to look back, but mastered the urge. *As long as their claws aren't in my spine, I'm winning.* In fact, he felt confident that he had quite a lead. Soon, he would reach the point where the sheep trail left the main path, and then he would leave them behind completely.

Storm struggled up a particularly steep section, urging himself on in spite of flagging muscles. *Almost there.* He topped the rise, a cry of triumph building in his throat...and skidded to a stop. Twenty lengths ahead, the familiar thread of the sheep trail wound enticingly away to freedom and safety. Between Storm and the sheep trail, however, lay Treace.

6

A Lecture

Storm's heart did a sickening flop. He wheeled to start back the way he had come.

"Storm!" The use of his name brought him up short. He glanced over his shoulder.

Treace had not moved. He stretched and rose slowly. "You're a remarkable foal, Storm. I'd like to talk to you—no tricks, just talk."

Storm hesitated. This was something new.

Treace took a step toward him. Storm took a step back. The foal was just beyond pouncing distance. Treace smiled. "This is a parley, not an execution. Sit."

Storm lowered his back end a little, but not enough to touch the stone.

Treace laughed. "That looks uncomfortable. Can you talk or do you only howl?" His voice was patient and friendly. Storm wondered if this could really be the same creature who had threatened Charder and mauled a ferryshaft so recently.

"What do you want to say?" asked Storm. He wondered if he could catch Treace enough off his guard to rush *under* his pounce. He'd done something like that with Ariand. At the same time, he wondered if the cat really wanted to talk and what he could possibly say that would matter.

"You've impressed us," said Treace. "Charder has grown old and foolish. We're looking for a new ferryshaft to put in charge of the herd. That's why Charder was arguing with me earlier. He's afraid that if we find you, we'll replace him. That's how we pick the new leaders, you know—the brave ones who challenge us."

Storm stared at Treace. "I don't believe you."

The cat flicked his tail. "We wouldn't expect you to—not immediately. But think about it, Storm. You could renegotiate the treaty—perhaps bargain for us to kill fewer ferryshaft. If you keep running away, we'll just kill you, but if you come with me...we'll tell you all kinds of things. I'm sure you've wondered about the war, about the treaty, how and why we conduct our raids..."

Storm knew the cat was lying, but he couldn't help but listen. Even the lies told him things he hadn't known. *They have rules about how they raid? Those rules are negotiated?*

Storm realized suddenly that Treace had edged forward, muscles tensing. Storm backed away quickly. "You think I'd believe that after watching what you did to those ferryshaft this morning?"

Treace gave a soft, nasty chuckle. "Wait until you see what I'm going to do to you."

Storm whirled and started to gallop back down the path, but he stopped after only a short distance. From this vantage, he could see much of the twisted trail below, including the rest of the creasia, well over halfway up and closing.

"Too late," said Treace softly.

Storm turned to the cat again, fearful of taking his eyes off him for too long. Treace stood with his head low, eyes narrow, edging forward.

Storm's stomach churned, and he felt light-headed. He couldn't breathe. *I can't go in either direction. I can't get past him. I can't...* All he could think about was the crunch of a ferryshaft's skull, the scream as the animal expired.

I won't die that way. I won't.

Storm glanced up: a sheer, gravelly wall with no footholds. He looked down. The cliff dropped away in a descent that was steep, but not sheer. *I might make it...if I don't stumble.*

He jumped.

If Storm had looked back, he would have seen Treace thudding to the ground almost on his tail. Treace peered over the precipice, growling. He had hoped to break the foal's legs and carry him back to Leeshwood alive. It might not impress Arcove, but the sight would certainly impress half the cats in every clutter. They would see the ferryshaft whom Sharmel and Ariand had been unable to catch, easily captured by Treace, and dying slowly on display.

It was a regrettable loss. However, Treace felt certain that he had succeeded in a broader sense. The foal couldn't possibly survive such a fall.

Treace watched as Storm dug in his heels, knee-deep in sliding rocks. The gray tail lashed wildly. Once he tripped, and Treace thought it was over, but then Storm righted himself. Treace's clutter arrived, but no one said anything. They could see well enough.

Finally, Storm reached the truly dangerous part. Fewer loose rocks interfered with his movements, but the descent was far steeper. Treace saw him jump amid a sea of slithering stones, and then he was lost to sight over the sheer drop.

All the cats ran back and forth, craning their necks to see, but it was no use. *We'll have to go to the bottom to find his body,* thought Treace. Then, impossibly, a streak of dust shot away from the cliff and, with it, a flash of silver-gray.

"You threatened them? All of them?" Arcove's stare was icy.

Treace looked angry, too. "They have broken faith and must be punished. If we can't catch the foal, perhaps his own race—"

"Treace," growled Arcove, "by your actions, you have admitted to the entire herd that we feel threatened by this foal. Before you spoke to them, they weren't sure. Now, they are."

Treace sputtered. "I hardly think that our cull will leave them feeling triumphant—"

"Secondly," continued Arcove, "a threat of that nature produces one of two results: either they turn on him, or they rally around him. I am not prepared to risk the second possibility at this point, as improbable as it may seem."

"They'll never—!"

"And thirdly, Treace, Charder is right. We cannot violate treaty stipulations at whim. Your breach was more severe than anything this foal has done."

"What are you afraid of?" spat Treace. "The ferryshaft? That race of talking sheep? Just because they gave you a bloody nose a generation ago..."

Arcove rose, and Treace's voice faded. All around the council circle, officers were staring at him. Arcove took a step closer, legs stiff, hackles raised. "Who is in charge here, Treace?"

For an instant, Treace's eyes locked with Arcove's. Then his gaze dropped. "You are."

"For a moment I wasn't sure."

Treace said nothing and kept his eyes down. After a pause, Arcove continued. "I understand your reasoning, councilor. I know what you were trying to do, but you lack experience. Ferryshaft are *not* talking sheep. In the future, you will break treaty code only at my direct orders. Do you understand?"

"Yes, sir."

An awkward pause. Finally, Sharmel spoke. "Arcove, can I try again?"

Arcove looked surprised. "You've already chased him once, Sharmel."

"I know, but I didn't understand the situation, and my clutter completely ignored my orders."

Arcove thought he understood. Ariand was the lowest ranking officer. Treace was next. They were taking turns at this problem by order of rank, and Sharmel wanted his correct position. "Go ahead. But don't threaten the herd."

Roup spoke. "I recommend not making a cull at all until you catch Storm."

Halvery rolled his eyes. "Here we go again."

Roup flicked his tail. "No, this is social logic." He looked at Sharmel. "If you begin to make a cull and the foal appears, you must chase him. The ferryshaft he saves will feel gratitude. Even if you return and make a new cull, the ferryshaft from the first cull will survive, and their loyalties will shift. In addition, those in the new cull may be inspired to follow Storm's example." He hesitated. "Besides, it sounds to me that Treace has performed a cull that will be sufficient for some time."

Even Halvery had to admit that this made sense.

"No cull, then," said Sharmel. "And I think I'll wait a bit, if that's acceptable." He glanced at Arcove. "We've been coming every few days. The foal is on edge. I'm sure he's planning his next escape even as we speak. I'd like to give him some time to get complacent."

"That's reasonable," said Arcove. "It'll give me time to sort out the mess Treace has created with Charder."

7

Threats and Apologies

It was as mild a winter as the island had seen in a decade. At no point did the snow entirely cover the ground, and the toughest bushes and grasses continued to peek through. Animals that were normally dormant came out of hiding. Rabbits and rock rats thrived, and so did the ferryshaft herd.

Charder reflected, as he browsed among the rocks at dusk, that not even the orphan cliques were likely to lose any members this winter. He doubted that a single ferryshaft had been reduced to covert cannibalism. A good year—or it should have been, if not for the creasia's recent alarming behavior.

Charder was not surprised when a shadow fell across his back, the outline of the head and ears towering above him. His heartbeat quickened, as it always did, but he didn't look up or turn around. "Are we at war, Arcove?"

"You tell me."

Charder raised his head and turned. Arcove didn't look like he planned to kill anyone. He appeared relaxed, but Charder could tell that he was watching minutely. "I came to apologize for the conduct of one of my officers."

Be careful, thought Charder. *Be very careful.* He allowed some anger to creep into his voice. "Treace threatened the herd. He asked for a specific individual. He culled without counting. His clutter left injured animals. Do you even know how many they killed?"

"I'm sure you'll tell me."

"Eighteen. Half of them died slowly over the following day. This is not how we agreed on culls."

Arcove inclined his head. "It is not. Treace acted outside my authorization and outside my knowledge. It should not have been done, and for that I apologize."

Charder watched him. *But...*

"But, he had a point. This foal, Storm, has violated the treaty and is therefore no longer under its protection."

Charder snorted. "Are ferryshaft supposed to stand still now and wait to be killed? The foal didn't attack your cats. Running away has never been a treaty violation."

Arcove's eyes narrowed. "And how did he know that, I wonder?"

Charder barked a laugh. "Arcove, the foals growing up now don't even know there is a treaty...or they didn't until Treace threatened them with it. Storm ran for his life. Your cats got sloppy. That's all."

"Howling is a treaty violation," said Arcove, his voice taking on that dangerously patient tone that Charder associated with threats. "Taunting us violates the spirit of the treaty if not the words."

"Then kill him," said Charder. "I'm not defending him. I'm defending the herd. They had nothing to do with this."

"Didn't they?"

"I don't know what you're implying, Arcove."

"I think you do, Charder."

"I've never spoken to Storm," said Charder. "All I know is that he's a low-ranking, half orphan. The herd ostracized him after his first escape from Sharmel. I believe some of them even tried to kill him. But if you can't, what makes you think they can?" *Don't smile. Don't laugh.*

But Arcove did. "Charder, sometimes you're not a very good liar."

"I'm not lying."

"No, you're just not telling the truth." All the smile went out of his voice. "Don't play games with me. You'll lose."

Charder looked at the ground. "You're wasting your time, Arcove. I don't know anything about Storm."

"You don't know why he called himself Vearil?"

Charder looked up. He thought for a moment. "The herd called him that."

"Ah. And which of the herd elders have been talking to him?"

"None that I know of."

"Again, I don't believe you."

"Then kill me."

"A tempting suggestion. You say you've never spoken to him. It's time you started. Tell him that many ferryshaft will die because of his actions if he persists. Tell him that if he publicly submits to our authority, I will let him live. That's the *only* way he's going to live. Tell him."

"As you say."

Arcove leaned forward and spoke almost in Charder's ear. "I promise you that I haven't forgotten how to deal with troublesome ferryshaft, Charder."

Charder swallowed. He had to exert all his willpower not to jerk away. "I have no doubt."

"Some of my advisers think you should be replaced. Should you?"

Charder wanted to say yes. *All these years, and I'm still afraid of him.* "I'll do what you want, Arcove."

Arcove stepped away. "Good. I'll see that Treace's performance is not repeated. You talk to the foal. I want this issue resolved by spring."

8

The Past

Storm hid for two days after the chase with Treace. He was bruised and shaken and a little afraid that the cats might have remained in the vicinity. When he did venture back among other ferryshaft, he found that no one was too surprised to see him. His precipitous descent had been observed by a number of ferryshaft on the ground, although there was a rumor going around that he was hiding because he'd broken a leg.

Most of the adults still wanted nothing to do with him, but the younger ferryshaft watched him with a kind of awe. Storm could see it in their faces, although they did not speak to him. *You think I'm something special,* he thought. *But anyone could do what I'm doing. In fact, you could have killed Treace.* He voiced these sentiments to his clique, but no one agreed with him.

"No, Storm," said Tracer, "anyone could *not* do what you're doing."

"I should hope not," said Kelsy, coming up behind him, "I like to think it took someone special to give me the slip every day for half a winter."

Kelsy had been hanging around a lot lately. Storm wasn't sure exactly why. In spite of his offer of mutual hunting, his clique was clearly breaking up, the process accelerated by the mild winter. Most members of Kelsy's clique were courting mates, and under the current conditions, it was easy for a pair of four-year-olds to find adequate food alone. Foals of that age didn't really need a clique this winter.

Kelsy, particularly, had no need of either hunting partners, or companionship, as he had three rues, who trailed him everywhere in an atmosphere of congenial mischief. Storm had seen high-ranking ferryshaft with two mates, but never with three. If they were jealous of each other, they gave no sign of it. In fact, they seemed to regard teasing Kelsy as a team sport.

"One of you really should find another mate," Storm had heard Kelsy remark on more than one occasion. "I don't know what I will do with all three of you."

"Oh?" Remy would say, wide-eyed and innocent. "Really? You don't know what you will do?"

Itsa would lean against him and echo Remy, "No idea? None at all?"

Faralee, always the cheeky one, would say, "But you figured out what to do with Remy last fall."

"Must not have done it right; she doesn't seem to be in foal."

"Oh, that's just because things weren't ripe yet. Here, let me check." And Faralee would stick her nose under his tail, causing Kelsy to skitter sideways, scattering laughing females.

Having them around was both entertaining and constantly embarrassing. Storm half expected Mylo to tell them to leave, but Mylo only watched with an air of puzzled suspicion. Kelsy regularly mingled with the highest-ranking ferryshaft in the herd, and he made a circuit of visits to various elders and cliques. However, he would usually spend part of the day with Mylo's clique. *He's increasing our status just by being here,* Storm realized. *And he's letting the others know that he approves of me. That may be why no one bothers me.*

For his part, Storm spent each day on edge. At any given moment, he could identify at least three escape routes. He was teaching himself more sheep trails. *Treace probably figured out where I'd go just by sniffing around the cliffs. I must have run up that same path a dozen times in the days before the chase. It was easy to figure out which trail I would use.*

He was surprised when four days passed, and no cats appeared. Then it was six days and then ten, and finally he lost track of the number of days since Treace's raid. The grass, barely suppressed by the light snow, began to poke up new shoots in sheltered places, and still no creasia came to trouble the herd. Storm tried not to become too relaxed, but it was difficult. The weather was fine, food easy to obtain, and all of his friends were in infectiously good spirits.

So-fet even came to visit him one evening. Storm was curled up half asleep between Tollee and Leep, listening to Tracer tell a story. He jumped up as soon as he saw his mother. Storm hesitated for an instant, then ran to her, tail waving, and she washed his face the way she'd done when he was very small. "Storm, I am so proud of you," she said quietly. "I know it must not seem that way, but I am."

"No, it's alright," said Storm as they walked away together. "I don't want the herd to punish you and Sauny if things go badly with me. You're right to keep away."

So-fet looked at him with such sadness that he felt suddenly awkward.

"Mother, I'm not dead yet."

She blinked. "No, no, of course not. I'm sorry I made you feel that way. I…I should go back."

Storm pushed in front of her. "But you just got here! And I wanted to ask you something. How old are you, mother? And what was it like when you were a foal…with the creasia, I mean?"

So-fet looked puzzled. "Like…? Oh, much the same as it is now, I expect. I'm six years old. I had you when I was four…quite young. Your father—his name was Alaran—he was much older."

Storm cocked his head. "And he was killed in a creasia raid?"

So-fet didn't quite meet his eyes. "Yes. I foaled when I saw him dead. That's why you were born early. Looking back, I'm not sure why I was so upset. I cared about him, but I didn't really love him. I guess I was afraid of being without protection."

Storm grew very still. "You were a ru?"

"Yes."

"What happened to your parents?"

So-fet thought for a moment. She spoke haltingly, her eyes flicking to Storm and away again. "My mother died foaling, so I never knew her. I suspect my father abandoned me. He probably thought I would die and didn't want to waste energy trying to feed me. By the time of my first memories at Chelby Lake, I was alone. I didn't stay that way, of course. I was someone's ru from that first summer on. There were several fights over me. I didn't end up with Alaran until I was two."

Storm cringed. "Mother...I'm sorry."

She smiled. "Things got better after you were born."

She started to say something else, but Storm interrupted. "How did you survive your first spring? With no one to nurse you or help you find food...? That seems impossible."

So-fet hesitated. "I think one of my mother's friends nursed me with her foal for a while, but...there was someone else. I have vague memories of him. Perhaps it was my father, although that doesn't seem right. He brought me food that spring and for a little while at Chelby Lake. Perhaps he was some relative. In my mind, he's just a shadow and a soothing voice, always with something to eat. I sometimes wonder what happened to him."

Storm had another surprise visitor early one morning, while planning one of his escape routes among the boulders. Charder approached from downwind, almost as quietly as a cat. Storm never saw him until he spoke from alongside. "Hello, Storm."

Storm wheeled to face the other ferryshaft. He fought down a ridiculous urge to run. Charder was alone and didn't look aggressive or angry.

"Walk with me," said Charder. "We need to talk."

"We do?"

Charder smiled—a small, crooked smile that did not touch his eyes. "Yes."

"Am I being disciplined, sir?"

Charder cocked his head. "Do you see half a dozen elders behind me?"

"No."

"Well, then, you have your answer."

Charder began strolling through the rocks. After a moment, Storm cautiously fell in beside him. "Does this have anything to do with the creasia, sir?"

"Of course. You can call me Charder."

"Are you angry with me, Charder?"

"I didn't say that."

"Then you approve?"

"I didn't say that, either."

For a few moments they walked without speaking, listening to the crunch and creak of morning frost beneath their hooves. The air smelled of thawing earth. "I have been directed," said Charder at last, "to give you a warning and an offer. You know, don't you, that what you are doing is unlikely to end well?"

"Yes," said Storm, and waited.

After a moment, Charder continued. "I know that you must feel that you've done well thus far, but you have only dealt with the lowest-ranking of Arcove's officers. More will come, and they will be better. Should you have occasion to deal with Arcove himself, you may wish that one of his generals had killed you. They are merely testing you to see if you are worth his time."

"I don't see that I have much choice," said Storm with a hint of irritation. "I suppose I could run away, try to live as an exile from the herd…but I'd rather take my chances here."

Charder inclined his head. "Your limited options have been taken into account. Arcove has offered to let you live if you submit to the creasia before the entire herd."

Storm stopped walking. He turned to Charder in astonishment. "He said that?"

Charder looked at some point over Storm's head. "Yes."

"And you believe him?"

Charder gave a faint, bitter chuckle, and his eyes dropped to Storm's face. "Oh, yes, I believe him. You can trust him to keep his promises."

Storm thought for a moment. "What does 'submit' mean?"

Charder grimaced. "Smart foal. It means that they'll do anything they want short of killing you—probably bite off your tail and your ears—certainly cripple you. They'll make sure you never run from them again. Every ferryshaft who looks at you will see a reminder of what happens when we challenge cats."

Storm felt cold. "I think I'll keep running."

"Suit yourself. Either way, it probably won't end well."

Storm frowned. "I thought…when you argued with Treace, I thought you were on my side."

Charder waved his tail. "Treace broke a treaty law. He made a mistake, but the creasia do not make mistakes often. If you depend on their errors, you will die. As for me: who says I'm not on your side?"

Storm looked at him in bewilderment. "You just said—"

"I said that you haven't much chance at winning."

So you are *on my side.* "Will you help me?" asked Storm softly. "If the ferryshaft would just fight when the cats come to raid, we could easily—"

"Careful," interrupted Charder in a strange, sing-song voice. "I can't be hearing this and not reporting it."

Storm gave an exasperated sigh. "So you'll tell them I'm breaking the rules and saying forbidden things? Like I'm not doing that already?"

Charder snorted. "Storm, if *you* break treaty law, it's on your own head. If *I* break treaty law, many more lives than mine will be forfeit. Maybe even the entire herd."

Storm thought for a moment. "I want to make things better, Charder. How do you suggest I do that?"

Charder looked surprised. He considered for a moment. Finally, he smiled—a real smile this time. "You survive."

9

A Strange Tunnel

Kelsy took a certain interest in Storm's search for new escape routes. "You really shouldn't limit yourself to the boulder mazes and the sheep trails," he said one evening, during his customary visit. "The woods at the top of the cliffs give good cover, and the Sea Cliffs have trails, too."

Storm pricked up his ears. "The trails on the Sea Cliffs are steeper," he said cautiously, "and the rock is more crumbly."

Kelsy acknowledged this. "But you're lighter than a cat," he said. "Never forget it."

"Why don't we all go to the beach tomorrow?" piped up Tracer. "We haven't been to the beach all winter because food is so easy to find this year. I miss the taste of those little rock creatures."

There were murmurs of agreement all around. Leep glanced at Mylo, who was always exceptionally taciturn when Kelsy was around. "Beach sounds nice," Mylo said, but he didn't smile.

Faralee stretched languorously beside Kelsy. "We could show Storm that strange tunnel. Might be useful to him, though I can't think how."

Kelsy frowned. "Tunnel? Oh! You're right. Storm, there's an odd…well, I don't know what to call it, but it looks like a cave that someone valued once. It's a ways south of here along the cliff top."

So, next morning, Mylo's clique, plus Kelsy and his three rues, made the trek to the top of the cliff. They browsed in the woods, rich with patches of early grass, leafy greens, squirrels, and rabbits, and then crossed to a trail down the Sea Cliffs. Kelsy told Storm about the four safe trails he knew. Of the four, Storm had only ever used two. He suspected that Mylo did not know about the others.

They descended to the beach and enjoyed the usual crunchy delicacies among the rocks. As often happened on these trips, they found an animal that no one had ever seen before in one of the tide pools—a bony-looking thing that curled and uncurled until Callaris bit it, and then it uncurled forever. Tollee never seemed to know how to behave around Kelsy's rues, but she was finally making cautious friends with Remy. Storm was happy to see her talking to someone. She'd been almost as quiet as Mylo ever since the chase with Treace.

As they moved up the beach, Mylo edged out ahead, and, after a moment, Kelsy joined him. Storm was surprised to see them talking. He was certain that Mylo was saying more words than he'd said in the last five days combined. Storm would have liked to hear their conversation, but the wind carried most of it away. He edged forward, but could only catch a phrase here and there.

Mylo sounded angry. "…your game?"

Kelsy had a patient expression. "…if Storm keeps getting away…"

Mylo's voice rose. "You're just using this to…"

Their discussion grew heated, and most of the other ferry-shaft became *very* preoccupied with hunting among the tide pools. Storm watched with his head on one side. Finally, Kelsy spun away. "Report me to the elders if that's how you feel," he shot over his shoulder. He approached Storm at a trot. "Come on, Vearil, let's go have a look at that strange tunnel."

Storm smiled at the epithet. He didn't say anything as they made their way back up the steep trail from the beach. Faralee and Itsa came with them, but Remy was still talking to Tollee, and it looked like the rest of the clique would be foraging for a while.

When they reached the top of the cliffs, Kelsy started south, still moving at a quick pace. "Why is Mylo angry?" asked Storm at last.

Kelsy snorted. "Because he's afraid."

"Of what?"

"Change. The creasia. Me." Kelsy laughed. "You just keep staying alive, Storm. Mylo will get over it."

They moved briskly in silence as the sun passed its zenith and started down the sky. Storm had just begun to think that this tunnel was really too far away, and they might not be able to rejoin the others before dark, when Kelsy stopped beside a thick stand of brush. "I think this is it," he said.

Faralee waved her tail. "This is it, but we're on the wrong side." She circled the thicket, which appeared to be impenetrable. Finally, she located a narrow game trail, probably made by sheep, and edged her way inside.

Itsa followed her, Storm and Kelsy behind. They emerged from the thicket on the edge of a broad opening in the earth, surrounded on all sides by brush. The ground was littered with the light, porous stone that Storm often found around cliff caves. "The first time, it looked as though someone had gone to some trouble to conceal it," said Itsa. There was a mass of branches piled around the opening, but it was rotting—probably several years old.

Storm peered into the cave. "Did you follow it back?" he asked.

"Oh, yes," said Faralee, pushing past him. "It's quite safe, but I'm not sure how useful it will be. You could get trapped here."

Storm remained cautious. He sniffed the air, but caught no scent of telshees. Itsa and Kelsy were already making their way down the passage, and at last Storm followed them. The tunnel slanted downward, but not steeply. Light from the entrance penetrated for quite a distance. Then the tunnel took a jog and became momentarily black. However, within a short distance, Storm saw the twinkle of daylight at the far end. To his surprise, he also heard and smelled the ocean.

He glanced at Kelsy, who just shook his head. "You'll see in a moment."

Storm realized that the tunnel opened onto a cliff face. He walked to the edge and looked down at a sheer drop to a strip of narrow beach. He realized, then, that he was in one wall of a small fiord. Storm could see the far wall a dozen lengths in front of him—farther than he could jump, even if there had been something to jump *to*. He looked up and saw the far ledge some distance above. He could not see the edge directly overhead, since the tunnel receded slightly into the cliff.

Storm studied the situation for a moment. The cliff walls to either side were smooth, without so much as a sheep trail. The fall to the beach would be deadly. "It does look like a good place to get trapped."

"You're probably right," said Kelsy. "But the way it was concealed seemed so strange."

"Also, the walls," said Faralee.

Storm looked in her direction and froze. The walls nearer this end were smooth, and they'd been covered with markings. Everything about the markings was unnatural, and Storm knew at once that they'd been made by an intelligent creature. However, they looked quite different from the lines and circles he was accustomed to seeing in caves. These looked more like the image of the telshee on the ceiling of the cave on Kuwee Island. Only, they were…

"Ferryshaft," he said slowly.

Faralee waved her tail. "They look kind of like us, don't they? Except, there's something on their backs."

Thinking about it in the right way, Storm could see that the cave wall was covered with images of ferryshaft and some other creature that seemed to be crouching on their backs. He even saw images of telshees at the bottom. "How…odd."

"Do you think telshees make things like this?" asked Itsa. "We are near the beach."

"I don't know," said Kelsy. "But someone made it, probably long ago."

Storm shivered. He remembered how the secret passage had opened at his back. *They could be here. They could be anywhere.* "We should go back to the others," he said. "We've come a long way south." He took another hard look at the cliff wall, gauging the distance with his eyes. An idea fluttered in the back of his mind. *I might be able to use this place after all.*

Emerging into the late afternoon sunlight, Storm felt a vague sense of unease. "Were you planning to stay on the cliffs tonight, Kelsy?"

"Probably. Did you have other plans?"

"No." The sky was overcast, and a light rain peppered their fur. Storm wasn't sure he'd ever been this far south along the cliff top. He was about to ask whether they might walk along the edge of the Red Cliffs on the way back so that he could get his bearings, when the wind shifted, and he caught the unmistakable scent of creasia.

The others caught it too. Storm saw the immediate rigidity in Kelsy's posture. Itsa gasped, and Faralee started to bolt. Storm ground to a halt and gave a fierce shake of his head. *Don't move!*

They didn't. No one said anything. They just stood with nostrils wide, breathing quickly. Storm looked in the direction of the wind—north and a little west. He couldn't see the cats, but they were certainly out there. *They must be looking for me. If I don't draw them away, they'll find my friends.* He forced himself not to think about what might have happened if they'd already found his clique.

He looked at Kelsy and gave a toss of his head towards the Sea Cliffs. *You go that way. They won't care about you in a moment.* Then, without looking back, he started towards the ominous scent.

Within moments, Storm caught a flash of brindled fur through the trees and hunkered down. *They're probably following my trail,* he thought, *we were returning in much the same way that we came. We would have met them head-on if the wind hadn't shifted.*

He wasn't sure where Kelsy, Itsa, and Faralee had gone, but he knew that he didn't want the creasia to stay in the area for a leisurely investigation.

So, he howled. It always seemed to work, and this time was no exception. Storm heard cries of excitement and the crackle of leaves underfoot. He saw a confusion of brown and black shapes coming through the trees, but he did not wait to count them.

Storm turned and fled. He was surprised to feel a sense of buoyancy and cautious optimism. The long days of uncertainty were over. He did not have to wonder how or where the next creasia attack would occur. The place was here, the time was now. He was well-fed and well-practiced, though not so much on this bit of terrain.

Time to change that.

Storm angled through the wood in the direction of the red cliffs. He would find a trail, and it would most likely be one he knew. With any luck, he could lose these cats before nightfall.

Storm burst out of the trees to rush along the edge of the Red Cliffs. All at once, his stride faltered. Why did he see so much green below? A terrible idea occurred to him. *Where is the Igby?*

One glance to the north confirmed Storm's suspicions. He saw the river winding eastward in a silver ribbon, but it should have been south of him, not north. Storm felt cold. He had crossed the river above the cliffs without realizing it. The deep green below was the Southern Forests: creasia territory.

Storm's thoughts raced, but he increased his speed again as the cats emerged from the trees not far behind him. The creasia were too close to allow Storm to turn around on the cliff top. *I don't know these sheep trails,* he thought. *I can't use them, but I could at least get to the bottom of the cliff.* The idea of taking a chase into creasia territory made Storm feel ill, but if he kept running along the cliff top, he would soon reach the Garu Vell—a dead-end.

I will go down the cliff, thought Storm, *and turn north. Soon I'll reach the Igby, and once I cross it, I know of dozens of places to hide. I'll stay in the rocks at the bottom of the cliff. I won't even go into the wood.*

Presently, he spotted a trailhead. Storm darted forward and down. He would have liked to go slowly, for he did not know the path, but he wanted a better lead on the cats, and so he took the unknown trail at a gallop.

10

Round 3: Sharmel

Storm barely saw the cats in time. They shot out of the boulders in front of him, almost blocking his escape from the cliff trail. *They must have been waiting.* Storm veered away, but his reflexes were slow. He'd been up and down the cliffs three times today. Evening shadows stretched among the rocks, and his panting breath left foggy clouds in the air.

Pain woke him up—points of agony as the cat's slapping paw twisted him into the air. Storm hit the ground upright and running, his fatigue temporarily washed away in a moment of panic. He ran with speed he hadn't known he could muster in the only direction available—into the trees. He felt warm blood coursing down his right foreleg. *Oh, no. No, no, no, no...*

In the space of a few heartbeats, all his plans had been dashed. Now he was running through creasia territory—an unknown forest—at dusk, injured, and leaving a blood trail. Panic and despair clamped down on his chest like the jaws of a predator. It was hard to breathe.

Storm raced on blindly as the wood grew darker, expecting to feel claws in his back at any moment. Finally, he stumbled. He couldn't catch his breath. He wondered if he was dying of blood loss. Storm pitched headlong into the leaves. He twisted around, completely spent, a quivering, terrified foal waiting for death.

In his glassy-eyed state, it took him a moment to realize that there were no cats immediately behind him. The twilight wood loomed all around. He heard only the sound of his own rasping breath and smelled only wet loam.

Storm tried to gauge how far he'd run, but couldn't say. The sun had set. He was no longer certain in which direction the Igby lay. *So I'm lost, too.*

Storm twisted around to have a look at his injury. One glance told him that, while he was certainly leaving a blood trail, he wasn't likely to die of it. The scratch was a superficial graze that ran along his right ribs. It would be of little concern if it hadn't passed over his elbow and upper right front leg. The act of running stretched the wound and caused it to bleed.

But I'm not bleeding to death, and the cats are not close behind me.

As though to qualify this point, a creasia call rose quavering in the night air. Storm shivered. The cat was close. *They probably didn't chase me hard because they knew I was leaving an easy trail. They probably wanted me deep in creasia territory.*

Storm rose, testing his shaky legs. He still felt that his chances of reaching the Igby were slim, but he wasn't dead yet. He quelled the urge to start running again as the creasia calls drew nearer. *I can't just keep running all night in random directions. I might be headed straight away from the Igby. I need to hide until morning. When the sun rises, I'll know which direction is north.*

But how to hide when I'm leaving a blood trail?

Storm's panting had subsided, and he was beginning to catch the more subtle sounds of the forest. Storm shut his eyes, held his breath, and *listened.* And there it was. The sound of running water.

In the chilly darkness just before dawn, a creasia bent over a stream to drink. He lapped at the ice around the edges. Water was running at the center due to the mild winter and to a hot spring farther upstream, and the cat didn't want to break through. He was not surprised, when he looked up, to see another cat three paces away. "Anything?"

"No." The other paused to drink.

"You think Sharmel will call it off? That foal's probably back with the herd by now...or sitting up on the cliffs laughing at us."

The first cat snorted. "You really think so?"

"There's not a whiff of him in the forest, Andrel. I went half-way to Chelby Lake; there's nothing. I say he followed the stream to the cliffs, climbed them, and he's long gone."

"Impossible," said Andrel. "You don't know how close we were when he found the water. Sharmel sent cats upstream immediately. There's no way he reached the cliffs."

"Well, he left the forest somehow."

"I don't think so. Neither does chief."

The second cat was quiet for a moment. "He disappeared mysteriously when Ariand chased him, too."

His companion growled, but he continued. "They say he went into a dead-end cave and never came out. They watched the place all night, but the next morning he was gone. He called himself Vearil—the ill-omen."

"Careful," muttered Andrel.

"Well, it happened!"

Andrel had stopped growling. He was quiet for a moment. Then he laughed. "Coden's ghost. Are we calling him that, yet?"

"Maybe."

"We'll find him," said Andrel. "He's not a ghost, and he's not an omen. He bleeds bright red. We'll find him."

"If you say so."

The creasia were still talking as they moved away. A night bird started to sing, then stopped as something moved in the tree overhead. Storm shifted as the first light of dawn touched the sky. He stared thoughtfully after the two creasia. *Who was Coden?*

11

The River and the Trees

Storm tried to stretch, but his situation in the tree made any movement awkward. *They still haven't figured it out.*

And why should they? Storm had never seen or heard of a ferryshaft climbing a tree. He'd simply guessed—correctly—that the long, torturous limbs would not be much more difficult to tread than a precarious cliff trail.

It *had* been a close thing. He'd struggled a short distance downstream over rotten ice, breaking through into freezing, knee-deep water, until he found a suitable branch that overhung the stream. He'd gauged his jump with the sound of approaching creasia wails loud in his ears. Every fiber of his being screamed *run!* The branch was high and the night black. It had begun to rain again. Storm had jumped three times before he'd managed to clamber onto the slippery limb, and the cats were so close that he feared the trembling of the branch would give him away.

Once the cats passed below him, Storm had worked his way to the tree's trunk. He dared not stay near his original point of departure from the stream. A cat might see the branch and suspect. The trees of the Southern Forest had stocky limbs and massive trunks, and they grew close together. Storm had found that, with care, he could walk from tree to tree. He had spent some time working his way along the stream in this fashion. At last, quivering with exhaustion, he had wedged himself in the crotch of a tree and fallen into a restless sleep. Creasia voices had woken him, and he saw that it was almost dawn.

Pain shot through Storm's muscles as he tried to stand. Never in his life had he felt so stiff and sore. The wound along his right ribs and foreleg throbbed. However, it had crusted over and did not seem likely to bleed again. His stomach growled, but he pushed that aside.

Storm listened carefully, then jumped to the ground. The air smelled pleasantly of woods after rain. He walked to the stream and took a long drink. For a moment, he stood perfectly still, savoring the water, thinking of the forest and the river that lay between him and safety. Then he turned and started north with the rising sun on his right shoulder.

When he wasn't galloping, Storm's footfalls were soundless on the forest floor. The ground beneath the trees was almost entirely free of snow, and he made good time at a swift trot. The first pair of creasia he encountered came from upwind, and Storm easily avoided them.

However, with so many creasia combing the forest, they could hardly avoid finding his scent trail. Suddenly the quiet woods began to echo with the yowls of an excited cat. Others answered, and their voices began to converge on Storm's trail.

Storm considered a flat-out race. He thought he must be close to the Igby. However, he couldn't be sure, and some of the cats might be between him and the river. If he ran in a straight line, they would intercept him. *They'll expect that,* he thought. *If I do what they expect, I'm dead.*

Storm listened carefully to the voices behind him. *What do they least expect?* He whirled and trotted south along his own trail, towards the calls of approaching cats. Storm moved toward the oncoming creasia until his nerve broke. Then he found a sturdy, low limb and jumped at it. On his second try, he landed on the branch and scrambled higher into the tree.

An instant later, he spotted the cats. Storm held his breath. When they weren't calling to each other, they were astonishingly silent. Storm crouched, tense and breathless, as five of them flowed like water beneath his tree. One cat paused and sniffed suspiciously at a shifting breeze, but then he dropped his nose to the trail and followed his companions. Storm heaved a sigh of relief as they disappeared from view.

The foal worked his way through two more trees, then hopped to the ground. For some time, he continued moving directly away from his original path on a course parallel to the Igby. When he was sure that he had gone far enough to escape any cat trying to intersect his original course, he turned and started trotting toward the river again. For a time, Storm felt safe and pleased with himself.

But it couldn't last. Soon a group of cats found his new trail and sounded the alarm. Storm performed his trick again and moved away. Once more, the pattern repeated. By the third performance, Storm realized that the cats had discovered his ruse. They seemed to be catching up quicker, not running all the way to the end of his scent trail.

However, Storm smelled water, and he knew the chase was almost over. He abandoned caution and *ran*. Soon, he caught a glimmer through the trees—sunlight on ice! In the same moment a large, gray creasia dropped out of the sky onto the ground in front of him. Storm dug in his heels and slid to a stop.

"We can climb, too," growled the cat. Beyond the trees ahead, the tantalizing glimmer still beckoned—so close.

Storm dodged to one side and pounded frantically towards the river. He was a little surprised when the creasia followed more slowly. He had a brief impression of the snowy riverbank, the light dazzling beyond the shade of the trees. In one bound, Storm propelled himself out onto the Igby and landed running. However, the previous day's rain had not frozen, and the ice was unusually slick. Storm had not skated in many days, and he went sprawling.

The river groaned. Storm's eyes widened, and suddenly he understood the creasia's lack of haste. A thousand things that he should have remembered flooded his brain—the mild winter, moving water in the little stream, the fact that no one had gone to the Igby to skate in more than ten days. *The ice is thawing.* Storm lay flat on his belly, afraid to move. Slowly, he turned his head to look over his shoulder.

The gray creasia had advanced a few lengths onto the ice, but he obviously had no intention of coming farther. A large number of other cats stared at Storm from the bank. If the ice creaked under a foal, it could not possibly support an adult creasia.

Storm allowed himself the leisure of studying their leader without fear of attack. He mustered a confident tone that he did not feel and said, "You must be Sharmel."

The cat cocked his head. He was dark gray—not Storm's near-white, but the color of wet beach sand. He had a frosting of white fur around his muzzle. Storm thought he must be older than most of the other cats. There was also something familiar about him. *Have we met before?* Aloud, Storm continued, "You look tired. Long night?"

The cat gave a brief, surprised chuckle. "Where did you learn that trick with the trees?"

Storm pulled his front feet under him cautiously, testing the ice. "Made it up."

"I don't believe that. Who's been coaching you?"

"Believe whatever you like." Storm focused his attention on his feet. The river creaked again.

"You've chosen an uncomfortable way to die," observed Sharmel.

Storm paused to squint at him. "You were in that group who chased me the first time, weren't you? Must be embarrassing to have lost me twice. I am just a foal, after all."

Sharmel's ears settled back, and his tail lashed. "You're going to die gagging for air, scratching at the underside of a frozen river."

"No," said Storm. "I don't think I am." He'd managed to get all four hooves under him. The river creaked loudly, but held. Storm paused, allowing the ice to settle. Then he began an agonizingly slow journey toward the far shore. At first he tried to walk, but the river growled with every step. At last, he gave up and propelled himself in gentle, sliding motions.

Suddenly a creasia yowl split the breathless silence, and Storm barely checked himself from a headlong plunge. Other cats caught on, and a bedlam of noise erupted from the creasia side of the river.

Storm's instincts screamed at him to flee. His exhaustion, frayed nerves, and lack of sleep made it difficult to think.

He turned back towards the creasia with a snarl and shouted, "Coden! He's the one who coached me!" He was rewarded with instant silence. "He comes to me in my dreams," continued Storm, inventing wildly. The consternation on their faces spurred his inspiration. "I am *Vearil*. I am Storm. I am the cloud before the Volontaro. I am your ill-omen, your bad luck. I am your doom!"

Some of them were actually bristling and backing away. Storm had become so enthusiastic over his performance that he forgot to distribute his weight evenly on the ice. He took several threatening steps towards the creasia, and a terrible snapping noise sent echoes skipping across the river.

Storm whirled and jumped.

Crack! He could feel the ice buckle and shift under his hooves when he landed.

Jump! The section where he'd been standing broke loose and flipped over.

Jump! This time, when he landed, he broke through, but he was only five lengths from the shore. Gasping in the frigid water, Storm managed to get his front hooves over the lip of the ice. His hind feet found the river bottom, and he gave one last surge. Moments later, he lay panting on the bank—wet and trembling, but safe.

"Well, I'm glad we let you try a second time, Sharmel," said Treace at council the next day, "what with the gossip now circulating among the common animals. Coden's ghost? That was a very productive outing."

"Storm was making it up," snapped Sharmel. "The clutter was taunting him, and he taunted back."

"Of course he was making it up!" laughed Treace, "but I'm not sure the subordinate creasia know that."

Sharmel wrapped his tail around his haunches defensively. "At least I wounded him. No one else has done better."

"Or worse," Halvery snorted. "A buck won't give you his haunch just because you wound him. This foal got lucky a few times, and you all panic! You're like cubs on your first hunt!"

"Storm is a foal, true," said Sharmel quietly, "but he's not lucky. He's resourceful, intelligent, and dangerous."

"*Dangerous!*" mimicked Halvery. "How many creasia has he killed so far? None. Oh, but of course, he's also injured...zero. Storm is only a danger to himself. Intelligent ferryshaft do not attack creasia. He's an impulsive misfit. He probably can't even attract a mate, what with his size and odd color, so he's doing this to get some attention."

"Well," said Roup brightly, "he's succeeded."

Halvery scowled at him.

Sharmel growled. "He used trees, Halvery. How many ferryshaft would even think of that, much less have the skill to do it?"

"Trees...?" Halvery hesitated. "Did you say that he used trees?"

"Yes! Have you ever heard of such a thing?"

"Once..." Halvery shook himself. "I still say that he's a foolish youngster, taking risks without a plan—certainly not a *danger* to a competent clutter."

"Well, now you have your chance to prove it," said Arcove.

Halvery grinned.

Roup and Sharmel shared a look over his head as the meeting broke up. *I do believe one of us is in favor of Storm's success in this instance,* thought Roup.

12

Round 4: Halvery

That afternoon, Storm lay sunning himself in his clique's favorite resting place, trying to banish the last of the river's cold from his bones. He'd told his story twice—once to his friends and once to his sister. Sauny had met him on the edge of the ferryshaft feeding grounds. She'd listened to every detail with absolute attention. When he talked about the river, she grinned. "I bet I wouldn't have broken through. I'm even lighter than you, Storm!"

Storm frowned. *And not quite a year old.* "Sauny, please don't try to do what I'm doing. Not yet."

"Someday?"

Storm hesitated. "Someday. Maybe."

"Will you teach me to run on the cliffs?"

Storm was surprised. He'd tried to teach his friends about the sheep trails, and they'd always refused. He looked at Sauny—small and fearless and too young to know better. "I'll think about it. You'll have to promise to do *exactly* as I say...and probably not tell your parents." *Dover will try to kill me if he finds out...again.*

Sauny capered around him. "Storm, we're going to kill creasia together!"

Storm laughed nervously. "*I* can't kill creasia, Sauny. You stay away from them."

That afternoon, as he lay in the sunbeam, Tollee came and sat beside him. She didn't say anything. The air was pleasantly warm and full of the drip, drip, drip of thawing snow and ice. Finally, Storm said, "Tollee, what's going on with Mylo and Kelsy?"

She shifted uncomfortably, but still said nothing.

Storm laughed. "I think everybody knows, except me. They all talk *about* me, but nobody talks *to* me. Not even you, anymore." *Maybe you really do want to be Mylo's mate.*

Tollee sighed. "Kelsy is trying to split the herd, Storm."

Storm was surprised. He'd expected something more mundane.

Tollee continued. "He wants to take a group of ferryshaft—this summer or next—and circle the lake. There is supposedly grassland on the far side, where no ferryshaft live. He thinks the cats won't bother us there."

Storm sat up. "And what do the other ferryshaft say? Why is Mylo angry about it?"

"Apparently, it's against the creasia's rules. There is only supposed to be one herd. The creasia choose the leader. Right now, that's Charder. If we leave, they'll come and slaughter us. Ordinarily, no one would even consider breaking their rules, but…because of you…ferryshaft are talking. If one foal can defy the cats and get away with it, what could a hundred adults do? Why do we follow their rules and let them kill us if they're so easily outwitted? The elders say that the hunting parties are only the tiniest part of creasia strength. If a large number of ferryshaft defy them, they'll come in great numbers and kill us."

Storm thought for a moment. "Has anyone mentioned someone named Coden?"

"Not that I've heard. Who is he?"

Storm shook his head. "Someone who died, someone who fought the cats. I think they feared him." He hesitated. "Does Mylo side with the elders?"

Tollee snorted. "Mylo says that Kelsy has always had his eye on herd leadership. But Kelsy knows that he can't lead *this* herd. The elders follow creasia rules, and only the creasia can decide who leads. When you got away the first time, Kelsy talked a little about fighting the cats, but the adults got so angry that he stopped. Instead, he started talking to the younger ferryshaft about forming a new herd. He can't have this one, so he's trying to create another.

"Mylo thinks he's just using you and your success to capture support and attention. He's not associating with our clique because he likes us or because he wants to give us status. It's the other way around. We—you, especially—are giving *him* status and leverage with the younger adults. Kelsy is *very* popular and one of the best fighters in the herd, but no one would listen to him about leaving if you weren't having such success. If the herd elders are right, he stands to get a lot of young ferryshaft killed."

Storm considered this. "What do *you* think?"

Tollee was silent for a long moment. "Ferryshaft are talking about things that haven't been discussed openly in our lifetimes. *I* didn't know there was a rule about only one herd. I didn't know that the creasia chose our leader. I didn't understand that the creasia rules are part of a treaty. I didn't know that, if we break the treaty, we could be at war with the cats. I didn't know we'd lost a war. I think it's important to know those things."

"What do you think about Kelsy and the idea of leaving the herd? Would you go?"

Tollee hesitated. "Would you?"

"Of course!" *It's probably the only way I could have you...if Mylo stayed behind.*

Tollee took a deep breath. "We're talking about most of the four to eight-year-olds in the herd, Storm. If you encourage them, and if you're wrong... Think about it."

"I have thought about it."

Tollee stood up and started away. "Says the person who's never lost anyone."

Storm felt a little angry. "You'd fight if it came to that." *You'd fight for me...wouldn't you?*

Tollee turned. She started to say something, then stopped. At last, she said, "Get Kelsy to teach you how to fight. He's better at it than I am."

"What's that supposed to mean?" But Storm had a sinking feeling. Somehow, although he'd won the race against Sharmel, he'd lost his friend.

Storm knew by the next day that he had lost his clique, too. No one would admit it. Mylo claimed that the clique had simply broken up. He would be five years old that spring and fully capable of defending Tollee on his own, given her willing assistance. Callaris and Valla were in a similar position. Leep and Tracer had both paired off with their prospective mates. They would be four years old and could make the transition to adulthood with a modicum of luck and cooperation. Tarsis had surprised everyone by fighting, and beating, the leader of another young clique and thereby advancing himself into a secure position.

Only Storm was left, at three years of age, to fend for himself. Tracer and Leep both invited him to hunt with them "from time to time," but no one told him where they were sleeping, and no one returned to the clique's old haunt. Storm could hardly blame them—a group of social misfits, caught suddenly and frighteningly in the midst of major herd politics. Rather than appear to sanction Kelsy's actions or to argue with him, they simply disbanded and attempted to get out of sight.

Still, Storm felt betrayed and rejected. Never had he imagined that success could feel so lonely. He wondered whether another clique would take him. Many probably wanted to, but he wasn't sure any would dare. He had a few things he wanted to say to Kelsy, but he never got the chance before the creasia attacked again.

They came in a typical raid pattern early one morning when most of the herd was grazing on the edge of the plain. Storm was deep in the boulder mazes when the raid began, and although he heard the screams, it took him some moments to reach the plain. When he arrived, the cats had separated a small group of ferryshaft—only three animals—from the herd and were pacing around them, waiting.

Storm felt reckless, and he strolled out of the boulders into the space between the herd and the cats without so much as a pause to identify their leader. "I expected you two days ago," he called. "Were you waiting to kill the newborn foals? Maybe you could catch *them*."

A dark brown creasia answered. He was a handsome animal with black points, though he had a curiously short tail. "The creasia kill when and where they please, foal."

"I have a name," snapped Storm.

"No one will remember it after today."

"On the contrary, I think that *you* will recall it vividly tomorrow." Storm spun away towards the boulders, expecting the cats to follow. However, as he clattered into the rocks, he heard the unmistakable scream of a mortally injured ferryshaft, cut horribly short. It was joined briefly, by snarls, the sounds of a struggle, and another desperate cry. He realized, with a jolt, that the creasia leader had stayed to kill the selected ferryshaft. *And I can do nothing about it. Some herd protector I am!*

For a moment, his stride wavered, but then he picked up his feet again. *No, I can do* one *thing.* The creasia's decision to sacrifice a few moments killing ferryshaft had been an act of calculated arrogance. Storm felt a flame of anger. *Are you so confident that you can afford to give me a head start? Well. Let us see what I can do with it.*

Storm suspected that the creasia leader would have posted cats near the major cliff trails to ambush him. There was no point in heading in that direction anytime soon. The plain, however, was recently free of snow, the grass still short, and the damp ground crisscrossed with the short-lived streams of spring snowmelt. It would provide any number of ways to confuse a scent trail. Storm angled in that direction, running south towards the river.

As he reached the edge of the plain, he glimpsed curb tracks in the soggy ground. Their trail ran in the same direction as his own. An idea blossomed in Storm's head. He slowed and spent a few precious moments finding the curb trail again. The tracks were definitely fresh.

Storm raised his head and looked out across the plain. He could not see the curbs, but that did not mean they were not close. Storm's explorations had taught him that curb tracks would generally be found in the troughs, where the curbs could stay out of sight of potential prey. He knew the dips in this area well, and had a pretty good idea of where the curbs must be.

Storm considered. He thought back to the time when he'd been attacked by curbs. *Tollee saved me. I was trying to save* her. The curbs were small compared to a creasia, but they were fierce, especially when they came in numbers.

The flame of anger still burned hot in Storm's chest. It mingled with the pain and frustration that he felt over his friends' recent rejection. He felt a little numb.

Methodically, ignoring the approaching yowls of cats, Storm began to follow the curbs' trail. His plan, he reflected, would be every bit as arrogant as the creasia's behavior and probably quite foolish. However, if it didn't work, he would only die.

Eyal looked over his pack once more before settling down in the short grass. He was a new leader, still wondering whether he'd made a mistake by volunteering for the long patrols. It was a position of unparalleled freedom and responsibility, so far from his queen in the Southern Mountains.

It was also a position of unparalleled danger. His predecessor had disappeared without a trace. Eyal had searched for him when he came north last fall, but the entire pack seemed to have vanished. He held out a small hope that the spring thaw might reveal their bodies beneath the snow, giving some clue as to how they had died.

But we already know that. While the forest and plain held many dangers for a lone curb, only one threat was likely to have eradicated an entire pack: other curbs. Specifically, lowland curbs.

The smaller, sleeker lowland packs dominated this half of the island. They cooperated loosely, although Eyal had seen them fight each other on occasion. However, they would viciously attack and kill highland curbs. The two clans had been at war for as long as anyone could remember.

Highland curbs had always been less numerous—larger and shaggier, but slower to breed. They lived in cooperative groups, all controlled by a single queen in the Southern Mountains. There'd been a time when highland curbs also controlled the foothills and parts of the surrounding plain, but the faster-breeding, less central- ized bands of lowland curbs had eventually driven them out until they held only the highest, most forbidding slopes.

Nevertheless, Myridia, their queen, still saw fit to send long patrols into the distant reaches of the island—her eyes and ears in foreign parts. Long patrols brought back word of the doings among other intelligent races, including alliances and power shifts, which might affect the highland curbs or their enemies. There'd been a time when several ferryshaft herds roamed the plain on both sides of the lake and kept the lowland curbs in check. Their absence this past decade was part of the reason for the highland curbs' decline.

Mortality among long patrols had risen alarmingly over the past few years, with whole packs disappearing without a single survivor. The patrols were now composed almost entirely of trou- blemakers—individuals that the queen did not wish to keep near her, but were too valuable as fighters to banish entirely. Females were never sent on the long patrols. They were too valuable to the survival of their race.

Four years ago, there'd been three packs of highland curbs living on the ferryshaft plains and reporting back to their queen. Last year, there'd been only one, and by the time Eyal arrived that summer, it had disappeared as well. Now, two seasons later, Myridia had still not sent another pack, nor even individuals to replace Eyal's subordinates who'd been killed that winter.

She has lost faith in me. Eyal remembered what he'd said to his queen as he stood beneath the great fir tree in the heart of their valley. "Give me a mate, my queen—only one, the lowliest of your bitches—and I will establish our tribe across the great river, beyond the flesh-eating forest on the slopes of the Great Mountain where the lowland curbs do not roam."

Bold words, thought Eyal bitterly, *and stupid.* He'd tried to scale the Great Mountain. He'd actually brought his pack safely to its foothills that summer. However, they'd been driven off by the ely-ary—enormous birds who ruled the mountain and did not tolerate other predators on its slopes. Eyal had been unable to parley with them and had returned at last to the plain, where his pack spent a miserable winter learning the territory and dodging packs of lowland curbs.

He'd come north with thirty animals—a large pack. By spring, he had nineteen. Eyal was not surprised when the snows melted and his queen sent no bitch to join him. This was no place to raise pups or establish a colony. *But if we don't,* thought Eyal, *if lowland curbs ever get past our guards in the mountains, if they ever find our dens in the valley...* It would take only one breach, one killing spree among the birthing dens, and his race would never recover. Eyal knew that they needed a second colony. His queen knew it, too, but as yet, no safe place could be found. So, Eyal watched and listened and waited.

On this particular spring morning, his pack was settling down to rest after a night of hunting sheep. Eyal had heard the cries from the ferryshaft herd not far away and had surmised that the creasia were raiding. This was nothing unusual.

Eyal was curious, however, as he'd noticed a recent disturbance in the pattern of creasia/ferryshaft relations. The raiding season had been predictably short this year due to the brief winter. Even so, the raids seemed to be coming extremely close together. In spite of this, his pack had found no ferryshaft bodies on the occasions when they'd tried to scavenge after raids. Odd. Eyal did not normally spend a great deal of time observing the ferryshaft, but over the last few days, he'd hung around the edges of the herd in an attempt to discover what was going on. He'd considered trying to capture and question a ferryshaft, but the potential loss of life to his irreplaceable pack made him waver.

Eyal cursed his own inexperience. He was certain that a more seasoned long patrol leader would have contacts among the ferryshaft and elsewhere who would already have alerted him to the situation. However, that knowledge had died with his predecessor, and every member of Eyal's pack was as green as himself.

Still, they were none of them so inexperienced as to all sleep at once. Consequently, about a third of the pack jumped up when a young ferryshaft bounded over the side of the dip into their midst. He flashed up the far side of the trench and was gone before Eyal could call an order. Eyal stood, bristling, and hesitated while the rest of the pack started up, asking their friends what had happened.

The foal was not far from the herd, but it did seem to be alone. Was it running in a blind panic from the most recent creasia raid? That seemed most likely, although the foal looked old enough to know better.

Perhaps we could capture and question this one. If nothing else, a youngster alone on the plain meant food. "We hunt," said Eyal, and the group turned to follow the foal.

At that moment, creasia poured over the side of the trench and plowed into the curbs. Eyal had no time to give orders, no time to prepare, no time to think. The curbs imagined that they were being attacked and retaliated. The cats were hot with running, and the scent of their quarry.

Eyal reeled back from the fight, shouting orders, but his subordinates ignored him. He collided with one of the cats as he bounded around the chaotic tangle of snarling bodies. "What are you doing?" sputtered Eyal, for the cat was obviously their leader. He was calling for order as loudly as Eyal and being just as thoroughly ignored. "When did Leeshwood declare war on the highland curbs?"

"We're not attacking you," snarled the cat.

"Oh, no?" The body of a curb sailed out of the fight to land in a limp sprawl some distance away. Eyal wanted to fly at the lead creasia, but he held his ground, seething. "Control your clutter!" he barked.

The lead creasia responded by wading into the fight himself and bellowing until the group broke up. When they finally separated, three curbs lay dead or dying. Not a single cat had escaped without injuries, and one looked seriously lame. The two groups continued to snarl at each other as the creasia leader herded his clutter up the far side of the trench.

"Stay behind that foal!" he ordered through clenched teeth. He came back and tried to apologize to Eyal, but the curb was still choking on bile. "My queen will hear of this!" he shot. "Arcove will hear of it! An unprovoked attack on neutral territory! Such a thing has not been done in living memory!"

The cat started to say something, thought better of it, and turned to follow his clutter.

Storm could hardly contain his merriment at the commotion behind him. His trick had worked better than he could have hoped. What was more, he felt alive for the first time in days. The numbness that had driven him to make this reckless gamble had vanished, and he felt giddy. Glancing back, Storm saw that he had a comfortable lead once more. *Now, let's see what I can do with this wet ground.*

13

Gone Swimming

The sun was halfway down the sky by the time Halvery reached the river. His clutter was tired, but still determined. They had followed Storm all day through the spring snowmelt, untangling one trick after another in a scent trail that backtracked and looped over soggy ground and through tiny streams.

Halvery was proud of his clutter. They'd made a mistake with the curbs, but as the day wore on, they behaved like the expert hunters they were—smoothly splitting up when the trail demanded it, solving problems quickly, calling to each other only when necessary in low voices. They'd all been wounded in the fight with the curbs, but no one complained. Even the cat who was hobbling on three legs tried to keep up until Halvery told him to go home.

We will run this foal to ground yet, thought Halvery. The incident with the curbs still made him bristle whenever he thought about it. *Roup will have fun with that in council.* Halvery was done underestimating Storm Ela-ferry. *No animal in the world is so lucky…and no animal will be so dead by the time I'm done with him!*

Halvery was certain they were closing in. Storm had spent too much time laying elaborate scent trails, which the clutter had solved with relative ease. These were not the young, hot-blooded cats that Ariand and Treace liked to recruit to their commands, nor were they the gray-muzzles who gravitated to Sharmel. Halvery's cats were seasoned hunters, all animals who'd fought in the ferryshaft wars, but none of them older than thirty. They could be unruly; Halvery had always valued aggression in his clutter. But they knew their business. Some of these cats had fought Coden beside Halvery on Turis Rock. They'd hunted wily ferryshaft and even telshees. They would not be daunted by a few scent tricks.

As they approached the river—running high and frothy with snowmelt—Halvery thought he understood how it would end. *Storm will turn west here, and it will be a race to the cliffs—a race he will lose. He's clever—more clever than I gave him credit for, but he's no fighter. Once we catch him, it'll be over quickly.*

Storm's trail did, indeed, turn west once he entered the belt of trees beside the river. Here he must have sensed they were closing in, for he ran straight without tricks through the little woodland, and Halvery's cats tore along his trail at top speed.

Then the scent trail ended.

Halvery was unconcerned. He had expected Storm to slow down and try to confuse his trail as he grew tired. The clutter fanned out to look for the missing scent. They should find it quickly.

But they didn't.

Time dragged on, and no new trail presented itself. The late afternoon sun dipped toward the horizon, and still the creasia searched. The clutter became restless and frustrated.

At last, Halvery sat down at the end of Storm's trail, and fifteen cats gathered round him. "Sir," began his beta, "we don't know where else to look." He did not add: *We're exhausted. We've run all day, fought with curbs, and haven't even stopped to lick our wounds.*

Halvery looked at their tired faces. "Where did he go?" he growled.

The other cat looked away. "The river?" he ventured.

It was a possibility they'd considered and discarded. Storm's path ended beyond sight of the river, and even if he'd found a way to reach it without leaving a scent trail, the roiling water, full of spring debris and chunks of ice, would be too dangerous. Halvery could not imagine an animal willingly risking it, even for a short distance.

The subordinate dropped his gaze. "I don't know, sir."

Halvery heard a mutter from one the other animals. "What was that?" he snapped.

The cat cleared his throat. "Some say he can float, sir."

"We all float, but not in that," said Halvery, with a jerk of his head at the river.

The others exchanged a look. "He meant, in the air, sir."

Halvery drew a deep breath. "And I suppose he can walk through stone, too? Because he's a ghost, right? Have you ever smelled a ghost, Omma?"

She would not meet his gaze. "I wouldn't know, sir."

Halvery let his voice turn savage. "I can't believe that *my* clutter would listen to such idiocy! The foal is clever, but he's made of blood and bones and gristle. He's tired just like you, and I think he's hiding. We can find him!"

A gloomy pause. Halvery's subordinates kept their eyes on the ground. They were too well-trained to suggest giving up. They would keep trying as long as he asked. But they did not know what to try next, and Halvery didn't know what to tell them.

Halvery licked his lips. *We are out of practice.* He would never have admitted it aloud. His clutter were expert hunters, yes, but how long had it been since they'd hunted anything more cunning than a buck? They'd killed one telshee after the recent Volontaro, but it had been injured—driven into the rocks and confused by the storm. *I used to run my clutter after foxes and oories to keep them in form. When did I stop doing that? Three years ago? Four?*

"Very well." He answered the unspoken request. "We will turn for home as soon as the sun touches the horizon." The sun was already very low. The tired cats sighed with relief.

Halvery turned and walked slowly along Storm's old trail. *I thought too highly of myself,* he admitted. *The foal is dangerous. Sharmel tried to tell me, and I didn't listen.* He thought of the cat limping home alone, who might not survive. *If we had not stayed to kill ferryshaft this morning, would Storm have had time to plan his trick with the curbs?* Halvery forced himself not to think of what Roup might say. *Concentrate! The day's not done.*

Halvery raised his head and looked around slowly. *I have missed something. The clue cannot be anywhere that we have already looked.*

A broken tree branch. Any creasia with his nose to the ground would have missed it. Halvery's eyes narrowed as he stared at the twisted limb, bent as if by unaccustomed weight. Sharmel's words rang in his head: *"He used trees, Halvery!"*

Halvery hurried into the forest to his left. Nothing. He moved to his right. Five paces, ten—another broken branch. The trail was difficult to follow. Storm had taken care to make as little disturbance as possible, but occasionally a dead limb had given way beneath his grappling hooves. Slowly, Halvery traced the evidence eastward, angling ever closer to the river.

Finally, on the edge of the water, he spied an evergreen tree—one of the few on this side of the river. It had a thick spray of needles in its upper branches. *It must have looked like a perfect hiding place,* thought Halvery. He gave a low cry, a summons to bring the other creasia. Then he slunk towards the tree.

Halvery's call awakened Storm, but it did not shake his confidence. The creasia had never managed to track him through trees before. Sharmel's clutter had only found him because he'd come down. Still, Storm recognized the sound as a rally cry, and the fact that it was nearby made him uneasy. *Maybe they're leaving.*

Thump. The whole tree trembled, and Storm gasped. Instantly he was on his feet, trying to climb higher, but he was already almost as high as his weight would allow. In an agony of uncertainty, Storm turned to look down.

The lead creasia grinned up at him. "Your games are over, foal."

Storm gulped and inched backwards. The cat climbed nearer. Storm found no refuge, save one slender branch, which hung over the river. He retreated onto the limb.

"You're smarter than I expected," murmured Halvery. "I've seen only one other ferryshaft climb a tree. He had more wit than you, but we still won in the end. We always do."

Storm's mind raced. Only a moment before, he'd been taking a much-needed nap, and it seemed the chase was over. Now, he was cornered. *The cat wants to talk,* he thought desperately. *Keep him going.*

"All the other leaders introduced themselves," Storm blurted as he risked a downward glance. He saw that the rest of the clutter had gathered on the riverbank. They were watching with shining eyes.

The lead creasia snorted. "I'm Halvery," he said indulgently.

"What happened to your tail, Halvery?"

It was, apparently, the wrong question. Halvery's voice dropped to a snarl. "I can kill you here, or you can go into the river. If the current doesn't dash you to pieces, I'll be waiting on the bank."

Storm glanced down again. Melting snow had transformed the normally sluggish Igby into whitewater. Storm thought he might be able to survive if he stayed near the bank on this side of the river. *But I'll never cross it. If I get swept near the center, I'm dead, and the cats will be waiting on this bank when I try to crawl out. Unless...unless they're distracted.*

Halvery was edging nearer.

Storm backed along his limb. His hopes rose for a moment. *Maybe he won't be able to reach me.*

Halvery did find approach difficult. Storm's branch refused to hold the weight of the cat, and a nearby limb groaned dangerously as the creasia advanced. Yet the branch did not break.

"Which will it be, foal?" Halvery took a swat at Storm and almost slashed him. One more step...

Storm made a decision. "I suppose I must risk the river. But in order to save yourself the trouble of running along the bank... why don't you come with me?"

In the same instant, Storm sprang, not into the current, but onto Halvery's branch. For one moment, the astonished cat stared into Storm's smirking eyes. But before Halvery could raise a paw, the limb snapped, sending them both into the churning water.

14

Fighting an Idea

"He dumped you in the river?" Roup looked like he was trying very hard to be serious, and that made it worse.

Halvery snarled at his old rival. He could take wounds without a whimper, but to appear foolish was intolerable. Sharmel turned away to smother his own chuckles.

"But at least he didn't injure anyone," continued Roup pleasantly. "Of course, the curbs did—"

"You laugh at the humiliation of your own race," snapped Halvery. "Do you enjoy watching the ferryshaft triumph, Roup?"

Arcove made a soft noise in his throat. "Enough. Storm escaped, and that is what matters."

"He may have drowned..." speculated Halvery, but his voice carried little conviction.

"Should we be worried about retaliation from the curbs?" asked Ariand. "It sounds like they lost some animals, and their leader was irate."

Arcove flexed his claws. "I think not. From what Halvery says, they were highland curbs. They've been declining for years. I doubt we'll see them in this part of the island much longer no matter what happens." He glanced at Halvery. "You can count yourself lucky for that. If they had been lowland curbs, we might have seen repercussions."

"I find it difficult to consider any of that lucky," muttered Halvery.

Treace uncurled with a yawn. "I still think we are trying to solve this problem the wrong way. Storm's tongue is sharper than his teeth. We can send a few cats to chase him and continue the raids. Prolong the killing. Take some of the newborn foals. *Punish* the herd. Either they will kill Storm themselves, or he will see the futility of his actions and cease."

Arcove waved his tail. "This problem is more complex than raids and dead ferryshaft, Treace. We are not fighting an individual so much as an idea—the idea that ferryshaft can oppose creasia without reprisal. We have to punish the lawbreaker, not the obedient. If we try to make the ferryshaft our enforcers, we will lose our hold on them. I would be surprised if some of them have not begun to break our rules already. If we appear to have despaired of catching Storm, it will only make them bolder, and our culls will spur further rebellion instead of quelling it."

"Then let them rebel," said Treace. He dared a challenging look at Arcove. "And, when they do, destroy every last one of them."

The other members of the council glanced uneasily at each other. Treace smiled. "I understand. No one wants to take responsibility for eradicating another intelligent species—loathsome pest though that species may be. I accept that responsibility. Send me and my clutter, Arcove. We will do this task for you, and then the council need never trouble itself over this matter again."

Arcove blinked.

Before he could speak, Roup said, "That sounds reasonable—"

Arcove shot him a warning look. "How many cats were you planning to take for this exercise?" he asked Treace.

Treace looked surprised. "A large raiding party. Perhaps thirty?"

Arcove chuffed. "You'd never come back. And we'd be at open war."

Treace sputtered, but Sharmel cut in. "Old ferryshaft allies might make an appearance as well."

"And if they did…" murmured Ariand, and shivered.

"In addition," continued Arcove, "if we break our word to the ferryshaft, we'd have difficulty making meaningful agreements with any intelligent species on the island. It would be a generation or more before anyone would trust the word of a cat."

Treace's lip curled. "You can't be serious! One raiding party is more than enough to destroy the ferryshaft herd. They don't know how to fight—!"

"They haven't the *will* to fight," growled Halvery, "but some still know how."

"Their alliances," continued Treace, "are dead. Fifteen years dead! No one would come to rescue them. Also, they have broken the treaty." He looked hard at Arcove. "Surely, sir, you could argue as much before any delegate from another species."

"Possibly," said Arcove, "although such an extreme response would stretch the terms of the treaty and certainly damage our reputation. If I *did* go to eradicate the ferryshaft, I would take half of Leeshwood. And I would go myself. One does not delegate such a task. Were you ever to lead Leeshwood, I hope you would do the same."

An awkward silence followed.

Arcove spoke again, his voice level. "We must kill Storm without making him into a martyr. We must show the Ferryshaft that we have *outwitted* their hero."

Halvery's mouth twitched. "I guess that means it's Roup's turn. Unless he's exempt."

Roup said nothing. His eyes flicked at Arcove.

"Roup will hunt Storm next." Arcove's voice brooked no argument.

Halvery's mood seemed to be improving. "Don't look so gloomy, Roup. We all know you've been wanting to meet the little pest. You can have a nice chat, perhaps hunt rabbits together, spend a day at the seaside…"

Roup's tail lashed. "Oh, but you already went swimming with him, Halvery."

Halvery's mouth snapped shut, and there was a ripple of poorly-disguised laughter from the others. As the meeting broke up, Arcove glanced at Roup and gave a flick of his head. With a sigh, Roup followed him away from the meeting.

Storm crawled from the Igby River muddy, bruised, and bleeding. He hadn't been in the water for long, but he'd still been carried quite a distance. He felt weak and disoriented. Storm clambered quickly into a tree, leaving very little in the way of a scent trail. He hoped that the creasia were too busy worrying about Halvery to track him. He slept most of the next day in the tree, and by evening he was sure they were gone.

Storm spent another day hiding and nursing his wounds before he attempted the long trek back to the herd. He found them migrating towards the spring feeding grounds, away from the Igby. He made no special effort to contact anyone. His friends had been mostly ignoring him, and he did not know where they were sleeping.

Sauny found him on the first night and told him that she'd been "practicing running" and finding hiding places in the boulder mazes. She renewed her request that he teach her to run on the cliffs. Storm felt uneasy, but agreed to take her up the next day. "Do not tell your father," he warned.

Sauny laughed. "I live with my clique, Storm. I don't even see Dover that often."

"Well, don't tell your clique, either."

Very late that night, he was dimly aware of someone lying down beside him. In his half-asleep state, Storm thought it must be Tollee and leaned gratefully into her warmth. When he finally woke late in the morning, he was shocked to see Valla nestled against him.

Storm stared at her. "Valla? Why—?"

She looked at him and tried to smile. "Callaris…" She began and tried again. "The creasia…"

Storm remembered the three ferryshaft that Halvery's clutter had separated from the herd. He remembered the screams as he started away. *I didn't even look at them.*

His throat closed. "Who else?" he managed.

Valla shook her head. "Nobody I knew."

"I'm so sorry." Storm didn't know what else to say. He wondered whether she blamed him. He felt irrationally guilty.

Valla's soft, brown eyes were not accusatory, only sad.

"You'll have no trouble finding a new mate," said Storm quickly. It sounded cruel, even as he said it.

Valla looked away. "I know. But I don't want to right now. Can I...can I sleep near you for a while? Everyone else from our old clique is busy with new mates."

That gave Storm a pang as he thought of Mylo and Tollee. He looked at Valla again and gave her a sympathetic lick on the top of the head. "Alright."

Arcove did not say a word until they had reached his own personal territory. Even then, he waited until they reached the cover of a hot spring before he turned to glare at Roup.

"'That sounds reasonable'?" The words were clipped and furious.

Roup drew a deep breath.

Before he could say anything, Arcove continued. "Roup, I do not expect you to back everything I say in council. You speak your mind, and I've always valued that, but I do not expect you to deliberately undermine me, either, and encouraging Treace to go get himself killed while destroying the credibility of our council is deliberately undermining me!"

Roup turned his head to one side and hunkered down a little. "I did not consider the effect on our reputation. You're right about that. However, I *would* like Treace to go get himself killed."

Arcove growled.

Roup maintained his submissive stance, but did not back away. "Arcove, he thinks that if he eradicates the ferryshaft, he will gain the support of the majority of Leeshwood—because he solved a problem you couldn't solve. He thinks you are too stupid to see this."

Arcove's growl died. He was still for a moment. When he spoke, his voice sounded tired. "As I've said, I could kill him in a fight. It will be decades yet before he could win. By the time that happens...maybe he will have learned to rule."

Oh, Arcove. You think he's like you...when you were that age and sat on the council and were so frustrated with the older cats. But he's not. He's not like you at all.

Roup raised his eyes. "Arcove, do you know why Coden died?"

It was not at all what his friend had expected. Arcove cocked his head and said nothing.

Roup continued. "He died because he expected everyone to behave honorably."

Arcove had the grace to look uncomfortable. Roup spoke again. "If Treace does not have the support of Leeshwood and he ambushes you with twenty other cats some quiet afternoon, the assembly will kill him because he did not win the position fairly. But if he has their support, if they believe that he would make a better king... Well, then, he may not fight fairly, and they may pretend not to see. Treace knows this. He knows it very well, and he sees an opportunity in this situation with the ferryshaft."

Arcove considered this, the steam from the hot spring curling around him. His posture relaxed a little. Finally, he said, with a trace of humor. "I suppose you'd better kill Storm, then."

Roup wrinkled his nose. *You would bring it around to that.*

"You *are* going, aren't you?"

"Do I have a choice?"

"Have I ever forced you to go on a raid?"

"Ah! Well, then, I'll be staying here. Let Halvery have another go. You know he wants to."

Arcove sighed. "Your making light of Halvery's misfortune does not improve his opinion of you."

"We both know he has never had an improved opinion of me."

Arcove lashed his tail. "Roup, if you don't go, it'll be all the excuse he needs to challenge you. No matter who wins, I lose."

Roup opened his mouth, but Arcove continued. "Let's assume for a moment that you win…and that you don't die of your wounds. Do you want to lead Halvery's clutter?"

Roup shut his mouth.

"They're the best fighters in Leeshwood," said Arcove. "They're also an unruly bunch who respect a sharp claw and a swift slap. Halvery keeps them in line. Would you? They won't follow Sharmel; he's too old. Would you rather they go to Ariand…or Treace?" When Roup said nothing more, Arcove added, "Halvery is a good lieutenant and a loyal officer. I wish the two of you would get along, but fifteen years of peace haven't mellowed either of you."

"I'll hunt Storm," said Roup quietly.

He must have sounded too dismal, because Arcove looked almost sorry. "There's no shame in not catching him. No one else has."

Roup laughed. He lifted his head and shook the condensation from his whiskers. "You're suggesting I just run him around a bit, and then leave him for you to deal with? No, Arcove. If I go to hunt, then I will *hunt.*"

15

Questions in the Dark

Valla slept beside Storm that night and for many nights after. Every day, he told himself that he should make her leave. And every day, he never quite got around to it. In appearance, Valla was as different from Tollee as any ferryshaft could be. She was a creamy buff color, and her fur was longer than average. It feathered prettily around her legs, and it had a silky sheen. Her ears were small and perfect—not a single nick or ragged edge. Her muzzle was un-scarred, her teeth unbroken. Valla was not the sort of female who fought with males. She was the sort of female whom males fought *over.*

She was also a year younger than Storm and would need help surviving the next two winters. *The best thing that could happen to her,* Storm told himself, *would be acceptance by one of the female cliques.* Unfortunately for Valla, she was more attractive than useful. She'd always been an indifferent hunter, and Storm suspected that the female cliques were unimpressed by a pretty face alone.

Still, for the spring, at least, no one needed a hunting partner. During the day, Valla sometimes foraged with Storm, although she just as often disappeared. Every evening, when he settled down to sleep, Storm expected that she would be gone—snapped up by a rogan or a female clique. And, every day, Valla would find him, usually after dark, and settle down beside him for the night.

He'd even caught her talking to Sauny. Valla was just as close in age to Sauny as to himself, and she might reasonably have approached Sauny's clique for acceptance. However, she seemed more interested in friendship with his sister than in trying to join her group.

Storm had begun teaching Sauny about the sheep trails. He took her out very early in the morning—from the time the sun first peeked over the horizon until it was fully up—when few ferryshaft were awake. He refused to take her out at any other time. He expected her to get tired of waking so early and frustrated with their brief sessions, but she did not. In fact, she quickly gained enough skill to begin practicing on her own. Storm felt a mixture of pride and anxiety over her performances. However, he told himself that at least she had a way to escape in the event of danger.

Danger that will probably arise because of me, he admitted.

Storm gave himself some time to recover from his swim in the Igby before seeking out Kelsy. It wasn't difficult to locate him, but it proved very difficult to catch him alone. Kelsy was constantly in the company of other high-ranking ferryshaft. Although Storm had no reason to think he would be unwelcome, he felt shy about approaching them.

Kelsy solved the problem himself by approaching Storm late in the afternoon beside a clear spring stream. "Is there any particular reason you're isolating yourself?"

Storm glanced at him and snorted. "You did that."

"Did I?" Kelsy bent his head to drink.

Storm felt like kicking him. Instead, he said, "You destroyed my clique."

Kelsy sighed. "I didn't know Mylo would react that way."

Storm said nothing.

Kelsy tried again. "You seem to be doing well. You've got an attractive mate, you flout the creasia, and your friends still seem reasonably friendly."

Storm turned in surprise. "Attractive mate?"

"Well…yes. That fluffy little female who follows you around. She appears to be yours."

Storm scowled. "She's not mine. She's from my clique. Her rogan was killed during the last creasia raid. She's just sleeping near me because she's lonely."

Kelsy's laugh rang against the rocks.

Storm didn't like being laughed at. He turned to leave.

Kelsy trotted after him. "Wait! Please, wait. I forget that you're only three years old. This female has obviously chosen you as her mate. Accept it, and be happy."

Storm sputtered. "Kelsy, I'm good at running away, not fighting. The first ferryshaft who challenges me over Valla will win."

Kelsy fell into step beside him. "I don't think anyone will challenge you. They're in awe of you, and many of them owe you their lives. But in case someone does, I'd be happy to teach you to fight.

I can't teach you anything about running, but I could teach you some things about fighting."

Storm turned to him suspiciously. "You just want to be seen talking to me, because then other ferryshaft will think I support you."

Kelsy cocked his head. "Do you *not* support me?"

"About splitting the herd?"

"About getting away from the cats. About ending the raids forever."

Storm hesitated. Tollee's words rang in his head. *"If you encourage them, and if you're wrong…"*

"At least hear what I have to say about fighting," said Kelsy. "If you think that'll give me too much status, we can meet secretly."

I'm already doing too many things in secret. "My little sister," he heard himself say, "will you teach her, too?"

Kelsy looked surprised. "I suppose. What's her na—"

"Good," interrupted Storm. "Meet us by this stream tomorrow just before sunrise." He smiled. "You might learn a few things, too."

That evening, Storm did not return to his accustomed spot to sleep. Instead, he found a little hollow beneath a rock, well away from other ferryshaft, and made himself comfortable. He wanted time to think. He wasn't sure why it bothered him that others thought Valla was his mate. *She knows she's not. I know she's not. What else matters?*

Tollee. The thought came unbidden. *What must she think?*

It doesn't matter, he told himself. *She's made her choice.*

Storm allowed himself to consider the possibility that Valla *did* want to be his mate. It was foolishness, of course. Some large, aggressive male like Callaris would claim her by fall. And, anyway, she did not want him. Still… He thought of her soft, brown eyes, always fixed so earnestly on his face whenever he spoke. He thought of her downy fur, her warmth pressed against him at night, the way she'd washed his face after he'd saved them all from the creasia the first time. He thought…

And then something enormous fell on him from above.

Storm tried to bolt to his feet, but they were pinned beneath him. He turned his head to snap, but there was suddenly great pressure against the back of his skull, forcing his chin to the ground. He could feel the points of contact against his head. He knew, in a flash of despair, that they were teeth, and that the jaws were too wide for a ferryshaft or a curb. A creasia was sitting directly on top of him, and it had his skull in its mouth. He wondered if he would even have time to feel his death. He tried to buck again and found that he could not move at all. His breath came short and quick through his nose. He was ashamed of the little whimper that escaped through his teeth as the cat shifted its weight, and he felt the prick of its claws against his back.

To his horror, a paw came down over his face, the claws a carelessly splayed crescent across his nose. *What is it going to do to me?* The pressure against the back of his skull loosened, but Storm dared not lift his head. One of the claws was directly over his left eye.

Hot breath stirred the hair above his ears. "Now," murmured his attacker, "I'd like to talk to you, Storm Ela-ferry. I apologize for this rude greeting, but I didn't think you'd stand still to be introduced."

The cat shifted his paw away from Storm's face. Storm raised his chin a little, and the cat did nothing. Storm had an idea that the cat expected him to say something. Instead, he tried leaping to his feet. The cat's weight was too much, however, even without its teeth pinning his head. He scrabbled uselessly for a moment before subsiding. The cat made a chuffing noise that might have been a laugh. "You're smart enough not to waste your breath screaming, but you don't have enough self-control not to waste your energy struggling."

"Easy for you to say," snapped Storm.

"If I was going to hurt you, I would have done it already."

"I get the idea." *Please get off me...before I really do start screaming.*

The weight was suddenly gone. Storm shot to his feet, stumbled, and almost ran straight into a boulder. His legs felt alarmingly wobbly. In that moment, he wanted to run out of sheer humilia-tion, but curiosity and his own shaking held him in place. Storm spun around to look at the creasia. It was sitting where he'd been resting—a male of average size. Its fur was tawny gold—glossy in the moonlight.

Storm blinked. He was certain that he'd never seen this cat before—not during any raid. He would have remembered that fur.

"Hello," said the cat, "my name is Roup. I'd like to ask you some questions. What would it take to get you to answer truthfully?"

Storm stared at the creasia. *Charder said they would get better. Still...* Halvery had been exactly Storm's idea of an alpha cat. Roup was...not.

"Do you have a raiding party?" he blurted.

Roup beamed. "An excellent idea! I will answer your ques-tions...truthfully...if you answer an equal number of my own." As though as an afterthought, he added. "You don't have to crouch over there. If I wanted to kill you, you'd be dead. You get tonight gratis. I do not promise I will not kill you tomorrow."

"Why didn't you kill me just now?" asked Storm.

"That's two questions, and I haven't even asked one. Yes, I have a raiding party. We call it a clutter. They're off that way." He jerked his head south. "They don't know I'm here. You needn't worry about them tonight. I didn't kill you because I'd rather talk to you."

Storm opened his mouth, but Roup continued. "My turn. Who's your father?"

Storm looked long and hard at the cat. He was reminded of Treace trying to capture him with pretty lies. But this felt different. This cat had already had Storm's head in its mouth for one thing. Storm thought about lying, but couldn't think of a good reason to do so. "My father's name was Alaran. That's all I know about him. Cats killed him before I was born."

"And your mother?" continued Roup.

Storm stiffened. *I shouldn't be playing this game.*

As though reading his thoughts, Roup said, "She's in no danger from me. In fact, I'll make sure no ferryshaft suffers for anything you say to me."

Storm sneered. "As though you could guarantee something like that."

The cat regarded him with honey-gold eyes. "I am, arguably, the second most powerful person on this island. So, yes, I think I can."

Storm stared at him. "You're—?"

"Who is your mother?"

"She's...she's nobody," Storm stammered. "Her name is So-fet. She was an orphan, raised by her rogan. She didn't know her own parents. Why do you care if you don't want to hurt her?"

Roup's mouth twitched up, and Storm knew that he'd asked the right question. The night was fully dark now, and Roup looked up at the stars. It was, Storm thought, a deliberately disarming gesture—carelessly exposing his throat. "Pretty night," said the cat.

Storm could hardly believe he was having this conversation. "Why?" he demanded. "Why do you want to know about my parents?"

"Because you remind me of someone I once knew," said Roup. "I thought you might be related, although I don't see how. All of his offspring died."

"Coden," whispered Storm.

Roup didn't look at him. "Yes. My turn. How do you know that name?"

"I overheard Sharmel's cats talking," said Storm.

Roup glanced at him, as though trying to decide whether he was lying.

"They said they thought I was his ghost," offered Storm.

Roup grinned broadly. "They *were* saying that. None of the ferryshaft mentioned him?"

"No. Who was he?"

Roup considered. "He was a ferryshaft. He tried to turn the tide of the war and almost succeeded. After the war, it was feared that his name and memory would be a rally cry for rebellion. So, ferryshaft were forbidden to speak of him or to name their foals after him."

His voice sounded so sad that Storm asked, "Was he a friend of yours?"

Roup's expression changed to something that Storm could not read. "It's not your turn," he said softly. "Who trained you?"

Storm hesitated. "I taught myself to run on the sheep trails."

"That's not what I mean. You're a small half-orphan, born to a young mother of low rank. Someone taught you survival skills. Who?"

Storm said nothing. He badly wished he had not let himself be drawn into this.

"If it's a ferryshaft, he's got nothing to fear from me," said Roup patiently. "If it's not a ferryshaft, I probably couldn't touch him anyway."

Storm was surprised. "Oh, it was a ferryshaft. It...it was Pathar. But he doesn't speak to me anymore. He certainly didn't tell me about Coden." Storm felt the desire to defend his old teacher.

Roup quirked a smile. "Pathar? Well, that is odd. The old barnacle hardly takes an interest in anything anymore."

"Who did you think might have talked to me...other than a ferryshaft?" Storm was intensely curious now.

Roup laughed. "Oh, that's not fair. I'm asking you about facts. You're asking me to speculate."

Storm grinned back. He felt silly, but he was enjoying himself.

Roup's tail twitched. "Any intelligent animal *could* have talked to you about the war—curbs, telshees, lishties, ely-ary... although the speech of ely-ary is difficult to understand if you're not accustomed."

Storm realized in that moment, that Roup had been speaking in flawless ferryshaft dialect throughout their conversation. Storm had become adept at parsing the creasia accent, so that he hardly thought about it anymore. However, Roup was not speaking like a creasia. He was speaking like a ferryshaft.

"About Coden—" began Storm, but Roup interrupted.

"It's my turn, and I'll stop there. Thank you for humoring me, Storm. I think we understand each other a little better, and that's never a bad thing."

Storm sat back on his haunches. He'd unconsciously moved forward, so that he was a comfortable conversational distance from Roup. His shaking had ceased. He fought down an absurd urge to invite the cat to come back and do this again sometime.

"You're a very strange cat," observed Storm.

"Halvery would agree."

Storm barked a laugh. "So he made it out of the river?"

"Yes. Sharmel was extremely amused."

Storm tried unsuccessfully to imagine his tormentors in a state of relaxed amusement.

"This truce ends at sunrise," said Roup as he turned to leave. "In the future, I'd advise you find a less accessible place to sleep. That, or make yourself less…conspicuous."

When Roup had gone, Storm went to Sauny's sleeping place and told her where to meet Kelsy in the morning. "I'll be busy," he said and hurried away before she could ask questions. Storm knew that he'd been given a reprieve, and he intended to use it.

He found Valla, curled up alone in his old sleeping spot. Storm felt a little guilty, although he was glad that she had not been present when Roup appeared. After a moment's thought, he invited her to join Sauny the next morning. *We'll see how good Kelsy really is. If he can teach Valla to fight, he can teach anyone.*

He then spent some time hunting and browsing until he had a full belly. At last, exhausted, Storm started up the cliffs. He moved along his favorite local sheep trail until he reached a roomy cave. At this time of year, the cave even boasted a trickle of water. Satisfied that he'd put himself beyond the reach of even Roup's dexterity, Storm lay down on the cave floor and slept.

16

Round 5: Roup

Storm stayed in the cave all day, dozing fitfully, and lapping up water from the trickle that ran down the cliff. He watched the herd ebb and flow through the boulders below him. He wasn't in a good spot to see the stream where he'd sent Sauny and Valla to meet with Kelsy. He wondered what they would say to each other and what they must think.

Last night was beginning to feel like a dream. *Did I really play question and answer games with a creasia? A creasia who talked like a ferryshaft?*

He waited for screams somewhere below, the thunder of hundreds of pounding hooves, the ripple of motion as every ferryshaft struggled not to be chosen. But nothing happened. It was simply a beautiful spring day. He even caught sight of a mother ferryshaft leading a wobbly, newborn foal from one of the birthing caves—a sign that the mother felt exceptionally safe.

Storm wondered how long he should stay in the cave if no raid occurred. Since the spring thaw, he had been unable to cache meat for long periods without it spoiling. He thought, belatedly, that he should have found some way to store roots or grass. By sunset, he would be hungry.

As the day wore on, Storm scanned the boulder mazes for creasia in a state of increasing frustration. Surely if they were down there, he would see them. *Could I have dreamed the whole thing?* Roup certainly seemed like a dream.

As the shadows lengthened, Storm found himself facing the same dilemma as when Ariand had trapped him. *If I go another day without food, I will become weak and slow. If I leave my sanctuary, I expose myself to attack.*

Of course, when Ariand had trapped him, he knew for certain that the creasia were waiting to pounce. In this case, he wasn't even sure they were still in the area…if they'd ever been in the area at all.

Storm made a decision. *If I go farther up the cliffs, I will be able to see more of the boulder mazes. Once I know where they're lurking, I can figure out how to find food while staying away from them.*

So he returned to the main path and proceeded up the cliff, keeping a careful eye on the visible portions of the trail, both above and below him. No one seemed to be following. He stopped frequently to look out over the boulder mazes. He didn't see how anything the size of a creasia raiding party—a clutter, Roup had called it—could hide from an aerial view. *They could be in a cave…* But most of the ground-level caves were in use as birthing chambers, and Storm was sure that the appearance of a creasia in a birthing chamber would cause a visible ruckus. He began to relax. *They're not here.*

Storm was three-quarters of the way up now, and the light was waning. He felt very hungry, and he'd not encountered so much as a lizard on the trail. On an impulse, he decided to go all the way to the top, rather than risk descending in the dark on an empty stomach. He could find something to eat, then perhaps return to the cliff cave for the night.

The light was still strong when Storm reached the top of the cliff. Indeed, it was much better than it had been on the eastern side of the cliff face. He was now too high to see details below. A cat could look much like a ferryshaft from this height, but he could tell that the herd was behaving normally.

Storm went straight into the trees and began to browse, hungrily ripping up mouthfuls of spring clover. He realized in that moment that he'd never traveled to the top of the cliffs by himself. It would mean a night alone, away from the herd. *Still, perhaps I should explore here more often…and along the higher cliff trails. A watcher on one of those trails could alert the herd to the approach of a creasia clutter long before a raid. A shout might not carry, but I think a howl would. Why don't we do things like that?* Storm snorted. *It's probably forbidden.*

It was twilight now beneath the trees, and Storm realized suddenly that it was also very quiet. *It's just that the daytime animals are going to sleep,* he told himself, but his fur bristled. Then, in the stillness, he heard a bird call. It was not like any bird Storm had heard before—a sort of chattering sound.

Storm turned in a slow circle. The chattering came again; he couldn't tell from which direction. A question occurred to him that he should have asked much earlier. *Would Roup expect me to go up the cliffs or down?* With mounting dread, Storm raised his eyes into the branches of the tree behind him.

A cat crouched amid the leaves. It chattered at him.

Storm *ran*. He wasn't sure whether it was the shadowy wood or the strange behavior of the creasia, but he'd never felt more frightened. He heard several muffled *thuds* as creasia hit the ground all around him. He wondered why the first cat hadn't tried to drop on him, then realized that he was now running in the direction of the Sea Cliffs, with their steeper, infrequent, and unfamiliar trails.

Stupid, stupid! You're letting him drive you. He has anticipated your every move; you're just reacting!

Storm zigzagged around a cat as he emerged from the wood. Putting on speed that he hadn't known he possessed, he pounded along the edge of the Sea Cliffs. Below and to his right, the ocean stretched endlessly, throwing back the faint light of the first stars. The rim of the sky glowed where the sun had set.

Storm remembered, vaguely, that Kelsy had mentioned a trail in this direction. He gritted his teeth, determined to hold his lead until he reached it. Pain started in his side and chest, but he forced himself to run faster.

Storm barely saw the trailhead in time. He darted sideways, nearly flipped over, and half skidded, half galloped down the path. Almost immediately he wondered whether he had made a mistake. The path was steep and narrow with loose shale that rattled under his hooves. Worse, the creasia dislodged stones in their descent, showering Storm on the back and flanks. Soon he was sliding more than running, and all the time the path grew narrower.

Storm realized that he was about to fall. He drove his hooves into the loose rocks and forced his body sideways. By the time he halted, he had spun completely around so that he was looking up the cliff. He saw that the creasia had stopped some distance above him. Storm thought that he should have found this reassuring, but he did not. Apparently the creasia deemed the descent too precarious. *And they're right.* But Storm had no choice.

He glanced down. He had perhaps half the distance yet to go. *I did something like this when Treace chased me.* However, this drop looked steeper and higher. The stones slipped and shifted around his hooves as he stood and continued. Soon he was coasting more than walking.

Roup did say that he didn't want to kill me. Is this what he decided to do instead?

One of his hooves caught on a stationary rock. Storm stumbled and thrust his back hooves into the ground, trying to regain his balance. Then a wave of sliding stones caught up with him, and Storm flipped sideways in a cloud of choking dust. He felt himself slithering over the cliff face. Then his head struck something hard, and he spiraled into blackness.

17

Seaside

Storm dreamed of singing—strange voices crooning in a wordless, melodic hum. It seemed to him that he fell into the song and drowned—floating sightless in a place without light or air, only a song that was as thick as honey and twice as sweet. Then the singing faded, and he heard the familiar beat of the sea.

Storm opened his eyes. It was night, without even a moon to light the sky. He lay with his hindquarters in a tide pool and his head on the sand...staring at a patch of white fur.

Storm froze as a familiar scent filled his nostrils—like brine and deep earth. He could not remember where he was or how he'd gotten here, but he remembered the smell of a telshee. Storm leapt to his feet and stumbled backward into flank-deep water. Almost immediately, he began to cough, gagging as he brought up sea water and a mouthful of grit.

When he managed to open his watering eyes, Storm saw that the telshee had not moved. It was watching him from the edge of the tide pool with large, blue eyes, gleaming in the starlight. The creature had a dark, leathery nose, framed in dense whiskers, and a face somewhere between an otter's and a seal's.

"Storm Ela-ferry." The telshee's disturbingly rich voice resonated against the rocks—probably female, though it was difficult to be sure.

Storm said nothing.

The telshee smiled—a horrible sight, full of teeth that belied its sweet voice. "You've come to us at last."

Storm swallowed. "No," he croaked. He remembered—Roup, the cave, the cliff. "I fell." *This is stupid. I should run.* But he didn't think he could get away. *At least my legs aren't broken.*

"We've been watching you," crooned the telshee, "for a long time. We'd like to talk. We could tell you things...so many things." The creature moved a little nearer, and Storm swallowed. What he'd taken for rocks was actually part of its coils. The animal was impossibly long.

Storm took a step back. "You should have thought of that before you tried to kill me in the cave last season."

The telshee cocked her head. "Kill you? My dear, we rescued you. You would have known that if you'd stayed to talk, but you ran away. I saved you again tonight; you would have drowned if I hadn't pulled you out of that tide pool."

Storm took another step back. "Or maybe you just now saw me."

The telshee gave a sorrowful shake of its head. "The creasia have done a masterful job with your herd. You don't even know who your friends are."

Storm thought of the strange tunnel that had opened at his back when Ariand trapped him in the cave. It *had* been the work of telshees, and it *had* saved his life. "If you're my friend, why didn't you talk to me in the tunnel?" demanded Storm. "You trapped me and attacked me!"

The telshee looked uncomfortable. "Is that how it seemed to you? I didn't have authority to speak to you. I wasn't sure my king would approve. But I and my drove would never have attacked you, Storm. We're on your side and always have been."

Somewhere in the distance, a cat's call sounded. The telshee's head swung towards the noise, and she growled. "I must go. The tide is rising, and at its height, our tunnels are not accessible. Come with me, Storm, and hear the answers to all your questions."

She moved back a little, and Storm discerned a low cave among the tumble of smooth sea stones, its mouth a darker shadow among the others. He was already shaking his head. "You must be insane if you think I'm going in there with you."

She smiled again, and her teeth flashed. "As you will. My name is Shaw. You'll come to us eventually, I think." Her voice faded as she melted back into the shadows around the mouth of the cave.

Storm waited until he was sure she was gone. Then he turned his back on the cave and hurried away. He wanted to run, but he didn't know where he was. The sculpted sea stone rocks were an alien landscape that he'd explored only briefly with friends. The changing tides added an additional level of complexity. Nothing looked familiar. *But surely, the cats think I'm dead. Surely that call I heard was only a rally cry as they started for home.*

Moments later, however, another quavering cry assured him that Roup had not given up. The cats were definitely somewhere at the bottom of the cliffs. Storm growled his annoyance. He stopped briefly to devour something crunchy from a rock pool, then headed south. The only safe trails that he knew up the Sea Cliffs lay in that direction. *I've got to get back to familiar territory.*

He wondered how long it would take the creasia to figure out that he'd survived the fall. He wondered if the scent of the telshee would detour them. *Probably not. Nothing seems to detour Roup.*

Storm shivered when he thought of the way the cats had chattered at him from the trees. *It's a clever way to communicate near prey—no yowling, no creasia sounds, just an imitation-bird call. I wonder how many times I heard it before I realized that it was unnatural.*

Storm wondered, uncomfortably, whether the creasia would call to each other in the usual way as they ran along his trail. *Probably not.* He ran faster.

Lyndi Ela-creasia moved like liquid shadow through the boulder mazes beneath the Sea Cliffs. She kept her part of the clutter together and did not call—not even in the chattering bird voices that Roup liked to use while hunting. Her cats were nervous. They'd all caught the scent of telshee near the place where they'd traced the ferryshaft's fall. It had shaken them. Most had believed the ferryshaft dead, but the desire to retrieve proof had driven them, slowly and carefully, to make the descent to the beach.

Roup never thought Storm was dead, though. He hadn't said it, but Lyndi could tell. *He was already planning his next move.*

But the scent of the telshee had shaken even Roup. He'd actually ventured a short distance into the sea cave—an action that horrified his clutter—in order to confirm that Storm's scent could not be traced within. "The telshee may have dragged him out of the water," he said at last. "Storm woke up and ran away from it. That's all."

Liar, thought Lyndi without malice. *You think it talked to him. You're worried about what it might have said.*

But it couldn't have said much, she reasoned. *We didn't take that long to come down the cliff.*

The rest of the clutter was more worried about where the telshee might be lurking, whether it had friends, and what they might do. No cat would willingly spend a night on the beach. But Roup's clutter was Roup's clutter for a reason. They were smart, and they did not spook easily.

Roup had split the group of sixteen animals—sending Lyndi with five others south along the foot of the cliffs, and going with the rest in pursuit of Storm. Lyndi listened for cries of alarm or aggression—some hint that Roup had either caught his prey or the telshees had attacked. But she heard only the sigh of the sea.

The waxing moon rose and improved visibility. It was halfway to setting when the clutter found what they were looking for—the foot of a cliff trail.

This one looked more navigable than the last. A quick inspection verified that Storm had not passed this way yet. Lyndi allowed the others to relax and catch their breaths. She remembered what Roup had said before they split. "This will be an endurance race in the end, so take rest and food where you can."

She turned to the others. "We watch in shifts—two at a time. The rest can either sleep or hunt for food. If you hunt, travel in pairs." They grunted their assent.

Soon, Lyndi was lying across the foot of the trail a few paces from one of her subordinates. Everyone felt better with an escape route from the beach at their backs, and she allowed herself to relax a little. *Roup knows what he's doing.*

But she wished he hadn't split the clutter—not with telshees about. Lyndi wondered, not for the first time, why they were really here. *Roup doesn't want to chase ferryshaft. He's never wanted to chase ferryshaft.* In the fifteen years since the war ended, Roup's clutter had not gone on a single raid. When asked about it, Roup would respond, "Peace means peace." They had been active during the war, though, often solving problems other clutters couldn't solve.

Arcove would rather take care of this foal himself, thought Lyndi. *We're out here because of Halvery.* Lyndi ground her teeth. She dearly wished that Roup would just fight him. "Beat him once. Soundly," she'd told Roup long ago. "Halvery will respect that."

"Why put anyone's life in danger for the sake of my pride?" Roup asked.

Lyndi didn't have an answer, except that the situation caused dissent. Roup had been Arcove's beta before Arcove won the leadership of Leeshwood. Arcove took it as a matter of course that Roup came with him. Unlike every other member of the council, Roup had not fought anyone for his position. Halvery had come along early in Arcove's administration, and he made it clear that, while he had every faith in Arcove's ability to rule the creasia, he did not feel the same way about Roup. Arcove sometimes spoke as though he had two equally ranking lieutenants but everybody knew who truly had his ear. It made Halvery furious.

Roup's unconventional behavior did not help. Arcove's other officers ruled over hundreds of cats, from whom they selected clutters when they went on a war hunt or other extended expedition. Roup only maintained about thirty, along with an array of mates and cubs. His core clutter had varied little over the years. They knew each other well, and they worked together like a single organism.

Their efficiency had impressed others during the war, but that was long passed. Now, it was only seen as eccentric, and it certainly did not garner the respect of cats like Halvery.

Likewise, Roup's choice to have only one mate. Arcove had five. Halvery, it was rumored, had nine. Roup's devotion to a single female smacked of weakness to a cat like Halvery, who regularly tested himself against other males in fights over mates. Lyndi suspected that Roup's choice to keep a female as his beta must also be viewed as peculiar, though no one had spoken to her openly about it in years.

Females normally came and went from a male's clutter as their fertility cycles permitted. It was a respected fact that female creasia made formidable fighters. However, once they reached breeding age, most females either established a den or joined an existing den as a lower-ranking member. They defended their den's hunting territory from other creasia and reared cubs. They did not concern themselves with the world beyond the wood or even beyond their territory when the cubs were young.

Creasia cubs typically needed their mothers for about three years. Depending on the availability of game and water, females might even nurse a second litter while the first were learning to hunt. However, mortality rates for cubs were high. Female creasia often found themselves unexpectedly between litters. When this happened, they might be included in a male clutter.

However, females did not become ranking officers in a male's clutter. Their presence was too undependable. Lyndi was an exception, because she was sterile. She did not know why. She had felt the mating instinct like all females at about six years of age and had joined the den of a male she fancied. However, she did not quicken.

After three seasons and no cubs, the females there made it clear that she should leave. In vain, she pointed out that she helped to hunt and that she cared for their cubs. Her investment was thought insufficient to guarantee her loyalty. She was suspected of poaching game for a nearby den. The females whispered that she mated with every male she could find in hopes that one would quicken her, and any cubs that she produced would not be of the den's blood. In spite of the three years she'd spent with them, Lyndi's lack of cubs made her an outsider, not part of their family. At last, she left.

For a time, she drifted aimlessly, poaching game from various hunting territories, risking reprisals, feeling lost and broken. She was in danger of becoming a rogue—the lowest ranking of creasia, usually short-lived—when Roup found her and offered her a place in his clutter. In truth, he had no real clutter—just a few hangers-on who were trying to impress Arcove. Roup was young, and he did not attract other creasia because of his odd behavior. Arcove, however, was a popular leader, rising quickly through the ranks of the council, and Roup was never far behind him. Lyndi watched and listened and kept her mouth shut. She performed so well that Roup soon made her his second.

It didn't take her long to learn to love him—her infuriating, inscrutable, soft-spoken leader. Because Roup's clutter was so small, they operated almost like a single family—denning in one area and rarely fighting over resources. Lyndi helped hunt for any den that was struggling, and they accepted her, treating her like one of the unmated males.

Lyndi fancied sometimes that Caraca—Roup's mate—was jealous of her. She wasn't sure why. Her relationship with Roup was purely in the role of officer. *Caraca should be jealous of Arcove*, thought Lyndi in rare moments of pique. *But, of course, no one is ever jealous of Arcove…except perhaps me.*

Storm felt comfortable with his lead as he started south below the sea cliffs. He wished the moon would rise so that he could see better. Nevertheless, he could see the cliff face well enough, even by starlight, to watch for a trail. The ragged scar of a good, safe trail would be visible from the beach.

Storm was not *so* vain of his lead that he felt comfortable running at the foot of the cliff. If he ran in a straight line, they could ambush him. Storm felt that the rocks and tide pools should have offered endless opportunity for subterfuge, if he'd only known what to expect around the next corner. However, he did not. He was reasonably confident that Roup and his clutter were equally ignorant of the terrain, so they could not capitalize on his mistakes.

The moon rose. Storm was beginning to feel the effects of a prolonged chase at a time when he would have normally been asleep. He told himself that if he could only reach the top of the cliffs with a comfortable lead, he would lay a false trail and catch a few moments of sleep in a tree.

At last, he saw what he was looking for—an irregularity in the cliff face that showed a trail. Gratefully, Storm turned his steps in that direction. He was so intent upon his goal that he almost didn't check himself in time when he saw the cats lying across the foot of the trail.

Fear forced all thought from his head as Storm executed an abrupt pivot and pounded back into the boulders. Behind him, he heard two sharp cries. They were answered an instant later by the creasia behind him—not so far to the north of him as he would have liked. *Those at the trailhead are telling those chasing that they've spotted me.*

Will they try to block the next trailhead as well? Storm didn't see why not. The cats could cover ground faster along the foot of the cliff than he could out here in the boulders. Storm wanted to lie down and whimper. More, he wanted to lie down and sleep. Instead, he *thought*, and as he thought, he ran.

18

Imitation

By the time the moon set, Storm had confirmed the distressing truth. The creasia had run ahead of him to the next trailhead. He considered trying to loop back to the previous trail. However, he suspected that they'd left one or two cats to guard it, and such an attempt would cost him most of his lead.

Storm was beginning to understand how a coordinated group of hunters could harry a single animal to exhaustion. Roup did not need to unravel all of Storm's scent tricks at great speed. He just needed to unravel them methodically, and keep coming. Meanwhile, the cats traveling along the foot of the cliff reached the trailheads ahead of Storm and had time to rest. Storm had no doubt that they slept in turns. He also suspected that they had switched out with some of the pursuers, giving everyone a chance to rest—everyone except their quarry.

Storm remembered something else—Roup's bright-eyed alertness in the boulders the night before, the things the cats had said and done during other chases, the way they squinted in bright daylight. *Cats sleep in the day,* he surmised. *The little oory cats do that, too. Night is their best time…and my worst.*

The sun had risen by the time Storm reached the third trailhead. He came only near enough to glimpse the waiting creasia before retreating. However, they must have spotted him, because he heard the now-familiar sharp cry, echoed moments later by the animals farther behind him. *That means they're sending more cats ahead of me to the next trail.*

Storm was weaving with exhaustion. Bruises from his fall had become a constant, dull ache. To make matters worse, he felt certain that he was approaching the headwaters of the Chelby on the far side of the cliff. *Even if I somehow get off this beach, I'll probably be in creasia territory.*

Water was a more immediate problem. The salty little animals he ate from the tide pools only made him more thirsty. He was sure that freshwater streams ran down the cliffs to the beach, but, unfamiliar as he was with the area, he'd stumbled over only one in the course of the night. Storm knew enough not to drink sea water, but he was tempted.

Soon, I'll just collapse on the sand. Then they'll come and kill me. I should have followed that telshee into the cave.

Stop.

Storm stumbled to a halt, head drooping, tongue lolling. He was in the midst of running through a tide pool to hide his trail—a trick that would only slow Roup a little. *What I'm doing is no dif-*

ferent from running in a straight line in a blind panic. More complicated, but no different.

Storm knew in his bones that he would never reach the next cliff trail. *I have to get up this one. I have to.*

Carefully, he turned and doubled back along his own path. Storm wondered how many creasia were in the clutter. *How thin are they stretched with cats left at three trailheads? How many are sleeping now that it's day?*

Storm found a likely looking tumble of sea rock—sculpted by wind and tide—and wedged himself into a curve. His pale fur blended nicely with the grays and whites of stone and sand. He knew he was gambling, but he felt this was his best chance, so he shut his eyes and let himself drift into a light sleep.

Storm dreamed of muskrat dens, hidden beneath the overhang of a riverbank. Except they were not inhabited by muskrats, but by telshees. He dreamed of underwater singing. He dreamed of birds that were not birds, but cats with wings, who chattered at him.

Storm's eyes snapped open. He was sure he had not been asleep for more than a few moments. The scent of creasia had woken him. They were passing barely two lengths away directly in front of him, flowing through the boulders along his trail. *If even one of them looks my way...*

But none did.

When they were gone, Storm rose on shaky legs. The brief nap had cleared his head. He thought he knew where he was. Something about the tide pools he'd passed recently seemed familiar. He had an idea...if he could only reach the top of the cliff.

Moving quickly, Storm retraced his steps to the trailhead. He held his breath and peeked from behind a rock. As he had suspected, only a single creasia stood guard. Storm wished, bitterly, that he knew how to fight and kill cats. His options were limited when even a single creasia presented an insurmountable obstacle. However, he suspected that now—dehydrated, exhausted, and battered from a fall down the cliff—was not the time to try to learn how to fight.

Something else, then.

Storm knew that he had only moments. Somewhere to the south, Roup would be realizing that his quarry had backtracked. Storm had sacrificed his entire lead for these few precious moments alone with this one cat at the foot of the cliffs.

What would make him leave the trailhead? Storm was pretty sure that simply showing himself would not be enough to draw the cat away. An image from his dream leapt in his mind—cats with wings like birds…chattering. A trick. An imitation.

Storm thought carefully, then drew a deep breath.

Roup was a little disappointed. Storm was clearly an intelligent youngster with moderate cunning and a natural gift for evading pursuers. However, that flash of intuitive brilliance that Roup had detected during their conversation had been absent. The foal had done nothing that a fox or an oory might not have done. *If he doesn't come up with something better than that soon, we'll be finished here.*

When the foal backtracked, Roup knew that he must be desperate. *Will he try to fight one of the creasia at the trailheads?* Roup thought it more likely that he would try to hide. However, that would be difficult on a beach that Storm obviously did not know.

As Roup neared the trailhead, his curiosity mounted. *Is Storm really going to trap himself between the guard and my pursuing clutter?* And then Roup heard…something.

He realized an instant later that his clutter was no longer around him. Roup stopped and looked back. They were frozen in place, eyes wide, bristling. Then he heard the sound of rapid footfalls coming towards them through the sandy rocks—a large animal running all-out. An instant later, Marakis shot into view. Roup growled. He was supposed to be guarding the trail.

"Telshee!" screamed Marakis as he saw them. "Telshee, telshee!"

Six of the eight animals with Roup turned and bolted. Lyndi—fresh after her rest at the last trailhead—hesitated. Rickle fixed his eyes on Roup, as though awaiting an order.

Roup wavered, concentrating. It had been a long time. Still… "That's not a telshee." He gave one ear-splitting rally cry, and then he was running for the trailhead, Lyndi and Rickle right behind him.

Roup was annoyed. He was also impressed. He realized, in that moment, that he'd been holding back…just a little. His clutter were tired—surely not as tired as Storm, but still exhausted from two days of watching and hunting and a night spent by the sea after the confirmed presence of telshees. Their nerves were stretched to breaking. And meanwhile, he'd been methodically testing this foal. *No more. This ends now, one way or the other.*

Roup tore up the cliff trail in the bright, morning sunlight. He was a predator, and he could see his prey—not too far ahead and above him, running hard for the cliff top. From somewhere below, Roup heard the calls of his clutter as they converged on the trailhead—letting him know that they had realized their error and were on their way. Lyndi and Rickle would be even nearer, but Roup didn't worry about any of them. He focused on Storm.

By the time he reached the top, Roup knew Storm must be nearly spent, because *he* was. He'd gained on the ferryshaft in the ascent, and Roup caught sight of him again as soon as he reached the crest. Storm had turned north. Strangely, he'd not gone into the trees. He was running along the cliff top in full view.

Roup wondered whether Storm even had a plan anymore. He seemed to be running at a wasteful, desperate speed—the way a deer runs just before the hunters drag it down. *So be it.* Roup took off after him, feeling the ache in his own muscles as he pushed them for that last bit of energy.

Then Storm seemed to vanish on what Roup assumed to be a downward slope. Roup did not slow down, and it almost cost him his life.

He came upon the fiord so suddenly that he sat down, flipped over, and ended with his back legs scrabbling off the edge. Gulping for air, heart hammering, Roup clawed his way back to solid ground. He saw that Lyndi and Rickle had almost reached him, bristling with alarm, probably for his safety.

Roup turned back to the cliff where he'd almost fallen. The rift was just wide enough that a cat could not jump it, and Roup was certain that Storm could not. Cautiously, he approached the edge again and looked down. The tide was out, and he could see plainly the white sand and rocks below. Storm's body should have been visible. It was not. Roup looked for a ledge where Storm might have landed, but the walls of the cliff were sheer and smooth.

Discounting nothing, Roup sent Lyndi and Rickle sniffing around the edges of the crevasse. *Maybe he really did jump it…or run along the edge where I couldn't see him.* But they found nothing.

At that moment, the rest of the clutter came running into view, sheepish expressions on their faces. Roup did not lecture them. He sent two back down the trail to investigate the crevasse from below and make certain that an injured Storm had not dragged himself beneath an overhang or into the rocks to die.

However, Roup was growing increasingly certain that they would not find anything. Roup watched his exhausted clutter as they sniffed fruitlessly around the edges of the fiord. *I guess Storm didn't need me to hold back after all.*

Arcove was among his hot springs on a foggy evening. The fog and the steam rolled around him in absolute silence. He walked, expecting to encounter a familiar tree or rock or riverbank, but nothing looked familiar.

He thought he heard the swish of fur over stone. He bristled. Surely, nothing could be stalking him here, among his own hot springs.

Something moved in the fog ahead, but when he reached the spot, it was gone. He heard a muffled laugh. "Show yourself!" he snarled. "If you want a fight I'm ready!"

"But I'm not," whispered a voice as smooth as honey.

Arcove took deep breaths, turning in slow circles.

"When I am, you'll know it," continued the voice. "Someday, when you think you're safe…I will come and take *everything.*"

Arcove blinked. He'd heard those words before. But not here. *This is a dream. Wake up!*

"Wake up."

Arcove opened his eyes. "Roup," he managed, and removed his splayed claws from his lieutenant's shoulder. "You're back."

"You drove him onto the beach?" snarled Halvery. "Were you *trying* to introduce him to the telshees, Roup?"

"You have divined my intent exactly," said Roup, but Halvery was not to be detoured with sarcasm.

"This fiord where he supposedly escaped—you didn't even figure out how he did it? He just vanished into the air?"

Roup cocked his head. "If I could have found him, I'd probably still be chasing him."

"He did the same sort of thing when I chased him," muttered Ariand.

"Sounds like he's gotten better at falling down cliffs and walking away," said Treace.

"And he's widening his knowledge of the territory," said Sharmel. "Arcove, we've tried."

Arcove looked around at them. "I gather that none of you will take it as an insult to your positions as officers if I personally hunt down this foal?"

"I'd like to come along," rumbled Halvery. "I'd like to tear off a piece of him!"

Arcove chuffed. "You'll all come. Bring ten of your best cats, and meet me here in three nights. Storm has challenged the creasia. He's about to learn what that means."

19

Experiments

"Well, it wasn't really a very good telshee," said Storm, although he couldn't stop the silly grin that crossed his face at the way Valla was beaming at him.

"Sounds like it was good enough," said Kelsy.

"They ran away like newborn foals at their first creasia raid," cackled Sauny, who was now a year old, and so had nothing but disdain for "newborn" foals. Her actual behavior did little to support her position. As they talked, she was splashing in a tiny pool, pretending to pounce on minnows. They were lounging on the edge of the plain among scattered rocks and lush spring grass. Small trees gave shade around the pool, and a stream ran tinkling away into the boulders.

Itsa stretched languorously amid the grass. "Perhaps we should all learn telshee songs."

"Perhaps," muttered Storm. He'd told them about Shaw, but his friends had dismissed the telshee's words immediately as a cunning trick. Storm wasn't so sure. He kept playing the incident over in his head. He hadn't told anyone how he'd ultimately escaped. *I need a few secrets.*

"Storm?" He looked up in surprise at the sound of Tracer's voice.

"Do I know you?" he asked politely.

Tracer made a face.

"Well, you don't know me," said the ferryshaft beside him. Storm struggled to remember her name.

"Mia?" he ventured.

She actually capered. Storm decided that Tracer had found the right mate. "I have been *begging* Tracer to introduce us," she enthused. "Here I find that he grew up with the most notorious ferryshaft in the herd, and he won't even let me say hello!"

Tracer looked uncomfortable. "Well, I never *stopped* you from saying—"

"Oh, but without an introduction? That would just be awkward. So, Storm, tell me all about yourself. I want to hear everything. And tell me all about Tracer, too, particularly anything stupid or silly he may have done as a foal."

Storm was laughing.

"Technically, he still is a foal," Kelsy pointed out.

"You're right!" said Mia. "That does explain so many things."

Tracer shoved her with his nose. "Storm, I just wanted to say congratulations on your continued success. I heard something about your imitating a telshee this last time, and I really do want to hear the story. I'm sorry I've been...not around much."

Storm smiled, then forgot what he was going to say as two more ferryshaft came out from among the rocks and approached them. He stood up. "Tollee?"

She stopped and looked uncertain for a moment, but then came on into the clearing. Tracer rolled his eyes. Storm ignored him. "Is everything alright?" he asked.

Tollee gave him an annoyed look. "Does anything have to be wrong for me to visit?"

Storm realized that he was behaving oddly, and everyone was looking at him. He sat down. "No, of course not."

From behind her, Leep's sarcastic voice chimed, "Well, hello, Leep! So good to see you."

Storm quirked a smile. "I thought you were just a shadow." Leep's spring coat was glossy black, showing off his elegant build to perfection. Storm noticed, with a pang, that Leep had not brought his mate. *Afraid to let your loved ones get too close to me?*

Tollee sat down awkwardly on the far side of the group, and Leep joined her. "I heard something about a telshee," said Tollee.

"News travels fast," said Storm. He forced himself not to ask about Mylo.

"Before you tell the telshee story for the hundredth time," said Kelsy, "I'd like to talk about something I discussed with your mate and your sister while you were off playing games with the creasia." Storm tried not to wince when Kelsy referred to Valla as his mate. No one else seemed to notice.

To the group at large, Kelsy said, "We were all going to meet for a little sparing practice—"

"Kelsy was going to teach everyone how to fight," interjected Sauny, still hock-deep in the pool.

Leep let out a snort of laughter. "Everyone…being who?"

Kelsy took this in stride. "Well, initially, just Storm, but he sent Valla and Sauny instead. I thought he was having a joke, but I figured, why not? We ended up talking for a long time about how a ferryshaft might fight a creasia."

Out of the corners of his eyes, Storm watched the group. This was a forbidden subject—something that could get them in trouble with the elders, perhaps even exiled from the herd, if anyone repeated it. Leep and Tracer looked uncomfortable, but nobody left.

"We figured," continued Kelsy, "that it wouldn't be too different from Sauny or Valla fighting with me, so we tried some things. Here's what we realized: if a ferryshaft is exceptionally quick and he catches a creasia by surprise, he might have a chance."

"He?" interrupted Sauny.

Kelsy flipped his tail. "He or she. If our hypothetical ferryshaft happens to be large, *she* has a better chance. However, under normal circumstances, no single ferryshaft will ever be a serious threat to creasia."

"Tell us something we don't know," muttered Leep.

"Alright, I will," said Kelsy. "With a little training, Valla and Sauny together could probably kill me."

That surprised everyone. "We don't fight that way," continued Kelsy. "For lots of reasons, we don't tolerate unfair fights. They don't mean anything. They don't prove strength or status. But war with another species is different. It's not about being fair. It's about winning."

"You're saying that a team of ferryshaft could kill a cat," said Tollee quietly.

"Absolutely," said Kelsy. "It wouldn't even have to be a very big team. If we outnumbered a group of creasia by two or three to one, I think we could kill them. It would depend on a lot of things, of course, but we're not *that* much smaller than a cat. Watch this."

He stepped into the center of the group, and Sauny and Valla bounded forward. They circled him, Kelsy striking out with hooves and teeth as they dodged nimbly away. Storm saw Tollee's eyes narrow. She was watching every move. Each time Kelsy tried to focus on one opponent, the other leapt in to distract him. If they'd been biting hard, Kelsy would have been badly injured. At one point, Storm was certain that Valla would have hamstrung him if she'd been trying. His reflexive kick landed with a solid thud. Valla rolled with the blow and bounced back up. Storm was impressed.

At last, Sauny—the smallest of the two—leapt onto Kelsy's back. If she'd been trying, her teeth would have fastened around his spine or the back of his neck. He bucked hard to dislodge her, throwing his head back. At the same time, Valla streaked in and fastened her teeth around his throat. They went down in a lashing tangle of hooves and fur. Valla must have been over-excited, because Storm heard Kelsy wheeze, "Alright, alright! We've made our point! Let go!"

Valla rose primly, tail high, and pranced off, ruffled and bristling. Storm thought she looked as proud as he'd ever seen her.

"Bravo!" called Itsa. "I'll have to teach Remy and Faralee for next time Kelsy misbehaves!"

Everyone was talking and laughing and cheering.

When they'd quieted, Kelsy said, "You see? It's not unlike the way a group of ferryshaft harry a cornered sheep. A little trickier, because you're dealing with an intelligent animal, but still not that different. Here's something else to think about: I believe we naturally out-breed the creasia. I think that they kill us to keep our numbers artificially low so that we cannot challenge them. If we could get beyond their reach for a few years, we would soon have a herd large enough to come back here and crush them."

Everyone went silent at that. Storm watched Tollee. She had an expression on her face that he could not read. Tracer shook himself. "Well, that certainly gives us something to consider. Now, about this telshee…"

Ever since Roup's chase, Storm had taken to sleeping in inaccessible places. At first, he decided that he would sleep only in caves along sheep trails, but Valla kept trying to follow him. "You teach Sauny to walk on the sheep trails," she observed reasonably, but Storm could already tell that Valla did not have the knack for it.

"If you fall, I will never be able to live with myself," he told her and tried not to see the way it made her smile.

In the end, Storm settled for caves too small for creasia. He was very selective. The cave must have two entrances, and he reserved one entrance only for emergencies, so that his scent would not betray its location. He found four such caves in the region of the spring feeding grounds and rotated through them, never spending two nights in a row in the same place.

Valla obviously thought this over-cautious, but she said nothing. Storm was tempted to tell her about Roup's visit so that she would understand. However, something stopped him. *Because I don't understand it myself? Because I'm afraid someone will tell me that Roup was only toying with me for information? That he probably lied? That I'm really nobody special?*

The possibility that he might be a relative of the mysterious Coden filled Storm with secret pride. His lack of status in the herd had been his bane ever since he'd been born. So-fet's confession about his father had not improved his view of things. Alaran was likely a bully who'd chosen his mother because she was young and defenseless. But Coden... Coden was a hero, the only ferryshaft whom the creasia appeared to fear. Storm wished that he could have met him. Just once.

Arcove did not hurry on his way to hunt Storm. The journey from Leeshwood to the spring feeding grounds of the ferryshaft herd could be made in two nights—a night and a day if a clutter pushed hard. Arcove took six.

Roup knew that Treace—and even Ariand—found the pace frustrating, but Arcove kept them busy with long scouting expeditions across the plain. He sent them all the way to the lake and back at several different points. "Remind yourselves where the dips are," he told them. "Familiarize yourself with the height of the grass and the lay of the plain, even the woods by Chelby Lake."

Roup knew very well that a few of Treace and Ariand's cats could not be "reminded" because they had never known. In all their lives, they'd come north only to raid and then only at the foot of the cliffs in the area where the ferryshaft wintered. Arcove knew it, too, Roup was sure. His king did nothing by halves. *Arcove will not lose Storm simply because the foal knows the land better than we do.*

Halvery was more circumspect than Treace and Ariand. He would have liked to travel faster, but he was a seasoned fighter who trusted Arcove's judgment and could appreciate what he was doing. Arcove sent Halvery and his clutter up and over the cliff, scouting out the trails and the belt of wood on top. When a cat had the nerve to complain that he'd been there recently, Halvery snapped, "Well, now you'll have been there even more recently."

"I do not want this hunt to land on the beach," Arcove told them. "In order to keep that from happening, we need to know the ways up and down the cliff—not as they were five years ago, or last year, or this winter. I want you to know what they are *now*."

To Sharmel's older clutter, Arcove gave the job of scouting the boulder mazes themselves. All of Sharmel's cats had come this way many times before, so they needed only to note recent changes and details.

Arcove kept Roup's clutter with him, sending them as messengers when needed. If there was a problem anywhere, he would send them as reinforcements. This had always been his preferred way of using Roup's small, but effective group of cats.

Arcove himself had no clutter, as was the custom. All of Leeshwood was his clutter. This way, it could not be claimed that he gave special favors to his own cats. Roup knew that Halvery would have liked to complain that Roup's clutter might as well have been Arcove's. *But he doesn't say it, because he doesn't want to fight with Arcove…just with me.*

So they traveled at a leisurely pace through the nights and often into early morning. Creasia felt most alert at dawn and dusk, and Arcove saw no reason to change their normal rhythms. "We raid in the daytime because that is when ferryshaft are awake, and we want them to see us," he told the clutters. "We are not going to raid this time. We are going to hunt Storm. We will probably attack at dusk."

Arcove himself chose to move along the top of the cliff for most of the journey, where he could keep an eye on the activities of the various clutters below and make his own assessments of the terrain. He came down into the boulders if he saw anything interesting and often during the day to sleep. Roup's clutter hunted small game and sheep. They slept fitfully outside their own territory, but the sunny rocks were pleasant.

On the third day, during one of these naps, Arcove said, "So what did Storm say?"

Roup opened his drowsy eyes. They were just out of earshot of the rest of the clutter. Roup's cats slept together like a pile of cubs when they were this far from their own territory. It gave them comfort. They would have welcomed Arcove, but he chose to sleep apart. Roup knew that they thought he did it to preserve his dignity, although Roup suspected that Arcove just didn't want to hurt anyone if he had a bad dream.

"Say?" Roup repeated.

"When you talked to him," said Arcove with excessive patience, "what did he say?" They'd been sleeping back-to-back—as they'd used to when they were cubs. Roup was reminded of those days when they'd slept by turns because they had so many enemies.

Roup refused to sit up and look at his friend. "What makes you think I talked to him?"

"You always talk to them."

Roup gave a sad chuckle. *More's the pity.*

"If you made him a promise, I'll keep it."

Roup sighed. He sat up. "You'd like him, Arcove."

"I'm sure I would. Fed on spring grass and seasoned with light running." It was a joke. Most creasia found the taste of ferryshaft unpleasant.

Roup laughed. "One conversation and you'd be friends."

"I doubt that."

"He doesn't know anything. No one's talked to him. He overheard Sharmel's cats talking about Coden. That's the only reason he knew the name. You should have seen his face—so young, so curious. He does remind me of Coden. He's a lot smaller, but he's the same color and…something about the eyes. I think they're related, but I don't know how. I'm not sure it matters."

"Is he a leader?" asked Arcove. "Do you think others will follow him?"

Roup thought about it. *Others won't even sleep near him.* "No. He's not like Coden that way. What little training he has, he got from Pathar. I thought that was odd."

Arcove cocked his head. "*Pathar?* That is odd." He thought for a moment. "Somehow, Storm *must* be Coden's. I can't see Pathar inconveniencing himself for anyone else's orphan."

Roup inclined his head. "That's what I thought, too. Charder…"

Arcove laughed. "You think he managed that? It would make him so proud—one small victory over me. Might be what's kept him going all these years."

Roup glanced at him. "I promised Storm that no one would suffer because of what he told me."

"Oh, I'm not about to kill Pathar," said Arcove, "or Charder. Pathar is too good at predicting the Volontaro, and it wouldn't do us any good anyway. He'd never tell me the truth, and I'd like to know." He hesitated. "What about the telshee? Did you recognize the scent?"

Roup could hear the change in his voice. *He doesn't want to talk about this, but Arcove was never a coward.* "Shaw," said Roup immediately. He'd always had a good nose and a better memory.

Arcove made a face. "Did you *have* to chase Storm onto the beach?"

"I wanted to test him on unfamiliar terrain. I suspected that he did not frequent the beach, and I was right. The fact that he ran from the telshee, rather than seek shelter with it, tells us a lot."

Arcove inclined his head. "I suppose."

Roup watched him. Arcove had not shared his plans for this hunt, and Roup still couldn't tell what he intended to do. Treaty code forbade them to ask for a specific animal, and Roup didn't think Arcove was ready to break treaty code, even with the possible excuse of Storm's behavior. "Assuming you don't kill him in the initial rush…will you turn him south, try to run him into Leeshwood?"

Arcove's tail twitched. "All the other chases have gone south. It didn't seem to work."

"And this time…"

"We go north," said Arcove.

Roup was surprised. "You'll drive him into the Ghost Wood?"

Arcove snorted. "Only if he's unlucky. If he's *lucky,* I'll kill him long before that."

20

Round 6: Arcove

"Storm!"

The rabbit he'd been stalking vanished in a spray of earth. Storm turned to see Sauny galloping out of the boulders. He felt the fear and excitement roll through him even before she spoke. "The creasia," she gasped.

"Where?"

"Everywhere," panted Sauny. "They just started turning up all over the place."

"Are they attacking?" asked Storm.

"No. They're ignoring everyone. I think they're looking for you."

At that moment, he heard a rally cry. *Well, they've found my scent. There must be enough of them who know it by now.*

"Sauny," he said quietly. "I want you to hide. I know that you've scouted plenty of hiding places around here. I will not be able to concentrate unless I know you're hiding. Will you do that for me?"

He looked into her eyes. He was afraid she was going to argue, insist that she could run with him or distract them or something even crazier…like fight. But the sight of the creasia seemed to have intimidated her. She was, after all, only a year old. "Alright."

Storm felt a wave of relief. He turned without another word and ran, intent on putting some distance between himself and Sauny. Evening shadows stretched between the boulders. Storm did not relish the idea of another all-night chase, but it seemed likely. He tried to concentrate on a strategy, on laying a confusing trail, on not trapping himself. The ferryshaft he encountered bolted at the sight of him. He saw mothers hurrying their newborn foals into caves, their movements panicky. Creasia never came at this time of year, and the mothers didn't know what to do. They could not flee as their instincts demanded, because their foals could not yet keep up. They shot accusatory looks at him as he passed.

Storm ignored them. Something Roup had said niggled uncomfortably at the back of his mind. *"I am, arguably, the second most powerful person on this island."*

So, Roup's superior would have to be...

At that moment, Storm heard another cat-wail—not from behind, but from above him. Storm looked to the cliffs. A quarter of the way up, silhouetted against the blood-red rock, he saw several creasia. One was black and a head taller than the others. *Arcove.*

Beside him, Roup's golden fur gleamed in the evening light. From another trail, Storm saw a line of cats bounding down towards the mazes. He recognized the large, dark brown cat in the lead with his strangely abbreviated tail. *Halvery.*

Storm felt a chill. *Have they all come this time?*

He realized a moment later that his own pale fur must show as distinctly as Roup's against the darker red rock. *Snow and beach sand are better cover for me.* The carrying call sounded again, and Storm realized that it was Arcove. He had spotted Storm and was directing the cats in the boulders to his location.

I can't stay near the cliffs. Storm felt as though an old friend had betrayed him. He remembered something else Roup had said. *"In the future, I'd advise you find a less accessible place to sleep. That, or make yourself less...conspicuous."*

Oh, you were just full of helpful advice, weren't you, Roup?

Storm turned towards the plain. The boulders thinned, and soon he was running on grass, which grew rapidly taller as he left the mazes behind. The plain, he reflected, would not be such a terrible place to lead a hunt at this time of year. The grass had grown to the height of his shoulders. Storm had only to crouch, and he was out of sight. In addition, the area was wrinkled with dips and ridges.

Motion to his right caught his attention. The grass a few lengths from Storm swayed, and a creasia shot into view. Storm veered away. Other clumps of grass burst into motion as the crouching predators sprang at him. Storm heard Ariand's voice, "Hello, Vearil! It is delightful to see you again!"

Treace's voice: "It will be even more delightful to devour your liver."

Storm barely registered their words. The ambush had been well-positioned. He shot away to the left in a sprint that cost him precious energy. The cats were *very* close. This hunt would end before it began unless he created a lead for himself.

Storm topped a rise and was, for an instant, beyond their sight. He dashed down the hill into the little pool where, only a few days ago, Sauny had been chasing minnows. There was one deep spot— deeper than it looked, beneath a scrubby tree at the far end. Storm splashed through the water. He took a couple of gasping breaths and dropped beneath the surface.

On the muddy floor of the pool, Storm found a twisted root and hooked one hoof through it to keep himself from floating up. He tried to calm his hammering heart and reminded himself that he could go a little while without breathing. The cats had been very close…hadn't they?

It seemed years, though, before he saw their shadows on the surface of the water. *They will think I followed the stream where it leaves the pool. That would be a good way to hide my scent. Follow the stream. Please.*

Storm clearly saw Treace's outline. He felt as though the cat was looking right at him. His heart hammered. *But the tree throws dappled shadows across the water here, and my fur matches the pale mud. Be calm. Be still.*

And then they were gone. Storm waited for what seemed an eternity, lungs burning. When he could stand it no more, he slipped his hoof from around the root and floated up. Even then, he did not shoot from the water, but brought only his nose into the air, forcing himself to breathe slowly. His ears broke the surface, and he listened. Nothing. Storm raised his head. Not a cat in sight!

Feeling a little smug, Storm bounded from the pool and started in the opposite direction from the stream. *You won't eat my liver this evening, Treace.*

"You see that?" said Roup. "Smart."

Arcove quirked a smile. "I see him."

The cliff trail was just high enough to give them a view of what had happened at the pool, but too far away for them to call to Ariand and Treace, who were fruitlessly combing the edges of the stream for Storm's point of departure. Roup's clutter paced nervously, anxious to be off on the hunt. Storm would soon be lost to sight on the dusky plain.

Roup glanced at Arcove. *It's been a long time since you matched wits with an opponent who could keep up with you. I think you're enjoying this.*

Arcove turned and started down the path at a flowing run. Roup bounded to keep up, and the clutter exploded around them. "He can muck about in the pools all he likes," said Arcove. "But in the end, he goes north."

Storm assumed that, like all the cats before him, Arcove would try to force the hunt into creasia territory. *But he'll have a long ways to go to do that.* The ferryshaft were currently at the farthest reach of their migration away from the Southern Forest. Storm angled north, putting even more distance between himself and cat country.

As the sun set, a plan began to form in his mind. *If I can just keep ahead of them all night across the plain, I'll reach Chelby Wood by morning. I'm sure I can lose them on the edge of the lake, and the trees will give me many options for hiding.*

The plain itself allowed him to create a certain amount of confusion. He backtracked and ran through streams and over boggy ground. He stayed in the dips, so that cats could not chase him by sight. Occasionally, he went to the top of a ridge for long enough to spot some of his pursuers. He would allow them to see him, start in a given direction, then get out of sight and go the other way. These things would slow the creasia, but not stop them. There was nowhere to hide on the plain.

As the moon rose, Storm got a couple of good views from the ridge tops. He was surprised to see most of the creasia off to the south. There was a knot of cats behind him, but he saw many more, strung out in a long line to his right. He had expected them to try to flank him on the left. Storm felt suddenly cold. *They're pushing me north...into Groth.*

High overhead, something screamed, and Storm hunkered down. He glanced up and saw, silhouetted against the moon, a bird. The cry had been like that of a hawk or eagle. Storm thought, based on the size of the silhouette, that the bird was low. However, he realized, after a moment, that it was actually quite high up. The bird was simply enormous.

"What is *that* doing out here?" muttered Arcove.

"What is it?" asked Nevin. He was the newest member of Roup's clutter, only seven years old and jumpy.

"An ely-ary," answered Roup.

"Why is it here?" asked Nevin.

"Be quiet, Nev," said Lyndi.

Roup and Arcove had picked up their pace and run a little ahead of the clutter. "You think Dora is taking an interest in this?" asked Roup. "Or is it just a coincidence?"

"Not sure." Arcove was running faster now, watching the gliding shape far overhead as it banked and flew off north. "I think I'd like to finish this hunt, though. Call in Sharmel's cats. Send a runner to have Halvery reinforce them. Make sure nothing slips between. Tighten the noose."

"And where are you going?" asked Roup as Arcove disappeared into the night, making speed as only he could.

His voice drifted faintly back. "To say hello."

Storm was running hard now in the deep shadow of a trench. He could feel exhaustion creeping up on him. *Perhaps I should start napping during the day.* His body was betraying him, insisting that he ought to be asleep.

Storm could tell that he'd grown since he'd challenged the creasia at the beginning of winter. His legs were longer and more muscled. He had an easier time staying ahead of a group of cats, and he was capable of great bursts of speed. Nevertheless, he had to admit that staying awake all day and running all night pushed the limits of his endurance.

In addition, the sight he'd glimpsed from the ridge filled him with fear. The cats were spread out in a line all the way to Chelby Wood. They probably weren't even running. Those farthest to the east looked as though they were simply lying in wait. *They are going to come together and trap me against Groth.*

Storm knew that he had to break through their ring. *But where? What won't they expect?* Instead of heading due south as his nerves urged him, Storm gritted his teeth, dropped into a trench, and started north at a dead run. *They won't expect me to move directly towards Groth or to travel within sight of it. I'll get as close as I dare, run along the edge, and reach Chelby Wood. That will give me the maximum amount of lead and the greatest possible time to hide once I reach the lake.*

The moon had begun to drift in and out of thick clouds as it moved towards setting. In the trench, when the moon winked out, it was very dark. Storm feared he might break a leg. Time seemed to stretch. He had no clear idea of how close he might be to Groth or to Chelby Wood, and he was afraid to move to a higher point of ground, lest the creasia see him.

He wasn't sure whether he should be pleased or dismayed when the clouds thickened, and a patter of raindrops began, growing to a steady thrum. The water would hide his scent, but it would also slow him down, and the darkness was now absolute. Storm could barely see where he was going.

A streak of lightning lit the plain suddenly, and Storm jumped straight up in alarm. Not ten paces to his left, in the deepest shadow of the trench, he'd glimpsed a huge, black cat. Storm bolted from the trench and out across the plain, heedless of the consequences. Lightning split the sky again, and he saw the sinister outline of Groth, directly in front of him. Closer still ran the black cat. He was keeping pace with Storm easily. Storm realized that the cat had probably been keeping pace with him for a while.

He stopped, panting. There was no point in running farther. Storm tried to catch his breath. "Aren't you…going…to introduce yourself?" he managed.

"I think you know who I am," said Arcove, raising his voice a little over the drum of the rain. He was so close that Storm could see the water dripping off his whiskers during the flashes of lightning. His eyes were as green as the spring grass, and his paws were as large as Storm's head. His voice was a rumble. "You've caused a lot of trouble."

"You've caused more."

Storm couldn't be sure, but he thought Arcove looked surprised. Then he laughed. "Maybe I have. But I'm not the one who's about to get caught by fifty wet and angry cats. You can still walk out of this alive. Do you want to?"

Storm's thoughts tumbled. He was trying not to let Arcove's size intimidate him, but it was difficult. He remembered what Charder had said: *"They'll do anything they want short of killing you—probably bite off your tail and your ears—certainly cripple you. They'll make sure you never run from them again. Every ferryshaft who looks at you will see a reminder of what happens when we challenge cats."*

At that moment, a wave of creasia surged from the trench to his left. Storm whipped around and saw another group approaching from the right. Cats were suddenly everywhere, their eyes eerily reflective in the flashes of lightning. Storm felt very young and very small. Everything was happening too fast.

I am choosing how I will die, he realized, and something inside him screamed, *No! I want to live! Please, please, please...* But he clamped his mouth around the words. *Not like that,* he told himself. *I don't want to live like that.*

But will I feel the same after he opens me with those claws?

Storm realized that a few of the creasia were edging between him and Groth. They were not attacking. They were clearly waiting for Arcove's signal, but they *were* trying to surround him. "I—" began Storm, and then he darted towards the plain. A cat leapt towards him, but Storm's movement had been a feint. Shoving his hooves in hard, and calling on every remaining bit of energy he possessed, Storm shot backwards, turned in the air, dodged between two startled creasia, and landed among the very roots of the carnivorous forest. Its sweet, heady scent overwhelmed him—at once both enticing and repellent.

Arcove had not moved. The other creasia formed a crescent around him. Storm caught sight of Roup and Halvery, then Sharmel, Treace, and Ariand. *They're all here to watch me die.*

"What will it be, Storm?" asked Arcove. "I've always given the ferryshaft choices, although they consistently choose the wrong ones."

Storm felt a moment of recklessness. "And what is the right choice now? What would you do, Arcove?"

Once again, Storm had the sense that he'd caught the creasia king off-guard. Arcove made a chuffing sound that Storm had come to associate with creasia humor. "No one will ever say you weren't brave, Storm. What would I do? I would fight and die. It is not in my nature to submit...or to run away."

"It is not in my nature to submit, either," said Storm. He took a deep breath. "But it's also not in my nature to die." He turned and fled into Groth.

21

Season's End

Roup settled down on the highest point of ground he could find on this part of the plain. He curled up in the wet grass and watched the Ghost Wood. Off to his right, he could just make out Lyndi's shadowy outline. Beyond her, his clutter stretched in an unbroken line, followed by Sharmel's clutter, all the way to the edge of the lake.

Roup did not think Storm would try to emerge from the Ghost Wood that night, but Arcove was taking no chances. He was with the other clutters now, going along the line, talking to everyone. Arcove had always been good at debriefing. He would visit with his officers and the subordinate animals, too. He would explain any part of the hunt that they had not seen. He would make sure that everyone understood what he had done and why he had done it. If any rumors were circulating that Arcove considered damaging or untrue, he would have an opportunity to correct them and to shape the story that would be told in Leeshwood.

If there was anything to be learned from the hunt, it would be dealt with as well. Roup suspected that Ariand and Treace would be encouraged to learn from what had happened at the pool. But, these things would be addressed privately, so as not to humiliate them in front of their peers or subordinates.

Thunder crackled again, and Roup got a momentary sharp view of the Ghost Wood with its tendrils, twisted roots, and enormous green and pink bowls, some large enough to hold an adult creasia. This close, the smell was overpowering. Roup shivered. He was glad that they were here to watch and not to sleep. He was afraid of what he might dream.

It was said that, long ago, when territories had been different and the creasia lived closer to the Ghost Wood on part of their range, cats had come here to die. If they could not come, their friends and relatives would drag the bodies here after death and deposit them in the bowls of the plants or among the twisted roots. Many of the old creasia still believed that the ghosts of such cats lived on—that the Ghost Wood had a mind, and that it was the mind of all the creatures who'd died there.

Some of the old creasia said that those who did not rest in the Ghost Wood did not rest at all, that their shades wandered in misery and confusion. It was not uncommon, even now, for cats to make the trek across the plain or through Chelby Wood with some token from a dead friend—an ear, a tail, a weathered bone—which they would deposit in one of the plants. Many of the younger creasia claimed that this was unnecessary. They said that, if an animal died anywhere on the island, that animal would be absorbed into the Ghost Wood, for its roots were everywhere.

And what of animals who fall from cliffs into the sea? thought Roup. *What of those whose bodies are never found? Do they wander the Ghost Wood, too?*

Roup knew that the ferryshaft had different stories. Their elders had once drunk, each year, from the bowls of the plants, and those who did not go mad saw visions. Some said they dreamed the future, others that the dead counseled them. Some wandered off into the Ghost Wood and never returned. The ferryshaft called the wood "Groth," which meant "eater" in their oldest, half-forgotten dialect.

Their interactions with the wood seemed to have ceased after creasia conquest. Arcove had not forbidden such things, but many of the ferryshaft elders had been killed. Stories and practices that had been passed down for generations had become garbled or forgotten. More importantly, the ferryshaft had lost faith in their traditions. They did not look to the past for answers to the future. Roup wasn't sure whether that was good or bad for the ferryshaft. He wasn't sure whether it was good or bad for the creasia.

He knew only that, if he'd met a silver-gray ghost out there on the wet hillside, he would not have known what to say. Except, perhaps, "I'm sorry."

Tollee woke before dawn to the sound of the spring rain drumming on the rocks outside the cave. She had a sick feeling in her stomach, and it took her a moment to remember why. *Storm.*

Mylo stirred as she rose, and she paused a moment to look at him—a big, rough ferryshaft with a scarred muzzle and ragged ears. He could be surprisingly gentle for such a brutish-looking beast. In all her days with him, she'd never seen him bully a female, and she did not think he would bully her if she tried to leave him. He was five years old this spring—fully adult—but he would have a hard time attracting a mate with his scars and broken front tooth. He'd survived as an orphan and a clique leader, but his friends had not. First Ishy had died, and then Callaris.

Mylo was not the sort to show pain or fear, but Tollee sensed his depression. He did not trust Kelsy, and Kelsy was fast becoming the most influential ferryshaft in the herd. Mylo had never been good at making friends. Now, he was trying to integrate himself into adult society, alongside others who had mocked and ostracized him as a foal. They might have forgotten, but he could not.

Tollee felt a great deal of sympathy for Mylo. She also felt the weight of her promise as a ru. She'd asked for his protection, and he'd given it. Since the day she asked him to be her rogan, she'd not been tormented by another male. She'd had enough to eat, and she'd had the companionship of others of her own age…like Storm.

Tollee shook her ears. She would serve her term as ru, because she'd promised. Mylo had kept his promise, and she would keep hers. There'd been a time when Tollee had resented that arrangement a great deal. She was sure it had shown in her words and looks, but age had given her perspective. She might have a foal next spring. Many four-year-olds did.

Would I want to have Storm's foal? With the life he leads now?

Tollee cursed herself for a fool. *Storm couldn't father a foal this year.*

But if he could, asked another voice in her head, *would you…?*

It doesn't matter, Tollee told herself. She could think of many reasons why it might not matter, but she wouldn't say them, not even to herself.

Tollee left Mylo sleeping and wandered out into the soggy dawn. She saw a few other ferryshaft, picking half-heartedly at the wet grass. They glanced covertly at her when she passed. *They'd like to ask me if I know where he is, whether he's back yet.*

She wanted to shout at them, *How am I supposed to know?!* Storm often disappeared for days when the creasia chased him. So far, he'd only been gone for a night. That was nothing.

But this time had been different. There'd been *so* many cats. Tollee shivered. She'd never seen that many in one place. She'd heard whispers that the creasia king, Arcove, had been present. "And when Arcove hunts a ferryshaft," said one adult, "that ferryshaft doesn't come back."

Tollee picked up her pace. She reached the cliffs and started up a trail. *Storm led them out over the plain,* she reasoned. *From the top of the cliff, I might be able to see something.*

It was midmorning before she reached the top. The things she'd been able to see as she climbed did not improve her spirits—shapes far out over the plain, towards the dark line of Groth. They were the right size to be creasia, although it was difficult to tell from this distance.

At the top of the cliff, she forced herself to stop and eat. There was clover beneath the trees and a kind of moss that ferryshaft considered a delicacy—thick and succulent with spring rain. Tollee ate her fill and then returned to the edge of the cliff. She was surprised to see several other ferryshaft emerging from the wood a little distance to the north.

Before she could slink away, one of them called to her, "Tollee!" Storm's little sister, Sauny, took a few steps towards her. "Tollee, have you seen Storm?"

Tollee sighed. "No." She gave up and approached the group. She saw Tracer, Mia, Leep, Kelsy, Kelsy's three mates, and a dozen other ferryshaft she didn't recognize—male and female. They were all about the same age, and she guessed that they were either cronies of Kelsy's or Leep's hopeful suitors. She also caught sight of Valla and had to struggle to hide her distaste. Valla was not at all the sort of female that Tollee would have pictured Storm choosing. *Surely he doesn't really consider her his mate—a delicate waif that can't even hunt properly.*

Several members of the group glanced at her, but they didn't say anything. Sauny broke the tense silence. "We came up here yesterday as soon as the creasia were gone," she said. "When the storm came, we saw part of the chase…in the lightning. It…it went near Groth." Her voice was too high and too tight.

Tollee looked at Leep, then at Remy. She liked Remy, in spite of the fact that she was Kelsy's mate. Remy was clever and quick, a good hunter. She'd also been a low-ranking ru before Kelsy claimed her. Leep wouldn't meet Tollee's eyes. Remy bent over and muttered in Tollee's ear. "We couldn't see details that far away, especially at night, but the lightning did show a little. All the cats came together in a knot right up against Groth. Then they separated and didn't seem in a hurry to leave. Look at what's happening now."

Tollee saw that things had changed since she'd gone to forage. The cats were coming across the plain in scattered groups. They seemed to be making their way towards the herd. As the sun rose towards noon, everyone continued to watch, saying very little. Sometimes, one or two ferryshaft would go away to eat or drink, but they always came back and sat down on the edge of the cliff. No one suggested returning to the boulders.

When the creasia reached the herd, they performed the familiar, bloody ritual that had been absent from herd life for most of the winter. They pushed the herd together, cut out a group, and killed them—a raid to make up for the many they had missed. No howl interrupted them this time. No streak of silver-gray intervened.

At this height, the animals below looked almost the same—just little spots of color that moved...or stopped moving. They couldn't even hear the screams this high up, just wind whistling among the rocks.

"Well," whispered Leep, "I guess that's it then."

Valla stayed with Sauny. When all the other ferryshaft had gone down from the cliff, she stayed beside the yearling foal, crouched on the edge, and said nothing. The wind painted ragged lines in Sauny's red-gold fur. She kept her eyes trained on the horizon as the afternoon slipped away—gray eyes, like Storm's. Valla watched, too. She watched for a familiar shape slinking across the plain—disgraced, perhaps, but alive.

They saw nothing.

Well, not nothing, Valla corrected herself. *The creasia haven't left.* Unlike Sauny, she continued to watch the tableau in the boulders. Valla couldn't be certain of the species of all the shapes, but she was sure that some were cats. *How long will they stay? All night? All tomorrow? All spring?*

As twilight approached, Valla said, "Sauny, we should eat."

Sauny shook her ears. "No, I want to watch."

"You can watch tomorrow," said Valla. She hoped her voice didn't sound as lost as she felt.

Sauny rounded on her. "He's not dead!" She looked like she wanted to argue, wanted to fight.

Valla had never known what to do with others who wanted to fight. "No, of course not," she agreed.

Sauny's face crumpled. "You don't mean that."

Be strong, Valla told herself. *She's only a foal.*

But so am I. Valla turned her head to the side and shut her eyes—a submissive gesture.

Sauny howled. It took Valla completely by surprise—a long, broken-hearted wail that reverberated off the cliff. Sauny's howl broke off abruptly as Valla knocked her to the ground and pinned her there, suddenly remembering some of what Kelsy had taught her.

"Are you mad?" she hissed. "There are still creasia down there in the boulders. I don't know whether they're punishing us or waiting for Storm to come back or whether they're just hungry for the taste of ferryshaft, but I know they're in a killing mood. Do you think anyone has told them that Storm had a little sister?" *A little sister with gray eyes just like his.*

Sauny was panting and struggling. "I'll kill them," she snarled. "I'll kill every one of them."

"Not right now you won't." Valla was glad that she was a year older than Sauny. She had to exert all her weight to keep Sauny pinned against the ground. "Right now, you will hide because they may be looking for you. Even if they're not, you don't want to remind them that you exist. You certainly don't want to go howling at them."

Valla was surprised at her own words and actions. She'd never forced anyone to do anything. *But I know I'm right. And I know I'm not going to let his little sister get herself killed.*

After a few moments, Sauny quieted. Her voice came out in a whimper. "When Storm was my age, he was outwitting Kelsy's clique. They told stories about him. I haven't done anything."

"Oh, Sauny," Valla let her up. "You will. I know you will. And Storm's not... He might not be dead."

Sauny looked at the ground.

"Come on," said Valla, "I know you haven't eaten all day. Let's get some food, and then we'll sleep up here in the wood. Maybe tomorrow the cats will be gone."

But they were not gone. Over the next few days, Valla made certain that Sauny stayed hidden. They remained on the cliff top until they spotted creasia in the wood one morning. Valla was all-but-certain that the cats had seen them, but they did not pursue. She found out later that the cats had been taking a census. Rather than accept the elders' estimate of the number of ferryshaft, the creasia went through the herd themselves and made their own count. They performed one more raid two days later. Apparently, Storm's activities had prevented them from killing the correct number of ferryshaft that winter, and the mildness of the season had also decreased the number of deaths.

Valla suggested that Sauny stay in a cave along one of the sheep trails. Storm had taught his sister to walk on those trails, after all, but Sauny seemed restless. She insisted on coming back down to the boulder mazes to check on friends from her clique. Valla was constantly afraid that one of them would say something indiscreet within earshot of a cat.

At night, she convinced Sauny to sleep in the caves that Storm had selected. Valla saw now the wisdom of his choices—inaccessible caves with two entrances. Valla thought Sauny might argue, but she didn't. Every night, Sauny curled up next to Valla in the place where Storm had once slept. Valla's own grief—buried deep inside her—loosened a little.

Days slipped past. Later, Valla would not be able to recall much of what she had said or done. Then the weather began to grow hot. Valla realized one day that she had not encountered a creasia among the boulders in some time. No one else had seen them either. Apparently, the cats had finally gone home.

It wasn't many days later before the elders announced the end of the spring season. The springs were drying up, the last of the foals were on their feet, and it was time to make the trek across the plain to Chelby Lake. As they jogged along to the thrum of a thousand hooves, Sauny turned to Valla with a brightness in her eyes that Valla hadn't seen in a while. "We're going to learn to fight this summer, Valla. The creasia are going to get a surprise next winter."

Valla smiled back. "I have no doubt." She glanced over her shoulder at the spring feeding grounds, at the pool where they'd once played, at the warm rocks and towering cliff—receding now into the distance. "Good-bye, Storm," she whispered.

Part III

Keesha

_____

1

Ghost Wood

It was as black as starless night beneath the carnivorous trees amid the pouring rain. Storm stumbled among the twisted roots and nearly screamed when he felt something move under his hoof. An image flashed through his head—the curb trap he'd raided with his clique two years ago, a dead sheep hanging from a tangle of vines, the feeling of the vine wrapping around his leg as he stepped over it.

They can move. I knew that. Don't panic. They're not alive, not really. Don't panic.

When Storm entered Groth, he had a vague plan—travel east towards the lake, find the edge of the water, swim south until he got well away from the creasia, crawl out of the water and hide. It seemed simple enough. However, a voice whispered in the back of his mind that escape would not be so easy. Ferryshaft and creasia feared Groth for a reason. *Arcove let you choose how you would die, and this is what you chose.*

Stop, he ordered himself. *Focus.*

Lightning seared the air, giving him a brief impression of tangled vines and roots; towering, fleshy leaves; and the grotesque shapes of the pink and green bowls. The lightning left him blinder than before, frantic as he tried to reconstruct the image. Had that vine been twisting towards him? Was he about to walk into one of the bowls, tipped half on its side? Had he glimpsed something hanging over his head?

Storm could definitely feel the vines moving underfoot. They did not move quickly, but he suspected that, if he stopped walking, he would soon be covered in them. Could they squeeze him to death? Drag him into the bowls of the plants? Smother him? Storm had no idea. He was beginning to realize exactly how much he did not know about Groth.

Storm was bumping into plants now as he tried to hurry. He realized that he no longer had any idea which direction was east. Dawn was still far off, and he was suddenly incredibly thirsty...

No, he told himself, *you're not. It's just this smell, this place. You'll find the lake soon.*

But there was water all around him, sweet and fragrant in the bowls of the plants, refreshed by the falling rain. Storm shook his head. *Focus!*

You will never find the lake, whispered a voice in his mind. *You will never leave.*

Storm stumbled on. His momentary alertness, born of panic, began to fade. Exhaustion reasserted itself. *I will sleep when the sun comes up,* he promised. *When I can see what's around me, when I know the direction of the lake. Dawn can't be far off, can it?* He found that he was walking with his eyes closed. *What does it matter? I can't see anything anyway.*

Storm tripped. This had become a frequent occurrence, but this time, he pitched headlong into one of the bowls. He came up sputtering and choking, the fluid stinging in his sinuses. He sat there for a moment, trying to hold his eyes open. Storm felt suddenly warm. The scent of the water was sweet and heady. The tension left his muscles. Without further hesitation, Storm lowered his head to the bowl and began to drink.

Storm dreamed of a wood—cool and damp, full of succulent moss, choice mushrooms, and the tastiest of greens. Sunlight dappled and danced on the loamy ground that smelled of rich earth and growing things. He wandered through vast meadows, dotted with velvety flowers—blue as a summer sky, yellow as sunlight, red as blood. Butterflies danced in the air above the grass, and little streams murmured in the hollows among mossy rocks.

Around one such stream, Storm encountered a group of ferryshaft. They were all talking and laughing. Storm thought that some of them looked familiar. He could almost remember their names. One of them—a spindly runt with a limp—came over and tried to engage him in a game of tag. Storm was distracted, though. He couldn't quite understand most of their words. He wanted to remember their names.

He wanted to remember his *own* name. Storm felt a moment of vertigo. *How did I get here? Who am I? What is my name?*

It seemed very important.

"Don't fight," he heard one of them say clearly. "It'll all be over in a moment. It doesn't hurt. Let go."

Storm turned and ran from them. He pounded away over the bright, grassy field. The wind in his fur was crisp and cool, and the sunlight nearly blinded him. *What is my name?*

Someone was running beside him. Storm turned to look at his companion—a ferryshaft with silver-gray fur so like his own that he stared and almost stumbled. The stranger was keeping pace with him easily. He was bigger than Storm—at least as tall as Charder— with battle scars on his muzzle and a proud carriage of his head.

Storm slowed. "You're... I know your name." But he couldn't remember.

The other ferryshaft watched him. "It's difficult to stand between," he said. At least, Storm thought that's what he said. His voice seemed to come from a great distance. "Do you want to stay here?" The voice was like wind.

Yes. "No," Storm whispered.

"Then walk with me otherwise," said his companion.

And Storm did. Somehow, they turned, and walked through the fabric of his dream, and he woke.

Storm raised his head, vision blurred, neck swaying. He lay in daylight—a balmy afternoon in cool shade. He was curled up in one of the bowls of the plants, neck-deep in sweet, deadly fluid. He had a feeling that his nose had just slipped beneath the surface, but he could hardly summon the energy to cough up the water. He wanted, stupidly, to put his head back under again, to take another long drink, to slip back into…

"*Storm!*" The voice was strained, as though from beyond a barrier.

Storm's head shot up. *My name! That's my name. I'm…I'm Storm. And I don't want to die.*

He struggled to a sitting position. It took more effort than he would have dreamed possible. All of his limbs felt as they were made of mud. His vision seemed to stutter in and out of focus—bright flashes behind his eyes. For one disconcerting moment, he thought he was back in the clearing beside the stream. A whisper: "*Don't fight. It doesn't hurt. Let go.*"

"No!" Storm struggled up again. This time, he managed to get his front legs out of the bowl. It felt horrible, as he imagined birth must feel—leaving a warm, comforting place for a harsh, uncomfortable world of pain and struggle. He cried out as he wrenched his hindquarters from the bowl, tearing its fleshy sides and opening a long rip in the shiny pink and green skin. It leaked fluid onto the forest floor as Storm lay panting.

He was alarmed to see—through his swimming vision—that he had blisters on his skin. Huge swathes of fur were missing. *Groth was devouring me as I lay there dreaming.*

Storm staggered up in renewed alarm. His muscles still seemed to work. He had all four limbs. His tail was present, though it was missing chunks of hair. He felt raw, and his skin burned. *Would the pain stop if I went back into the water?*

When he tried to stand, the little vines curled around him. Their embrace was not tight or rough. Under normal circumstances, Storm would have had no difficulty shaking them off. However, in his weakened state, they were all the excuse he needed to lie back down. Storm rested there, panting, with the little vines curling over him, and the bowl of the plant tipped half on its side—inviting. He felt thirsty, so thirsty. "*It doesn't hurt.*"

He drank.

"*Storm, get up.*" That voice again, from far away. Storm raised his head and saw, through his stuttering vision, the gray ferryshaft from his dream. He squinted at the stranger, trying to decide whether he was real. "*That's enough! Get up!*"

It was enough. In fact, the drink seemed to have helped a little. The pain and burning of his injured flesh had eased. However, the flashes behind his eyes had intensified. Storm rose on wobbly legs. He felt as though he were floating. The gray ferryshaft turned and started away. Storm followed him.

He could not say how long they walked through a wood that swayed and flickered and swam in and out of focus. The stranger didn't slow down. The vines seemed to ignore him, while they wrapped around Storm at every opportunity. Storm struggled on.

Finally, the stranger stopped. "*Here.*" His voice was faint, but clear. He was standing in front of a bowl, and Storm approached gratefully. *He wants me to drink again…to ease the pain.*

He was disappointed, however. The bowl the stranger had indicated contained no liquid. It was old and shriveled. The pink and green of its interior had faded to leathery brown. A thick, slimy muck stood in the bottom of the plant. Storm shuddered to imagine what might be dissolved in that muck. Instead of a sweet scent, the plant gave off a faintly musky odor of decay.

Storm wrinkled his nose, but the stranger stood there beside the bowl and would not move. Storm sat down. He was tired. He was fairly certain that he was hallucinating. He wanted another drink.

He looked at his companion and closed one eye so as to keep him in focus. "I want to be just like you," he murmured.

The gray ferryshaft smiled. "*I'm dead.*"

"Aside from that." Storm could tell that he was slurring his words. It was hard to talk properly.

The gray ferryshaft looked sad. "*Don't be like me, Storm. Find another way.*" He looked down at the bowl again.

Storm followed his gaze. This time, he saw something in the muck at the bottom—a glossy curve that caught the light. His vision grew fuzzy, cleared for a moment, grew fuzzy again. Carefully, because his depth perception had grown poor, Storm lowered his muzzle into the bowl and nudged the object. It rolled a little in the muck.

Curious now, Storm tried to grasp it with his mouth. It was round and slippery, and the muck had a foul taste, but after several tries, he managed to lift it. Something slithered from the mud along with the object, and Storm dropped the whole mess gingerly onto the ground.

The object appeared to be a round stone—more perfectly round than anything Storm had ever seen. It was about the size of his hoof. The interior was black, but it seemed to be encased in a layer of clear blue. It reminded Storm of something, though he couldn't think what.

The stone was affixed to a string of linked circles made of something harder than bone, yet delicate. They reminded Storm of vertebra. The string was ingenious and far beyond the ability of any creature of Storm's acquaintance to create. "What is it?" he whispered.

No one answered. Storm looked up. He was alone. He felt suddenly bereft. *Please, don't go. Don't leave me here.* "Coden!" he shouted. His voice sounded unnatural in the heavy silence of the carnivorous forest. "Coden!" he shrieked again. Then he howled.

Moments later, a huge shadow passed over him. Storm started up in alarm. He snatched up the delicate string attached to the strange stone and bolted with it through the tangled forest, stumbling and tripping, struggling through the lazily moving vines.

He didn't get far.

2

Telshees

"Storm? Can you hear me?"

Storm opened his eyes. He had a vague memory of doing this before. He was in a sea cave. He lay in a pool—very shallow at one end, but deeper towards his tail. He could feel the gush and roll of waves. He was floating in brine, pushed gently like a dead thing. A thin sheet of water flowed across the cave floor into the pool. It must have come from a hot spring, because the water of the pool was a perfect temperature. Wisps of steam rose up where the spring water met the brine.

Something in the water gave off a faint green luminescence. By its light, Storm saw the telshee—huge and pale and furry, its eyes as blue as...as a stone. A stone he remembered.

Storm tried to sit up. "Where...?" he asked weakly. His mouth felt parched and gummy.

He heard a murmur and turned to see several more telshees, all watching him. He heard one say, "Well, that's new." His head spun with the slight movement, and he closed his eyes.

"You're in a sea cave," said the telshee nearest him. "You've been mostly unconscious for days."

"Shaw?" Storm ventured.

"Yes." The telshee sounded pleased to be remembered.

"Did I...did I fly here?" Storm's memories were hazy—flashes of light and color.

"You did."

"An ely-ary..." murmured Storm. It had snatched him up. He had thought it would crush him in its talons, but it had only held him firmly as it rose up and up over the vast, swaying forest of Groth. He remembered the sun in his eyes, flashes of Lidian from the air. The whole island had been laid out below him as the giant bird rose even higher than the cliffs. Storm had seen the plains of his birth, the southern forests of the creasia, and more plains beyond. He saw the entire ring of the island—toothy mountains in the south and the Great Mountain to the north. He remembered these things as still images, interspersed with blurs of color and flashes of light.

"It…brought me here?" asked Storm. He couldn't remember that part.

"Yes," said Shaw. "When I heard that Arcove had gone to hunt you, I was afraid we had waited too long to help. I tried to rouse my king, but he refused to take an interest. I have some friends among the ely-ary, so I sent one to watch over you—a weak gesture, I know, because he would not have done anything to provoke war with Leeshwood. When he found you alone in Groth, he plucked you up and brought you to the beach. You were unconscious then, injured by the Ghost Wood. We carried you to our healing pools and hoped for the best. You should count yourself lucky. Many sleep thus and never wake."

Storm blinked. He still felt like he needed to remember something. "Did I have a stone in my mouth? A strange string with a stone on the end?" He felt a moment of panic. What if he'd dropped it during the flight? What if it had never been real?

Shaw grinned, showing her mouthful of teeth. "Indeed." She shifted, and Storm saw the stone lying on the ground beside her—clean now, and even more striking than before. "And for that, Storm Ela-ferry, you will get an audience with my king…as soon as you are well enough. He will be curious to know how you got it."

"You know what it is?" asked Storm in surprise.

"Yes," said Shaw. "It belongs to us. But it had been lost these many years. The 'string' is called a 'chain.' It's made of metal, which is sort of like stone. You're meant to wear it around your neck. That way, you'll be less likely to drop it next time an ely-ary snatches you up."

Storm's vision was beginning to blur again. He shut one eye to keep things in focus. "Did telshees make it?"

"No," said Shaw. She lowered her head towards the water flowing across the cave floor and lapped up a mouthful. "You can drink this. You've done it before; you just don't remember."

Storm was too exhausted to ask more questions. He leaned forward and turned his head on one side to reach the spring water. It was oddly warm, but not salty. He took a long drink, his tongue lapping against smooth stone. Then he sank back down and rested his chin on the shallow incline of the pool. As he shut his eyes, he heard the telshees begin to croon. They sang softly to each other—wordless melodies, indescribably beautiful, and Storm felt as though the music itself eased his hurts and held him floating in a warm half-dream.

Storm opened his eyes again. He could not say whether it was moments or days later. He saw that the telshees had brought him a fish. "What *are* you?" whispered Storm.

Shaw raised her head. Storm thought she might have been asleep. He had no clear idea of the passage of time, but the fish looked fresh. He saw that the other telshees had left the cave.

Shaw yawned, and Storm tried again not to notice exactly how many teeth she had. "We've been called many things," she murmured. "Siren…sea snake…monster…mermaid…dragon. We are none of these…or perhaps we are all of them. On Lidian, we are telshees."

Storm understood very little of this. He watched Shaw with his head on one side. "Are you male or female?" He thought it might be a rude question, but he still wasn't sure.

Shaw laughed. "Both and neither."

"Is that your answer to everything?"

"I still lay eggs from time to time, so you may call me female. The oldest among us are exclusively male. There are very few, and they are often asleep."

"But you've all been both?" Storm was fascinated. *No rues here…or rogans, either.*

"Eat," Shaw told him. "We can sustain you without food for a time, but not forever. Eat and grow strong, so that you can make the journey into Syriot."

"What is Syriot?" asked Storm.

Shaw smiled. "Our kingdom. This cave is but the threshold. Eat, and you will see."

Storm ate, and he drank the warm spring water. He slept and woke and ate and slept again. Shaw began to encourage him to move about—first to kick and swim in the shallow pool—and eventually to move about on the cave floor. The first time he rose from the water, Storm was shocked at how much his own body seemed to weigh. It was all he could do to take a few steps up and down. He was also horrified to see that his lower half—the part that had been submerged most deeply in the plants of Groth—was nearly hairless.

"It looks better now than when you arrived," said Shaw. "You were covered in blisters, then—seeping pus and blood."

Storm could see that fur was beginning to grow back, but it would be some time before his coat returned to its former luster. In the meantime, Storm talked to Shaw and, occasionally, to the six other telshees who came and went from the cave. The others were all smaller than Shaw. The largest was about the size of a creasia, and the smallest was no bigger than a ferryshaft foal. Shaw called them all "pups," and they deferred to her. They were shy around Storm, talking with eyes averted.

"Why does the water glow green?" Storm asked.

"A tiny jellyfish," Shaw told him. "We call it acriss. We telshees like a little light. Light drives away the lishties."

"What are lishties?"

"Our cousins," said Shaw, "and our mortal enemies. They are the sea snakes of the deep dark. Their fur is almost translucent. Their eyes are slitted and green. They are poisonous—one bite would kill you. We have some immunity, but not enough."

Storm considered this. "I think ferryshaft have mixed the two descriptions. I remember hearing foals say those things about telshees."

Shaw inclined her head. "After the war, Arcove forbade the ferryshaft to have any contact with telshees. I believe the adults told the foals lies about us to keep them away."

Something caught Storm's eye—a mark on the wall behind Shaw. It was the same strange stick marking that he'd seen in some caves. "What is that?" he asked. "Is it a telshee sign?"

Shaw looked horrified. "So it's true," she whispered. "They've stopped teaching the foals to read. Syra-lay is right. The ferryshaft are not what they once were."

Storm felt a little irritated. "I'm sorry that I'm so unsatisfactory. If you told me what you meant, maybe—"

Shaw shook herself. "Forgive me. This is not your fault. Perhaps there is still time—for you and for your people. Those markings are writing, and you interpret it by reading. I think telshees may be the only animals left who practice such things on Lidian. Each vertical stick represents a word, and each symbol along the stick represents a sound."

Storm considered this.

Shaw continued. "The word you see scratched on the wall says, 'Healing'." She moved to the symbol and showed Storm the markings for each sound.

Understanding bloomed suddenly. "Oh! I thought it just… *meant* something. I didn't realize…"

Shaw smiled. "You thought that someone had to tell you what it meant before you would know, but that's what makes reading special. If a young telshee, lost or injured, wandered into this cave, she would know the value of this pool. If we lose this territory to lishties or some other disaster and are gone from this place for a thousand years, our children, returning, will find these marks and know our opinion of this place."

Storm felt a surge of excitement. "I've seen those marks in caves all through the boulder mazes."

Shaw looked pleased. "You are observant. If you know how to interpret them, those words can tell you many things. Sometimes, they indicate a tunnel that leads into telshee territory. Sometimes, they show a hiding place, a spring with freshwater, or a cool, dry cave for storing meat. They may be cryptic, though, if it was thought that an enemy might see them.

"Other words may not be intended for you or for posterity—a message left for a friend, a memorial after a battle, the spot where someone died. Writing fades if it's not refreshed, and the ferryshaft have not used the craft these many years. I suspect that the markings you find may be only half readable."

Storm thought about that. "Why would the ferryshaft stop teaching their foals to read? It seems useful."

Shaw growled. "Treaty law. I'm sure Arcove forbade it. He does not want the ferryshaft to remember their past."

As soon as Storm was able to stand and walk easily, Shaw declared it was time to leave the healing pool and go deeper into Syriot. Storm was a little sad to leave. He'd felt safe here. Shaw was teaching him to read. "But Syra-lay will be happy to do that...I hope."

"You keep mentioning him," said Storm as they walked. The tunnel was dark, and he crowded close to Shaw. "Is he your king?"

"As much as telshees have kings, I suppose. When she was young, we called her Keesha." There was no mistaking the fondness in Shaw's voice.

Storm cocked his head. "Was she...he...your mate?"

Shaw laughed. "He might have fathered a few of my pups. I might even have fathered a few of hers."

Storm shook his ears at the strangeness of this.

"When our pups hatch," Shaw continued, "they drink our milk and play in our dens, and when they are strong enough, they go away into the sea. The most adventurous swim down into the roots of the mountain where there are otherways. Most of our pups never return. Many die in their travels. Others find a home on distant shores and forget the place of their birth. However, the strongest return after many years, to breed. Our eggs only seem to quicken in this place, in the warm, deep pools among the acriss."

She glanced back at her drove—the group of telshees trailing behind them. "Lothlia and Thul have come back to us. This is their first returning. It may be their last, or it may not. They are the largest of this group, and they will lay eggs before they leave again. The others have not yet taken their first leaving."

Storm was fascinated. "You swim to other places...other islands?"

Shaw smiled. "Why do you think we call this island 'Lidian'? Why call it anything if it is the only place? No, Storm, there are many places—lands so huge you can hardly imagine. Lidian is a small place. A special place."

"Why is it special?" Storm could think of nothing more ordinary than his own home.

Shaw laughed—a smooth chuckle that reverberated in the dark tunnel. "You land creatures! You live here in the mouth of an ancient volcano on a fault line between the worlds. You flicker in and out of phase in a thousand realms, and every now and then, the old volcano belches a little magic. You are fantastic and amazing and only half real...and you don't even know it. You live out your petty lives, never guessing the impossible truth. Any sailor can find Lidian...any sailor in a thousand worlds. But only if they have one of us to guide them."

Storm did not understand, but he wanted to. "What are the others places like?"

Shaw was silent a moment. "Ask Keesha that question."

3

A Minor Problem

It was a warm summer evening in Leeshwood, and Arcove and Roup were engaged in the time-honored tradition of offering their offspring marginally unhelpful advice. "You're pouncing where it *is*," called Roup. "You need to pounce where it's *going*."

"I *am* where it's going," sputtered his daughter.

"No, you're where it *was*."

The mouse had, indeed, passed her.

A smug friend returned it to the circle a moment later, only to lose it immediately upon deposit. Her brother pinned the mouse, then lost it as Roup's cub barreled into him. The training was, if nothing else, vastly entertaining.

"This whole exercise would be easier if you did not work at cross-purposes," called Arcove. "Cooperate."

"We are cooperating!"

"If you say so."

The three yearling cubs were scampering around a circle scratched in the dirt. It was, perhaps, two of their lengths across. Within the circle, a mouse darted in first one direction and then another. The cubs were supposed to keep the mouse in the circle without injuring it. So far, the mouse had been out more often than in.

"Whaf if I jus hol it in my mouf?" asked Arcove's son.

"I don't see how you'll learn much about hunting that way," said Arcove.

The cub dropped the mouse in the circle, and it escaped immediately. His sister pinned it under one foot, then another, then executed a flip as she tried to follow it.

"Bat," said Roup, trying to choke down laughter. "You bat it, not step on it. Or you could just keep running into each other."

"Or you two could just go away!" shouted his daughter. "I think that would be *really* helpful."

There was a squeak and an unhappy crunch as Arcove's son landed too roughly. All three stopped at once, and Arcove came over to assess the damage. The offending cub tucked his tail and turned his head to one side. "Sorry." The injured mouse moved weakly. Arcove scooped it up, chewed once, and swallowed.

There was a chorus of unhappy voices. "Aw, Dad! Come on! One more? Please!"

"You can have all the more you want," said Arcove. "The meadow is that way."

"But—"

"Practice again tomorrow. If you perform to our satisfaction, we'll help you catch more mice. In the meantime, go try to do it yourselves."

The cubs padded away, grumbling. They were at an age when they badly wanted meat, but their parents insisted they learn to catch it themselves.

The wind shifted, and Roup looked around. Another adult creasia was sitting among the trees a little distance away. He stood and came padding over.

"Halvery," rumbled Arcove. "It's good to see you. How are things by the lake?" Halvery's territory extended along the edge of Chelby Lake, and it was a popular spot at this time of year when the weather was hot.

"Evening, Arcove." There was an infinitesimal pause, and then he added, "Roup."

Arcove twitched his head in the direction of the clearing. "Walk with us. We promised to keep an eye on those three, little as they think they need it."

Halvery smiled. "There's nothing more fearless than a yearling cub with a belly full of milk."

"True. You're welcome to bring one or two of yours. We could have a massive mouse-circle."

Roup and Halvery laughed at the same time. "Maybe if we start them early enough, they'll get along," said Roup with a twinkle.

Halvery ignored that. "It's a long walk for a yearling," he said. "I came to see you about something else. Have you noticed any irregularities with game lately?"

They'd reached the Great Clearing—the largest in the wood, where the rare assemblies took place. The three cubs were engaged in a mock battle a short distance away in the long grass. "Mice!" called Roup. "You're here for mice! You can chew on each other back at the den!"

Three heads popped up. "We are, Dad!"

"You are what? Chewing on each other?"

"No, we're hunting!"

"Forgive me. I must have forgotten what that looks like. Carry on."

Behind him, Halvery said, "The deer are scarce this year—scarcer than I've ever seen them. There are fewer fish than I'd expected as well. The lower ranking members of my clutter are feeling it. I was wondering whether you'd noticed anything up here near the cliffs."

Arcove frowned. "Actually…yes. I hadn't taken a count, but—" He glanced at Roup.

"I mentioned it yesterday," said Roup. "It looks to me like too many of the pregnant does were killed this winter. They didn't throw enough fawns. Right now, those fawns should be feeding us, and they're not, so creasia have been killing more adult deer than usual, which only adds to the problem."

Halvery looked relieved. "I'm glad it's not just my clutter. I had been lecturing them about their hunting practices, but they all swear that they haven't been doing anything out of the ordinary. No one has seen signs of sickness in the deer, either. We haven't found them dying of disease. They're just…gone. I talked to Sharmel on the way here. He said that some of his oldest cats died this spring, and starvation was a factor. It wasn't the only factor, but—"

"But that's troubling," said Arcove. He watched his lieutenant for a moment. "You have an idea of what's causing it?"

"Yes." Halvery wasn't normally one to hedge, but he seemed uncomfortable. "Some of my cats claim to have seen Treace's cats pulling down a pregnant doe."

"Ah." Treace had the most remote of the officer's territories. It was the largest, but also the most game-poor, located in the far southeast corner of the wood. It adjoined Halvery's territory near the lake. "You think Treace's cats have been practicing poor game management?" asked Arcove.

"He's been taking on a lot of rogues over the last two years," said Halvery. "They disappeared from my territory, and for a while, I thought they'd died, but later I started seeing them in his. Many of those cats were rogues for a reason. They were rejected from dens and clutters because they're unstable. They disobey orders. I'm thinking that Treace took them because he wants to have the biggest clutter in Leeshwood. What young male doesn't want that? But now he can't handle them, and it's becoming a problem."

Arcove and Roup were silent for a moment. In the distance, the cubs squealed with laughter.

"Technically," continued Halvery, "Sharmel is his superior officer, and should go talk to him, but—"

"But Sharmel is getting gray around the muzzle," finished Roup, "and Treace *wants* to fight him. He's next in line."

"Exactly," said Halvery, "and I want to address the game problem, not orchestrate a fight. So *I* am going to speak to him, but I thought I would talk to you first."

"Thank you for that," said Arcove. "Did you ask Ariand whether he's noticed anything? His territory adjoins Treace's as well."

"No. I wasn't sure whether that would be…productive."

"They seem to have made up after their fight," said Roup in a speculative voice. "They were quite friendly at the last council meeting. Do you think Ariand would relay whatever you said to Treace?"

"Possibly," said Halvery. "In any case, Treace now outranks Ariand, so even if he knows there's a problem, it's not his place to address it."

"I could call a council meeting…" offered Arcove.

"Respectfully, sir, I think I can handle this."

"No," said Roup abruptly, "you can't. I'll go check on Treace. Stay in your own territory, Halvery."

Halvery looked surprised. Roup made endless snide remarks, but he *never* pulled rank. Never. His voice didn't sound snide now, though. It sounded like an order.

"Excuse me?"

Roup looked at him levelly, "I will check on Treace. If I think there's something you can do about him, I will let you know."

Halvery began to bristle. "You think I can't take that little rat's pizzle in a fight?"

"I think you can't take his whole clutter," said Roup calmly.

Halvery exploded. "The day I can't walk into another officer's territory and deal with a…a minor game problem—!"

"Will be the day you die, yes; that is what I'm worried about."

Halvery was bristling all over now. Arcove watched them without a word.

"Halvery," said Roup, employing the same tone he used with the cubs. "Treace sees you as a threat. He does not see me as a threat."

A shadow passed over them.

"That's because you're not," snapped Halvery.

"I hope Treace shares your opinion."

A snarl interrupted them. Roup and Halvery turned to see Arcove bounding across the clearing at the same moment that an ely-ary dropped out of the sky. They went after him at a run, but Arcove reached the cubs an instant before anyone else.

He was just in time. The giant eagle checked its dive and flapped for a moment above the ground, talons outstretched, beak open in a thwarted scream. Arcove crouched below it—his ruff standing as high as his ears, teeth bared to the gums. He tried to slap at the ely-ary, but his claws fell short, and he could not move without exposing the cubs. He roared, and the cubs shrieked and cowered beneath him.

For one second, the ely-ary appeared ready to strike Arcove. Then Roup sprang at it from the side, knocking the startled eagle from the air. The ely-ary screamed in surprise, snapping at Roup with its beak. It could not bring its deadly talons into play, as it was trying to stand on them. It flapped its massive wings and bounced up, hissing, but before it could strike again, Halvery came at it from behind. He landed on its back, and his jaws closed around its neck.

The huge bird gave another cry, this time of anguish, and tried to launch itself into the air. It succeeded for a few beats, Halvery clinging doggedly to its back, and then they came down hard. Roup and Arcove were waiting. They each latched onto a wing, and spread the creature between them, its talons thrashing uselessly as Halvery crushed the life from it.

When the bird was finally still, they all stood panting. The cubs stared wide-eyed. Arcove turned to them, still bristling. "Cooperation," he thundered. "That's what it looks like. You can do it…even if you're acting like cubs." He said the last to Roup and Halvery, neither of whom met his eyes.

Roup was bleeding from the chest where the bird's beak had caught him. The wound was not deep, and he said so. Halvery was limping a little from the fall. "It's amazing how high they can get with an adult creasia!" he muttered, licking his paw.

The cubs had gathered around the dead bird, exclaiming and taking experimental nips in the long feathers. "Can we eat it?" one asked.

"You can try," said Roup. "You're not going to like the way it tastes. Not unless you're *very* hungry."

"These things have gotten aggressive lately," said Halvery, glaring at the eagle. "Only a few days ago, one plucked a two-year-old cub out of the lake. By all the ghosts, I hope this is the same one."

Arcove frowned.

"We were teaching several cubs to swim," continued Halvery. "The most precocious had paddled a little ways out, and the ely-ary dropped down and took him. Not a thing we could do but watch."

Roup looked at him more closely. "One of yours?"

"Yes," snapped Halvery.

"I'm sorry."

Halvery just growled. "The females say not to name cubs until they're three," he muttered. "Useless advice when they name themselves."

Arcove paced around the bird, studying it. "Fully adult," he said, "but young, I think. Hard to tell the sex. It's in good condition—not sick, not old, not wounded. I wonder whether they're expanding their territory."

Roup frowned. "Perhaps we're not the only ones having problems with game?"

"Perhaps."

"I think I'll be on my way," said Halvery. He looked at Arcove. "Unless there's anything else."

"No."

Halvery looked unwillingly at Roup. He didn't say anything.

"I'll stop by and let you know about Treace," said Roup. "Unless, of course, you want to bring your cubs to that giant mouse circle."

Halvery smiled. It was as close to a reconciliation as anyone could expect. When he was gone, Arcove and Roup started back towards the dens. They walked slowly, the cubs scampering ahead. Arcove spoke in a low voice, "What are you doing, Roup?"

"What any good officer does—keeping my subordinates alive."

"You really think Treace would ambush Halvery? And risk the retaliation of Halvery's entire clutter?"

Roup sighed. "I don't know. I know that Treace sees Halvery as a threat that he will have to deal with before or after he deals with you. He doesn't see Sharmel that way. He'd like to beat Sharmel in a fight just to move up in the council, but he doesn't really see him as a threat. Me..." Roup laughed. "He sees me as an extension of you—someone who will cease to matter once you're gone. But Halvery would remain a problem, and Treace is a little afraid of him. So, yes, I do not want Halvery wandering around in Treace's territory with little or no escort. Accidents happen."

"You could have explained that."

"I did. You heard me."

Arcove's tail lashed. "May I make an observation?"

"I know you're irritated when you ask my permission."

"You both came to me within a day of each other with the same concern."

"That's because we're both doing our jobs."

"Just so."

Roup sighed. "If I wanted Halvery dead, I'd let him do as he likes."

Arcove relented. A smile crept into his voice. "I thought your interference had more to do with the way Halvery is likely to handle the situation."

Roup snorted. "That too. I won't go in there bellowing and giving orders. I'll just look around. I'll let you know what I see. If I think the problem can be solved with a conversation, I'll solve it."

Arcove said nothing for a moment.

Roup glanced at him. "You disagree?"

"Don't overestimate your own cunning, my friend."

"And by that, you mean?"

"Don't be so sure that you've got everyone fooled, Roup. You're not planning on going alone, are you?"

Roup thought for a moment. "If I walk in there with half my clutter, it'll be perceived as an act of aggression. We've already escalated this by two levels of command. How paranoid would you like to look?"

"If you go alone, then you are *alone*," said Arcove.

"I'll take Lyndi. Just me and my beta, out for a visit."

Arcove thought for a moment. "Alright."

Roup butted his head against Arcove's shoulder. "Why so dour? You're the one who keeps insisting that Treace is just a headstrong cub who needs firm leadership."

Arcove looked a little pained. He didn't say anything.

"I'll be careful," said Roup.

4

Syriot

Storm had no clear idea of how long they traveled through Syriot, but it must have been days. Shaw told him that the ely-ary had brought him to the beach in the far north—well away from ferryshaft or creasia territory. The telshees moved sometimes through night-black tunnels, but more often along the banks of underground streams, glowing faintly with acriss. Storm was certain that the telshees could have moved much faster—both in the water and out of it. They were going slowly for him, but they did not complain.

Sometimes the walls of the caves glittered with color—blue, green, red, or a clear crystal that threw back the light in rainbows. Sometimes the riverbank disappeared, and they had to swim. Then, Storm would put his front legs over Shaw's body, near her head, and hang on as she undulated through the water.

They traversed vast, echoing caverns, with ceilings lost in shadow, and along the banks of rivers as wide as the Igby. Pale fish swam there, along with tasty little shrimps—almost transparent. Some of the caves were completely black. The acriss, Shaw explained, could not live in freshwater. However, the little jellyfish thrived in salt and brackish water, especially where it was warm. "Hot streams bubble out of the heart of the mountain," Shaw explained. "They're all over Lidian, but even more common down here." The sea often mingled with the hot springs, so that some of the rivers appeared to have tides.

Storm had no sense of day or night. The telshees slept when they grew tired and moved on when they woke. *All my friends must think I'm dead.* That gave Storm a pang, but also a sense of relief. He felt freed of all obligations…except, perhaps, to his rescuers.

Twice, the drove encountered the scent of lishties. Then they would grow agitated and restless and travel in silence until the next meal or nap. When their rivals did not appear, they relaxed again.

Storm got the idea that the telshees did not often come this way. Shaw was certainly their leader, but even she frequently had to cast about to decide their route. Storm did not like to bother her when she seemed to be concentrating. However, when the going was easy and straight, he would ask her questions, or she would teach him writing signs.

"You sing to each other before going to sleep," he observed. "Why?"

Shaw had to think before answering. "Do ferryshaft never sing together?" she said at last.

Storm smiled. "Sometimes. When we're trying to entertain one another, we sing stories. But you don't usually sing words at all. You sing…" He searched for a word and couldn't find it. "Feelings. Sensations." He gave up. "Did you heal me with your singing?"

"We helped," she said. "It's easier when you're in our pools."

One of the other telshees spoke up. She was the smallest of the pups, no bigger than Sauny, and quite shy. "Shaw healed you," she whispered. "We only sang with her."

Shaw laughed. "Your songs will be powerful, Ulya. Just give it time."

"So older telshees can do more powerful things with their singing…" said Storm slowly.

Shaw inclined her head. "Our pups leave and return to breed," she told him, "and many return only once. A few return again. A *very* few return to stay. These are the telshees of Lidian. Most of us are either quite young—and not yet ready to leave—or quite old and have seen many shores. I am an old telshee, but Keesha was swimming the deep mountain when I was no older than Ulya. His song is like nothing you've ever heard."

"You asked why we sing before we sleep," said Ulya. "It comforts us. Also, Shaw is teaching us songs. Sometimes, we practice them together."

"Aren't you afraid that lishties will hear you?"

Ulya giggled. "Oh, they're more likely to run away if they hear us. Lishties don't like telshee songs."

All this talk of songs put the drove to humming. They often did that—not a full-mouthed song, but a harmonized humming as they moved along. It was a little eerie. Far more eerie was their ability to speak while humming. They could carry on a conversation without breaking their hum, although if the discussion required concentration, they often stopped. Once, during a song, Storm could have sworn that Shaw was harmonizing with herself in two voices. Storm thought he understood why their songs might frighten lishties. In full cry, the drove sounded much larger than seven animals. Listening to them, Storm could have sworn there were fifty or more.

"I frightened a creasia once by pretending to be a telshee," he said.

Of course, they had to have the story. The entire drove was delighted and begged Storm to demonstrate his telshee song, but he was overcome by sudden shyness. "It doesn't sound anything like you," he said. "Really, the cat must have been half-deaf."

"You must tell Keesha that story," said Shaw. "He will be terribly amused."

Storm had noticed how the other telshees looked at each other whenever Shaw talked about Keesha. He wasn't sure what it meant, but he didn't think it meant anything good. "Is Keesha sick?" he asked.

"No," said Shaw, a little too clipped.

Storm tried again. "He's one of the old ones, though—one of the males. Is he the oldest?"

"The oldest that wakes," said Shaw. "He does not lay eggs anymore, and I cannot remember the last time he could be bothered to sire a pup. We call him Syra-lay. It means Lord of the Deep—not just the deep ocean, but the deep and secret ways beneath the mountain."

"And he wants to meet me?" asked Storm in a small voice.

Shaw sighed. "He will. You have something that belongs to him…and you will remind him of a friend."

Storm looked down at the blue stone with its black core. He was still wearing it around his neck. "Coden was friends with Keesha?"

Shaw inclined her head. "No one knows how long a telshee may live…if she manages to avoid all the dangers of the sea and land. But we do know that old telshees enter periods of torpor—like hibernation. They sleep, sometimes for years. Eventually, they never wake. Keesha was sleeping a great deal when Coden first started coming here.

"Telshees and ferryshaft have an ancient history, but we had not been much involved with one another for generations. Coden would sit and talk to our Syra-lay. He always called him Keesha—to remind him of his youth. Eventually, Keesha started listening. Coden would ask him questions about other lands, and Keesha would tell him."

Shaw shook her head. "I think he told Coden things he won't tell us! They made plans—mad, insane plans—but it made Syra-lay happy. Coden talked of traveling the ways of the deep mountain. Preposterous! I don't think a ferryshaft would survive in the otherways—"

"Otherwise," murmured Storm. "*Walk with me otherwise.*" "Did they do it?" he asked aloud. "Did they leave Lidian?"

"No. Arcove had become a threat, and the ferryshaft chose Coden to lead them. Coden was well-liked, known for his tricks. He convinced Keesha to help in the war."

"Why *was* there a war?" asked Storm. "I asked Pathar once, and he said that ferryshaft and creasia have been fighting forever. Is that true?"

Shaw considered. "Near enough. Creasia have always been the largest land predator on Lidian. Our stories say that they were the last to learn to speak—because cats are stubborn and hate change, and they would rather fight than talk. They do not write, as far as I know.

"Other species banded together to protect themselves from creasia. Ferryshaft went into the forest every spring and killed most of the cubs. Creasia were not well-organized. They fought among themselves and even killed their own cubs frequently. They are a vicious species. Their king was the cat most capable of beating all the others in a fight—a bully, not a leader."

"But Arcove was different?" asked Storm.

Shaw's lip curled. "Different, yes. They say he killed a member of the creasia council when he was only a cub himself. He was certainly very young when he came into his power. He began organized attacks on the ferryshaft almost at once. By the time he was finished, there were hardly any ferryshaft left. The entire southern plain is empty now, except for lowland curbs, which I hear have become numerous. The ferryshaft were overconfident, it's true, and their leaders at the beginning of the war made many mistakes. By the time they put Coden in charge, it was all-but hopeless. It *would* have been hopeless without us. Keesha let Coden use our tunnels and secret caves to hide and to ambush. He sent telshees to fight alongside ferryshaft.

"We can be fierce, Storm, but adult telshees have never been numerous. Lidian is our nursery. We come here to rest, to make love, to raise our young, to share our histories, and to die. We are not a warring race. We had not involved ourselves in a land war since the days of the humans, but Keesha did it for Coden, and we did it for Keesha.

"Many telshees died in the fighting—too many. We lost knowledge, lost history, lost pups and lovers and friends. In the end, we lost the war and Coden. I thought Keesha might grieve himself to death."

Storm didn't know what to say. "But he didn't?"

"No. He went to sleep. And he hasn't woken much since."

Over the next sleeping and waking cycles, they began to encounter more telshees, and Storm could see that the drove relaxed. "We are unlikely to meet lishties here," Shaw explained. "The telshees we just met are a border patrol. This territory is ours."

"You came a long way for me," said Storm.

Shaw smiled. "Yes."

"The ely-ary...he's your friend?"

Shaw gave a noncommittal motion of her head. "Ely-ary and telshees have an understanding. We are the only two species who leave Lidian. They do not travel as far as we do. However, I have encountered the occasional wind-blown bird alone on the vast sea, and I have guided those creatures home. Ely-ary remember such debts."

They were coming now to a series of caves amid a confusing mixture of underground rivers and hot springs. Curtains of steam billowed between fantastic, lacy walls of stalactites and crystal—all lit by the faint, green glow of the acriss. Shaw navigated this maze with ease. The telshees were clearly home. Others called to them as they passed, splashing out of pools and uncoiling from the shadows and out of side passages.

For the first time since telshees had rescued him, Storm felt nervous. Their scent was very strong in the cave, and it triggered instinctive fear. It didn't help that they all stared at him—not quite hostile, but not quite friendly, either.

Storm remembered what Shaw had said. *"We lost knowledge, lost history, lost pups and lovers and friends. Keesha did it for Coden, and we did it for Keesha."*

I wonder if they wish they hadn't.

Shaw stopped abruptly. Peering around her, Storm saw another adult, almost as big as Shaw. She blocked the way, bristling, and Shaw moved forward to speak to her. Storm heard the other telshee say, "You've got some nerve! Bringing *that* here."

Shaw answered more quietly. Storm heard the other's response, "Well, it's none of our concern if they're dying! *We* will be dying if we're not very careful, or haven't you noticed?"

More muttered conversation. The pups who'd traveled with him formed a little ring around Storm, keeping the other telshees from coming too near. Storm felt small and vulnerable. He heard the other adult's voice again, this time with a sneer, "Good luck with that. He hasn't stirred in a year at least."

"He has," snapped Shaw, her voice finally raised in anger. "I spoke with him recently."

The other telshee sniffed. "Why does no one else ever hear these conversations, Shaw? Keesha sleeps the final sleep. He will never sing again in waking life. We should name a new Syra-lay."

"And who would that be?" growled Shaw over her shoulder. "You?"

The other telshee lowered her head a little. "Of course not. Emyl, if she ever returns." She hesitated. "You, perhaps. You may have all the charm of a leopard seal, but you are at least awake." She said this last like a joke and a peace offering.

Shaw snorted, but didn't turn around. "Come, Storm. You others, well done. Take your rest." The drove dispersed immediately, talking in low voices. They did not look back. Storm felt very alone. He followed Shaw into a passage that sloped steeply downwards. It was dark, and they walked for so long that Storm began to grow tired and wished for something to eat and drink. The air grew very warm. At last, he saw the familiar green glow ahead and surmised that they were about to enter a cave with water. He heard something, too—a low, melodic hum that made his skin prickle.

Shaw turned to him, her face in shadow. "Storm, what you are about to see is not for ferryshaft eyes. Coden was here, it's true, but no other creature, other than telshees. Not even our pups are allowed to come here until they have gone away and returned twice."

"You don't have to—" began Storm, but Shaw hushed him.

"It may take some time to get his attention. I want you to be patient. I saved your life, remember?"

Storm bowed his head. He understood now. *Somehow I am supposed to save your friend.* "I will do my best, Shaw."

"Thank you." She stopped a little farther on before the opening to a side passage. The hum had grown loud. Shaw raised her voice a little over the weird music. "Welcome to the Dreaming Sea."

5

Syra-lay

Storm found himself looking down into a large cavern that was mostly underwater and must have connected to the ocean, because it was rising and falling gently as though with a tide. The water steamed, so that Storm suspected hot springs beneath the surface, and it glowed green with acriss. The ceiling was only half visible, lost in steam and shadow.

A number of extraordinary creatures lay in the water—telshees of immense size. Their furry coils looped across the floor, entwined with each other in a confusion of soggy white. Storm spotted one's head. It could easily have fit Shaw's head in its mouth.

Shaw beckoned him from the water below. "Do you want to jump?"

Storm wasn't sure. It would be a long jump. "How deep is the water?"

"It varies," said Shaw. "The bottom is solid rock and slippery. Will you let me lift you?"

Storm swallowed. He tried not to think about all of her very sharp teeth. "Could you sing me down?" he joked.

Shaw did not laugh. "Perhaps. You wouldn't like it much."

Storm shut his eyes. "Just do it."

He was surprised at how gently she scooped him up. She did not use her mouth, but a coil of her neck. A moment later, he was on the floor in warm, flank-deep water that smelled faintly of minerals and strongly of telshee. Shaw was already sliding away, her body making a faint swish as she navigated the coils of the sleeping giants.

Storm followed her, sometimes walking, sometimes swimming. He stared as they went. The telshees looked dead, and some even had green mold and barnacles crusted in their fur. One had coral growing around him. There were all kinds of fish in the water—not just the white cave fish, but reef fish and crustaceans. They scurried and swam to get away from Shaw and Storm.

Storm knew that the telshees weren't truly dead, no matter how they might look, because they were humming. The sound was low and melodic, and now that Storm moved among them, he could see the vibration on the surface of the water and feel it in the stone beneath his feet. The sound was incredibly soothing. Listening to it, Storm thought that he would not mind lying down here among the coral and the brightly colored fish in the soft glow of the acriss and going to sleep…

"Storm!" said Shaw sharply, and he realized that he'd sat down and rested his chin on a coil of white fur. "Do not go to sleep here," she admonished. "It would take me days to wake you!"

"Sorry," muttered Storm as he staggered up. "I didn't realize…" He shook his head and blinked hard. "Talk to me. Why are they all here? Are they really still alive?"

Shaw sighed. "We have a saying in Syriot—that if the world doesn't kill you, it will break your heart. I suppose only the truly ancient understand. I didn't used to, but…I'm beginning. Keesha told me once that they dream of the past—that they relive their long lives, sometimes making changes as they wish. I admit, there are moments when that sounds pleasant."

"Aren't you afraid they'll drown?" asked Storm.

Shaw laughed. "A telshee's nostrils close without conscious effort when her head is underwater, and we can hold our breaths for a long time. If these grow uncomfortable, even in their sleep, they'll shift their heads." Storm saw that most of the telshees had their heads resting on several loops of their bodies.

Shaw stopped before a hump of white fur. "Storm," she said softly, "this is Syra-lay—Lord of the Deep, oldest of those who wake, and Keesha-that-was."

Storm spied the telshee's head. He was perhaps a third again the size of Shaw—a huge creature, but not so immense as some of the others in the room. He was coiled more neatly than the rest, and his fur was cleaner. Storm thought his humming was a little louder, although it might only be that he was closer.

"Keesha," continued Shaw. "This is Storm Ela-ferry. He has brought you the Shable and some stories that I think you will like. Arcove has been hunting him."

Storm thought that the tone of Keesha's humming changed at the mention of Arcove. The great sides moved in a noticeable breath. Shaw looked pleased. She began to hum along with Keesha. The song mingled in a hypnotic aural dance. It did not make Storm want to sleep. It made him feel restless, which he was sure Shaw intended.

How long this continued, Storm could not have said. He grew hungry enough that he went a little distance away, caught a fish, and ate it. Shaw did not stop him or even acknowledge his leaving. When Storm returned, Keesha was breathing more noticeably, his sides rising and falling as though running a race. He uncoiled, twisting a little in the water as though in discomfort. A growl escaped his lips, and, at last, his great eyes opened. At first, Storm could see only his third eyelid, but then he blinked several times, and the arresting blue of his pupils flashed into view. Keesha groaned and yawned—huge, pink tongue and sharp, white teeth.

"What do you want, Shaw?" His voice was a melodic rumble in the cave. He was still humming, and he did not sound pleased to see his friend.

Shaw answered without breaking her own hum. "I have brought someone to see you."

"I don't want to see anyone," growled Keesha. "I am composing a song. Go away."

Shaw's voice was full of practiced patience. "You've been composing that song for fifteen years. I'm sure you can pause long enough to meet the ferryshaft who's been running Arcove in circles."

"Arcove..." murmured Keesha. "Please tell me he's still alive."

"As far as I know," said Shaw. Storm got the idea that they'd had this conversation before.

"Good," said Keesha. "It would be a great disappointment if someone else killed him."

"I'll help you look for him right now," said Shaw slyly. "Let's go."

Keesha huffed. "You're not serious."

"I am. Let's go find him and kill him, and then you can stop sleeping down here and singing songs full of pain."

"We would probably die," said Keesha.

"Perhaps. I am willing to risk it."

"It wouldn't be enough."

"No revenge is ever enough to bring back the dead," said Shaw. "But I have brought you the next best thing."

Keesha wasn't listening to her. "No, I mean, I have something else in mind for Arc—" He stopped. He'd seen Storm.

Keesha stared. He stared for so long that Storm became uncomfortable. "Hello. Shaw says you…you might want to meet… me."

Keesha moved forward, shifting a little clumsily, as though he'd forgotten where all his coils were. He bent his head and sniffed at Storm's ears. Storm held his breath. *He won't eat me, he won't eat me, he won't…*

"Who is this?" he whispered.

"As I told you," said Shaw with excessive patience, "this is Storm Ela-ferry. I have been telling you about him all winter, but you have not been attending. He's only three years old, and he's been giving the creasia grief since the river froze. Arcove chased him into the Ghost Wood this spring, and I sent an ely-ary to fetch him out. He came as you see him."

Storm realized that Keesha's gaze had fastened on the stone around his neck. "Where did you get that?" whispered the telshee.

A ghost gave it to me. "I found it in Groth."

Keesha's eyes shot to his face, disbelieving. Storm felt a little frustrated. "What *is* it exactly? Shaw won't tell me. She says it belongs to you."

Keesha moved back a little, blinking. "It doesn't exactly belong to me."

Storm felt baffled.

"Although," continued Keesha, "I suppose that if it belongs to anyone, it's me. We call it the Shable. It opens Kuwee Island."

Storm was surprised. "The little island in Chelby Lake beside the summer feeding grounds? The island we're not supposed to visit? But there's nothing there anyway...except a cave with a telshee on the ceiling."

Keesha laughed in delight. "You've visited it?"

"Yes," said Storm. "I swam out once. There were old bones and a hill with a cave on top and that...that likeness of a telshee on the ceiling."

"It's called a painting," said Keesha, "or a picture. Did you notice anything interesting about it?"

"Well, the telshee was missing one...eye." Storm looked down again at the blue stone with its black core. "Oh."

Keesha smiled. "If you give the telshee her other eye, the cave opens."

"Opens?" Storm was fascinated.

Keesha inclined his head. "Kuwee Island is a fortress—the place where the humans used to live. There are things in Kuwee that even I don't understand."

"What are humans?" asked Storm.

"An intelligent animal that no longer lives on Lidian," said Keesha. "They were very clever. They made things—all kinds of things."

Storm squinted down at the stone. "Like this?"

"Yes," said Keesha. "They were telshee allies once...in the days before ferryshaft and creasia learned to speak. But humans were treacherous and much too powerful. In the end, we had to kill them...or perhaps we drove them away. Some of the telshees sleeping here could probably tell you...if they ever woke."

Keesha shook himself. He reached down, caught the edge of the chain deftly in his teeth, and lifted it from Storm's head. "Thank you for bringing this back to me. I should never have let it out of Syriot. Kuwee Island is a place that should stay locked, and I am glad to know that Arcove does not have the key." Keesha curled up again, tucked the stone somewhere in his coils, and shut his eyes. "I will show my gratitude by not eating you. Please leave now."

Storm made an indignant sputter. He had come to think of the stone as his. "Coden gave that to me, not you."

Keesha opened one huge, blue eye. "Excuse me?"

"When I was lost in Groth," said Storm, "a ghost showed me where to find it." *And then he left, and I howled, and the ely-ary came. Would it have found me if I hadn't howled?*

Keesha blinked at him. "You saw—"

"Start at the beginning," said Shaw, who'd been listening with signs of mounting impatience. "Tell him what you've been doing all winter."

Storm glanced between them. "Everything?" Not even Shaw had heard the whole story.

"You think you saw Coden's gho—?" began Keesha again, but Shaw interrupted.

"Everything from the beginning, please."

Storm took a deep breath. "Well, if I don't tell you about Kelsy, the rest won't make sense. So I guess I should tell you how I learned to run away."

6

Misdirection

Roup chose to visit Treace in the early morning. The wood was soft with pre-dawn light when he and Lyndi began to pass the tree-scratches and scent markings that denoted the edge of Treace's territory. They found two separate sets of marks—one for the broader territory and one for the individual den that claimed this patch of wood.

Roup had not sent a messenger to announce his coming, and he did not call out as they passed the markings. "Sir?" began Lyndi. She was already bristling a little. All cats found this sort of trespass uncomfortable, doubly so as they came unannounced. The markings around Treace's territory were particularly aggressive—deep gouges, as though the cat who'd placed them had an abiding hatred for trees.

"Let's just have a look around," said Roup. "They'll find us when they find us."

They encountered the first den a short time later. Treace's territory had very little in the way of natural caves, and the den was dug into the side of a hill amid a thicket. Roup did not approach it, but watched from upwind. A number of cubs were playing around the edge of the thicket. Lyndi tried to count them, but kept losing the number in her agitation. "Shouldn't we go down there and introduce ourselves?" she whispered. "I'm sure one of them knows where Treace is likely to be found at this time of day."

"No," said Roup without looking away.

So it's like that, thought Lyndi with a sinking feeling. She'd wondered why Halvery or Sharmel had not been sent on this errand. *You wanted to sneak, oh my crafty leader, and sneaking is dangerous.*

They watched for a little while longer and then padded away. Roup was paying attention to everything—ears twitching at every sound, nostrils flaring, eyes scanning the ground. Lyndi was watching, too, but mostly for other cats, who might attack them for this unannounced intrusion.

They encountered another den sooner than Lyndi would have expected. Once again, a number of cubs were playing around the entrance. Roup sucked in his breath sharply when he saw them.

He hunkered down as though he definitely did not want to be seen, peering from around a tree. "Is that what I think it is?"

Lyndi squinted. The cubs were playing with something—long and reddish. At first, she thought it was a small animal, but as she watched them toss it into the air, she saw the shape more plainly. "A…ferryshaft tail?" It was much too long to be a fox tail.

"That's what it looks like," muttered Roup.

Lyndi frowned. This was not the raiding season, and even during raids, she'd never known creasia to take trophies back to their dens. It had been done in wartime, of course, but now… What pride could anyone take in the possession of a ferryshaft tail?

They passed three more dens, and still Roup made no move to speak to anyone. Lyndi was sure they would have been apprehended by now if not for the time of day. *Perfectly chosen, Roup.* Many of the creasia were dozing off. They would have full bellies from a night's hunting. *Still, someone is bound to cross our scent-trail eventually, and I don't think they'll be pleased.*

Roup broke into her thoughts. "Did you see those tracks back there?"

"Sir?"

"Curb tracks," said Roup. "Lyndi, please pay attention. I brought you for your eyes and nose."

You brought me because Arcove wouldn't let you go alone. "Sorry, sir. I'm too busy watching for cats coming to kill us."

Roup gave a low chuckle. "You think they'd dare? Well, maybe you're right. Things here are more complicated than I expected." He stopped suddenly, and Lyndi jumped, her nerves strung taut.

Roup muttered something under his breath. Following his gaze, Lyndi saw a deer hanging at least two lengths in the air. She blinked. A thick tendril of vine looped around the deer's neck and upper body. Its hindquarters were quivering. As they watched, the animal thrashed a few times. It was choking, but not quickly.

"Impressive, isn't it?"

Lyndi spun around, head down, already preparing to meet an attack. Three creasia stood behind them. She recognized the one in front, and this did not ease her nerves. *Moro.* He was Treace's brother and his beta—a cat almost as black as Arcove, but with pink nose leather and strangely pale eyes. He did not often leave the clutter's territory, but there were disconcerting rumors about him.

Roup turned smoothly and without surprise. "Good morning, Moro. Are you having problems with curbs of late?"

Moro smiled. The two creasia with him had fanned out. *Three against two isn't such bad odds,* thought Lyndi, but she did not like that smile.

"I don't know about curbs," drawled Moro, "but we certainly seem to be having problems with trespassers."

Roup refused to be baited. "We've been looking for Treace. There have been complaints about game management over the summer. However…" Roup jerked his head at the struggling deer. "If curbs have been setting these traps in your wood, I can see why it's happening. I've heard that lowland curbs are becoming populous on the southern plains, so it makes sense that they're coming into your territory."

Lyndi watched Moro. *Roup is giving you a graceful way out. Say it's the curbs and that you'll look into it. It doesn't have to be your fault…even if it is.*

Moro cocked his head. He didn't say anything. The two cats with him had circled Roup and Lyndi completely. *They're not even going to pretend to have a conversation,* thought Lyndi.

Roup had apparently come to the same conclusion, because his ears flattened, and he growled. "Think about what you're doing, Moro. Think about what it will cost."

One of the two subordinates leapt at Roup. Roup dodged the charge easily, catching the other cat with a slap across the face. However, as Roup came down, the earth opened beneath him, and he vanished.

Lyndi was so startled and horrified that she missed the other subordinate cat, who charged her, knocked her off her feet, and pinned her with his teeth around her throat. He was savvy enough to pin her cross-wise, so that she could not slash his belly with her back claws. For a moment, Lyndi panicked, struggling as he cut off her air. Black spots flashed across her vision. Some logical part of her brain told her, *He hasn't ripped your throat out. This is a threat, not a death grip.* She went limp.

An instant later, the other cat's grip slackened, and she was able to get a breath. Her vision cleared. Lyndi craned her neck upward, disoriented and desperate. *What happened to Roup?*

Half upside down, she saw Moro and the other cat, standing on the edge of a partially covered hole. Suddenly, Lyndi understood. *They dug a pit and covered it with slender sticks and leaves. A trap.* She had never heard of creasia doing such a thing, though she grasped the concept immediately. *Are they doing it all over the wood? No wonder they're catching pregnant does!*

Moro was talking into the pit, which gave Lyndi hope that Roup was alive. A moment later, Roup shot out onto the half-caved covering of the pit, but it gave way beneath him, and he dropped again. Next instant, he tried to clamber over the far side of the hole, but the edges were crumbly, and Moro's subordinate knocked him back.

"I suppose we are having trouble with curbs," Moro was saying, "and these new traps of theirs. How unfortunate that you fell into one. I suppose it must have caved in and buried you alive. Oh, if only we had found you in time!"

"Perhaps, he died of thirst," offered the subordinate who kept thwarting Roup's attempts to jump out. "Trapped here for days."

The cat pinning Lyndi spoke up. "Do you think they both fell in? Perhaps he killed and ate her before he expired." Lyndi forced her fear down. *I will not die without a fight.* She rallied herself for a final effort, but then she heard another voice.

"Moro… What is this about?"

Lyndi craned her neck again and saw Treace pace into view.

Moro did not look at all guilty or concerned. "We have trespassers," he said.

"So I heard," said Treace in a speculative voice. "Though it would be a shame if this misunderstanding resulted in the death of Arcove's…"—he allowed the briefest of insulting pauses—"beta."

Moro gave an exaggerated expression of surprise. "Oh! Is that who it is? He might have said so. Let him out, Pons."

The cat above Lyndi let her up as well. She was fairly choking on rage. *As though anyone in Leeshwood could fail to recognize Roup!*

Roup scrambled out of the hole a moment later. It was apparently just deep enough that he could not gracefully clear the edge, and he struggled for a moment before getting his back legs over the lip. He was dirty and bristling, but when he spoke to Treace, his voice was even. "How many of these have you set in the wood, Treace?"

Treace cocked his head. A tiny smile curled the edge of his mouth. "You never lose your temper, do you, Roup?"

You'd like to see that, thought Lyndi.

Roup repeated himself, "How many?"

"The curbs set them," said Treace. "As you say, we have a problem."

So you overheard the whole thing, thought Lyndi. *Did you just want to frighten us? Or were you trying to decide whether to let Moro kill us?*

Roup shook himself, sending twigs and dirt flying. The other cats stepped back from the spray—all except Lyndi, who came to stand beside him.

Treace appeared annoyed at the dirt on his coat. Before he could say anything, Roup spoke again, "Stop setting them. You're catching female deer. We eat fawns in the spring and summer, bucks in the fall and winter. We do not eat does unless we are desperate. This is the oldest rule of game management."

Treace inclined his head. "Duly noted. May I ask who was complaining?"

"No, you may not," said Roup, and for the first time irritation crept into his voice. "I trust Arcove will not have to address this problem himself?"

"Of course not," said Treace.

"One other thing: why are your cubs playing with ferryshaft tails?"

This seemed to catch Treace by surprise, which Lyndi was sure Roup intended. The briefest flicker of a glance passed between Treace and Moro.

Roup waited.

Moro spoke up. "Ferryshaft wander into the wood from time to time. You can't really expect us to spare them."

"Wander into the wood?" repeated Roup.

Lyndi shared his skepticism. To reach Treace's territory, a ferryshaft would have to "wander" all the way through Halvery's or Sharmel's. While a desperate ferryshaft might forage on the edge of the wood, this degree of penetration sounded extremely unlikely. Nevertheless, she wished Roup would stop talking. *We already know they have no respect for tradition. Let's leave…and not return without the entire clutter.*

"Yes," said Treace, "I had heard that a few had wandered in. They grow bold of late…what with that foal that Arcove took so long to deal with." Before Roup could say anything, he continued, "But I'm sure they'll soon settle down, now that the problem has been resolved."

Roup looked hard at Treace. "I'm sure they will…and I'm sure we'll hear no more complaints about deer." He turned and walked away, back towards the edge of Halvery's territory. Lyndi was shaking just a little, but she followed him with her head held high, tail up. *You won't see us run, you arrogant sheep turds.*

But as soon as they were out of sight, Roup picked up his pace.

"Sir," began Lyndi.

"Not now," said Roup. His voice was low. "We need to get out of here."

"I was going to say that they didn't offer us an escort out of their territory. Doesn't that seem odd?" *Unless they're going to try to kill us again.*

"Find water," said Roup.

"Excuse me?"

"Water!" he snapped, and she knew then that he was anxious. "They can't dig pits in water."

It didn't take them long to locate a stream, they walked in it all the way to the lake, which they reached near midday. Lyndi had to keep shaking her head to stay alert. Roup went all the way out into the lake, where they paddled along until near evening. Lyndi thought several times that she saw cats moving along the bank, just out of sight amid the trees.

They were both drooping with exhaustion when they finally pulled themselves from the water. Lyndi thought that the scent and scratch marks of Halvery's clutter had never looked so attractive. Roup began calling as soon as they emerged from the lake—long, loud yowls that cats customarily used to announce their presence. They were soon answered.

Roup turned to Lyndi before any of Halvery's clutter arrived. "Don't speak to anyone about what just happened. Let me tell this story...or not tell it."

"Yes, sir." She hesitated. "Why do you think they're doing it? Just lazy? They don't want to hunt properly?"

Roup hesitated. "I think..." he said slowly. "I think we're being misdirected."

At that moment, several members of Halvery's clutter arrived. "I need to speak to Halvery," Roup told them. "And then we need a place to sleep for a while."

Lyndi looked back towards the lake as they started away. She could have sworn that she saw the flash of a pink nose and pale eyes amid the evening shadows.

7

Brothers

Storm thought at first that Keesha might curl up and go back to sleep while he told his story. The enormous telshee closed his eyes and hummed and didn't seem to be paying attention, but Storm could tell by his breathing that he was awake. When Storm got to the part about Ariand's chase, Keesha gave a little snort that might have been a laugh. For the first time, he interrupted.

"You told them your name was Vearil?"

"Yes," said Storm. "It upset them more than I expected."

Keesha grunted. "Arcove won the war at the full of the hunter's moon. They always called him lucky."

"I didn't know," said Storm. "I guess *I* got pretty lucky that time. Shaw saved me from Ariand, although I didn't know to thank her."

Keesha glanced at Shaw with a frown.

"He trapped himself in one of our tunnels," said Shaw. "I heard about it. The least I could do was come and let him out."

"The very least," agreed Storm. "I thought you were trying to kill me."

Keesha opened his mouth, but Shaw interrupted. "I did speak to you about him, but you don't listen lately, Keesha. Storm, keep talking."

So, he did. He told them about Treace and Sharmel and Halvery. Keesha had his eyes open now. He laughed aloud when Storm got to the part about Halvery and the river. "I heard that Coden shortened Halvery's tail for him the last time they fought," said Keesha. "I do hope it's a source of discomfort."

When Storm got to the part about Roup and their strange conversation, Keesha grew very still. Storm could tell that he had the telshee's full attention. "Roup is an odd cat," said Storm. "I don't think he really wanted to kill me."

"I'm sure he didn't," said Keesha. "But he's ultimately Arcove's creature, so don't trust his mercy too far."

Storm looked at Keesha curiously. "Why is Roup so different from the others? Do you know?"

Shaw snorted. "Oh, we know." She glanced at Keesha. "Are you going to tell him?"

Keesha looked between them. Storm realized suddenly that Keesha had stopped humming. His eyes looked bright, alert...and angry. Keesha turned to Shaw with a low growl. "Do you think I don't see what you're doing?"

"I am seeking your counsel for a ferryshaft who badly needs it," said Shaw calmly. "Storm's enemies are our enemies."

"You are trying to make me wake!" snarled Keesha, and his voice reverberated off the water of the Dreaming Sea. He rose up, bristling. "You could tell him all of this yourself! Tell him our histories back to the dawn of days! Tell him every secret you know and go start a war! Just leave me out of it!"

"It was *your* war!" shouted Shaw, matching his height, long neck swaying. "This is your story, Syra-lay, not mine!"

Keesha dropped down a little. There was something sharp and brittle about his eyes. *Pain,* thought Storm. *Grief.*

"They were *your* friends," said Shaw more quietly. Her voice grew pleading. "And you were *my* friend, and I miss you, Keesha."

Keesha looked away. His mane settled. There was a moment of silence, during which he seemed to compose himself. Finally, he raised his head and looked at Storm. "Roup was raised by ferryshaft."

Storm blinked. "How—?"

"I will tell you the story as Coden told it to me," said Keesha. "At that time, there were several herds, both north and south of Leeshwood. Ferryshaft controlled the creasia by killing cubs every spring. Adult creasia are difficult to deal with, as you well know. They killed ferryshaft at every opportunity, but they were neither numerous, nor organized, so the ferryshaft kept them in check. Creasia do not read or write. They do not often parlay with other species or form alliances. From a telshee's point of view, they have barely learned to talk.

"Apparently, during one of these spring raids, a ferryshaft elder got the bright idea of learning more about the creasia by studying one of their cubs. So he spared one and brought it back. He chose the cub at random because it had an interesting color of fur."

"Roup," said Storm softly.

Keesha inclined his head. "One of the males had a mate who had recently foaled, and she was persuaded to nurse the cub along with her own foal…who also happened to have an unusual coat color."

Storm's mouth fell open. "Coden?"

"Yes."

"So…Roup and Coden were…?"

"Coden considered him a brother," said Keesha. "They used to meet, even after Arcove escalated the war, just to visit."

Storm licked his lips. "Then how did…? Doesn't that make Roup a…?"

"A traitor? Well, I suppose he had to decide whom to betray. No easy choices there, and Roup wasn't exactly well-treated by the ferryshaft. They wanted to see how he developed as compared to a ferryshaft foal. They didn't really know much about creasia, and they were curious. They did all kinds of things to him. Making him run all day to see how long he'd last, throwing him off ledges to see if he'd survive the fall, forcing him to swim for great distances, feeding him strange things.

"Coden was afraid they'd kill Roup eventually, and when they were both three years old, he helped Roup run away. They parted at the edge of the forest and promised to meet at the same spot in one year.

"Coden didn't really think Roup would survive. Cats were known to kill cubs who were not their own, and Roup smelled and spoke like a ferryshaft. But they both thought it was the only chance Roup had. Coden was delighted when his 'brother' met him again a year later at the appointed spot. Roup had a black cub with him—a year younger. That was Arcove."

Keesha's voice took on a peculiar timbre when he said Arcove's name. It made Storm bristle uncomfortably. He shook himself and tried to concentrate on the story. "That's amazing! They knew each other? The three of them?"

"Oh, yes. That's probably the best-kept secret in Leeshwood. Roup and Coden met secretly for years. Arcove joined them a few times, but I don't think he and Coden ever got along." Keesha thought for a moment. "I'll give Arcove this much: he never used Coden's friendship with Roup as a weapon. There were never any ambushes when Coden came to visit, and Arcove kept Roup's secret from the other creasia, who would surely have killed him for it.

"Coden tried to keep Roup out of his dealings with Arcove as well. He made me promise once that I wouldn't harm his 'brother' to get at Arcove. I've kept that promise so far...although there are times when I wonder whether Coden might still be alive if I hadn't...or how much one is bound by promises made to the dead."

Storm watched Keesha's dark expression. "You really hate Arcove, don't you?"

"I have good reasons," murmured Keesha. "We have a blood debt, he and I. Someday, he will pay it."

"Because he killed Coden?"

"Not just Coden," said Keesha. "Let me tell you about the Battle of Chelby Lake."

8

The Battle of Chelby Lake

"The ferryshaft elders asked Coden to take over their leadership one fall—most of them, anyway. A few small herds didn't acknowledge him, but most of the leaders came to the fall council where they chose Coden. He was a war-time king—a king to unite all the herds. Coden had no herd of his own, although he'd grown up in Charder's. He was cunning and had friends among the telshees. The ferryshaft hoped that he could save them from Arcove. They swore fealty until the end of the war, and their leaders became his officers."

"You *know* they were afraid," muttered Shaw, "to agree to set aside their pride like that."

"They were terrified," agreed Keesha. "Arcove was killing them with alarming speed. He made a policy of leaving dismembered ferryshaft bodies where they could be found. He targeted herd leaders, along with their mates and foals. His cats were organized and persistent. No one had seen creasia behave this way before.

"Coden put a stop to it, at least for a little while. He united the herds on the southern plain, and formed a defensive system among the caves that riddle the cliffs in that direction. They baffled Arcove for a time, throwing back several large-scale attacks and killing the nightly assassins he sent among them. I do not think they lost many ferryshaft that winter. Arcove contented himself with killing the small, scattered herds and individuals who'd refused to join Coden.

"We telshees offered our help that spring. Coden had done well even without us, but he was having a hard time protecting the birthing females and their newborn foals. Creasia were catching them daily around the caves. I gave Coden the Shable and allowed him to use Kuwee Island. This put the foals and their mothers beyond the reach of Arcove's cats. The rest of the ferryshaft could leave the island in groups, attack creasia, and then return to hide in an unassailable place.

"Kuwee gave them a great advantage. It also gave telshees a place to hide on the mainland. The fortress beneath Kuwee does not connect to Syriot, but we could move to and from the sea via the river and the lake. We began assisting the ferryshaft in their raids. The creasia were clearly disconcerted by our presence and the ease with which we killed them. I suspect that we would have won the war by fall, if..."

Keesha trailed off. Shaw watched him without a word.

"If what?" prompted Storm.

Keesha shook himself. "That summer was brutally hot. No one could move without panting. The streams dried up. Even the Igby River grew so shallow that we couldn't swim it without being seen and possibly attacked by cats. I and about fifty other telshees chose to stay on Kuwee with the ferryshaft for the summer. The rest went back to Syriot.

"Cats watched us from the shore, but no one really thought they'd attack. It would mean heavy casualties for them, and we could simply retreat into unassailable caves. Then one day, the Igby River dried up. One day it flowed. The next, it didn't.

"I found out later that the cats had been busy in all that heat. Arcove dammed the river. He flooded part of the forest to do it, but, because the water was already so low, it worked. He couldn't drain the lake, of course, but he didn't have to. Kuwee Island is close to shore. The water between the island and the mainland was already shallow enough that a ferryshaft could walk across. After Arcove dammed the river, the water level fell rapidly. On the island, ferryshaft and telshees started to panic."

Keesha stopped talking again. Storm listened to the low, hypnotic hum of the ancient, sleeping telshees and thought about what it must have been like...watching the water sinking and the lines of cats coming closer.

When Keesha spoke again, his voice sounded tired. "Coden and I both felt that fleeing the island would be a mistake. The cliffs were the next best place to hide, and they were a day's journey away. In crossing the plain, the ferryshaft herd would be vulnerable to attack. Most of the young foals would not survive. We believed that we could outlast the drought.

"Some of the ferryshaft elders disagreed with us, including your teacher, Pathar. They took about half of the herd and struck out swimming across the lake. They intended to come out near Groth, and travel along its edge to the cliffs. I heard later that most of them made it, although nearly all of the young foals drowned or fell to cats. Nevertheless, they were the most fortunate of us all.

"By the next day, we no longer had their options. The water of the lake had become shallow enough that creasia could walk all the way around the island. At this point, I had to admit to myself that we might be trapped and overrun. There are no springs on Kuwee, and there would soon be no water that we could reach.

"We agreed to parlay with Arcove. It did not go well. His terms would have put the ferryshaft completely at the mercy of the creasia for the foreseeable future—a future you are now living. He wanted telshees off the mainland forever. Coden would not agree to it.

"That night, I told Coden to take a small group and sneak off. I wanted him to go to Syriot and tell the other telshees what was happening. The trap had closed so quickly that I was sure none of them knew. We would need reinforcements to fight our way out.

"Coden was the ideal candidate for this. He was good at hiding, good at tricks. But he was not the sort to abandon his family and friends.

"In the end, his mate talked him into it. He was extremely fond of her. She went with him, leaving their two-year-old foal with the others on Kuwee. They insisted upon bringing the foal who'd been born that spring—a female named Lirsy. She was strong, and Coden was sure that her best chance was with her mother. They also took Charder—Coden's old herd-leader and friend. Charder was about ten years older than Coden, and he was one of Coden's most level-headed officers. Charder could fight; he was known for it. They took the Shable as well, so that, if the worst happened, Kuwee Island would not become a huge cat den.

"My telshees created a diversion, attacking the cats on the back side of the island. In the confusion, Coden and his party escaped. At least I didn't have to watch them die." Keesha fell silent again.

Shaw stared morosely at the water. "If I'd been quicker, no one would have died."

Keesha snorted. "I doubt that." He looked at Storm. "Coden did reach Syriot, and he did manage to contact Shaw. Shaw discovered the dam when she tried to come to our aid. Her drove tried to break through, but in that shallow water, just a few cats made the job difficult. In the end, she couldn't reach us in time."

Keesha's voice sank to a murmur. "The foals died first, including Coden's two-year-old. He'd played in my pools in Syriot when he was a yearling—a bright, happy little thing. When the headache grew unbearable and his tongue swelled so that he could hardly talk, I knew there was no hope. So I sang him to sleep...him and many others.

"The youngest of the telshees started to weaken soon after. In their confusion and delirium, we could not always prevent them from darting out across the dry lake bed towards water. We could see it there, glittering beyond the creasia. *They* had plenty to drink and eat with so many fish stranded in shallow pools. Any ferryshaft or telshee who made a dash for the water was torn to pieces. Occasionally, a little rain fell, and then everyone struggled around the puddles. It was impossible to keep order. They were so thirsty.

"We were soon starving, as well. Every bit of game on the island had been eaten. The ferryshaft were stripping the trees of needles and bark, but we telshees couldn't eat that. We told each other that help would come...if we just held on.

"Telshees can go for a long time without food, but not so long without water. I think Arcove knew that. I don't think his attack on Kuwee Island had much to do with ferryshaft at all. I think he was trying to take *us* out of the war."

"Well, he did *that*," muttered Shaw.

"Many of the older telshees entered torpor to avoid death from thirst," continued Keesha. "When the final attack came, they could not be roused. The creasia killed them where they lay sleeping—old friends, mostly." Keesha had started to hum beneath his own monologue. Storm thought it was a kind of self-comfort—an unconscious thing, like wrapping one's tail around one's feet.

"Those telshees knew shores and seas and creatures that these dim, bloody-minded cats will never dream of in their short, brutal lives," growled Keesha. "But a life of learning and exploration is no defense against calculated savagery. By the time Arcove chose to attack, even those who were awake were too weak to put up much of a fight. The cats crept in very quietly one night, killing the weakened sentries as they went. By the time anyone shouted an alarm, creasia were already inside the fortress of Kuwee, slaughtering ferryshaft and sleeping telshees.

"The strongest of us managed to rally enough of a defense to drive them from the caves. We shut the entrance, leaving the wounded to their lonely deaths. By then, I had with me only four other telshees and perhaps fifty ferryshaft. I thought we could at least reach the water of the lake. I didn't know how far we would have to go to find deep water, but I felt we had a reasonable chance.

"In this, I was mistaken. There were over a hundred cats swarming across the island, and they all converged on us as we tried to reach the water. They pulled down one animal after another in a bloody frenzy. A very few of us did reach the new edge of the lake, and, Storm, you should have seen how they bent to lap it. They could not restrain themselves—bleeding, dying, with cats all around, they stopped to taste the water and were killed.

"I alone kept going—out across the shallow lake with only the barest sliver of a moon to light my way—and it was *much* farther than I expected. Indeed, I despaired of ever reaching deep water. But I am not called Syra-lay for nothing. I was quick, even in my exhaustion and thirst. I did not stop to drink.

"Cats are slower when running through water. Arcove was the only one who could keep pace with me, and he harried me all the way across the lake. At last, I turned and we *fought*. I was hot with grief and anger, and I saw a chance there without his escort around him." Keesha's eyes flashed. "He never would have fought me fairly if I'd asked, but out there in the shallow lake, I had as good a chance as I was likely to get."

Keesha was bristling with the memory. His hum had grown resonant with a darker tone. "Only it *wasn't* fair," he muttered, "because I was starving and so thirsty that when I got a mouthful of his blood, I almost stopped fighting just to lick it off my whiskers. In the end, I had to turn, as his followers approached, and flee again.

"At last, near the very center, the water became suddenly deep. I wish I'd had the presence of mind to create the illusion that it was still shallow and lure him in. Then I really might have made an end of Arcove Ela-creasia on the night of his great victory. As it was, I splashed into deep water and finally allowed myself a few mouthfuls to wet my dry throat. Then I turned back for a last word with my enemy. Arcove was quite close—well ahead of his escort again—and I called to him. I told him that I would kill him. I told him that no matter how long I had to wait, I would see vengeance for those who died on Kuwee."

9

A Difference of Opinion

"They would have killed Halvery. No question."

Arcove had listened in silence while Roup recounted his experience of two days past. Roup could see that he was angry. "I'm tempted to send Halvery with half his clutter and orders to bring back Moro…in pieces."

"I'm not sure that would be productive."

"They threatened my messenger," growled Arcove. "I know you think I'm angry because it was you, but it shouldn't matter—"

"He'll say he didn't recognize me. And it's true that I didn't introduce myself. I didn't think of it."

Arcove gave a dismissive huff.

"And," continued Roup, "Moro leaves their territory so infrequently that his excuse might sound plausible."

"Do you think it's true?"

"Of course not. But he didn't actually hurt me. And I *was* trespassing."

Arcove's tail lashed.

Roup continued. "Besides, I think an overreaction would only fuel the discontent that Treace is trying to muster."

Arcove frowned at him. "Last season, you wanted me to kill Treace. Now you're afraid of him? Of his brother?"

Roup said nothing for a moment. "What do you know about Moro?"

Arcove considered. He visited the other territories more frequently than Roup did. "Quiet," said Arcove at last. "He has a reputation for innovation…but also for cruelty."

Roup snorted. "He demonstrated both traits in quick succession for me."

"He's Treace's brother from a younger litter. Smart, but not very likeable, or so I've heard. Treace has the charisma. There are some who say Moro has more intelligence, although I've never gotten the impression that Treace is stupid."

"No," muttered Roup. "Unfortunately, he is not."

"At least we know what's been happening to the deer," offered Arcove. "Did you tell Halvery?"

"I told him he was correct," said Roup, "that I'd found evidence of does being killed and that I spoke to both Treace and Moro about it. I told him that they claimed to have a curb problem. I asked him to watch for inappropriate hunting activity, as well as for signs of curbs."

"You didn't mention the traps…or the threats?"

"No. I thought Halvery might try to go in there and do something about it. I figured I'd let you decide how much to tell him."

"Those traps could easily harm creasia," said Arcove. "I wonder how many they're really setting."

"I wonder that as well." Roup licked his lips. "The more I think about it, the more I think that they can't be setting very many. It doesn't make a lot of sense."

Arcove cocked his head. "How so?"

"Whatever else he may be, Treace is not lazy. Why hunt with pit traps? They're a danger to his own cats. Then there's the vine trap. We *know* those are set by curbs. I wouldn't know how to make a trap like that, and I can't imagine that Treace does."

"You did see curb tracks…" said Arcove. "Maybe they really do have a problem. Maybe the curbs are killing the deer?"

Roup shook his ears. "Maybe." He did not sound convinced.

Arcove waited.

"There's the ferryshaft tail," continued Roup after a moment. "What's that about? I think they may be poaching ferryshaft. Why?"

Arcove did not have an answer.

"I do think I know what's happening to the deer," said Roup, "and I don't think it has anything to do with traps."

Arcove looked surprised.

"How many creasia do you think we have in Leeshwood right now?"

"About fifteen hundred," said Arcove. "I counted them at the last Volontaro."

"I think it's closer to two thousand," said Roup. "Possibly more."

Arcove's eyes narrowed. "The dens you passed—"

"Were too close together. At first, I thought the mothers might be related, or perhaps the males are friends like you and I, but the scents were wrong for that. I don't think those cats have any special fondness for each other; I think they're just crowded. Also, every one of those dens had at least fifteen cubs playing outside. That's more than any den should have if they're following your breeding restrictions."

Arcove drew a long breath. "Well...that does explain a lot." He thought for a moment. "I always said we would have this problem eventually. Overpopulation and starvation—the punishment for success."

"Good game management and breeding restrictions would have prevented it," said Roup.

"Most of the dens actually like the breeding restrictions," muttered Arcove. "Bitterleaf makes the females come into season faster...and they don't seem to object to being in season...or to *not* having a litter every two years. It's less work for the den to feed fewer mouths—"

Roup snorted. "I don't think it's about that. I think Treace wants...well, what Halvery said—the largest clutter in Leeshwood. Truth to tell, I think he already has it. I think he likely has twice as many adult males as any other clutter."

Arcove grew very still.

"I think the time to force Treace to do anything may have passed," said Roup. "I'll tell you this much: if Halvery goes in there, he won't come out."

Arcove growled. "The Volontaros..."

"I know," said Roup, "we should get an accurate count during those storms, but not everyone runs for shelter, Arcove. The lowest ranking muddle through the storm down here in the forest. We did it once, remember?"

Arcove chuffed. "How could I ever forget?"

"I think Treace has been leaving his excess population behind to fool you. Some of them die, certainly, but not all. From what I saw, I suspect he's been working on this for several years."

Arcove scratched an ear. The fleas were particularly bad this summer. "Do you think the females would put up with that? I'm surprised I haven't heard from the dens about it."

Roup considered. "What do you know about Treace's alpha female? Iska? Is that her name?"

"Yes…" Arcove thought for a moment. "I've only met her once, but…now that you mention it…my chief impression was 'young and inexperienced.'"

Roup grimaced. "That's what I remember, too. It's a strange choice of alpha female for a ranking officer like Treace…unless…"

"Unless he doesn't want her to know any better," finished Arcove. His tail lashed. "I'll talk to Nadine. She'll know something if anyone does."

Roup inclined his head. Nadine had been alpha female to the two previous creasia kings. Arcove had won her along with the leadership of Leeshwood. Nadine was ten years Arcove's senior, and Roup suspected that she'd been more than a little disconcerted to find herself with a seven-year-old mate who knew far more about fighting than about females, dens, or cubs. All things considered, Nadine had been quite gracious. Her knowledge of the state and bloodlines of the various dens of Leeshwood was unparalleled.

"Do you think they've been poaching ferryshaft out of hunger?" asked Arcove. "Perhaps using the pit traps for the same reason?"

Roup looked unsatisfied. "Possibly."

"So what happened to Roup?" asked Halvery when Arcove came to visit him a few days later.

Arcove looked at him quizzically.

Halvery's short tail twitched. They'd met by the edge of the lake in the pleasant cool of evening. A deer had been killed a little distance away along the shore. The highest ranking members of the den had already fed, and now the lower ranking and juvenile cats were gathered round, occasionally snarling at each other or fighting over a choice morsel.

"Roup looked like something had chewed him up and spit him out by the time he dragged himself into my territory," continued

Halvery. "I think he and Lyndi swam all the way back. Of course, he wouldn't tell me anything. Did he fight with Treace and Moro?"

Arcove considered. *Don't make me regret this, Halvery.* "No, he fell into a pit trap they'd dug."

Halvery looked surprised. "A pit trap?"

"Yes. He thinks that could be why they're catching does. Treace claimed that curbs set the trap. What do you think?"

Halvery flexed his claws against the muddy bank with a thoughtful expression. "We do see curbs here from time to time, especially along the edge of the lake. They're usually hunting mice and rabbits—not our level of game. I let them pass. I figure we're not at war, and I've never seen one take a cub. Occasionally, a loner tries to feed at one of our kills and gets himself a broken back for his trouble, but mostly we just ignore them." Halvery hesitated. "Would you prefer that we do otherwise?"

"No," said Arcove. "Do they set traps here?"

"Not often. I'd hunt them for that. I've only found curb traps in my territory a couple of times since the war. A pit...that's not even the kind of trap curbs set. It sounds more like something Moro would try—just to see whether it works. He's like that. I doubt he's setting them all over the wood, though. Roup was probably just unlucky."

"Moro threatened to kill him," said Arcove.

Halvery glanced up quickly. For all he did not like Roup, Halvery had no patience with insubordination. "Are you going to do anything?"

"I considered burying Moro in his own pit. There's a bigger issue here, though." Arcove told him Roup's suspicions about the size of Treace's clutter. "I talked to Nadine, and she confirmed that the dens in Treace's territory favor very young females. They don't mingle their blood very much with the other dens."

Halvery looked skeptical. "Arcove...do you really want to hear what I think?"

"Of course." *Unless it's just more complaining about Roup.*

"I know Roup doesn't like Treace," said Halvery, "but Roup doesn't like anyone other than you."

Arcove decided that a debate on this point would be unproductive.

"Roup *does* like ferryshaft," continued Halvery, "as a species, I mean. I don't know how else to say it. He positively likes the vicious little beasts, and he has always favored more lenient policies towards them." Arcove opened his mouth, but Halvery risked interrupting him. "And I *know* Roup is loyal. There's not a cat in Leeshwood who would get between you and danger faster than Roup, but he has this one quirk. Treace doesn't like ferryshaft. He has always favored more aggressive policies towards them. Roup looks at Treace and sees something more sinister than is warranted."

"He thinks Treace and Moro would have killed you," said Arcove quietly.

Halvery's ears flattened. "He must not think much of my ability to defend myself. Arcove, Treace can't take you or me in a fight. He knows this. Truthfully, I doubt he could take Roup, although Roup would get more respect if he demonstrated his abilities more often. I think Treace will eventually fight Sharmel, and he'll probably win. He'll stop there for a while. I don't think he's plotting to take over Leeshwood. I *do* think he's collecting a lot of rogues and possibly overpopulating, although not to the degree that Roup imagines. Treace has more power than he knows what to do with right *now*."

"And your dens? What kind of exchange goes on between them?"

Halvery snorted. "Well, the leftovers always trickle to the bottom, don't they? Until recently, Treace's territory *was* the bottom. No female in her right mind wants to go to the lowest ranking officer. When females decide to leave my territory, they try Sharmel's. Until recently, they would have tried Ariand's. Ghosts help them, they even try Roup's, although he hardly ever takes anyone...and if you're looking into inbred clutters, I suggest you start there."

Halvery saw Arcove's tail lash and spoke quickly. "It was a joke!"

Don't push your luck.

When Arcove said nothing, Halvery continued. "So, yes, the females who leave my territory for Treace's do tend to be inexperienced misfits. That doesn't mean they're unaware of the breeding restrictions. Only a few of his females are accepted into my dens because we can afford to be picky. My dens get excellent offers from Sharmel and Ariand's dens all the time."

Arcove decided that further dissection of this issue would be fruitless. "How often do Treace's cats move through your territory?"

Halvery flicked his ears. "We let them pass along a couple of common routes. It's the Ghost Wood, you know? Some cats just aren't happy unless they can make that trek to the Wood with part of a dead friend. I understand that. As long as they stay on those paths through my territory, I don't pay much attention to them."

He hesitated. "I still say we should extend our territory along the edge of Chelby Lake all the way to the Ghost Wood. It makes cats uncomfortable—not having that connection."

Arcove shook his ears. "Charder doesn't think the ferryshaft will survive without access to Chelby Lake in the summer. Most of the springs near the cliff dry up. They're already on the most game-poor stretch of plain."

"So let their territory overlap with ours," said Halvery. "What does it matter?"

Arcove snorted. "What does it matter if they see us outside the raiding season? Teaching two-year-old cubs to swim and setting up mouse circles?"

Halvery smiled. "Point taken."

"I don't want them anywhere near cubs," said Arcove. "The sooner they forget how easy it is to kill cubs, the better. The less we're seen outside the raiding season, the more they'll fear us."

"So you think the problem with Treace has been dealt with?" asked Halvery. "He's been warned, and whatever inappropriate hunting techniques he's been using will cease?"

"I'd like to think so," said Arcove.

"Roup should challenge Moro," said Halvery with a growl. "Only blood will solve that problem."

"Possibly." Arcove stood up. "Were you planning on talking to Treace yourself?"

Halvery made a grumbling noise. "You don't want me over there, do you?"

"No."

"You think Roup is right?"

"I have not yet decided what I think, but a warning has been given. Let us see how they respond." Arcove watched him. *Don't make me regret it, Halvery.* He decided to add incentive. "Roup didn't tell you because he thought you might go charging over there."

Halvery made a face. "Oh, that's precious. I don't know how I survive my daily activities without Roup to protect me. Of course, I will do as you ask, Arcove."

10

A Conference Concluded

"Did Arcove really win the war that night?" asked Storm.

"Truthfully…yes," said Keesha, "although Coden and the ferryshaft fought on for another season. I was hurt more badly than I'd realized—fighting with Arcove in my weakened state. First the bleeding wouldn't stop. Then the wounds festered. It took me half the summer to find my way out of the lake and back to Syriot. Most of the telshees thought I was dead."

"I never did," said Shaw, and Keesha smiled.

"When I did find my way home, I fell asleep in a healing pool. I was sick in body and spirit. Old friends were dead because they'd followed me. I drifted. I do remember that Coden came to visit me once."

"He visited several times," said Shaw. "He was happy to find you alive."

"He tried to give me back the Shable," continued Keesha, "but I wouldn't let him. I pointed out that Kuwee Island might be of use to them again that winter, when rivers cannot be dammed. He agreed, mostly, I think, to pacify me. I tried to ask him about the war, but he was vague. He seemed…sad…not himself. He wanted to talk of other shores. He wanted me to tell him stories of places he'd dreamed of visiting. I think he knew, then, that he would never see them."

Keesha's hum had become so sorrowful that Storm grew restless. He half-swam his way over to a loop of Keesha's great body and laid his head across the coarse, white fur. Keesha seemed startled by this gesture. Then he smiled—a sad expression. "Ah, foal." He brought his body around in a loop that cradled Storm and brought him half out of the water. "You are not afraid of me? I, who could crush you in one breath or sing you to sleep forever?"

Storm laughed. "You, who sacrificed so much for my herd? Who still mourn them? Why should I be afraid of you?"

Keesha looked pleased by this answer. After a moment, he continued. "Coden and his party rejoined the ferryshaft who'd gone with Pathar. They fled over the cliffs, along the beach, and back to their caves on the southern plains. The war went poorly for them after that. Coden's mate was killed—a thing that must have broken him; he loved her so much.

"Coden died one night in fall—the night of that famous hunter's moon. The rains had come again. The rivers had risen, and I believe he was trying to reach Kuwee Island to see whether it might be used once more as a sanctuary for the desperate ferryshaft. The creasia had all-but trapped them in their caves. They were starving.

"Coden never reached Kuwee. The story goes that Arcove chased him and killed all of his companions. Coden fled and hid for three days before the creasia caught him. I dared to send a telshee pup into the rivers of Leeshwood, just to see if we could do anything. My spy did catch a glimpse of Coden crossing a river. He had the Shable with him at that time, which is why I'm surprised that you found it in Groth.

"Coden and Arcove fought on Turis—a high rock on the cliffs above Leeshwood that overhangs the sea. I'm told it was an impressive fight, but the outcome was certain. Shortly before that fight, Arcove killed Lirsy—Coden's only surviving foal—as Charder was trying to bring her to me for protection."

"Charder," muttered Storm. He'd made himself comfortable in the loop of Keesha's body. "He's the one who surrendered to Arcove...and agreed to his terms?"

"Yes," said Keesha. "Charder didn't have many choices by then. I don't think he can be blamed for what happened."

"You haven't seen those raids," muttered Storm.

"Tell him what happened after Roup talked to you," prompted Shaw. "Tell him about your...singing." She grinned.

So Storm told Keesha about his flight from Roup on the beach. He told him about his telshee song, which met with great amusement. He even told them how he ultimately escaped—a thing which he'd told no one else. He talked about his friends, his sister, his mother. He talked about that terrible evening when Arcove and all his officers had appeared and chased Storm out onto the plain—how he'd run all night through the dark and rain and had ultimately been trapped against Groth.

"It's often called the Ghost Wood," said Shaw quietly.

"Pathar took me there once when I was little," said Storm. "He said that those who drink from the plants dream the future, but that's not what I dreamed. I dreamed of a meadow and a wood where the dead played. And I saw Coden. He asked me whether I wanted to stay, and I said no, and then...somehow I followed him out into the real world. Everything hurt, and half the time I was seeing double. I couldn't walk straight. All I wanted to do was crawl back into one of those plants and go to sleep. But he kept calling me, and I followed him…and he led me to this old, withered plant with the Shable in it. Then the ely-ary grabbed me."

Keesha and Shaw looked at each other. Storm glanced between them. "Do you think he was real?"

Keesha didn't answer.

"Well, you found the Shable, didn't you?" offered Shaw. "I still wonder how it ended up there."

"Did he say…anything else?" asked Keesha.

Storm was tempted to invent something comforting, but couldn't bring himself to lie. "Not much. I can't remember very well. It's all jumbled together in my head."

"That's the Ghost Wood," said Shaw, "trying to make a ghost of *you*."

Storm looked at Keesha. "That's all I've known, Syra-lay. All winter—just running and hiding and trying to understand." He laughed. "And *everyone* trying to make a ghost of me. Even my own herd."

Shaw snorted. "If you can baffle Arcove, a few ferryshaft elders won't stand much of a chance."

"I didn't exactly baffle him," said Storm. "I would have died if you hadn't sent the ely-ary."

"Perhaps you would have been better off," muttered Keesha.

Shaw looked at him sharply. "Keesha!"

Keesha sighed. "Forgive me. At my age, one has seen history repeat itself too many times. But not always. Sometimes something new happens." He shook himself. "Shaw will show you the Cave of Histories. That might be of interest to you. You're welcome to live in Syriot if you like, but I've never been able to interest ferryshaft in that proposition before…not even to save their lives."

Storm shivered. The idea of living in this chilly, damp, shadowy place was not appealing. Already, he missed the sun intensely.

"You are welcome to anything I have," said Keesha. "In time, I will be able to help you a great deal. But not yet. For now, you must let me sleep." He straightened the loop of his body, and Storm slid back into the water.

Shaw raised her head. "The lishties have been aggressive these last few years. We could really use your assistance."

Keesha shut his eyes. "I told you: I am composing a song."

Shaw's voice grew exasperated. "Telshees are dying…"

Keesha's eyes snapped open. "And they died under my leadership fifteen years ago."

Shaw's head drooped.

"I think rather more died than if you had been in charge," Keesha continued.

Shaw looked dejected. "Are you punishing yourself or the rest of us?"

Keesha shut his eyes again. "I'm not punishing anyone. I am composing a song. It is almost finished. Then I will come and help you. I am not ready to sleep the final sleep, no matter what the rest of Syriot thinks. In the meantime, you are more than capable of doing whatever can be done about the lishties."

"I have never heard of a song that required fifteen years for composition," muttered Shaw under her breath.

Keesha didn't answer.

11

Death and the Cave of Histories

Shaw spoke very little as they made the long trek back up to the more populous caves above. Storm, too, was lost in thought. He *did* miss the sun. He wondered, for the first time, how Sauny must have taken his death. He hoped she had not done anything foolish. The more he thought about it, the more worried he became. *Is it still spring? Summer? Surely I can't have been down here all the way into winter!* But it felt like an age since he'd smelled fresh wind or tasted grass.

"Shaw, you've been more than kind, but I think I need to go home now. Did I…did I do what you needed me to do?"

Shaw shook herself. "Yes, Storm, you helped. The things Keesha told you…he's never spoken of them since the war. I know this is difficult for you to understand, but, for Keesha, the war was not so long ago. He's been asleep for most of those fifteen years. The friends he lost, the enemies he made…that all seems quite recent to him."

"Will he wake again?" asked Storm.

"I think so. I wasn't sure for a while, but after listening to the way he spoke to you…yes, I think he will. He's planning something. I don't know what, but if you can stay alive until he's finished, I think you'll find you have a powerful ally."

Storm smiled. "I think I already do."

"You mean me?" Shaw snorted. "I'll try, Storm. It's been all I can do lately to keep our eggs and pups safe and to continue our training rituals. Speaking of which…I agree that you should visit the Cave of Histories. It might interest you or at least give you a reason to return. Afterward, I or one of the drove will gladly show you the way to the surface."

Storm did see the Histories, but only after he'd had a rest and a fish and a drink of fresh water. Shaw provided him with these things in what was clearly her sleeping cave. Telshees at home were not solitary creatures. Storm dozed between two pups, who couldn't have weighed much more than himself. The gentle, melodic hum of contented telshees filled the labyrinth of tunnels. When Storm woke, Ulya was there with orders to show him around.

She took him through a baffling series of winding passages. Once, they had to ford an underground stream with a ceiling so low that Storm could barely keep his nose above the water. When they arrived at last, Storm was not surprised to find himself in an enormous cave with walls covered in writing. He was not even surprised to find it partially flooded with sea water that moved like the ocean. He was a little surprised to find it flooded with daylight, as well.

"We're near the surface," Ulya explained. "This cave is a deep column. At the top, you would find an opening in the cliff face of the Garu Vell. The water won't reach the top, though, even at high tide, and only sheep could reach it from the outside."

Storm clambered onto one of the many rocks that jutted out of the water. The soft sunlight showed more colors than the acriss glow to which he'd become accustomed. The rippled walls of the cave were surprisingly beautiful with bands of umber, red, yellow, and pink stone. The stick-lines of telshee words covered them. Storm squinted. Beneath the lines of writing, he could see things buried in the stone itself—shapes of ancient bones and sea creatures.

"This cave already contained a history," said Ulya softly, "even before we chose to write here. Some of the bones in the walls look like nothing that has swum the seas in living memory."

Storm focused on the writing—thousands of words, running up and up the walls. "How...?" he began.

"In the beginning," said Ulya, as though she were reciting a lesson, "telshees wrote in the sand with their bodies—short messages, washed away by the tide. Later, they left pebbles in the shapes of words, and this was better, but still temporary. Finally, they discovered that some rocks left marks on other rocks. They studied such things until they identified the best materials for leaving lasting marks.

"Here, in the Cave of Histories, we go a little further. Upon reaching ten years of age, each telshee must trace each word in this cave. She takes a stone in her mouth and traces the lines. In this way, she learns the history of her people, and she makes the marks a little deeper. We have done so years without number until the old marks are very deep. Most telshees perform this ritual again on their first returning to Lidian. If they leave and return three times, they are permitted to add their own words to the histories, and pups will trace them for ages to come. It is difficult to write in stone, so we choose our words carefully."

Storm turned in a slow circle. The undulating walls of the cave, covered in undulating lines, were mesmerizing. He could see that the marks near the bottom were worn deeply into the water-polished rock, whereas the marks became fainter farther up. Ulya followed his gaze. "We started at the bottom," she explained. "One can only reach the upper levels at high tide. There are a couple of other caves where we write as well, but this is the oldest."

"Is everything you know written in this cave?" asked Storm, a little awed.

Ulya laughed. "Not everything! That would take too many words. It would be too difficult. We sing to each other, and that is how we learn. But these are the Histories—the things that happened to us and to Lidian. Some of the Histories are difficult to understand—just a few lines from a single telshee to account for all the deeds of her long life. Some of the words at the bottom have become confused, and we're not sure what they mean anymore. But we keep tracing them in case, one day, we need those words."

Storm felt small in the presence of so much wisdom. "Shaw said that ferryshaft used to write, but I don't think we ever wrote like this."

"Maybe not like this," said Ulya, "but you had caves for writing. Shaw told me that the ferryshaft used to collect a stone that made marks on the rock of the Red Cliffs. They kept their words in cool, dry caves to the south. She said that the creasia filled in the caves after the war and scattered the rocks for writing."

Storm gave a bitter sigh. "I suppose that makes sense. They don't want us to remember anything."

Ulya watched him. "What has been done to your people, Storm…it has never been done to an intelligent species…not in all the histories written here on these walls. It can't last. The creasia will suffer for it."

"I hope so."

"You can stay here as long as you like. If you need me to explain anything, I will do my best." She'd become less shy on their journey, and she seemed immensely proud of the cave.

"How old are you, Ulya?" asked Storm. "Have you traced these words yet?"

"I traced them last year." The little telshee was practically preening. "That's why Shaw wanted me to show you. It is a great honor to trace the Histories. It means that I can leave if I wish, but I am not ready. I do not know enough songs."

Storm smiled back at her. *You're more than twice my age, but you're more of a foal than I am. Telshees live at a different pace, I suppose.*

"Can I come back another time, Ulya? I miss my herd…and I have forgotten what it feels like to be dry."

Ulya laughed. "I hope to never be dry. Of course, you can come back. You can come and stay if you want. Shaw said that ferryshaft won't live in Syriot, but I don't understand why."

"We're creatures of the sun and wind and plains," Storm tried to explain. "It would be hard for us…in the dark and wet." He thought for a moment. "Do we have to come out in the Garu Vell?" For the first time, Storm felt apprehensive about his return to the mainland. "That's in creasia territory."

"Oh, no," said Ulya, "Shaw said to bring you back to her before you left, and I think she'll send you out onto the northern plains. The Garu Vell has several entrances to Syriot. It's not really creasia territory, but it's right against the Southern Forests, so I understand why you wouldn't want to leave that way."

We've got a long way to travel, thought Storm. He was beginning to feel impatient. *I'm alright, Sauny…Mother, Tollee, Valla, Tracer, Leep… Even Kelsy! I hope you haven't done anything stupid in my absence.*

By the time they reached Shaw's sleeping cave again, Storm had almost changed his mind about being deposited in the Garu Vell. "Just send me to the surface," he told Shaw. "No one will be looking for me. No one will know I'm alive. The herd will be down by the lake, so I've got a long run ahead of me no matter where you send me out."

Shaw frowned. "I didn't save your life only to send you carelessly into harm's way, Storm. Let us at least put you out of our caves somewhere far from Leeshwood."

So, they started north with ten other telshees. They slept and woke and slept again. Shaw seemed in no great hurry. She asked Storm more questions about his herd and the current state of life among the ferryshaft. Storm tried to answer patiently, but he did not feel patient. *Let me go, Shaw. I've done what you asked. Now let me go.*

Storm thought of what he would do when he left the caves. He felt fit enough. All the walking and swimming had restored the tone of his muscles. Even his fur had grown back. *I'm more than three years old,* he thought. *In less than a year, I could even take a mate...*

He was so intent upon plans for his return that he wasn't paying much attention to the behavior of the telshees. Consequently, Storm could not have said when they stopped talking and the tone of their humming changed. He *did* notice when the acriss dimmed. Suddenly, the tunnel—half filled with water—grew much darker. Several of the telshees hissed. Shaw stopped abruptly and whipped a loop of her body around Storm. It caught him off guard, and he almost panicked, half smothered in white fur. There was a cry and a confused sound of thrashing from the front of the party.

Shaw's coil tightened. Storm thought it was involuntary and gave her a kick to remind her of his presence. "Shaw, what's happening?"

She didn't answer, but scooped him up abruptly in her mouth. Storm gasped. He didn't dare move amid her teeth. Shaw shot forward faster than he would have believed possible. Storm got a glimpse of a side passage surrounded by telshees struggling furiously, but he couldn't tell what they were fighting.

Then something shot out of the water right in front of him. Storm thought at first that he was looking at a small telshee. It was long and pale and somewhat like a seal. It did have white fur, although patches were missing. The skin beneath was almost translucent. The eyes that focused on him were green…green and slitted and slightly filmy. Storm was so terrified that he couldn't breathe. The creature looked *dead.* It even smelled faintly of death.

The dead thing opened its mouth, pale lips peeling back from bloodless gums. Storm saw that it had another set of needle-sharp teeth behind its incisors. He got a *very* good view, as he was on eye-level with the creature, due to his position in Shaw's mouth. The lishty hissed.

Shaw dodged backwards with blinding speed, and Storm felt his neck snap painfully forward and back. The lishty's strike missed. Shaw brought a loop of her body around the side of the creature even as her head dodged back. She caught the lishty behind its own head, pressing it down into the water. Her coils closed in an instant, and the water roiled as the animal thrashed beneath. Storm *heard* its back break.

Then they were racing on up the passage so fast that Storm felt wind on his face. Shaw did not slow down or set Storm on his feet until they'd left the water behind and zigzagged up a dry tunnel. Storm knew they must be near the surface. They went up steeply for a time, and then, at last, he saw a shaft of sunlight ahead.

Shaw stopped. She placed Storm gently on his feet and then leaned against the rock, panting. He knew she was exhausted, because she didn't even hum. Storm himself was shaken. "Shaw?"

"Mmm?"

"Are you alright?"

She squinted at him. "Better than that lishty."

Storm shuddered. "Was it even…*alive?*"

Shaw's lip curled in an expression of disgust. "That's a topic of debate. They can talk, although they don't do it often. They don't sing. They are very difficult to kill. I'm not even sure that I killed the one in the tunnel, although it will probably die of its wounds eventually."

"Its wounds…?" repeated Storm. "You broke its back!"

"Yes," said Shaw. "You'd be surprised how they can keep striking at you with a broken back."

Storm shivered again. "What a horrible creature. You said they're poisonous?"

"Yes." Shaw's eyes snapped fully open. "It didn't bite you, did it? I thought I dodged—"

"No, no." Storm smiled. "*You* bit me a little, but that's all."

Shaw sank back. "*I,* at least, am not venomous."

"I'm sure you saved my life...*again.* What about your drove?"

Shaw looked weary. "I'll soon find out. It looked to me like we were winning, but I wanted to get you away." She gave a jerk of her head towards the light at the top of the tunnel. "You'll find a crack in the rocks up there. You'll be able to slip through, although most telshees couldn't. You'll be in the boulder mazes, well north of creasia territory."

"Thank you," said Storm. He tried to convey the depth of his feeling.

Shaw smiled. "If you return a few times, you'll soon learn your way into Syriot. In the meantime, you can always come to the beach and howl. One of us would probably hear you."

12

Riddle on the Wall

Storm stood, blinking, in mid-day sunlight among the rosy rock of the boulder mazes. *Summer.* The air smelled of mature grass, warm earth, and the comforting scent that emanated from these rocks in the heat of the day.

Storm shut his eyes and breathed. He turned his face into the sun and felt the dry wind move through his damp fur. "I'm home," he whispered, and then, more loudly, "I'm home!" He capered in a circle, forgetting all his three-year-old dignity. "Do you hear that, Arcove! You didn't kill me!"

Storm tore away through the boulders, leaving a red plume of dust. He wanted to run and run and never stop. He soon got his bearings. He was about two-thirds of the way from the Igby River to Groth. As Shaw said, he was quite a ways from the Southern Forests. *I'm quite a ways from anywhere.* Storm startled a rabbit and soon had something to eat. *Something that's not a fish!* His fur dried quickly.

With his belly full, Storm hopped onto a tall, flat rock. He stretched out in the warm sun and shut his eyes. All of Syriot's dim grandeur seemed like a fantastic dream. *But it wasn't a dream. I'll have so much to tell the others when I find them. But first...I just want to feel the sun.*

Storm woke to an ululating cry—a warble that ended in a series of yaps. He sat up with a jerk, disoriented, and almost slipped from his perch. The sun had set behind the cliffs, and evening insects were singing among the scrubby plants of the boulder mazes.

Storm shook himself and looked around. *That noise...* He'd heard curb cries before. Somehow, they sounded more intimidating when one was not surrounded by friends. Storm realized that he'd never been this far from the herd alone. His friends would be by Chelby Lake at this time of year. He'd had a vague plan to start in that direction next morning. The mazes were a better place to spend the night than the open plain.

Still... *What was I thinking? I should have slept somewhere safer.* But he had an uncomfortable feeling that caves, which would have protected him from creasia, would not protect him from the maker of that cry. *Curbs can get into small spaces.*

Storm realized something else, too. *I haven't passed a single stream.* He tried to remember where he'd found water in this area before. *But, of course, there was snow on the ground, then. Even if I go north into the spring feeding grounds, I'm not sure how much water I'll find. We leave for Chelby Lake when the streams start to dry up.*

Storm wasn't unduly worried, but he did feel more cautious. He tried to remember the sheep trails in this region. He could think of a couple. *Dare I walk them at night...after being gone for a whole season?* Besides, those trails didn't have any caves or ledges on which to sleep.

Storm knew of a few caves at the foot of the cliffs. He wasn't sure how much protection they would provide from curbs, but... *It can't be worse than sleeping on a rock in the open.*

Moving quietly, Storm jumped down and made his way towards the cliffs. The twilight had deepened by the time he found a cave. Its shadowy mouth did not look inviting. *Might curbs sleep in caves, too?*

Another warbling cry made up his mind, though, and he started into the blackness. Storm stopped again just beyond the entrance to allow his eyes to adjust. The last of the dusky light showed a rocky room with nowhere to hide. Moving towards the back, Storm saw that the cave narrowed to a tunnel that continued on out of sight.

He had a vague memory of his mother telling him not to play in these caves because foals had gotten lost and starved to death. Even when hiding from Kelsy's clique, Storm had always avoided deep, lightless caves with too many branching passages. He wondered if the cave connected to Syriot. More likely, it was just a dark warren of narrow tunnels. If he'd been hiding from the creasia, he needn't have gone more than a short distance inside. However, hiding from small, nimble curbs was trickier. *I could stay awake and keep moving... But, then, how safe would I be crossing the plain tomorrow with no sleep?*

Storm took a deep breath, commanded himself not to think of lishties, and was about to plunge into the night-black passage, when he noticed something on the wall above: unnaturally straight, white lines. Storm squinted. Then he caught his breath. Telshee words had been scratched into the rock just above a low ledge. *No,* he corrected himself, *not telshee words. Ferryshaft words!*

Storm moved closer to the wall in the dim light. He licked his lips and concentrated, struggling to remember Shaw's instructions. Slowly, he sounded out the symbols. "Look...back."

That was all it said. Storm walked around the cave, scanning the walls for the rest of the message, but found no more words. The night was completely dark now with only starlight to aid his search. A curb yipped again. It sounded disturbingly close, and Storm shivered. He remembered that time with Tollee on the way to Groth—how curbs had almost killed him.

Storm returned to the back wall. He stared at the words again. *I don't even know why I'm doing this. Didn't Shaw say that most of the words I found in the mazes would be nonsense? The rest of the message has probably dissolved with time. And how could it help anyway?*

But he kept looking. A natural rock shelf seemed to underline the message. It was so low that Storm could easily put his front feet on it—not a suitable hiding place. On an impulse, he jumped onto the shelf anyway just to have a closer look at the words. "Look back."

Storm turned around. Then he laughed.

The hiding place was in the ceiling—a shallow, second cave with a wide, flattened mouth that opened towards the back of the lower cave. From anywhere on the floor, the ceiling looked smooth. Only by standing on the shelf and looking back towards the entrance did one achieve the right angle to see the second cave.

Storm tried three times before he managed to jump from the shelf into the cave in the ceiling. When he finally succeeded, he found that he was not the only ferryshaft to have visited the hiding place this year. Someone had stuffed the back of the little cave with summer grasses, which had dried in the heat. Storm had seen hay before, although it was usually claimed by upper-level members of the herd. It was a food source that would last for some time if it did not become wet. *This is some elder's winter cache,* thought Storm. *Well, I hope he or she doesn't mind sharing with me.*

Soon, Storm was nodding off again, well-fed once more, feeling secure and comfortable amid the sweet scent of summer hay.

Storm woke to a bedlam of noise. His heart gave an unpleasant skip and then pounded for a few moments while he lay perfectly still, wondering if some predator had discovered his hiding place. The noises coming from below sounded like fighting—snarls and roars and yelps. When no grappling paws appeared in the opening of his sanctuary, Storm inched forward and peered cautiously over the edge.

Curbs were fighting in the cave below, their bodies illuminated by weak, dawn light. More curbs than Storm could easily count were thrashing around the room in a seething mass of blood and snarls. As he watched, one group rallied and managed to form a defensive circle. Storm saw that these were a bit larger and shaggier than their opponents. The smaller, sleeker curbs danced around the outside of the ring, flashing in to snap at flanks and hamstrings. The circling curbs made a determined rush forward, and the smaller animals fell back before them, calling insults and threats even as they retreated. "Breathe while you can, stinking rat spawn! We'll taste your blood by nightfall!"

The larger curbs made one more rush, and the group disappeared from Storm's view. There was a moment of silence, and then he heard the panting of the curbs again. The larger curbs seemed to have driven off their attackers, but they had not left the cave.

"Sir—" began one.

Another answered, "I know, Cohal."

Storm jumped again when one animal set up a keening howl. Storm peered down and saw that the curb was standing over the body of another, dead or dying on the stone floor. "No, no, no, no…"

"Shut up!" barked another. "Just shut up!"

"Oh, let him be. We're all dead anyway. What's the difference?"

"We could try these caves. Might be another way out."

"I doubt it. More likely, we'd just get lost and starve underground…or be killed by telshees."

"I think I'd rather be killed by telshees…just to spite Quinyl."

"All of you, be quiet," growled one. He had the tone of a leader. "Can everyone still walk?"

"Everyone who's still breathing," muttered one.

"Alright, then. Maenie and Nof, check these tunnels. Do *not* get lost. I just want to know if we can get out that way. Quinyl will try to keep us in here until she's gathered another pack or two. I doubt they'll attack before nightfall. Go on."

Storm watched with interest and a degree of pity as the two curbs scampered away into the blackness. The rest settled down to mourn their dead and wait. *They're trapped,* thought Storm, *and so am I.*

13

Curbs

The two curbs who'd been sent into the passages returned by midmorning. "Well, it's a good place to get lost and die in the dark," said one, "but I don't think it leads to the surface. Not a breath of fresh air or even a trickle of water."

Storm was sorry to hear this. He was getting thirsty.

"We'll have to take our chances with whatever's outside, then," said their leader. "Best try in the heat of the day when they're likely to be napping."

They did try, but they were driven back. The curbs outside did not attempt to press their attack into the cave, but seemed content to trap their opponents within. Storm could see the back third of the cave from his hiding place, and he'd gotten a good look at the trapped pack. There were eight of them, along with three dead that they'd dragged into a corner. The bodies were beginning to stink.

Storm kept hoping that they would make a successful drive into the mazes—at least long enough for him to escape—but they always returned within moments. He got the idea that they were severely outnumbered and hesitant to risk further losses. Storm tried to remember everything Pathar had told him about curbs, everything he'd ever heard from Tracer or Leep or Tollee. But he couldn't think of anything helpful.

As evening approached, the pack's desperation faded into resignation. They stopped trying to escape. They stopped pacing. They lay on their bellies, heads up, and waited. Two or three groomed each other. They did not speak. Outside, the yips and howls started. It sounded like hundreds of curbs, although Storm doubted it was more than twenty. *I suppose I could just wait until they're all dead. At this rate, it won't take long.*

He knew when the attacking curbs came into view at the front of the cave, because all of those below him stood up. They did not leap to their feet. They stood with tired dignity and moved into a defensive crescent, putting the furthest wall of the cave at their backs.

"Can we talk about this?" asked the foremost curb below Storm—the one he'd identified as the leader.

"There's nothing to talk about," came a smooth, female voice from the front of the cave. "You are in our territory. We will not suffer it."

"Your territory grows by the year," said the curb below. "We are all curbs, Quinyl. We share blood. Why must we fight?"

"Your predecessors said such things, too, when their backs were to a wall or a cliff or a river," she said. "But when they were not desperate, those curbs raided our caches, killed our young, and dismantled our traps. We are not the same blood, you and I. And after today, our plains will be free of your stench."

The attacking curbs had moved into Storm's line of sight. He'd been right about the number—twenty at least, maybe a few more. They outnumbered the larger curbs by more than two-to-one, and they were obviously fresher. The female who'd been talking stood towards the back of the group. The foremost appeared to be a large male, almost as big as his opponents. He was moving in a slow stalk towards the leader of the defending curbs, dancing a little this way and that to keep the other off balance.

If the attackers move a little farther into the cave, I could jump down behind them and run, thought Storm. *They wouldn't follow me. They're too intent on killing these others. That's what I should do. That, or wait until the fight is over.*

Instead, he moved to the lip of the upper cave, far enough out that he could be seen by those at the back…if they happened to look up. Storm looked directly at the leader of the trapped curbs. *One chance. One chance, because I have a weakness for trapped, outnumbered creatures. And because someone saved my life recently… when she didn't have to.*

Storm thought for a moment that the leader would not see him, that the attacking curbs would pass below, and the battle would carry on to its inevitable conclusion.

Then the leader stiffened. His eyes met Storm's. Storm read a moment of pure astonishment. *Think fast. I can't help you if you're slow or stupid.* Storm looked down sidelong at the foremost attacker and jerked his head.

The leader moved forward. As though he and Storm had planned it all along, he leapt at his opponent, drawing the largest attacking curb into a position directly beneath Storm's perch. The attacker followed, bared his teeth, and would have sprung…if Storm had not fallen on him like a stone from above.

Storm felt his front hooves connect with a satisfying crunch against the back of the curb's skull, and he landed with a final, solid thump on the broken body. Already, he was turning, lashing out in all directions with his hooves and teeth. He'd grown taller since the last time he had dealt with curbs, but surprise was his greatest weapon. They were so astonished and bewildered that he'd killed two more before they scattered, yelping and calling confusedly to each other.

The beleaguered party took full advantage of the situation to tear into their opponents. *But we can't stay here.* Already, Storm could hear those who'd fled outside sending up a frantic yapping. He remembered what the leader had said about Quinyl calling other packs.

The moment Storm saw a clear space, he bounded out of the cave. The defending curbs ran with him. "You're highland curbs, aren't you?" shouted Storm without preamble.

"Yes," panted their leader, struggling to keep pace beside him. "Who are—?"

"Can you run on sheep trails?" demanded Storm.

Their leader looked confused. "Yes... Maybe."

"The answer is yes or no," shot Storm. "Follow me."

They did—all the way up a winding path with a snarling pack of lowland curbs rallying on their heels. Storm was determined to reach the sheep trail before the last of the evening light faded. The going was slower than he would have liked. He'd been gone for so long that he dared not take the trail at a run. However, when he took a moment to look back, he was pleased to see the highland curbs, picking their way along behind him over the uneven thread of rock. He felt an additional moment of satisfaction when he glimpsed their pursuers, milling about in confusion where the real path ended.

"I guess they're called 'lowland' for a reason," he said over his shoulder.

The leader of the highland curbs laughed. Storm thought it was the first time he'd heard a curb laugh. "I think I've seen you before," he told Storm.

"Oh?"

"You led a clutter of creasia into my resting pack last spring."

"Oh." Storm slowed a little. He wanted to glance back to gauge the curb's expression, but he needed to watch his feet. "Sorry about that. I was desperate."

"They killed two of my pack-mates," continued the curb.

"Does that make us enemies?"

"I think you just saved our lives, so I suppose you've made up for it. My name is Eyal, and I think mine is the last pack of highland curbs this side of Leeshwood. You're the one they call Vearil, aren't you? The one Arcove supposedly killed last season."

Storm smiled. "Yes. I'm not very good at staying dead. You can call me Storm."

14

Return

The sheep trail ended at the top of the cliffs. Quinyl and her pack would have a long detour to reach them, if they managed to figure out where the trail emerged at all. Storm expected that he and the curbs would go their separate ways after reaching the cliff top, but Eyal seemed in no hurry to be rid of him. He offered to show Storm a spring that was still flowing at this time of year—information that Storm did not possess and badly needed.

So, they traveled southward through the night, and Storm was glad of the naps he'd taken in the cave during the day. "What are you doing so far from your herd?" asked Eyal. "Has Arcove made you a fugitive?"

"Oh, no," said Storm, "I was with the telshees."

He wondered after he said it whether he shouldn't have, but the curbs did not seem surprised. "So the old alliances are not dead," said Eyal's second, a curb named Cohal. "This news will not please Arcove."

"Well, I don't think anyone is going to tell him," said Storm, a little apprehensive. "I didn't know about the old alliances until the telshees saved me…although I suppose it was really the ely-ary who saved me."

"An ely-ary saved you?" asked Eyal in open wonder.

Storm found himself telling them the story in bits and pieces. He hoped he wasn't making a mistake, but he badly wanted to tell *someone* about his adventures. He knew it should have been Tracer and Leep and Tollee, but the curbs seemed both friendly and interested.

When Storm stopped for breath, Eyal said, "You are an amazing creature, Storm Ela-ferry."

Storm laughed. "Not really. Sometimes I think I *am* an unlucky omen."

"Only for those who hunt you," said Eyal. "Here's the spring."

It was cool and deep, flowing in a trickle towards the cliffs. Storm had never seen it before, probably because it was frozen and under snow in the winter. When he'd quenched his thirst, he lay down beside the water, his eyes sliding shut.

The curbs were obviously wide awake and ready to search for food. Eyal watched Storm in amusement. "You are a day-time creature," he observed.

Storm yawned. "What gave it away?"

"Are you going back to your herd, Storm?"

He opened his eyes and tried to focus. "Yes. I need to get back as soon as possible. I'm afraid my friends and family must think I'm dead."

"Would you like an escort across the plain?" said Eyal.

Storm cocked his head. "You'd do that?"

"Of course," said the curb. "We owe you a debt." He paused. "And I would value your friendship."

Storm smiled. "You're not afraid of making Arcove angry?"

"Arcove is not the one killing us," said Eyal. "Ferryshaft used to keep lowland curbs in check. Now that your people have been so reduced, the lowland curbs have become numerous. They have driven us off all the southern plain and even off the slopes of the Southern Mountains. We have only one high valley left where our females feel safe to breed, and I worry that even that may soon be gone. There are rumors that lowland curbs are negotiating an alliance with the ely-ary. The great birds will expand their range into our mountains, and together they will hunt us to extinction." Eyal looked suddenly very tired. "So, no," he continued, "annoying Arcove is the least of my concerns."

Storm felt a stab of pity. He'd assumed that the ferryshaft were the most endangered of the intelligent species on Lidian. "I'm sorry about leading the creasia into your pack," he said, this time with sincerity.

Eyal gave a toss of his head. "You didn't owe us anything."

"Is Quinyl your chief enemy?"

"Not exactly. Lowland curbs are not organized. Their packs sometimes fight each other, but Quinyl has been campaigning to unite the packs. Part of her claim to such leadership is the fact that she and her pack have hunted down and killed most of the highland curbs on the northern plain in the past few years. The other packs admire this. She now has loose control of about five packs.

"They managed to kill my predecessor before I was able to speak to him. We used to have friendly contacts among the ferryshaft, the creasia, and even the ely-ary. But I did not receive any of that information when I arrived, because my predecessor and all his curbs had died." Eyal's ears drooped. "I've had only the chatter of songbirds and mice to help me make my decisions—not enough, I'm afraid."

Storm cocked his head. "The chatter...of mice?"

"Do the ferryshaft not listen to the half-awake?" asked Eyal.

Storm was lost.

"The other animals," Eyal tried to explain, "the ones who don't talk. They still have things to say if you know how to listen. We call them the half-awake. But they are no substitute for actual contacts among the intelligent species."

"No, but they sound useful all the same." Storm made up his mind. He'd trusted the curbs this far. He might as well trust them a little further. Perhaps he could even learn from him. "I'd like to travel with you, Eyal. I'm not used to being in this part of the island in the summertime, and I don't know where to find water. If we're attacked…well, you'll have one more set of teeth." He hesitated. "I don't have many friends, either. Not really."

Eyal smiled, his incisors flashing in the starlight. "You have one more."

Storm traveled with the curbs for the next four nights. They came down from the cliffs well south of their previous location. When there were no signs of pursuit, they started across the plain towards Chelby Lake. Storm tried to fix in his mind the sources of water that they showed him—sometimes no more than a boggy patch, where one could lap relatively clean water off the top of a puddle if one were careful not to disturb the ground.

Eyal also tried to show him how to listen to the birds, mice, foxes, rabbits, and even the insects—not just their voices, but the messages in their tracks, the complexity of their scents, their bodies when they were caught and eaten. "Creasia have passed this way recently," Eyal said as they stood listening to the birds one evening.

Storm was startled. "In summer? Why? Do they know I'm alive?"

Eyal listened for a while longer and then shook his ears. "I can't tell. Probably just a trip to the Ghost Wood."

"Ghost Wood," repeated Storm, "that's what the telshees called Groth. Why would creasia go there?"

"To leave a token of their dead," said Eyal, watching Storm curiously. "This is how they honor lost friends. Do ferryshaft really not know such things?"

Storm felt embarrassed. "I'm sure the elders know, but we don't talk much about the creasia."

On the third night, they reached the lake. They were not so fortunate as to stumble immediately upon the herd, but they did find evidence that ferryshaft had passed that way recently. After casting around for a bit, Eyal and his curbs announced that the ferryshaft were headed south. They would probably find the herd by tomorrow evening, possibly sooner.

Eyal recommended a rest and a hunting session, and Storm agreed. The curbs spread out along the edge of the lake, looking for small game. Storm caught sight of Kuwee Island away across the water to the east. The sight reminded him that Keesha had not returned the Shable.

Storm realized, as he stood on the edge of the calm, sparkling water in the moonlight, that he had not thought much beyond this moment. He had imagined returning to his friends and family, and resuming the life that had been arrested that day on the ice when he'd run from Sharmel's clutter. But was such a thing even possible? *Would the elders try to kill me again? Would they threaten my friends? Would Charder tell the creasia I'm alive? Would I survive another encounter with Arcove?*

He thought about what Shaw had said of Keesha: *"If you can stay alive until he's finished, I think you'll find you have a powerful ally."*

Maybe I should do that, thought Storm, *just survive.* He had never truly considered surviving away from the herd, but now that he'd been gone most of a season, it did not seem so difficult. He liked the curbs. *Would they let me stay with them?* He thought it possible.

"Storm!" He turned at the sound of his name. Cohal stood, bristling, looking back over his shoulder. "Eyal sent me to get you," he said. "We found something to the south. You'd better come and see."

Mystified, Storm followed Cohal away through the trees at a trot. The curbs had spread out while hunting, and it was some time before Storm caught sight of Eyal. He was running low to the ground. When he saw them, he stopped, and waited.

"What is it?" whispered Storm when they met. Before Eyal could answer, Storm caught a scent on the wind—creasia…and blood. Storm's stomach gave a sickening lurch. He plunged forward through the trees. *Are they raiding in the summer now? Is it because of me?*

The curbs did not speak or try to stop him. Storm caught a flash of fur through the trees ahead. He saw moving shapes, though it took him a moment to grasp that they were not creasia. Storm bounded around the last thicket and stopped so suddenly that he almost sat down.

A ferryshaft was standing there in the moonlight, its fur dark with blood. A body lay on the ground beneath it—large and dark and feline. The ferryshaft raised its head, and Storm gasped. It was Sauny.

15

Control

Roup was awake during the day…again. He'd wandered over to the hot springs because he found the heat comforting, even in summer. He was near the junction of Smoky Branch and the stream they called Crooked Tail. The steam was thick here, where the warm water of the Branch met the cool water of the Tail. Roup sat in the fog, letting it condense on his whiskers.

The problem with the deer was not going away. As far as he could tell, it was getting worse. Many of the lower-ranking creasia were turning to small game for their mainstay. That would work for a while…until the small game succumbed to the same pressure as the deer.

Arcove had called a conference two days ago. Treace had been there with three of his officers, though not Moro. Various explanations had been bandied about, chief of which was the increasing number and boldness of the lowland curbs, as well as their possible alliance with ely-ary seeking to establish a population beyond the Great Mountain. No one, however, seemed willing to accept what Roup thought was obvious—too many mouths to feed.

Treace had offered a solution which Roup found unsettling. "We could try to manage the deer more closely," he'd said. He'd looked around at their blank expressions. "Keep them in one area, protect them from curbs, monitor breeding. Over time, we could probably figure out which sort taste better and encourage those to breed."

"Sounds like a lot of work," Halvery had grumbled.

"Sounds impossible," Sharmel had said. "The deer won't breed well with us following them around."

"The highland curbs do something of the kind with the sheep in the mountains," said Treace, "or so I've been told."

"Sheep live in flocks," said Roup. "Deer don't."

"Ah, true," said Treace, his green eyes sparkling. "If only we had a food animal that lived in groups and was easy to control. If only we could just tell the deer what to do."

No one had responded. After a moment, Halvery began to complain about the ely-ary again. Roup had glanced at Ariand, who was keeping very quiet. Roup had always gotten along well with Ariand. He tried to talk to him after the conference ended, but Ariand slipped away the moment Arcove called a conclusion.

Afraid, thought Roup. *That look in his eyes was fear.*

Roup sorted through the pieces in his head again. *What am I missing?*

He almost missed a ferryshaft, picking its way cautiously across the river in front of him. Roup rose in a half crouch, all his

---

senses alert. *What is a ferryshaft doing in the heart of Leeshwood? In Arcove's territory, no less?*

He was about to pounce first and ask questions later, when the ferryshaft turned, and Roup got a good look at his profile. "Charder?"

The animal froze, scanned his surroundings once, scanned again, and caught sight of Roup, well hidden among the steam and long grass. Charder didn't move, but waited for Roup to stand and come towards him. "I need to speak to Arcove," he said, his voice tight.

Roup approached him warily. He half wondered whether Charder had developed the foaming sickness, but he didn't look ill—only exhausted. Roup sniffed at him. "What are you doing here?"

Charder shied away. "I need to speak to Arcove," he repeated.

"He went to visit Sharmel," said Roup. "He'll probably be back later tonight."

"I'll wait then," said Charder.

Roup thought of how far he must have come—all the way from Chelby Lake and then through creasia territory almost to the foot of the cliffs. On rare occasions, when it seemed necessary, Arcove or one of his messengers, had visited Charder when the ferryshaft resided by Chelby Lake. On no occasion had Charder ever attempted to bring a message to Arcove.

Roup watched him. Charder's jaw was tight, and he was breathing in a deep, even pattern that looked like forced calm. "Would you like a place to rest?" asked Roup.

Charder looked around. "I can wait here."

Roup considered this. "I think not. If someone finds you, they'll kill you."

Charder said nothing.

"Come with me," said Roup. "I'm afraid I must insist."

Charder gave a bitter snort. "Then I'm afraid I must come."

Roup had a sudden, vivid flashback of a much younger Charder, telling him to follow. Roup had to look up at him back

333

then, and he'd struggled to keep pace with Charder's long strides. They'd attended a conference, where a dozen ferryshaft had talked over him as though he couldn't hear, poking and prodding and suggesting things that made Roup tremble. He remembered that Charder had defended his continued existence by pointing out that he was hardly worth eating.

After the war, Roup had never spoken to Charder outside of a council meeting. He'd let Arcove deal with that. *I know you must think I hate you, but I don't…not anymore. I'd tell you that if I thought it would make any difference.*

"Is the herd well?" asked Roup.

"As well as can be expected," muttered Charder.

"You're not going to tell me what's wrong, are you?"

Charder glanced at him. Roup noticed more gray around his muzzle than he remembered. "Is that an order?"

Could we make this any more awkward? "No."

Charder clearly had a good idea of where Arcove's den was located. It had been the den of high-ranking creasia for generations. Roup decided there was nothing to be gained from trying to make Charder wait somewhere else and brought him right up to the cave, where the roots of ancient trees twisted amid old stone. They were accosted three times on the way by Arcove's mates and half-grown cubs, who stared, but turned away when Roup told them all was well.

Seeka was dozing across the threshold when they entered, and she barely opened one eye as they passed. Nadine raised her head from among her den-mates and cubs. She glanced from Roup to Charder, flicked her elegant ears, rolled her eyes, and went back to sleep.

"Well, that's sorted," said Roup cheerfully. "You can sleep anywhere."

"Sleep?" echoed Charder.

"Yes, you look like you're about to fall over."

Charder just stared at him.

"Well, lie down, at least. Don't pace about, or someone may kill you out of sheer annoyance."

When Charder woke, it was dark. He knew he'd slept hard—much harder than he had intended. He could smell creasia, but that seemed appropriate. He felt a lingering sense of desperation, but it took him a moment to remember its source.

When he did, he started up. "Arcove—?"

"Charder." Arcove's rumble, no doubt about that.

Charder tried to focus in the gloom. He could see the outline of the mouth of the cave, and the silhouettes of two cubs tussling. An adult came and went past the entrance—its movements quick and alert. *They're hunting,* he thought.

"Charder," repeated Arcove, and Charder turned towards the darker back of the cave. He saw Roup's pale shape and Arcove's night-black form silhouetted in front of him. "In all the years of our acquaintance, I don't think you have ever expressed a desire to see me." Arcove's voice held a note of amusement, but also of uncertainty.

"I can't see you now," grumbled Charder. He could hardly believe he was making a joke, but his nerves were on edge. He felt as though he might start laughing hysterically at any moment.

"Come outside," said Arcove. "You were sleeping so sweetly, we didn't want to wake you."

Charder rose stiffly. Arcove and Roup padded past him towards the front of the cave. A cub darted in front of Charder and almost ran into him. "It's a ferryshaft!" he heard one whisper. "It's a live ferryshaft!"

At least for the moment, thought Charder.

Outside, in the starlight, Charder could see a little better. Arcove moved away from the front of the cave. When a cub followed them, obviously curious to listen, Arcove turned and said, "Away from here. Go."

When they were out of earshot of the activity around the mouth of the den, Arcove turned to Charder and said, "How did you even get here? Roup said he found you by Smoky Branch."

Charder gave a weary sigh. He wanted to go back to sleep. "There are some things I can still do, Arcove."

"Clearly. Will you be sleeping in my den often? Shall we make a nest for you?"

"I didn't know how else to contact you," said Charder. Arcove's reaction was making him feel a little better. *But it could all be for show. He and Roup may know exactly why I'm here. These cubs may pick my bones by dawn.*

"Are we at war, Arcove?"

"I don't think so."

Charder peered at him in the gloom. It was difficult enough to read Arcove's expressions in broad daylight. Dealing with him at night felt like running blind. "Are you still punishing us for Storm?"

"No," said Arcove slowly. "Should I be? Charder, clearly someone has broken the treaty. You might as well tell me what's happened so I can deal with it. Have you been ousted from herd leadership? Who is in charge in your absence?"

"Sedaron," said Charder, "with Pathar to advise him. The elders agreed that I should come. There's been no change in leadership." He took a deep breath. "Creasia have been raiding over the summer." He watched for a change in expression, but Arcove was perfectly still. "I thought… perhaps you were sending them to punish us…but it wasn't a normal raiding pattern. Ferryshaft just disappeared—no public spectacle. We found creasia tracks and scent, but nothing else. Bodies turned up half-eaten. When the cats *were* seen, ferryshaft reported just one or two—not a clutter. One observer swore that they carried a foal off alive. This sort of thing went on for half the summer, and then…then some of the younger ferryshaft started fighting back."

Storm and Sauny stood frozen, gaping at each other across the body of a dead creasia. Storm was dimly aware of voices rippling around them, ferryshaft rushing up to him, but not quite touching. "Storm?! Storm, is that really you?"

"Is it really him?"

"It can't be."

"It is!"

"It's me," said Storm, still without taking his eyes off Sauny. Then bodies were all around him—pushing, sniffing, licking, shouting. He heard Kelsy's exuberant laugh and Tracer's jubilant yip, but Sauny didn't move. After what seemed an eternity, she walked slowly around the body of the creasia. The other ferryshaft grew quiet. Storm stepped forward, and Sauny sniffed noses with him.

She swallowed and finally tried to smile. "I knew you weren't dead," she whispered.

No, you didn't, thought Storm.

But Kelsy was speaking beside him. "She did. She kept saying so."

Sauny came right up to him and rested her head across his shoulders. Storm could tell that she was fighting the urge to rub her face in his fur just to convince herself that he was real. She was trembling. "Please talk," she whispered against his ear. "Please talk to them."

Storm didn't know what to say, but he knew that Sauny needed him to fill the awkward silence. "What happened here?"

"They've been coming all summer," muttered Kelsy, "sneaking around the edges of the herd at night, grabbing orphans and loners and young foals who wander. Everyone said it was a new kind of raid—a punishment because…well, because of you."

Storm stared at the body of the creasia—its fur a deep ocher, stained black with blood. "How did—" he began. "How did this—?"

"Sauny thought of it," said Kelsy.

For the first time, Storm looked around at the little crowd of ferryshaft. "Thought of what?"

"She said that if they were coming alone, we could kill them. She was right."

More than a dozen ferryshaft were gathered round them. Storm didn't recognize all of them, but he had caught sight of Kelsy's three mates, Tracer, and Valla. They were staring at him as though he had grown a second head. "I can't believe you're alive," whispered Tracer.

A ferryshaft whose name Storm did not know gave an abrupt whoop. "This is it!" he exclaimed. "This is what we need to move the herd! Storm alive? They'll fight now!"

A babble erupted from the others. Ferryshaft began shouting and laughing and prancing with excitement. "The foal that Arcove couldn't kill!" someone called. And another threw back the cry. "The foal that Arcove couldn't kill!" They were pushing forward again to touch him, to lick him, to congratulate him, to ask questions.

Storm felt overwhelmed. He caught Valla's eyes over the press of bodies. She grinned at him, but he thought there was hesitation behind her smile. "Please, everyone calm down!" he said, but they wouldn't listen.

"Vearil," someone shouted, "the doom of cats!"

"Vearil, the doom of cats!" chimed the others.

To his consternation, Storm realized that the crowd was growing. "Come on!" Sauny seemed to have mastered her shock at his appearance. She was beaming now. "They need to see you. Come on, Storm!"

Storm looked around for the curbs, but they had vanished. Kelsy and Sauny stayed right beside him as the group swept them along with its momentum. "That's only the third creasia we've killed," Kelsy tried to explain, shouting in Storm's ear. "The group was already excited. You just walked up at the right time."

"We've been practicing," Sauny said from his other shoulder. "We've gotten about thirty foals and young adults involved, but we need more." Sauny turned to the pushing crowd and shouted. "Get back! Give us room to walk!"

To Storm's shock, they obeyed her. *They didn't listen to me. Or even to Kelsy.* He glanced sideways at his sister. She'd grown taller, though she was still obviously a foal. Her tail had filled out, and she held it high as she walked. Her red-gold fur was almost the same color as Kelsy's, but her eyes, when she turned to look at him, were pale gray…as gray as those Storm had seen in the Ghost Wood. *What are you becoming, Sauny?*

Their riotous company began to pass little groups of sleeping ferryshaft, who stared at them blearily from their grassy nests. "Storm has returned!" chanted the group. "The foal that Arcove couldn't kill! The doom of cats!"

Charder stared at Arcove in the gloom, his voice pleading. "The way these raids happened…it was almost as though we were being baited. Cats coming alone? Cats raiding in secret? Carrying off live foals? Were you trying to—?"

Arcove finally spoke. His voice was flat. "I didn't send them."

Charder let out a breath that he hadn't realized he'd been holding. "I thought—"

"Assume for a moment that I am not trying to bait your herd into fighting so that I can annihilate it," said Arcove. "Because I'm not."

Before Charder could fully appreciate his relief, Arcove started talking again. "How many cats have they actually killed?"

"Only one that I know of," said Charder, "but these raids happen so secretively that there might be more—"

"Did you recognize the cat?" cut in Roup. "Did you recognize any of them?"

"No," said Charder. "The ones I saw looked like young adults, but I didn't see most of them. The dead one was…mauled. Don't ask me who killed it, because I didn't see that either. The situation is getting out of my control. The younger ferryshaft are very angry." He didn't think he needed to point out that opportunities to kill lone creasia would only increase their confidence, skill, and determination.

"Are they still talking about Storm?" asked Roup.

"Yes," admitted Charder. "They whisper about him. These odd raids have gotten a lot of them asking whether Storm might have had the right idea."

Roup was muttering furiously in Arcove's ear. Charder thought that, behind his calm façade, Arcove looked worried. Charder raised his head and dared to be blunt. "You asked me whether I've lost control of my herd, Arcove. Have *you* lost control of yours?"

16

Homecoming

Storm talked until sunrise amid a comfortable nest of clover and long grass by the lake. In spite of the fact that it was midnight, so many ferryshaft came to listen that several fights broke out on the edges of the group among those straining to hear. Storm implored them to calm down. He would tell them everything if they were patient.

I'll try, anyway. During the long, dark days in Syriot, Storm had frequently imagined himself sitting comfortably with half a dozen friends in the sunshine, gleefully relating his adventures. The idea that he might have to tell his story to a shoving, chattering crowd in the middle of the night had not figured into this vision.

Storm felt like running. Instead, he held his head high, raised his voice, and told the story as best he could. He talked about stumbling through Groth, about finding a strange blue stone, about being rescued by an ely-ary. He told them about recovering in the care of telshees, how the telshees were their allies and not their enemies. He told them about Shaw, about Keesha, about the Battle of Chelby Lake and the fortress that lay locked beneath Kuwee Island.

Most of those who sat listening to him were young—less than ten years old. He recognized many of them as Kelsy's friends and supporters. They were clearly riveted to his story—shocked by things they had not known. However, Storm also caught sight of a few older ones in the crowd—even an elder or two. They did not look surprised, only grim. *I'm not telling you anything about the past that you didn't already know,* thought Storm.

When he paused for breath, one high-ranking female of perhaps thirty years stood up and said loudly, "It's a lie."

The whole group went quiet. Many turned to stare at her. "Rocks that open caves, ely-ary that rescue ferryshaft, telshees that heal wounds with singing, secret codes scratched in stone…" Her voice was heavy with contempt. "It's a fine story by a fine trickster."

A low rumble of talking broke out, but she continued more loudly. "Storm Ela-ferry, we all know how you escape from hunters. You hide. You're good at it. You hid from Arcove, and it was quite an accomplishment. However, you left *us* to take the punishment for your tricks. We've been punished all summer because of you. You were too afraid to return here and face the creasia, so you've been hiding while we suffered. You've had plenty of time to work on this story, and now you think it's safe to return and tell your fable. You think we'll welcome you like a hero after all the death you've caused."

An angry murmur swept through the group. Storm went rigid. *Here it comes. This is the part where they try to kill me.* He spoke desperately. "You know that's not true. You're old enough to know. Why do you want to keep these things from the young ferryshaft? Do you think it will make us safe? It hasn't for fifteen years."

The female looked at him with an expression of undisguised hostility. "If your story is true, where's the proof? Where are these curbs that you supposedly returned with? Do you have a single telshee, ely-ary, or mysterious blue stone about you?"

Storm had to raise his voice over the mounting babble from the crowd. "I think the curbs were frightened by a group of ferryshaft capable of killing creasia!"

Storm knew, as soon as he said it, that the cat's death was news to the older adults. The female's eyes went round. "You are fools, all of you."

"No, you are!" someone shouted. Storm realized with a jolt, that the hostility building in the crowd was not directed at him. The younger ferryshaft were glaring at their parents and elders. "Storm isn't the coward who stood by while the creasia killed us for years! You are!"

"Death to cowards!" a voice screamed. "Death to cowards!"

Oh, no. "Stop!" Storm shouted. "Please, everyone, calm down!"

Beside him, Kelsy was shouting, too, but it was Sauny who waded into the maddened crowd and got between several young males and the older female who'd been speaking. "Enough!" she barked. Valla had very quietly inserted herself beside Sauny, and Storm saw several other members of Sauny's clique coming forward. "*All* of us have been cowards," said Sauny, "but it's creasia we must kill, not ferryshaft. The next time they come to raid, we will be waiting. We have killed them before; we will kill them again. They could not kill Storm, and they will not stop us!"

"They could not kill Storm! They will not stop us!" chorused several excited foals. "We have killed them before! We will kill them again!"

"And we'll kill anyone who gets in our way," snarled one of the young males, staring over Sauny's shoulder at the elder.

Storm felt a thrill of excitement. *This is really happening.*

Charder woke to the sound of his name. Dawn light was streaming into Arcove's den. Arcove stood silhouetted against it.

He dropped something on the floor in front of Charder—a dead rabbit. "I'm sending you back," he said. "I've assigned a cat to go with you and make sure no one attacks you. Eat that, and you can be on your way."

Charder scrambled to his feet. He'd gone to sleep last night with the mutter of Arcove and Roup talking in the background. They sounded almost as though they were arguing. Charder had never heard them argue before, and he did not think it was a good sign. "What are you—?" he began.

"I have sent for my officers," said Arcove. "We will travel to the ferryshaft herd and attempt to capture one of these raiding creasia. I will learn what is going on and deal with it."

Charder felt a measure of relief. "The cats who were killed—"

"If your herd was only defending itself from unlawful raids, I will ignore that," said Arcove. "If they seem inclined to continue breaking the treaty, I will make an example of some of them. First, however, I need to know why this is happening. We will probably leave tomorrow evening. I think you should be gone by then."

It was as generous an agreement as Charder thought he was likely to get. Still… "*All* of your officers?" That seemed excessive. Arcove didn't usually bring all of his officers unless he wanted them to witness something. *Like Storm's death.* He surely didn't think he needed all of them to catch one or two rogue creasia or to deal with a few angry foals.

"You think one of them is behind this." Charder spoke his thought aloud. He did not voice the following thought. *You really have lost control of your subordinates.* Ten or fifteen years ago, the idea would have filled him with vengeful glee. Now, however, Charder thought it unlikely that civil war in Leeshwood would have a good outcome for the ferryshaft.

Arcove did not answer. "Eat that," he repeated. "Before a cub does." Several cubs were, indeed, eyeing the rabbit.

Charder glanced down. In their long acquaintance, Arcove had never offered him food. He started to say that summer grass was plentiful, but thought better of it. Grazing took time. Eating meat was quick—a fact that Arcove had surely considered. *He wants me well away before his officers arrive.*

Charder devoured the rabbit in a few bites, crunching through the smaller bones, but leaving the head and part of the back legs. He tossed the remainder to a hopeful-looking black cub. *You better hope your father knows what he's doing. Or you won't eat many more rabbits.*

Changes of power in Leeshwood were legendarily bloody. The officers of an ousted king were often killed, along with their young cubs. Sharmel was the only officer in Arcove's administration who'd served under the previous king. Charder gathered that the cats thought this innovative and unusual. He wondered if a new creasia king would keep Arcove's promises to the ferryshaft. He did not want to find out.

For Storm, the following days passed in a blur. He'd become so accustomed to living in the dark with telshees and staying awake at night with curbs that he found the return to a daytime existence jarring. If he'd been allowed to readjust in peace, he might have taken delight in the summer sun and found peace in the waters of the lake, but there was nothing peaceful about his days as an endless stream of ferryshaft came to stare at him and follow him about.

At any given time, Storm was surrounded by at least fifty ferryshaft—most of them young adults and foals—all straining to hear his every word. Kelsy, Sauny, Valla, and a collection of Kelsy's friends stayed close and kept the crowd from actually harassing him, but Storm found the situation unnerving.

Tracer told him loudly—and at length—that his own quest to acquire a second mate had met with success "because I grew up with the infamous Vearil, doom of cats!" Tracer then seemed to forget that Storm was a year younger than him and proceeded to tell him far more than he wanted to know about his recent first attempts at mating.

Leep turned up on the second day, grinning, to introduce his awed mate, Silfa. *You were afraid to introduce her to me before,* thought Storm, *but now I'm a status symbol.*

He wanted to say, "It's just me, Leep! Tracer, we used to race across the ice. We used to joke about how we'd never get mates. Don't you remember?" But their eyes looked so bright and dazzled that he couldn't bring himself to say it.

Very late on the third night, Storm woke when someone lay down beside him. He thought, at first, that it was Valla, because she draped her head across his shoulders, but then he woke up a little more and recognized the scent. Storm's eyes snapped open, though he didn't move. "Tollee?" he whispered.

She gave a little sniff that was hardly an answer. Storm thought that she must have crept in with extraordinary stealth to avoid waking any of the others.

Storm didn't know what to say. He was afraid that if he moved, she would disappear. "I didn't see you earlier," he ventured. "Were you in the crowd?"

"No," her voice was barely a murmur. She said nothing for a long moment. "But the whole herd is talking about you. Such stories… You must be tired of repeating them."

"I'm not," Storm heard himself say, although he certainly was.

Tollee let out a long sigh against him. He couldn't see her face at all, but he felt the warm stir of her breath against his fur. "Tell me?"

Storm did—in his softest voice, unhurried, and without the pressure of staring eyes or eager strangers. He told her things he had forgotten himself—how he'd felt, what he feared, and the wonder of it. Occasionally, she would give a soundless laugh or a snort of disgust or amazement, but she mostly just listened. Towards dawn, her breathing changed, and Storm realized that she'd fallen asleep. He wasn't offended. For the first time since he'd rejoined the ferryshaft herd, Storm felt as though he'd come home.

17

Respite

Later, when he looked back on that period, Storm realized that he had been happy. If he had known, then, what a brief period it would be, he might have reveled more.

Storm was the darling of his peers. They treated his every observation as though it were wisdom carved on the walls of Syriot. They told and retold his stories. Storm grew so tired of correcting their exaggerations that he finally stopped and let them think what they wished. He heard repeated assertions that he'd fought with Arcove and won. That story bothered him, but most ferryshaft listened to the truth with an indulgent expression—as if they thought he was being modest.

Sauny was euphoric. Indeed, she often stayed up talking to her friends and allies late into the night. Storm worried that she did not sleep at all. "We have to be ready," she told him. "When those cats we killed don't come back, Arcove will send a bigger group. We have to be ready for them."

Sometimes she sounded so old that Storm wanted to ask her where his little sister had gone. On other occasions, she sounded distressingly naive. "Sauny, killing a clutter of creasia will be very different from surprising and killing a lone cat. You realize that, don't you? I want it as much as you do, but you do realize how difficult this will be...right?"

"That's why we've got to practice!" she told him. "We can kill a clutter, Storm. We can kill Arcove. I know it."

Sauny brought Storm to the evening sessions in which young ferryshaft attempted to learn how to kill creasia. Upon Storm's arrival, these sessions swelled from about thirty to well over two hundred, with more showing up every day. An activity that had previously been covert now became public. No one dared tell them to stop.

The youngsters who had actually participated in successful creasia killings went through the group, organizing them into small packs, assigning roles, and giving critiques. Kelsy and his mates were always about, and Storm had to admit that they were good teachers. Some of their students had become proficient. Storm suspected that if they survived their first few encounters with creasia, they would become quite deadly. *If...*

Valla was Sauny's lieutenant and constant shadow. Storm saw her quietly remind Sauny of various ferryshafts' names on more than one occasion. When Sauny was in the midst of animated discussion, Valla made certain that no one threatened her. This was necessary, as Sauny would go into parts of the herd where she was not welcome and talk loudly to anyone who would listen. Her enthusiasm was infectious, but it also angered some of the more conservative and powerful members of the herd.

"She got hurt earlier this summer," Valla told Storm one day. "She told one of the high-ranking males that you weren't dead, and he knocked her down and told her that the cats should have killed her, too. Her clique came running, but I got there first. He didn't say it twice."

Valla had never been exactly shy, only quiet. Now her silence had a grim confidence behind it. In addition, she was distractingly lovely. Her blond fur had darkened just a little—cream with a touch of red—still longer than average and glossy when the sun hit her. She had a wonderful scent, and the males all raised their heads when she passed. Storm didn't think any of them would try to make her a ru, though—not after they saw her practice with Faralee, Itsa, and Remy. Sauny told him that Valla had delivered the killing bite to the second of the three cats who'd died. Storm believed it.

In spite of their fierce purpose, there was an air of frivolity to the evening practice sessions, with a great deal of joking and dark, playful humor. Storm often caught sight of ferryshaft he hadn't expected to see, including Pathar, watching from a distance one evening. Storm tried to speak to him, but he vanished before Storm could make his way through the crowd.

So-fet even shocked him by turning up at one of the sessions. After effusive greetings, he ventured, "Where is Dover?"

So-fet tossed her head. "Dover will not be my mate this fall. He no longer suits me."

Storm felt a strange mixture of satisfaction, guilt, and pride. "Did you have someone else in mind?" *Someone who doesn't treat you like a ru and me like a disease?*

So-fet smiled, as though she could read his thoughts. "I have two incredible foals," she said. "I do not think Lidian is ready for another just now." Storm washed her face, as she had done so many times when he was little. They were the same height now. "If you'd like to learn to tear the throats out of creasia, I believe Remy is offering tips over there," he said.

Sometimes, at night, Storm would hear curbs yipping out across the plain. He even thought he recognized Eyal's voice on several occasions. He hoped the highland curbs were alright. *I know you were only repaying a debt. Still, I like to think we were friends.*

And some nights, very late, Tollee would come to him. Storm never asked her whether Mylo knew or cared. She would curl up against him, and he would tell her about his day and his thoughts and even his fears that he dared voice to no one else. She would listen. Very rarely, she would offer advice. Storm wished she would tell him about her life in his absence. She seemed vaguely sad, though she never offered an explanation.

Then, one day, it all ended.

18

Waiting to Blink

The leaves had just begun to turn to orange and gold, when a young ferryshaft woke Storm and his friends with the breathless words, "They're here."

Sauny was on her feet in an instant, bristling with excitement. "Where?"

"Last night," panted the youngster, who'd obviously run from a distant part of the herd. "In the woods near the marshy part of the lake—a creasia attacked and killed a spring foal. The cat carried off the body. The mother looked for it in the morning, but found nothing but blood and fur."

"They're eating us now," muttered Valla in disgust, "as though we were deer or sheep!"

"Who was the mother?" asked Kelsy.

Sauny shot him an annoyed look.

Storm had noticed a degree of tension between Kelsy and Sauny since he arrived. He wasn't sure that anyone knew who was the true leader of their group. However, they had so far avoided open confrontations. Kelsy was consistently more interested in the social status of their allies, while Sauny refused to admit that it mattered. Storm knew that Kelsy was hoping that the dead foal had high-ranking parents. It might galvanize the older members of the herd, who were trying to separate themselves from the youngsters.

"Low-ranking," said the foal who'd brought the news. "That's why she was sleeping apart. Her mate was killed last winter, and he was nothing special. The foal was sickly. The mother's friends thought she should not have nursed it to begin with. This morning, she was in distress and talking about the death to anyone who would listen."

That could have been me and Mother three years ago, thought Storm.

Sauny frowned. "She's not one of ours?" By this, she meant that the female had not been coming to their training sessions.

The messenger flicked his ears. "No. I tried to get her to come with me, but her friends had rallied by then to give her some comfort. She'll be welcomed back into their clique now that she's without a sickly foal. I don't think she wants to jeopardize what little status she has by coming over here."

Sauny was already headed towards the lake. "Let's get tracking."

Tracking was a more familiar skill than fighting, since most ferryshaft had to track game in winter. Better yet, Sauny had assured Storm that the creasia coming to raid were careless and made no attempt to disguise their trail.

She was correct. They tracked the cat easily through the marshy delta where several small streams emptied into Chelby Lake. They didn't even need to use their noses, but followed the enormous prints in the mud. Soon, the creasia was joined by another. "This one killed as well," muttered Sauny. "I smell the blood in the footprints. I wonder who it got? A lone adult, perhaps? Or an orphan who hasn't been missed?"

"If we're lucky, it was one of the elders," muttered Kelsy.

Sauny snorted. "If so, we'll never hear about it. They'll pretend it didn't happen."

Storm was looking ahead. "Quiet," he murmured. "Up there—that's where I'd sleep if I were a creasia far from home."

They all followed his gaze to a thicket on the edge of the marshy ground. It was just far enough into the trees to be dry beneath. Faralee and Itsa came forward at once, running low like foxes. They were absolutely silent, in spite of the sucking mud, stepping daintily around the wettest patches. They circled the thicket and returned to the group. "Storm is right," whispered Itsa. "They're in there. You can't see them. The thorns are too dense, but there's a bit of fur on the brambles and no fresh tracks leading out."

Kelsy and Sauny were both quiet for a moment. Then they both tried to talk at once.

Storm spoke up instead. "Ambush?" *I ought to know how this works. Usually I'm the one in the thicket.*

"Yes," hissed Sauny before Kelsy could open his mouth again. "We can't attack them in the thicket. We need room to work a creasia in order to kill it."

"*And* we need as many ferryshaft as possible to see this," cut in Kelsy. "Most of them haven't actually seen us kill a creasia. Let's circulate the word about what will happen this evening. When those cats emerge, we'll fall on them with a hundred ferryshaft or more. The creasia will be dead before they get the sleep out of their eyes, with the whole herd watching."

Sauny quirked a smile. "Why kill them quickly, Kelsy? Like I keep saying: we need practice."

Roup drifted in and out of uneasy sleep in the warm afternoon. Two of his cats had complained privately to him the evening before that they were hungry and homesick. Roup told them that they had come to do a job and would leave when it was finished. However, he was privately inclined to agree. Being away from home territory was beginning to wear on him.

How long can Arcove keep us out here? Arcove had always been a hunter of infinite patience, and he'd shown no signs of being ready to give up. *During the war, we would have thought nothing of this,* Roup reminded himself. *Perhaps we've all become a little too accustomed to regular meals and a solid day's sleep. That, or never un*accustomed. The sour looks on the faces of the younger cats said plainly that they wished they had not been chosen for this mission.

It had all started well enough. They had crossed the Igby on the second night and made their way to the mouth of the river by the fourth. Arcove had been methodical in his examination of the bank—looking for evidence of recent creasia passage. On two occasions, they'd found tracks and scent, but Sharmel had identified one as a cat from his own clutter who'd recently lost a mate and would be visiting the Ghost Wood. Ariand had identified the other as a similar case. They were well west of the ferryshaft herd, and Arcove had accepted these explanations.

On the banks of the Igby, beside Chelby Lake, Arcove set sentries and lingered. Roup knew that Halvery had identified this area as the spot where Treace's cats usually left his territory to travel to the Ghost Wood, using the scattered sandbars of the delta for an easier river-crossing. Arcove made no mention of the fact, but Treace and Moro could not miss it. Arcove sent scouts north through Chelby Wood to locate the ferryshaft herd, which was not far away. However, he did not send cats near it again. Roup lost count of the days as they patrolled...and waited.

If Arcove felt as uncomfortable as the others, he hid it well. He slept every day beside Roup, as soundly as he'd used to when they were cubs before the war. During the night, he circulated through the various clutters, hunting with them and listening to them. *You've pulled them all out of their territories and given them practically nothing to do,* thought Roup. *You're making them uncomfortable on purpose...waiting for someone to make a mistake. You think it's Treace, but you're not sure.*

Roup had to admit that Treace was nearly as good at hiding his discomfort as Arcove. *He has to be on edge.* But he didn't show it. Arcove had assigned a rotation of cats from Roup and Halvery's clutters to watch Treace's clutter at all times. They were to report any unexplained departures. They were circumspect, but Roup had no doubt that Treace realized he was being watched.

Moro was clearly angry that he'd been made to come on the trip. Arcove had requested his presence specifically and had spoken sharply to him on the first day. It was a plain invitation to challenge or attack if that's what Moro wanted, but Moro had flattened his ears, tucked his tail, and turned his head—all perfectly correct submission, though delivered with bad grace.

Roup suspected that Arcove had spoken—and perhaps more than spoken—to Moro in private on the third day, because he suddenly became extremely deferential to Roup. His sullen glares were replaced with downcast eyes. Roup wasn't sure it was an improvement. At least, when Moro was glaring at him, he had a better idea of what Moro was thinking.

Roup figured that if Treace had direct control over these raids, he was racking his brain for a way to get a message to his cats, ordering them to cease their unlawful activities. Arcove's summons had included no details on the nature of their mission until the officers and their clutters arrived, after which the group had left immediately. If Treace was particularly prescient, he might have guessed the nature of the mission and given orders to stop terrorizing the ferryshaft even before responding to Arcove's command. If that was the case, then their mission would be fruitless, and Arcove would be made to look ridiculous.

However, Roup suspected that Treace did not have direct control—that he'd allowed a situation to develop by indirectly encouraging the behavior and then turning a blind eye. In that case, he probably did not even know whether any of his cats were harassing the ferryshaft herd at the moment.

Roup had no doubt that he would plead ignorance. The only way to demonstrate otherwise would be to catch the offending cats alive and get an explanation from them. *In that case, he's as likely to kill them as to warn them.*

As days passed and no danger or problems presented themselves, the officers and their clutters grew restless. Small birds and fish were plentiful along the edge of the lake, but difficult to catch. Less tasty small prey, like frogs and salamanders, were also in abundance, though one had to hunt all night to fill one's belly with them. Turtles could be caught, but they took half an evening to chew and presented little meat for the effort. Cats who were not on patrol spent most of the night looking for food, and they still often went to sleep hungry. Roup thought that he detected a smug expression on Treace's face when they met in council. *You know we're not finding what we're looking for, and you couldn't be happier about that.*

Roup took advantage of the long, quiet nights to reacquaint himself with Ariand. They'd gotten along well during the war, and Ariand's territory bordered on Roup's. They'd never been close, but they'd certainly never quarreled. Roup suspected that something had happened with Treace to make Ariand afraid. After several nights hunting together, Roup finally managed to pry the story out of him.

"You remember Dustet?" asked Ariand, when he was sure that they were completely alone amid the tall river grass of the delta.

"Of course," said Roup. Dustet had been Ariand's beta during the war. They were the same age and had been cubs together. They shared a den. Several years ago, Dustet had lost a fight to another cat, whose name Roup could not recall. He was no longer Ariand's beta, but he was still a ranking member of Ariand's clutter.

Roup frowned. "Where is he?" Arcove had asked for all of his officers' betas. He'd not specified other members of the clutter, but it suddenly seemed strange to Roup that Dustet hadn't come.

Ariand licked his lips. "What about Sandry? Do you remember her?"

This time, Roup had to think longer. "One of your mates?" he ventured.

"The first. Our...first mate. She didn't stay alpha for long, but..."

But you loved her. Roup was beginning to get a sick feeling in the pit of his stomach. "What happened?"

Ariand swallowed. His eyes darted around nervously. "Sandry's sister lives in a den in Treace's territory. They visited each other from time to time. One day, Sandry didn't come back. I sent inquiries and learned that she'd gotten into a fight with Moro, and he...he killed her."

Roup made a face. "Why?" Fights between males and females were rare in Leeshwood. Fatal fights between the sexes were almost unheard of.

Ariand swallowed. Roup could see that the death still pained him. "I still don't know. Treace and I had been getting along well—better than I'd expected after he beat me. I really thought we were becoming friends. I demanded an explanation, but he only said that she had challenged his beta. I could not imagine Sandry doing such a thing! I think she saw something, Roup. I have no idea what, but I think she saw something she wasn't meant to see, and they killed her for it.

"I was furious. I intended to publicly challenge Moro, but before I got the chance, Parod challenged Dustet."

This time, Roup drew a complete blank. "Parod?"

"Yes," said Ariand as though he had to force the words from his throat. "Parod is an eight-year-old who joined a clutter in my territory two years ago."

"He came originally from Treace's clutter?" guessed Roup.

"Yes," said Ariand. "Dustet was my third-in-command, and Parod challenged him, beat him…and killed him."

Roup had anticipated this part of the story, but he still flinched. In a fight over dominance, the survival of the loser was entirely at the discretion of the winner. No den or clutter would punish a victor who fought fairly and chose to kill his opponent. It was his right. Still, it wasn't common—not anymore. The only reason to kill an opponent was the expectation of trouble from him in the future. Often a victor found it more troublesome to deal with the resentment of his rival's surviving friends than to simply let him live.

"You think it was a warning?" asked Roup. "To make you drop the issue about Sandry?"

Ariand snorted. "Oh, I know it was a warning. And I…I guess it worked."

"And now you're afraid of your own third-ranking officer," muttered Roup.

Ariand flicked his tail. "He's my beta now. He fought and beat Nissir, although he didn't kill him. It was all very technically correct."

Roup growled. "You do not have to take this, Ariand."

Ariand rounded on him with a resentful expression. "No? Well, explain how I can avoid it, Roup. Treace outranks me. His cats outnumber mine. They join my dens and clutters, and I think they spy for him. It's easy for you to stand up to Treace with Arcove at your back; I'm not that lucky."

He stalked away, stiff-legged. It was rude behavior from a subordinate, but Roup couldn't bring himself to hold anything against Ariand. *He's still grieving over close friends.*

He told Arcove about the incident when they lay down to sleep that morning. "Sharmel is worried, too," said Arcove.

"Why? Has Treace been killing his friends and mates?"

"No, but he thinks that Treace will challenge him soon and probably kill him if he wins."

"He didn't kill Ariand."

"Ariand is younger."

And more likely to be seen as useful. "Point taken."

Roup did not say, *How difficult do you think it would be to turn a frightened cat?* He knew it was an unworthy thought. Sharmel had been nothing but loyal since the day Arcove invited him to remain on his council. Still... *If the officers start to suspect that Arcove can't handle Treace...will that loyalty hold?*

Roup thought of these things as he drifted in and out of uneasy dreams. *We're all watching each other. Waiting to see who blinks first.*

"Arcove! Roup!" The words came in an urgent whisper. Roup's head jerked up, and Arcove went instantly tense beside him.

One of Sharmel's subordinates was leaning over the top of the riverbank, an excited expression on his face. "Two cats!" he whispered. "Crossing the river delta just now, going north."

Arcove was up and over the riverbank in an instant, Roup close behind him. They followed the sentry at a swift trot through the trees beside the Igby, towards the broad mouth of the river. It was late afternoon. Roup felt a surge of excitement. What creasia would choose to travel at such a time of day...unless they were hoping to avoid other cats?

They found the tracks easily enough—evidence of the recent passage of two young males. Roup knew as soon as he caught the scent that they were Treace's cats. However, identifying broad territory by the scent of tracks alone was tricky and easily mistaken. It was not the full proof they needed.

"You are relieved," Arcove told the sentry. "Don't wake everyone else or speak about this until I do."

"Well, your patience has been rewarded," Roup observed when the sentry had gone.

Arcove didn't say anything. He followed the tracks far enough to confirm that they were going towards the ferryshaft herd. Then he sat down in the sun and considered. "If we intercept them before they do anything, this will all be a wasted effort."

"Agreed," said Roup. "They'll say they were just going to the Ghost Wood." He thought for a moment. "So give them a night to get their claws bloody, then go after them tomorrow evening. And don't tell Treace."

Arcove inclined his head. "My thoughts exactly. Tomorrow evening, we'll hunt them down and get our answers."

19

Blood and Water

By evening, the ferryshaft herd was thrumming with excitement. Storm could feel it prickling along his skin—like the sensation before a nearby lightning strike. "They're all here," whispered Sauny gleefully. "Even the elders and the high-ranking cliques. They pretend that they don't care, but the herd is closing up around that thicket. Around us! They all want to see what's going to happen."

Storm felt a deep sense of conflicted pleasure. *One of my friends could easily die this evening,* he kept reminding himself. Still, he thought they had a good chance, and he *wanted* to see a ferryshaft kill a creasia. *If the whole herd believed we could do it…what would that be like? Could we stop the raids? Move to the southern plains? Kill enough creasia to make them hide in the forest and never bother us again?*

Kelsy and Sauny managed to keep enough order to prevent the excited foals and young adults from warning their quarry. Most of the ferryshaft remained on the edge of the trees, while a few kept watch near the thicket. When the first cat emerged, a two-year-old foal showed herself and ran towards the plain. The cat took the bait, chasing after her.

"He must think himself lucky," murmured Sauny as the animal lumbered past the spot where she, Valla, and Storm were crouching among ferns. The creasia was, as Kelsy had predicted, still shaking the sleep out of his eyes. Storm glanced back towards the thicket, and Sauny followed his gaze. The other cat had not made an appearance.

Moments later, there was a startled shout from the direction of the plain and the sound of snarling. Sauny took one more uncertain glance at the thicket and then ran through the trees towards the sounds of fighting. Storm and Valla trotted after her. *One at a time might be easier,* thought Storm, although he was already having second thoughts.

The trees thinned ahead of them, and the muddled roar grew louder. They burst onto the plain to the welcome sight of a creasia surrounded by young ferryshaft. The cat looked dazed and baffled as the youngsters took turns leaping in to snap at him. He couldn't seem to decide whether he should attack or run away.

Well, no one's gotten hurt yet.

The herd was certainly taking an interest. More ferryshaft than Storm could easily count were trotting around the group, straining to see. *No raid has ever looked like this before!*

The three of them had almost reached the edge of the circle. Sauny was jumping over other ferryshaft to get through. All at once, the cat leapt forward and barely missed mauling one of the foals who was dancing around him. *We've got to do more than just torment him,* thought Storm. In the same moment, Kelsy darted from the other side of the circle, and his jaws snapped down on the back of one of the creasia's legs.

The cat gave a high-pitched snarl of pain. He whirled, but Kelsy had already leapt away. As the cat turned, it was clear that damage had been done. His left hind leg crumpled beneath him, and he almost lost his footing before finding it again on three legs.

"Hamstrung!" shouted Sauny. "He's ours, friends! But don't be too hasty! Show the herd what you can do!" With that, she leapt in, fox-fast, and snapped off the latter half of the creasia's tail. He screamed again in pain, but the other foals were running around him in a blur, slashing and darting and leaping. The cat was soon bleeding from a dozen wounds, turning in circles, nearly falling over, slapping at the air and snapping his teeth where a ferryshaft had been moments before.

The circle opened up. The youngsters were euphoric. They could have killed their quarry ten times over, but no one moved to do so. The cat staggered, half blinded by blood, hissing with every breath, and they began to nip at him, chasing him. Now he was in full retreat, but the foals directed him easily—running him, limping and stumbling, through the herd.

"This is what you were afraid of, elders!" someone shouted. "Does it look so scary now? Have a mouthful of blood and see what it tastes like!"

Storm raced behind them, riding the tide of excitement. Around him, he saw some of the adults running, too. They were shouting to each other, the herd rippling, moving. *They'll tear him apart,* thought Storm. *The anger of fifteen years will come scalding to the surface, and the entire herd—elders and all—will rip him to pieces.*

"What—is—this?" The voice had thunder in it. It carried, somehow, over the riot of the herd. Storm knew that voice.

The group of ferryshaft, who'd been chasing the cat stopped and looked around. The hunted creasia crouched, belly to the earth, panting, and tried to blink the blood out of his eyes. Storm craned his neck to see through the crowd. His heart sank. On a little rise of the plain, a number of creasia were standing. The foremost was huge, silhouetted against the sky, and black as midnight. His eyes swept the scene before him. "What is this?" repeated Arcove, his voice sharp and carrying. He was speaking very clearly, with hardly a trace of creasia accent. He started down the slope toward the ferryshaft.

Storm saw even more creasia coming into view over the rise—first five, then seven, then twelve, then he lost count. He saw the flash of Roup's golden fur and the brief silhouette of Halvery's shortened tail. *They're here,* he thought numbly. *They're all here. For me?* He felt paralyzed with fear.

"This is vengeance," snarled a voice. "This is your doom!" To Storm's absolute horror, Sauny shot out of the crowd and plowed into Arcove. It happened so fast that even Arcove seemed surprised. There was a brief scuffle, and then Storm saw his sister's body flip like a broken blade of grass into the air.

"No!" someone shrieked, and then Valla shot past him in a blur.

Storm felt his legs unlock. The mind-numbing fear melted away, and there was only Sauny's still form on the grass and Arcove turning towards it. Storm never knew how he reached the front of the herd so quickly, but an instant later, he landed, snarling, between his sister and Arcove.

Time seemed to slow down as he stared into those summer-green eyes. He saw a flicker of surprise, and it gave him courage. *You didn't know I was alive. None of this was about me.*

"Keesha sends his love!" shot Storm. He had not known what he was going to say before he said it, but he saw the surprise melt into something else—an instant's hesitation. *Could it be there's something you fear, Arcove?*

Storm leapt back as Arcove's deadly claws cleaved the air where he'd just stood. He darted in the other direction and managed to get a glimpse of Sauny. His heart gave a leap. *She's not dead.* Valla had pulled her to her feet, and they were in the act of melting into the crowd. The other creasia were running forward, tails twitching, ready for a fight, but not sure who to attack first.

Storm found his voice again. "Are you going to fight the entire herd, Arcove? Did you bring enough cats for that? I doubt it."

Somewhere behind him, someone shouted. "So says Vearil, doom of cats! Listen to him, ferryshaft! They could not kill Storm, and they will not stop us!"

The herd behind Storm erupted. Ferryshaft all around him leapt forward at the creasia. The startled cats fell back under a wave of outraged ferryshaft. Blood and fur flew in all directions. It should have been a glorious moment, but all Storm could think about was Sauny. *How badly is she hurt?*

A scream pulled him back into the present. A gutted ferryshaft was stumbling towards him, tripping on his own intestines. Storm blinked. It was Tracer.

No. Oh, no, no, no. A cat caught Tracer before he quite reached Storm and broke his neck with one crunch. Storm shot forward, landed on the cat's back, and buried his teeth just above its shoulder blades. The animal leapt and twisted beneath him, but Storm set his jaws and hung on.

The numbness settled again, this time devoid of either hope or fear. Storm felt his teeth scrape bone and bit harder. The cat rolled over, scratching and shrieking, and Storm was finally wrenched away with a bloody mouthful of fur. He was up again in a moment and flying at another feline form. The same cat? A different cat? He had no idea. His teeth ripped through an ear, and claws grazed his face.

A paw caught him, and sent him sailing through the air. Storm rolled with the blow. Distantly, he felt the sting of the claws over his ribcage. He hit the ground so hard that, for a moment, he couldn't breathe. He tasted blood and thought it might be his own.

Storm forced his eyes open, expecting to see a creasia coming to finish him off, but he was lying alone in a patch of long grass. He struggled to his feet and turned towards the fighting. What he saw made him sick. The herd had put a great deal of space between itself and the small battle.

And the battle was *small*. The only ferryshaft who'd come forward were the youngsters—the core group that Sauny and Kelsy had trained. The rest, even those who'd come to their practice sessions, had not moved.

Storm caught sight of Kelsy a little distance away. He was just standing there. Then Storm saw the body at his feet—Faralee. Kelsy was looking at her as though he could not quite understand what had happened. He looked up at the battle again, glassy-eyed. The last of their supporters were either running or dying.

Sauny. Storm made himself get up. He could see that he was bleeding, but he couldn't feel the wounds. He forced speed into his movements and reached Kelsy. "Where are Sauny and Valla?" he demanded.

Kelsy looked at him vacantly, as though he did not recognize him. Storm felt cruel, but he gave Kelsy a shove with his nose and practically bellowed in his ear. "Sauny and Valla! Where did they go?"

Kelsy blinked. "The lake," he managed.

Storm shot away. He reached the edge of the herd and darted over and around ferryshaft towards the trees. He paid no attention to the looks they gave him. They were just obstacles now—things between him and his sister.

As he entered the deepening shadows beneath the trees, he realized that two other ferryshaft were trying to follow. He glanced back and was shocked to see Tollee and Mylo. "She's over here," said Tollee, before Storm could speak.

"Sauny?"

"Yes, follow us."

He did—north through Chelby Wood and along the edge of the lake as the last of the sunset faded from the sky and the air cooled. All the while, he expected to hear the sounds of pursuing creasia. *They'll want me, of course. And I'm sure Arcove hasn't forgotten who attacked him.*

They soon found a blood trail, but it was a ways farther on before they finally caught up to Valla and Sauny. Storm's stomach gave a flop when he saw them. Valla was streaked with blood—bright crimson on her creamy fur—and it was not her own. Arcove's claws had left a track of destruction from Sauny's shoulders to her hips and deep into her left foreleg. Her skin gaped open along multiple fissures with every step she took.

To Storm's surprise, Sauny's spirits appeared unchecked. "I'm alright," she kept saying. "It doesn't hurt. I just need to hide somewhere so that I can clean the wounds and let the bleeding stop. Don't look at me like that, Storm. I'm alright."

She paused at one point to ask, "How is the battle? Are we winning?"

Storm didn't think he could bear to explain. "I don't know, Sauny. I needed to make sure you were safe."

She frowned at him. "But they need to see you! The foal that Arcove couldn't kill. They need to see you, Storm."

He almost lost his temper, then. "Sauny, I just saw my oldest friend disemboweled and killed in front of me. Please, stop asking questions."

She was quiet after that.

"Do you think the creasia are following?" whispered Valla.

"I don't see why they wouldn't," muttered Storm.

"Do you think we have time to stop and let the blood clot?"

It was an excellent question. Sauny's wounds pulled and bled with every step. *If she's to have any chance at all, she needs to lie still for a day or more,* thought Storm in despair.

"Yes," he heard himself say. "Yes, let's stop and clean the wounds."

They did—with the last traces of twilight to guide their efforts. They cleaned Sauny's wounds carefully, trying not to disrupt any of the clots. Sauny had begun to shiver. She flinched when Valla probed a gash for sand. "Is it starting to hurt?" asked Valla gently.

Sauny gritted her teeth. "A little."

A lot, thought Storm. His own wounds were beginning to pain him, although the bleeding had mostly stopped. He had one deep scratch over his nose that kept obstinately dripping. Every time he shook his head, he speckled his friends with blood.

Tollee and Mylo were silent shadows. Storm snuck glances at them. He hadn't seen Tollee in daylight since his return, and he hadn't seen Mylo at all. Tollee had grown and lost her baby curves. Her coat had darkened to loam with flecks of ash. She would never be a beautiful ferryshaft, but she had a hunter's grace. Mylo had grown into a massive, barrel-chested beast. His ragged ears and scarred muzzle still spoke of too much fighting for too few meals, but he seemed quietly confident.

"Thank you," Storm told them humbly.

"Don't thank us yet," said Mylo. "We're leaving too much of a trail. You need to swim."

Storm knew he was right. Water would be the only way to disguise their blood trail, and the lake was convenient. *But how far can Sauny possibly swim?* Night had fallen, and the water looked dark and cold.

"I think—" began Storm, and then Tollee spun with a snarl. It was all the warning they got as two creasia leapt from the shadows. Mylo met one and threw him back with surprising ease. Tollee danced in to strike at the other. Storm had not seen either of them at any of the organized practice sessions, but they had clearly considered how to do this.

"Go!" shouted Mylo over his shoulder.

"Now, Storm!" snapped Tollee.

Storm wanted to say, *I can't leave you.* But he wasn't sure that Valla could protect Sauny alone. *What is the right thing to do?* He glanced back and saw that Valla and Sauny had made it into the water and were paddling away. A moment more, and they would be lost to sight in the darkness.

"Storm, please!" There was a note of desperation in Tollee's voice as she backed away from the circling cat.

Storm swallowed a whimper, turned, and plunged into the lake. As he paddled away, he heard a ferryshaft scream from the shore. It seemed to go on for a long time, and, when it ceased, Storm felt as though his world had ceased with it.

20

Parting Ways

Roup knew from the moment he smelled the ferryshaft herd that something was wrong. There was a scent of blood in the air, along with freshly trampled grass and turned earth. Even so, he was unprepared for the sight that met them from the top of the ridge— a large group of ferryshaft harrying a cat that they had crippled and obviously intended to kill. The crowd had worked itself into a frenzy, and Roup was a little worried when Arcove elected to walk right down into them before the bulk of the other clutters caught up.

He was fairly certain that Arcove intended to speak, not to the herd, but to the creasia they'd cornered, when a foal bolted out of the crowd and attacked him. The attack was sudden, as was Arcove's reflexive defense. None of this surprised Roup, but he was thunderstruck to see a pale gray ferryshaft bound into the space between Arcove and the foal.

By all the ghosts. Storm Ela-ferry.

Arcove kept his composure, but to Roup's eyes, he looked rattled. He seemed caught for a moment between the urge to speak to Storm and the urge to strike at him. Then Storm said something that Roup didn't catch. It made Arcove hesitate and then lash out—too late. Another ferryshaft had already dragged the wounded foal from the field, and now all the clutters had arrived. They were twitching with the smell of blood and the palpable battle tension in the air.

Storm shouted a challenge, and that was all it took to send the most aggressive of the ferryshaft hurdling at the creasia. Roup spent a moment, lost in the fighting, before he realized that their attackers were all young. He did not see a single herd elder, nor any of those old enough to have participated in the war. It filled him with a mixture of relief and sadness.

The end result was predictable—a patch of blood-soaked earth, and twenty or more dead ferryshaft. Roup was more surprised that there were also two dead creasia and three seriously injured. *The foals planned this. They just didn't plan to be abandoned.*

Several of the creasia were starting into the herd in pursuit of fleeing youngsters, but Arcove bellowed a rally cry that brought them reluctantly back. *Good call,* thought Roup. *The herd is on edge. How much more would it take to get the older ones to fight?*

Roup saw that, amid the tumult, someone had ripped the throat from the unfortunate creasia the foals had been tormenting. He growled. The wound looked too large for a ferryshaft mouth. Roup shot a glance at Treace and Moro, who were watching with a degree of serenity that Roup found perverse.

Halvery had just come dashing up to Arcove, and Roup heard him say, "—headed towards the lake. That one who attacked you was his sister. They're leaving a blood trail."

So we're going to chase Storm again, thought Roup wearily, but as they started into the trees, Sharmel came running up. "We found where the raiding creasia were sleeping," he said. "The second one seems to have come to the edge of the trees, probably saw what happened to his companion, and then started off south recently."

Roup looked at Arcove. *Storm going north. Our quarry going south. Which will it be, my friend?*

Arcove shut his eyes and drew a long breath. "Halvery, are any of your cats already in pursuit of Storm?"

"Two," said Halvery. "I thought you'd want—"

"That'll have to be enough. Please verify what Sharmel found and then catch up with us. We deal with our own problems before dealing with ferryshaft." As the sun set, Arcove turned south, along the trail of the fugitive cat.

Storm focused on Sauny. *If I think about the rest, I'll start screaming and never stop.* She was already struggling to keep her head above the water. Her breath came short and quick. Storm and Valla got on either side of her. Storm tried to decide how he would hold her up if she became exhausted. It would be impossible to get a good grip behind her head without pulling at her wounds.

Storm thought of Keesha's story about the Battle of Chelby Lake. *Sauny's would not be the first ferryshaft bones to rest on the bottom.*

No! That will not happen. I will not let it happen.

"Up ahead." Valla's voice was surprisingly calm. "There's a place to rest. I saw it before the light faded."

Storm was about to ask what she meant, when he made out a darker shadow on the water ahead. *A clump of trees. I'm glad one of us was paying attention.*

It wasn't a true island. There was no soil, just the twisted, scrubby trees that grew along the edges of the water. Pathar had told Storm once that these trees rooted in the lake during periods of drought and could survive prolonged submersion. "Don't mistake them for land, though. Never swim out to them."

But Storm was glad of them now. Sauny was almost spent. She managed to keep her head up long enough to get her front legs hooked around a tree branch, and then drooped, nose barely above the water, breathing in chattering rasps. Valla and Storm could have clambered completely out of the water. Sauny, however, was too weak to follow them and too injured for them to lift her. Storm was certain that, without their assistance, Sauny would lose consciousness and drown. So they all stayed on lower branches, half-submerged in the chilly lake. *This will be a very long night.*

"When dawn comes, we can swim back to shore," he told them. "The creasia will have probably gone north, searching for our scent along the edge of the lake. They won't expect us to still be out here." Storm rambled on, speculating on their strategy and trying to drown the awful images in his head.

Valla did not interrupt him. She inched over alongside Sauny and tried to curl around her. "She's cold," Valla said, when Storm paused for breath.

Storm was glad that they could not see his expression in the dark. He paddled around Valla and got on the other side of Sauny. She was, indeed, cold, and her breathing had become shallower. Storm tried to share the warmth of his body. "Sauny?" He was afraid to speak her name, afraid she would not answer.

"Storm," she said thickly. A long pause. "We lost, didn't we?"

Storm shut his eyes. "We're not dead yet. That's all that matters."

"I will be soon."

"No." Storm could not keep the pleading note from his voice. "Sauny, please don't give up."

She tried to raise her head to look at him, but she only succeeded in dropping her chin heavily on his shoulder. "I really thought we could do it."

We could have…if the others had fought.

"You'll kill them one day, brother." Her voice sounded so small.

"Sauny—"

Valla interrupted. "Storm, why don't you tell us about telshees."

Storm peered at her over Sauny's slumped shoulders.

368

"Tell us a story," said Valla softly, and, for the first time, he heard her voice falter.

Storm started talking again. He was sure that Sauny and Valla had heard him recount the tale of his adventures in Syriot at least a dozen times, but they listened now as though they'd never heard it before. Storm found himself dwelling less on the violent moments of his adventure and more on Syriot itself—the caves of many-colored crystal, the rooms that hummed with telshee song, the strange pools with stranger creatures.

At one point, he felt Sauny relax, and his throat clenched, but Valla only reached out to balance Sauny between them and make sure her head was above water. "Asleep," she whispered. "Just asleep."

Storm was about to start talking again, when he heard a soft splash that made him jump. *Could the creasia have swum out here?*

Then, to his astonishment, someone quite close said, "Storm?"

Storm and Valla both craned their necks to see through the branches. Storm answered hesitatingly. "Yes?"

A pale head rose from the water directly in front of them. Valla gasped.

"Ulya?" whispered Storm.

The small telshee blinked at them, her eyes like dark pools amid the shadows. "I heard your voice," she said. "But I didn't think— Why are you out here?"

"Why are you?" blurted Storm.

"Shaw sent me to watch and try to find out how you were getting on. I've been around the edges of the lake for several days. There was some commotion this evening, but I couldn't tell what it was about."

"There was a battle," said Storm bitterly. "We lost. This is my sister, Sauny, and my friend, Valla. Sauny fought with Arcove and was badly hurt."

Ulya's eyes widened. "This tiny thing…fought with Arcove? Truly, you ferryshaft are great warriors."

Storm was sure, then, that Sauny was more than just asleep. He was certain that, under normal circumstances, she would have woken to dispute the word "tiny." *And she's not tiny...not for a yearling.* His throat clenched again. *Only a yearling.*

"I think she's dying, Ulya. She lost consciousness a little while ago, and she's lost a lot of blood."

Ulya came forward and rested her head against the side of Sauny's chest. She looped a coil of her own body under Sauny's chin as well, shut her eyes, and appeared to listen intently. When she opened them, her expression was grim. "You're right, Storm. We might be able to save her in Syriot, but I would have to take her there at once and swim as fast as I can." She thought for a moment. "I might need one of you to help me. I can't carry all three of you, though. I wouldn't be able to swim fast enough."

"Let me go," Valla spoke before Storm could. She glanced at him. "Please." She drew a quick breath and spoke again before Storm could think what to say. "Besides, you need to find out what happened on shore."

No. I don't ever need to find that out. "Alright," he heard himself say. "I'll meet you there as quickly as I can cross the plain."

So Ulya made a curve of her body, and Valla helped hold Sauny in place. "I could carry her in my mouth," said Ulya, "and I'll probably have to at some point, but I don't want to make her wounds worse."

Ulya was surprisingly quick, in spite of the awkward loop of her body and the extra burden. Storm watched them glide away. Then he was alone with his thoughts and the darkness.

21

Good-bye

Arcove's party caught up to the raiding creasia a little after full dark. Roup felt almost sorry for him. The cat had clearly run after seeing the ferryshaft attack his friend, and he had no idea that Arcove and the entire council were on his trail.

The cat gaped as Roup's clutter swept around him. They were running a little ahead of the others, trying to keep pace with Arcove. "Stop!" Arcove snarled, and the creasia came to a quivering halt, glancing about and blinking.

He might have been surprised, but Roup did not think he was innocent. An innocent cat would have begun sputtering questions. This cat didn't say a word. He waited with an uncertain expression, watching Arcove.

Arcove didn't say anything else until all of the other clutters arrived. Treace's came last. Roup was sure that Treace hoped Arcove had killed the fugitive creasia in a fit of rage. *Unfortunately for you, your king knows better how to direct his anger.*

About fifty creasia from all over Leeshwood were soon gathered around Arcove and the raiding cat, who had hunkered down, tucked his tail, and lowered his gaze. "What is your name, and who is your commanding officer?" demanded Arcove.

"Rasit," mumbled the offending creasia. "Treace."

"And what were you doing out here, Rasit?"

"Going to the Ghost Wood," said Rasit, without taking his eyes off the ground.

"Halvery, what did you and your clutter find in this creasia's sleeping spot?"

"The remains of a half-eaten ferryshaft," said Halvery briskly. A dozen creasia murmured their agreement.

"We were hungry…" said Rasit.

"Do not lie to me!" thundered Arcove. "You and your friend came here to kill ferryshaft, not to visit the Ghost Wood. Will you admit this, or do I need to bring further evidence?"

Rasit swallowed. For the first time, he glanced at Treace. "You told us... You said that we could..."

Treace looked furious. Moro was keeping his eyes carefully downcast.

Arcove's voice grew cold and level. "Your commanding officer told you that you could hunt ferryshaft out of season?"

Rasit looked relieved. "Yes."

"And are you aware of my rules about this? Rules that have been in place since before your birth?"

Rasit said nothing.

"We made a promise. You broke it."

Rasit dared to lift his eyes, and Roup saw that sullen flash of insolence that he'd come to expect from cats in Treace's clutter. "*I* didn't make any promises. I can't break what I didn't—"

Arcove interrupted him. "No, you didn't break your word. You did something much more serious. You broke *mine.*" He glanced at the cats behind Rasit. "Kill him."

If Rasit had not been expecting it, the other creasia certainly were. The sentence was carried out with brutal speed and efficiency.

Arcove turned to glare at Treace before his subordinate had even stopped twitching. "Treace Ela-creasia, what do you have to say for yourself?"

Treace had not moved, but the creasia standing between him and Arcove had melted away. A larger circle re-formed around the two of them.

Treace lifted his chin and seemed to come to some decision. He met Arcove's gaze levelly. "They're edible," he snarled. "Ferry-shaft meat is unpleasant when the animals are eating flesh, but they are as edible as deer when they're on grass or milk. You've made us raid in winter to keep us from knowing it."

Roup was surprised. He had expected Treace to deny every-thing. He'd not expected a real argument. He had particularly not expected Treace to puzzle out this little fact. Roup felt suddenly uncertain.

Arcove, however, looked unimpressed. "So, you admit that you willfully broke treaty law, without consulting me or the rest of the council, putting our reputations with all other species at risk?"

"I admit that I took liberties with an archaic agreement that has remained unrevised for fifteen years and which has no parallel in all known history of sentient species relationships!" Treace was shouting now, talking too fast, as though he were afraid Arcove would silence him at any moment. Arcove was, indeed, advancing on him, tail lashing.

"I sent animals to test my theory, and I was right," continued Treace. "Ferryshaft are an appropriate food source. You say they're dangerous. Very well. I'll grant you that." He was backing away now, head low and defensive. Arcove's hackles had risen, making him look even bigger. "They're dangerous in their current condition. Look at what happened today! They attacked us. They killed creasia. Ferryshaft should be either used or destroyed. Right now, they're just a burdensome winter task, waiting to become a serious problem. Look at Storm! One foal! And not even you can kill him."

Roup didn't think he'd ever heard Treace speak so many words at once. *He's actually got a point. It's a point I've been making for years...except our solutions are different.*

"Enough!" snarled Arcove. "You do not respect my decisions or my leadership. I consider that a challenge."

He closed in a flash, and the two of them flipped over in a blur of black and tan. Roup felt a sense of relief. *Finally. Shut him up.*

Arcove had never been one to needlessly prolong a fight. His first blows were usually devastating, and if they did not kill, they at least ensured that his opponent could not win.

The two cats separated, both panting. Arcove's claws had caught Treace across the face. Treace's left eye might be ruined, and he was probably having trouble seeing out of either through the mask of blood.

To Roup's surprise, Treace continued to waste precious breath on words. "We all know you can fight, Arcove! Everyone knows that! You say we raid to keep the ferryshaft afraid of us, but they're not afraid of us! They're afraid of *you!* Even Charder. Do you think he will bend his neck to the next creasia king? Not likely. You've created an unnatural situation, which will last exactly as long as you live. Then it will break, and *someone* will have to clean up the mess!"

His words were cut short as Arcove managed to catch his right foreleg and snap him around. Treace came to his feet with a grimace. Roup wasn't sure whether the leg was broken or dislocated, but either way, Treace was now wholly at Arcove's mercy.

Treace stood there, swaying, half blinded by blood and said, "I have not challenged you, Arcove Ela-creasia. You'll kill me in cold blood for disagreeing with you. I doubt I'll be the last."

The gamble was breathtaking. Roup shot a glance around the circle of faces. They were far more conflicted than Roup would have liked. He wished, suddenly, that Arcove had not brought so many witnesses.

As Arcove advanced, Treace hunkered down, put his chin on the ground, and waited. *Treace is really going to make Arcove kill him in cold blood,* thought Roup. *Will he?*

In a voice so quiet that the listeners had to strain to hear, Arcove said, "I was once a young cat on the council. I was frustrated with the way things were done. But when I disagreed with my king, I challenged him. I did not break his word behind his back."

"Only because you knew you'd win that fight," said Treace, his voice small and flat. "Does strength guarantee wise decisions?"

There was a moment of perfect stillness.

Then Arcove let out a long breath. "You are no longer one of my officers, Treace. You will answer to Halvery. He and Ariand will split your territory. They will examine it to see what other of my policies you may have...*disagreed* with. I will tell you when, if ever, you may return to my council."

374

The entire circle of creasia let out its collective breath. Roup watched their faces. He wasn't sure Arcove had made the right decision. He wasn't sure Arcove had made the wrong decision. At that moment, Roup wasn't sure of anything.

Storm swam to shore with the first light of dawn. He'd slept for a brief period during the darkest part of the night, wedged into the crotch of a branch just above the water. Still, he felt immensely tired, stiff, and unrested. The water seemed to suck the last traces of warmth from his bones, and the scratches across his ribs and face stung fiercely.

Ashore, he inspected the ground where the creasia had attacked. He found a great deal of blood, but no bodies. Storm found no fresh creasia scent or tracks, either. It was hard to be certain, but he did not think they'd come back this way during the night. He hoped they'd continued on around the edge of the lake. Perhaps they'd even decided to investigate one or more of the small islands just off shore. That would take a long time.

Storm started into the trees, not sure what he intended to do. He knew what he *wanted* to do—get across the plain as fast as possible and down to Syriot. *But what's the rush? Sauny will either live or she won't. It's out of my control now.*

He'd almost reached the far side of the wood when he came upon a mound of fur, lying on a patch of earth dark with blood. At first, Storm thought he was looking at two ferryshaft bodies, side-by-side, and then one raised its head.

Relief hit Storm like a hoof-blow to the gut. "Tollee."

She stared at him, her eyes wide and wild. Finally, she staggered to her feet, and Mylo's head flopped from where it had been lying across her front legs. Storm's mouth went dry. He saw, then, that Mylo had been slashed nearly in two—blood and entrails smeared across the leaves where he'd dragged himself.

Storm took a step back. "Tollee, I—I'm sor—"

"He died near dawn," she said. "I ran away, but they caught him. When I came back, they'd gone, and he was— I stayed with him, talked to him. He—" Tollee's voice broke. She gave a long, low moan—almost a howl—a sound of unutterable sadness.

Storm didn't know what to do. He tried to lick her face in comfort, but Tollee jerked away. "This was my fault."

"No," said Storm. "No, it wasn't." *If anything, it was mine.*

"You don't understand," wailed Tollee. "I didn't love him! I stayed with him because I thought it was my duty, but he would have let me go. He could have found someone who cared. He shouldn't have been here helping me...because...because of you." She rocked back and forth, whimpering. "He didn't deserve this."

Guilt rushed over Storm like a wave. He remembered that time on the ice, when he'd hoped Kelsy would kill Mylo. He remembered thinking that, if only Mylo died, he and Tollee could be together. Looking at her now, he wasn't so sure.

"I thought I was doing the right thing, but I did the wrong thing," she moaned. "Wrong, wrong, wrong. And now it's too late."

"Tollee..."

She opened her eyes and stared at him miserably. "I might be carrying his foal. What do you think of that, Storm?"

Storm wanted to say, "You're too young to have a foal." *But my mother was carrying me at that age...and she was a ru, too.*

"Come with me," he heard himself say. "Across the plain to Syriot. We'll leave the herd forever. That's where Sauny and Valla have gone. I'll help you raise Mylo's foal. I don't care..."

But she only shook her ears. "No, Storm. No." Tollee turned and walked away from him—a bit unsteady, her tail low.

Storm wanted to call after her. *You're only punishing yourself! Punishing me!* But he didn't. He looked at Mylo's body and held his tongue. *Maybe if I'd ever actually asked her to be my mate, she would have left...and Mylo wouldn't be dead. Too late, Storm. Always too late.*

He thought that he should go into the herd to ask who had survived the battle. Instead, Storm fell asleep in a sunbeam. He made no attempt to hide, but the creasia did not come. When he woke, his fur was dry, and it was evening. Storm headed out onto the plain, going north and then west. He avoided the few ferryshaft he came upon. Farther and farther he ran, through the long grass, browning now in the fall chill. He found a ridge with a few scrub trees, sat down, and began to yip. He imitated the warbling rally cry of the mountain curbs as best he could. He yipped until the moon rose and the stars came out. Finally, someone answered him.

A little while later, Eyal and his pack came trotting through the grass up the ridge. "Have you gone mad?" panted Eyal. "A few calls will do! We came as fast as we could, but we were far to the south. You're lucky you didn't attract other attention!"

Storm waited impatiently for him to stop talking. "I need to get to Syriot. Will you go with me back across the plain?"

Eyal thought for a moment. He spoke briefly with his beta. "Yes, we will go with you." He looked closely at Storm. "Is something wrong? You smell of blood and lake water…and grief."

Storm looked at him dully. "How can I smell of grief, friend?"

Cohal spoke up. "You have a deep scratch across your nose, Storm. It will probably leave a scar."

"I'm lucky I don't have worse."

"I think you do," said Eyal.

"Can we go?" Storm demanded.

Eyal said nothing for a moment. Then he turned and called to his pack. "Kiera, Maeoli, come and meet Storm Ela-ferry."

Storm was confused. "Did your queen finally send you fresh pack members?"

Eyal did not answer as the two new curbs came forward to lick Storm's muzzle in greeting. Storm realized, with a jolt, that they were female. "Eyal! You're going to have your den?" He would have expected to see more joy over the prospect.

"Kiera, tell Storm the message you brought."

The female looked up at Storm with sad, golden eyes. She was very thin. "My queen told me to find Eyal's pack on the northern plains, if it yet lived. She sent this message: 'We are overrun. The dens of your birth are full of dead pups, and our valley is lost to us. I send you these three of my daughters. I can do no more for you. Good hunting, friend. I doubt that we will ever meet again.'"

The curb dropped her gaze as her rehearsed speech ended. "We were three when we fled, but we were only two by the time we found Eyal's pack. If any of our kin live, they are scattered in the mountains."

Her voice fell silent, and Storm watched the other curbs. *They can never go home,* he realized.

Eyal turned and started away. "The cliffs will offer better hunting at the turn of the season," he said, "and safer hiding places." His voice had a desolate note that Storm found oddly comforting.

You will not try to cheer me. Good. I do not want to be cheered.

So, Storm ran west across the plain with the highland curbs. Unlike all the previous times when he had wandered, he did not feel the pull of the herd at his back. He thought of Faralee, laughing as she teased Kelsy. He thought of Tracer—how he'd befriended Storm that first day on the ice, all the games they'd played, all the hopes and dreams they'd shared. He thought of Mylo, accepting him when no other clique leader would have him. *Mylo didn't trust Kelsy. He thought Kelsy would get a lot of young ferryshaft killed. And wasn't Mylo right about that in the end?*

Ah, but who encouraged them, made them dream of killing creasia, set them an example of defying cats? Me. If I hadn't been in that crowd, if I hadn't shouted a challenge at Arcove, would the foals have attacked? Storm wasn't sure, but he was certain that he was at least as much to blame as Kelsy.

Good-bye, Storm told them all quietly. *Good-bye friends, living and dead. Good-bye, mother. Good-bye, Tollee. Good-bye, home. We are better off without each other.*

Part IV

Teek

_____

1

The Next Generation

Charder woke at first light to the unpleasant, prickly sensation of being watched. He raised his head from his nest of grass and looked around. Several old friends were curled up nearby, but none of them were awake. Instead, Arcove was watching from the shadow of a tree a few paces away. *Well, it's about time.* It had been more than twenty days since the disastrous incident with the raiding creasia.

Charder got to his feet. Arcove had already turned and started towards the lake. Charder followed him, yawning. "I expected you days ago." Indeed, he'd expected a visit—likely an unpleasant one—immediately after the pitiful battle. However, there'd been no signs of creasia since then. The herd had slowly regained its collective footing.

Arcove grunted. "I thought you told me that Storm hadn't turned up."

"He hadn't!" said Charder. "Not before I left. After I came back, yes, but I didn't know how to find you then." *Not that I would have considered that something worth finding you over.*

Arcove stopped beside the lake. "Where is he now?"

"I don't know," said Charder. "Truly, I haven't seen him."

He expected more probing, but Arcove moved on. "How has the herd responded to the fighting?"

Charder thought for a moment. "Well, they're calling it the Foal's Folly, if that tells you anything."

"How are the surviving foals? Have they been ostracized?"

"Not...exactly," said Charder. "I don't think they're anxious to fight with you again, though." *Please don't ask me to identify them. We've had enough killing. Summer is supposed to be a peaceful time.*

"Do they have a leader?" asked Arcove.

Charder considered. "Sauny—Storm's sister. I believe you killed her."

Arcove looked surprised. "She was rather young. Anyone else?"

Charder sighed. "Kelsy. A popular five-year-old."

Arcove watched him closely. "How popular?"

Charder gave a non-committal wave of his tail. "A lot of the adults like him," he admitted. "Or *did*. Now they're a little afraid to associate with him." *But that will change if nothing terrible happens in the next season or so.* "He lost a mate in the fighting," added Charder. "He had three."

"Three?" Arcove was surprised. "Isn't that a lot for a five-year-old ferryshaft?"

It's a lot for any ferryshaft. "Yes, well, he's a popular five-year-old."

Arcove quirked a smile. "Is this who the herd would choose to lead them…if they chose such things?"

Charder looked out across the water. "Possibly. Are you looking to replace me?"

"No, but I think perhaps I have been remiss in not meeting the next generation. I'd like a word with him."

"Now?"

Arcove answered with an impatient flick of his tail.

"Alright," said Charder. "But give me a few moments to find him." He hesitated. "Did you… Did you learn why the raids…?"

"Treace is no longer one of my officers," said Arcove. "There will be no more out-of-season raids. I will send someone to check on you from time to time and make sure this is true. Now, go find Kelsy."

Arcove watched the lake as he waited for Charder to return. Kuwee Island lay off to the right in the mist. *Young cats fighting young ferryshaft. Just when you think you've put a stop to it, it starts all over again.* Treace had, indeed, been overpopulating. Halvery had admitted, grudgingly, that Roup's estimates were correct, perhaps even a bit conservative.

"The problem is complicated," he told Arcove. "As we've gone around to the various dens, we've found that bitterleaf is scarce in Treace's territory—completely absent from some den sites. We're not sure why. *I* think that Treace has been encouraging the males to destroy the plants, but nobody will admit this. If that's the case, though, it started more than five years ago, before he even became an officer. One or two years of persistent destruction would make the plants hard to find, even if the practice is no longer ongoing.

"We've also learned that many females are incorrectly identifying a different plant as bitterleaf. Since they often come to Treace's territory young, they may never have tasted it before, and they easily confuse it with a similar-looking weed. Again, I think someone coached them incorrectly, but the lie has been passed from mother to daughter. Some of them have stopped even trying to prevent overpopulation, because they don't think bitterleaf works. They're nursing one litter while pregnant with the next. It makes them old before their time and too tired to care."

Arcove thought Roup had made an admirable show of looking interested without saying, "I told you so."

Ariand had looked happier than Arcove had seen him in several years. "We'll get this sorted," he had said cheerfully. "We'll carry bitterleaf over there and seed it ourselves if we have to." Arcove also heard that Ariand had picked a fight with his own beta and killed him—the cat from Treace's clutter who'd killed Dustet.

Arcove had expected complaint from Roup over his own decision not to kill Treace, but Roup had been quiet about the fight. His only comment had been, "Why did you tell him that he might *ever* come back to the council?"

"Because a cat like that needs a goal," said Arcove. "Hope gives him a reason to behave."

Roup had sighed. "He'll have to behave for a very long time before I'll be interested in giving him anything beyond hope."

Arcove turned away from the lake at the crunch of a leaf. A tall, red-gold ferryshaft on the cusp of adulthood was making his way cautiously towards him. Arcove could tell, just by watching Kelsy move, that the ferryshaft knew how to fight. Charder came behind, picking his way around wet spots. When they reached him, Arcove said, "Kelsy Ela-ferry?"

Kelsy was bristling with anxiety, but he carried himself well. "Yes."

Arcove glanced at Charder. "Leave us."

Charder looked a little disappointed, but Arcove turned and ignored him. Kelsy's eyes were dilated to near-blackness. He had not quite tucked his tail, but he looked like he wanted to.

Arcove decided that causing panic would be counter-productive. "I won't kill you," he said. "Yet."

Upon reflection, it was not the most reassuring thing he could have said. Kelsy's expression did not change, but he raised his ears a little. "Charder says you are his likely successor," continued Arcove. "We'd best get to know one another."

"I won't help you kill ferryshaft," blurted Kelsy, in what must have been an act of considerable bravery.

Arcove sniffed. "Charder says you are popular. Are you popular enough to control them? If you tell them not to breed, will they listen?"

Kelsy looked surprised. He said nothing.

"If you can keep their numbers within my parameters, there'll be no need for culls," said Arcove. "But I doubt you can. Charder never could."

"Ferryshaft do not take direction in that way," said Kelsy carefully.

"I've noticed."

Kelsy was silent. His ears flicked nervously.

"You were among the group who attacked my cats some days ago," said Arcove. "That happened because one of my officers was raiding without my knowledge. That cat has been punished, and the remaining raider killed. It should not have happened, and so

I will overlook your behavior. If you *ever* attack me again, I'll kill you. Do you understand?"

"I understand," said Kelsy softly.

"Now, as for Storm Ela-ferry—"

"Storm is my friend." Kelsy met Arcove's eyes. "Nothing you say will change that."

Arcove smiled. "Well, you're not a coward. If you're also not a fool, we'll get along fine."

This seemed to confuse Kelsy.

"I was going to say that I would like to speak to him."

"Speak?" repeated Kelsy with obvious disbelief.

"Yes," said Arcove, "I won't hunt him—not for at least a day and a night afterward. Longer, if he feels the truce is insufficient." He hesitated. "If he won't talk to me, he could talk to Roup. He might find that less intimidating. I know you don't understand, but Storm will. Tell him."

Arcove thought that Kelsy might question the validity of his truce, but Kelsy only sighed. "I don't know where Storm is. I haven't seen him since the battle. No one has."

2

Injuries

Deep in the caverns beneath the cliffs, amid the soft green light of the tiny acriss jellyfish, Storm sat and watched curbs stalking small, pale fish and crustaceans in the shallows. Shaw watched with him. She wore a resigned expression.

"Well," she asked with a degree of sarcasm, "is it satisfactory?"

"I think so," said Storm. "They seem happy this time."

Eyal came splashing through the water towards them. "It is extremely satisfactory, and we owe you a great debt, Shaw Ela-telshee."

She inclined her head. "Yes, you do."

Storm frowned at her. "They are my friends, Shaw, and they've helped me."

Shaw sighed. "In my youth, I was not in favor of telshee involvement with land animals. I said it would lead to wars and death, and I was right. I argued with Keesha for days over his decision to get involved with ferryshaft matters. It will amuse him no end to learn that I am now providing denning arrangements for a pack of curbs."

Storm smiled. "You must have been desperate when you sent that ely-ary after me."

"I was," agreed Shaw.

Eyal observed this exchange in respectful silence. He did not seem offended by Shaw's rude behavior. "We are grateful for your folly," he said, when Shaw paused.

That made her laugh. "As long as you understand that's what it is."

"How soon will you have pups?" asked Storm. "Do you have them only in spring like ferryshaft do, or…"

"We will have our first litters as soon as the females have gained enough weight to come into season," said Eyal. "Right now, they are too thin. It won't be long, though, on this kind of diet."

"Will they both…be your mates?" Storm had been curious about this from the start, but uncertain of how to ask. He'd seen no fighting among the curbs as they crossed the plain, even though there were only two females and eight males. He'd wondered whether Eyal received mating rights by default because he was the leader.

Eyal cocked his head. "We are a pack. The pups will be pups of the pack."

Shaw snorted above Storm's head. "Curbs believe a pup can have eight fathers," she said. "Perhaps *their* pups can...but I doubt it."

A look of annoyance crossed Eyal's face. Storm thought he would have liked to say something rude to Shaw, but held it back out of gratitude for her gifts.

"Curbs are very odd animals," continued Shaw airily.

Storm turned to stare at her. "You...who lay eggs and are both male and female...you are calling someone else an 'odd animal'?"

Eyal gave a bark of laughter.

Shaw looked irritated at both of them. "Wait until you see their pups," she told Storm. "You will understand what I mean."

"Our pups will be charming and delightful," Eyal assured Storm, still grinning. "Now I will help the others gather bedding material. Thank you again, Shaw."

Storm watched as several curbs trotted away up the long, steep passage that lead, eventually, to the boulder mazes. The curbs had refused to stay in Syriot without some sort of path to the surface, and they'd been shown four caves before approving this one. Storm had used every appeal to Shaw's good will to get her to allow it. "We can barely protect ourselves!" she had argued. "How are we supposed to protect a pack of curbs?"

"They don't need protection," Storm had said. "They just need a place to hide from the lowland curbs while they have their babies."

"They will be having babies indefinitely!" exclaimed Shaw.

"Well, until there are more of them, then."

"And what happens when your friends get killed by lishties? I won't be responsible for that."

"They think they've got a better chance down here," Storm had said. "Please, Shaw."

Storm hoped he'd done the right thing. The curbs certainly seemed grateful. Almost unwillingly, Storm said, "I should go see Sauny."

Shaw hesitated. "It will be a while yet before we know—"

"Yes," said Storm, trying to keep the snap out of his voice. "You've said that." The brief joy of seeing the curbs settling into their new home evaporated, and he felt suddenly tired and cold. *But it's not Shaw's fault.* He thought of trying to apologize and decided it would be better to just remove himself.

"I know the way," he said over his shoulder. He was relieved that she did not try to escort him. In spite of her concerns about lishties, this part of Syriot was telshee-dominated territory not far from the Cave of Histories. From what Storm could gather, lishty sightings here were rare.

He followed the tunnels deeper into the earth, sometimes wading through shallow water, occasionally swimming small rivers. Sometimes the acriss lit his way, and sometimes Storm walked in darkness. He'd gotten used to that—to finding his way by feel and smell and memory. He did not think he would ever get used to never feeling the sun on his face. *But Sauny may have to.* That thought chilled him.

Storm passed telshees occasionally in the caves. They'd grown accustomed to his presence and paid no attention to him. The distant strains of their humming mingled oddly and echoed from far off in the caverns. Storm heard the healing cave before he reached it—a low, throbbing, harmonized hum that made him feel simultaneously wide-eyed and sleepy.

The pool where they'd placed Sauny was not deep. It was barely large enough for her body, though it connected to a larger pool nearby. *A pup's pool,* Storm found himself thinking. *Well, she is a pup, isn't she?*

He was pleased to find her awake today. Valla was talking to her quietly. Sauny did not appear to be attending. She was staring vacantly at the floor, her head draped over the side of the basin. Storm sat down opposite Valla. "Hello, Sauny."

Her eyes flicked at him briefly and then away.

"Do you remember what I told you about the curbs?" asked Storm. "Well, they finally found a cave they like. They're going to have their babies down here. Would you like to play with curb pups?"

Sauny didn't answer. Valla glanced at Storm over Sauny's head. Her eyes looked tired.

"Have you tried to stand yet today?" asked Storm, refusing to be dismal.

For answer, Sauny heaved herself up in the water. She tottered there for a moment, balanced on three legs, trembling with effort and grimacing with pain. Her mangled left foreleg moved clumsily and did not support her weight. Half-healed wounds all along the left side of her body continued to gape and ooze. Sauny flopped back down in the water, facing away from Valla and Storm. "Leave me alone," she muttered.

"I think that's better than yesterday," Valla tried.

"No," interrupted Sauny, "it isn't. I want to sleep. Please let me sleep."

"You've slept for days," said Storm. "You need to move around."

"You should have let me die," whispered Sauny.

Bleak helplessness descended on Storm as it had so often over the last few days. The telshees didn't think that Sauny would ever walk normally again. When she'd first arrived in Syriot, they'd wanted to snip off her leg with their teeth—an idea that had horrified Valla. The telshees said that the leg would never work properly and that the wounds might poison the rest of Sauny's body. Valla had insisted that Sauny would rather take the chance. Storm thought she was probably right, although a lame leg wasn't much better than a stump in the end.

She will never again run on cliff trails, he thought. *Never play tag on the ice, never hunt properly, never win another fight.* The thought of his vivacious, beautiful sister limping her way painfully through life made him want to sit down and howl in desolation.

To make matters worse, Sauny was smart enough to understand the implications of her situation. Storm had not seen her smile once since he arrived. Last season, Sauny would have been thrilled to meet a telshee and fascinated by Syriot. She would have asked endless questions. Now, she said nothing and barely raised her head.

Valla admitted that, when Sauny woke, she'd insisted on hearing the truth about the battle. Valla had told her what little she knew, including several deaths of foals in Sauny's clique. Storm did not know these ferryshaft, but Sauny took the news hard. Storm did not want to tell either Sauny or Valla about Faralee or Mylo, but they eventually pried the truth out of him.

Since his arrival, Storm had spent at least as much time trying to arrange a denning site for the highland curbs as he'd spent with Sauny. He did not think he could bear sitting in that drowsy cave, thinking about everything he'd lost. Valla did—somehow. She'd gotten one of the humming telshees to teach her to read and sometimes practiced making their signs with little lines of pebbles on the stone floor.

When Storm stopped to puzzle out what she was writing, he found she'd written the names of dead friends…over and over. *We all mourn in our own way.*

Storm tried to get Valla to come with him to see the curbs. "We'll leave the cave for a while," he told her, "hunt outside."

"No," said Valla without looking at him. "Sauny can't leave. I'll stay with her."

"But she wants to be alone right now," said Storm. "She's safe here with the telshees."

Valla's eyes snapped up to Storm's. For the first time, he heard her growl. "I said *no,* Storm."

That was when Storm realized that he'd not only lost Tollee. He'd lost Valla, too.

3

Bargain

"Well, you wanted a chance to see him fight. I hope you got a good look." Treace opened his left eye with an effort to stare balefully at Moro. He'd dragged himself above ground for the first time in many days and was lying beneath a fir tree near the stream beside his den. He was still shivering a little in spite of the warm sun, but not so badly as he'd been a few days ago.

"You're improving," commented Moro. "Do you even remember the last time I was here?"

"No," muttered Treace. "Did I walk all the way back? I don't remember a lot of that, either."

"You did," said Moro, "without stopping to rest…much to the admiration of the entire clutter. Iska says you may not lose the eye."

Treace grunted. "I can see light and shadow out of it. Maybe that'll improve with time. The leg is a little better, too."

"I told you it wasn't broken," said Moro. "You'll be walking straight again by midwinter. The fever was what worried me, but it sounds like that's better."

"Yes. Dare I ask what's been happening while I was lying in the dark, delirious and shivering? Are Halvery's cats pissing themselves over the breeding infractions?"

Moro flipped his tail. "They're making some noise about it, but they've got no stomach for killing cubs, so there's not a lot they can do…except try to seed our territory with bitterleaf. Whether Arcove calls you an officer or not, you have more cats than any other clutter in Leeshwood. If you told them to attack, I think they would. We might even win."

Treace made a face. "And kill half the males in every clutter. I want their loyalty, not their corpses."

"Well, you made an impression with that speech on the plain. It was quite a risk."

"Not really. If I'd kept fighting, he would have killed me."

"I thought he was going to kill you anyway."

"So did I."

Moro smirked. "You should have seen the look on Roup's face when he didn't. Oh, that was not the way he planned it."

Treace gave a laugh that hurt his ribs and made him wince. "Pity I missed that."

"It won't be the last time."

Treace said nothing.

"I started a rumor that Roup's cubs are really Arcove's," said Moro.

"Oh?"

"Yes, they never look like Roup. He's sterile and requires his friend to do his breeding for him."

Treace chuffed. "Roup's cubs don't look like him because his color doesn't breed true."

"Yes, I know, but it makes a good rumor."

Not really. Treace thought for a moment. For a cat of such great inquisitiveness, Moro could be remarkably uncreative when it came to divining the possible motives of others. *The most damaging rumors have a little bit of truth.* "I've heard it whispered that Roup would rather lie down for Arcove than mount any female in Leeshwood." Such friendships were not uncommon between males who'd spent their bachelor years together. However, failure to sire one's own cubs certainly was uncommon. Such a thing would garner the immediate disdain of every alpha male in Leeshwood.

Moro snickered. "He's forgotten how to be on top?"

Treace shut his eyes. "If he ever knew. Anyway, that's a better rumor." *It might even be true, although I doubt it.* "Roup should share Arcove's den and not his council. His clutter is Arcove's, and everyone knows it. I suppose his cubs might as well be."

"And he hates you," put in Moro.

"And he hates me," agreed Treace.

"Do you know why they *don't* share a den?" asked Moro.

Treace snorted. "Because Nadine doesn't like competing with Roup for Arcove's attention?"

Moro cocked his head. "That's what I thought, too, but I got some of Halvery's older cats talking when they were over here. Apparently, Nadine and Roup are cozy as cubs in a litter. But she told Arcove from the beginning that Roup shouldn't share his den because Arcove would need him on the council, and officers always have their own clutters."

Treace scowled. "Females have no business meddling in clutter affairs. If Roup weren't on the council, Arcove might listen to my ideas." He thought for a moment. "I wonder whether Nadine was so free with advice to the last king."

"I doubt it," said Moro. "Or maybe he was just wise enough not to listen."

Treace shook himself. "I look forward to pinning her down and reminding her of her place."

"And killing every black cub in that den," said Moro with a flash of teeth.

Treace stretched. "I'll leave that to you. I'm sure you can find something interesting to do with them. And while we're on happy topics—has anyone caught Storm?"

"No. I'm not sure Arcove has even tried."

That made Treace chuckle. "There's one ferryshaft for whom I have nothing but good will. Long may he run free...and make Arcove look a fool."

"I am sorry to hear you say that," came a voice from across the stream.

Treace's head jerked up, and Moro spun around. So far, Halvery's inspecting cats had not been so rude as to invade Treace's personal den during his recovery. Treace tried to struggle to his feet, outrage mixing with fear in his belly. How much had they overheard?

But the animal who stepped from the bushes was not a creasia. It was a curb. She came boldly to the edge of the water—easy pouncing distance. "Rumor has it," she said. "That you have been asking to parlay with us."

Moro started to say something, but Treace talked over him. He still felt weak, and his head was spinning from standing too rapidly, but he *was* the alpha, and he was determined to act like it. "We've been trying to parlay with you for two seasons. We haven't made much progress."

The curb smirked. She sat down. "Rumor has it, you ask for secrets. Secret things come at a price."

"What is your name, curb, and what is your price?"

"My name is Quinyl."

Moro's ears perked. "I've heard of you."

She looked pleased. "I am the leader of the lowland curbs north of the forest."

"And your price?" asked Treace.

Quinyl's ears settled back. "Storm Ela-ferry. He has convinced the telshees to harbor my enemies. They are creating a den on the northern plains. I will not suffer it."

Treace licked his lips. "You want us to kill Storm for you?"

"Yes. He is the only reason telshees would do such a thing. I am certain that we will be able to destroy the last of the highland curbs without his interference."

"And in exchange—" began Moro.

"I'll tell you what you want to know," said Quinyl. "I'll help you kill Arcove."

4

The Conference Again

Storm ran with the highland curbs. He hunted with them and fought alongside them when they encountered other curb packs. On the beach one day, they cornered an adult seal that had been injured, probably from an encounter with a shark. The seal was fiercer than any of the prey the curbs normally hunted, and they circled it, leaping and snapping without making much progress. Finally, Storm managed to catch the creature in the side of the head with a hoof blow. He whipped in before the animal could regain its balance and caught a mouthful of the rubbery flesh of its throat.

Storm set his teeth and jerked back. His mouth filled with blood, and he heard the seal bellow. Its thrashing shook him this way and that, but he held on. As soon as he got an opportunity, he ripped loose a chunk of flesh and then another. The wound widened, and the spurting blood slowed.

Distantly, he heard the curbs calling to him. Finally, Eyal's voice broke through the fog of the hunt. "It's dead, Storm! Dead! You can stop now."

Storm raised his head and blinked blood out of his eyes. He saw that the seal's head was half off. The curbs were staring at him. "We'll have plenty to eat for a few days," Eyal said.

Storm didn't share their meal. He wasn't hungry.

Sauny still didn't want to talk to anyone. She'd left the healing pool and begun to move around the caves. As Storm had feared, her walk was a hopping limp—dragging the injured leg. Shaw had allowed her to visit the Dreaming Sea. Storm didn't know whether Syra-lay had woken enough to talk to her, but Sauny certainly liked spending time snuggled up in his coils. Storm feared that she would fall under the trance of the sleeping telshees' song and drown. Sometimes he thought that was what she wanted.

Valla divided her time between Sauny and the Cave of Histories. She had become fascinated by telshee script. If all Sauny wanted to do was sleep, then all Valla wanted to do was read. She would spend hours staring at the ancient, half eroded symbols, or quizzing Ulya about them. Neither Sauny nor Valla had much use for Storm.

"You should go back to the herd," Valla told him. "I'm sure everyone is wondering whether you're dead…again."

"I doubt they care," muttered Storm. "Besides, they didn't fight. They left Sauny and the rest of us to die. I don't want to be a ferryshaft anymore." He wished he could dispel the hollow sensation that filled his belly when he said those words.

Valla looked past him at the lines of text on the wall above his head. "Then go be a curb, Storm."

He gave a bleak snort. "And will you and Sauny be telshees?"

Valla did not smile. "Maybe."

So Storm ran with the curbs. He tried not to notice when the last of the leaves fell. The wind grew sharp, and his fur thickened. He tried not to notice, but Eyal would not let him forget. One evening, he invited Storm to hunt with the pack in the boulder mazes. They headed south. They passed several likely places to look for sheep, but Eyal didn't pause. Around midnight, they were trotting along a lower cliff trail, when Storm glimpsed the silver gleam of the Igby River ahead in the moonlight. Along its banks and among the nearby boulders, he saw irregular shapes darkening the grass and mazes.

Storm stopped walking. He turned to Eyal with a glare.

The curb looked up at him innocently. "The ferryshaft appear to have completed their winter migration."

Storm scowled. "What a coincidence."

"They just arrived," continued Eyal, "so I doubt they have the energy to attack anyone they might have reason to dislike."

Storm said nothing.

"Perhaps we should go down and look for this…uh…Tollee person."

Storm's scowl deepened. "You've been talking to Valla."

"Or someone named Kelsy?"

"They don't want to see me!" snapped Storm. "I don't want to see them." He took a deep breath. "I just want to be a curb, Eyal. Can't I just be a curb?"

"Of course," said Eyal. He thought for a moment. "In that case, we should go down and look for stragglers. Weak foals, old adults—probably exhausted and sleeping. Excellent hunting down there."

Storm was horrified. "You're not serious."

Eyal looked at him without a trace of guile. "I am. It's what curbs do...unless, of course, our friend is a ferryshaft."

Storm sighed. He looked back down at the herd. "It's the conference," he muttered. "Every year after the migration, Charder meets with Arcove, and I guess...I guess they decide how many of us the creasia will kill that winter. I didn't completely understand before."

"Maybe you still don't," said Eyal.

Storm gave him a withering look.

Eyal refused to be drawn. "My pack will not help you attack a creasia clutter, Storm. Certainly not one with Arcove in it. We'd die. We *will* help you find out what's become of your friends and make sure your herd doesn't try to kill you...if that's what you want."

"I just told you it isn't what I want," muttered Storm, but his voice carried little conviction.

Eyal turned and started towards the ground. Storm trailed behind. The moon was setting by the time they found their way to the foot of the cliffs, and dawn had erased the stars by the time they reached the outskirts of the herd among the boulders. Most of the ferryshaft were still sleeping, huddled in small groups on the frosty earth and stone. The area around the river was foggy at this time of morning. Storm remembered that. He remembered the excitement of sliding on the ice for the first time. He remembered how Sauny had squealed with delight when he'd shown her how to do it two years later. *She'll never be able to do that again.*

A ferryshaft loomed out of the mist ahead, only to take one look at the curbs and flee. The same thing happened again a moment later. Storm remembered something. *Tollee's parents were killed by curbs.* She hadn't responded when he'd told her about the highland curbs that fall. Still... He turned to look at Eyal. "Maybe you should let me do this on my own."

For the first time, Eyal looked uncertain. "Are you sure?"

"Yes," said Storm. *I'm here. I might as well see my mother and tell her that her children are not entirely dead.* "I'll meet you back at your den in a day or two." *But if you're waiting for me to thank you for pushing me into this, you'll be waiting a while.*

Eyal inclined his head. "As you wish. Any ferryshaft who can tear the head off a seal is able to take care of himself. But if we don't see you in a few days, we'll come looking."

"Do that," muttered Storm. When they were gone, he hopped onto a rock, worked his way to a vantage point, and watched the dawn. He watched the mist melt away and the herd wake. Ferryshaft passed beneath his perch without glancing up. He didn't see any of the ones he was looking for, so he said nothing. It took him half the morning, watching the ebb and flow of the herd, occasionally dozing, before he spotted one of the females that had belonged to So-fet's clique. He hopped down and followed her at a distance.

It was near noon when he finally approached his mother in the woods beside the river. So-fet was so overcome when she saw him that, for a moment, she could not speak. Storm felt instantly sorry for his failure to contact her earlier. He hurried forward and looped his neck over hers. "Sauny is alive, but she's crippled." He had not meant to blurt it out that way, but the words came, and he couldn't stop them. "She's with Valla in Syriot...the place with the telshees... She—"

"Shhh..." said his mother, and Storm realized that he was trembling. He felt weak and hated himself for it. "I'm glad you're alive," whispered So-fet. "I'm glad you're both alive. I hoped... but—"

"I should have sent a curb to tell you," said Storm. "I'm sorry, mother."

"A curb?"

"Yes, I've been with the highland curbs…and the telshees."

"I see." So-fet gave him a critical sniff. "You certainly smell like it."

Storm didn't want to talk about that. "My friends—my ferryshaft friends—do you know what's happened to them?"

So-fet spoke carefully. "You mean Kelsy?"

"Kelsy and Tollee." He thought for a moment. "Leep." *Although he's one of the ones who didn't fight.*

"I heard that Tollee had taken up with Remy," said So-fet. "They're old enough now, and they can both hunt… They'd do better if they joined a female clique, but I think they stand a good chance of surviving the winter even if they don't."

"Remy?" echoed Storm. "Kelsy's Remy?"

"Yes. She and Kelsy had a falling out after Faralee died…and over other things. At least, that's the rumor. These are your friends, Storm, not mine."

Yes, but everyone in the herd knows Kelsy.

"Was Itsa hurt in the fighting?" asked Storm with a new sinking feeling.

"No," said So-fet. "Itsa and Kelsy are still together as far as I know. Remy is carrying his foal, but I don't think she's speaking to him. Tollee…"

"Tollee is carrying Mylo's foal," said Storm dully. He clamped his mouth shut to keep from saying more.

So-fet watched him. "There were rumors that it was…yours."

Storm felt a new kind of guilt. "No," he said softly.

"I offered to help her," said So-fet, "for your sake, but she seemed to be doing well enough."

"Tollee is a survivor." Storm thought for a moment. "Why isn't Remy speaking to Kelsy?"

So-fet looked uncomfortable. "You know that the creasia meet with our leaders at this time every year, don't you? Charder goes, often Pathar, sometimes other elders."

"Yes," said Storm. He had not actually *known* that Pathar attended these meetings, although it didn't surprise him when he thought about it.

"Well," continued So-fet, "this year, Kelsy went. With Charder, of course, and Pathar, too, I think."

Storm gaped at her. "He...he went to—"

"Arcove met with him after the battle in the fall. The rumor was that they got along pretty well and that Arcove is grooming Kelsy to be the next herd leader. Creasia have been monitoring the herd since the attacks, although there hasn't been any fighting. Kelsy was invol—"

"'Got along pretty well'?" Storm couldn't believe what he was hearing. "Arcove killed Faralee! He maimed Sauny! He sends creasia to slaughter ferryshaft every year—"

So-fet gave a bitter snort. "I'm not sure that's the way Kelsy sees it. But I wouldn't know. I'm just a low-ranking, unmated female, Storm."

Storm felt as though he'd swallowed something vile. *I should never have let Eyal talk me into this.*

As he turned away, he heard his mother say, almost timidly, "Where will you be sleeping, Storm?"

"I don't know." He glanced over his shoulder. "In Syriot by tomorrow."

So-fet looked stricken, but Storm was too numb to care. "I can't stay with the herd, mother. Not anymore. I'll try to come see you now and then."

He'd expected her to argue with him, but, instead, she said, "Be careful, Storm. We came west in a hurry this year because Pathar and some others thought a Volontaro was coming. Now they've changed their minds, but creasia came from all over Leeshwood to stay in the Great Cave for the storm. They're mostly on the south side of the river right now...but be careful."

5

_____

The Calm Before...

Storm's anger carried him away from the river at speed, but he hadn't gone far into the boulders before a sense of bewildered betrayal almost overcame him. He stopped. He couldn't even decide where he was going. *Kelsy. How could he? I thought he and Sauny were friends. I thought he and I were friends! Mylo never trusted him. Tollee tried to tell me. I wouldn't listen.*

He thought of looking for Tollee, but couldn't bring himself to do it. *What if she's got something even worse to tell me?* Storm realized suddenly that he'd been awake for most of a day and a night. He could not recall the last time he'd been above ground at noon. The sun seemed to glare down out of a blinding sky, and he felt exposed with no shadows in which to hide.

I should go sleep somewhere. Perhaps, when I wake, I will know what to do.

This stretch of boulders and cliff were among the most familiar to Storm. He went a little distance north—just enough to be beyond the bulk of the herd. Then he selected a sheep trail and walked until he reached a little cave where he'd used to stash game.

Storm lay down, conscious of how the cave seemed to have shrunk. He wondered whether he'd even be able to use this cave by next year. *Not comfortably.* Storm thought about the seal. *I could never have killed something like that last year.* He decided that he would gladly trade access to some hiding places for the size and power to kill a creasia. With that thought in mind, he drifted off to sleep.

Storm woke to the chirp of evening insects. Far out across the plain, the rays of the sinking sun shone golden on dying grasses. The foot of the cliff was already in cool shadow. Something about the light seemed odd to Storm. He scooted to the lip of the cave and squinted upward. The sky looked almost green, and the clouds made odd, tortured patterns overhead. Far away to the north, he could see sheets of rain sweeping the plain, although the sun shone directly behind him.

"Storm!"

He turned towards the shout. Someone was standing at the junction of the sheep trail and the main path. Storm thought he knew who it was. He considered going back into the cave.

"Storm!" The other ferryshaft took a few tentative steps onto the sheep trail.

"Ghosts take you." Storm started towards his visitor with a growl. *Please don't fall off before I get a chance to push you.*

Kelsy backed onto the main trail again as Storm picked his way towards him. "I thought you'd show up when we reached the cliffs," said Kelsy. He seemed pleased with himself.

Storm stopped a few lengths away, not yet on the main path. He said nothing. He wondered how many ferryshaft had seen him among the boulder mazes and then down by the river. Word of his arrival had obviously traveled. *I should have taken better care.*

Kelsy's smile faltered. He watched Storm for a moment and waited for him to speak. When he didn't, Kelsy said, "Is anyone else with you?"

"If you mean Sauny," said Storm, "then, no, she's with the telshees and likely to remain there. Her left foreleg is so badly maimed that she'll never walk straight again."

Kelsy winced. He started to say something, but Storm interrupted him.

"Or perhaps you mean Valla? Since you're looking to replace a mate? They seem to be interchangeable to you. But she's in Syriot as well. Lucky for you, since I'm sure she'd kill you if she could see you now."

Kelsy shut his mouth. Storm glared at him. At last, Kelsy said, "What did you hear?"

"I heard that you and Arcove are great pals now!" Storm exploded. "I heard that you're looking to take over the herd with his blessing! That's all you ever really wanted, isn't it? You thought you could get your own herd by defying the creasia, but now it turns out that the easiest way is to serve them."

Kelsy bristled. "It's not like that, Storm."

"No? Well, tell me what it is like, Kelsy. You're willing to make common cause with Faralee's killers? Did you love her at all? And Sauny! Was she anything more than a stepping stone to you?"

Kelsy sat down on the trail. "Do I get to talk, or are you just going to shout at me?"

"Talk," spat Storm.

"Arcove did not send the summer poachers," said Kelsy. "One of his officers did that without his knowledge. The officer was injured and nearly killed for it."

"Nearly," mocked Storm. "My oldest friend, Tracer, was *completely* killed for it."

"The officer was demoted," continued Kelsy, "and the other poacher that we tracked that day by the lake was killed. I do not think those kind of raids will happen again."

"Just the winter kind," said Storm bitterly, "with a crowd of onlookers and bodies ripped open in the snow."

"I am trying to negotiate about that," said Kelsy, his voice exasperatingly calm.

"Negotiate?" Storm thought of Keesha—the pain and fury in his fathomless blue eyes. He thought of the Battle of Chelby Lake, of Coden, of the countless ferryshaft who had died in the fifteen years since the war. "There is no negotiating with Arcove."

"He'd like to talk to you," said Kelsy quietly. "He wanted to talk to you right after the fighting."

Storm laughed. "And by 'talk,' you mean 'disembowel'?"

Kelsy smiled. "That's what I thought at first, too. But if he says he wants to talk, then that's what he wants. If he plans to kill you, he'll tell you plainly." Kelsy hesitated. "Storm, it would help to have you at those meetings."

Storm nearly choked. "You can't be serious."

"I am. Fighting is not the only way to solve things. There are other ways, better ways."

"Never," snarled Storm. "The only way to solve what's happened between our two species is with a lot of dead cats."

Kelsy's ears flattened. "That's never going to happen, Storm. I *do* understand how you feel. I think about Faralee every single day. I wake up, and she's not there, and it *hurts,* but getting even more ferryshaft killed won't bring her back! Remy is angry with me for the same reasons you are, but I can't fix that, either. Yes, I want to lead the herd, and that means I've got to think of what's best for all of them, not what would bring me the most satisfaction.

"Arcove isn't going away. You can't kill him. I can't kill him. But he does seem interested in avoiding future conflict by parlaying with us if we can meet his terms. We could make things better for everyone if we just—"

Storm's lip curled. "I can't believe I'm hearing this. You wouldn't even be alive if I hadn't broken all the rules."

Kelsy looked hurt. "I know that." He hesitated. "But you can't run away forever, Storm. They *will* catch you."

Storm snorted and took a step back onto the sheep trail. "You're threatening me? I think we've had this conversation before."

Kelsy shut his eyes. "I didn't mean it that way."

Storm turned and started back towards the cave. Kelsy called after him, talking fast. "Storm, please listen! There's a Volontaro coming! I came up here to warn you. We're all going to the Great Cave. I was hoping… There's a truce in the cave. We could talk…" His voice was lost to the wind as Storm continued on along the trail.

In the Cave of Histories, Valla inched her way up a rock with little attention to the rising water. She had moved around the cave in response to the tides for so many days now that she'd stopped thinking about it. Her favorite was low tide—when she could almost see the oldest writing in the cave near the bottom of the ancient wall. The very oldest writing was never above water, and Valla had begged Ulya until the telshee had agreed to hold her still beneath the surface so that she could view the ancient text herself.

Ulya didn't like doing it. "You're not a sea creature, Valla," she had complained. "I'm afraid you'll drown. Can't I just tell you what it says?"

"You don't know what it says," countered Valla. "I can hold my breath for a little while."

The bottom line of text was pure gibberish to the telshees—circles and lines that did not represent any known sounds or words. The oldest writing that could be read was simply a series of names. Then came simple sentences. "I have been Rog." "I have been Nysi." "I have been Cathul." The "have beens" went on for some time, and then became a little more complicated. "I have been Terra, who survived the famine." "I have been Olla, who swam the deep mountain." "I have been Solon, who fought with great beasts."

Then, quite suddenly, the structure of the sentences changed. "I am Mirra. I am awake." "I am Tosla, who spoke with humans." "I am Kavith, who saw a hundred shores." Eventually, they became brief stories—a record of the telshee's most notable exploits.

Valla was fascinated by the vast spans of time represented on the wall. She was particularly fascinated by the points where the style of the record changed. *What made this telshee decide to write something different from the last five generations? Why change "I have been" to "I am"?* Some of the stories spoke of creatures unknown to Valla or to any of the telshees now living. *What are harpies? What are dragons? What are fauns?*

She was having trouble reading today because the afternoon light had been inconstant—with brief sheets of rain and strong gusts of wind. The wind had begun to make a strange whistling in the chinks overhead. Valla was surprised when she looked down and saw that she was standing on the very tip of the rock. It was one of the highest rocks in the cave. She'd never seen it underwater.

She was still puzzling over this when she heard a splash from the entrance. She blinked when she saw Sauny—paddling madly through the water towards her. "Valla, you have to get out of here. Keesha says there's a storm coming."

"Keesha?" Valla had never seen the huge telshee stir, though Sauny claimed that he sometimes woke. "You're swimming!" Valla had not seen Sauny swim since the injury.

"Yes," exclaimed Sauny impatiently. "The caves are in an uproar—telshees trying to move all the pups and eggs to safe places. I figured they probably forgot about you. Come on!"

Valla leapt into the water and paddled towards her. The wind moaned in the chinks overhead, and the tide was as high as she'd ever seen it. Her skin prickled. "Is this a Volontaro, Sauny?"

"I think so." Sauny was paddling unevenly, but still making good headway. Valla thought that she might actually be faster in the water than on land.

They reached the spot where the rising tunnel should have brought them to dry ground, but there was only more water. They were swimming in complete blackness now, without even the little acriss jellyfish to guide them. The water had begun to heave. Valla had never noticed waves in this part of the caverns before. It made her a little sick. The sounds of their splashing echoed in the dark tunnel, so that Valla wasn't even sure Sauny was still ahead of her. She bumped suddenly into a wall, lost her bearings, and went under.

Valla kept her head enough to avoid gulping sea water, but when she surfaced again, she was completely disoriented. "Sauny!" She knew her voice sounded panicky. "Saun—!"

"I'm here." Sauny was right beside her, nudging her forward in the black water. "We'll be able to stand soon. We've just got to keep going until we reach high ground."

Valla felt her stomach settle a little. This was the old Sauny— the Sauny who followed her brother over sheep trails when she was only a year old, who was confident and quick, who sometimes did the wrong thing, but always did *something*.

Sure enough, Valla's hooves brushed the bottom a moment later. They swam-walked for what seemed like an eternity before the water level dropped low enough for running. Sauny couldn't run, though. Valla had almost forgotten. She adjusted her pace to Sauny's limp. "Thanks for coming to look for me."

"If it was me, you would have come," said Sauny.

Valla smiled in the darkness. "Do you think Storm is alright?" she asked.

Sauny snorted. "He's with the curbs. I'm sure he's fine."

6

The Storm

Storm returned to the cave and lay down, fuming. *I really will become a curb,* he thought. *I'll leave the herd forever. If Eyal wants to hunt ferryshaft after the winter migration, I'll do that, too. They're no more than sheep to me. I'm not one of them.* He knew he was being ridiculous and did not care.

The wind was picking up. Far below and off to the south, he could see a milling mass of animals pushing their way up the trail that led to the stone bridge and the Great Cave. It looked even less organized than what he remembered from the previous Volontaro. Storm squinted. He thought he saw both ferryshaft and creasia, all packed together on the trail. Those on the ground pushed and shoved for their chance to start up. As he watched, one of the climbers—he could not tell what species—fell from halfway up the cliff.

Stupid ants. "I'm glad the herd has such organized and thoughtful leaders," he announced to the wind.

The rational part of his brain pointed out that the storm had come up suddenly, after the danger had seemed passed. Conditions on the trail would be nightmarish—panicked animals struggling along a steep and increasingly narrow path. Foals would be trampled or separated from their mothers. Anyone who was careless or unlucky would be pushed over the cliff. The bridge itself would be the worst—single-file over a thread of stone, animals piled up waiting to cross, an endless stream coming up behind them, pushing…

Storm gave an involuntary shiver. *That can't be the best plan for a Volontaro.* He wondered whether the elders had invented or exaggerated the danger of the storm. *Because the creasia require it? So that they can get an accurate count of our numbers?* Volontaros were the one time when the creasia were guaranteed access to the entire herd. *But, then, why risk bringing all of their own species? It seems dangerous for them as well.*

Storm shook his head. *Doesn't matter. I'm not a ferryshaft. I can wait out the Volontaro right here. Even if the mazes are underwater, I should be safe. It only lasted for about a day last time.*

Below him, the occasional straggler pounded past. Storm watched with indifference. The sky had darkened, and it had begun to rain—stinging darts that hurt when they hit his nose and eyes. The wind was making an eerie noise as it gusted among the rocks. Storm saw the scrubby trees among the boulders laid almost flat. He was grudgingly impressed. The clouds overhead looked like a bruise—purple and violet and black. Lightning bounced between them.

Storm knew that he should scoot to the back of the cave, where he would be most sheltered from the elements. However, each time he moved away, he returned to the lip moments later, unable to drag his eyes from what was happening outside. The light had almost gone. He heard a sound that he could, at first, not identify. Then he recognized it. *The sea.* The waves must be tremendous if he could hear them breaking from this side of the cliff.

A niggle of doubt began in the back of his mind. *Maybe staying here wasn't such a good idea…*

In a flash of lightning, Storm saw something out across the plain—a gray column as tall as the cliffs. One flash, and then it was gone. Storm blinked in the shadows. His heart pounded. *What was that?*

Thunder crashed overhead. The wind howled like an animal in agony. It was growing louder. Storm backed into the farthest corner of the cave. It was too dark to see anything outside, and he no longer wanted to.

Then the rock shuddered under Storm's feet as something slammed into the cliff. For one moment, he was completely submerged in water. He came up gasping and sputtering. Something slick and wet was thrashing against his flank. Lightning lit the world again, and Storm saw water gushing from the cave he was now sharing with a tentacled monstrosity the color of day-old meat. Storm swallowed a scream as the world plunged into blackness again. The thing in the cave writhed. *Octopus? Squid? Something else?* He'd never seen anything like that in a tide pool. *Can it bite, sting?*

He couldn't get away from it in the small space, so he tried to kick it towards the mouth of the cave. He'd barely begun this effort, when he heard a noise that he would never forget. He'd imagined that noise before, heard it in nightmares, strained for it during winter storms, but never heard it in reality...until now. It was the sound of a massive rockslide.

The telshee caves were in chaos. Everyone was scrambling to snatch eggs and young pups from the pools. Valla did not see any of the telshees she recognized. "Where are you going?" she tried to ask, but no one seemed interested in stopping to answer her.

"They go to deep caves with air pockets," Sauny said. "It's less dangerous than the higher caves during the storm, but we can't dive that deep. We'll go to the Dreaming Sea. I *know* they don't drown."

"But they can hold their breaths for a long time," said Valla doubtfully. However, she didn't have a better answer.

As they started towards the passages that lead into the deep mountain, the water level of the pools began to drop sharply. Sauny saw it and frowned. "Oh, that's not good. That's not good at all."

Every ferryshaft old enough to have visited the cliffs had heard about rockslides. They were the most dangerous disaster one was likely to encounter. Rockslides could bury dozens of animals in the time it took to draw breath, and they could hopelessly trap ferryshaft in caves or on trails. The only warning was generally a rumble and a plume of dust. Fortunately, large slides were rare, and every ferryshaft who climbed the cliff took care not to needlessly disrupt stones.

Storm had seen small slides, and he'd heard the characteristic rumble, which died immediately as a minor slide subsided. The noise he heard now was not minor. It grew to a roar that drowned the wind, and then the opening of his cave vanished in a deadly curtain of falling stone. The tentacled creature was swept away, and Storm cowered in the back of the cave, expecting it to collapse and crush him at any moment. After what seemed like a lifetime of terrifying noise, the outline of the cave mouth came back into view, and the grinding roar was replaced by the howl of the wind and the splatter of hail.

Storm staggered back to the cave's mouth. *Well, aren't you more clever than everyone else? What a fantastic idea—staying up here for the Volontaro.*

He waited for the lightning. When it struck, he saw with relief that most of the sheep trail seemed to be intact. However, a huge portion of the cliff to his right had been wholly ripped away. *Lucky. For once. Don't expect it twice.*

Storm had seen something else in the flash of lightning—two more gray columns swaying across the plain. *I have to get out of here.*

7

No Different

Storm did not think about the sheep trail. He knew that if he thought about it, he would fall. He waited for the lightning, got one good look at where he had to land, and then bounded to the head of the main path. He teetered only once on a shelf of stone that was half-missing. He was certain that his memory had not betrayed him. That bit of cliff had simply been washed away.

Storm hit the path running and almost slipped over the edge. Another jagged shaft of lightning showed him a gaping wound across the main trail. Again, he did not stop to think, just jumped, scrabbling at the far side, and then he was running again. Water gushed along the trail, spilling in cataracts from the edge. The rock was slick, and he forced himself to slow down as he reached the steepest section. Rain was coming in torrents now.

Storm jumped the last few lengths from the trail and landed in hock-deep water. *Ghosts and little fishes.* The mazes were already flooding. It would be like running through mud. In desperation, Storm leapt atop a boulder, then to another, then another. He was not far from the trail to the bridge, but it seemed like an immense distance as he measured the space between boulders in the flashes of lightning and felt the solid rock shift beneath his weight as the water rose higher. He heard another rumble from the cliffs.

Another rockslide? How close? Off to his left, something enormous was thrashing in the water. *A shark? A lishty? Something larger?*

Storm almost missed the trail to the bridge, in spite of his desperate scanning of the cliff face. In the darkness and flood, nothing looked as he remembered. He would not have recognized the trail if he hadn't caught the silhouette of a dead foal, lying half in and half out of the water. He splashed down and swam the last few lengths to the foot of the cliff. The trampled foal was clear evidence of the panic here earlier, but nothing was stirring now.

Storm raced up the path. He noticed things that he had not considered in his youth. The path was set into the cliff. It had been worn so by countless animals, and the overhang sheltered climbers from wind and falling rock.

Storm had never traveled this trail during his explorations. It led only to the bridge, and he'd considered it a potential trap. He wished now that he'd made its acquaintance on sunnier days. He was forced to slow as the path narrowed, growing steeper and taking turns with which he was not familiar. He came up one such switchback and spotted another animal bounding along ahead of him, higher up, caught for a moment in a flash of lightning. A creasia.

Storm felt a jolt of…something. It was the first time he'd come near a creasia since the battle by the lake. He found that he was not afraid.

Storm focused on running. The path was growing narrower, the switchbacks steeper. He caught intermittent flashes of the creasia up ahead. He was gaining on it. He was certain that it had not seen him.

Storm was flying over the stone now. He felt almost as though he were floating—the terror of the storm distilled into white-hot speed. He had not run so hard in…how long? *Since Arcove chased me?* For the first time since leaving Tollee beside Mylo's ravaged corpse, Storm felt truly alive.

He mounted the last steep switchback and saw the narrow straight-away that lead to the bridge. The creasia was there, squarely ahead of him, running as fast as it could, but not fast enough.

Storm closed with a burst of a speed that should have cost him, but he was too excited to feel the strain. He jumped—just a little to the cliffward side of the cat—and lashed out with a back hoof. He caught the creasia with what must have been a numbing blow to the shoulder, and the animal went head over heels. Storm thought that it was going over the edge, but then the cat managed to catch itself on the lip of the precipice.

Storm darted forward before the cat could regain the trail. It was clearly having trouble with the shoulder he'd damaged. It scrabbled desperately without managing to pull itself over the edge. The cat looked up at him, wild-eyed. "Truce…during…the storm," it managed.

"Is there?" asked Storm. He leaned forward, and the cat gave another desperate surge, almost as though it expected him to help pull it onto the path. Storm remembered the seal. His jaws closed around the creasia's throat. He set his back legs and jerked.

The animal's scream, so close to his ears, nearly deafened him. It broke off with a wet crunch, and then Storm stumbled backwards against the cliff face with a mass of fur and meat between his teeth. The creasia hung on for a moment longer. It opened its mouth, but only a spray of red droplets came out. Its eyes, still fixed on him, lost their focus. Then it fell.

The rain ran red over the edge of the cliff in front of Storm. He stood there a moment, staring. Then he dropped the evidence of his first creasia kill without looking at it. He turned and ran for the bridge.

Sauny tried to run for the tunnels that lead to the Dreaming Sea. She tried, but Valla could tell that Sauny's uneven gait would soon exhaust her. To make matters worse, the drop in water levels had created an unfamiliar landscape of deep chasms and steep climbs over wet stone slick with cave mud. Most of the acriss had vanished when the water levels dropped. In the darkness, with the pools all confused, Valla wasn't certain they were even going in the right direction.

"Sauny, maybe we should just climb to the highest spot and wait. There doesn't seem to be any immediate danger."

Sauny's voice in the darkness sounded winded. "Keesha said that when the water levels drop like this, sometimes they come back—"

There was a sudden loud gush and grinding noise. Water swirled around Valla's legs.

"Fast," finished Sauny in a whisper. "Valla, just swim. Try to find something to climb on and wait and…and thank you for being my friend."

The water was rising with terrifying speed. In desperation, Valla sloshed towards Sauny's voice in the darkness. "Shaw!" She shouted. "Ulya! Keesha! Anyone!" Her voice echoed weirdly in the tunnels, but nobody answered. "We are not going to drown," she informed Sauny as the floor dropped away beneath them. "You're a strong swimmer. I'm a strong swimmer. We're smart."

"Then save your breath and look for high ground," flashed Sauny.

Storm hesitated when he reached the bridge. The night had grown, if possible, even blacker. *Waiting won't make it any easier. One look. Just one, and then I'll go.* One look was almost too much. Lightning lit the sky from rim to rim, and he saw what he remembered—a thread of stone, impossibly narrow, slick with rain and without shelter from the wind. *Now,* he commanded himself. *Go now before you lose your nerve.*

Storm staggered when he moved from the lee of the cliff. He paused, readjusted his balance, and then stepped onto the bridge.

This is where you don't hurry.

There were no animals shoving behind him this time, no ferryshaft backside inching along in front of him. *Take your time.*

He did—careful step after careful step over the wet stone in the dark, leaning just a little into the wind, and making himself as flat as possible against the stone bridge. Storm was well over halfway and congratulating himself, when the pitch of the wind changed. The howl rose an octave. *Oh, no.*

Another flash of lightning, and he risked a glance away from his feet towards the sea. Something was coming up the Garu Vell—a wall of wind and water.

Storm abandoned caution. One, two, three desperate leaps. And then it was on him. Storm plastered himself instinctively to the stone. No good. He was slipping. *I did not survive Arcove to be killed by my own namesake!*

Storm scrabbled for purchase, anything. Still slipping. Something Pathar had said long ago flashed through his mind. *Don't fight the wind. Use it.*

Storm slipped over the side of the bridge...the windward side...on purpose. Instantly, the force of the gale pressed him against the bridge. He was able to stop struggling and catch his breath. He was half-off the bridge. If the wind stopped now, he'd fall. However, he was, for the moment, not slipping. Storm inched forward again. He knew he had to be near the cave. He might be mere lengths away in the darkness. Just a little farther.

An irregular shape came into view on the path ahead, perhaps half a length in front of him. Storm squinted. He thought he saw wet fur. *A body?* That couldn't be. Anything lying on this slick rock would be instantly swept away. But the shape wasn't moving. Storm was almost on top of it now.

And he saw what it was. A cub—hardly bigger than a rabbit—pressed flat to the bridge, every claw extended, hanging on, but barely. Beyond the cub, Storm glimpsed the massive outline of the Great Cave.

The wind dropped a fraction, and Storm inched quickly back towards the center of the bridge. It gusted, and he barely managed to shift his weight to the windward side. If the gale began to change its intensity, he would not be able to find a balance. Unlike the cub, he did not have claws to aid him.

Storm considered. The cub did not seem to be moving, and he could not get around it. He thought that a mere tug on its tail would probably break its fragile grip. Lightning struck again. The cub was not well-nourished. Storm saw clearly the shape of its ribs beneath its saturated fur. It was smaller than he would have expected. Ferryshaft were never born so small. *Not even me.*

What am I waiting for?

He found himself wondering what happened to creasia orphans—whether they had cliques, how they found food, whether adults helped them or hindered them.

No matter. This cub will grow up to kill ferryshaft just like all the others. I just killed a creasia. This is no different.

"No different," Storm reminded himself softly. "No different at all." He took a deep breath and inched forward.

8

Out of the Storm and into the Surf

Kelsy lay beside Itsa, feeling miserable as the Volontaro howled outside the Great Cave. He wondered if Storm would have come for shelter if he had *not* approached him. *Probably. I made him angry.* Common wisdom said that mortality for animals who remained outside the Great Cave during a Volontaro was around fifty percent.

Storm has survived worse odds. Still, Kelsy felt responsible, and this particular storm looked bad. He'd lain down within sight of the bridge, hoping to see Storm come in along with the rest of the stragglers. But the last light had died, the wind had grown fiercer, and Kelsy hadn't seen any stragglers in a while. He couldn't even see the bridge anymore. *I hope you're safe in your cave, Storm.*

Kelsy's eyes had started to drift shut when a silhouette materialized at the spot where the bridge met the cave. Kelsy started up. For a moment, he could not make sense of the shape, although he caught the gleam of pale fur. Lightning streaked across the sky, and Kelsy glimpsed the startling image of Storm flinging away a creasia cub...as though he had been carrying it by the scruff. Kelsy blinked in the new darkness. Storm's silhouette staggered, shook itself, and then bounded away into the shadows. An instant later, Kelsy thought he saw a smaller silhouette following after.

Valla wondered, as her nose brushed the ceiling of the cave, whether any other ferryshaft bones rested in Syriot. Surely not many. *Will Ulya carve a few characters for us in the Cave of Histories? 'They were Valla and Sauny, ferryshaft who lived among Telshees.' Is that too long?* Valla tried to work out how the characters should fit together. It was easier than thinking about how she would soon not be able to breathe.

Light! Valla blinked. A faint glow had begun in the water. "Sauny! Sauny, do you see that? The acriss have come back. Maybe we can find... Sauny?"

No answer. Valla panicked. She swept the surface of the water, but could not see Sauny, and the light was very dim. In desperation, she plunged her head beneath the surface, opened her eyes, and saw...

Acriss. A perfect trail—like glowing green bubbles—all the way from the surface near Valla to the bottom of the cave. They disappeared into the mouth of a smaller cave or tunnel that must have been at the bottom of the pool when it was at normal levels.

Sauny was following the acriss—swimming down through illuminated water, past what would have been the surface of the pool, deeper and deeper towards the opening at the bottom. Valla stuck her head up, got two more gulps of air, and then followed Sauny into the glowing sea.

Storm tried to dismiss his experiences on the trail and the bridge as he hurried into the Great Cave. *Hide.* He did not know what creasia would do if they encountered him, but he did not wish to test the limits of their Volontaro peace treaty.

The Great Cave is large, he reasoned. *Plenty of places to get lost.*

This might have been true, but the ferryshaft side was strewn with sleeping bodies—thickest in the sandy area in the front of the cave, where the ground was most comfortable. Storm picked his way quickly among them, hoping to go unrecognized in the darkness.

His progress seemed to evoke more muttering and growls than he would have expected. Finally, after hearing a snarl in the wake of his passage, Storm glanced back and saw, to his surprise and disgust, that the cub was following him. *I spared your life; isn't that enough? Now please get out of my sight and allow me to forget you ever existed.*

The cub's presence was drawing more attention than Storm would have liked. With a rising temper, he picked his way to a patch of boulders. He settled into a crevice and waited for the cub. He saw its silhouette approaching a moment later, walking quickly on its short legs—jerky and anxious and sometimes stumbling. Its head craned around in a panicky manner.

"Why are you following me?" Storm hissed from the shadows.

The cub stopped, peering into the crevice of rock. It sniffed the air. "You," it began timidly. Storm thought that it was male. "You carried me off the bridge."

"You may express your gratitude by leaving me alone," snapped Storm.

The cub hunkered down, tucked its tail, and lowered its ears—gestures almost pitifully conciliatory. "Thank you," it stammered. "Only, since you were behind me...I wondered if you might have seen my mother." He swallowed, almost overcome with anxiety. "She fell right at the beginning. Everyone was shoving, and they pushed her off the edge, but we weren't very high, and I saw her land. I think she was alright. I thought she would...would come at the end."

Storm felt as though he'd dropped from a warm, sunny cliff into a dark, icy pool. "Your...mother."

"Yes, did you see her on the trail?"

"No." *No, no, no, no, no...*

The cub deflated against the ground. He looked very small. "She made me promise to keep going," he whispered. "No matter what happened."

Storm darted out of the crevice around the crumpled cub. He dashed through the sea of ferryshaft, not caring if he stepped on legs or tails. He ran until he reached the comforting tangle of boulders at the back of the cave. He located a high shelf of rock along the back wall and jumped up. Storm tucked himself out of sight, flipped his tail over his face, and tried to forget the world.

Valla's lungs were already starting to burn when she reached the mouth of the tunnel where Sauny had disappeared. *We're going to die in here. We're going to die in here...* But at least they would not die in the dark. Valla pushed her head into the tunnel and saw the line of acriss illuminating it clearly for three or four lengths before the tunnel took a sharp upward turn, and the trail of tiny jellyfish veered out of sight. Sauny was nowhere to be seen.

Even in her fear and air-hunger, Valla could not help marveling at the acriss. She'd never seen or heard of acriss behaving in such a way. Valla suspected that Sauny had intended to explore the tunnel and return with news of whatever she found. *But if it goes much farther without reaching air, this is a one-way trip.*

The tunnel *might* reach air, of course. Their current cave obviously had a leak, which was why it had filled with water. If they found an airtight cave, they would not have this problem. Valla clambered inside the tunnel. Acriss swirled around her as she disturbed them with her passage. She thought that Sauny must have done the same, yet they had reformed behind her. Odd.

Valla reached the curve in the tunnel and looked up. She let out an involuntary gasp of bubbles as she saw the high column of water overhead, and, at the top, the unmistakable flat mirror of a surface. Sauny was treading water up there, and the acriss swarmed in bright clouds, driven by the movement of her legs. Even as Valla struggled upward, she saw Sauny's front half disappear and realized that there was a way to get out of the water.

We're going to live!

Valla's head broke the surface. She gulped in a dizzy breath of air, her head spinning. Small cave. Not flooded. A few telshees. Sauny panting beside her, half out of the water.

"Well, that—" began Valla, but Sauny made a choking noise, and she stopped.

Valla looked at her friend. Sauny had frozen on the edge of the pool. She was staring at the telshees. Valla followed her gaze. She noticed an odd smell in the room—almost like death. One of the telshees was coming towards them. It looked fish-belly pale, its fur almost transparent. Its eyes were not blue, but green. Green as the acriss…with the same kind of luminescence.

Valla's mouth went dry. She was just drawing a frantic breath to dive back into the water, when the lishty spoke. "Hello," it said. "I have been Kos."

9

Boundaries

Storm woke to a low, sustained growl. His eyes snapped open, and his brain did a scrambling assessment. *Don't move*, he reminded himself. *You're on a narrow ledge.* Storm looked out over the Great Cave in the weak morning light. It was still raining outside, but lazily. A stiff wind whipped the rain in misty droplets around the cave and moaned in the rock chinks, but it was nothing like the predatory howl of the Volontaro the night before.

Storm heard the growl again, followed by a hiss. He looked directly down from his perch and saw the cub. It had backed into a corner of rock just beneath him. It was bristling hugely, tiny ears flat to its head, lips peeled back in a snarl. Five young ferryshaft foals had cornered it and were circling cautiously, muttering and giggling to each other.

"Is it really a creasia?" Storm heard one foal say.

"I haven't heard it talk."

"It can't be a creasia! They're never so small. It's an oory, right? It must be an oory. Can you eat an oory?"

"I think so."

"Leave it alone," said Storm from on high.

The clique glanced about, startled, until one looked up and saw him. "It's Vearil!" breathed the foal. "The ghost spawn!"

Is that what they're calling me now? "Leave it alone," repeated Storm.

"I'm not an oory," said the cub in a voice so tiny that Storm felt certain he'd made his position more precarious rather than less.

The clique's attention shifted back to the cub. "It talks! Oories don't talk. But it can't be a creasia; it's too small."

The youngest of the foals, surely not even a year old, piped up. "My dad says milk-fed cubs are delicious." Everyone looked at him, and he looked suddenly anxious. "But I wasn't supposed to tell."

The clique's apparent leader, probably a two-year-old, whirled on the cub, eyes bright. "Are you a milk-fed cub?" he wheedled, inching nearer.

The cub responded by bristling and giving a hiss that sounded more terrified than aggressive. Storm dropped from the ledge, scattering the clique. "I said leave it!" he barked.

They were already gone, racing into the boulders that jumbled the back of the cave. Storm turned to the cub. "Why are you still here?" he demanded.

The cub lowered its eyes and licked its lips. "I still can't find my mother."

And you never will. "Don't you have a father?" *No, don't answer that. I don't want to know.* "Any other relatives?"

The cub looked at the ground. Its voice came in a hesitant mumble. "We were low-ranking in our den. I don't think… I don't know if they would want me…"

"Well, *try*," said Storm impatiently. "There must be cats over there who would know how to help you. I don't. Now get out of here before some other ferryshaft decides that 'milk-fed cubs are delicious.' This is *our* side of the cave."

The cub looked at him, uncomprehending, and Storm realized that he couldn't possibly be a year old. *Do creasia have cubs in spring? He can't be any older than that.* Which meant that this cub had never been through a Volontaro before, never visited the Great Cave. He'd probably never seen a ferryshaft until last night.

Last night… The scene on the trail played over and over in Storm's head with cringe-inducing clarity. Had the creasia been male? Female? He had no idea. His memory of the voice was genderless. *It wasn't his mother,* Storm told himself stubbornly. *She probably died when she fell the first time…or was injured and drowned in the mazes.* But he kept seeing the creasia's desperate eyes, illuminated by flashes of lightning. Was it his imagination, or did the cub's eyes look the same?

No. This is not my fault. This is not my problem. Wasn't Valla orphaned in the last Volontaro? It must happen to creasia, too. Somehow, they deal with it.

The cub's timid voice broke into his thoughts. "You saved me."

No, that is not what happened. I should just tell him. Then he'll leave. "I—"

"Storm!"

Storm turned in exasperation. Kelsy had come trotting out of the tangle of boulders. "I thought I saw you come in last night."

Storm drew a deep breath. *But if not for the stupid cub, you'd never have found me.* "What do you want?"

Kelsy's eyes had shifted to the cub. He looked confused. "We're not supposed to hunt creasia in the Great Cave, although if you found it on our side…"

"I'm not hunting it," snapped Storm. "Just ignore it, please." *Ignore it, and maybe it will go away.*

To his relief, Kelsy did. "There's a meeting this morning. I was hoping you would come."

Storm felt cross and reckless. He opened his mouth to say no. Instead, he heard himself say, "Certainly. I have thought of some questions I would like to ask." *Like how to get rid of cubs that I may have orphaned by accident.*

Kelsy peered at him. "Was it difficult, getting across the bridge? It looked impassable."

"Oh, you know me," said Storm blithely. "I walk on air. Where is this conference of yours?"

Kelsy was silent a moment. Storm could tell that Kelsy did not like his tone. "You're not planning on attacking anyone, are you?"

"Not unless they attack me first."

"Are you bringing that cub to threaten it? Because I don't think that's a good idea."

"What cub?" said Storm.

Kelsy sighed. "This way."

Storm did not look back to see whether the cub was following. He decided that completely ignoring it would be the best tactic. *I can't really ask anyone about it.* The obvious solution was to snap its back with one shake. How could he admit that Vearil, ghost spawn, doom of cats, could not bring himself to do this? *I* will *do it if he keeps following me. But this conference will be near the boundary line, I expect, and that will give him a chance to see his side of the cave. He probably just doesn't know where to go.*

The conference did, indeed, appear to be near the boundary line—not the current line, but the old one, directly under the large stone with the telshee character. Storm could read it now: Boundary. *How convenient. We meet on what is now creasia territory, but it used to be neutral ground.*

No one challenged them as they splashed through the little stream, stopping briefly to drink. The ground was uneven, with boulders strewn everywhere. Storm could see that they were headed towards the boundary stone, but he didn't see the animals underneath it until they were almost on top of them. Arcove was sitting at the base of the great outcropping of rock, looking out towards the swirling mist of rain at the cave's mouth. Roup lay beside him, and Halvery was pacing a few lengths away. Sharmel and Ariand sat a little further off towards the creasia side, chatting to each other. There were five other creasia that Storm did not recognize. Charder was there, along with Pathar, and four elder ferryshaft—two female and two male. Storm could not remember their names. They were all talking in low voices, but stopped abruptly when they saw Storm and Kelsy.

Kelsy smiled madly, addressing himself to Arcove. "Well, you said you wanted to see him."

Arcove half stood. Everyone looked some shade of startled or horrified. Storm realized that this particular venue had not been Arcove's idea.

Storm shot a sidelong glance at Kelsy. *Well, you've still got nerve.*

Kelsy pretended not to see their expressions and continued addressing himself to Arcove. "He's not that easy to corner. If you don't want to see him, I'm sure he'll be happy to go away."

Arcove sat slowly back down, his eyes fixed on Storm—unreadable. "Stay," he said. The talking slowly resumed. Storm realized that the animals he did not know were weather experts like Pathar—a rare gift, allowing them to sense minute changes before others sensed them. They were discussing why the storm had come up so suddenly and why they'd failed to identify the danger until such a late stage.

Kelsy went forward to join the group. Storm did not, although he stayed near enough to catch snippets of the conversation. Arcove was saying nothing, just listening. Roup looked asleep, but Storm saw the slit of one golden eye open, watching.

"What I'd like to know," said Storm loudly, "is why this rock in the middle of the cave says 'Boundary,' but we ferryshaft are kept on the far side of the stream, in an area that is considerably smaller. Why, I wonder, is that?"

The group went dead quiet again. Storm wasn't sure which they found more shocking—his words or the revelation that he could read. "You stay over there because that's where we put you," snapped Halvery. Storm glanced at him. Halvery's hackles had risen, and his dark eyes looked dangerous.

Storm thought that it would be easy to bait him into a chase, but he wanted to say something more. He turned his full attention to Arcove. "My sister is alive; thank you for asking. She is learning all kinds of things in Syriot. Keesha is also well. He has not forgotten you. In fact, he seems to think of little else."

In the stillness, Storm could hear the wind keening among the rocks outside and the distant gurgle of the stream. Arcove's voice came at last, a murmur lower than the wind. "Are you warning me or threatening me?"

Storm matched his tone. "What do you think?"

"Because," said Arcove, as though Storm had not spoken, "I do not respond well to threats."

"Really? I was hoping you would."

Kelsy looked ready to eviscerate him. "Storm!" he hissed.

"I was thinking," continued Storm. "This cave makes good shelter, but it would be a terrible place to get trapped. That bridge could blow away at any moment. One day it will surely just crumble. There's no approach from the cliff. Trapped up here… After we had all finished fighting and eating each other, we'd die. Did our ancestors never think of that?"

Arcove had risen and paced slowly forward. Storm did not back away.

"I think they did," he continued. "I think there's another way into and out of the Great Cave—a tunnel somewhere among the rocks. But you'll never use it, will you? Not unless you're desperate. Because it goes through Syriot. Who wrote that word on the stone, I wonder? I think it was a telshee—maybe one of those enormous males, sleeping now in the Dreaming Sea."

Arcove was looking directly down at him. Storm stared into his implacable, green eyes. "How badly do you want to die, Storm?"

"You won't kill me," said Storm with confidence. "You keep your word, don't you? And besides, you're in a telshee cave, and you know it, and it scares you—at least, it should."

Halvery was growling, and now he shot forward.

"Don't," said Arcove and Halvery checked, almost on top of Storm.

Storm kept his eyes on Arcove. "When you're ready to talk to me like an equal, I'll be ready to listen. Maybe. If Syra-lay hasn't killed you by then."

He turned and forced himself to walk, without hurrying, away from the boundary stone.

10

Follow

Storm headed for the bridge. There might be flooding outside, but he could deal with it. He'd rather deal with it than with anything in here. He'd just crossed the stream that marked the current boundary and started up the rise towards the sandy portion of the cave, when a furious snarling and hissing broke out behind him.

Storm turned to see an older adult ferryshaft grabbing at, and narrowly missing, the cub. The tiny cat had instinctively flipped onto its back and flailed with all four clawed feet. It was a ridiculous defense, but it had the desired effect of making his antagonist withdraw for a moment. However, the ferryshaft was only deterred for an instant. He circled quickly, the cub on its back, flipping awkwardly this way and that to keep the predator in sight. The contest would be over in a matter of heartbeats.

All of the pent up energy of his showdown with Arcove came boiling to the surface and Storm gave a snarl that was more like a roar. "Leave—it—alone!"

The adult ferryshaft was so surprised that he sat down. He looked at Storm. A dozen other heads turned in their direction.

Storm came forward, seized the unresisting cub, and hurled it along his intended path towards the bridge. "That is mine! I am saving it for later! If anyone else touches it, I will rip out their guts and feed them to telshees. Do you understand?"

"I—I didn't know," began the adult.

"Do you understand?!" repeated Storm.

"Yes."

Everyone in earshot understood. They were all staring. Storm whirled away, conscious that a crowd was forming, and stalked towards the bridge. Out of the corner of his eye, he saw the cub pick itself up and fall in behind him. This part of the cave was crowded, but the ferryshaft made way for him. Storm avoided their faces. He didn't want to recognize anyone. As he started onto the bridge in the misty rain, he heard the rumble of talking begin.

Oh, I have given them something for this evening. What will they say about me? Vearil, the bad luck omen. Vearil, who leaves the herd for a season and only returns out of the heart of the worst Volontaro in a generation. Vearil, who attends creasia conferences and returns with a cub for an evening snack.

Storm almost giggled. He was starting to feel shaky. *There were a lot of ferryshaft at that conference. Someone will repeat what I said to Arcove. What will they think of that?*

Storm shook himself. *They'll think what they think. They'll say what they say. What did Kelsy tell me last year? That I'd be a legend?*

He'd already crossed the bridge and gotten halfway down the trail, when he came out of his thoughts enough to remember the cub. Storm looked back. It was still following, although it had lost some ground. It already looked winded and was beginning to pant.

Euphoria vanished. Am *I going to eat it?*

The cub reached him and flopped down at his feet. Storm heard himself say, "What's your name?"

"Teek," he panted. "My mother—said—it wasn't—proper—to name—"

I don't want to hear about your mother. "Do you know how to hunt, Teek?"

The cub looked at him in surprise. "I— I ate a mouse once," he ventured. "But Mother killed it."

Storm was horrified. "You mean you're not even—" *Of course. Of course he isn't. He may not live no matter what I do.* It was almost a relief.

Teek leaned against his leg. Storm pulled away. "You could still go back to the cave," he said. "You don't look like you can keep up with me."

"I can," said Teek. "They won't want me back in the cave. I know they won't. And I'm afraid of the black cat."

Storm looked at him curiously. "The black cat... Arcove?"

"No, not him. The other one." Teek shivered. "He likes to hurt rogue cubs."

Storm was lost. "What's his name?"

"I don't remember." Teek was trembling—whether from fear or exhaustion, Storm couldn't tell.

Send him back. Send him back while he still has the strength to reach his own kind. "I have to go now," said Storm. "You should go find your mother's friends. I'm sure she had some."

"She didn't."

Storm stepped away from him and continued at an even trot down the path. *He'll never keep up. All I have to do is behave normally, and he'll go away.*

The trail ahead looked suddenly familiar. The Volontaro had washed away the dark stains, the scratches in the crumbling stone, the grisly matted blood and meat... But Storm recognized the spot anyway, as though a ghost looked on and screamed, "Look! Look!"

Storm moved a little faster.

Much later, after an exhausting day of struggling through mud and water over slick rock, Storm settled down in a cave to sleep. Nothing stirred in the twilight outside—not even birds or small animals. Storm wondered where the lowland curbs went in such a maelstrom. He wondered whether the highland curbs were alright.

The boulder mazes he'd traversed bore little resemblance to those he remembered. Storm had found his way by following the cliffs, by recognizing a canyon here, the outline of a rock there, but in between was chaos. He tried several times to find his way to the top of the cliffs, but on each occasion, he returned to the bottom after only a brief effort. Too many trails had washed away, and the cliff face was unstable. Now and then, he heard the distant, but still frightening, sound of a rockslide.

Give it a few days to settle. Then I can start learning my way again. He felt certain that the boulder mazes would also be more recognizable and more passable in a few days. *There's a reason why the herd stays in the Great Cave for a bit longer.* Parts of the mazes were still flooded. Sediment and lose rock had buried other sections. Time and again, he had to backtrack because slot canyons were blocked or the low places were too flooded or unstable.

Storm had thought that one determined day's journey would see him back to Eyal's den, but he was forced to admit that it would take two, possibly three. In the twilight, he lay gnawing on a freshly dead fish he'd found in one of the pools, listening to the whistle of the wind.

Storm had not seen the creasia cub since morning, and he tried not to think about him. *He got discouraged and went back to the Great Cave. As he should. Encouraging him would have been cruel.*

You're a fine one to talk of cruelty, said another voice in his head, but Storm ignored it. He should have fallen asleep easily after such a long day, but he didn't. The moon rose. Every time Storm began to drift off, the wind seemed to morph into voices, muttering just beyond his comprehension. At last, exhausted, he slept.

Storm dreamed of wind and blood and desperate eyes illuminated by lightning. The wind whispered, *"You killed me when I'd done you no harm, and you left my cub to die alone. You killed a friendless mother...and her little one...and we will be here each time you close your eyes...Vearil."*

Storm twitched awake. He was panting. He saw silhouettes outside and realized that it was almost dawn. Storm struggled to his feet. "Teek!"

He bounded out of the cave, shaking sleep from his head. *You're mad,* he told himself, but he shouted again, "Teek!"

He followed you. You know he did. He was never going to stop. In spite of his own thoughts, Storm was astonished when he heard a high, frantic mew.

"Teek!"

The sound came again—hoarse and fragile. Storm followed it, retracing his steps from the day before. He hadn't gone far when he reached a fin of rock, bounded by steeper slopes. Storm had cleared it in a single jump on his first journey. Teek lay at the bottom on the far side.

Storm jumped down beside him. The cub tried to stand, but failed. His paws were bleeding, and he seemed exceedingly weak.

"You came all that way?" muttered Storm.

Teek didn't answer. He was breathing hard. Storm realized that Teek had *not* been sleeping at the base of the rock. He'd been following all night, and he was still trying—bloody and too weak to stand. Storm thought of all he'd been through the previous day—the pools he'd swum, the slopes he'd climbed, the knee-deep mud and shale. The cub had both remarkable tracking skills and remarkable tenacity. But he was at the end of his strength now. Storm saw blood-flecked foam at the corners of his mouth.

Gently, he picked Teek up by the scruff, as he'd seen oories and foxes carry their babies. Teek went completely limp, and Storm's heart dropped into his stomach. He put the cub down again, expecting to find a corpse, but Teek roused himself and raised his head to lick Storm's muzzle. Storm picked him up again, and again the cub went limp. *A natural response?* It certainly made him easier to carry.

Storm gave a great bound and cleared the fin of rock once more. He trotted back through the mud and pools to the cave where he'd spent the night. *You almost made it,* he thought. *It was just that last hurdle you couldn't clear.*

He put Teek down. The cub lay on his side, eyes closed, breathing ragged. Storm went out and hunted around the pools until he found another fish. He returned and laid it beside Teek. It was almost as big as the cub. Teek raised his head and sniffed. He licked at the fish.

Storm thought of something. "Did you drink the water in the pools?"

Teek raised filmy eyes. "Yes…" he croaked.

Storm shook his head. "It's brackish from the Volontaro. We passed one clean stream, but everything else is half sea water."

Teek's eyes slid shut. "I know. Just…so thirsty."

Storm tore a chunk out of the fish. Blood pooled in the fish's body. "Drink," he commanded.

Teek hesitated, then lapped at the blood. After a moment, he pushed himself up on his forepaws and took a bite of the rubbery flesh. It seemed to take him forever to chew it. Storm wondered whether he had all of his teeth.

"I don't have any milk for you," said Storm miserably.

Teek said nothing. He swallowed the mouthful of fish. Then he tottered up and took a couple of steps to lean against Storm's flank. Storm didn't know what to do, so he lay down. Teek curled into the crook of his body—bedraggled, but warm. Storm lay there while the sun came up and Teek slept with his small head on Storm's foreleg. After a while, Storm dropped his own head. He dozed, and his dreams were peaceful.

11

Cubs and Pups

"You want us to do…*what?*"

"Just let him stay here for a little while," said Storm, trying to ignore Eyal's horrified stare. They were standing in the rocks near the entrance to the long tunnel that led, after many branches, down to the curbs' den. Teek lay at Storm's feet with his head on his paws, apparently unconcerned.

"Just…until he's old enough to fend for himself," said Storm. Eyal's mouth hung open.

"You're the one who wanted me to socialize," Storm muttered.

"I sent you to find out what happened to your friends in the herd!" exploded Eyal. "And you come back with a creasia cub?"

"You should be happy I came back at all," snapped Storm. "You left me right before the worst Volontaro in—"

"I know, I know," muttered Eyal. "We thought we'd killed you. We would have howled for you if we hadn't been so busy trying not to drown. The tide rose in the caves… It was bad. We lost Fael. And on top of everything else—"

"Eyal?" One of the other curbs had come to the den entrance. He seemed to forget whatever he'd been going to say—staring at Teek.

"Not now," growled Eyal.

"Teek wasn't quite weaned, and now his mother is gone," persisted Storm. "He drank a little of the brackish water in the mazes two days ago. He was vomiting yesterday, but he seems a little better today. I found fresh water for him, and I gave him some fish, but I don't know if that's right. What should I feed him?"

Eyal rolled his eyes. "Better ask what you should feed him *to.*"

"If you're not going to help—"

Eyal looked down at the cub. "Open your mouth, cat."

Teek looked at him, round-eyed. "Go on," said Storm.

Teek obeyed.

Eyal bent to look into Teek's mouth. "Milk teeth," he pronounced. "You can see the permanent ones are coming in, though. Did you say he's 'not quite weaned'? More like 'not at all weaned.' This one is hardly a season old, Storm."

Storm said nothing.

Teek cut his eyes at him, tiny jaws still agape. "You can close your mouth," said Storm.

Eyal nosed the cub around roughly. "Underfed. Sickly. He was either born very late in the season, or he's a runt; he shouldn't be so small this late in the year." Eyal looked at Storm. "Creasia cubs have a high death rate. They're very competitive. This one probably wasn't going to survive."

Teek looked at the ground.

"That sounds a lot like what the herd told my mother." Storm's eyes locked with Eyal's over Teek's head.

Eyal sighed and turned away. "Curbs have no particular quarrel with creasia. I won't kill it, and I can make sure my pack doesn't kill it, but I can't vouch for your telshee friends. And as for anyone else taking care of it—"

"That's fine," interrupted Storm. *He probably won't survive anyway. Even Eyal thinks so.*

They started towards the mouth of the cave, Teek close on his heels. "I heard a story about a creasia who lived with ferryshaft once," said Eyal over his shoulder. "I don't think it turned out very well."

Roup. Storm wished suddenly that he hadn't been so rude at the conference. *Maybe I could have asked him what to do.*

Could you? mocked a voice in his head. *Could Vearil Ela-ferry, doom of cats, have asked that?*

No, thought Storm, *probably not.*

"We had extra excitement during the storm," continued Eyal, "because Kiera birthed her pups."

Storm was astonished. "I didn't even realize she was pregnant!"

He could hear the smile in Eyal's voice as they proceeded down the dark, twisting passage. "Curbs don't stay pregnant for long, and we don't give birth in quite the same way as ferryshaft. You'll see. We were afraid she'd lose the pups with all the scrambling and swimming, and she may have lost a few, but three of them are secure."

Storm was baffled. *How could you not know how many she lost?* "So you were all carrying them as you—?"

Eyal laughed aloud this time. "Wait and see."

Teek crowded close against Storm's legs in the darkness. When they got to the steep part, Storm picked the cub up by the scruff and carried him. When the path finally evened out, and they began to glimpse weak acriss light, Storm stopped and set Teek on his feet again. Eyal watched and shook his head. "You are placing yourself in the path of so much trouble, my friend."

"And nothing else I've done has caused me trouble," quipped Storm.

"Maybe it is your nature. Maybe you cannot help yourself."

"Maybe."

The curb who'd tried to speak to them at the den's mouth was waiting by the stream that ran through the cave. The normally gently-flowing water gushed at a furious rate, and it was twice as wide as Storm remembered. "The telshee Shaw came to us this morning," he said to Storm. "She was distraught to learn that you were not here. I returned to reassure her, and she's waiting for you now at our nest."

"Well, I'm alive," said Storm, "no thanks to any of you." *And hardly thanks to myself.*

Eyal made no comment as they followed the stream to the little cluster of rocks where Kiera was apparently keeping her babies. The pack was resting in and around the rocks. They looked exhausted. Storm caught sight of Shaw hovering on the edge of the pack. The telshee grew completely still when she saw them. Her eyes locked on Teek. *Here we go.*

"What—is—that?"

Storm stepped in front of her. Teek had wisely chosen to stand directly underneath him, peering out between his front legs. "Why, yes, I survived the Volontaro. Alone. Would you like to know how I did it? Of course you would—"

"I said, what is—"

"No? Well, if you don't want to hear the story, I am anxious to see these new curb puppies. Please get out of my way."

Shaw just stared as Storm moved around her and into the rocks. He nearly tripped on Teek, but he pretended not to notice.

Kiera lay in a scant nest of tan and brindle fur. "You must think us very poor parents," she said when she saw Storm. "But our magnificent nest of seal fur and bird down washed away, and we must make do with our own fur."

Storm laughed. "Ferryshaft don't nest at all. I'm certain that I was born on the hard ground." He hesitated, not wanting to be rude. Everyone looked so proud. "Where are the puppies?"

Kiera smiled. "You are a special ferryshaft, Storm, for us to show you such things—"

She stopped abruptly as she caught sight of Teek, peeking from between Storm's legs.

"It's alright," said Eyal. "The creasia cub is with Storm. It's very young. Just ignore it."

Kiera's gaze shifted to Eyal's face. "Our pack is becoming very strange."

"Indeed," said Eyal dryly. "But we will soon have a bigger pack. Let Storm see. We owe him our home and safety."

Kiera rolled onto her back, and Maoli, who'd been sitting quietly beside her, nosed at the fur on her lower belly. "Look," she said softly.

Storm bent, puzzled and fascinated. What he'd taken for the swollen teats of a nursing mother were actually tiny nubs no bigger than the tip of Teek's nose, yet recognizably distinct creatures. They had stubby, ill-formed limbs and blobby heads with just the suggestion of a darkness where the eyes should be. They squirmed now and then in a disturbing display of independence, yet their tiny mouths were each locked around a teat in a way that seemed irreversible.

Storm stared, open-mouthed. "What—? How—?"

"I told you curbs are very odd," said Shaw from high overhead. She seemed to have found her voice, and Storm was relieved to hear amusement. *She's not too angry about Teek to say, "I told you so."*

Kiera rolled back over. "Our babies are born after only a brief period inside us," she explained. "We often do not even realize that we are pregnant, and sometimes we don't realize when they are born, although an experienced mother will know. They must crawl through our fur and attach themselves to a teat. There are usually more pups than teats, and the weak or the slow do not survive. I have four teats, so I am sorry that a fourth pup did not manage to latch on. They were born during the storm, so I was climbing and swimming. I'm a little surprised that any managed to latch on at all.

"We try to avoid too much activity when the pups are bound to us," said Maoli. "The most dangerous time comes when they are a little bigger and heavier. They still need to be latched on to survive, but they're heavy enough to fall off. At that point, a mother needs a pack to feed her. It doesn't last long. After a short while, they drop off, and then they nurse the same as any ferryshaft foal until they are weaned."

"Lowland curbs are born much as ours are," said Eyal, "but they have a pouch—a flap of skin that keeps the pups from falling off. Their females can run and hunt during all stages of the process, so they do not need a den to bear their young. They only have one or two pups at a time, but they are not as vulnerable as we are. It is probably the reason that they are driving us to extinction."

"Storm?"

Storm recognized the voice. "Sauny?" He turned and moved quickly out of the sheltering rocks, Teek scampering after him. Storm caught sight of Valla's cream and honey-colored fur down near the water and Sauny's smaller, red-gold form beside her.

Shaw had already circled the rocks and started towards them. "Valla, Sauny…I am relieved to see you."

Storm frowned at Shaw. "You mean you didn't know where they were?"

Shaw looked uncomfortable. "Water rose very quickly in the caves, Storm. Many of us were separated. I'm still looking for three of my daughters. They're probably just—"

"Your daughters are telshees!" exploded Storm. "We're ferryshaft, Shaw! We can't hold our breaths for so long—"

"We're alright," interrupted Valla. Storm had reached her, and they sniffed noses. She had a tense, expectant expression. "We found—"

"An air pocket," interrupted Sauny. "We found an air pocket, and we stayed there until the end of the storm."

Valla shot her an odd look. Sauny had a defiant expression, but she seemed more engaged than Storm could remember since the battle by the lake. "It…sounds like quite an adventure," he offered, willing to dismiss even Shaw's negligence for a chance to see Sauny excited about something.

"Not really." She didn't quite meet his eyes. Then her ears stood straight up. "What's *that?*"

Storm turned with a sigh. Teek was peering around his back legs.

"A snack," said Shaw cheerfully. "I don't think it's one of Arcove's, but we can pretend."

Valla was staring, too. "Storm, you…you brought a—"

Storm spoke quickly. "His name is Teek. He's an orphan. I saved his life by accident on the bridge, and for some reason, he thinks I'm his friend. Watch him for a moment while I have a word with Shaw." He looked down at Teek. "Stay here for a moment. I'll come back."

Teek looked like he wasn't going to obey, but then Shaw dropped her huge head to the ground directly in front of him and bared her formidable teeth. "If you put so much as a paw anywhere that you're not invited, I will devour you in a single gulp," she hissed.

Teek arched his back, his thin coat bristling. He turned sideways to Shaw in an effort to look bigger. What came out his mouth was more of a squeak than a hiss, but Storm still had to admire his courage. *Shaw could chew once and swallow, and there'd be nothing left of Teek but a little red on her whiskers. But does he run away? No. He stands there and hisses.*

Of course, answered a mocking voice in Storm's head. *He's a creasia—the fiercest land predator this island has ever known. His instincts are telling him that one day he'll be big enough to rip out Shaw's throat. He's practicing.*

"Stop it," snarled Storm. "There's no need for that."

"Oh, there obviously is," said Shaw without taking her eyes off the cub. "You don't seem able to control him. How do you know he's not a spy?"

"Because he isn't. Because he's hardly a season old. Just…come here for a moment."

Storm moved away among the rocks. Shaw followed with an angry snort. "Storm, I am disappointed in you."

"I know." *I am, too.*

"After everything we've told you about the creasia, after the way they've treated your herd, after all that we've suffered—"

Storm turned abruptly. "I think I killed his mother," he said in a miserable whisper.

Shaw looked unimpressed. "I fail to see how that—"

"On the trail up to the bridge over the Garu Vell, during the Volontaro…I killed a cat. She even asked me for help, and I—"

Shaw shook her head. "You don't owe them anything, Storm."

"I hear her ghost in my dreams." His voice came out smaller than he'd intended.

There was a moment of silence. Shaw's ruff settled a little. "Storm," she said gently, "female creasia go on raids, too. Think about that. Think about the last raid you watched and ask yourself whether those creatures deserve your pity. That cub—if he survives countless fights with other cats—will grow up to become one of those predators. Before the war, ferryshaft hunted creasia cubs every spring, because that is the one time in their lives when creasia are easy to kill. If you don't kill them then, you have to deal with them later."

Storm looked at the ground. "Teek probably won't survive. Everyone says so. He's a runt, and he wasn't even weaned. He trusts me. I don't know why, but he does. Can't you let him die comfortably instead of ripping him to pieces? Then maybe the ghost of his mother will be appeased."

There was another long silence. Storm could feel Shaw's eyes on him, but he did not raise his head. At last, she sighed. "Die comfortably? Alright. Provided he remains in the curbs' den cave, and he promises to be dead by spring."

"Shaw!"

"If he comes any farther into Syriot, you'll need to speak to Syra-lay. Do you really want to have this conversation with him?"

Storm considered. *Keesha hates Arcove, but I'm not sure he'd care about some random cub...not anymore.* He didn't say anything, though. *Shaw will be the next Syra-lay. She feels responsible for what could happen.* He wondered whether Coden and Keesha had had a conversation like this about Roup.

Shaw broke into his thoughts, "Why don't you go talk to your old mentor, Pathar, about this? I'd wager he'd have a few things to say about ferryshaft raising creasia."

Storm was surprised. "Pathar?"

"Yes…" Shaw's eyes had a nasty gleam. "Yes, talk to Pathar about it. He might even be able to give you some useful tips."

12

Friendly

Storm and Shaw emerged from the rocks to the unlikely sounds of giggling. Storm caught sight of Teek on the edge of the stream in the act of executing a half-flip. He came down with all four paws spread, tail fluffed, glancing about wildly. He began to lift one paw at a time, looking cautiously under each as though expecting to find something sinister. Valla and Sauny were standing to either side, along with a couple of the curbs.

"What on earth—?" began Storm.

Shaw did not volunteer a comment.

Storm trotted towards the stream. The giggling appeared to be coming from Valla and Sauny. Teek jumped straight up in the air, and Storm saw that he'd caught a small fish—hardly larger than a minnow. He danced around it as the fish flipped this way and that. He tried to follow it under his belly and did a somersault. Then he got distracted by his own tail and chased that instead for a moment. It was the most absurd "hunting" that Storm had ever seen.

Valla was laughing openly. Sauny looked like she was trying not to, but couldn't help herself. Storm sat down beside them. "You could just eat it," he said to Teek.

Teek looked up, eyes dilated, ears flat. "But it's not dead!" He leapt up again as the fish wriggled underneath him.

"So kill it," snickered Valla.

"How?"

She blinked. "You mean, you've never…?"

"He wasn't weaned," said Storm in a tired voice. "I think he'd eaten exactly one pre-killed mouse when I found him."

Teek caught the flipping fish under one paw. Storm saw that he didn't even have his claws extended. He took a deep breath, as though working up his nerve. "Do I have to?"

"A creasia who's never killed anything," said Valla in wonder. "Not even a minnow."

Sauny limped forward suddenly. She nosed under Teek's paw, lifted the little fish deftly, and tossed it back into the stream. "No, you don't have to."

Teek looked both relieved and disappointed.

"He has to learn to hunt sometime," said Storm.

"Not today," said Sauny. "He doesn't have to kill anything today." Storm watched her. He had been afraid that Sauny would see in Teek the source of her maiming, and maybe she had at first. *But you only need to spend a few moments with him before…*

Teek had become distracted by the twitching tip of his tail again. He flopped onto his side, swatting at it madly. *Before he does something like that.*

440

Storm said he would go and talk to Pathar, and he meant it. But, somehow, the days passed, and he did not go. The winter storms came and then the snow. Storm hunted with the curbs in the deep drifts or, just as often, in the icy tide pools along the beach. This winter was not the gentle chill that had visited last season. This was a winter of ice storms, of freezing rain and fog. Some days, they were reduced to bringing back seaweed from the edge of the tide pools, though Eyal warned Storm that he must drink plenty of water when eating it. Too much salt was poison.

Maoli gave birth shortly after the winter began. The curb puppies grew into fuzzy appendages beneath the bellies of their mothers and finally dropped off. The female curbs—lean and sharp-eyed—were able to rejoin the hunt.

Valla joined the pack, as well. The water in the Cave of Histories had grown so icy that she could not tolerate it for long, and the search for food had become more important than the search for knowledge.

Storm learned, with some dismay, that most of the telshees went to sleep for the winter or left the island for warmer seas. "It is an uncomfortable time of year," Ulya told them with a yawn. "If you could sleep through it or go somewhere else, wouldn't you?"

Storm was not sure whether Shaw had entered torpor or left the island, but he did not see her after the onset of the snows. He knew that she felt betrayed in the matter of Teek and was, perhaps, regretting her renewed involvement with land animals. Storm himself stayed away from the telshee caves for fear that Teek would follow him. The cub tried, with his every fiber, to obey Storm's instructions, but he was young, and he sometimes forgot.

Storm considered speaking to Keesha about Teek. If he could convince Keesha of Teek's harmlessness, he felt sure that Shaw would come around. He suggested the idea to Sauny, who had spent more time with Keesha than had Storm.

"Leave it alone, Storm," she told him. "Shaw is right about Syra-lay, no matter what the other telshees say. He's not ready to sleep forever. He'll wake one day, and then everything will change. Until he wakes, though, he won't involve himself. Just leave it alone."

Sauny had been surprisingly even-tempered since the Volontaro. She was sleeping less, but that might have been because there was no one to feed her. After a short period when Valla attempted to feed both of them, Sauny stopped accepting food from anyone else and declared that she'd either starve or learn to hunt again.

Storm feared that she would starve in truth, but she established a circuit of the tide pools near telshee caves, and, though she grew very lean, she did seem to be surviving. "Starfish don't run very fast," she told Storm, as they lay in the rocks near the curbs' nest one evening.

"But they taste horrible," piped up Teek.

"The lame can't be choosy," said Sauny.

"Why are you lame?" he asked.

Sauny went quite still. Storm held his breath. "Because I picked a fight with someone bigger than me," she told Teek.

"Did you win?" he asked.

Valla barked a laugh.

Sauny looked annoyed. "How could you think—?"

"Well, he could be dead," Valla pointed out.

Sauny rolled her eyes. "No, I didn't win. Although…sometimes I think surviving is winning."

Yes, thought Storm. *Sometimes surviving is the best kind of winning.*

On a day in early winter, Roup meandered down through a tumble of roots and boulders to a gem of a pool all-but-underground, with a beam of light streaming in overhead. The water was just cool enough to drink, though it had a mineral taste that some found unpleasant.

Roup still remembered the first time he'd seen this cave. He'd been predisposed to hate it, as he'd just learned that he and Arcove would not share a den. But Nadine had walked him down here—a pleasant walk, closer to the king's den than Roup had any right to expect—and introduced him to her daughter, Caraca.

Caraca was the smallest adult creasia that Roup had ever met—barely larger than an adolescent cub, with brindled brown and gray fur and eyes so dark they looked almost black. She was nine years old, yet she had not taken a mate or chosen a den. Instead, she'd claimed this little cave on the edge of her mother's territory. It was rumored that she'd kept a warren of rabbits alive in the cave, bringing them food until they'd become impervious to creasia presence and would gamble about her on the floor. When a Volontaro took them one year, she replaced them with oory cats—a practice that other creasia found even more unsettling because the little animals were so creasia-like, and yet without speech.

Caraca had innumerable observations on the coloration patterns from generation to generation of her rabbits and oories. In her way, she had a body of knowledge as great as that of her mother. However, Nadine's knowledge covered the bloodlines of the dens of Leeshwood, while Caraca's covered the smaller and more controlled world of her willing captives.

Before Arcove's rise to power, Caraca had expressed no interest in establishing a den or joining one. Many said—though not in Nadine's hearing—that Caraca had been spoiled. She occasionally ate at her father and mother's kills. She produced no cubs, nor did she help care for the cubs of others. If she'd been anyone else's daughter, she would have become a rogue and probably met a swift end.

Knowing what he knew now, Roup suspected that Caraca had never been deeply averse to joining a den. However, she feared that a den would curtail the strange projects that were her chief joy in life. In this, she was probably correct.

Nadine had introduced Roup and Caraca shortly after Arcove killed Ketch, the previous King. Caraca's immediate interest in

Roup had, he suspected, more to do with his unusual coat color than with anything else. However, Roup needed a mate to establish his legitimacy on Arcove's council, and Caraca could not go on forever being half a rogue. Nadine feared, naturally, that the new king would not be so indulgent of his dead rival's daughter.

Caraca would not have thrived in a large den, and Nadine assumed, correctly, that Roup would not want one. In the end, they got on well together. Caraca did not complain of Roup's frequent visits to Arcove's den. She seemed more puzzled by his strange partnership with the sterile female, Lyndi, who was his beta. Caraca and Lyndi were never quite sure who outranked whom. They had come near blows on more than one occasion. Mostly, they avoided each other.

However, on the whole, Roup was an ideal mate for Caraca. He took no other mates, allowing Caraca the unprecedented freedom of being a high-ranking female with no underlings to manage. Roup had a high tolerance for unconventional activities and was unperturbed by Caraca's oories, rabbits, and rock rats. Roup was so friendly with the rest of his small clutter that Caraca could easily share maintenance of her cubs with other females. When that failed, Caraca's cubs were always welcome in Arcove's den, and Roup would take them there himself if Caraca was too preoccupied to do so.

The bulk of Roup's clutter had moved long ago to a location beyond the edge of Arcove's territory just to preserve the look of the thing. However, Caraca still maintained a colony of rock rats in this cave. Roup found her among them on this particular day, lying quite still, and watching their activities along the edge of the wall.

The tamest of her oories—an unusual creature with white fur and pink eyes—had come with her. Caraca had nursed it along with her own cubs and tried in vain to teach it to talk. The oory could clearly understand some words, although its mind did not seem to function in the same way as a creasia's. Caraca called it Friendly. Creasia outside Roup's clutter quietly called it an abomination.

Caraca and Friendly both turned as Roup jumped down into the cave and padded towards them. Then Caraca turned back to the rock rats. Roup lay down beside her without saying anything.

After a moment, Caraca darted forward, startling even Friendly. She caught one of the rats in her teeth, and killed it with a single shake. Friendly came cautiously forward, and Caraca gave him the dead rat.

"What did that one do?" asked Roup.

Caraca yawned. The other rats had scattered. "It was afraid of me...more afraid than the others."

Roup cocked his head. "It seems to have been justified."

Caraca snorted. "I've been working on this colony for a while. It's gotten more and more docile."

"You think docility is in the blood?" asked Roup.

"I don't know," said Caraca. "But if I kill the shy or aggressive rats, the whole group seems to become more...friendly."

Friendly turned at the sound of his name and gave a conversational little mew. He reminded Roup in some ways of a perpetually young cub.

"Hmm..." Roup stared, unseeing, into the pool.

Caraca came up beside him and butted her head against his chest. "What's wrong?"

Roup sighed. "I just came from breaking up that three-day fight on the edge of Ariand's territory."

"They were still at it?" asked Caraca in surprise. "I thought it was just a scuffle between some four-year-olds."

"Oh, they'd gotten Mardin and Paslo involved by the time I stuck my nose in. Five of my cats and six of Ariand's. I think they were prepared to hunker down and make a winter-long siege. Ariand called me in to help. We finally got it sorted, but..."

"But what?"

"I'm still not sure what it was about. I couldn't get a straight answer out of anyone, but it was my impression that some of Ariand's cats said something disparaging about me or my clutter and it escalated. Everyone was too kind to tell me what was said, but I can guess."

Caraca considered. "Were they really Ariand's cats?"

Roup flicked his tail. "Two of them used to belong to Treace." He scowled. "Sometimes I think that breaking up his clutter was like dispersing the flies on a carcass. You get them off your food, but then the whole cave is full of them."

"What do you think they were saying?"

"Oh, the usual. My cubs are not my cubs. My clutter is Arcove's. My place on the council is unjustified."

"Those rumors have gone around before," said Caraca.

"I know," said Roup, "but then no one listened. No one cared, except a few trouble-makers."

"And now?"

"Now, when I come upon a conversation, everyone stops talking," said Roup. "When I surprise cats in the forest, they give me strange looks."

Caraca considered. "Are you sure it's not because they're saying something that they wouldn't want Arcove to hear?"

"That's possible. Does that make it any better?"

"I suppose not."

They were both silent a moment.

"Caraca, why *don't* my cubs look like me?"

She gave a nervous laugh.

Roup flicked his tail. "Oh, I'm not saying— I know they're mine. But if anyone knows how color is inherited, it's you."

Caraca smiled. Roup thought she was flattered and trying to hide it. "If you bred to one of your daughters, you might get a golden cub."

Roup gave her an odd look.

"I'm just telling you...and I could be wrong...but that's what I've seen with the oories and the rabbits. Unusual colors are hidden inside some of us...in the blood. But when the right two animals come together, you see it in the fur. There could be all kinds of colors hiding in other females, but I know for sure that they're hiding in your cubs…if that makes sense."

Roup licked his lips. "Sort of."

"Have you seen Mist and Percil's litter?"

Roup grinned. "I have." Mist was Roup's daughter, and Percil was Arcove's son. They'd established their first den a little to the north. One of the cubs was black with golden eyes.

"That's your blood," said Caraca. "But proof isn't what these gossips want. They want to make trouble." She thought for a moment. "Is Treace causing it?"

"Directly? Probably not. Indirectly? Almost certainly."

"Have you thought about fighting him yourself?"

"What would that accomplish? I already outrank him."

Caraca flipped her tail. "You could kill him."

Like one of your aggressive rats. Roup sighed. "I have thought about it." His mouth twitched up. "And wouldn't that shock Halvery?"

Caraca laughed.

"But Arcove spared Treace. And for me to pick a fight… It wouldn't look right." *And I don't even want to think about what Arcove would say.*

"Doesn't matter how it looks, so long as it works," said Caraca. "Everyone knows you don't get along with Treace." She thought for a moment. "But it might not work. The problem might already be bigger than that. Why don't you go talk to my mother? She's been mate to three kings. I'm sure she'll have a few ideas."

13

Instinct and Reason

Storm taught Teek to stalk mice and rabbits on the edge of the boulder mazes. He was wary of taking the cub too far from the caves. *What would I do if we met a creasia clutter?*

But they saw no sign of creasia. The herd passed twice in the vicinity of the curbs' den, and each time Storm kept Teek away until they were gone. It was just as well, because the ferryshaft herd left no food in its wake. Even the ground beneath the snow was scraped clean. Storm wondered what it must be like for foals born two springs ago. Their first winter had been mild. This one must come as a cruel shock.

Teek slept curled in the crook of Storm's body. Storm tried, on several occasions, to get him to sleep with the pile of curb puppies, but he always came creeping back. Like the curbs, Teek seemed most alert in the early morning and late evening. Storm was hunting with the pack, so he adjusted his sleep schedule to fit theirs.

On sunny days, Teek would beg to be allowed to sleep on the warm stone outside. The curbs were leery of this, afraid to be caught away from their nest when their pups were still small. Storm, however, began making tentative forays above ground during daylight. He missed the mazes and the cliffs. Little-by-little, he began to reacquaint himself with his old haunts, including the sheep trails. Teek came right along behind him. A voice in Storm's head whispered that, if Teek were ever to lead a creasia clutter, he would prove a deadly opponent. *But, he'll be too big and too heavy to run on sheep trails by then,* Storm reasoned.

On rare days when the sky was cloudless, Storm and Teek would find a rocky ledge where they could stretch out, sun their bellies, and dream the day away. Occasionally, Teek would twitch and whimper in his sleep. Once, he lashed out with a clawed paw. Teek's claws were still just tiny pricks of pain, but the event reminded Storm of what they would become. For a long time, he could not get Teek to tell him the nature of his nightmares. He was afraid to probe too deeply. *What if it's the ghost of his mother... showing him how she died?*

But one day, still dreaming, Teek whimpered, "The black cat, the black cat…" and woke with a gasp. Then Storm remembered what Teek had said that first day when he'd followed Storm from the Great Cave.

"Who is the black cat?"

Teek rose and curled up against Storm's flank. He was bigger now than he'd been at the start of winter—still short-legged, but less bony, closer to the size of an oory than a rabbit. When he was at peace, he sometimes made a throbbing noise. Storm had never heard anything like it before, but he'd come to associate it with comfort. Teek tucked his head against Storm's side and began to make the noise, as if trying to reassure himself.

Storm tried again. "What did the black cat do, Teek? What did you see?"

After a moment, Teek muttered. "I was exploring away from my den...not very far...I don't remember. It's like a dream."

Storm washed the top of Teek's head the way that he'd seen curb mothers groom their puppies. After a moment, Teek said. "They'd caught a rogue cub. Older than me… And they tore open his belly, and they put snakes in."

Storm was mystified. "Who are 'they'?"

"The black cat," whispered Teek, "and another cat and…" He struggled for a moment. "Curbs. There were curbs. One said, 'You have to give it the blood of its prey.'"

"Snakes?" echoed Storm. "Like the black snakes near the river…?"

Teek tucked his head again. "I don't want to talk about it."

Storm thought for a moment. "Teek, who was your commanding officer? The highest ranking cat in your part of the wood. Do you know?"

Teek was silent a moment. "I think his name was Treace."

Nadine was feeding at a kill when Roup arrived, and she graciously invited him to join her. Several hungry-looking females and adolescents were hanging around nearby, but Nadine took her time as befitted her rank. She listened as Roup spoke, pitching his voice for her ears alone. He'd finished and was tearing a few bites off the deer's flank, when Arcove joined them. "Well, I think a lot of cats will be hungry this winter, but I don't think we'll have mass starvation. If we manage the game perfectly and don't have many cubs this spring, I think next winter will be easier."

Roup glanced at him sidelong. He knew Arcove had been preoccupied with the deer-count, the cub-count, and their implications. He felt disloyal for raising another issue.

"I'm glad to hear it," said Nadine. "Roup was just telling me that there's been a lot of fighting lately between the males."

"He's not wrong," said Arcove. "Halvery broke up a serious fight just before I left. If they would challenge each other to single combat as is traditional, we wouldn't have to get involved. But several dozen cats were quarreling over a kill, and cubs were on the ground in the middle of it. One three-year-old was already dead, and two others had wounds they can't afford. Everyone is hungry, and it's stirring up tempers."

"I think *Treace* is stirring up tempers," muttered Roup. "How many of the cats fighting were previously under his command?"

Arcove sighed. "A few."

"I want to hear what Nadine thinks," said Roup. "She's been doing this longer than we have."

Nadine smiled. "Ah, Roup. Always the sweet one."

Arcove gave a rumbling chuckle. "You could have had him in your den."

"I know. It is such a shame that you needed him on the council."

Roup felt slightly embarrassed. "Maybe we should give the rest of your den-mates a chance to eat?"

"They are getting impatient, aren't they?" said Nadine. "Let's go talk where it's warm. We might as well be comfortable…because neither of you will like what I have to say."

Roup followed, wondering, as she led the way through the trees, along a trampled path between drifts of snow, to a bend of Smoky Branch. Nadine turned at last and looked at Arcove amid the curling steam. "I can't tell you what to do, but I can tell you what your predecessors would have done. They would have killed Treace, but not *just* Treace."

Arcove growled. "Oh, I'm sure."

"Ketch would have taken a clutter over there and slaughtered every male in that den and anyone else who was unwise enough to raise a paw. Masaran would have made the officers fight him one-by-one and *then* killed their cubs."

Arcove opened his mouth, but Nadine continued.

"This would have provoked a brief, but bloody war. Some of Treace's cats would have fought back. Perhaps they would even have won. Here's the important thing: they would have fought. We are creatures of struggle, Arcove. Creasia are born to fight. We fought with the ferryshaft for as long as anyone can remember. We fought with the telshees. When we weren't fighting with them, we fought with each other.

"You gave us peace. Sixteen years of peace. Everyone said it couldn't be done. You did it. But you can't keep that battle-hunger trapped forever. If you don't give them something else to fight soon, they'll fight you."

There was a heavy silence.

When no one said anything, Nadine continued. "Roup, I think you are right that some of this unrest is coming from Treace—or, at least, from cats who are dissatisfied over his demotion. Arcove, I think you are right that simply killing him won't solve it—not unless you make the kind of example you don't want to make. But

I don't think either of you see the larger issue, and that's because you didn't live as adults under previous kings."

"You think, as a species, we're incapable of peace?" asked Arcove.

Nadine sighed. "I don't know. I *do* know that you cannot break an animal of its nature. Caraca cannot teach her oory to talk no matter how hard she tries. Perhaps you cannot teach the creasia not to fight."

Arcove gave an unhappy rumble. "I didn't win the war to let them kill each other over petty squabbles. I didn't stop them from killing each other's cubs so that I could begin doing it myself."

"I know," said Nadine. "But perhaps you have been too gentle with them. When you won their leadership, we were desperately outnumbered. You needed every creasia alive and fighting, and that remained true for a long time. But it's not true anymore, Arcove. You'd never tolerate the kind of behavior from Charder that you've tolerated from Treace."

"I will not rule the creasia the way I rule the ferryshaft," growled Arcove. "I didn't win the war to do that, either."

"Won't or can't?" said Nadine.

Arcove was bristling. Roup watched them. He'd never had more respect for Nadine, but he hoped she hadn't pressed too far.

"Your loyalty is to your den and your cubs," said Arcove after a moment.

"Yes," agreed Nadine. "Most of them will not outlive you, and I do not think I will have a fourth mate, either."

"Can't or won't?" asked Arcove with a smile and Roup relaxed.

Nadine chuffed. "I was counseling kings when you were still at your mother's teat, oh confident one."

"And did any of the others let you keep your cubs when they took your den?"

Nadine's gaze dropped. "You know you have my loyalty, Arcove. And I can't tell what you should do. You're on an untrod path and always have been. I can only tell you what was done in the past and why it worked. Excuse me now. I need to go make certain that everyone gets a share of the kill. As you said, we are all a little hungry."

When she'd gone, Arcove stretched out with his head on his paws. Roup thought he looked tired. "Maybe I shouldn't have—" Roup began, but Arcove gave a hard flick of his tail, as though to dismiss the apology.

After a moment, he muttered, "Perhaps I shouldn't have eliminated all the fractious little herds of ferryshaft after the war. Then I could send the young cats out to fight with them."

"You haven't sent out any raiding parties this winter," ventured Roup. He hated to bring this up as a solution, but he also saw the wisdom of Nadine's words.

"No," said Arcove. "And I won't."

Roup was surprised. "Why?"

"Two reasons. I keep ferryshaft numbers at half of ours, and we are considerably more numerous than I thought. Also, these cats are hungry. Treace has already put it into their heads that ferryshaft are an acceptable food source. I don't want to tempt them. Under normal circumstances, creasia would rather eat deer, and by next winter, most of them will be doing that regularly again."

Roup lay down beside him and draped his head over Arcove's shoulders. "We are *not* incapable of peace."

Arcove chuffed. "I know *you're* not." He seemed to perk up suddenly. "There is another way… I was always averse to the idea before, but…maybe new problems require new solutions."

"What would those be?" asked Roup.

"Let me think about it a little more."

"That's what you say when you know I won't like what you're thinking."

Arcove's tail twitched, but he said nothing.

14

Spring

Deep beneath the earth, in the heart of a warm and glowing pool, an egg half the size of a ferryshaft foal began to undulate. Valla and Sauny watched from the edge of the pool as two telshees circled the egg—anxious, but not ready to interfere. Their bodies flickered beneath the surface in the green light of the acriss. The egg itself glowed as if lit from within. Half a dozen other eggs lay on the bottom of the pool as well, and they all had a faint, green luminescence.

"Do you think—?" began Valla, but Sauny shushed her. She leaned over, concentrating, trying to see through the distortion of the water.

However, when the moment came, it was not easily missed. The egg tore—not cracking like a bird's egg, but tearing like a turtle's egg. A flood of luminous fluid poured forth. *Tiny jellyfish,* thought Valla, although they were too small to distinguish as such. An instant later, the newborn telshee pup writhed into view, splitting the fleshy skin of her egg in all directions. She thrashed there amid bright clouds of jellyfish spore, until the adults bore her to the surface. She choked out water, drew in her first gasping breath, and squalled in several voices. The adults immediately began to sing, and she quieted. They curled around the pup in a confusion of furry coils.

Valla and Sauny moved respectfully to the far side of the cave. Their presence here was not entirely welcome, but Sauny had been determined to see how the telshees were born. As spring warmed the seas, the telshees had begun to wake, and so, too, had their eggs.

Sauny had been watching this egg for days as it grew brighter. "I think it's because of the shell," she told Valla. "All the eggs have jellyfish inside, but as they get closer to hatching, the shell grows thinner, and the egg gets brighter."

"So you think the lishty was telling the truth?" asked Valla in a low voice.

"I haven't been able to find anything to prove otherwise," said Sauny.

"Except actually asking anyone," said Valla.

Sauny said nothing.

Valla took a deep breath. "So…you're still thinking about… doing what it said?"

"It came to see me again a few days ago on the beach," muttered Sauny.

Valla shuddered. "Aren't you afraid of it?"

"Kind of. But, then, other animals would be afraid of *me*…if I did what it said…wouldn't they?"

"I don't think you should. But if you do…I'll go with you."

Sauny gave her a hard look. "You mean you'll change with me?"

"Yes."

Sauny thought for a moment. "Is this your way of trying to stop me? Because it won't work."

Valla said nothing for a moment. "You're my herd leader," she said at last.

Sauny peered at her. "I'm only three years old. And I'm lame."

"Nevertheless."

"And I'm an outcast. And I don't know how I'll ever kill another creasia…unless I do this."

"Do you think we'd still be ourselves?"

"I don't know," said Sauny. "Sometimes I don't like being myself."

Valla swallowed. "So why haven't you done it, then? If you're so convinced?"

Sauny looked at the ground and seemed a little smaller. "I'm scared." She licked her lips. "Valla, do you think Teek is really a creasia?"

Valla laughed. "Of course he's really a creasia! What else could he be?"

"I don't know. He doesn't act like a creasia. I think he must be different from the rest."

"How do you know what creasia act like when they're not hunting?" asked Valla.

Sauny said nothing for a moment. "He brought me a bird the other day. It was the first bird he'd managed to kill, and I don't think he'd eaten in about two days, but Storm said he wanted to bring it to me."

Valla smiled. "He's an odd little beast."

"That can't be what the others are like. There must be something wrong with him."

This is what's stopping you, thought Valla with a jolt. *Not fear. Hope.*

"Ulya told Storm to get Teek out of the caves before Shaw wakes up," said Valla. "She said Teek was only supposed to be here until spring, and now it's spring, and she's afraid Shaw might do something to him."

Sauny tossed her head. "She wouldn't dare!"

"Don't be too sure," said Valla. "I think Storm is considering rejoining the herd."

"He can't," muttered Sauny. "Not with Teek." More softly, she added, "Not without me."

"You're walking better," said Valla.

Sauny snorted. "No, I'm not."

"I think you are."

"Nonsense." She thought for a moment. "You just want me to leave Syriot to get me away from lishties."

Valla grinned. "You've caught me." Her expression turned more serious. "If you want to see Teek, you should take the opportunity over the summer. I know Storm thinks he can keep him forever, but I don't think so. Eventually Teek will have to go back to Leeshwood."

To her surprise, Sauny bowed her head. "I know," she said softly. "I know, and it makes me sad."

Storm felt as though he might be sick as he approached the spring feeding grounds. Teek seemed to sense his anxiety and padded along without saying anything. They passed pleasant streams and grassy expanses dotted with flowers between the boulders.

Storm remembered. *Tracer and Leep and I played tag here when I was only a yearling. Sauny chased minnows over there a year later. Tollee and I lay for hours in the mud on a hot day and talked until the sun set. And over there, just beyond that rise, is the pool where I hid from Arcove's cats.*

Sunlight dazzled on the little streams, and it made Teek blink and yawn, but Storm felt as though he were wide awake for the first time in ages. He knew where he had to go. He'd visited last night and sniffed around. But he wanted to come in daylight. *Like a fer- ryshaft. Not like a curb or a telshee or a creasia.*

Storm rounded a boulder, and there they were—half a dozen female ferryshaft and a confusion of tottering foals. The adults were talking between mouthfuls of spring grass, and the foals were exploring cautiously.

Storm forced himself to keep walking until they saw him. He didn't know what he expected after that. He thought they might scream and run at the sight of Teek…or even at the sight of him. In fact, they did neither, although everyone stopped talking. Several stopped chewing with grass still dangling from their lips.

Then one dark, brindled female separated herself from the group and came towards him. Storm was relieved to see that she had a twinkle in her eyes. "That's quite a scar," said Tollee.

Of all the things she could have said, this was not what Storm had expected. No one had mentioned the scar across his nose from the creasia battle in so long that he'd almost forgotten it. He fumbled for words, "It…doesn't hurt."

A little sand-colored foal struggled after Tollee. It stopped and peered uncertainly around its mother's legs.

"And who is this?" asked Storm.

"I've called her Myla," said Tollee. "After her father."

Storm bent to sniff the foal's nose. She smelled of Tollee and spring grass and, faintly, of blood. She smelled like life.

Tollee's expression changed when she spotted Teek. Storm realized that the others probably hadn't seen him in the long grass. "Remy owes me a rabbit," said Tollee smugly.

Storm stared at her.

"I knew you wouldn't kill it," she said. "The cub who followed you from the cave, I mean."

"Am I that predictable?" asked Storm.

"Maybe not to everyone." She hesitated and glanced at her clique, who had moved a little distance away, shooting covert glances over their shoulders. "*Obviously* not to everyone."

Teek stared up at Tollee, his posture uncertain. "She's a friend," said Storm. "And," he added, "a *very* good hunter."

Teek's ears came up. He was always impressed with superior hunting.

"I don't know whether you should say that after this winter," said Tollee. "The oldest of our clique starved to death. We thought she was getting enough, but…we woke one morning and she was dead. When we examined her, we realized that she was a lot thinner than we thought…under her winter coat. Her foal died in her belly, poor thing."

Tollee herself looked fit enough. Like all the ferryshaft, she was in the process of shedding her winter coat, and she had patches of sleek brindled fur between heavy, dense wads of winter fluff.

"But Remy's alright?" asked Storm.

"Oh, yes. She's actually spending time with Kelsy and Itsa again. There were no raids this winter, you know. Remy thinks maybe she was wrong about Kelsy rolling over for Arcove. Maybe it did more good than fighting, in the end."

Storm was impressed. "No raids? Really?" He felt suddenly that he should have known this, should have been paying more attention to what was happening to his herd. Before Tollee could answer, he said, "I should have been here."

"Why? I wouldn't have let you help me."

Storm smiled. "You never needed my help."

"But I did miss you."

Storm thought that this might be the nicest thing he'd ever heard in his life.

Tollee's voice grew wary. "How are Sauny…and Valla?"

Is that jealousy? "They're fine. They're practically telshees now. They—"

Storm broke off as Teek leaned forward to sniff noses with Myla, who seemed equally curious. Tollee stood perfectly still, legs braced as though she might need to strike. Storm held his breath.

Then Myla sneezed. Teek jerked back, but he only shook his head. He glanced up at Storm and said, with absolute seriousness, "She's just a baby."

Storm did his best not to laugh. "She's one year more of a baby than you."

Teek came forward again and proceeded to wash Myla's face.

Tollee gave a surprised snort. "Well…" she said in a wondering voice. "It's a new year, I guess."

"I guess it is," said Storm.

15

Solution

On the evening Arcove went to visit Treace, he took Halvery and a dozen of his cats, but he did not tell them what he intended to do. He told Roup, although he wouldn't let him come along. "I should be there," complained Roup. "If this works, it may be the most important thing you do as king."

"You don't get along with Treace," said Arcove patiently, "and he's just enough of a cub to resent your presence. Let me do this."

When they reached Treace's territory—now restricted to his immediate den-site, Arcove was not entirely surprised to find a mock-fight in progress. Treace was sparring with one of his clutter members. They were going at it just aggressively enough to be mistaken for a real fight at first glance. However, the relaxed attitudes of half a dozen females and adolescent cubs in the vicinity prevented any experienced cat from making that mistake.

The other den members scattered when they saw Arcove and Halvery. Arcove wondered how many of them thought that he'd come to do as Nadine had suggested. The two combatants were so focused that it took them a moment to realize what was happening. When they finally broke apart, Halvery's clutter had circled them.

Treace's officer gave a nervous hiss, bristling all over, but Treace didn't make a sound. He tried to catch his breath, eyes darting around the group.

"Well, that was interesting," said Halvery. "Your leg seems much improved."

"Oh, he's practicing," said Arcove. "He's not good enough yet, though."

"Won't be for a long time," said Halvery. "If ever."

Treace said nothing, just watched them.

Arcove turned away. "Come on, Treace. I'm going to treat you like an adult for a moment. Try to act like one."

He didn't look back, but he heard Halvery say, "Well, go on. You want to take a swipe at him? Now's your chance. We'll stay here. So will your clutter, of course."

A moment later, he heard a soft footfall and knew that Treace was following. His footfalls were slightly uneven. *He's still limping, but not much.* His eye also seemed to be functioning, although he had a scar across his face.

Arcove slowed down and let Treace catch up. They were approaching the southern edge of the forest and the plains beyond. "Did you know that Roup and I used to live near here?" asked Arcove.

Treace gave him an odd look. The limp and the scar had taken the edge off his characteristic poise, but Arcove could tell he was adjusting.

"A little to the west," continued Arcove, "beside a stream that was too small to have a name and has probably changed course since then."

"Why—?" began Treace.

"Because we were rogue cubs, and this is the most game-poor section of the forest," said Arcove. "I wouldn't bend my neck to anyone, and not even other cubs wanted to call a two-year-old their alpha. So here we stayed for more than a year, barely surviving."

There was a long pause. Finally, Treace said, grudgingly, "They say you killed one of the king's officers when you were two."

"I did," said Arcove. "That's why I was a rogue." *But you'll wait a long time before I'll tell that story.*

They'd reached the edge of the southern plains, and the open sky stretched in a vast, star-dappled dome above their heads— fading to pink along the horizon where the sun had set. "There weren't many cats in Leeshwood back then," said Arcove. "About a hundred males, I suspect, although no one was counting."

Treace turned to him with a look of astonishment. *Now I've got your attention.* "There were many small ferryshaft herds on both plains. They killed us at every opportunity, and we killed each other almost as often. When males fought, they fought to the death. When a male took another male's mate, he killed her young cubs. The female would come into season faster that way, and he didn't have to raise his rival's offspring."

Treace seemed to consider. *You thought you were returning to something more natural when you stopped them from eating bitter-leaf, didn't you? But the old way wasn't quite what you envisioned.*

Arcove drew himself up to his full height and turned to glare at Treace. He dropped all the velvet from his tone and gave it claws. "You grew up in *my* Leeshwood, Treace. You would not even recognize what was here before. You are making trouble in *my* wood."

Treace licked his lips. "I didn't—" he began. "I haven't—"

"You think you want to rule?" demanded Arcove. "You think you can do it better than I can?"

Treace stood perfectly still and did not meet Arcove's eyes.

"Answer me."

"If I say anything, you'll kill me," whispered Treace.

"Not tonight," said Arcove. "Perhaps tomorrow, but not tonight." *Tell me I can't treat him like Charder, Nadine.*

Treace's eyes flicked up and back down. "You won the war when no one else could," he admitted. "But you're right; it's a different world now. You won when such things were decided by strength. Now, they are decided by cunning."

Arcove had to force himself not to laugh. "Well, so far, your cunning has gotten you a limp and a scar...although I may have done you a favor with the scar. You look considerably fiercer than you actually are."

Treace bristled a little. He forgot to keep his eyes down. "If the creasia do not move forward, they will move back! The ferryshaft are a relic of—"

"Ah, yes, the ferryshaft. Your main point of contention. Do you know why I don't kill them all?"

"Because Roup doesn't want you to," snapped Treace.

"No. Try again."

Treace seemed taken aback. After a moment, he ventured, "Because you're afraid something worse will replace them?"

"Getting closer," said Arcove.

Treace stared out at the plain. He seemed genuinely puzzled.

"I think," said Arcove, "that we will eventually have war with the telshees again. If I had managed to kill their king on Kuwee Island, this might not be true. But I didn't. And I don't think he's forgotten. I think he's biding his time while their numbers improve."

Treace looked skeptical. "Then why don't we strike first?"

"You wouldn't say that if you'd ever fought with telshees in their own tunnels," said Arcove. "Because we wouldn't win, that's why."

"What does that have to do with the ferryshaft?"

"Telshees were ferryshaft allies. If I eradicate the ferryshaft, Keesha will feel that, to have his revenge, he must eradicate the creasia." *Instead of just me.* "Telshees have long memories. I don't want that sort of blood-debt between us."

Treace thought for a moment. "Why are you telling me this?"

Arcove looked out across the plain. "Tell me about Moro."

Out of the corner of his eye, he could see that he'd caught Treace off-guard. "About..."

"Moro, yes, your beta, tell me about him."

Treace licked his lips. "He's my brother. Half-brother. I raised him. There's not much else to tell."

Arcove peered at him. "You raised him? That's interesting. Why?"

Treace had recovered his composure. "Our mother asked me to. He got into a fight with another cub when he was three, and the den rejected him." Treace looked at Arcove levelly. "I'm sure you can understand that, sir."

Arcove let the silence stretch, but Treace was good at waiting games. He said nothing. "That's unusual," said Arcove at last, "for a den to reject a cub for fighting. Exceedingly unusual. It's what cubs do."

"I agree," said Treace.

"However, cubs who kill other cubs in unprovoked attacks... Cubs who kill much younger cubs... That certainly draws the ire of a den mother."

Treace said nothing.

"Does he still like to kill cubs, Treace?"

Treace took a deep breath. "As you have pointed out, sir, I allowed them to overpopulate. There were an excess number of cubs and more rogues than in other clutters. Sometimes, they stole from—"

Arcove interrupted. "I would get rid of him, if I were you."

"Moro is a loyal officer and very clever, sir."

"Funny, that's what I used to say about you."

Treace gave a startled snort of laughter.

"Good officers are like claws," said Arcove. "A claw stays sharp because you can retract it. When a cat cannot retract his claws, they grow dull. They can catch on things, tear, and bleed. They can get you into trouble. Make sure you can retract all your claws, Treace."

Treace actually smiled—a genuine smile, Arcove thought. "Why are you trying to give me helpful advice, Arcove?"

"Because I think you'll need it."

"In order to rule my little 'game-poor' patch of forest?"

Arcove hesitated. "There aren't many creasia who can lead. There aren't many creasia who *want* to lead. Creasia kings don't get old, Treace."

Arcove let that sink in. "You have to *want* it. You have to want it more than you want a long life. You have to be *that* certain that you could do a better job. I think you do want it, and I think you are certain. And that's rare. That kind of ambition doesn't come along very often. It's why I haven't killed you. I think your ideas for Leeshwood are completely misguided, and that you'll destroy my wood if you have your way. But I do think you're something special."

Treace flicked his tail. Arcove thought he was flattered and trying not to show it.

"In addition," continued Arcove, "you've generated a certain amount of loyalty. Your cats are not happy that you've been removed from command. They're picking fights and causing trouble. In a way, that speaks well of their devotion, if not their judgment. Your cats are young, Treace. They're like you. They've never seen a war, and they don't know what they're asking for."

"I don't want a war," said Treace. The words tumbled out. "I want to fight you and win."

There was a moment of perfect silence. Treace drew a quick breath. "But as you keep pointing out, I can't."

"That is correct," said Arcove. "You can't have my Leeshwood, but perhaps you can have your own. I have discouraged cats from leaving the wood in the past, but perhaps now it's time."

Treace stared at him. "You mean exile…"

"No, I mean a new…" Arcove realized that he didn't have a word for what he meant. "A new Leeshwood. A new kingdom. I am proposing that you take any cats who want to call you chief, and make a new home for yourselves out across the plain. There are forests at the foot of the southern mountains. I know. I was there once. It's about three days' journey, more if you're traveling with cubs, but you can get there.

"The lowland curbs will fight you. They think of that region as their home territory, but with courage and diplomacy, you can make a place for yourselves. I believe there are deer in those woods, although I am not certain. I know there are sheep in the mountains and perhaps other animals. I do not think there is enough game on the plains to support a creasia den year-round, but I could be wrong about that. The plain might be another option. I think it's time we find out."

Treace's eyes darted back and forth. This was not what he had expected. "So…would that make me one of your officers again?"

"No," said Arcove. "It would make you my equal as far as I'm concerned. A king in your own territory. You would be my subordinate if you came here, but I'd be yours if I went there. I propose

465

we make an agreement to offer each other assistance if we are in dire need. Otherwise, we need not trouble each other."

Treace peered at Arcove's face as though trying to decide whether he was serious. "I— I have to think about this."

"Of course you do."

"What about…what about the Ghost Wood? Some cats won't like being separated from it."

"You can make a new Ghost Wood," said Arcove. "If you have enough control, you can give them new traditions. If not…I believe you can approach the Ghost Wood from the other side if you continue to follow the edge of the lake. I've never been that far, but the Ghost Wood must have a northern border."

Arcove rose and shook himself. "Think about it, Treace. If you stay here, you'll need to take a more active role in redirecting the tensions that you've caused. I know you're not personally starting all these fights, but I am confident that you could personally stop most of them if you wanted to. If you keep this up, I'll have to make an example of you just to keep peace." He paused and looked Treace directly in the eyes. "And if you challenge me again, you'll die with my teeth in your throat, I promise."

Treace held his gaze for a moment, then looked away. "When do I need to make a decision?"

"I'll give you ten days," said Arcove.

Treace looked alarmed. "Ten days? That's hardly—"

"It's enough time to consider your options and to rally your supporters. It's enough time to cross the plain and establish a den site before any of your pregnant females give birth. It gives you plenty of time to settle in before winter."

"You've thought about this," said Treace after a moment.

"Yes, I have. Now it's your turn. If you're not gone in ten days, I had better see an improvement in the behavior of the cats previously under your command."

16

Poison and Marrow

Later that night, Treace sat on the edge of the lake and stared, unseeing, towards the little island where Moro sometimes tested new ideas. Two of his officers had expressed concern after the visit from Arcove, but Treace hardly heard what they said to him. He wondered who had spoken to Arcove about Moro's history. He'd lost control of some of his cats as they'd shifted into other clutters.

Treace remembered the first time he'd seen Moro—not a particularly large cub, black as a shadow, hunched in a tree, looking small and alone. He'd actually been a year and a half old, not three. Even their mother had abandoned him, but she'd had just enough feeling for the cub to send for Treace—her only living offspring. "Go talk to him," she had said without meeting his eyes. "See what you think."

She had not begged him to save the cub. Just consider it.

Moro had killed a litter of youngsters barely old enough to totter away from their den. He'd led them into the forest and then drowned them one-by-one in a deep puddle—three cubs, too frightened and young to escape. He'd made no attempt to hide the bodies or his own scent trail. He was discovered the next day, picking through the innards of one of his victims. It was unclear whether the cub had been completely dead when Moro dragged him out of the puddle and opened his belly.

The mother of the cubs would have killed Moro on the spot, but he'd climbed into a tree where no adult could reach him. The den mother had tried to question him from the ground, but his answers proved unsatisfactory. His father had died earlier in the year, and his own mother made no attempt to question him—a detail that other adults found significant. The cub was deemed unfit to live. He'd been in the tree for two days when Treace arrived, and thirst would soon claim him if one of the adults did not.

Moro had peered down at Treace with those strangely pale eyes.

"Why did you kill them?" Treace had asked.

"I wanted to see what was inside," Moro whispered.

"Did you think anyone would be angry?"

"No one got angry when I looked inside squirrels," said Moro.

"Creasia aren't squirrels," said Treace, although he felt an odd leap in his chest.

Moro said nothing. "They weren't doing anything important," he said at last. "They didn't even talk very much."

"Are you sorry?" asked Treace.

"No."

"You have to act like you're sorry," he said. And he thought, *You're like me. You've got the same thing. Whatever it is that makes us different.*

Moro looked confused. "How?"

"Say it was an accident, that you were frightened when they drowned, that you got scared and tried to make them live again. That's why you gutted that one. You thought you could help him."

"But I didn't," said Moro.

You've got it worse than I do, thought Treace. "You have to pretend," he said aloud, "or the others will kill you. When you say it, you must lower your head and your tail, and avert your eyes."

Moro looked uncertain.

"I'll do it," said Treace, surprising even himself. "Come with me." He'd never done anything like this before, never saved anyone before. But, when he looked at Moro, he felt something he'd always wanted to feel—kinship. *This is how I'm supposed to feel about my own cubs,* thought Treace. He'd tried with that first litter. He'd tried very hard, but when he looked at his cubs, he felt nothing.

Treace understood Moro. He was better at hiding his own dark side, but he understood.

When Treace planned his fight with the leader of his clutter, Moro had said, "Sharpen your claws in sashara berries."

Treace had stared at him. "They'll know—" he began, but Moro continued.

"The poison will slow him down, and you'll kill him in the fight before anyone sees the signs."

"But the berries stain purple," objected Treace.

Moro had smiled. "So fight him in the mud."

Treace had. And he'd won.

A year later, when the bitterleaf started mysteriously disappearing from their den site, Treace had said nothing. More cubs meant a larger clutter. If a few disappeared now and then, what did it matter? Moro got what he wanted, and so did Treace.

He was more concerned that Moro didn't seem interested in taking a mate. When he finally did, Treace thought he might kill her. He left such bite marks on the back of her neck each time they mated that the other den members started giving him nasty looks.

"You have to stop that," Treace told him. "If you've got to kill a cub or a rogue now and then to feel right, then do it, but you can't mistreat your mate."

"I'll try," Moro had said. Next season, she disappeared. Moro took no more mates, although one or two young females disappeared every year.

Arcove's words echoed in Treace's head. *"Make sure you can retract all your claws."*

"I can," Treace said aloud. "I can control him."

"Control who?"

Treace looked around and spotted the pale flash of Moro's nose in the water, swimming in from the island. Moro clambered up the bank, and shook himself.

"Arcove was here," said Treace. "He's offered to let us leave... to take anyone who wants to go and make a new kingdom in the forests of the southern mountains."

Moro snorted. "Are you serious?"

"He seemed serious."

"He's offering you exile. How generous."

"He said I'd be a king in my own territory."

"You must be making him nervous...if he's willing to say things like that."

Treace said nothing.

"Coincidentally," said Moro, "I had a visitor, too."

Behind him, a pale head rose out of the lake. Treace flattened his body instinctively, legs spread, ready to attack or flee. Everything Arcove had said about telshees flashed through his mind. Then the animal opened green, luminescent eyes and looked at him. Treace blinked. He'd seen only three telshees in his life, two of them dead after a Volontaro. This one looked...wrong. Its smell reached him, and he took a step back. It smelled of death.

"Hello," said the creature in what Treace supposed was meant to be a friendly voice. "I have been Kos."

"If it works, I'll say you were right," said Roup.

It had been twelve days since Arcove's visit to Treace's den. Arcove and Roup were walking the edge of Arcove's territory. "As far as I can tell, it has," said Arcove. "Treace and Moro are definitely gone. It sounds like they took about a hundred and fifty cats with them—mostly young adult males, although there were twenty or thirty females."

"That'll make for some fights."

"Yes, but it could be managed. That group is the core of his old command. If they have strong enough bonds with each other, they'll sort things out."

"Treace wouldn't have been my first choice for such an expedition," said Roup, "but he might be the only one with enough followers to make it work and enough ambition to volunteer." Roup thought a little more. "He's starting with about the same number of cats that you did."

Arcove smiled. "I thought of that."

"His going won't eliminate all the troublemakers. The bullies and gossips aren't that brave. I'm sure they stayed behind."

"But without a rally point, they'll be easy to deal with," said Arcove.

"Agreed."

"If we do have another war, this will give us greater numbers."

"*If* Treace comes to help us," said Roup skeptically.

"And if he doesn't, we're no worse off than we were before." Arcove stopped to sharpen his claws on a log, leaving behind his own distinctive scent. "War with the telshees may not happen again in our lifetimes. It may be something our cubs must deal with. Then they may be glad of their cousins across the plain."

Roup sighed. "So…I suppose you were right about letting Treace live."

Arcove waved his tail. "They may all die—fighting with curbs or fighting with each other. I tried to give Treace some advice, but I couldn't tell whether I made an impression."

"At least you sent them in the opposite direction of the ferryshaft herd," said Roup.

"Yes, I thought you'd appreciate that." Arcove paused on a little rise to look out over the treetops of Leeshwood. "Treace and his cats can flourish or perish by their own lights. Whether they're the marrow of the next generation or deadly poison, at least they're out of my wood." He took a deep breath. "Now, I just have to decide what to do about Storm."

Roup cocked his head. "Have you had news about him?"

"Yes. I sent Sharmel to check on Charder a few days ago. You will not believe what he told me."

Teek and the Curbs

On the day that Storm left the cliffs, he came to the curbs' den to say good-bye. He'd not been hunting with them for most of the spring, but they greeted him warmly and introduced him to seven puppies, who were now beginning to hunt outside the den. Storm could not tell most of the puppies apart, but Teek remembered a few of their names, and they seemed to remember him.

Sauny and Valla came up while Teek was talking to the puppies. "Are you sure you won't come with me?" Storm asked. "I think the herd would accept you. There've been no raids this winter. No one's seen any creasia at all...except for Teek."

Valla looked unhappy, but it was Sauny who spoke. "No, Storm. Not yet. I have to..." She looked away.

"Have to what?"

"I have to think about something."

Storm glanced at Valla, but she only said, "What are you going to do about Teek, Storm?"

"I was planning to take him to the summer feeding grounds ahead of the herd," said Storm. He knew he was speaking a little too quickly, but hurried on. "Then he'll know his way around in case of trouble. I thought we'd travel to the edge of Groth, and I could talk to him about it."

"And after that?"

"We'll stay a little apart from the herd the way we've done all spring. Teek and Myla like each other. They play together."

"They play together," said Valla flatly. "Storm, you're not answering my question."

Storm didn't meet her eyes. "I don't know what you're asking, Valla."

"You want to be with Tollee," said Valla. "You always have. And this fall, you'll be old enough. What will happen to Teek when you rejoin the herd in earnest?"

Storm opened his mouth, but she continued. "Let's say that you convince Tollee to live with you away from the herd—unlikely, but let's say you manage it. What happens in a few years when Teek wants a mate? What happens when he's too big to live on small game in the summer? He can't eat grass like we can, and there's not much large game in the summer feeding grounds. What happens when—?"

"I don't know!" exploded Storm. "What do you want me to say, Valla? I don't know." He took a deep breath. "Have you seen Shaw yet?"

"No. But if you think you're going to convince her to let him stay with us in Syriot, you're delusional."

Storm screwed his eyes shut.

"You need to find a way to send him back to Leeshwood," said Valla quietly. "The longer you wait, the harder it will be for him to fit in…and the harder it will be for you to let him go."

"I can't just send him back," muttered Storm. "He thinks the other cats will kill him. He's probably right…especially now that he smells like me."

"I know," said Valla gently. "I know you can't abandon him. But if a way presents itself…think about it, Storm."

Tollee and Myla almost came with Storm and Teek on their journey to the lake. In the end, Tollee decided that it would be an unwise risk with a very young foal. A few days later, Storm had reason to be glad of her decision.

He woke alone one morning in the little hollow where he'd been sleeping with Teek. He could hear angry voices. Storm struggled up in the long grass and crept towards the sound. When he raised his head, he saw a pack of lowland curbs—about ten of them—in a ring around Teek.

"—a long way from Leeshwood," one was saying. "Such a little cat to be so far from home. Why are you out here, little cat?"

Teek wasn't speaking to them. He was bristling all over, and his eyes darted around the group.

"We heard a rumor," said one of the curbs, "that our enemy is traveling with a creasia cub. Do you know who our enemy is, little cat?"

"If you mean me," said Storm, suddenly standing up, "then perhaps you should bring your quarrel over here."

The whole pack turned to look at him, and their leader snarled. "Storm Ela-ferry," he murmured, "champion of highland curbs."

Before the leader could say anything else, Teek darted forward and savagely attacked the hindquarters of the nearest curb, who'd turned to look at Storm. This was clearly not what the pack had been expecting from a yearling cub, and it threw them into confusion. About half of them bolted, while the rest tried to attack Teek in a bedlam of snarling and yelping.

Storm bounded forward, got a mouthful of curb flesh, and shook the animal as hard as he could, slamming it against the ground as he let go. At the same time, his front hooves came down in a solid blow against another curb's skull. He felt jaws latch onto one of his back legs and kicked out viciously, flinging away his attacker.

All of this happened in an instant. In the next instant, Storm saw Teek jump straight up out of the pile of struggling bodies. Teek landed on one of the curbs' backs, all of his claws extended. The curb gave a screaming yelp. He bolted out of the group, jumping and twisting in the air. He writhed briefly on the ground, but when he came up again, Teek was still there. The little cat appeared to have locked his teeth as well as his claws in the curb's spine.

The curb gave another panicked scream and tore off across the plain. Storm took off after them without waiting to see how many curbs he'd killed or what the rest were doing. The curb was running at a speed born of mortal terror, Teek still clinging to his back in what must have been a state of nearly equal terror. Storm soon lost sight of them.

It took him a quarter of the day to catch up. Storm was certain that he would find Teek's corpse at the end of his search. Instead, he found Teek beside the body of the curb. Teek was trying, half-heartedly, to groom his own ruffled fur.

When he saw Storm, he dashed up to him, trilling a desperate greeting and making that odd throbbing noise between breaths. He butted his head against Storm's front legs. "I thought they were going to kill you."

"I thought the same about you," muttered Storm, staring at the curb. "How did you…?"

"I don't know," said Teek. "I don't know, I don't know. Can we run away before they come back?"

"I don't think they'll come back." When Storm examined the curb, he realized that Teek must have instinctively set his jaws in the curb's neck just behind the head. The animal could not reach him or dislodge him. An older cat—even an older cub—would have broken the curb's neck in short order. However, Teek's jaws were not yet strong enough for that. Instead, he had slowly crushed the curb's neck bones as the animal ran howling across the plain.

Storm shuddered. He glanced at Teek, now calmly grooming himself. *I never taught him that. It was pure instinct. What else will his instincts teach him?*

Teek seemed to sense Storm's eyes on him and looked up. He studied Storm's face. "Did I do something wrong?" He sounded genuinely concerned.

"No," said Storm. He tried to smile. "You may have saved my life."

Teek padded back to him quickly and rubbed around his legs. "Can we go now? Please?"

Storm felt suddenly tired. *This is the sort of thing I'll have to deal with all the time if I want to live away from the herd. Could Tollee and I have protected Myla if we'd been attacked alone?* He could feel bruises on his legs where the curbs had tried to latch onto him. "Yes," he said aloud. "Let's get to the lake. I'd like to hear frogs this evening."

18

Mistakes of the Past

Over the next few days, the ferryshaft herd drifted in, and Storm almost forgot his worries for the future. The air was warm and the water of the lake delightfully cool. Frogs and insects filled the evenings with sounds that Storm associated with contentment and plenty. Fireflies winked under the trees at night. The grass was sweet and tender, and small game was plentiful in Chelby Wood.

Storm taught Teek to swim and then to fish. Teek wasn't very good at fishing yet. Storm wondered whether fish were a normal part of a creasia's diet. He was beginning to realize exactly how much he did not know about cats. Teek had, at least, grown proficient at catching the rodents that whisked about under the leaves, and young birds were also in abundance. He tried, repeatedly, to eat grass like a ferryshaft, but it only made him vomit.

Storm stayed out of sight of the herd on most days, but Tollee and Myla made frequent appearances. Myla was learning to talk, asking a thousand questions. Teek tried to teach her to hunt, which proved comical.

"I won't take a mate this fall," said Tollee one day out of nowhere. "I don't think it would be fair to Myla."

"You're probably right," said Storm. "My mother didn't take a second mate until I was a year and a half old."

They were silent a moment. "I really am sorry about Mylo," said Storm.

Tollee looked out over the plain. "Well, we made our trade. I had his foal…and he saved your life."

Storm winced. After a moment, he said, "I'm only four years old. I'm not even sure I could father a foal."

Tollee smirked. "But you'd like to try."

"You'd like to let me." Storm couldn't believe he'd said it aloud, but now that the words were out of his mouth, there was nothing to do but try to look confident.

Tollee snorted a laugh. "You think so?" Her hackles were up, but so were her ears and tail—mixed signals of aggression and play.

She's flirting with me, thought Storm with a jolt.

Near the tree line, Teek was trying to get Myla to chase him, dancing around her and nipping at her ears and tail. Myla would play along briefly, and then become distracted by a blade of grass or a dragonfly.

"I'd stay," Storm said. "Even if you don't want to risk getting pregnant this year. I'd be your mate and help take care of Myla next winter." *I'd never treat her the way Dover treated me.*

Tollee started to say something. Then her expression changed. "Storm…"

He turned around. Three ferryshaft were coming towards them from the direction of the herd. Storm recognized all of them. He stood up. "Maybe you should go."

Tollee snorted. "So that a bunch of males can decide my fate?"

"I don't think it's your fate we'll be deciding."

"I'm staying right here."

Charder walked a little in front of the group, Kelsy almost abreast of him, and Pathar picking his way along behind. When they came within hailing distance, Kelsy trotted out in front, tail waving. "Storm!"

Storm did not smile. "Kelsy."

"You're looking well," said Kelsy.

"And you're looking like trouble. What do you want?"

Kelsy gave him a wounded expression. "If anyone's got a right to be unfriendly, it's me. You behaved very badly the last time I invited you to a conference."

"I never promised to behave well," said Storm.

"We'd like to speak to you alone," said Charder more quietly. "Can your...uh...friend watch the...um..." He glanced towards Teek and Myla.

"I think his mate deserves to know what you want," said Tollee. "The foal and the cub are fine."

Mate? Storm had to exercise every bit of his self-control to avoid turning to see whether she looked serious. She *sounded* serious.

Before he could think what to say, Charder said, "Very well. It has been suggested—*strongly* suggested—that you, Storm, should come to the fall conference with the creasia this year."

"Haven't they learned better than to invite me to conferences?" asked Storm.

"Furthermore," continued Charder, "you are to bring the cub. They will take him back to Leeshwood and guarantee his safety *if* you come and talk to them."

Storm drew a deep breath. "What if I don't want to send him—?"

Pathar spoke for the first time. "Do you want him to grow up, Storm? Because this is probably his only chance."

Before Storm could answer, Charder said, "If you agree to this, I will tolerate the presence of a creasia cub around my herd this summer. If you do not agree, I will make your life here very difficult." His voice had grown icy. "I know you think me impotent, but I assure you that I am capable of enforcing exile on a ferryshaft who has become a threat to my herd. You've walked that line for most of your life, and now you've crossed it."

Storm felt himself bristle all over.

Kelsy stepped between Charder and Storm. "Stop it," he snarled at Charder. "I told you to let me talk." Before Charder could answer, he turned back to Storm. "There were no raids this winter because the creasia are having overpopulation problems. Now, a number of cats have migrated south—something that Arcove has never allowed before. Things are changing, Storm. This is our chance to renegotiate the treaty. You started this. Please come and be a part of it now that we're finally getting somewhere."

Storm's eyes flicked around the group. "Why me?" he said at last. "I haven't really accomplished anything. Is it just because of Teek?"

Kelsy barked a laugh. "'Haven't really accomplished anything'? Storm, you beat Arcove."

Storm smiled. "I did *not* beat Arcove. I barely survived."

"How many animals on Lidian can say that they survived when Arcove tried to kill them?"

"You're trying to flatter me."

"Is it working?" Kelsy grinned. "Or should Charder try threatening you again?"

Charder rolled his eyes. "That was not a threat. It was a promise. A creasia cub in the ferryshaft herd is a bad idea."

Storm peered at him. "Because it's been tried before?"

Kelsy looked confused. Behind him, Charder and Pathar glanced at each other.

"Oh, so you haven't told Kelsy about Roup?" asked Storm.

Kelsy looked at his elders. "Told me what about Roup?"

"That he was raised in the ferryshaft herd," said Storm.

"That's enough," hissed Charder.

"Is that why you're worried about Teek?" asked Storm. "Because Roup grew up to be—"

"Come with me," interrupted Pathar in the tone he'd used when Storm was a spring foal and behaving badly. He started away towards the lake.

Storm glanced at the others. "Go," said Charder, his eyes narrowed to slits. "Before you make me regret asking him to train you."

Storm blinked. "*You* asked Pathar to—?"

"Now, Storm!" thundered Pathar from the edge of the trees.

Myla and Teek had stopped playing and were staring uncertainly at the adults. Storm started after Pathar. "It's alright," he told Teek as he passed. "I'm not going far. Just stay with Myla."

Pathar turned at the edge of the lake, completely out of sight of the others. He didn't look angry anymore. He looked haunted.

Something clicked in Storm's head. "You were the one who took him," he whispered. *Keesha didn't mention that detail...but it makes sense.*

When Pathar said nothing, Storm continued. "You took Roup to...experiment...because you've always been the curious sort... haven't you, Pathar?" *The sort who'd drink from the poisoned waters of Groth just to see what would happen.*

"Who told you?" asked Pathar.

"Does it matter?"

"Yes, because there are several sides to that story."

"Well, tell me the side that doesn't involve you torturing a baby to satisfy your curiosity."

Pathar shut his eyes. "I did not bring him back to the herd to torture him. I just wanted to watch him develop." He took a deep breath. "There were so many things we didn't know about creasia. Some still claimed that cats could only learn to talk if they were weaned on the blood of a talking animal. Some claimed that they couldn't learn to read because they lacked the necessary intelligence. I didn't think that was true. I wanted to know what *was* true."

Pathar's eyes looked dark and sad in the pale-frosted fur of his face. *Frosted with age?* Storm had always assumed so, and Pathar was certainly very gray around the muzzle. Still... "Are we related, Pathar?"

"Coden's father was my brother."

"That doesn't answer my question."

"I brought Roup back from a hunt, and Akea offered to nurse him with her own foal. That was mercy, wasn't it? All the rest of the cubs we found that day were killed and eaten."

"The version I heard didn't sound very merciful."

"Many of the herd elders took an interest in my little project. It affected the safety of the herd, so I couldn't very well refuse them."

"So every idiot who had an idea got to try it?" asked Storm. He couldn't help thinking of Teek—wide-eyed and trusting, trying so hard to do whatever Storm told him.

"They fed him all kinds of things," muttered Pathar, "poisonous plants, dirt, rotten meat—it's amazing that he grew up at all. He was often sick. He hardly ever complained, though." Pathar looked as though he'd swallowed something bitter. "Coden figured out what we were doing when he was still quite young. He was always a bright one. There were others who didn't like to see Roup hurt, but in the end, Coden was the only one willing to risk anything for him."

Pathar drew a deep breath. "We thought we were studying Roup during those three years, but sometimes I think it was the other way around. Arcove certainly seemed to understand ferryshaft to a degree that his predecessors had not. I'm sure Roup told him things."

Storm listened in silence.

"Do you think I don't regret what happened?" whispered Pathar. "We paid for it. Paid and paid. All the herd elders who hurt Roup died in the war."

"Did Roup hunt them down?" asked Storm.

"No, but Arcove did." Pathar shuddered. "I'm sure I'm only alive because I'm good at predicting the Volontaro. I am telling you this, Storm, so that you will not make my mistake."

"Your mistake wasn't saving him, Pathar. It was what you did afterward."

Pathar shook his ears. "I had good intentions. So do you. But it won't end well. Our two species don't mix."

"Coden and Roup were friends."

"And Coden died when he was fifteen years old," said Pathar, "while Roup *watched*. Remember that, Storm, when you look at this cub."

Part V

Treace

1

Winter Conference

Storm walked along the Igby beneath the tall riverside trees, through mounds of fall leaves, and *thought*. It was a perfectly clear day with a fathomless blue sky and a crisp breeze that parted his winter coat in ripples. Teek bounded along ahead of him, scattering leaves and pouncing on anything that scampered or fluttered out of them. He was as large as a lamb now—robust and healthy with a dense winter coat of his own.

"Is this where you dumped Halvery in the river?" he asked gleefully.

Storm gave a crooked smile. "Not quite. It's a little farther on."

"You'll tell me when we get there?"

"I suppose."

Storm was regretting his decision, earlier that summer, to tell Teek and Myla about some of his more exciting chases. They had both sat enraptured while he recounted his struggles to survive. After that, he was not permitted to sleep in the evenings until he recounted a chase. When he ran out of stories, they made him repeat them. Teek now had what Storm could only describe as an unhealthy familiarity with Arcove and his officers—more as legends than as real animals.

Storm could never decide, when he told these stories, whether Teek identified more with him or with the cats. Teek certainly liked to hear about Storm foiling his pursuers, but he also seemed intensely interested in these larger-than-life hunters. Storm had avoided vilifying his old enemies in Teek's hearing. He did not want the cub to feel more conflicted than necessary.

Storm watched Teek dash through a ray of sunlight, whirling dust moats and dried leaves into the air, and he braced himself for what was coming. In two days, the ferryshaft herd would journey to the cliffs, and the winter conference would commence.

Kelsy was right. This is an opportunity that might never come again—for me, for the ferryshaft, for Teek.

He remembered what life had been like this time last year—the bitter despair of the foals' failed attack on the creasia, his grief at Sauny's horrific injuries, the helplessness and desperation. He would never have considered attending a creasia conference then. *Would I have been able to see another way without Teek?*

Storm didn't think so. He watched Teek race halfway up a tree for the sheer joy of it and then drop to the ground in a shower of leaves. *You gave me my life back. Now I have to give you yours.*

He was distracted by a flash of movement off to his left. He craned his neck, trying to see through the trees. Throughout the summer, he'd noticed the unsettling presence of lowland curbs skulking in the distance wherever he went. They had not approached him since the attack on the way to the summer feeding grounds. They never came close enough to force a confrontation or even a conversation. They were just there—on the skyline, in the distance, beyond the next ridge. Storm hardly ever saw an entire pack. Usually, it was just one or two individuals, watching.

Is this meant as a threat? Are they trying to play on my nerves? Are they afraid of me, or are they trying to make me afraid of them?

He had not pointed out the curbs to Teek, although the cub had noticed them on several occasions. Storm didn't think Teek was aware of their near-constant stalking, and he couldn't see a reason to mention it.

Teek burst into his thoughts. "Is this it?" He was looking at a great tree that overhung the river.

"Yes, I believe it is," said Storm.

Teek clamored up the tree, as agile as a squirrel. "I bet I can get out on the end of a branch."

"I bet you can," agreed Storm. "And if you fall, I bet you can swim to shore."

Teek appraised the view from a limb that might very well have been the spot where Storm had taken a nap two years ago. "The river had ice in it when you and Halvery were here," said Teek.

"Yes," said Storm. "It was extremely cold."

"Was Halvery mad?"

Storm snorted. "Wouldn't you be?"

Teek looked down at Storm through the branches. "Do you think he's still mad?"

I'm certain of it. "If you see him, you probably shouldn't ask him about it."

Teek giggled. "Oh, I'll never see him."

"Don't be so sure," muttered Storm.

Three days later, they sat in the trees near the headwaters of the Igby, where it rushed in a half dozen waterfalls from the cliff. Storm felt ill with anxiety and angry with himself for feeling this way. Tollee had insisted on waiting with him. She would not be deterred, and he eventually stopped trying to convince her to go away.

Myla provided a good distraction for Teek in any case. Storm had told him nothing, but Teek seemed to sense Storm's anxiety. He kept asking why he couldn't go into the boulder mazes and begin exploring.

The weather was clear. According to Pathar, there were no signs of a Volontaro. Under these conditions, Arcove and Roup usually came to the conference with a single clutter and sometimes one or two other officers. Charder warned Storm that all the officers might come this year, due to the unusual nature of the conference. "However, there is an explicit agreement of no hostilities for three days before or after the conference," he told Storm. "You do not need to be worried for your safety."

And yet you keep telling me how all of this is unprecedented, thought Storm. *What exactly can I do if they attack me?* He wished, belatedly, that he'd tried to contact the telshees the day after he had reached the cliffs. It would have been comforting to know that Shaw was lurking in the headwaters of the Igby.

But would she have come? Storm had had no news from Syriot all summer. It seemed likely that Sauny, Valla, Eyal, and the rest were still thriving, but he would have liked to know it. He would also have liked to know that Shaw still felt well-disposed towards him in spite of Teek. *As soon as this is over, I'll visit,* he promised himself. *I'll go down to the Dreaming Sea, too, and check on Keesha. Maybe I'll even take Tollee and Myla. As soon as this is over.*

Storm finally finished the thought that he'd been avoiding all summer. *When Teek is gone.*

He knew, objectively, that it was for the best. The herd was not friendly to Teek. Storm had no doubt that, if anyone else had adopted a cub, it would have been harassed and tormented to death. Only his reputation, and his caution, kept Teek safe.

As Teek grew older, he would become harder to kill, but he would also become harder to hide and feed. Pathar assured Storm that, when Teek reached breeding age, he would become more aggressive and a new set of problems would present themselves.

"He will probably go back to Leeshwood eventually no matter what you do," Pathar had said, "but if he goes back as an adult, he'll be a rogue—a cat with no clutter or den. He'll have to fight his way into a clutter if he wants to avoid a life of loneliness. He'll have poor social skills by creasia standards, and he may not be able to manage the transition. Creasia are social animals like ferryshaft. You don't want to doom him to a life of isolation and misery, Storm. He won't thank you for it in the end."

There's something else he won't thank me for, either, thought Storm. *If he ever finds out.*

The herd remained close together along the edge of the Igby River, as was traditional during the conference. Storm could see a few of them from where he sat among the rocks. He was pretty sure that the council ledge gave a good view of the whole area. *So that Arcove can count us? Surely not. Charder and the other elders must count them during the migration...unless Arcove's cats do it before the conference starts.*

That idea made Storm glance around nervously. He'd grown so accustomed to Teek's scent that he might easily miss the subtle distinction of a different cat.

Tollee was being very quiet. Storm suspected that she felt almost as conflicted as he did about Teek's departure. She'd never argued about it, though. *She thinks it's the right thing to do,* Storm told himself, *just like everyone else. It is the right thing to do.*

"Do you think Teek will ever come on a raid?" she asked, so softly that Storm hardly heard her.

"Surely not."

"Surely," agreed Tollee.

Will I kill him one day? Will he kill me?

"Don't be afraid."

Tollee jumped and Storm's head whipped around. Roup had come up so quietly that neither ferryshaft had noticed. His glossy golden fur gave good camouflage amid the fall wood. Storm scowled at him.

"At least I didn't pin you to the ground this time," said Roup with a twinkle.

Storm had had some vague notion that his comfort around Teek would ease feelings of anxiety in the presence of adult creasia. That idea was immediately dispelled. Roup was easily a head over Storm in height and probably four times his weight. Storm's every instinct screamed, *Predator!* He glanced at Tollee and saw that she'd crouched, ears flat, breathing quickly, hackles raised.

Roup looked away from them, towards Myla and Teek, playing tag among the tree trunks. Storm had gotten better at reading creasia expressions over the summer. He thought Roup looked sad. "What's his name?"

"Teek," said Storm. A sudden fear gripped him. "You're not going to take him right now, are you?"

Roup looked at him, and now the expression was unmistakably pity. "Of course not. Does he know?"

Storm looked at the ground. "No."

Roup looked back towards the youngsters. "Whose foal?"

"Mine," said Tollee. Her hackles had settled a little, but her voice was not friendly. "Her father was killed by creasia."

Roup did not pursue this. "Teek will go into my clutter," he said at last. "We don't raid."

Storm tried to hide his relief.

At that moment, Kelsy came trotting out of the trees. "Storm, it's time for— Oh."

Roup stretched in what Storm was sure was meant to be a disarming gesture. His claws fanned in enormous crescents. "I just came to say hello."

"You've said it," said Tollee. Storm could tell that it would take a lot more than one friendly conversation to make her trust an adult creasia.

Kelsy's raised voice had attracted the attention of the youngsters. Teek caught sight of Roup and came to a stop with his mouth agape. His eyes darted to Storm for threat assessment. The moment he saw Storm's relaxed posture, he came trotting forward. "You're Roup Ela-creasia," he breathed.

Roup cocked his head. "So I am."

"Storm made you think he was a telshee."

Roup looked startled and then made a chuffing sound. He glanced sidelong at Storm.

"He likes stories," Storm mumbled.

"Do you have hunting stories?" Teek asked, still eyeing Roup.

"I have a few," said Roup. The corner of his mouth quirked up, and the tip of his tail twitched. "I think Arcove has more."

Teek's eyes went round. "Is Arcove here?"

"Yes," said Roup.

Teek looked worried again. He glanced at Storm. "Will he hunt us?"

"Not today," said Roup. "Today, he just wants to hear your stories."

Teek came all the way up to Roup and sniffed noses with him. Then he ran around the whole group in an excited circle. "We're going to meet Arcove! We're going to meet Arcove!"

Roup shot Storm a bemused look. "What *have* you told him?"

Myla, who'd hung back, became suddenly bold and came up to sniff noses with Roup as well. Storm was relieved that Tollee didn't decide to kick him.

"Can I come, too?" Myla asked.

"Not today," said Roup.

Tollee said, "No," in the same instant.

Myla looked disappointed.

"I'll tell you all the stories," said Teek. "I'll come back and tell you."

Tollee glanced at Storm with a look that said, *Please go, before this gets any harder.*

"Come on, Teek," said Storm wearily. "Let's go meet Arcove."

2

The Truth at Last

The traditional council ledge was on the ferryshaft side of the waterfall. The trail ascended the cliffs from a point just north of the trees and climbed to a ledge about a third of the way up.

Storm followed Roup and Kelsy out of the trees and across a grassy patch of plain to the boulder mazes. He glanced back once and saw the ferryshaft herd scattered over the plain to the east. He turned towards the trees and saw Myla, looking small and alone, and Tollee, a darker shape behind her. *It's for the best,* he told himself again. *Our species don't mix.*

Teek was scampering ahead, stopping to wait impatiently, and then dashing forward as soon as they reached him.

"What *did* you tell him?" repeated Roup.

"Everything except the raids," snapped Storm. "I figured I'd let you explain that."

Roup said nothing.

Liar, said a voice in Storm's head. *There's one other thing you didn't tell him.*

Arcove and Charder were waiting at the foot of the trail. Teek would have dashed up to them, but Storm checked him with a word. The cub came running back and sat down at Storm's side. Roup looked impressed. "Friendly *and* obedient. Maybe you should start raising mine."

Arcove finished whatever he'd been saying to Charder and turned to give them his full attention. "Storm Ela-ferry." He had a faint smile in his voice, which Storm found annoying.

"Arcove Ela-creasia."

"Last time you were invited to a conference, you seemed inclined to make trouble...and then you left with something of ours." He was looking at Teek.

Storm didn't want to talk about that. "How do I know you won't kill me?"

"There's a peace treaty."

"So I've been told, but I want to hear it from you."

"I won't hunt you for three days," said Arcove. "I give you my word. Ask anyone on Lidian if I've ever broken it."

Storm relaxed a little. At his side, Teek was glancing from Storm's face to Arcove's as though this were the best day of his life.

"And Teek?" demanded Storm.

"I don't kill cubs," said Arcove quietly.

Storm sighed. "In that case...there's one who'd like to meet you."

Teek darted forward, but he became shy at the last moment. Storm couldn't blame him. Arcove would have made a leopard seal shy. Teek tucked his tail, bristling a little, and crouched. "Hello," he whispered.

"He has apparently been weaned on stories of Storm's chases," said Roup.

"Oh?"

"Yes, don't be surprised if he asks you to explain your failures."

All the ferryshaft laughed. Charder, in particular, seemed thoroughly amused.

Arcove took it in stride. He looked down at Teek. "So...am I the hero or the villain in these tales?"

"Both, I think," said Roup.

Arcove cocked his head at Storm. "Well. That is interesting." He bent and gave Teek's head a lick that nearly knocked him over. "Hello, Teek Ela-creasia."

That seemed to unstop Teek's mouth. "Storm says you can run really fast!" he said, bouncing up and down. "Have you ever been in Groth before? Did you know that an ely-ary—?"

"That's enough," interrupted Storm. *Although I'm sure he'll repeat it all later.* "Let's get this over with."

The hike up to the council ledge was steep, but relatively short. It was a sheltered path worn into the cliff, almost a tunnel, with a rock wall that obscured their view of the plain until they reached the top. They had to go two-by-two, and the noise of the waterfall made conversation impossible.

However, by the time they reached the council ledge they were high enough above the waterfall that they could easily hear one another again. Kelsy got right to the point. "There are about eleven hundred ferryshaft down there."

"There should be about a thousand," said Arcove.

"At least a hundred will die of natural causes this winter," said Kelsy.

"And more than a hundred will be born this spring," said Arcove.

Kelsy licked his lips. "I think I can control the breeding this fall."

Charder rolled his eyes. "No, you can't. I have tried everything you're thinking, and, trust me, you can't. Let him take a hundred. It will be less painful in the end."

Teek sidled over to Storm. "What are they talking about?" he whispered.

"I'll tell you later," Storm said and hated the lie.

"Let me try with my own herd," said Kelsy quietly. "I'm certain we can figure something out."

"No," said Arcove. "One herd. That's not negotiable. I will entertain your breeding experiments, so long as it results in a thousand animals by this time next year. If not, the cull will be larger, and you will have a very bloody winter."

Charder spoke quietly. "What will you do with the ones who breed out-of-turn, Kelsy? Because they will. More than you think."

Kelsy sighed. "I suppose we could cull *just* those."

"So you'll do it yourselves?" asked Arcove.

"No, of course not."

"So, you'll tell us who to kill? That will certainly make you a popular leader."

Kelsy made a noise of exasperation. "The cull is *already* uneven. The lower ranking animals are more likely to be taken. They're more likely to be hungry, to run slowly, to be on the edge of the herd. It's obvious why the elders agreed to the cull. *They* are hardly ever killed."

Storm's head came up sharply. Suddenly, a great many things made more sense.

Arcove flicked his tail. "You are now one of those 'elders.' Yet you argue for something more fair. I think that speaks well of you, Kelsy, but you're not telling me anything that seems likely to produce fewer ferryshaft by this time next year."

Roup spoke. "What do you think, Storm?"

Storm was staring out over the plain. *The herd certainly looks smaller from up here.* "I think you're creating a problem where none exists." He turned to look at Arcove. "We don't need you to regulate us. Leave the herd alone."

"No," said Arcove. "Anything else?"

Storm shut his eyes. The waiting seemed intolerable. *Why can't this just be over?* "Why am I here?" he demanded. "So that I can watch you convince Kelsy of what you convinced Charder a long time ago? This isn't a real conference. You have all the power. What do you want from me?"

There was a moment's tense silence.

Arcove's voice dropped to a murmur. "Tell me about Syriot."

Storm felt that he should have seen it coming, but he hadn't.

"You've been there recently," continued Arcove, "as you keep reminding me. How many telshees are down there now, and what do they plan to do?"

"I'm not your spy," spat Storm.

"No, but you would like me to do something for you," said Arcove. "I'll take the cub, and I'll make sure he's safe, but you need to give me something in exchange."

Teek, who'd been looking confused, sat bolt upright. "What?"

Roup gave Arcove a frantic shake of his head.

Arcove looked surprised. "You mean he doesn't—?"

"Take me where?" Teek whirled to face Storm. "What's he talking about, Storm?"

Storm looked at Teek. Half a dozen lies struggled to come out of his mouth, but they all stuck in his throat. "You're going back to Leeshwood, Teek."

Teek's big, dark eyes darted over his face. "No," he whispered. "No, no, no."

"Yes." Storm tried to put both finality and compassion into his voice. "You're not a ferryshaft, Teek. You won't be happy in the herd. You don't belong there."

"But I am happy!" Teek's voice had risen an octave. "I'm happy with you! I'll go wherever you go, Storm."

"The creasia will have all kinds of hunting stories," Storm began, but Teek interrupted him.

"I don't want their stories! I want your stories!" He was growing frantic in the face of Storm's calm determination. "Why do you want to get rid of me? What did I do to make you want to get rid of me?"

Storm felt his composure slipping. "I don't want to get rid of you, Teek. I just can't keep you."

Teek started backing away from him. "I won't go. I'll run away. I won't come back until you say you'll keep me."

Storm followed him. "Teek, stop it."

Teek was whimpering. "You don't want me. You've never wanted me. You always tried to get rid of me. What did I do? What did I do, Storm?"

"It's not what you did; it's what I did," Storm heard himself say.

"I'll always be good," Teek pleaded. "I'd never hunt you, Storm. I promise! I promise! Please—"

"I killed your mother!" Storm shouted. The words felt as though they'd always been there, crouching in the back of his throat, a hideous monster waiting for a chance to spring free. Storm wanted to run after the monster, to cram it back inside him, but he couldn't.

There was a moment of perfect silence on the council ledge. Teek's eyes had dilated until they looked completely black. He took another step away from Storm and stumbled.

Storm's voice broke. "That's why she never came for you after the Volontaro. I felt responsible for you. I felt...sorry for you. But I can't keep you, Teek!" *And I don't deserve to.*

Teek took another step back. He opened his mouth, but didn't make a sound. Storm felt certain that the expression of hurt and betrayal on Teek's small face would haunt him as no ghost ever could. Teek whirled and bolted down the trail.

Roup stepped in front of Storm before he could follow. "Let him go," said Roup quietly. "I'll track him down later. I doubt he'll go far. For now...just let him go."

Storm inclined his head. He didn't dare look at any of their faces. "I don't know how many telshees are in Syriot," he said. "I don't think Shaw plans to attack you anytime soon. I don't think she wants anything to do with you. But if Keesha wakes…you'd better look out."

"He's asleep?" asked Arcove, and there was a note in his voice that made Storm raise his head. Caution? Fear?

"He's been asleep since the end of the war," said Storm. "He woke up and talked to me, though."

"I'll bet he did," muttered Roup.

"What did he tell you?" asked Arcove, his voice still guarded.

"Only what you did on Kuwee Island," said Storm darkly. He hesitated. "I found—" *Should I not tell them this? But I don't see how it can hurt anyone. And they seem to want some piece of information in exchange for taking care of Teek. Maybe this will be enough.* "I found Coden's blue stone in Groth. The Shable, Keesha called it."

That brought them all to attention. Even Charder turned from where he'd been looking over the plain. Arcove spoke. "You found…the Shable…in Groth?"

"Keesha and Shaw seemed as confused as you are," said Storm. "I'd tell you that Coden's ghost gave it to me…if I thought you'd believe that."

Roup looked like he wanted to know more, but Arcove spoke again. "So Keesha has the Shable now."

"Yes." Storm took a deep breath. "Is that enough? Will you take care of Teek?"

"We'll take care of him," said Roup quickly. "You can even come and visit if you like."

Arcove shot him a warning look as though to say, *"We'll discuss this later."* He turned back to Kelsy. "So. Raid or not raid, Kelsy? I told you I'd let you try this year, so it's your decision, but there will be a lot of killing next winter if you can't control them. And if you try to start a new herd without my blessing, I will kill you and every one of your followers. Do you understand?"

Kelsy seemed untroubled by the threats. "I understand, and I'd like to try to control them without raids."

"So be it," said Arcove and, behind him, Charder gave a deep sigh.

"Storm," said Arcove, and Storm fancied he could feel the weight of Arcove's gaze like a heavy rock on his shoulders. "I would like you to rejoin your herd."

Storm watched him warily. "What do you mean?"

"I mean exactly what I said. I do not approve of rogue ferryshaft. They tend to be the seeds of new herds. Is your sister still in Syriot?"

"As far as I know," said Storm carefully. *No need to mention Valla.*

"Then I would like her to rejoin the herd as well. Tell her."

"And if we don't?"

Arcove's tail lashed. "If you don't, I will send creasia to hunt you. However, if you rejoin your herd and do not incite them to break treaty laws, I will treat you as any other ferryshaft." He glanced at Roup. "Perhaps you might even come and see Teek."

You're going to use him to control me, thought Storm with a sinking feeling. *At least you haven't threatened him. Yet.*

"I'll think about it," he said.

"One of our rules stipulates no contact with telshees," said Arcove.

"I heard what you said," grated Storm.

"As long as you understood what I meant."

"Do you always get your way?" Storm demanded.

"Usually," said Arcove. "Charder, you're being very quiet. Do you have anything to add?"

"No," said Charder. "And I think we should go down. The herd is behaving oddly."

Storm followed his gaze, but the plain looked as it had before. Only now he understood what Charder meant. The herd looked small because it *was* small. Most of the ferryshaft must have gone into the belt of trees by the river. There were not nearly enough shapes on the plain to account for eleven hundred animals.

Arcove was looking down as well. "Agreed," he said after a moment, and Storm thought he sounded puzzled.

They all started along the path, walking just a little more quickly than was necessary. They were halfway down when they found the first body.

3

Run

A young male creasia lay sprawled across the path, eyes glazed, chest soaked with blood. Deep scratches cut into the muscle and meat of his flanks. Roup bounded forward. "Nevin?"

The cat did not answer. Roup was bristling all over as he bent to sniff him.

Arcove growled and started running. "Roup!" he bellowed over his shoulder. "With me! Now!"

Roup was still crouching beside his subordinate's body. Charder had frozen in the middle of the path. Storm and Kelsy pushed around him. Arcove whirled farther down the trail and shouted back at Roup. "They're fighting; you can't help that one. Come! Now!"

Roup broke away from the corpse with a visible effort and flashed down the trail after Arcove. Charder, Kelsy, and Storm were all running now. "This is bad," panted Charder. "Creasia fighting at the winter conference…? It's never happened before. That's probably why the herd went into the trees—anxious to get away from the fighting." He turned to Kelsy with a snarl. "If this has anything to do with your lot—"

"It doesn't!" Kelsy exclaimed. "I didn't hear so much as a whisper about fighting from any of the young cliques."

"A ferryshaft didn't kill that cat," said Storm. "Only creasia leave scratches like that."

Arcove and Roup had disappeared around a switchback. Storm felt numb. *What about Teek? Did he run into the middle of it?*

They'd almost reached the bottom, when they had to jump over the bodies of two more creasia. Storm didn't recognize any of them, but they'd clearly died of cat-inflicted wounds, and their blood slicked the rock beneath his hooves.

Storm pushed ahead of the other two and burst out of the enclosed portion of the trail a little before they did. Finally, he had an unobstructed view of the plain from about ten lengths above the ground, and the sight hit him like a physical blow—bodies everywhere, the red rock glistening redder. In the grassy area between the boulders and the riverside trees, he spotted ferryshaft bodies—the shapes that he and Charder had seen from the ledge. Nothing was moving.

At least, that's what Storm thought until he actually reached the foot of the trail and spotted Ariand. Arcove was crouching in front of him. Roup paced around them with the desperation of one who seeks to help and can do nothing. Storm could see blood, and he could tell that Ariand was badly hurt, but he'd almost reached the creasia before he realized what he was looking at.

Ariand had been disemboweled and his entrails tangled in a thorny bush. He could not pull away without ripping out more of his own insides. Blood-loss and the shock of his injuries had done the rest. Storm thought that he was dead, but as he watched, Ariand blinked his filmy eyes. He tried to speak and only sprayed Arcove's whiskers with blood.

Storm heard Kelsy's sharp intake of breath at his side. "What—happened?"

Charder came up beside them. He hesitated for a moment, then went right up to the group of creasia. Arcove didn't stir. He was almost nose-to-nose with Ariand, who was trying desperately to say something.

"Treace," managed Ariand at last.

Roup gave a snarl so savage that Storm flinched.

Arcove didn't move. "How?"

"Attacked just after you left," croaked Ariand.

"While we were passing the waterfall," murmured Charder. "It would have drowned out sounds from below."

"Halvery and Sharmel?" asked Arcove.

"Don't know," whispered Ariand. "Didn't see." He drew a breath that sounded wet. "Treace said to tell you he'd be waiting in the Great Clearing...to fight."

Roup stopped pacing. "You mean he left you like this on purpose?"

Ariand didn't respond. He was trembling with effort and, Storm suspected, with pain.

Charder's eyes flicked around the rocks as though expecting an ambush. Storm had to agree that this seemed like the perfect set-up.

"He took the ferryshaft herd," continued Ariand softly. "Drove them across the river."

Storm felt cold.

Kelsy had gone perfectly still.

"Where?" demanded Charder.

"Don't know," said Ariand. "Some of them fought. I wouldn't... wouldn't take the most direct route to the clearing if...if I were you." He screwed his eyes shut as though each breath required concentration.

Arcove spoke almost against his ear. "Do you want me to end this?"

"Please." He gulped in air. "Roup, will you...take me...to the Ghost Wood...when this is over?"

Roup stopped pacing. "Of course."

Arcove whispered, "We will miss you, councilor." His broad, pink tongue ran from Ariand's nose to the top of his head, as a mother cat might wash a cub. Then his jaws closed behind the other cat's skull. Storm looked away at the last moment. There was an audible crunch. When Storm turned back, Ariand's trembling had ceased.

Arcove stood up. He had been the picture of unshakeable calm during the ordeal. Now, he looked vacant.

"We have to go after the herd," whispered Kelsy in a voice that sounded far from certain.

Charder said nothing. He was watching the creasia.

Storm shouted, "Teek!" And he thought, *Tollee, Myla, Mother...*

"They can't all be dead," muttered Roup, staring at Ariand.

"Dead or turned," said Arcove, his expression still flat.

"My clutter would not turn," spat Roup. "Neither would Halvery's, and Sharmel—"

"Well, they're not *here.*"

"No, but we are."

Storm looked up and saw a curb perched on a nearby boulder. He snarled. "Quinyl."

"Ah, you remember me!" she murmured. "Good. I have certainly not forgotten you."

Three more curbs joined Quinyl. Out of the corners of his eyes, Storm saw a dozen more emerging from the scrub and rocks. Then two dozen, then more...and more...

Storm felt as though he couldn't breathe. *When did the lowland curbs grow so numerous?*

Arcove was growling low in his throat.

Quinyl glanced at him. "We've no quarrel with you, rulers of Leeshwood-that-was. Your fate is waiting for you in the Great Clearing. And you, Charder and Kelsy, rulers of a conquered people. Your herd is on its way into the deep forest. You should go and find it. But you, Storm Ela-ferry. We've a blood-debt to settle with you."

One of the curbs behind Storm set up an ululating howl that made him dance in a nervous circle. Quinyl laughed. "Yes, run. You're good at that. I think I would like to watch. Run away, little ferryshaft. Run as hard as you can. You'll go down kicking and screaming soon enough."

Arcove's rumble cut across her. "You are interrupting my council meeting, curb."

Storm glanced at him. Arcove's eyes seemed to be focusing again, and he looked like he wanted to kill something.

Quinyl looked at Arcove with a neutral expression. "Your council is over, cat. Many things are ending today."

"Such as my tolerance for lowland curbs," grated Arcove. "You are walking very close to war, little hunter."

Quinyl cocked her head, and now her expression was undisguised contempt. In the distance, Storm heard the faint sound of a creasia rally cry. From the way Arcove and Roup's ears flicked, he knew they heard it, too.

Quinyl sneered, "Now, who do you think that could be? Your cats...or Treace's? Think quickly, creasia king. You can have a fight in the clearing with witnesses, or you can have a fight out here... with us...and whatever is coming."

Arcove's lips peeled back in a terrible, gleaming snarl, and the fur along his spine rose, making him look even bigger. Roup was bristling, too, but his eyes kept skipping around the rocks. Storm guessed there were over a hundred curbs, and Roup probably didn't like the odds...especially since those rally cries were coming nearer.

A part of Storm wanted to flee—to take his chances with the curbs and look for Teek. *But Teek is either dead or safely hidden. And Arcove could have left me to die. He didn't.* Storm fought down his own instincts and backed up beside Arcove. "Do you remember what you told me in front of Groth?"

Arcove took a moment to respond. His whole attention was fixed on Quinyl. *He's really thinking about jumping up there and taking on the whole pack. He might even win...if there weren't other creasia coming.*

Storm guessed that the shock of what had just happened was affecting Arcove's judgment. *He just killed his own officer of...what?*

Twenty years? Thirty? That would rattle anyone. And besides, the sun is directly overhead. Teek was always a little fuzzy at noon, even when Storm had him on a daylight schedule. *For him, it's the middle of the night.*

"I asked you what you'd do with your back against a wall," continued Storm, "and you said you'd fight and die before you'd run away."

"I remember," snapped Arcove.

"I think you should reconsider," said Storm, and he couldn't help but add, "because I think you're about to *really* not get your way."

"If you have an idea, Storm," murmured Roup, "say it."

"I know a place to hide." Storm spoke softly and quickly. "Not a telshee cave; a different place. But we have to go now. Before those cats get any closer. I think the curbs will try to follow us, but they're not all that anxious to fight you. If they were, they'd already have attacked. They're waiting for Treace's cats."

Arcove was still looking up at Quinyl, Ariand's body cooling at his feet. "Arcove," said Roup softly, "I think we should do what he says."

Arcove didn't move.

"You're not thinking clearly," said Storm. "I know. It's daytime. You need to sleep."

Arcove shifted his attention from Quinyl to glare at Storm. *What am I doing?* thought Storm. He was suddenly conscious of how closely they were standing. *If he loses his temper... One swipe...*

"Arcove," said Charder. He took a deep breath. "I'll... I'll tell you..." He couldn't seem to get the words out.

Arcove's hackles settled a little. He glanced at Charder. "Tell me what?"

Charder took another breath. "I'll tell you how Storm is related to Coden...if you come now."

There was a pause. Finally, Arcove made a little snort. "Charder..."

"You'll come? Good," said Storm, and he darted away. He'd already planned the route in his mind. He knew the others were following when the circle of curbs moved with him instead of closing in.

Then Arcove sailed over his head and landed on a curb who hadn't moved fast enough. The animal didn't even have time to scream. The next one did, though, as Arcove's claws caught him and flipped him into the air in a spray of blood. Roup thumped down beside Arcove, slapping at scampering animals, and then the circle of curbs broke apart.

Storm ran all-out towards the headwaters of the Igby. It was the easiest place to cross, where all the tributaries had not yet converged, and large boulders from the cliffs provided staging points.

Behind and around him, he could hear the curbs yipping and howling. *They'll follow us and try to guide pursuing creasia. But it won't matter if we reach our destination.*

In the trees, when they'd gained enough distance to avoid being overheard, Roup called, "Storm, are we going to that fiord?"

"Yes."

"The one where you lost me when I chased you?"

"Yes." *I told Teek about it, so there's no point in keeping it from you. He'd tell you eventually...unless Treace's cats... Unless Teek...*

Storm shook his head. *Run,* he told himself. *Just run.*

4

The Fiord

Their run took them along the foot of the cliffs into creasia territory, through mazes that Storm did not know well. Roup said that this was technically Sharmel's territory, though it was riddled with telshee caves, so close to the Garu Vell. No cats denned here.

Arcove said almost nothing, but he obviously knew his way, and he took the lead through the boulders. He led them to a trail that ascended the cliff in dizzy switchbacks, and they spent the rest of the afternoon climbing. Three quarters of the way up, they got a good look at their pursuers—a mixture of cats and curbs, bounding along the lower trail. Arcove and Roup stopped for one hard look.

"I see at least three cats from Ariand's clutter," said Roup quietly.

Arcove grunted.

So it's not just the cats you sent away with Treace, thought Storm. *Other cats have gone over to them. That can't be good.*

Or can it? What would be best for the ferryshaft? Could we use this to somehow get free of the creasia forever? Storm didn't know, but he knew that a Leeshwood ruled by Treace would certainly not be better for anyone.

When they reached the top of the cliff, Roup struck out in a straight line for the fiord. Storm could hear the ocean now and smell the sharp tang of brine. They burst out of the trees above the Sea Cliffs, and Storm caught a glimpse of the jagged line of the fiord up ahead. He could not help but feel smug. "Been wondering about this, have you?"

Roup just lashed his tail.

"You shouldn't feel *too* stupid. It's all-but-impossible to see—"

"Just tell us how it works," snapped Arcove.

Storm scowled. After a moment, he said, "There's a cave in the opposite cliff wall. You can't see the opening from the top, but you can just make out the lip. That's where you aim when you jump. The cave is a tunnel that comes out in a thicket north of here. Without a scent trail leading there, it's nearly impossible to find."

Kelsy's head came up sharply. "I showed you this! A couple of years ago. Itsa and me...and Faralee."

"Yes," grinned Storm. "You did."

"I'd never have tried jumping to it from the cliff, though," said Kelsy. "If you miss, you're dead."

"Well, Roup was about to catch me the first time I tried it," said Storm, "so it seemed like the better option."

The fiord opened suddenly in front of them. "I almost went over the edge here," muttered Roup. "Lyndi was—" He stopped and shook his head.

"It's actually easy once you know where you're aiming," said Storm. "You see that line? It looks like a tiny shelf of rock not even wide enough for standing, but that's the lip of the cave mouth. You just can't see the opening from this angle."

Arcove studied the cliff. "Clever," he muttered.

"Yes, I shouldn't be showing it to you," said Storm.

"Well, I did just save you from a pack of curbs," said Arcove.

"So we're even." Storm backed up, took a running start, and jumped. He could not suppress an instant of fear as the cliff wall rushed up to meet him. Then a dark opening yawned abruptly, and he landed, with a clatter of hooves, in the hidden cave.

The others soon followed. Storm had been a little worried about Charder. He was the oldest and not in fighting shape, or so Storm had thought. However, Charder made the jump so neatly that Storm wondered whether he'd done it before. Kelsy, by contrast, nearly fell. He landed, scrambling, on the edge, and then bolted into the cave, bristling with anxiety. Roup came next, sniffing and looking at everything, and finally Arcove, who, for all his size, landed silently.

"Oh," murmured Roup, when he saw the odd figures on the walls. "This is an old ferryshaft cave." Sunset light streaked the ancient images of ferryshaft with odd creatures on their backs.

Arcove grunted.

Roup was examining the images minutely. "Very old. From the time of the humans."

Arcove padded past him down the passage. Storm doubted that he would rest until he'd seen every bit of the cave. *Just as well.*

506

I haven't been here in more than a season. I hope the exit hasn't collapsed.

Storm wished that the cave had water or anything to eat. They'd passed a stream earlier in the afternoon, and everyone had taken a few gulps, but Storm was thirsty again. Still, the cave had the essential thing—safety. Arcove was still gone when there came a rustle of activity on the ledge above—creasia voices and calls, the yip of curbs.

Sounds carried easily in the fiord. Everyone sat very still. Arcove came stalking back, and waited, saying nothing, while the clamber continued above. After a while, the sounds died away. However, the fugitives took the precaution of moving farther back along the tunnel before speaking or settling down. Arcove and Roup curled up back-to-back. They were talking in voices too low to understand, but their tone sounded grim.

"I'll take first watch," said Kelsy suddenly.

"Second," said Storm.

"Wake me when you get tired," said Charder. He glanced at the creasia. "You two, sleep. We'll wake you if there's anything to kill."

Neither of the creasia responded.

It's not so easy—staying awake all night and running all day, is it? Storm shut his eyes and tried to sleep. However, all the fears that he'd managed to suppress during the day came flooding into his brain. *What would Tollee do if creasia tried to drive her into Leeshwood? She's a fighter. Was her body out there on the plain? Would Myla survive the river crossing? It's a long swim for a spring foal. How many drowned?*

More than anything, Teek's expression of pain and betrayal hung like a ghost before his mind's eye. *Were those his last moments?*

"Storm?"

Storm's head jerked up. Roup was looking down at him. "I thought you might like to know—I did a quick run around the trailhead before the rest of you reached the ground. I was trying to identify all the creasia bodies. I didn't see Teek or smell his blood."

Storm swallowed. "The curbs might have chased him before they killed him."

"They might have," agreed Roup. "But they seemed focused on us. I think he got away."

Storm felt his insides unclench a little. "Maybe."

Roup hesitated. "That cub loves you, Storm."

Storm could not meet Roup's steady gaze. "Not anymore."

"No," said Roup in a tired voice, "he still does. You never really stop loving someone like that…no matter how hard you try." Roup turned away before Storm could respond and went back to lie down beside Arcove.

Leagues below, in the twilight of the Dreaming Sea, a pair of blue eyes opened, fully alert for the first time in decades. Syra-lay raised his snowy head, scattering brightly colored fish and crabs. His coils rippled and uncurled, snapping off crustaceans and bits of coral. He yawned hugely, shook himself, and laughed. "My song is finished."

5

Loyalty

In the chilliest time of night, just before dawn, Charder crouched on the cold stone near the northern mouth of the tunnel. He wrapped his tail around his legs and tried to stay awake. He was thinking that this all felt familiar—as though the past and the future were colliding. *I have waited, hungry and cold, in such caves before.*

Then a darker shape—a little blacker than the shadows—came gliding around him.

Charder managed to repress his instinctive flinch. "We don't need anything killed yet."

Arcove sniffed at the breeze blowing in from the mouth of the tunnel. Charder already knew that it smelled of woods and sea, but not of other animals. Arcove yawned and lay down on his belly, closer than Charder would have liked. The cat put his head on his paws and shut his eyes. "Tell me."

Charder swallowed. "Tell you what?"

Arcove smiled without opening his eyes.

Charder fidgeted. "Don't you want to wait for Roup?"

The tip of Arcove's tail twitched. "If I wait for him to wake up, I'm not sure I'll have time to kill you."

Charder said nothing.

Arcove's green eye opened a slit. "You never know when I'm joking, do you?"

Charder concentrated on breathing. "I would not presume to guess."

"Are you trembling because you're cold or frightened?"

"Both."

"Well, let me see whether *I* can tell *you* what happened. Lirsy survived…somehow. That's the only thing that makes sense. Storm's mother is her…daughter? Granddaughter?"

"Daughter." Charder felt a strange relief as the secret left him. "Lirsy didn't fall from the cliff. She jumped into a tree that overhung the edge. I found her…after." *After I watched you kill Coden, and I couldn't abandon his foal, Arcove. I couldn't. No matter what I'd promised.*

"So you hid her from me…and lied to me about it for fifteen years."

Charder laid his head on the ground and shut his eyes. *Please use your teeth and not your claws.*

"You did this even though you're scared to death of me. That is remarkable loyalty, Charder."

"Don't you think Roup would have done the same if you'd died and it had been your cub?"

There was a long silence, during which Charder hardly dared to breathe.

"Yes," said Arcove at last, "I suppose he would have." He didn't actually sound angry. Charder dared to open his eyes. "Peace," said Arcove. "I've lost enough officers lately."

You think of me as one of your officers? The world seemed upside down and backwards.

"Is she still alive?" asked Arcove. "Lirsy, I mean?"

Charder cleared his throat. "No. She took a mate, but had several miscarriages. She died when So-fet was born. A friend nursed the foal, and I fed her and protected her during her first two seasons. Then I distanced myself. I was afraid you'd notice."

Arcove said nothing.

"Would you...would you have killed her...if I hadn't run with her?" Charder wasn't sure which answer would be worse, but he *had* to know. *She was never quite right after the war. I'm sure she would have lived a longer life if she hadn't been on the cliff that night.*

Arcove thought for a moment. "If I had caught her, I would have used her to threaten Coden into surrender...to get him down off Turis Rock alive. I would have preferred to keep him in charge of the ferryshaft. They would have obeyed him more readily, and things after the war would have gone more smoothly. I had no plans for his foal beyond that."

Charder bowed his head.

"But," continued Arcove, "the assumption that I intended to kill her was not unreasonable, given the circumstances. In your position...I won't say I would have done the same, but I would have considered it."

Charder gave a bitter laugh. "In my position, you would have fought beside Coden and died."

"I am glad you did not," said Arcove. "Your herd should be glad of it, too."

Charder didn't know what to say to that. After a moment, he muttered, "It is difficult for low-ranking ferryshaft now. Ferryshaft herds were never meant to be so large. There aren't many resources left over for those at the bottom. Kelsy is right when he says that the low-ranking animals are most often killed in raids. He's correct, too, that it would be easier to manage things in a smaller, more natural-sized herd."

"I will not be outnumbered and surrounded *again*," growled Arcove.

"Too late," said Charder and wondered where his new bravery had come from.

Arcove gave a sad little chuckle.

Charder had stopped trembling. *I am old enough to be your father, and when we met, you were hardly more than a big cub. A cub feeling his way along in the dark. Why did I never see that?*

"This thing with Treace," said Charder, "I always knew something like this would happen eventually." He hesitated. "I thought I would enjoy it more."

"Well, the irony might be sweeter if you weren't in here with me," said Arcove.

"No," said Charder, "I don't think so. Arcove...what if I could get the herd to fight for you...for your cats?"

The twitching tip of Arcove's tail grew suddenly still. *You weren't expecting me to say that.*

"It would put you in my debt, of course," continued Charder with no small degree of smugness.

Arcove was silent for a long moment. "You've learned from me too well," he said at last. He thought for a moment. "I don't think you could get them to do it."

"But if I could," persisted Charder. "Would you stop the raids and let the herd split up?" *Would you trust us?*

Arcove was perfectly still. At last, he said, "Is that your advice, then, councilor?"

"It is." *You're going to have to trust* someone *before this is over.*

A clatter of hoofbeats sounded in the passage. Charder and Arcove rose quickly as Storm dashed out of the shadows, Kelsy and Roup on his heels.

"We may be discovered," said Storm in a frantic whisper. "I heard— I thought I heard—"

"We heard voices on the ledge overhead," said Roup more evenly. "Indistinct voices."

"It was Teek," said Storm miserably. "I think he was telling them how to get in. He knows. I told him."

Kelsy looked bleary-eyed and skeptical. "Storm, you couldn't even understand what they were saying—"

"I know his voice," snapped Storm.

"I don't think your cub would do that," said Roup.

Storm only shook his head.

"Quiet," muttered Arcove.

They all sat perfectly still. In the silence, Charder realized that the night birds outside had stopped singing. *So much for loyalty. This tunnel would be a terrible spot to get trapped. But if we bolt, and Treace's cats* haven't *found us...we could lose our hiding place.*

Arcove was listening intently. And now Charder heard it, too—low voices, not far away.

Suddenly, Roup came stalking right up to the cave's mouth. He reared, so that his head was above the opening, and made a chittering noise. Arcove cocked his head, but he didn't say anything. Roup did it again, and this time, there was an answer.

Roup looked like he was ready to jump out of the cave then, but Arcove said, "Wait."

"It's someone from my clutter," hissed Roup. "Has to be. No one else would answer that call." He was pacing back and forth in the spill of moonlight at the cave's mouth.

"Wait," repeated Arcove.

The chittering came again, much closer. Arcove crouched, eyes fixed on the lip of the cave's mouth. Then the silhouette of a creasia's head popped into view. "Roup?" it whispered—a female voice.

"Lyndi." Roup's voice was undisguised relief.

She jumped down into the cave's basin. "Oh, boss. We've had a rough night."

Behind her, two larger shapes thumped down into the cave. "Halvery?" Arcove rumbled in surprise. "Sharmel?"

"Arcove," came Halvery's tired voice. "By all the ghosts… I was beginning to think we'd never see you again."

Arcove chuffed. "Likewise."

"Treace attacked us with at least three times our numbers," grated Sharmel. "They killed Ariand—"

"No," snarled Roup, "they left Ariand at the foot of the cliffs, dying, with his guts tangled in a bush, as a *messenger*. I haven't seen anything like that since the war."

Sharmel sagged visibly, and Halvery growled beside him. "We should have gone back for him. We shouldn't have run—"

"Yes, you should have," said Arcove. "If you hadn't run, you wouldn't be here."

"We wouldn't be here anyway," said Halvery, "if not for this little fellow."

A smaller shadow detached itself from Halvery's and came hesitantly towards Storm. "I knew who he was," whispered Teek. "Because of his short tail."

6

Council in Hiding

"Treace's followers killed the sentry at the foot of the trail to the council ledge first," said Halvery, "to prevent Arcove from getting a warning. Roup and Ariand's clutters were stationed in that part of the boulders. I'm sure Treace's cats were trying to kill them quietly. They probably ambushed a few before anyone knew what was going on, but Lyndi saw what was happening and ran to get me."

"They'd already surrounded the foot of the trail," put in Lyndi. "They were killing anyone who tried to get near it. I thought going for reinforcements made more sense."

The group had moved a little back into the tunnel, where their voices wouldn't carry. In the darkness, Storm could hardly see the outlines of the others. He kept glancing over to the puddle of shadow that was Teek, but the cub had lain down about halfway between Storm and Halvery. He'd grown so still that Storm thought he might be asleep.

"The waterfall really did work to their advantage," said Halvery bitterly. "I was stationed up there, and I didn't hear a thing until Lyndi came running out of the trees, shouting that Treace's cats were killing Ariand and his clutter. I had just enough time to give a few rally cries. Then the world went mad."

"They stampeded the ferryshaft herd," said Sharmel. "They were well-organized—driving the ferryshaft together in a mass and then pushing them towards the headwaters of the Igby. It was the easiest way to get them to cross the river, but it also sent a thousand panicked ferryshaft directly into my clutter and then Halvery's. As nearly as I can tell, four of my six creasia were killed—either trampled to death or injured and then finished off by Treace's cats."

"They had it easy," growled Halvery. "They just came along behind the ferryshaft, killing whatever limped out of the dust. Five of my ten cats are dead or missing. The rest of us ran. It was that, or be trampled."

"Did you see any lowland curbs?" asked Arcove.

"Not at the time," said Halvery, a curious note in his voice, "but later, as we tried to regroup and fight our way back to the council trail, we did see a few. They appeared to be helping Treace's cats."

"He's made friends in the Southern Mountains," said Arcove. "Continue."

"We tried to get back to you," said Halvery. "But, by the time we managed to separate ourselves from the ferryshaft herd and regroup, we were well south of the Igby, and Treace's cats were hard after us. I decided that it made most sense to split up. We needed numbers. I sent what remained of our clutters to our respective dens to warn them and to rally our commands. We had two cats left from Roup's clutter besides Lyndi, and I sent them home, too. I told everyone to come to Arcove's den, since I think it's the most defensible."

"Also, the most likely to be attacked," muttered Sharmel. "Treace's creasia are not playing by the rules."

"Do you think your messengers got through?" asked Roup.

"I don't know," said Halvery. "I…I really don't know. As night fell, we finally managed to put some distance between ourselves and our pursuers by climbing the cliffs. We headed back north, determined to find you or your body. Lyndi insisted on coming with us. We were excited when we finally crossed your trail, but then it ended at this fiord."

"Which, of course, I remembered," said Lyndi. "I figured that, if you were still with Storm, you must have gone wherever he went. But these two didn't believe me."

"It's not that we didn't believe you," snapped Halvery. Storm could tell that he was very tired. "We just couldn't figure it out. Treace's cats had obviously been following Arcove. Their scent and tracks were mixed up with everyone else's. There wasn't any blood, but we thought they might have pushed you off the cliff. Then we met this cub…"

Everyone paused and looked towards Teek. After a moment, Storm saw a stir amid the shadows. "There was a dead creasia in the trail when I ran down," said Teek, his voice creaking with exhaustion. "So I looked for someone to tell. But then a curb saw me, and he chased me, and there were a lot of them." Teek hesitated. "So I remembered some of the places that Storm and I went last year, and I remembered that lowland curbs don't like sheep trails, and I went to the trail that's near the crooked tree spring, and I lost them."

Storm sat up. "You ran that trail…after being gone for a season?"

Teek's voice held a note of defiance. "I ran the trail."

"You're lucky you didn't break your neck," said Storm.

"*You're* lucky I didn't break my neck."

That made Storm shut his mouth.

"I got to the top of the cliff," continued Teek, "and I couldn't go back because of the curbs. While I was watching, everyone came down from the council ledge, and I saw the curbs chase you, and I tried to follow, but I couldn't keep up." Teek drew a deep breath. "So, then it was night, and I'd been awake all day, and I was really tired, but there were still curbs around, so I was afraid to stop anywhere to sleep. I kept walking south, hoping I'd see you. Finally, I saw these creasia coming the other way. And I hid from them, but then I saw Halvery's short tail, so I knew who he was."

"You can stop mentioning that part," cut in Halvery.

"It's not his favorite feature," said Roup with a hint of mischief.

"He knew about the tunnel in the fiord," said Halvery, "although it took us a while to find the southern entrance."

There was a moment's heavy silence.

"What does Treace want with the herd?" asked Charder.

"He wants to eat them," said Roup.

Kelsy drew in a sharp breath.

"He wants to groom them as a food source," said Arcove more evenly. "He's not going to eat them right away."

"I thought," stammered Kelsy, "that creasia didn't like eating ferryshaft."

"You don't taste good when you're eating meat," said Halvery with a nasty smile in his voice.

"Why do you think I send the raids in winter?" asked Arcove. "I do not approve of talking animals eating each other. If I wanted you all dead, I'd kill you and leave you for the birds and the foxes." He hesitated. "You would not believe how your elders complained of that in the last war."

"You left bodies so they could be found to inspire fear," snapped Charder, and then closed his mouth quickly and looked away.

"At least I didn't eat them," said Arcove in a dangerous murmur.

"I think," ventured Sharmel, "that some of Ariand's command has gone over to Treace."

"I think most of them have," muttered Roup. "Treace has been working on Ariand's command for years. He's put a lot of cats into those clutters and dens. They share blood ties with his cats, and most of them are less than twelve years old. They didn't fight with us during the ferryshaft wars. They didn't see Arcove kill Ketch or...anyone else."

"If that's true," said Sharmel softly, "we were outnumbered two-to-one before he even attacked us."

"I would put one of my forty-year-old creasia against two of Treace's ten-year-old's any day," scoffed Halvery, "and watch mine tear his to pieces."

"I'd bet on yours, too," said Roup, "in a fair fight. But maybe not if they were surprised."

"*Even* if they were surprised," returned Halvery. "My cats actually go on raids, Roup. They still know how to kill things."

"You think killing panicked ferryshaft is good practice for war?" flashed Roup.

"We killed a telshee two Volontaros ago—"

"Enough," growled Arcove. "Halvery, Sharmel, you're in no state to fight right now. Sleep. We'll leave in daylight, after our pursuers have exhausted themselves. I suspect we will have to fight our way into my den."

Storm wondered whether Arcove was worried that Treace had killed his mates and cubs. If so, his voice gave no sign. As the others spread out along the passage to find comfortable sleeping places, Storm inched towards the spot where he'd last heard Teek. The cub had gone, and Storm followed his scent along the tunnel to the darkest corner—a place where no ferryshaft eyes could pierce. His nose told him that Teek was there, somewhere in the shadows.

All year, I've tried to get you to sleep alone. And every night you've come crawling over to curl up beside me. And now...now it's the other way around.

"Teek?" he whispered.

For a long moment, Storm thought he wouldn't respond. Finally, he heard fur shift over stone. "What?"

"Aren't you cold?"

"No."

Storm took a step back. He felt as though someone had filled his legs with cold sea water—heavy and numb. Storm curled up against the wall. *Should I go with Arcove's cats tomorrow? Why? Should I try to find my herd? Won't I just get killed?* Storm felt a faint brush of fur against his hip. He turned in the darkness, but he could see nothing. Cautiously, he leaned over to sniff...and then recoiled as something hissed and eye-watering pain shot down his muzzle.

Storm yelped. All his muscles tensed and he suppressed the urge to jump up, to lash out, to bite, to kick. Instead, he laid his head on the ground and took slow, deep breaths through his stinging nose. *He scratched me pretty good.* Storm tasted blood in the back of his throat. Teek came to him then and burrowed up against his neck.

"I'm sorry," whispered Storm.

Teek didn't say anything. He curled up against Storm's neck and chest. He was trembling with exhaustion and, perhaps, Storm hoped, with relief. A moment later, Teek was asleep.

Roup was restless, but knew he mustn't disturb the others. He allowed himself one circuit of the tunnel before settling down. On his way back, in the darkest corner, he saw the outline of Storm and Teek, sleeping. The cub was cuddled up to Storm's chest, his head resting across the ferryshaft's shoulders.

Roup felt a mixture of warmth and apprehension. *Maybe it won't end badly this time. Maybe.*

Although things aren't looking so good right now. Roup did not have a large clutter. He knew every one of them—every one that had died today. *Mourn them later, fight for the ones still alive. That's what Arcove would say.*

He passed Lyndi, curled up near the entrance. *At least you're alright.*

Arcove sat just within the cave's mouth. The sky outside was growing lighter. "My turn," said Roup. "You sleep."

Arcove didn't argue, but he didn't go anywhere, either, just laid his head down on his crossed paws. "I should have killed Treace," he muttered, and now Roup could hear all the doubt that never entered Arcove's voice in council.

"I agreed with you about sending him away," said Roup. "So did Halvery. I thought Treace would make trouble if he stayed in the wood, but I never thought he'd come back and do this. If I had seen it coming, I would have told you. I didn't."

"Ariand—"

"Was suffering," said Roup.

Arcove gave a little snort. "I didn't kill him when I broke his neck. I killed him when I didn't kill Treace."

"You'll kill Treace," said Roup.

They were silent a moment. "Roup, how long did Ketch rule?"

Roup considered "Three years, I think."

"And Masaran?"

Roup didn't like where this was going. "I don't know. Maybe eight."

"And the king before that?"

"Arcove, stop it."

"Creasia kings don't get old," murmured Arcove. "Twenty-three years is a long time."

"You're not old," said Roup. "Do you know how many cats will die if you don't win this? Ferryshaft, too."

Arcove's eyes flicked up and he gave a little smile. "Charder suggested they could help us...in exchange for ending the raids."

Roup laughed. "I think that's a good idea."

"The day I need ferryshaft to fight my battles for me is the day I'm done ruling Leeshwood."

Roup didn't agree, but he was relieved to hear the spark return to Arcove's voice. "And, besides, they wouldn't," continued Arcove.

"Don't be so sure."

"I'm sure." Arcove stopped suddenly and cocked his head. "Roup, do you...hear something?"

"Something?" Arcove did not seem inclined to elaborate. Roup listened. "A few morning birds." He shut his eyes and concentrated. "Nothing else."

Arcove was bristling. "You're sure?"

"Yes." Roup peered at him. "What did it sound like?"

Arcove laid his head back down on his paws. "Nothing."

Roup frowned. *You know exactly what you think you heard. You just don't want to say.* Roup listened again, but he heard nothing.

Into the Dark

Midmorning found them all trotting groggily back to the cliff trail. There had, indeed, been searchers out last night. Fresh creasia and curb tracks crisscrossed their own. "I heard voices on the ledge again at dawn," said Charder.

"That cave is a good hiding place," muttered Halvery. "I think I remember losing Coden there once, but it's been years since I came that way."

"Well, they don't call me his ghost for nothing," said Storm with a hint of insolence.

Halvery glanced at him. He had completely ignored Storm since he'd arrived. "They don't call you his ghost at all," he snapped. "They call you Vearil."

"That, too." Storm knew he was more cheerful than he had any right to be. Teek was trotting along at his heels, darting shy looks at the adult creasia.

They were about halfway down the cliff when Halvery asked, grudgingly, "Whose cub?"

"Not sure," said Storm. "He came from Treace's territory, and that's about all he knows."

Halvery peered at Teek more closely. "Might be Treace's cub. They're about the same color."

"I'm Storm's cub," said Teek with a defiant lift of his chin.

"You are an unnatural abomination," said Halvery, but with no real malice.

Storm was surprised. *Was that almost a smile, Halvery?*

Teek trotted up beside the adult cat. *Please don't ask him about the river,* thought Storm.

"Do you remember when you chased Storm and he—"

"Teek, why don't you ask Halvery about his own cubs." Storm wasn't sure why he said it, only that it might divert Teek from an unpleasant conversation.

Halvery's head jerked around at Storm, and he almost stopped walking. He turned back to the trail with a huff.

Storm felt taken aback. "Well, I assume you have some."

"He has a lot," called Roup from the front of the group.

"But I don't talk about them to ferryshaft," said Halvery.

Storm was about to say that he would only be talking about them to Teek, when he heard a soft sound—as though the cliff itself gave a sigh. Storm's heart dropped into his stomach.

He turned around and looked up. Far above them, a plume of dust billowed over a wave of sliding rock that grew wider and louder as it rushed downward. Along the lip of the cliff, Storm saw the silhouettes of dozens of curbs. He could almost hear Quinyl's smug voice. *Try to run on a sheep trail now, Vearil.*

Arcove shouted something that Storm could not understand over the building roar. Then Arcove turned and leapt over the edge of the path. They couldn't hope to get beyond the radius of the avalanche by running. Their only hope was to get down the cliff first.

Halvery whipped around and grabbed Teek by the scruff before he jumped. Storm could have licked his nose for it. Then they were all bounding and sliding down the cliff in a controlled fall. Choking red dust rose around them. Storm coughed as he slid knee-deep in loose rock, falling occasionally where the cliff went sheer. He could see Arcove at the head of the group, tail lashing in an attempt to balance. Kelsy and Charder were keeping up. They were already more than three quarters of the way down. *We'll make it.* Little rocks started to clatter around them, then bigger ones.

The ground was coming up fast. Then the roar grew deafening as boulders started to crash past. Arcove, Roup, and Kelsy reached the bottom, but then the sliding rocks caught up, and Storm lost sight of them. Charder lost his balance, slid sideways, and flipped over in a maelstrom of dust. Halvery hit the ground, Teek flopping helplessly in his mouth, and then they disappeared amid the choking red cloud. Something hit Storm from behind, and he lost his footing. The earth reeled, and dust stung his nose where Teek had scratched him. Then he fell into blackness.

Arcove woke in a ghost-world. The air was thick with dust, and he coughed until he gagged. He could not remember where he was or what he was supposed to be doing. He thought he must have water in his ears. He thought, for a moment, that he must be *under*water. He needed to swim to the surface. He needed to breathe. He needed to find…something…someone….

He stumbled along, boulders looming out of the haze. "Roup?" he whispered. *Please wake me up. Please. I'm in my nightmare.*

He could finally hear something—a song. A terrible, beautiful, merciless song. It set its claws in his gut and *pulled*. Arcove whimpered.

He was going into a cave. Into the darkness. The world washed around him like a dream—a dream from which he could not wake.

Storm dragged himself to his feet. The dust was so thick that, for a moment, he thought it was evening. "Teek!" he balled and then remembered the curbs. *Well, they won't be coming down that trail anytime soon.* Storm threw back his head and howled.

To his surprise, someone answered. Storm moved towards the sound as quickly as his shaky legs would carry him. He was bruised, but nothing felt broken. *We were almost at the bottom. So close.*

Charder found him a moment later. He was limping. Kelsy was with him.

"Curbs?" gasped Storm.

Charder shook his head. Storm took this to mean that Charder hadn't seen any curbs hunting them through the rubble. It was difficult to talk with so much dust. Storm heard the sound of frantic digging and hurried towards it, grumbling as he weaved and tripped. Through the haze, he caught sight of Halvery, gray and red with dust, digging through the loose shale. Storm gave a sigh of relief when he saw Teek, struggling ineffectively to help.

The three ferryshaft came forward and helped dig. A moment later, Storm caught a glimpse of dark, matted fur—very still. He thought, for a moment, that it was Arcove. Then Halvery got a grip on the body and dragged it free. It was Sharmel, his dark gray fur made darker by dust. He lay unmoving, with bloody froth around his lips.

Halvery backed away, cursing. He gave a wailing rally cry. Somewhere off to their left, someone answered, and Halvery ran in that direction. Charder crouched by Sharmel's head. "He's still breathing," he murmured. "Storm, go help Halvery. We'll stay here."

Kelsy glanced at Charder, but he didn't argue. Teek trotted after Storm. They caught up with Halvery a moment later, running towards the base of the cliff. They were angling a little north, away from the main path of the avalanche, and the dust began to clear. Storm was about to ask where they were going, when Halvery pushed through a stand of gnarled trees, and Storm saw Roup and Lyndi. They were peering into a rocky crevice.

Halvery called to them as he approached. Roup whipped around, bristling all over. His nose was bloody, but he seemed otherwise unhurt. "Arcove went in here. I followed his scent trail. But…it doesn't make sense."

Storm reached Roup and peered into the narrow cave. He sniffed at the cool, still air. *This one goes deep.*

Halvery snuffled around in front of the cave. "Well, you're right; he went in here."

"Of course I'm right!" snapped Roup, his voice taut.

Halvery stuck his head into the cave. "Arcove!" he bellowed.

"I already tried that," said Roup. "I went quite a ways in, and then the tunnel goes straight down. I'm not sure I could get back up. I'm not sure—" He bit off whatever he'd been going to say.

"Did you see him?" Halvery sounded confused.

"No," said Roup. "I woke up, and he'd already gone."

"Without you?" Halvery sounded incredulous.

Roup said nothing.

"He must have hit his head," said Halvery

"Arcove wouldn't go into a cave," whispered Roup. "Not if it might be a telshee cave. He—he *wouldn't*."

"Well, obviously he did!" said Halvery.

Roup shook his head, still bristling.

"You think he was dragged in there?" asked Halvery. "Did you smell any telshees?"

"No," said Roup.

"Then he walked in for…for some reason." Halvery craned his neck as though that would help him see into the blackness.

"I'm going after him," said Roup, "but I don't think you should wait for me. Get everyone to the den site and we'll meet you there if—"

Halvery gave a frustrated snort. "I'm not going anywhere."

"Greetings, rulers of Leeshwood-that-was."

Everyone whirled to see half a dozen creasia advancing towards them out of the trees. Storm didn't recognize any of them, but Halvery bristled to his tail tip. His lips peeled back in a bone-rattling snarl. The other creasia halted. "We come as messengers," said the lead animal, tail and chin high. "We come in peace."

Storm was surprised to hear Teek's much smaller growl beside him. The cub arched his back and hissed. At the same time, he pressed himself against Storm's flank. Roup and Lyndi didn't make a sound. They waited, watching the other creasia.

"We have come to bring a challenge to Arcove Ela-creasia. Where is he?"

"We'll take your message," said Roup. "Speak."

The other cat seemed to consider. Finally, he said, "Treace waited for you all night in the Great Clearing with over a hundred witnesses. You did not appear. It would seem that our king is afraid."

He waited for some response, but no one spoke.

"Or," continued the messenger slyly, "perhaps he is just enjoying his time in the company of the ferryshaft known as Vearil—an animal who has challenged creasia authority on more than one occasion. Perhaps Arcove is too busy meeting Vearil's demands to answer a challenge from another cat."

"We answer to no one," grated Halvery.

The younger cat looked at him coolly. "If Arcove is no longer among us, Treace will meet the challenge of any who wish to fight him this evening. He will also graciously accept your surrender and your recognition of his dominance if you wish to live."

"Oh, he'll get a fight," said Halvery. "I promise you that."

"Very well." The messenger's lip curled. "If we spend another night waiting for you to appear, we will take it as evidence of your cowardice. Our king does not have endless evenings to spend chasing his tail. Cowards who refuse to surrender will be hunted down by all of Leeshwood. Like rats."

"Well, I'm glad you haven't been hunting us like rats yet," said Roup, his voice bright and brittle. "Tell Treace to go chase his tail while he still has it. You are dismissed." He turned deliberately away from them.

The words of an alpha, thought Storm. He glanced at Halvery. He could sense that there was a confusion in the hierarchy here. *Who is really in charge if Arcove is gone?*

Before either Roup or Halvery could say anything, Storm spoke. "I'll find Arcove," he said.

In the surprised silence, he turned to Teek. "You stay with the creasia."

Teek opened his mouth, but Storm talked over him. "No arguments. It's not safe for you; it's safe for me." *I think. Unless Shaw really hasn't forgiven me.*

He turned to see Halvery glaring down at him. "If you have anything to do with this… If you know what's happened—!"

"I don't," said Storm. "But I can go in there, even if there are telshees. I'm the only one here who might be able to get Arcove back if they've caught him." Storm thought of offering terms, but he could tell by the fury on Halvery's face and the anxiety on Roup's that now was not the time. *First see whether I can do it. Worry about gratitude later.*

"I'm going with you," said Roup.

"No, you're not," said Storm. "Your presence will make it harder to get what we want. Every moment I delay makes it less likely that Arcove will be alive when I find him. Don't argue with me."

Roup's mouth snapped shut.

"Sharmel isn't dead," continued Storm, "at least he wasn't a moment ago. Charder and Kelsy stayed with him. He'll need help getting out of here, though."

Without waiting to see what they would say, Storm plunged into the blackness of the cave. He was relieved when nobody followed.

8

Song and Storm

Storm followed Arcove's scent easily along the winding floor of the cave. Roup was right. No other animals' scents crossed the trail. *Why did you come in here, Arcove?*

After looping downward for several moments, the trail came to a vertical drop. Storm strained his eyes and ears in the blackness.

Somewhere far below, he could hear the rush of water. *This is not the sort of place one would go if one were trying to avoid telshees.*

Storm danced nervously back and forth along the lip of the hole. He found one spot that seemed to offer a bit of an incline, rather than a sheer drop. He took a deep breath and slithered down...and down...and down...

Storm splashed into a stream with a gasp. The water was icy and as high as his chest. He took a cautious lap and found it brackish. Somewhere ahead, he saw a faint greenish glow. *Syriot. Arcove can't have been pleased about landing here.*

Storm sniffed around the wall, looking for evidence that Arcove had tried to climb back up. He found nothing. *So far, so strange.*

In one direction, the underground stream dove beneath the airless rock. In the other direction, he could see the acriss light. *Well, I'll guess that he didn't go underwater. Although it would make as much sense as anything else he's done since the avalanche.*

Storm walked upstream, following the light. When he finally found a spot to climb out, the acriss was swarming brightly in the water, and Storm could see Arcove's enormous, wet tracks on the bank. Storm had never visited telshee caves south of the Garu Vell, closest to creasia territory. He knew, in theory, that they existed, and he remembered that Roup had noted an abundance in this area.

However, it wasn't until he'd gone well into the deep cave that he finally caught the scent of a telshee crossing Arcove's path. Storm followed with trepidation. He could tell that Arcove was running now. The trail became confused. Arcove circled several times. He took branching paths, but always returned to the main tunnel, always going deeper into the cave. *Why?*

Storm had a suspicion—a poorly-formed idea that loomed in the back of his mind. Then he heard splashing ahead, accompanied by low voices. Storm put on a burst of speed, came around a corner, and the cave broadened out. He could hear the distant sound of waves and thought that he must be almost on the far side of the cliffs.

He saw the silhouettes of a dozen or more telshees gathered in a circle around what looked like a pit. Acriss light glowed up from it. One of the silhouettes was enormous, as big around as the largest tree trunk in Leeshwood. Storm had last seen that form surrounded by coral, sleeping in the Dreaming Sea.

He wasn't sleeping now.

"Keesha!" Storm trotted up to him, panting.

Keesha turned, his great seal's face with its enormous blue eyes lit from beneath by the acriss glow. He looked down at Storm and smiled—an unnerving sight. "Storm! Well, this does complete the circle. I'm glad you're here."

Storm glanced around. He saw Shaw, looking at him with surprise and uncertainty. He saw Sauny and Valla, their faces expressionless in the eerie glow. He saw telshees that he didn't recognize, and he followed their gazes down into the hole. It was a tide pool—a deep one with smooth sides.

Arcove was treading water at the bottom. There was no place to get out or stand up, and he was moving with the deliberate slowness of an exhausted animal trying to conserve his strength. However, Storm was relieved to see that he didn't look injured.

He turned to Keesha. "I need him back. Do you know what happened on the mainland yesterday?"

"No," said Keesha without interest. He was watching Arcove's slow circuit of the pool.

"Treace attacked the herd. He's taken them away into Leeshwood. He wants to…to eat them." Storm still choked on the words.

Sauny and Valla looked up in alarm.

"Who is Treace?" asked Keesha in a bored voice.

"One of Arcove's officers," said Storm, "the youngest, born after the war."

"Then I have no quarrel with him," said Keesha.

"You should!" said Storm. "He is trying to destroy my herd, and he'd be no friend of yours if you met him."

"Creasia doings are none of my concern," said Keesha.

"What about ferryshaft doings?" Storm shoved his shoulder against the arc of Keesha's neck. *Look at me! I know I remind you of your dead friend, and maybe it's wrong to play on that, but right now, I'll take whatever I can get.*

Keesha's head whipped around, and he hissed. Storm sank down on his belly. "You told me once that you'd help me," he said softly. "Now, I'm asking you to do that."

Storm had expected a shouting match, but Keesha only turned and slid a coil into the tide pool. Arcove paddled away from it, but not quickly enough. Storm thought that Keesha was going to scoop Arcove out of the water. Instead, the coil whipped around him and shoved him under. The water roiled, but no part of Arcove broke the surface.

Keesha turned to Storm, his expression leisurely again. "You are telling me that Leeshwood is in the midst of one of its little power struggles, and you would like me to let Arcove return so that he can kill a rival whom you find distasteful?"

"Yes," said Storm with mixed relief and uncertainty. "Yes, and you're drowning him." Already, the stirring of the water had slowed.

"Oh, he won't drown," said Keesha. "He may suffocate, but he won't drown." He thought for a moment. "Shaw tells me that you have adopted a creasia cub. Did you listen to nothing we told you?"

"I listened!" exclaimed Storm, frustrated beyond words. "Can we talk about this later? I promise I will come back and let you shout at me all you like, but right now, let him go." The water of the pool had grown completely still, save for the muted lap of waves.

Keesha made a sound that was almost a giggle. "Oh, very well."

He jerked the loop of his body suddenly out of the pool and flung Arcove's limp form onto the cave floor. A murmur went up from the circling telshees. Storm understood then what Keesha had meant. He must have crushed the air from Arcove's lungs when he pushed him underwater. Arcove couldn't have drowned, even if he'd wanted to, because he couldn't get a breath. The cat's hollow sides lay still, his great jaws slack, eyes open and unfocused.

"You've killed him," said Storm miserably.

"Yes," said Keesha, "but I am willing to kill him again." And then he sang. It was the most distinctive song that Storm had ever heard, yet he could not remember a note of it a moment later. The song vibrated in the roots of his teeth and the joints of his bones. Storm felt as though he'd sliced himself open on a sharp rock—a mortal wound—and he was watching the blood well up, waiting for the pain, hovering in that moment between trauma and agony. But the agony never came. At least, not for Storm.

Arcove's body jerked and he sucked in a lungful of air. He convulsed briefly, kicking, struggling as though he were still drowning. He flipped onto his belly and grasped the stone with splayed claws, breathing in quick, panicked gulps.

"Arcove," murmured Keesha, and Arcove's whole body flattened at the sound of his name. He opened his eyes and glared up at Syra-lay. "Storm has some use for you. Do what he says, and I won't hunt down every one of your mates and cubs. That's generous, I think. More generous than you ever were. We'll meet again soon."

Arcove's muscles went taut. His bared teeth flashed in the dim light, and he looked as though he would spring.

Keesha hummed a single note. And again, Storm felt the hair rise along his spine. He had the peculiar certainty that someone had dealt him a terrible blow that he could not quite feel. He could tell that the telshees sensed it, too. Behind Keesha, Shaw dipped her head and turned to the side with a grimace.

Arcove made a low, guttural sound, the like of which Storm had never heard. He backed away, lay down, and tried to curl in on himself. Storm could hear him trying to pant through clenched teeth.

"That's better," said Keesha. "Keep that in mind next time your tiny, predator's brain prompts you to attack me."

"You're hurting him," said Storm, who'd grasped that much. "I need him to fight."

Keesha yawned. He'd stopped singing, although Arcove was still curled in a ball on the cave floor. "Storm, you do realize that it probably won't matter who wins this fight, don't you? Leeshwood has these bloody power shifts every few years. These cats will fight and fight, and *that* will help your herd more than anything. It's the one redeeming feature of creasia: they kill each other."

Storm felt angry, but he wasn't sure why or at whom. "Can I take him back to the surface now?"

"By all means," said Keesha. "*I'm* certainly not going to do it."

Storm looked around desperately, but the telshees were melting back into the shadows. Shaw was gone without speaking to him. He couldn't see Sauny or Valla. He felt utterly alone.

"Arcove?" he said. He was a little afraid to get near him. "Let's go."

Arcove stirred at the sound of his name, but he did not raise his head. Keesha's nose darted out and gave him a shove that sent him head-over-heels. Arcove came up hissing. "There you go!" said Keesha. "Back to normal."

Storm had to disagree. Arcove staggered side-ways, as though his legs weren't working properly. Storm wondered how long he'd been treading water. He was bristling, but his tail was tucked under him. Storm had never expected to see Arcove tuck his tail.

Keesha turned away. "He might take a bit to get his legs sorted out, but he should be mostly functional by this evening. I make no promises after that."

"Come on," whispered Storm desperately. *Before he changes his mind.*

Arcove's eyes were so dilated that Storm could hardly see any green. They seemed to look right through him. Storm gathered his courage and came to within a length of Arcove's face. "Arcove," he tried to keep his voice even. "Get up. We have to go."

Arcove's eyes seemed to focus. "Coden?" he said, in a voice so small that it could have been Teek's.

532

Storm swore to himself, then and there, that he was going to hear the creasia side of this story. "No, it's Storm. Can you follow me?"

Arcove shook himself as though to clear his head. "I don't know." He was slurring a little. "You're hard to follow."

"Not today. Today, I promise to be easy. Come on."

Storm was relieved when Arcove finally got up and staggered after him.

9

Arcove Delirious

Keesha was right about Arcove's ability to walk straight, although Arcove kept ignoring the fact. He tripped. He slipped in puddles. He walked into walls. *You'll never win a fight like this,* thought Storm.

At last, Storm said, "Stop."

Arcove kept walking until Storm got right in front of him. "You need to rest," he said. "We'll have to climb at the end; you'll never make it like this."

Arcove squinted at him. "Roup?"

Storm sighed. "No, it's Storm. Why don't you lie down?"

"Confused." Arcove's voice sounded plaintive. "I'm…I'm not making sense. I know I'm not making sense."

"I think it will get better," said Storm. *I certainly hope so.*

Arcove squinted at him. "Why are you here?"

"Lie down, and I'll tell you."

Arcove hobbled over to the cave wall and collapsed. He arranged his head on his paws with effort.

Storm hesitated a moment, then came to within a length of his shoulders.

"I came because I think you're better for the ferryshaft than Treace, but I want you to promise me you'll stop the raids if we get out of this alive."

"I won't," said Arcove, his eyes barely open to slits.

Storm felt frustrated. "You won't stop the raids after—"

"No, I won't get out of this alive."

Storm felt a chill. "Like you said, you're not thinking clearly."

Arcove's voice seemed steadier, now that he didn't have to walk and talk at the same time. "Where's Roup?"

"Probably waiting for you," said Storm. "You wandered off into a cave after the avalanche. Why did you go in there?"

"Avalanche..." repeated Arcove. "I remember that. And then... then I woke up in my nightmare."

"Keesha called him." Storm looked up as Sauny drifted like a shadow out of the boulders. "Keesha woke up and left the Dreaming Sea. Then he sat in this cave for a day and a night and *sang*. And, oh, Storm... I'm glad he's stopped."

"Sauny!" Storm felt a wave of relief.

Arcove cocked his head at her. "Sauny Ela-ferry?"

Sauny looked at him warily.

"You're the one who acts like him," said Arcove.

"Acts like who?"

"Coden. Storm looks like him...but you act like him."

Sauny glanced at Storm uncertainly. "He's confused," said Storm. "He keeps thinking I'm other animals."

Arcove did not dispute this.

Sauny sat down in front of him. "You hurt me. You killed my friends."

"I've killed a lot of friends," agreed Arcove.

That isn't exactly what she said, thought Storm.

"Keesha's going to kill *you*," said Sauny.

"He was always going to do that," said Arcove. He squinted at her. "Didn't *I* kill *you*?"

"No, you just…"

And then Storm remembered the way she'd walked out of the rocks. "Sauny, you're—"

She grinned at him. "You were right. I *was* getting better last spring. Shaw kept saying it was too early to tell if the damage was permanent."

"Yes, I—I remember." Shaw *had* said that. Over and over. *But I thought she was just trying to ease the blow.*

Sauny trotted a ring around Storm. Her limp was gone. She turned back to Arcove. "You're not as big as I remember."

"You're bigger."

"Let him sleep," muttered Storm. "He'll never win a fight like this. He's running into things and repeating himself. What did Keesha do to him?"

"I'm not sure," said Sauny in a guarded voice. She was still watching Arcove. "He doesn't *sound* confused."

"Arcove, do you know my name?"

"Storm," said Arcove quietly. "You were going to tell me why you're here…or did I just forget?"

Storm sighed. "Because I need you to kill Treace. Because I'd rather deal with you and your cats than with his."

Arcove said nothing.

"Why did you save me from the curbs?" asked Storm.

"Because Treace needs to prove to Leeshwood that he can do what I can't…or didn't."

"Kill me?"

"Just so," said Arcove. He thought for a moment. "What happened after the avalanche?"

"You're repeating yourself," said Storm.

Arcove grimaced. He laid his head down on his paws and stopped talking.

Sauny was watching him with an unreadable expression. Storm wondered whether she felt avenged. He couldn't blame her for wanting to see Arcove hurt, but he couldn't say that he'd enjoyed it. He wasn't sure why. He felt that he *ought* to have enjoyed it.

Storm tried to picture the raids. Instead, he saw a pair of desperate green eyes, illuminated by flashes of lightning, a scream so close to his ear that it nearly deafened him, fur and blood in his mouth. Storm shook his head. His nose still stung where Teek had scratched him. *And then...then he forgave me. How could anyone forgive that? Did he not understand when I told him?* But Storm remembered the look on Teek's face when he'd blurted out the truth on the council ledge. *He understood perfectly.*

Arcove had grown very still. Storm had to look closely to see that he was breathing. *The telshees chased him. Then he tread water for who-knows-how long. Keesha held him under and he struggled until he passed out. Or died. Is that what happened back there? Did Keesha bring him back to life?* Storm shivered.

Storm sat with his sister in awkward silence, watching Arcove sleep. Sauny stretched out on her belly and rested her head on her hooves. Storm wanted to ask her questions. He wanted to tell her things. But he didn't dare. After a while, he put his own head on his hooves and dozed.

Storm woke to Valla's excited voice. "Sauny, we found it!"

Storm jerked to his feet, blinking, before he quite knew what was happening. Valla and Shaw were both beside them in the tunnel. Sauny was dancing back and forth between them. "Thank you, thank you!"

"Don't thank me," growled Shaw, "just go before Keesha notices it's missing." Storm saw that Valla was wearing a familiar glossy blue stone around her neck.

Arcove had staggered to his feet, and he snarled at Shaw, white teeth bared to pink gums. Shaw took one look at him and turned away with a dismissive sweep of her head. She didn't even bother to bristle. "Storm," she said, "for the sake of the friendship between us, I will do this for you, but in return, I ask that you do something for me."

Storm was bewildered. "You'll do...what?"

"The herd," said Sauny. "You said that Treace wanted to eat them."

"He does," said Storm. "He's taken them away into the forest. No one knows where. Arcove and Roup said that he wants to make them into a food source for creasia."

Shaw dipped her head. "You may use the Shable to open Kuwee Island. Send the ferryshaft there and make them safe while the creasia are at war with each other. When the blood stops flowing, you may be a free people again. But this thing between Keesha and Arcove—stay out of it."

Storm took a step back. "No."

Shaw growled at him. Storm didn't think he'd ever seen her look at him that way. "Why?"

"Because this is *our* business," said Storm. "This is land-animal business, not yours."

"You don't know what you're talking about," said Shaw.

Storm did not relent. "The creasia war affects the place where *I* live. Whoever rules Leeshwood will have a direct impact on me and my herd. You can come back here to Syriot when it's over or swim to distant shores and forget about it; I can't!"

Arcove spoke behind him. "He has a point, Shaw." Storm felt at once relieved and alarmed to hear the focus back in Arcove's voice. When he glanced over his shoulder, he saw that the sharpness had returned to Arcove's eyes, and he was holding himself with the poise Storm remembered.

Shaw *did* bristle then. "You are a dead thing," she growled.

Arcove stretched, his long claws flexing against the stone. "Not yet." He smiled at her, and Shaw hissed. Arcove turned away. "Let's go, little ferryshaft, Coden's foals. I believe you wanted me to kill someone for you."

Storm trotted after Arcove. The creasia was moving with near-perfect coordination. "Do you remember the way out?" asked Storm.

"No, but I can follow my own trail."

"You'll go straighter if you follow me." Storm was a little unnerved by Arcove's sudden return to lucidity, although he told himself that it was a good thing.

"And who might you be?" asked Arcove as he slowed to let Storm go ahead. He was looking at Valla.

She bristled nervously and danced back.

"She's my beta," said Sauny.

Arcove snorted. "Two years old and you have a beta. You are very like your sire, and you definitely need to return to the herd."

"I liked you better when you were too weak to stand," Sauny commented.

"Likewise," said Arcove.

Storm thought that that might make Sauny too angry to talk, but she piped up again a moment later. "Why do you keep calling us Coden's foals? Storm and I didn't even have the same father."

"He was your great grandsire," said Arcove as he jumped over a pool. "His foal, Lirsy, was your mother's mother."

Storm was astonished. "How do you know that?"

"Charder," said Arcove. He was all-but-running now, and Storm saved his breath. When they reached the final stream, all three ferryshaft were panting. Storm explained that they would need to walk upstream for a distance and then climb. Arcove considered this. Before stepping into the water, he hesitated. "Am I—" He licked his lips and did not look at Storm. "Am I still repeating myself?"

Storm felt sorry for him. "Not since you woke up."

Arcove splashed into the stream.

10

Decisions to Be Made

Here it comes, thought Lyndi, after Storm had disappeared into the cave. *Roup and Halvery, decisions to be made…and no Arcove.*

"Go to Arcove's den and see what kind of support we have there," Roup said in a tight voice. "I'll wait here."

"Don't you even want to see how badly Sharmel is injured, *sir?*" snapped Halvery.

Lyndi couldn't remember ever hearing Halvery call Roup "sir," before, and it didn't sound like deference now.

Roup rounded on him. "If you've got something to say, say it, Halvery."

Storm's cub, Teek, looked between them, wide-eyed. Lyndi considered how to get him out of the way if they leapt at each other. She growled to remind Halvery of her presence. *If you engage now, Halvery, it'll be two against one. Don't think for a moment that I won't help my alpha.*

Halvery hissed at her to show his disdain for her gesture. He was making a low, sustained rumble. *Fine,* thought Lyndi. *Let's do this.*

"Halvery." Sharmel's voice.

Roup, Halvery, and Lyndi did not take their eyes off each other, but Lyndi saw Sharmel limping towards them out of her peripheral vision. The two ferryshaft—Charder and Kelsy—were with him. "Halvery, a word," said Sharmel, his voice weak but persistent.

Halvery did not stop growling, but he cut his eyes sideways at Sharmel. Lyndi risked a glance at him as well. Sharmel looked wobbly, and he had dark stains around his mouth and chest. He would not be much use for fights in the near future…or perhaps ever again. *He's old,* thought Lyndi. *Cats have been whispering for years that Arcove should replace him. Perhaps they were right.*

"Halvery, please," Sharmel's voice was even. "A moment."

Halvery turned away from Roup and Lyndi, walking stiff-legged, and still bristling. He and Sharmel retreated a little distance and began muttering. Roup turned his back on all of them and returned to the mouth of the cave. He'd already stopped bristling. *He doesn't care,* thought Lyndi. *He never cared about rank. But he could win that fight with Halvery...even without me...if he wanted to.*

The two ferryshaft appeared to be having their own argument off to her right. Lyndi inched towards Halvery and Sharmel, straining to hear what they were saying. She caught Sharmel's strident whisper. "If you kill Roup, Arcove will grieve himself to death. Do you think we'll survive if he doesn't? Don't you dare, Halvery!"

"*I* can kill Treace if Arcove doesn't come back," snapped Halvery.

"And if it comes to that, do you really think Roup will fight you for the leadership? Do you think he wants it?"

Halvery said nothing.

"Wait and see," muttered Sharmel.

Halvery's answer was too soft for Lyndi to hear, but she could tell by his posture that he'd calmed down. She glanced back towards Roup and saw that Teek had gone to sit next to him. When she looked back around, Halvery was almost beside her. Lyndi took a swift step back. Halvery snorted as he passed. "Do we need to recap that for you, Lyndi? Did you hear enough?"

Lyndi growled. "You don't want a fight."

"I *do* want a fight," said Halvery. "But not right now."

Roup didn't even turn around when Halvery and Sharmel approached him in the mouth of the cave. "We'll go to Arcove's den," said Halvery. "We'll rest if we can, and if we have reasonable support, we'll go to the Great Clearing this evening. If you and Arcove don't join me, I'll fight Treace."

He waited, as though he expected Roup to say something, but Roup didn't even look at him.

"And that will make me king if Arcove is gone," persisted Halvery. "Unless you would like to fight me for Leeshwood. Roup, are you listening?"

"I'm listening. I wish you joy of your fight," said Roup. "I do not think you will survive it."

Lyndi could tell that Halvery was trying not to grind his teeth. He swallowed whatever he wanted to say and turned away. Sharmel followed him wordlessly through the boulders, heading south towards Arcove's territory. A moment later, the two ferry-shaft trotted after them. "Teek," said Lyndi gently, "you should go with them."

"No," said Teek. "I'm waiting for Storm."

Roup didn't argue, so Lyndi didn't, either. The sun was climbing up the sky, and she felt as though she hadn't slept in days. Roup seemed to sense her exhaustion. He looked away from the cave mouth for the first time since the argument with Halvery. "Sleep. I'll watch."

"I can watch," said Teek softly. "I sleep at nighttime."

Roup glanced at him and gave a crooked smile.

Are we going to trust this cub from the ferryshaft herd? wondered Lyndi.

"Alright," said Roup to Teek.

I guess we are. Lyndi stretched out beside Roup, facing the opposite direction. The sun was shining warm on their backs, and the wind sighed through the fir trees. In spite of everything, Lyndi felt a sense of peace. She put her head on her paws, shut her eyes, and was asleep in moments.

It was late afternoon by the time Storm saw daylight. The climb had been difficult. Storm suspected that Arcove was still not quite as coordinated as usual, although it was impossible to tell for sure in the darkness. When they reached the tunnel, Arcove started running again.

Storm caught sight of the entrance a moment later and a pair of creasia silhouettes, getting to their feet. Roup's voice called, "Arcove?"

"Here."

Then they were in the sunshine. Teek ran to Storm, beaming. "I knew you'd get him back."

Storm smiled uncertainly. *Don't thank me yet.*

Arcove paused long enough to sniff noses with Roup, but then he started off immediately, going south and angling into the trees. "Storm says we're expected in the Great Clearing at evening."

"Yes." Roup kept pace with him. "Arcove—" Storm could hear the relief in Roup's voice, but then Roup seemed to collect himself, and when he spoke again, his voice was level. "You smell like telshees and sea water. What happened?"

Arcove, Storm, Sauny, and Valla were all wet from the river and gritty from the climb. Sauny and Valla jogged along beside Storm, blinking and looking around. Storm suspected they had not seen this much sunlight in quite a while. Roup's beta—Storm could not remember her name—eyed them all suspiciously.

"No time now," said Arcove.

"You've acquired more ferryshaft," said Roup. His eyes slid over Valla and then flicked back. He blinked. "And the Shable."

"Yes," said Arcove. "They were just leaving."

Sauny sputtered. "You need our help."

Arcove glanced at her. "I was under the impression that you needed mine." He'd slowed his pace a little, and in that moment of divided attention, he stumbled on a root. It was a tiny mistake, instantly corrected, but Roup noticed. Storm could tell by his look of surprise.

"Keesha—" began Storm, but Arcove talked over him.

"Roup, this is Sauny Ela-ferry, Storm's sister. Coden was their great grand-sire. That other one is her beta."

"My name is Valla," piped up Valla.

Roup looked at Sauny with an expression that Storm could not read.

"They are hoping to hide their herd on Kuwee Island while we all kill each other," continued Arcove.

"Not an unreasonable plan," said Roup mildly.

"However, they are sufficiently worried about Treace that they would like him dead by this evening, which is where I come in…I think. Did I get that all right, Storm?"

Storm let out an exasperated breath. "Well, you're mixing up things I said with things Shaw said, but—"

"But that's the gist of it," said Arcove. "Now, we have to run if we're going to reach the Great Clearing before this fight. I assume Halvery is going to fight him if I don't turn up?"

"Yes," said Roup. "He and Sharmel went to your den to see what kind of support we've got. They'll meet us at the clearing." He was watching Arcove minutely. "Are you alright?"

"I'm fine."

"You don't look fine."

"I look wet," said Arcove. "I'll dry."

Sauny trotted up beside Storm. "What are you going to do?" she whispered.

"Stay and see how the fight turns out," muttered Storm. "Decide after that. Are you going after the herd right now?"

Sauny thought for a moment. "No. I'll stay, too. See how the fight turns out. How did you end up with the creasia, anyway?"

Storm sighed. He dropped back a bit and watched Teek to make sure he was keeping up. Arcove was moving quickly, but, in spite of his words, he wasn't running with the speed that Storm remembered. *Because he's conserving his strength? Or because of whatever Keesha did to him?*

Storm looked at Sauny and Valla. "Here's what happened," he began. He talked quickly, trying to tell them only the parts of the story that really mattered. However, as the tale unfolded, he had to keep going back to fill in details that he'd left out. In the end, nearly everything seemed important. By the time he'd finished, they'd reached the Great Clearing.

11

Cheat

Storm understood instantly why the creasia called the clearing "Great." This had to be the largest open grassland in the forest, and it was presently surrounded by cats. They were lying or sitting in the shadows just under the trees, their eyes winking in the dusk like eerie fireflies, tails twitching, waiting.

Halvery came to meet Arcove within moments of his arrival. Storm gathered that all the cats on the eastern end of the clearing were Arcove's supporters.

"Well, at least we're not alone," Storm heard Roup mutter.

Storm couldn't tell whether Halvery was relieved or disappointed not to be fighting Treace himself. He greeted Arcove warmly, although, like Roup, he got a puzzled expression after they sniffed noses. *We probably all smell like telshees,* thought Storm.

Arcove barely stopped for long enough to exchange a few words with Halvery. Then he moved beyond the last of the waiting creasia, into the open clearing. Arcove stopped there in the last rays of the setting sun. His fur had dried completely, and he looked formidable. The sunset painted the fall grass red around him, and his shadow stretched out towards his enemies, dark and immense. "Treace Ela-creasia!" he bellowed. "You have challenged me, and I am here."

A murmur went up from the waiting cats. On the far side of the clearing, a fawn-colored shape detached itself from the rest and moved across the grass towards Arcove, head and tail held high. Storm remembered the way Treace's clutter had mauled the herd when Treace had come to hunt him. He remembered the way Treace had tried to trick him with lies when he'd cornered Storm on the trail. *I've done the right thing,* Storm assured himself. *Arcove is dangerous, and we'll have to deal with him after Treace is gone, but at least we can trust what he says.*

"Storm, come here." Storm looked to his right and saw Roup standing beside Halvery on the very edge of the clearing. Roup jerked his head and tail impatiently. "Come."

Storm looked uncertainly at Sauny, Valla, and Teek. All three of them were glancing nervously at the cats. However, Arcove's creasia seemed wholly focused on what was happening in the clearing. Roup's beta spoke up. "They'll be fine," she said. "Go talk to Roup."

Storm walked past the last rows of cats to the very front of the group. No one so much as glanced at him. "What happened?" hissed Roup when Storm stopped beside him.

In the clearing, Arcove and Treace were circling each other. Arcove made several swift lunges, but Treace dodged nimbly out of the way. "Well, he learned from the last fight," muttered Halvery. "This one won't be over so quickly."

"Storm…" repeated Roup.

Storm licked his lips. "Keesha caught him," he whispered. "Keesha…called him…somehow. And did something to him; I don't know what."

"Did something?" repeated Roup, his voice and eyes probing.

Storm looked away. "He held Arcove under the water. Arcove passed out. I got there; I talked Keesha into letting him go." *That's not all that happened, but that's all I know how to explain.*

Now Halvery was listening, too. He shot Storm a dark look around Roup. "Did Keesha break ribs?" He looked back out at the field. "That would explain the way Arcove is moving."

"Maybe." Arcove hadn't complained of anything like that. *But would Arcove complain to me? Probably not.*

Arcove was trying and failing to close with Treace. The smaller cat kept striking and dancing away. He wasn't really causing any damage, but neither was Arcove. The creasia along the edge of the trees were beginning to murmur.

"He wasn't quite himself on the way here," whispered Roup to Halvery.

"He was running into walls right after it happened," muttered Storm.

Roup looked horrified. His eyes darted to the field and back to Storm. "Why did Keesha let him go?"

"Because Keesha promised me a favor," said Storm.

Roup looked as though he didn't believe it. Storm couldn't blame him. He hardly believed it himself. *What really happened back there?*

"Something's wrong," whispered Roup. "Something more than broken ribs. I should have made him tell me on the way here."

"Well, there's nothing you can do about it now," said Halvery.

Roup was on his feet, tail twitching.

Halvery looked alarmed. "Roup," he whispered in a near-snarl, "if you go out there, if you help him, it's cheating. You can't interfere in a king's fight with a challenger! The assembly will kill you and Arcove, too. Then we'll have a bloodbath. Sit—down."

But Roup did not sit down. The creasia were talking softly all around them now. Even Storm, who'd never seen Arcove fight with another cat, could tell that Arcove did not possess his usual devastating speed. Arcove was huge and powerful, but not as quick as Treace, who had begun to take real advantage of the fact. He dashed around Arcove and closed suddenly, hitting his opponent in the flank and knocking him over.

Roup was picking up his feet one at a time and setting them down again in a state of great agitation. "Treace will think Arcove was injured in the avalanche," he said, apparently to himself, "but would Treace take that kind of risk? He wouldn't know about the telshees. I don't think so. Treace is a planner, not a risk-taker. There's something else. Something we haven't seen."

Abigail Hilton

"Shut up," muttered Halvery. "Just shut up and watch. It's all you can do."

Treace and Arcove were flipping over in a blur of black and tan. Arcove came up on top, and, for a moment, Storm thought he would rip out Treace's throat. However, he'd pinned Treace directly underneath him, and Treace kicked up with his back legs. Arcove jumped to the side to avoid being disemboweled, and Treace wriggled away.

Roup and Halvery were both pacing now. Many of the cats around Storm were doing the same. "Almost," muttered Halvery. "Arcove is definitely not himself, but if Treace will close with him one more time, I think it'll be over."

Arcove seemed to think so, too. He pursued Treace aggressively across the clearing, nearly catching him twice, while Treace dodged and danced away. Storm suspected that Arcove was nearing the end of the strength provided by his nap in Syriot. Whatever was wrong was getting worse, and Arcove needed to finish the fight quickly. "Did you want to fight me, or play hide-and-hunt?" snarled Arcove as Treace dipped and weaved almost into the trees on the southern end of the clearing.

Roup had stopped pacing. He was standing perfectly still, neck craning high to see. "The deer," he whispered. "Oh, ghosts and little fishes! It wasn't the pit we should have looked at. It was the deer."

Treace and Arcove were weaving in and out of the trees now. Roup set off at a dead run across the clearing towards them. Halvery's teeth snapped on empty air as he made a grab for Roup's tail. "Blood and gristle!" he bellowed. Then, to Storm's surprise, he tore off after Roup.

Shouting broke out on all sides. Some cats started forward. Others began backing away. Storm wondered, later, whether Halvery had intended to kill Roup to prevent him from interfering in the fight. Or perhaps Halvery just wanted a better look at what was about to happen.

At any rate, the two creasia were about halfway across the clearing, and the crowd hadn't yet decided how to respond, when

Arcove disappeared in a shower of leaves and then shot straight into the air, thrashing. Something thick and green curled around his head and upper body. Storm gasped. "A curb trap?"

He heard a moan beside him, and looked down to see Teek, pressing against his flank. "The snakes," he whispered. "The snakes...the black cat..."

Sauny and Valla had come up beside him as well. All around them, cats were surging forward, snarling. "Storm," whispered Valla. "Storm, I think we should leave."

"Not yet," muttered Storm. He couldn't take his eyes off the field. Treace's cats had moved to surround the trap. It was difficult to see, properly, but Storm thought that a pit had opened beneath it, preventing Arcove from touching the ground in spite of his weight.

If Roup had started running a moment later, he would never have been able to fight his way through. However, he reached the spot just a little ahead of all but a couple of Treace's cats. One of them jumped at him, but he dodged, and leapt over their heads. He scrambled up Arcove's body to tear desperately at the vines with his teeth, while the whole trap swayed wildly. Then Roup and Arcove both fell into the pit. Halvery barreled into one of Treace's cats an instant later, and they flipped over in a cloud of leaves. Storm saw a spray of blood, and then Halvery was up again, jaws crimson, lunging at the next cat.

Storm lost sight of them, then. The entire assembly of creasia had flung themselves at each other, and the dusky clearing was full of their struggling bodies. Cries of "treachery!" and "cheating!" filled the air, hurled from both sides. A cat rose up suddenly out of the dusk, wild-eyed, head covered in blood, and made a slap at Storm with splayed claws.

Storm leapt out of the way, but Teek was not so quick. The creasia's claws went over Teek's head, but then it lurched down to snap at him with its jaws. Teek screamed, and then Roup's beta slammed into the strange cat. She landed on its back and crunched down behind its skull.

She raised her head, bloody and bristling. "Go!" she snarled. "Arcove's den! Go!"

Teek ran and Storm followed. *I don't know how to find Arcove's den.* "Sauny!" he shouted. "Valla!"

"Here!" Storm spotted them running through the twilit trees ahead of him. Kelsy and Charder were with them. They slowed for long enough to let Storm and Teek catch up. "Follow me," said Charder.

12

Exhaustion

Tollee thought, when the stampede began, that some of the youngsters from last fall must have attacked the creasia. There'd been no violence for more than a year, and her first impulse was anger at whoever had started it now. However, as the panicked animals around her became thicker, and Myla started to mew in terror, Tollee realized that something else was happening.

The crowd was suddenly too packed to ignore, and she was forced to run with them. She shouted at those around her, demanding an explanation, but their fragmented responses were confused and made no sense. To her astonishment, Tollee tripped on the fallen body of a creasia. She got a brief glimpse of another, obviously wounded, struggling to rise, and then disappearing under frantic ferryshaft hooves.

She heard a hair-raising wail, followed by snarling—cat sounds, but she didn't know what they meant. The thunder and shouting of the ferryshaft herd made it difficult to pay attention to other noises, but she caught one noise that she knew—a noise from her childhood that still woke her from sound sleep sometimes at night—the tremolo of yipping curbs. Not one or two, but many curbs.

Tollee felt cold. "Myla!"

"Mother!" Myla was right there at her side, but Tollee dared not take her eyes off the animal in front of her.

"No matter what happens, you stay on your feet. If we get separated, you keep running. Do you understand?"

"Yes, mother," whimpered Myla.

As though to mock her words, there was a splash ahead of them, someone pushed Tollee so hard from behind that she stumbled and went head-over-heels into the river. She opened her eyes underwater, trying to find the surface, while hooves crashed down all around her. Someone kicked her in the belly, punching the last of the air from her lungs. The current caught her, and then...then someone had her by the back of the neck, and her head broke the surface. Tollee gagged in air, her legs kicking instinctively, swimming with tightly packed animals.

"Mother!" Myla's frantic voice trilled in her ear. "Are you alright?"

Tollee laughed in spite of herself. "And if you can't run, you should swim," she choked. "Did...did Storm teach you that?"

"No, Teek taught me," panted Myla. "When we were swimming alone one day, and I got scared and went under. He pulled me up like that."

Of course. Cats have a scruff.

"Do you think he's alright?" asked Myla.

"I think he's probably safer than we are right now," said Tollee, and she almost believed it. *What is happening? Are the creasia fighting with each other? With the curbs? With us?*

Whatever was happening, it seemed to involve the whole herd. On the far side of the river, they started east into the forest. Tollee finally got a glimpse of what was driving them—creasia, certainly, but also curbs, racing around the edges of the herd. She heard the screams of animals who fell behind—unmistakably ferryshaft sounds. Some of the elders tried to talk to the cats, but this only resulted in savage attacks. Tollee looked for an opportunity to disengage from the stampede, but there was none.

Soon, exhaustion overpowered curiosity. The herd slowed, but the cats and curbs kept nipping at their heels. The ferryshaft had completed their annual migration only the day before, and the whole herd was already tired. Now, they seemed to be headed roughly back towards the lake. Their tormentors allowed them to slow to a pace barely sustainable for the foals. They ran all day without stopping for water or food. Tollee was tremendously proud of Myla. The foal stayed on her feet, though many others fell.

The herd was allowed to rest at evening, and Myla was so limp with exhaustion that Tollee didn't even consider trying to sneak away. By this time, the elders had given up asking questions. The cats did not speak, not even to each other, within earshot of the ferryshaft.

Tollee and Myla tried to grab a few mouthfuls of grass, but their immediate vicinity was soon picked clean. Tollee tried to catch sight of animals she knew, but those nearby were strangers, and the creasia growled every time anyone stood up or tried to move around.

In the middle of the night, they were roused again and hurried on through the forest. The journey in the dark felt surreal, running on stiff and painful legs, dizzy with thirst. Myla tripped repeatedly, and Tollee had to drag her to her feet. Tollee knew, from her time with Teek, that cats could see better in the dark than could ferryshaft. They were also more alert at night. She did not think escape under these conditions was possible.

By dawn, they'd reached the shores of the lake and were allowed to splash down to the edge to gulp water and tear at the fibrous reeds. It was poor forage, but it filled their bellies. Soon they were hurrying on again, along the edge of the lake, going south, away from ferryshaft territory.

Are they taking us to the southern plains? It seemed like a senseless thing to do, but nothing the creasia had done since the conference made any sense to Tollee. It was clear to her now that the ferryshaft were being herded by a relatively small number of cats—perhaps a dozen, aided by an indeterminate number of curbs.

We could get away, she thought. *If we made an organized effort.* But the cats wouldn't let them talk to each other, and exhaustion was a powerful deterrent.

We're too tired and too cowardly. Tollee considered the very real possibility that she would never see Storm or her home plains again. *I don't want my daughter to lose her mother the way I did—seeing her eaten alive by curbs.*

Chelby Lake contained a variety of small islands—many undoubtedly without actual soil. At evening, the creasia broke their silence for the first time and began ordering the ferryshaft into the lake, insisting that they swim to one of these small islands. Tollee was relieved to see the animals at the front of the group struggling out of the water. The foliage came down right to the edge of the island and she had thought, for a few horrified moments, that they were to be stranded, clinging to tree limbs in the middle of the lake.

Tollee could see that Myla was at the end of her strength. She had to drag her foal out of the water and through the weeds into the trees, where the herd was shaking itself off and getting its collective breath. Looking back, Tollee saw that the curbs and creasia lined the shore, but they had not swum across. In spite of everything, she felt a moment of immense relief. Ferryshaft were calling to each other, daring to raise their voices to locate their families and friends.

Tollee lay down beside Myla. The foal dropped her head on her hooves and lay insensible while the herd milled around them. Amid the chaos, Tollee saw other mothers and foals. She saw lone foals, too—some calling, some huddled still and silent. The herd was too exhausted to sort itself out properly, and most animals lay down as soon as they'd had enough water to take the edge off their thirst. Tollee was asleep before her head quite touched the ground.

Arcove's den was a warren of packed-earth caves among the roots of enormous, ancient trees that twisted among boulders. Storm was surprised and impressed by the hot springs that warmed and humidified the air. They sent up tendrils of pearly steam that created hazy curtains wherever the warmer water met colder air or other streams. Storm smelled pine and the peculiar odor of the springs. If not for the sounds of fighting in the distance and the nearer moans of wounded animals, it would have been a delightful place.

Sauny was impressed, too. "This is where they live?" she whispered.

Charder huffed over his shoulder. "Did you think creasia kings would live somewhere unpleasant?" After a moment, he added, "There are hot springs like this in the boulder mazes south of Leeshwood, in territory where ferryshaft used to roam."

They were challenged on their way in, but Charder came boldly to the front of the group and told the sentries who they were and why they were here. Arcove's creasia seemed suspicious, but ultimately more concerned about other cats than about ferryshaft. When they reached the main cave, a large, nut-brown female with dark points on her paws and nose came out to meet them. She seemed to know Charder, and she directed them all to the back of the main cave.

"Stay here," she said. "I cannot guarantee your safety anywhere else."

"Nadine!" someone bellowed. Not far away in the night, cats were screaming. Storm couldn't tell whether it was a threat or a sound of agony.

Nadine whirled away.

"That's Arcove's mate," said Charder quietly, "the highest ranking, the den mother. We can probably trust her."

"Storm..." whispered Teek, and Storm looked around to see several dozen anxious faces peering at them out of the shadows. He almost laughed.

She's put us with the cubs. That's a strange turn-around. Storm was fairly certain that Arcove's mate was old enough to have seen cubs killed by ferryshaft.

A couple of them looked to be about Teek's age. Most were a little older, and there was a small, fluffy pile of those who were a year younger.

A big cub with night-black fur approached, stiff-legged, watching Teek. Teek backed up against Storm, bristling. Most of the cubs seemed cowed by the awful noises coming from the forest and the agitation of their mothers. Wounded were beginning to trickle in, and some had truly horrific injuries. Storm didn't see any cats that he recognized, although it was difficult to tell in the shifting shadows. He wanted to ask someone about Arcove, but all the creasia seemed busy.

Sauny and Valla had lain down side-by-side, watchful, but willing to rest. Charder had lain down and put his head on his hooves as well. Kelsy seemed more restless. He paced. Storm fell asleep, listening to the back and forth clip-clop of Kelsy's hooves.

13

The Next Morning

Storm woke, disoriented and thirsty. Someone nearby was keening. The chilly air was rank with the smell of blood and offal. Storm raised his head, blinking in the pre-dawn light. He could see the confused shapes of dozens of creasia curled or sprawled on the floor of the cave. Sauny and Valla were still sleeping. Charder and Kelsy had gone. Teek was curled up against Storm. Storm managed, gingerly, to extract himself without waking the cub.

Most of the other cubs had left the back wall of the cave. Storm caught sight of some of them as he picked his way around the sleeping creasia. The keening was coming from the far side of the cave, where a cub nuzzled desperately at the unmoving form of a female.

As Storm made his way towards the entrance, he spotted others who would never rise again. Some were clearly sleeping, exhausted, but here and there Storm saw the unnatural stillness of death. Cats lay with their innards oozing out of gaping belly wounds, their blood thick and sticky on the cave floor, open eyes glazing. Some had all-but-lost legs. Some had died convulsing in their own vomit, and they lay in twisted shapes among their sleeping companions.

The bodies continued outside. Storm estimated that over two hundred creasia were sleeping in and around the caves. He tried to count them, but kept losing track. *I can't tell how many are alive, anyway.*

The first creasia Storm recognized was Halvery. He was lying beside the entrance, his fur stiff with blood, but clearly alive. He looked at Storm balefully in the wan light.

Storm hesitated. "How many did you lose?" he asked softly.

"What's it to you?" snapped Halvery, his voice rough with weariness.

Storm did not speak or move for a moment.

Finally, Halvery muttered. "This is why kings and challengers fight. One fight. Two cats. In order to avoid…all of this." The last words came out in a whisper, and he laid his head back down on his paws.

Storm inched around him and kept going. He took a drink at one of the streams, though it seemed strange to be drinking warm water. It had an odd taste, but he'd seen creasia drinking from it the night before, so he felt safe. Storm's stomach rumbled, and he realized that it had been two days since he'd eaten.

On the edge of the hot spring, in a little bend of the stream, Storm finally found Arcove. He thought that it was an odd place to sleep, although the caves were certainly crowded. The female from the night before, Nadine, was lying between Arcove and the other animals, fast asleep. Roup lay half curled around Arcove with his head draped over Arcove's back. He opened his eyes as Storm approached. Storm saw that Arcove was shivering. He was lying so close to the hot water that steam was condensing on his whiskers, and yet he was shivering as though he'd been lying in snow.

Roup got up, awkwardly, and Storm saw that he'd been raked from nose to tail by claws. The bloody tracks were stark against his pale fur. Storm couldn't tell how badly Arcove might be wounded from the fight. His black fur showed nothing. Storm suspected that the worst wounds were invisible.

"Arcove?" whispered Storm.

Arcove's eyes opened to slits. Storm didn't think he'd been asleep. He did not look at Storm, but stared blankly into the river. "What do you want?" His voice was so low that Storm had to strain to hear.

Storm sat down on the riverbank. He glanced at Roup, but Roup said nothing.

"You should go find your herd," said Arcove, his voice still whisper-soft. "The advice Shaw gave you was…accurate."

Storm didn't know what to say. He was saved from this dilemma by the sound of a not-so-distant ululating yip. Roup jerked up and looked around, but Arcove didn't even raise his head. Storm suspected that Roup was thinking of hundreds of lowland curbs charging into their sleeping company. Before Roup could sound an alarm, Storm said, "Wait." He listened hard. "That's not lowland curbs." He couldn't help but smile. "That's highland curbs. They're calling me."

Storm backed away from Arcove, Roup, and Nadine. He trotted west along the river until he found a spot narrow enough to leap across. The sky had brightened into dawn, but the sun had not risen yet over the cliffs when Storm found Eyal and his pack. He was not surprised to find Sauny and Valla already talking to them. He was delighted to see that they'd killed a pair of sheep, and everyone had obviously eaten their fill. Storm sniffed noses with Eyal and then tore into the food. He wished he'd brought Teek and made a mental note to take some back to him.

"Rumors are flying about you, my friend," said Eyal while Storm ate.

"Aren't they always," mumbled Storm around a mouthful of liver. "How are your puppies?"

Eyal grinned. "See for yourself."

Storm raised his head. Looking more closely, he saw that the pack included animals he did not recognize—a little lankier than their elders, but just as tall. "They grew fast!" exclaimed Storm.

Eyal beamed. "We have five new pack members. We lost two, but such is the way of things. We have you to thank for our safety over the winter, and we have not forgotten. We heard that you might be in some trouble."

Storm sighed. "The creasia are in trouble."

Eyal peered at him. "So I gathered. Why do you not leave them to their fate? Last we spoke, you seemed anxious to see Arcove feeding the vultures."

Storm looked at the ground. He felt tired of repeating the events of the last few days. Every time he thought about them, he came to a different conclusion. He glanced at Sauny. She was wearing the Shable this morning. The smooth, blue stone with its black pupil gleamed amid the red-gold fur of her chest like a third eye. "They're very brave," she offered.

"Creasia are brave," agreed Eyal. "It is a trait that curbs admire. However, they are not good at making friends among other talking animals. If you help them, they may not reciprocate later."

"Arcove keeps his promises," said Sauny.

Storm was surprised. *Little sister, you have been growing up this summer. Maybe I have, too.*

"And has Arcove made you any promises?" asked Eyal.

Good point.

"No," said Sauny.

"The lowland curbs helped to drive my herd somewhere into the forest for Treace," said Storm aloud. "We need to go after them soon. Can you help us with that?"

"That I will do gladly," said Eyal.

A curb began to growl suddenly, and Eyal's ears flattened. In the same instant, Storm caught the scent of brine and a smell he associated with darkness and deep caves. A moment later, he saw Keesha's enormous form gliding through the forest like water pouring down a hill. Seeing Keesha outside of Syriot was even more alarming than seeing him in it. He carried his head at half the height of the average tree, and yet he moved with the speed of a summer snake. Shaw was with him, as well as half a dozen other telshees that Storm didn't recognize. The curbs stopped growling, but they looked uneasy, in spite of all the time they'd spent on the borders of Syriot.

Keesha looked utterly serene. His bright, blue eyes flicked around the group, and he lowered his head to a more friendly height just above theirs. "How is Arcove?" he asked genially.

"Unwell," said Storm. "He lost the fight. What did you do to him?"

"I was afraid that might happen," said Keesha. "But I'll sort it out. Where is he?"

"His cats are in and around his den," said Sauny cautiously. "You're not going to stroll in there, are you?"

"Of course I am," said Keesha, "unless one of you would like to tell him to come out and see me. He can see me there or see me here: his choice."

"I'm not sure how far he can walk," said Storm.

"That bad?" said Keesha. "Well, I will wait patiently. If he's not here by noon, I'll come and find him...and kill anything that gets in my way."

14

Poison

Arcove floated in and out of a fever dream. He knew Roup was there and that Roup was desperately worried. That knowing was worse than anything, but Arcove couldn't fix it. He knew that Nadine and Seeka and his other mates were already grieving for the cubs that would die tonight or tomorrow, but he couldn't fix that, either. He thought Charder came to see him, and that seemed odd. Charder, at least, should not expect him to make anything better. And yet, there he was, speaking words that Arcove couldn't quite follow.

The one thing he did understand with agonizing clarity was that he had lost a fight. Arcove had never lost a fight. He knew the consequences for losing fights. Leeshwood did not forgive such things. Not for a creasia king.

Arcove had never thought beyond losing a fight. It seemed particularly cruel that he should still be alive, watching his friends and followers grieve and struggle, trying to make decisions, when there could be no good outcome for any of them. He told himself that it was always going to end this way, that he'd known from the beginning that this day would come.

"Was it worth it, Roup?"

Roup's worried face swam into view. "Arcove? Are you awake? Halvery wants to talk to you."

Arcove tried to think of an answer, but he couldn't concentrate. "Was it worth it?" he repeated.

"What do you mean?"

Arcove spoke in a whisper. At least, he thought he did. He wasn't entirely sure whether he was speaking aloud. "We could have shared a den, two or three females, had cubs and never even known whose was whose. I'm sure we could have kept them safe from ferryshaft and other cats. We could have had smaller lives… longer lives… Your brother would probably still be around."

He knew he'd spoken out loud, then, because Roup's face crumpled. "Please don't talk like that."

"But I need to know," whispered Arcove.

Roup took a deep breath.

Anyone else would just tell me yes, thought Arcove, *but you'll tell me the truth.*

"Do you think you could have done that?" whispered Roup. "Walked away from the council? Knowing you *could* be king?"

Arcove shut his eyes.

"Am I sorry we didn't grab something for ourselves when we could have made things better for everyone?" continued Roup.

"Did I make things better?"

"You gave them sixteen years of peace."

Arcove didn't say anything.

Roup put his head down against Arcove's. "I don't think you're capable of walking away from a challenge like that, and I'm not sorry I followed you, Arcove." His voice broke. "I have never been sorry for that. Now, *please,* focus; we need you."

But Arcove could not focus. He was unbearably cold, and he kept trying to crawl into the hot spring. Roup and Nadine kept stopping him. "Just for a moment," he told them.

"It is going to snow," he heard Nadine say. "You shouldn't keep getting wet; you'll freeze."

"I'm already freezing," whispered Arcove, but he was fairly certain that he did not say it aloud, because they didn't seem to understand him. He felt nauseated and tremendously dizzy. He remembered feeling this way after fights when he'd lost a great deal of blood. *Did I bleed that much? I don't remember it.*

"Arcove." He opened his eyes, and there was Coden, looking at him with those sea-gray eyes.

Am I in the Ghost Wood? Do I have to fight you again?

"Arcove," repeated Coden, only this time some foggy part of Arcove's brain informed him that this ferryshaft was not Coden. He was too small and too young and he looked much too concerned.

"Keesha wants to see you," whispered Storm. "He says if you don't come out to him, he will come here and kill anyone who challenges him. I think you'd better come."

That registered. Arcove's head jerked up. The world rocked around him, but he saw, as though through shattered vision, the shapes of creasia—*his* creasia, through the curtains of steam. *Keesha...cubs...Nadine...Roup...wounded...no.* Storm pushed something at him—a bloody hunk of meat. Arcove thought, for a moment, that it was a dead cub, but then his nose told him that it was part of a sheep. "Eat," said Storm. "Eat. It might help."

Arcove tried to tell him that it wouldn't, but he couldn't make his mouth work, and at last he bent his head and devoured the meat in a couple of bites. He felt instantly nauseated and thought he might vomit. Storm was dancing nervously back and forth. "Come on," he whispered. "Come on before Roup gets back."

"Where is—?" Arcove managed.

"I got the curbs to bring your cats some food," said Storm. "Roup has gone to help make sure everyone gets a fair share. We've only got a few moments. Let's go. Unless you want Keesha in your den."

Arcove staggered to his feet. He felt as though he was standing on a log, floating down the Igby River, and the log was heaving up and down and back and forth. He'd only gone a few paces before he vomited up the meat.

Storm sighed.

They moved along the steamy edge of Smoky Branch to a narrow point, and then Storm jumped across, but Arcove splashed through the stream. He paused and considered lying down in the water, but Storm dared to give him a nip. "Hurry!"

Insolent foal. Arcove considered swatting him, but didn't think he could balance on three legs. He could barely balance on four.

Weaving crazily, he managed to follow Storm through the forest until he spotted the immense form of Syra-lay, like a snowy, fallen tree, up ahead. Bile rose in the back of Arcove's throat. Half-remembered nightmare images fluttered and stirred in his mind.

Keesha's voice sang out merrily. "Ah, there you are. I was about to get bored."

Suddenly, he was *right* there, inches from Arcove's nose. Arcove thought that nothing so big should be able to move so quickly. *Or is it just that I am moving so slowly?*

Arcove resisted the urge to jerk away. He stood his ground and looked the monster in the eyes. "What have you done to me?"

Keesha gave an unnerving chuckle in several voices. "I poisoned you...with a song."

Arcove tried to make sense of this. Keesha had started to hum. His voice dropped to a hiss. "I took your name and the taste of your blood and the fire of my pain. I took the memory of every friend that you murdered, every foal and pup and telshee and ferryshaft who died on Kuwee Island. I took all that, and I made a song...just for you. It took sixteen years. I hope you appreciate it."

The hum rose and *engulfed him.* Arcove had one clear thought—*If I scream, my cats will hear and come running. They'll be killed.* He was on the ground without knowing how he got there. The world spun wildly, and then he was falling—sickening, panicked free fall. There was a live rat in his belly. It was chewing its way out. *Don't scream, don't scream, don't scream.* He was retching helplessly, convulsing. He couldn't see, couldn't hear, couldn't smell. He was lost in his own head. He was falling, and then he hit the bottom. Pain shot through him in every direction, and then he blacked out.

Tollee woke to the sound of Myla whispering in her ear. "Mother? Mother, please wake up. I'm scared."

Tollee opened her eyes. The air had that first breath of winter in it, and she shivered. The world around her was limed in pre-dawn light. The brightening sky looked clear, but Tollee thought she could smell snow on the wind. Her fur had partially dried, but she was still a little wet. If not for the warmth radiating from so many other bodies, she would have been quite cold.

"Mother..." repeated Myla and Tollee blinked. The world around her was not simply aglow with dawn light. It was *glowing*. Many of the trees' limbs or leaves had a speckling of green luminescent points of light. They were not immediately obvious, since the whole wood was green, but, upon close inspection, there was certainly something odd here.

The ground was so thick with sleeping ferryshaft that Tollee could hardly see a place to walk, but, here and there, she saw others waking, getting to their feet, staring. A few were hesitantly grazing, although they shied away from things that glowed.

"They're just plants," she whispered to Myla. "Just...odd plants."

Myla did not look convinced. "That one has snakes."

Tollee squinted. She saw, with a new chill, what Myla meant. One tree appeared to have the same sort of tentacles as the plants from Groth, growing out of an otherwise normal limb. They dangled lazily overhead, swaying in the occasional breeze.

Tollee swallowed the lump in her throat. *Poison,* she couldn't help thinking, *this wood has been poisoned.* Aloud, she said, "Let's get a drink." Tollee and Myla had not gone more than a few paces from the water's edge the night before. Tollee was certain that the island was not large, else the ferryshaft would have spread out more. She rose now and inched down to the waterline, Myla following. While she drank, Tollee examined the far shore. It seemed invitingly close.

As she watched, several creasia moved along the bank. To her dismay, three of them slipped into the water and started paddling out towards the island. Tollee retreated with Myla back to the cover of the thick foliage. She noticed, now, that much of it

563

looked strange. Familiar plants looked warped—as though they were trying to grow tentacles…or bowls. A poorly-formed suspicion niggled at the back of her mind.

Many of the ferryshaft were stirring now. Tollee picked her way around and through them, towards the center of the island. She'd gone only a short distance, when she ran into Remy and Itsa. Tollee was relieved to see that Remy's foal, Teedo, was still with her.

"Tollee," breathed Remy. "Have you looked around?"

"Not much," whispered Tollee, "but these plants…"

"We know," said Itsa. "We've been all around the edges of the island. It's tiny, and all of the plants are deformed. In the center…"

She was cut short by the arrival of the three creasia. Ferryshaft scattered before them as they came up the bank, although they didn't strike at anyone or give any orders. The lead cat was shadow-black, and Tollee thought, for a confused moment, that it was Arcove. However, as the cat came nearer, she saw that it wasn't big enough to be Arcove. This creasia had pink nose-leather, and his eyes looked oddly colorless.

The three creasia walked through the sea of ferryshaft, who parted for them like leaves before a wind. Then, because they clearly weren't sure what else to do, the ferryshaft followed the cats towards the center of the island. Tollee, Remy, and Itsa looked at each other. Then, hesitantly, they joined the throng, their foals trailing behind them.

There was no pushing this morning. No one was especially anxious to be in the lead. However, they'd gone only a short distance when they encountered a clearing. "This is the center," muttered Itsa. "It really isn't a large island."

The grass in the clearing looked more palatable than the foliage of the wood, but not many ferryshaft had tried to eat it. The reason stood in the center of the clearing—a small stand of what were unmistakably the carnivorous trees of Groth. They weren't very big yet—about the height of an adult ferryshaft—and the pink of their inner bowls was still pale. It had not yet deepened into the opened-mouth color that Tollee associated with the carnivorous

forest. However, the smell was the same—sickly sweet, both alluring and repulsive. The trees would have been unsettling enough by
themselves. However, Tollee could see the strange points of green
light glowing through the thin plant-skin of their bowls. *What is
that?*

The black creasia stopped beside the broad leaves and gently
swaying tentacles of the deadly plants, flanked by his escort. He
turned and looked at the cautious, frightened faces peering at him
from the edge of the clearing. "Hello, ferryshaft."

He did not speak loudly. Tollee had to strain to hear.

"My name is Moro," continued the cat, "and I am your new
master. This," his gaze swept the clearing, "is your new home. I
know it seems a bit crowded at the moment. But I'll help with
that." Tollee felt herself bristle. She did not like this cat at all, but
she found herself moving forward, straining to hear him. The rest
of the herd was doing the same.

"This island isn't big enough for a creasia den, let alone the
entire ferryshaft herd," said a female near the front. Tollee recognized her as an elder. A murmur went up from the herd—emotions
of frustration and anger, previously held in check by fear and weariness—came surging to the surface. "Where is Arcove?" demanded
the elder. "Did he order this? Where is Charder? He is our herd
leader. If he has been replaced, we deserve to know."

Moro grinned—more of a flash of teeth than a true smile.
"Arcove has been deposed," he said. "Treace is the new creasia king.
Charder is dead or soon will be. There is no need for a herd leader
anymore. *I* am in charge of you."

The murmuring in the ferryshaft herd grew louder. "That's not
part of treaty law," growled a big, dark-colored male. Tollee knew
that he was Kelsy's father.

"No," agreed Moro. "The treaty is void and meaningless. You
are a conquered people. What need have we of a treaty?"

The growling and grumbling deepened as the ferryshaft closed
in around Moro. Tollee felt a mixture of apprehension and hope.

Can he really be this stupid? If the treaty is void, then we have nothing to lose by killing him.

From among the plants behind Moro, something rose up—a slender thing with patchy hair, fish-belly pale. Its slitted eyes glowed green. The ferryshaft near the front of the group tried to retreat so quickly that they ran over their companions. They pressed back, and Tollee thought, for a moment, that they would stampede again. She heard a foal squeak, "What is it?" And someone shushed him.

"That's better," purred Moro.

"This is Kos. It just wants to learn about you. We're going to kill some of you, of course, but we want to be fair about it, so we thought we'd let you do the choosing. I'll come again this evening. If you don't provide me with a subject, I'll choose ten. One dead ferryshaft or ten. Your choice."

15

Something Extraordinary

Arcove's eyes snapped open. The echo of pain was still intense, but his head cleared. He looked around and saw, in addition to the telshees, three ferryshaft and a number of highland curbs, all staring at him. Arcove struggled to his feet, and the world did not spin. The nausea was gone. His limbs obeyed him.

His head snapped around at Keesha, and he snarled.

Keesha yawned. "So predictable. I just fixed you. Aren't you going to say thank you?"

With an effort, Arcove controlled his instinctive growl. He shut his eyes and took a deep breath. He could remember everything from the last day, but the events took on new meaning. *I didn't lose the fight...not exactly. Treace used a curb trap. But I wasn't fighting correctly. I was sick and dizzy. Keesha...*

Arcove opened his eyes. "It won't last...will it?"

Keesha grinned at him, showing all his teeth. "Now you're catching on! That tiny predator's brain does puzzle things out in the end!"

"He'll get sick again?" piped up Sauny, but Keesha ignored her.

"I have the poison and the cure, and the poison *is* the cure. You cannot fight this...although I know you'll try."

"What do you want?" asked Arcove tightly.

"Is that your idea of begging? You're not very good at it."

"What do you *want?*"

"To watch you die in great pain, obviously. You'll do that when I finish the song...and you'll die if I don't finish it, too. The whole thing is a little redundant, but I *can* drag it out. You should be flattered. Do you know how hard it is to make a song like that?"

"If you think threatening me will allow you to control—"

"Oh, I have control," said Keesha. He hummed a single note, and Arcove flinched. The rat stirred in his belly. "I've put an invisible cord around your neck," hissed Keesha, "and when I yank it, you will come. If you don't, I'll yank you right out of your head. You'll do whatever I want."

"You haven't told me what that is," said Arcove through clenched teeth.

"Is there anything Coden could have said to keep you from tearing him apart?" asked Keesha. "Did you make him beg before the end?"

All kinds of things, thought Arcove. *And Coden would never have begged.*

"How did the Shable end up in Groth?" asked Keesha. "I thought I knew what happened that night, but maybe I need the story from an eyewitness."

"I don't know," said Arcove. *I could guess, but I don't know.*

"Liar."

Arcove said nothing.

When it was clear that he was not going to respond, Keesha said, "I want the ferryshaft herd free. I want Leeshwood under ferryshaft control. If they choose to be more merciful to you than you were to them, that's their business. I wouldn't expect too much if I were you."

"I do not currently have control, either of Leeshwood or the ferryshaft herd," said Arcove.

"Well, that is unfortunate," said Keesha. "Storm seems to think this Treace person is more repulsive than you are. I can't imagine that I'd want to deal with such a cat. And I don't have a song for him. I might just have to kill all of you if he ends up in charge."

Arcove could hear the blood beating in his ears.

"I won't kill Roup," continued Keesha, "because I promised Coden I wouldn't. So I'll spare him. Do you think he will be lonely all by himself, the only creasia left on—?"

"Shut up," grated Arcove. "You've made yourself clear." He turned away and was relieved that his legs did not betray him.

Keesha called after him, his voice merry again. "When you begin to feel ill, come and see me. I'll be around."

I will choke on my own vomit before I come and see you.

"When you're ready, you'll ask for my help," continued Keesha. "Ask nicely."

Arcove stopped, but did not turn. His voice came out savage. "You were an evil-tempered thing on Kuwee Island, and sixteen years of sleep have not improved you. *You* got your friend killed, Keesha. Coden would still be alive if you hadn't been there."

Arcove didn't turn, but he heard Keesha's low hiss and earth-throbbing snarl. *Go ahead. Tear me apart. That might be best for everyone.*

But Keesha did not attack. He didn't even hum. However, as Arcove started moving again, the low, furious voice called after him. "I will sing to you again when you *beg*. Not before."

Arcove spun around. "Is that a promise?"

Keesha's mane was bristling, making him look even bigger. "Oh, yes."

And you've said it before witnesses. Arcove felt a measure of relief. *At least I get to choose how I die.*

Storm watched in dismay as Arcove disappeared into the trees. He had suspected that Arcove's illness was Keesha-induced. He'd expected Keesha to address the problem and to make threats and demands. However, the scope of the situation had exceeded Storm's expectations by several orders of magnitude. He glanced sidelong at Sauny. She looked just as uncertain as he felt.

"Keesha…" began Storm.

"Yes, yes, I know you are going to ask about that cub," said Keesha, still watching the place where Arcove had disappeared. "I'll make some allowance for him. And if you truly want to manage a small population of creasia here, then I suppose I'll allow that, too." He turned to look at Storm and Sauny. "But this struggle between your two species has gone on long enough. It is a source of constant turmoil on my island. You have an opportunity here to get the creasia under control and to free your people. I suggest you take it."

"And by 'get the creasia under control,' you mean kill all of them?" asked Storm.

"Most of them, yes," said Keesha. "Do you have a better idea?"

None that you'll like.

The telshees with Keesha were looking around uneasily. Storm didn't think they'd spent so much time above ground in a decade or more. "We'll be back at evening," said Keesha. "I'm told there's going to be a creasia battle. Will you foolishly stay for that, or shall I send some telshees with you to find your herd? I suppose that if you simply wait long enough, most of the cats will be dead. It might be easier to collect your herd then."

Storm hesitated. "We need to…think about it."

"Think fast." Keesha turned away towards the cliffs. His telshees trailed after him, although Shaw lingered a moment. Storm thought that she wanted to say something, but then she shook her head and followed Keesha.

The curbs, who'd been inordinately quiet, began to pace. "Your friend is very powerful," muttered Eyal. "That song—"

"We know," said Sauny. She retreated a little distance from the curbs. Valla was muttering in her ear.

Storm followed them. "What are you thinking?" he whispered.

"I'm thinking Arcove-in-our-debt might be better than Arcove-dead," said Sauny.

"But Keesha says he'll die anyway," Valla pointed out.

"Do you trust everything Keesha says to Arcove?" asked Sauny. She hesitated. "Or about him?"

Valla was quiet.

"Arcove is *stubborn*," said Storm. "I tried to make him promise to stop the raids after I got him away from Keesha in Syriot. He was practically blind with pain, and he still wouldn't say it. Kelsy tried, too, on the council ledge. I think Arcove likes Kelsy as well as he likes any of us, but he wouldn't say it then, either. If he lives, we can't control him. Even Keesha can barely control him."

Sauny was silent.

"I heard the creasia talking," whispered Valla. "They are certain that Treace will attack tonight, and there's a good chance that they'll be overrun and killed. They're badly outnumbered. They're going to die unless something extraordinary happens."

Sauny's mouth twitched up. She glanced at Storm. "How angry do you think Keesha would be if we…" She jerked her head, making the Shable bounce against her chest.

Storm laughed. "Pretty angry."

Roup expected to find Arcove *in* the hot spring upon his return. Arcove had been trying to crawl into it all day. Roup didn't think

Arcove was delirious enough to drown, but he worried about the snow. Fat flakes had begun to drift from a sky that had turned gray with clouds, darkening to purple along the horizon like a bruise. *It won't matter,* Roup thought. *Nothing will matter by nightfall.*

Halvery was organizing their defenses as though he were already the new king. Roup let him. *King for a day.* However, Roup did want to make sure that the tattered remains of his own clutter got something to eat. *No need to spend their final evening hungry.*

Caraca had not come to Arcove's den. Roup had not expected it. Females did not normally involve themselves in male squabbles. It was not their duty, nor would it have been good for Leeshwood.

Roup was surprised that so many females from Halvery and Sharmel's dens *had* joined their mates. He was fairly certain that such numbers were unprecedented and he wondered what it would mean for the creasia population in the coming years if so many females were killed in the fighting. *Surely Nadine and her den mates don't mean to fight with us. They are being polite because we are trapped here, but when the fighting starts, they will retreat to their caves.*

Roup was surprised, when he headed back to the hot spring, to meet Arcove coming in the other direction. He knew immediately that something had happened. Arcove's eyes were bright. His hackles were up. He was moving with that surety and grace that Roup had thought never to see again.

"Arcove?"

"Where's Halvery?"

"He's…" Roup pulled himself together. "He's eating. Storm's curb friends were kind enough to bring us several sheep. Did you… did you talk to them?" Roup sniffed over Arcove, who shied away. He didn't smell as he had after returning from the deep cave. Still… "Keesha," growled Roup. "Where is he?"

Arcove glided on into the press of sleeping or resting animals around the caves. Roup had to trot to keep up. "Where is he, Arcove? I want to talk to him."

"Stay out of it, Roup." There was a warning in his voice.

Oh, no. That might work with everyone else, but not with me. "This is all his doing, isn't it? The fight, the way you've been acting... I want to speak to him."

"Well, you can't," said Arcove without looking at Roup. "We don't have much time. Let it be."

They topped a little rise behind the caves and caught sight of the bloody remains of the curbs' gift, stark against the new-fallen snow. The sheep had been rapidly stripped down to bones, and cats were now cracking those to get at the marrow. Ordinarily, they would have fed by order of rank, but in this case, the officers had attempted to ration the food evenly. No one was satisfied, but no one was faint with hunger, either.

Halvery was crunching through a sheep femur when they found him. His eyes widened at the sight of Arcove. "You look... better," he said cautiously.

"How many?" asked Arcove without preamble.

Halvery licked his lips. "As near as I can tell, we had about two hundred and fifty males going into the fight yesterday evening. The battle was poorly-planned—"

"How many?"

"We've got maybe a hundred and fifty who can fight well," said Halvery. "Another fifty or so are wounded, Sharmel among them. They'll try, of course."

"Of course."

"We estimate that Treace had about three hundred and fifty going into the fight, and I don't think he lost as many as we did. His cats were expecting a battle. Some of them actually circled around behind us while you were fighting. They attacked from the front and from the rear." Halvery hesitated. "That curb trap..."

"What about it?" Arcove's voice was unreadable.

"It was cheating, sir," said Halvery. "I think so, and I fully support you, but..."

"But the subordinate animals disagree?" asked Arcove.

"They are divided," said Halvery. "There's no traditional rule... It was an innovation." He hesitated again. "The first cat to actually touch one of the combatants was Roup when he chewed you loose." Halvery very carefully did not look at Roup.

"And they're saying I cheated because of that?" asked Arcove.

"Not loudly and not to me," said Halvery, "but I've heard rumblings. I'm sure it's what Treace is telling his lot. We've had a few desertions. I think we'll have more shortly unless something changes."

Arcove thought for a moment. "Treace probably has about three hundred cats. We have half that."

"Ours are more experienced," Halvery pointed out.

"But Treace also has lowland curbs," muttered Roup.

Halvery cleared his throat. "One other thing. A surprising number of females have come to your den. Some of them even joined in the fighting yesterday. I'm not sure how much we should depend on them, but…there are at least a hundred, maybe more."

Arcove frowned. "I'll talk to Nadine."

All three of them sat in silence for a moment. Roup noticed that Halvery kept studiously avoiding his eyes. At last, Arcove said, "We attack. The sooner the better."

"That's what I thought," said Halvery. "Treace's cats will come at evening, prepared for a bloody stand-off in these caves. We'll kill a lot of them, but they'll win that fight in the end. Right now, they're sleeping, tired from yesterday. We have had an unexpected meal, so we're feeling a little fresher. The desertions are only going to get worse, and we're only going to get hungrier. Things won't get any better than they are right now."

"Our odds are terrible," muttered Roup.

"Do you have a better idea?"

"*I* do." They all looked around to see Storm and Charder almost upon them, sound and scent muffled by the falling snow. Storm was wearing the Shable—bright blue against his pale fur. "Like Roup says," continued Storm, "your odds in a fight are terrible."

Arcove was looking suspiciously between the two ferryshaft. Charder had on his political face. Roup couldn't tell what he was thinking, but he thought he detected the hint of a smile.

"This isn't the time for fighting," said Storm. "This is the time for running and hiding. Which is what I'm good at."

"Creasia kings do not run and hide," growled Halvery.

"What are you saying, Storm?" asked Roup.

"Sauny and I are offering to open Kuwee Island for you," said Storm.

Roup saw his own shock mirrored on Halvery's face. Arcove, however, didn't even blink. "If...?"

"No if," said Storm.

They were all silent, watching each other. "Where *is* your sister?" asked Arcove at last.

"She and Valla and Kelsy have gone to find our herd," said Storm. He hesitated. "When I came to your conference, I trusted you. Now, trust me."

Something like hope stirred inside Roup, then died instantly. *Arcove will never do it.*

"Kuwee Island is far away beyond an encircling line of enemy cats," said Arcove.

Storm grinned, so that points of light danced in his gray eyes. "Well, I can't tell you what to do. But I know what *I* would do."

"Stop being coy," said Charder. "Arcove, it's snowing. Have you seen what it's doing to the hot springs?"

Roup thought for a moment. "Oh..." Even from here, they could all see the clouds of steam, rising lazily into the gray sky.

"You want us to walk in Smoky Branch..." said Arcove slowly.

"Yes," said Storm. "Find the deepest water and move quietly. I think you'll pass right through those lines of sleeping cats and on down to Chelby Lake. By the time you reach cooler water, you'll be past the danger. Then you'll have a long run to warm up."

"That might actually work," muttered Roup. He glanced at Arcove. *It's not your style. But please...*

"Alright," said Arcove.

Roup thought that Halvery looked just as surprised as he felt.

Charder looked relieved. "You'll need to leave as soon as possible to get ahead of—"

574

"I'm aware of that," said Arcove. He started back towards the cave. "Roup, Halvery, get the clutters ready to move."

Roup looked after him uncertainly. He knew he should feel relieved, but he didn't. *Something is still wrong.*

16

In the Water

"You don't have to come," Arcove told Nadine. He watched her for a moment. *Let me rephrase that.* "You *shouldn't* come."

"Why not?" Nadine looked tired. She was staring into the tendrils of steam.

"Because king's wars are male things," said Arcove. "You didn't die with Masaran. You didn't die with Ketch. You should not die with me."

"Are you so certain that you're going to die?"

"If I don't, then I will come back, and things will be as they were."

Nadine looked at him. "I invited ferryshaft to shelter with my cubs last night, Arcove. *You* are about to run away from a battle— No, don't interrupt me. For what it's worth, I agree with the ferryshaft about this. If you accept their help, it will change everything. Things will never be as they were."

Well, that is true enough. "You have been den mother to half of Leeshwood," said Arcove. "Either way it goes, they will need you to—"

Nadine turned on him almost savagely. "Yes, I have been den mother for many a season, but I see fewer turn-overs than the average den. Do you know what the old females say? The ones who survive one new clutter after another?"

Arcove did not know.

"They say that you only love every other mate," said Nadine. "You love the first, and you never quite forgive his killer, no matter how kind he is to you. The third mate avenges the first, and so you love him, but the fourth you hate again, and so on. Each time, you love the cubs a little less, because you cannot afford to love them too much. And you love the males a little less, too, because if you love them too much, you'll die of a broken heart. You love your female den mates; they are all you can afford. And this is the way it has been for as long as we have stories of our past. It is our nature. It is our way."

Arcove was silent. She'd never spoken to him this way—not in all their years together.

Nadine drew a deep breath. "Do you remember the first thing you said to me when you walked into my den?"

Arcove did not remember. He remembered that Roup had been pacing anxiously outside.

"You looked at my cub—Ketch's cub—and you asked, 'What's his name?'"

Arcove did remember then. He remembered her dignity and the resignation on her carefully blank face when she responded, 'Does it matter?' Arcove had said, 'How else will I know what to call him?' He'd not been sure, even then, whether she thought his behavior weak or merely eccentric. She'd started giving him advice, though. It had taken him years to realize how unusual that was.

"You said that," whispered Nadine, "and I knew. Before the war. Before Kuwee. Before Coden. I knew you were going to change everything." She took a deep breath. "If males can stop killing cubs, then females can start fighting wars. We're coming with you."

And they did. While Treace's creasia slept, and the snow fell thick and fast, a silent procession of cats paddled or waded down the center of Smoky Branch. A few scouts went first, creeping cautiously past every bend in the river, noting the places where their enemies were sleeping close to the bank or where the rocks turned easily under foot.

They reported back to Arcove, Roup, and Halvery at the head of the line. Behind them, came the fighters most prepared to handle trouble in their path. Among them were quite a few females. Towards the back, many were carrying cubs. Even the smallest were quiet, limp in an adult's mouth.

Sharmel came near the rear. He'd volunteered to oversee the wounded. They limped or wobbled along, sometimes buoyed up by the chest-deep water, occasionally dragged by their companions. Adolescent cubs swam alongside them, excited and trying not to chatter.

At times, they passed almost under the noses of their sleeping enemies or heard them stir just beyond the steam. Then, they would hold their breaths and hope that nothing splashed, not even a fish.

Storm felt surreal, walking and swimming among them. Charder had elected to move near the front, but Storm stayed with the cubs. Teek was so excited that he could hardly contain himself. They were on a grand adventure with all of his heroes.

Storm tried not to think about Sauny and Valla and Kelsy. *They have the curbs with them; they'll be alright. After all,* he reasoned, *Treace's main strength is here. He can't have left much of a guard around the herd with so many needed for the fight this evening. How dangerous can it be?*

Tollee had to admit that Moro's strategy was brilliant. *The only thing more demoralizing than killing random members of the herd is making us select the victims ourselves.* She couldn't imagine anything that would more effectively prevent the ferryshaft from working together to escape. *Even the lowest ranking animal has friends and family. If we do this, it will create resentment and distrust that will never die.*

But if we don't do it... Tollee doubted very much that Moro's cull would stop at ten animals. *He said he was going to make us comfortable on this island. How many would he have to kill...?* Tollee shivered. *We have to escape. We* have *to.*

The herd began bickering as soon as the cats departed. Tollee noticed some of the elders eyeing young orphans. *Trying to decide which have the fewest friends?*

Some wanted to take a vote, but the entire herd had never voted on anything before. They couldn't even effectively have a discussion. Tollee could hear animals quarreling in raised voices through the trees.

She looked at Itsa and Remy. Then, without speaking, they moved towards the lake-ward side of the island. As Itsa had said, the island wasn't large. However, at the point where they emerged from the trees, they were out of sight of the mainland. Tollee could see what might be several other small islands in the distance. *Or they might just be stands of trees with no soil.* It had begun to snow, although it wasn't quite cold enough for the snow to stick.

"Do you think they'll swim after us if we just leave?" murmured Itsa.

"Well, they'll definitely *see* us," said Remy. "Once we get beyond the shelter of the island, we'll be swimming in plain view. They could easily follow us along the shore."

"We could swim to one of those islands," persisted Itsa, "stay there until they lose interest, then swim to another island when they seem preoccupied."

"Unless they just swim out after us," said Tollee. She licked her lips. "I've fought with curbs. I've killed them in the water. I think the three of us might be able to make it...if the creasia don't take an interest...but..." She cut her eyes at Myla and Teedo, who were chasing minnows in the shallows.

Remy looked stricken.

578

Our foals will never make it, thought Tollee. *I'm not even sure they would make the swim…if we had to swim all day…if there was nowhere to get out of the water. Certainly if our enemies came after us and we had to fight for our lives… Our foals would never make it.*

"I'm not going," said Remy at once. She turned to Tollee. "I'll keep Myla if you want to try. Maybe…maybe we'll meet again… and if not, then you were right to go, because we can't protect them here, either. But I'm not going."

Tollee licked her friend's nose. "There has to be another way."

"I don't think so," murmured Remy.

"Tollee…Remy…" Itsa's voice sounded strained. They turned to look and saw her staring at Myla and Teedo. The foals seemed to have discovered something in the water. They were standing still, rearing up a little, necks arched as if they wanted to look at it, but were afraid to get too close. Itsa had gone just a little farther along the bank towards them. Suddenly, the thing moved, and the foals dashed back to the bank.

"Mother," whispered Myla, "it's…like Teek…under the water."

The thing rose up. Remy gasped. Tollee thought, at first, that she was looking at a muddy creasia cub who had somehow been lurking in the shallows. The animal was a little bigger than Teek, perhaps a year older. However, as mud slithered from its body, it became clear that something was *very* wrong. Loops of slimy, dull gray tissue were trailing from the cat's belly. Here and there, a flash of pink appeared, but the wounds looked old and rotten. The cub opened its eyes, and they were *green*—as green as the lishty's eyes among the carnivorous plants.

The animal took a staggering step towards them. All five ferryshaft retreated up the bank so quickly that they nearly ran into each other. Below them, the little cat opened its mouth impossibly wide and hissed. Tollee felt cold. The cub appeared to have grown a set of long fangs behind its incisors.

Myla whimpered. "Mother, what is it?"

"I don't know," said Tollee.

"Is it dead?" asked Teedo.

"I don't know," said Remy.

"It smells dead," said Myla.

"I think it *is* dead," whispered Itsa. "Like we are all going to be."

Tollee rounded on her. "Don't say that!" she hissed, but Itsa was looking out along the bank.

"Look," she whispered. "Look at them."

Tollee's stomach did a sick flop. She followed Itsa's gaze. Lumps and hillocks that she had taken for piles of mud or rock were half-covered bodies. She could see, now that she knew what to look for, the shape of an ear here, the tip of a tail there. Most were cubs or adolescents. All of them, if she watched long enough, were moving just slightly—trembling, jerking, twitching.

Tollee *hoped* they were dead.

17

Hide and Hunt

Kelsy watched the curbs uneasily as he trotted behind Sauny and Valla. He had a sense of having lingered too long away from his herd and mates. Ever since that moment on the plain, after they'd come down from the council ledge and seen the corpses, Kelsy felt as though he'd been moving underwater. The sight of those still forms had brought back memories of agonized moments by the lake more than a year ago.

Kelsy remembered Faralee's warm body—so limp as he'd tried to drag her to her feet. *I kept telling her to get up. And that was the last thing she heard. Me shouting at her to get up.* In that instant,

Kelsy had understood what war meant, and he knew that he *never* wanted one.

Focus! They had run wide of Treace's cats—back towards the cliffs and then looping northeast. The highland curbs had only a vague knowledge of this part of the forest. The ferryshaft didn't know it at all. However, their luck held as they ran on through the trees. No one challenged them. There was no sound of yipping at their heels.

They crossed the trail of the ferryshaft herd near noon. It was easy to follow—a broad swath of broken ground and bent saplings. The going was easier after that with a clear trail and underbrush beaten flat. They ran at the fastest pace they could maintain.

Kelsy was surprised that they did not encounter any dead animals. He smelled traces of blood, and it was evident that the herd had been moving at panicked speed. He even found offal in several places, but no bodies. *Did the curbs and creasia eat them so quickly?* It seemed impossible. Kelsy glanced at Sauny and Valla. They were clearly focused on the goal. He thought of mentioning the strange lack of bodies, but decided to save his breath.

The sun was slipping down the sky, and the cool air had grown cold by the time they encountered the first lowland curb. They came upon the animal suddenly—a scout, perhaps. The highland curbs fell upon it before it even had time to yip. Twilight was deepening towards dusk and the snow had started to stick by the time they encountered the second curb. They killed that one, too, but it had a companion. Kelsy caught a glimpse of the second curb darting away through the trees.

Eyal turned to Sauny and Valla. They were all panting from their long run. "I think we're close," began Sauny. "I smell the lake, and I think—"

"Agreed," cut in Eyal. "We'll go after that curb, try to kill it before it finds its companions. In all likelihood, we will fail, and they will be after us. I suggest we split up. You go find your herd. We will distract the curbs and any creasia who join them."

"Thank you," said Valla. "Be careful, Eyal."

He gave a flash of teeth, and the curbs were gone.

Kelsy could smell the lake, too…and something else. *Feces? Frightened animals?* "We should get off the trail," he said aloud, but he let Sauny take the lead, due east, angling away from the trail of the ferryshaft herd and straight towards the lake. They came out of the trees just as the first series of excited yips reverberated through the wood behind them.

Kelsy felt his heart begin to pound. Sauny and Valla struck out south along the lake, since that was the direction the herd had been going. Kelsy blinked. Up ahead, one of the little islands near shore was…glowing.

Sauny and Valla saw it, too. "What in the deeps?" murmured Sauny.

"It looks like acriss," said Valla.

"It does." Sauny's voice sounded strained. "Do you think—?"

And then there was a snarl behind them. Without pausing to look back, all three of them broke into a full gallop. Kelsy felt a sharp ache in his muscles—sore from a long day of running—but he ignored it. They tore along the edge of the lake at top speed in the last of the fading light. *We can't keep this up for long.*

But it didn't matter, because the breeze shifted, and he caught the scent of the ferryshaft herd—massive and earthy, complex with sweat and fear. *On that glowing island…*

Kelsy risked a backwards glance. Their pursuers were not as close as he'd feared. The island drew nearer. Without pausing to consult the others, Kelsy veered sideways and launched himself into the lake. He hit the water paddling furiously. An instant later, he heard a splash behind him and knew that Sauny and Valla had followed.

I'm coming Remy, Teedo, Itsa. I'm coming. Even if I'm only coming to die with you.

Treace was stunned. He stood in the largest of the ancient caves that had been den to creasia kings time-out-of-mind. He'd expected to fight a battle here—a bloody, difficult battle, but he'd expected to win. His cats—lean and young and fierce—paced around the caves, growling and muttering. They were well-rested, their blood was up, and they wanted to fight.

Treace stood in the empty cave and tried to re-order his thinking. *Arcove ran away? I didn't know he had it in him.*

Not only had Arcove and his clutters run, they had taken females and cubs with them. *Unbelievable!* Treace had heard rumors that females fought in the battle the previous evening. *Just Roup's freakish beta,* he had thought, *not true females.* Now, he wondered.

They even took their wounded. Or killed them. The only bodies left around the den were stiff and cold. There were quite a few of those, at least. *They're outnumbered, that's certain.*

"Sir," growled one of his officers, "the subordinate animals… You need to speak to them."

Treace licked his lips. *They want a fight, and I don't know where to point them.* He wracked his brain. *Arcove must have gone towards the cliffs. We would know if he went into the forest. But… there's nothing for him at the cliffs! Nothing more defensible than here.*

"What are the scouts reporting?" he asked aloud.

"Nothing, sir."

Arcove's cats are traveling with cubs and wounded. The only way they could avoid leaving a blood trail would be…

Treace spun around. He could feel the comforting warmth of the hot spring even from this distance—a spring he'd hoped would be his own. The snow drifted down serenely. *Of course. It's what I would do.*

"They went in the hot springs," said Treace flatly.

"Sir…?"

"They walked out under the cover of steam in the rivers that flow from the hot springs!" Treace was angry now. "They walked out practically under our noses!" He'd been sleeping less than two lengths from that stream.

His subordinate backed away. Treace shut his eyes and took a deep breath. "Rally the clutters. I'll speak to them."

He lingered a moment in the cave, thinking. *It's what I would do, but it's not Arcove's way at all. There's something else going on here, and I'm not sure what, but it has Storm's sneaky little hoofprints all over it.*

A strategy was forming in his mind as he trotted out of the cave and climbed up the tangle of roots, into the lower branches of the massive tree that sheltered the den. His cats were gathering below him, their eyes reflecting the red light of sunset, white teeth flashing. "Friends, we have been tricked," began Treace. "Our former king has run from us. He and his few supporters have hidden themselves in steam and walked through our midst."

A murmur began below him.

"Strange behavior for a king," continued Treace. "Strange behavior for Arcove, who was known for his bravery in his younger years, but I can tell you why he did it."

The cats below quieted.

"This has the mark of the wily ferryshaft known as Vearil," said Treace. "This is not Arcove's plan at all, friends. He has made a bargain with the ferryshaft to save himself. What do you suppose he has promised them in exchange for their help? Half a dozen cubs every spring? Half a hundred?"

The murmur below rose to snarls and roars.

"The ferryshaft leader, Charder, was also here last we knew," continued Treace. "I will give you these beasts as your food animals. Arcove would give them to you as your masters. Which do you prefer?"

"We are with you!" roared one of the cats below. "We have always been with you!"

"Death to cowards!" shouted one.

"Death to ferryshaft and their allies!"

"In addition," continued Treace over the racket, "Arcove has encouraged our females to behave unnaturally—fighting with males, carrying their cubs away from their dens. This will result in fewer mates for everyone. It will result in fewer cubs. This cannot be tolerated!"

Some of the cats below were already racing off in the direction of the hot springs. Treace jumped down from the tree. "We hunt!" he cried. "And what we catch, we kill!"

18

Choose

Storm had hoped that they would reach Kuwee Island before dark, but they were still quite a ways out when dusk began to settle on the landscape. Arcove's creasia were flagging. The snow had begun to pile up, and the air felt icy on partially wet skin. For a time after they left the stream, Storm worried that the water had been too high a price to pay for escape. Those who could not run to get warm fell behind first. Some of the wounded died. The cubs under three were not able to sustain the pace, but they grew cold when they were carried. Storm insisted that Teek run from time to time, but he could tell that the cub was exhausted.

And we still have to cross the Igby.

Once they reached the big river, Arcove elected to run east towards the lake along its bank, rather than cross immediately. Storm suspected that he intended to cross at the delta, where the water was shallowest. It would make their entire journey a little longer, but it would avoid the brutal swim that would otherwise claim many of his followers.

As darkness fell, Storm began to imagine that he could hear wailing creasia rally cries behind them. *How long will it take Treace to realize he's been tricked? How long to realize where we've gone?* Once Treace figured it out, Storm had no doubt that he would come after them more quickly than they could run away. *He's not traveling with cubs and wounded, and his cats are the youngest males in Leeshwood.*

Storm was surprised, as he jogged along in the dark, to find Arcove suddenly beside him—a shadow of a shadow. The moon was peeking over the cliffs behind them—nearly full and yellow as a cat's eye. "Is that your luck or mine?" asked Storm.

Arcove chuffed. "We may need both tonight." He hesitated. "Walk with me a moment."

Storm felt uncertain, but he angled away from the group, into the edge of the trees. "Do you want us dead?" asked Arcove.

Storm thought it was a strange question, considering the circumstances. "If I did, I wouldn't be out here."

"You want peace?" asked Arcove. "No more raids? And creasia still alive on Lidian?"

Do I want peace without revenge? That's what you're asking me.

"Yes," said Storm. He was surprised that the answer came so easily.

"Because of the cub?" asked Arcove.

"Yes," he said again, although the real answer was more complicated.

He could feel Arcove's eyes studying him in the darkness. Storm kept his own eyes on the ground ahead. "I can't see as well as you can," he ventured after a moment. "Can we get back out from under the trees before I trip on a root?"

Arcove ignored his request. "Roup will probably ask you what happened in Syriot...and afterward. If you want what you claim, don't tell him. Never tell anyone. Will you promise me that?"

Storm did peer at him, then, but there was nothing to see. Even the reflection of his green eyes was lost in darkness with the moon shining behind him. "Are you…alright?" asked Storm. *Are you already sick again?*

"Yes or no?" persisted Arcove.

"I won't tell him," said Storm. "I can't vouch for what Sauny will do, and Charder—"

"I've already spoken with Charder," said Arcove. "I would appreciate it if you would talk to your sister." Then he was gone, gliding back into the light of the hunter's moon as it rose above the cliffs.

Tollee thought that the elders had made a decision. She did not know what. She did not care. She had decided that, at noon tomorrow, when most of the creasia were napping, she would try for one of the small islands. She would take Myla, and if they died, so be it. Her friends did not agree with her. Remy was unwilling to risk Teedo's likely death. Itsa flatly refused to go into the water after seeing the things along the shore.

"What if they're in the lake?" she asked. "What if they can swim? What if there are more lishties?"

"They don't seem very mobile," replied Tollee carefully. "I think lishties prefer sea water, and we don't even know whether the dead cats can hurt us."

"Did you see the fangs on that cub?" demanded Itsa. "I think it could have come after us if it had wanted to. I think it's guarding the edge of the island."

They quarreled on and off as they tried to find food for themselves and their foals. There was still enough forage without risking the carnivorous plants at the center of the island. *But if we're here for more than a few days, we'll strip this place clean,* thought Tollee. *We have to run now, before we grow weak with hunger, before we start fighting with each other over food.*

Moro came at dusk. This time, he brought eight creasia, and they herded the ferryshaft together around the clearing. Tollee told herself that she would not watch. She was glad that Myla was too small to see over the backs of those in front of her.

"Well?" drawled Moro, when the herd had quieted. "Which ferryshaft are you going to give me...or shall I choose?"

"They choose me."

Tollee had promised herself that she would not look, but the words brought her head up anyway. She was far back in the crowd, and the light had grown weak. She did not, at first, recognize the ferryshaft who stepped away from the others and walked calmly towards Moro and the ominous, glowing plants.

Then she blinked. His grizzled fur was familiar, even at a distance. *Pathar. Storm's old teacher.*

"I have always valued knowledge," Pathar said, his voice soft, but clear. "What is it you're hoping to learn from killing me, Moro?"

Moro's body language registered displeasure. "A volunteer," he said icily. "Oh, no. We can't have that."

He turned away from Pathar, but Pathar continued placidly. "I think what you are doing here is unwise. Lishties have goals that you could not possibly understand. Are you trying to wake Groth? I think that is exceedingly foolish."

Moro spun around. "Silence!" he snarled. "You will speak only when spoken to."

"Why?" asked Pathar. "Will you kill me twice?"

Moro's teeth flashed in the dim light, and Tollee shivered. "Maybe."

He turned back to the crowd. "It seems I've got some choosing to do. Where are those two who were seen talking by the water?"

Tollee wasn't sure whom he was addressing, but then a cat on the edge of the crowd behind her called, "They're over here."

To Tollee's horror, Moro started in her direction. She saw Remy trying to back away, but the ferryshaft weren't letting her through. They closed up tightly behind her. Everyone looked at the ground. They were pushing each other without meeting anyone's eyes. *Cowards, cowards, cowards!* thought Tollee, but she was trying to back away as much as anyone else.

She looked up and saw Moro right in front of her, his pale eyes gleaming in the light of the rising moon. *He's going to choose me. He's going to do something horrible to me.*

His eyes fell to Myla, cowering at Tollee's feet. *No, no, no, no...*

"Which shall I take," he asked. "This foal...or that one?" His head whipped around, and Tollee saw Teedo, trying to crawl between Remy's front legs. She met her friend's horrified eyes beneath Moro's gaze. "Well, be quick," he said. "I'm giving you a choice. Your foal or hers? Or shall I take both? Come, I haven't got all night."

This is meant to divide us, thought Tollee hopelessly. *And it will work.*

She opened her mouth, but no sound came. She tried again. "I—"

At that moment, there was a commotion on the far side of the crowd. Animals were stirring and muttering. From the trees beyond the clearing, Tollee heard creasia yowls and rally cries. Moro looked around. "What's going on?" A subordinate came up suddenly and started whispering in his ear.

Tollee took advantage of his distraction to slip quietly into the animals behind her, who'd begun to mill about. Moro moved back towards the center of the clearing, muttering to his officer. There was more commotion among the herd. Tollee wished she could see what was causing it. She could feel her heart thudding against her ribs, and she felt certain that her ordeal was not over. *How to get away, how to get away, how to get away...?*

And then she saw them—three ferryshaft slipping quickly through the press, speaking here and there. Tollee caught her breath. *Kelsy... Valla? And Sauny!*

Most ferryshaft believed Sauny was dead. Many of the younger ones regarded her as the tragic hero of their attempted rebellion. Rumors that she was alive among the telshees had persisted, but few really believed them. Now, not only was she among them, but she was walking—not limping, not hobbling, but running and walking as smoothly as anyone else.

"This is very interesting." Tollee looked back towards the center of the clearing to see Pathar peering into one of the plants' bowls. They were glowing more strongly now in the dim light. "They're more active after dark," he continued. "They don't like the light, do they?" Pathar caught at a tendril suddenly with his teeth and jerked, tearing part of the plant.

"Get away from that!" snarled Moro.

In the same instant, the plant shuddered and the tendril coiled in a clumsy, reflexive fashion. Pathar danced away. "They're quicker than the ones I'm used to, but not exactly implacable."

"Get away from that!" roared Moro again. He was trying to reach Pathar, but the agitated herd was getting in his way. Everyone wanted to see what was happening, and the ripple of excitement that followed Sauny and her companions created even more chaos.

Several wet and panting creasia were racing around the edges of the herd or trying to push through it. "We're in pursuit of three rogue ferryshaft!" one shouted. "They just swam over. We think one of them was at Arcove's council."

"Well, they're here now," snapped Moro as he shoved past the last of the ferryshaft into the center of the clearing. Pathar had ducked into the stand of plants, but he backed out suddenly as Kos emerged.

Tollee stared in horrified fascination at the lishty's nearly transparent skin, green in the light from the surrounding plants. It cocked its head at Pathar. "This one is old and ailing," it said. "A poor host. Unsuitable."

"I know that," growled Moro. "But we still can't have him tearing up the ghost plants." With casual brutality, he lunged forward and crunched through one of Pathar's front legs. A collective moan went up from the watching ferryshaft, but Pathar didn't make a sound. He staggered sideways, looking more surprised than hurt, and sat down heavily. Crimson blossomed down his mangled leg and began to pool on the ground in front of him.

"I'll deal with you later," growled Moro.

He turned back to the ferryshaft herd, his tone brusque again. "Well, you are fortunate this evening! It seems your choice is obvious. Give me the newcomers."

The noise in the herd died away. Tollee held her breath. She could no longer see Sauny, Valla, and Kelsy, but she had an idea of where they had vanished into the crowd. She didn't dare look in that direction. Treace's creasia were shoving in among the ferryshaft, who parted for them, but remained silent.

There was a sudden shriek at the far edge of the crowd, and Tollee was jostled by a ripple of shoving animals. She thought, at first, that they'd parted to reveal Sauny, Valla, and Kelsy, but, instead, three of the muddy creasia from the island's bank lurched into the faint glow from the plants.

"Ah, here's some incentive!" said Moro. "Shall I just let them start biting? I think they'd like that."

The cub that Tollee had seen earlier opened its mouth like a snake and hissed. Then, horribly, it spoke. "I have been Serka," it said thickly, as though it was not quite accustomed to its tongue. "This body…is…strange…to us."

"You'll get used to it," said Moro. "Or perhaps you can try a ferryshaft."

The herd was talking. Their voices rose in a frightened babble around Tollee. A few had simply curled up on the ground and buried their faces in their tails.

"They're just jellyfish!" shouted a voice. A ferryshaft was bounding over the others, trying to get to the front of the group. Tollee thought, for one moment, that it was Storm—fluid as a deer—and then she hit the ground, and it was Sauny Ela-ferry in the center of the clearing, glaring at Kos. The fur bristled along her spine. "Poisonous jellyfish!" she spat. "You can get inside dead animals and control them, but you're just jellyfish!"

Kos hissed at her. "You…" it murmured. "We trusted you."

"You lied to me," said Sauny. "But that's not important now."

Moro was advancing on her, tail twitching. "Is this a good specimen?" he asked Kos. "Young? Strong?"

"Yesss," hissed the lishty.

Tollee looked at the ferryshaft around her. They were trans-fixed, hardly breathing. *Do something!*

"You're not going to hurt me," said Sauny, although she was backing away. "My herd won't let you."

"Your herd is a cowardly prey species," said Moro. "They will stand and watch."

Another ferryshaft struggled through the press to stand beside Sauny. Tollee wasn't surprised to see Valla. Kelsy came out on the other side of the clearing. He was shouting something, although it took Tollee a moment to understand what he was saying at that distance. "Are you going to let this happen?" Tollee heard him say. "It's now or never, ferryshaft!"

He was interrupted by a long, lonely sound that rose quavering in the air. Tollee took a moment to recognize that it was a ferryshaft howl—deeper and longer than the sound the curbs made. It took her another moment to realize that Pathar was the one howling. He sat where Moro had left him, although he looked like he was having trouble holding himself up. He'd tilted his head back, and the haunting sound carried over the clearing.

Far back, on the edge of the crowd, someone answered. Their song created strange harmonies. It didn't sound like two ferryshaft. It sounded like three or four.

And then it *was* three.

And then it *was* four.

And then it was hundreds of hundreds.

Tollee had never howled with a group before, but it seemed instinctive. It stirred something in her blood—a beast that woke and feared nothing. A beast that sang for blood.

Moro seemed to sense the change in the herd. Several more ferryshaft had come forward to stand by Sauny, but Moro veered away from them. In two bounds, he reached Pathar, caught him by the throat, and ended his song forever.

Kos was hissing, and the dead cats were showing their fangs. Tollee heard snarls around the edges of the herd as creasia attacked howling ferryshaft. But it did not matter. The ferryshaft herd had had enough.

19

The Telshee's Eye

Storm stood in the cave at the top of the hill on Kuwee Island, panting. In the near-distance, he could hear the rally cries of Treace's cats. The waxing moon had risen a quarter of the way up the sky, casting sharp-edged shadows. Arcove and Halvery stood beside him in the cave. Below them, creasia were filing up the hill, putting one weary foot in front of the other. Roup had stayed by the edge of the water to count the cats who were still swimming over.

It was unclear how many they'd lost in the run. Those who couldn't keep up had simply dropped back and hidden. If they were lucky, Treace's cats might pass them by in favor of more meaningful conquests. However, Storm had heard the snarls and screams of those who were *not* lucky. Treace's cats were closing in, killing the stragglers whenever they found them.

Storm stopped in the center of the cave and shrugged off the Shable stone. It looked at home here, with the rougher blue crystals jutting from the walls. Arcove and Halvery watched him. Storm could hear a faint rattle in Arcove's breathing. He didn't dare ask how he was feeling.

"Well?" demanded Halvery. "How does it work?"

"Just a moment," muttered Storm. He scanned the ceiling of the cave for the strange shape—the painting. As before, it took his mind an instant to sort out the lines. There was the telshee, its enormous white outline sprawling across the ceiling of the cave, its pink tongue, and its one blue eye staring down at him.

Halvery seemed to make sense of the painting in the same moment. "Ghosts," he muttered and hunkered down a little. "I don't remember seeing that before."

Arcove looked down the slope at the cats staggering through the trees. "It was there."

Storm caught the metal string of the Shable in his teeth and swung the blue stone into the air. He didn't understand how it was supposed to wedge into the empty socket of the telshee's eye. The indentation didn't look deep enough. The Shable struck the ceiling and fell with a clatter. Arcove whipped around. "Don't break it."

Storm felt embarrassed. "I—I'm not exactly sure…"

Arcove came over and picked up the blue stone in his mouth. He reared up on his hind legs, craning his neck, and he was as tall as Shaw like that. He pressed the Shable stone into the empty socket of the Telshee's eye and sank back to the floor.

To Storm's fascination, the Shable stuck there, suspended, the chain dangling. "It's lightning stone," said Arcove. "It's made from the same rock as this cave. Lightning stone sticks to itself."

Before anyone could ask questions, there was a deep creak from the ceiling and also from somewhere underground. The entire section of the ceiling containing the telshee painting dropped gently towards the floor of the cave. Storm, Arcove, and Halvery scrambled out of the way. In the front of the cave, creasia were gathering. They did not speak. They watched.

A rectangle had opened in the ceiling, and the piece that had fallen formed a ramp up to it. Storm tried to understand. *It's like a jaw,* he decided. *The piece that opened is the bottom jaw, and the roof of the cave is like the top. The weight of the stone sticking to the bottom was enough to make it open.*

Of course, that means we've got to go down its throat.

Nothing moved in the dark void at the top of the ramp, but Storm thought he could feel a faint, warm breeze. He took this as a positive sign. *If air is moving, we won't suffocate.*

Arcove padded up the ramp. He stopped in the dark opening, sniffing, and then disappeared. A murmur went up from the watching creasia. Storm was certain that many of them did not like the idea of taking refuge in a cave that had been a fortress for ferryshaft and telshees and humans, but never for creasia. However, their king had gone in, and where he went, they would follow. They began to file up the ramp.

Beside him, Storm heard Halvery give a sigh of relief. "Even if we can't close it, a few cats could hold off hundreds in that small opening."

"I think we can close it," said Storm. "Didn't they close it when you laid siege to Kuwee?"

Halvery hesitated. Everyone had avoided mentioning the siege. "Yes," he said at last. "But they had telshees."

Creasia were filing past them—some with cubs in their mouths, exhausted three-year-olds, limping wounded, grim-faced fighters. One of the females stopped beside Halvery. She laid the cub she'd been carrying carefully down between them. It was one of the young ones—less than a year old. Storm saw that it was not moving.

Halvery nosed at the cub. He licked it, but it did not respond.

The female licked the top of Halvery's head. "She's been cold since the river, Halvery. But I thought you'd want—"

"Yes," he said quickly. "I'll— Yes."

He picked up the small body and stalked out of the cave.

"What will he do with it...with her?" asked Storm.

The female glanced at him. Storm did not think she would deign to answer, but then she said, "Hide the body. Take her to the Ghost Wood when this is over...if we live."

There'll be a lot of trips to the Ghost Wood, thought Storm, *if we live.*

Off to the south, Storm heard the unnerving wail of hunting creasia. He looked back at the line of cats. *Hurry.*

Storm trotted out into the moonlit night and then beneath the boughs of the shadowy trees. Bones loomed up out of the soil ahead of him, gleaming white where the moonlight touched them. Storm felt an uneasy prickling along his spine. *The last animals to take refuge here ended badly.*

He'd left Teek with Roup on the edge of the water. Storm had been hurrying ahead to open the cave, but now he felt he should get the cub out of harm's way. He did not want Teek involved in the fighting if the foremost of Treace's cats met the rearmost of Arcove's.

The rush of incoming creasia had slowed to a trickle by the time Storm found Roup. Only a few heads bobbed on the moonlit ripples. "Are they almost all here?" asked Storm.

"Almost," said Roup. He hesitated. "Almost all of those who are coming, anyway." He was watching the swimming cats and the far shore. Teek lay at his feet, asleep.

"How many?" asked Storm.

"Two hundred and thirty-four adults have swum over."

Storm winced. "You lost a lot of the wounded."

"Not as many as we would have lost if we'd stayed at the den," said Roup. He stopped to call to a struggling swimmer who was getting off course. "Here! Come ashore here!" Roup glanced back at Storm. "Do your telshee friends know where we are?"

Storm licked his lips. He thought about lying, but he didn't think that would be helpful. "No."

"Will they figure it out?"

"Maybe."

Roup considered. Storm expected a reprimand. Instead, Roup said, "If Keesha turns up, I want to talk to him. No matter how angry he is, I want to speak to him."

Storm said nothing.

"What is wrong with Arcove? He's more than tired; I can tell."

When Storm still said nothing, Roup growled. "Charder wouldn't tell me, either. Do you think everything will resolve in your favor if Arcove dies?"

"I'm not trying to get him killed," said Storm.

"You're not trying *not* to get him killed, either."

Teek stirred at Roup's feet. "I want to get Teek back to the cave," said Storm. He hesitated. "Where's Charder?" It occurred to him that he hadn't seen the older ferryshaft in a while.

Roup turned back towards the far shore. "He's one of the ones I'm waiting for."

"Oh."

They sat in uncomfortable silence for a few moments. A few wet and limping cats dragged themselves out of the water and started into the trees, following the scent trail left by their companions. Finally, Roup said, "Did you ask your curb friends about that trap Treace used during the fight? I've never seen a curb trap latch onto a creasia like that."

Storm shook himself. He *had* actually asked Eyal before he left. "Highland curbs don't make traps," he said slowly, "but they know how traps are constructed. They said…" He hesitated, remembering something Teek had mentioned last summer. "Curbs bite off long tendrils from the…the ghost plants. They put the cut ends in the blood of the species of animal they wish to hunt. Usually, they place them in the belly of a recently killed sheep or deer. The plants soak up the blood and…remember."

Teek was awake now, looking at him. "Give them the blood of their prey…" murmured Storm. "I think Teek saw them practicing on a cub. It's one of the reasons he followed me from the Great Cave. He grew up in Treace's clutter, and bad things happened to orphaned cubs there."

"The snakes," whispered Teek.

Roup looked down at him. "Snakes?"

"He has nightmares about a cub with snakes in its belly," Storm explained. "I suppose they were vines." He grimaced. "Would Treace's cats really do that to a cub?"

"Moro would," said Roup. "I found one of their early tests with a pit and a vine trap. I thought they were just catching deer to feed their overpopulating dens."

Storm stood up suddenly. In the moonlight, he saw a ferryshaft dash out of the trees on the far shore, run along the bank, and splash into the water. At the same time, he heard a creasia rally cry from the same direction, frighteningly close. There was still one more cat paddling towards them, but Storm could see no others.

Roup stood up, too, tail twitching. "Storm, get Teek up to the cave."

It was good advice, since Teek could not sprint as quickly as the adults. Teek kept glancing back all the way through the forest. "What about Roup?"

"He's coming," said Storm.

"So are Treace's cats," whispered Teek.

"Roup will get here first." Storm hoped that he was telling the truth as they stood in the cave, shivering, and waited. Creasia faces looked down from the opening at the top of the ramp. *They're expecting a fight,* thought Storm. He wondered again how to shut the entrance. He had a nagging fear that he would not like the answer.

Teek seemed to read his mind. "Will someone have to stay outside to close it?"

"I don't know," said Storm.

His hopes rose as a creasia came racing up the hill, but it was only the final swimmer. Storm heard another creasia rally cry, and it sounded so close that he thought the animal *must* be on the island. He was about to trot up the ramp to the entrance, when two shapes broke out of the trees at the bottom of the hill and darted up the slope. Charder nearly collapsed when he reached the cave. "I—am getting—too old—for this," he gasped.

"Oh, surely one is never too old to trap oneself on Kuwee Island," panted Roup with more sarcasm than Storm thought necessary.

"Charder," said Storm, "how do we close it?"

"By leaving someone outside to die, of course," said Charder. He looked around at their serious faces, then caught his breath and laughed. "Joking. Go on up the ramp."

Roup looked as confused as Storm felt, but he backed onto the ramp. Storm and Teek followed him, and the creasia who had been watching from the top retreated out of sight. "Go on," repeated Charder. He stepped onto the bottom of the ramp, then leaned over the side and nosed around beneath the edge. "Why do you think it's on a chain?" he muttered. Then his teeth closed around the silver thread, and he pulled the Shable up over the side of the ramp.

Nothing happened immediately, although, as Charder walked towards them, Storm felt a subtle shift in the stone underfoot. Behind Charder, in the moonlight, Storm saw the first of Treace's cats emerging from the trees. Storm backed up quickly towards the dark opening. Charder came on, and as he did, the ramp began to lift from the ground. Without either their own weight or the weight of the Shable to hold it open, the "jaw" was closing.

Clever. Storm thought, wistfully, that he would like to have known the humans. Then he turned and filed with the others into the dark fortress beneath Kuwee Island. The "jaw" clicked shut.

Sauny felt euphoric. The wood around her was in bloody chaos, and she had caused it! Ferryshaft had turned on creasia and trampled them or ripped them to pieces. Even the lishties—and they were all lishties as far as Sauny was concerned, even the ones who looked like creasia—even they had fled or been trampled. In the midst of the madness, Kelsy had shouted by her ear, "We need to lead them!"

Sauny had spat out a mouthful of cat fur. "Then do it!"

But that was not so easy. The moment the herd had eliminated the immediate threat, they began plunging into the lake, swimming for the mainland. It was a bright night, but as soon as they got beneath the trees, it became difficult to see what was happening. Animals were shouting to each other, running this way and that. Sauny wondered whether any of the lowland curbs would be unwise enough to make an appearance. If so, she didn't see them. She didn't see any highland curbs, either.

"I don't think they're going to listen to anyone!" Valla had to shout to be heard, even though she was right beside Sauny. Kelsy had been lost somewhere in the shadows up ahead.

"But we're running in the right direction," said Sauny. "Back towards the northern plain—towards home."

"Do you think they'll actually do what we want once they get there?" asked Valla.

"I don't know." For the first time that evening, Sauny felt uncertain. "I guess we'll find out when they stop."

20

The Worst

Storm woke in a shaft of sunlight. Some sleepy part of his brain informed him that this was odd. Near his ear, a small voice said, "Storm! Storm, wake up and look..."

Storm opened his eyes. He was lying in a little cave with no ceiling, inside the bigger cave. In the confused dimness of last night, he'd sensed dozens, perhaps hundreds, of these. *It's like a beehive,* he'd thought.

In the morning light, that notion was reinforced. However, he could see better now, because sunlight fell in bright streams from tiny openings in the ceiling of the vast cavern. Everywhere, crumbling walls formed corridors that ran much straighter than the slot canyons to which Storm was accustomed. They formed little rooms, some with walls only as tall as a cub, and others with walls that even Arcove could not have looked over. A few had roofs, although many did not. Towards the back of the cave, these structures became more complex and rose like an anthill of rooms piled on top of each other, some with walls falling down, but most intact.

Storm had settled in a little room partway up the mound of structures, and he had a good view from the entrance. It was clear to Storm that these structures had been created by living creatures in an organized effort. He could not imagine how.

All of this would have been astonishing enough, but Teek was staring at something else—paintings like the one of the telshee at the entrance. Nearly every wall was covered in lines and images. Some seemed to be senseless. Others were clearly animals, trees, rivers, and plants.

Teek was walking around the little room in which they'd slept, staring. "Storm, look! That's an oory. And that...that's a rabbit. Storm, is that a ghost plant? Storm, look!"

"I see, I see." Storm stretched luxuriously. The air in the cave was decidedly warmer than the outside air. He felt both comfortable and safe for the first time in days. Well, almost comfortable. He could tell that hunger was waiting to pounce on him the moment he began to move around.

"What are they?" asked Teek. "Who made them?"

"The telshees call them paintings," said Storm. "I think the humans made them. Humans disappeared from Lidian hundreds...maybe thousands of years ago."

"I wish they were still here," said Teek without taking his eyes off the paintings.

Storm had had more time to think about that last night. *An animal so clever could also be very cruel.* He wondered if humans had ruled the island in their day, whether they had culled other species, whether they had gone to war.

Teek finally tore his gaze from the wall. He looked at Storm almost guiltily. "I'm hungry," he whispered. "But I know there's nothing to eat."

Storm winced. He remembered Keesha's story of watching Coden's foal and other friends die of hunger and thirst in these caves. He remembered the pain in Keesha's voice and in his humming. *I hope I don't learn how he felt.*

Storm hopped up onto the crumbling wall as though it had been a sheep trail. From here, he had a view of almost the entire cave. He could see into some of the little rooms farther down the slope where cats were resting. He saw mothers nursing cubs, clutters sleeping in heaps, cats grooming themselves and each other. *Almost like a herd,* he thought. *They're social animals...like ferryshaft. In so many ways, they're like ferryshaft.* He did not see Arcove or Roup.

As Storm's gaze shifted upward, he was surprised to catch a brighter rectangle of light. "The door is open!"

"What?" Teek clambered up beside him.

Storm squinted. He saw a few cats coming and going near the entrance, but nobody looked alarmed. "Let's go down and find out what's happening."

Arcove was dizzy by the time he woke that morning. The feeling was familiar now—vertigo and waves of nausea. Nevertheless, he got up and organized a party of the strongest fighters to go out and drive their enemies from the island. It was a critical move, as the cave was only a death trap without control of the rest of Kuwee.

As Arcove had expected, Treace did not waste much effort in trying to hold the surface of the island. His cats had doubtless slept uneasily in the open last night, expecting an attack from the cave at any moment. It was easier and safer for Treace's cats to lay siege from the bank, where they could see enemies swimming over long before they arrived. Arcove's creasia would eat up most of the food on the island within a few days, so it would be an easy waiting game.

Nevertheless, Treace's creasia put up a token struggle before they were driven off—a test, no doubt, to see how much of their opponent's strength remained. Arcove killed two in spite of his spinning head. He knew he was behaving recklessly. *There is one more thing to do…although dying in battle might be preferable.*

However, when the dust settled, he was hardly more than scratched. *Time enough for dying later.*

On his way back to the cave, Arcove ran into Storm, poking cautiously around the entrance. "They're off the island," he said. "Hunt if you like. Halvery is setting up a perimeter patrol."

Storm squinted at him. Arcove wondered whether he was swaying. He felt like the floor was heaving up and down. *Don't you dare ask.* Arcove turned quickly and made his way into the ruins. He went up, layer after layer, until he found a room near the very top. Diffuse light streamed in through chinks in the porous stone above. He curled up in the farthest corner and slipped into uneasy dreams.

Valla woke on the plain north of the Igby. The sun had come out and melted the thin layer of snow. The sky was bright, and she felt like singing. Sauny was plucking at the grass nearby. Not far away, Kelsy, Remy, Itsa, and the foal, Teedo, were curled over and around each other, warm in spite of the frost. The ferryshaft rested or grazed. For the first time in sixteen years, they were not doing what cats had told them to do. *And it feels good,* thought Valla.

But… "Sauny?"

"Hmm?"

"Are we still going to find Storm…and Arcove's creasia?"

"Of course."

Valla sat up and joined her friend in the search for food. "If they reached Kuwee—" she began.

"No if," said Sauny.

"Alright, *when* they reached Kuwee, Treace will have followed them."

"I know," said Sauny. "He'll lay siege on the bank. They'll need us to break it."

Valla was relieved to hear that Sauny had thought this through. "It would be easier if we could coordinate an attack with the creasia on the island."

"I think they'll see us," said Sauny. "The entire ferryshaft herd attacking more than half of Leeshwood? That'll be hard to miss. They'll come out and join in."

It seemed reasonable.

"How many ferryshaft do you think we've lost in the last few days?" asked Valla.

Sauny stopped eating. She sighed. "I don't know. I was thinking I should go around and take a count."

"Better start talking to them, too," said Valla. "I don't think this is going to be easy."

"Leave the talking to me," said Sauny.

At that moment, Valla heard snarling from the direction of the river. She peered out towards the edge of the herd and saw curbs—big curbs—trying to avoid several ferryshaft. "Get out of here!" she heard one of the ferryshaft shout. "We're done running from you! Go!"

"Eyal!" called Valla. She and Sauny ran towards the curbs.

"It's alright," Sauny told the ferryshaft. "They're highland curbs; they helped us. It's alright."

When they reached the curbs, Valla searched for Eyal, but did not see him. The foremost was Eyal's beta, a curb named Cohal. He looked considerably battered—one ear ripped so badly that there was barely anything left, bite wounds over his chest and shoulders. The rest of the pack looked no better. Sauny sniffed noses with him. "Thank you for what you did yesterday," she said. "Our herd is free because of you."

The curb inclined his head. "We owed a debt," he said. "It is paid."

Valla felt a chill. "Where is Eyal?"

Cohal's soulful, brown eyes met hers. "He died last night in the fighting. He said to tell Storm Ela-curb that this year, borrowed from death, was the best of his years."

Oh, Eyal. Valla glanced at Sauny, who'd gone very still.

At last, Sauny said, "Will you howl for him?"

"Of course," said Cohal.

"Would you...would you wait for Storm?" asked Sauny. "I think he would like to howl with you."

This seemed to please the curbs. "We will wait for Storm," they agreed.

"We came to tell you something else," said Cohal. "The dead things—the lishties—are coming. The new four-legged ones are not so fast, but they are coming."

Sauny recoiled. "Those dead cats?"

"Those and others," said Cohal. "Every animal that fell in the fighting. This is strange to us. Lishty bites normally kill any animal other than a telshee. But the bites of these creasia lishties seem to infect four-legged animals, even those who are freshly dead."

"Now we *really* need to find out how many we lost," muttered Valla.

Arcove woke, disoriented, near noon. Someone was licking his ears and shoulders. The pleasure of being groomed created a strange counter-point to the pain in his belly and joints. Finally, he opened his eyes, "Roup?" He tried to lift his head. It felt much heavier than he remembered.

Roup came around in front of him. Arcove saw that he'd brought a dead rabbit. "Have you eaten since this started?" Roup asked. "Truly?"

"Yes." *I threw up afterward, but I did eat.*

"You look gaunt."

I feel gaunt. "The cubs will weaken the quickest without food," said Arcove. "I can wait."

"You mean, 'Don't waste food on me, because I'm dying,'" said Roup.

Arcove said nothing.

"What *happened?*" whispered Roup. Frustration and despair played tug-of-war with his voice. "Why won't you tell me?"

"I think that curb trap may have been poisoned," offered Arcove.

Roup snorted. "You're a terrible liar."

"I don't have much practice," Arcove admitted.

Roup waited a moment, but Arcove said nothing. Finally, Roup spoke, his voice thick. "So that's it, then? Everything we've been through, and now you've decided you're going to die, and you won't even tell me why?"

I can't, thought Arcove, *and that's the worst part. Would it help if I said so? Probably not.*

21

A Shadow on the Past

Arcove drifted in and out of delirium. He thought that Teek came to see him. The cub wasn't really looking for Arcove. He was looking at the ancient human paintings, following their lines around the ruins. The wall of the room where Arcove was sleeping contained a large image. Arcove hadn't paid any attention to it. Paintings were not creasia things.

However, as the cub walked back and forth in front of it, Arcove did look. The image included telshees and ferryshaft with odd, spindly beasts on their backs. He thought he saw curbs at their feet and ely-ary overhead.

"Where are *we?*" asked Teek. He sounded distressed. "I can't find us. I can't find us!"

Arcove thought that he might be dreaming. However, when the cub did not disappear, he scanned the wall and finally found the outline of trees and bushes in a bottom corner. A pair of eyes glared out from the forest. He saw the suggestion of claws and teeth. "There," he muttered.

Teek stared. "Is that supposed to be us?" He scanned the image again. "Why are we all alone?"

"Figure that out," muttered Arcove, "and you'll understand everything you need to know about ferryshaft and creasia."

He shut his eyes again, but he thought he heard scratching—like a stone over stone. *Scratch, scratch, scratch…*

When Arcove opened his eyes again, Teek was gone. He told himself that the despair he felt was an effect of the peculiar torture that Keesha had inflicted on him. *I had a plan. It was a good plan. It will work. Stick to it.*

Keesha came in the afternoon. When Arcove tried to stand, he staggered gracelessly sideways and fell over. *I can't feel my feet.* His body felt three times heavier than normal.

Keesha regarded him coldly from the entrance to the room. Arcove caught sight of Storm, looking anxiously in behind him. "Well," growled Keesha. "I hope you're pleased with yourself."

Not yet. "I want to talk to you alone," said Arcove.

"Are you really so afraid that anyone will hear you beg?" asked Keesha. "I certainly listened to enough begging in these caves, although mostly, it was for water. You have no right to take refuge here."

"Alone," repeated Arcove.

Storm's head disappeared from the entrance. Arcove hoped no one else was outside. Keesha glided into the room, most of his body trailing out the door. Arcove tried to get away from him and then gave up. Keesha didn't try to touch him, though. His great head hung over Arcove like a shark hovering over a smaller fish. "Well…?"

Arcove swallowed. "Put Roup in charge of Leeshwood," he said, his voice barely above a whisper. "You won't have to coerce him to stop the raids or to work with the ferryshaft. He'll want to. He's always wanted to. He'll be good at it."

Keesha looked unimpressed. "You are really bad at begging."

Arcove plunged on. "He will give you the kind of peace you want, but you can't tell him what happened to me. He won't work with you if you do. Let him think you tried to save me and failed. Or make up a better story. Anything. Just don't tell him."

Keesha looked incredulous. "Please tell me you're not about to ask me to help you win this war."

"Not me," said Arcove. "Roup...and Storm...and cats who will listen to you when this is over because they'll be in your debt. But you can't tell them about—"

"I heard you the first time," snapped Keesha.

Arcove sank back down. The intense purpose of delivering his message began to dissipate. "When future generations are born, you can tell them I was responsible for the war," he whispered. "Blame me for the raids, make Coden their hero. Let them hate me or forget me. Let me be a shadow on their past." *Every group needs a monster to hate,* he thought. *Claws in the forest. Teeth in the dark.* "You and Storm and Charder will have your peace and your revenge, and Roup and Nadine and the rest will survive."

Arcove waited for Keesha to say something, but for once, he didn't. Arcove felt too heavy to move. "And you're right," he said at last. His voice sounded small in his own ears. "I'm not very good at begging."

Keesha was silent and still for so long that Arcove finally decided to try raising his head. Keesha's face didn't tell him much. Arcove had never been good at distinguishing telshee expressions. Keesha was not snarling, and that was all he knew for certain. At last, Keesha said, "Do you want me to sing to you?"

"No," said Arcove. "If you come in here, and I'm alive and then you leave and I'm dead? No, that will never work. Maybe you can tell their cub's cubs about your song, but right now—"

"I don't mean to sing the *end* of the song," interrupted Keesha.

Arcove finally lost his temper. "No, I don't want you to keep taking me apart and putting me back together until you grow bored! No."

"You'll die," said Keesha. "Soon."

"Good."

"It will hurt."

"So does your singing."

Keesha was silent again. "Very well," he said at last and Arcove thought he heard grudging respect in that sonorous voice. *Although that's probably just the delirium.*

Roup felt as though he could have ripped off Storm's head without a shred of remorse. "I told you I wanted to speak to him!" he snarled.

"You'll get to," said Storm desperately. "Calm down."

"Arcove is trapped up there with his worst enemy!" thundered Roup. "Do not tell me to calm down!"

"Keesha can help him," said Storm.

"Oh, I'm sure he can," said Roup, "but I doubt that he will. I doubt that very much."

They were standing in a large room a level down from the top. This one had a ceiling. Shaw was blocking the only entrance to the steep path that lead to the final level.

Roup had been on the far side of the island when he'd heard the news that telshees had come ashore. By the time he'd reached the cave, they'd already entered. The creasia on watch were pacing back and forth in a nervous quandary. No one really wanted to tackle Shaw and Syra-lay. Storm kept insisting that they were not here to cause trouble.

For once, Roup wished Halvery had been present with his quick temper and strike-first-ask-questions-later mentality. But, Halvery had been sleeping—a reasonable activity, since he'd been fighting all morning. Sharmel had hardly moved since dragging himself into the cave the night before.

They'd both roused themselves, though, when they'd heard about the telshees, and now all three officers were growling and pacing in front of Shaw's immovable glare. Even Charder had come up the steep, winding corridors to see what all the fuss was about. He sat in the back of the cave and watched.

After what seemed an eternity, Keesha came gliding back down the passage. Roup took advantage of Shaw's momentary distraction to wriggle past her. He met Keesha head on. "You and I need to talk," he snarled.

"Oh, we'll be doing plenty of that, I expect."

Roup felt ill as he struggled around the telshee, cursing and tripping on his coils. *No blood?* Keesha's coat looked as white as new-fallen snow. Roup raced up the passage to the room and confirmed that it was not smeared with the gore and entrails of his friend. In fact, Arcove didn't look as though he'd moved from the last time Roup had visited. Roup stayed just long enough to see him take a breath and then whipped around and charged back down the passage.

Halvery was standing at the bottom, looking up. "He's fine," said Roup quickly. Keesha was talking to Shaw and Storm. As he turned to go, Roup blocked his path.

"Oh, no," he said. "We are going to spend some time here."

Keesha looked weary. "And what are we going to do during this time?"

"I am going to talk. You are going to listen."

Keesha rolled his eyes at the ceiling. "All the wrong people want to beg me for things today."

"I'm not going to beg you for anything," said Roup. "I'm going to tell you a story. It's not one I tell very often, so make yourself comfortable. It may take a while."

"As I said, we will have plenty of time for—"

"Do you want to know why you lost the war, Syra-lay? Truly? I promise you haven't heard this."

Keesha froze, watching him. *Well, I finally have your attention.*

"Do you want to know how the Shable ended up in Groth?" asked Roup. "I can tell you that, too."

Now, he definitely had the full weight of those fathomless blue eyes. Keesha moved away from the exit to the room. "I'm listening…"

Moro woke among the broken and trampled ghost plants. The sun seemed blinding as he dragged himself out from under the wreckage of his work. *No, no, no…*

The plants that he'd cultivated with so much effort had been destroyed. Their juices squished under his feet as he staggered over and through the bent and shredded bowls and the woody bases that had been pounded into pulp. Even the fluorescence that had given him such joy when it had first begun to glow in the stems had darkened into lifelessness.

Not too late.

Moro blinked hard. He looked around for the voice, but nothing seemed to be moving in the clearing. When had the sun grown so bright? It was difficult to see properly.

Better under the trees. Better at night.

"What?" croaked Moro. He shook his head. He felt like a swarm of bees had taken up residence there. He realized that he was limping, although he felt no pain. Moro looked down and was shocked to see that something had apparently gnawed on his left foreleg. He could see white bone peeking through. He could also see places were fur had been ripped away, bruises where ferryshaft had trampled him. He could see, but he felt nothing.

I'm in that space after injury when the body shuts down, he thought. *I need to hide and rest.*

No. And now he distinctly heard the response as something separate from himself. *We must find new hosts. We must hurry.*

"Lishties," said Moro aloud.

You are fortunate, said the thing in his head. *We welcome you.*

Moro flinched. He could feel the thing rifling through his memories. At the same time, he had a sense of darkness and endless seas, of waiting, of longing, of hunger for sight and touch and sound. *These are its memories,* he realized.

The sensation did not please him. To his horror, he had a sudden, intense memory of a cub he had killed a few months ago... only this time, he was in the cub's head, and its terror nearly overwhelmed him. Moro shrieked. He toppled over and thrashed on the ground for a moment.

Stop! shouted the lishty. *You are harming this body! Stop!*

"You said," panted Moro, "that we would live forever."

You will, said the voice in his head with terrible sincerity. *We treasure all our memories. But yours are strange to us. We must study them.*

Moro was not reassured. "Am *I* my memories?" he asked aloud.

To his further distress, he found that he was walking towards the lake without meaning to. "No," he said, "stop. What are you doing? Stop!"

We must find the others, said the voice in his head. *We must find new hosts.*

Something was breaking through Moro's gums. He could feel the points with his tongue, and this *did* hurt. "I need to rest," he insisted. "I need to heal. I don't want you in my head. We haven't done enough tests yet. We don't know if this is safe."

We are satisfied with the tests, said the lishty. *We have crossed into four-legs. We are pleased with you.*

Moro wanted to scream, but he seemed to have lost the use of his voice. He was swimming. Once he reached the far shore, he staggered up the bank without shaking the water from his coat. He was dimly aware of deep, visceral pain, as though his insides were undergoing some wrenching change.

Moro whimpered. His vision was flashing on and off. He walked. The wound on his leg opened wider, showing more bone, but he kept walking.

Treace, he thought. *Need to tell Treace this was a bad idea.*

The fangs pushing through his gums sent saliva and blood trickling down his chin. He did not lick it away. He could not.

Moro died. And he kept walking.

22

Tell It All

"I was raised by ferryshaft," said Roup, "but you know that." Keesha knew, but Roup was certain that at least one person in the room didn't. Out of the corner of his eye, he saw Halvery stiffen. *Well, now you have a name for the thing about me that you've always hated.*

Sharmel didn't react. Roup had always suspected that Sharmel knew or guessed his origins. Sharmel had been an adult when the rest of the officers were all cubs, and he might have heard rumors that Halvery would have missed. He'd been paying more attention than Halvery, too, in those early days when Roup had still made the occasional slip in accent or behavior.

But here's the part that even you probably don't know, Sharmel. "Pathar brought me back to the herd after a raid because he wanted to learn about creasia," continued Roup. "My eyes weren't even open. Coden's mother agreed to foster me, so I grew up right beside him."

Keesha looked impatient. "I knew all this long ago. It does not make me well-disposed towards you. You got your 'brother' killed while he protected you. Did you know that? He made me promise not to kill you."

Roup winced. *Of course. Of course he did.* "I am telling a story," said Roup. "Shut up and listen."

Keesha huffed. From behind him, Roup heard Shaw snicker. It made him feel a little better. "I had a few friends among the ferryshaft," said Roup, "or at least I thought they were my friends. I realized later that most of the ones who seemed kind were simply curious or anxious to test me. Hardly a day passed when a ferryshaft did not threaten to kill me, so I valued those who seemed friendly. They encouraged me to eat things that were not food to see whether I would survive, abandoned me in lonely places to test my tracking skills, dropped me into a tide pool once and let me tread water until I started to drown, and subjected me to a daily series of tortures which, at the time, seemed normal."

Charder stirred from where he was sitting against the wall. "For what it's worth, I'm sorry about that. I wasn't in favor of it, even back then."

"It was your herd," said Roup.

"I know," said Charder. He didn't seem to know what else to say and looked at the ground.

Roup felt a twinge of guilt. *Arcove has already made you sorry enough.* "Coden was the only one who truly had no agenda with me. He defended me when others attacked me and kept me company in my loneliness and during those times when I was injured or sick. We both knew the adults would kill me before I grew big enough to be a serious threat.

"When I was three years old, Coden helped me run away. He took me to the edge of the forest and left me there. We promised to meet again in a year. I could tell that he did not think I would survive. He'd heard all kinds of terrible things about creasia, but I knew almost nothing about my own kind.

"Arcove found me by a stream. It was the middle of the day, but I was on a ferryshaft schedule. Arcove didn't even try to talk to me. He knocked me down. We fought. He won.

"Afterward, I asked whether he had a clique. I meant a clutter, but I didn't know the word. He said, 'I do now.' Then he asked why I sounded like a ferryshaft. I told him. I figured that if he wanted to kill me, he would have done it during the fight. I knew it might be dangerous to tell, but I didn't understand until later *how* dangerous.

"Arcove didn't comment except to tell me not to talk to anyone else. We went off and found a hiding place to sleep. He curled up around me like I was his only friend in the world. I guess I was."

Roup hesitated. No one said a word. Even Keesha was just listening. "It took me several days to piece together what had happened the night before. Arcove's mother was an attractive female, which doesn't always work out well for females. Not now, and certainly not then. Another male challenged Arcove's father over her. They fought, and Arcove's father was killed. The victor proceeded to kill all of his opponent's cubs."

Storm raised his head. "He…did what?"

Halvery spoke for the first time. "That happened a lot back then."

"Yes," said Roup. "It makes the female come into season faster. Also, it was considered a mark of weakness in those days to raise the cubs of another male. So he killed Arcove's brother and sister, but Arcove turned and fought."

Halvery smiled. Early in their acquaintance, he'd tried to get Roup to talk about Arcove's first fights, and Roup had been standoffish, afraid that he would reveal too much of his own past. Roup's apparent unfriendliness had set the tone for their relationship. *Maybe I should have just told him.*

"All of Leeshwood knows this story," said Roup, "but it's grown a little in the telling. This part is true: Arcove was only two years old, and he killed a fifteen-year-old adult. Arcove was a big cub, almost as large as some three-year-olds, but he was still just a cub. I've heard cats say that Arcove only won his fights because he's exceptionally large. That's not true. He fought and killed cats many times his size at an age when most cubs are still at their mother's teat."

615

Halvery was enjoying the story. "The one he killed was an officer, right?"

Roup shifted. "The adult he killed was an officer of the king, yes, and that's where the trouble started. Cats say that Arcove won his seat on the council when he was only two, but they forget that he didn't claim that seat until he was four. At the time, it almost got him killed.

"If the dead cat had been anyone else, the den would have praised their cub's skill and bravery. But many of the officers were bullies, and they were all friends. The den mother feared retaliation, so she drove Arcove away. It was as good as a death sentence for a two-year-old cub.

"That's why Arcove was awake in the middle of the day when I wandered into Leeshwood. He'd never been alone in his life. Now his siblings and his father were dead, his mother had abandoned him, he'd been driven from his den, and he thought high-ranking adults might try to kill him."

Roup took a deep breath. "Then he found me, and I was nothing but a liability. Arcove wouldn't let me talk to anyone else for months. He coached me until I could sound like a creasia. We hunted together—poached game because, with no territory, we didn't have a choice. We lived alone for almost two years. No one wanted to call such a young cub their alpha, and Arcove wouldn't bend his neck to anyone.

"Arcove started forming a clutter a little before he turned four, mostly from rogues. All of them were older than we were. Arcove fought and beat them one by one, and they followed him. He didn't trust them, though. He couldn't afford to."

"But he trusted you," said Storm thoughtfully, "because he knew your secret."

"He knew my secret," agreed Roup, "and eventually I knew all of his. We used to sleep in turns because so many cats wanted us dead. When he turned four, Arcove went to a council meeting and announced that he was claiming his place, having killed Cranow—the one who'd killed his father and siblings. The officers

616

were surprised and amused. Arcove ended up fighting one of them before they'd take him seriously. After that, it was three frustrating years on the council. He knew they were doing everything wrong, that they would never win the war. They didn't even seem to think it could be won…or that it was a war.

"There were only about a hundred adult males of fighting age in Leeshwood back then, and I swear to you that Arcove fought and beat every one of them at some point. Cats call him lucky, and he often was, but he fought for every scrap of their loyalty. When he turned seven, he challenged Ketch, the current king, and fought him to the death in the Great Clearing with everyone watching.

"Arcove's first act as king was to threaten death to anyone who killed a cub. He didn't think he could stop them from killing each other over mates, but he told them that if they killed a cub, he would personally hunt them down. He said we needed every single cub, and he was right. He had to enforce that rule a few times before they understood that he meant it. Since that time, it's become common for a male to raise his rival's cubs if he wins a mate in battle. Mortality in fights over females has also decreased. When Arcove escalated the war with the ferryshaft five years later, we had more young creasia than anyone had ever seen."

Roup stopped talking abruptly. Arcove was leaning in the mouth of the passage to the upper level. He looked like he'd dragged himself there, mostly with the aid of the wall. Everyone was staring at him, but he was looking only at Roup. In the perfect silence, he said, "What are you talking about?"

"My cub-hood," said Roup.

"It sounded like mine."

"Hard to talk about one and not the other."

"I wish you wouldn't."

"If you will not explain yourself," said Roup, "then I will."

"There's nothing to explain."

"I disagree."

Arcove looked like he'd swallowed something unpleasant. He pushed himself off the wall and walked with only a slight weave across the floor to Roup, where he collapsed, as though he'd just swum the Igby in flood. "Don't make excuses for me," he said in a low voice. "Please."

Roup looked down at him. "Since the day we met, you've stood between me and the whole world, Arcove. My turn."

Arcove dropped his head on his paws with a defeated expression.

Trust me, thought Roup. *I am not telling your secrets to hurt you.*

"It may sound strange," continued Roup, "but none of this stopped Coden and I from meeting once or twice a year—usually at Turis Rock. Sometimes we just spent a day talking and hunting, but occasionally we made long excursions. Arcove usually came with us. One summer, we went all the way to the Southern Mountains. Coden and Arcove would both say later that they never got along, but it wasn't true. They had some friendly rivalry, but mostly they got along fine."

Keesha drew a long breath. "That didn't stop you from betraying Coden when it was time to choose sides."

Roup considered. "I suppose I did not think that *Coden* would choose sides. He'd left Charder's herd by then. He and his mate were rogues.

"When we started to engage the ferryshaft herds in earnest, I told Arcove everything I could think of. Their social and migratory patterns, their hiding places, the way they lived, the personalities of their leaders. These days, the ferryshaft have no secrets, but back then, there were many things about them that creasia didn't know or understand.

"But Coden was...not like anyone else." Roup struggled. He didn't know how to say the next part. "Maybe there was something wrong with him. Or maybe it was something right. He wanted to roam from the Great Mountain to the seas beyond the Southern Mountains. He wanted to learn to speak to the ely-ary and swim to distant shores with telshees. He wanted to unravel the secrets of the humans and drink the poison waters of Groth and dream the future. To me, most of the other ferryshaft seemed like bullies and cowards, but Coden…"

Roup shook his head. "I saw Coden kill a shark once. It was trapped in a tide pool—probably chasing a seal—and Coden just waded in and went after it. I kept shouting at him to get out of the water, but he just laughed the whole time."

"Did he kill it?" asked Halvery in wonder.

"Yes!" exclaimed Roup. "And he didn't do it to show off. I'm sure he would have done it even if nobody had been around—just to prove to himself that he could. When he was in those moods, it was like nothing could touch him. He thought he could do anything, and often he did. I suppose that's why the herds chose him as their war-time king, but I never saw it coming. I can't tell you how sick I felt when I found out. I suppose Coden was feeling invincible that day."

Arcove spoke at last, his voice a raspy rumble near Roup's feet. "He paid for those highs on the other side."

"Yes," Roup admitted. "When he was down…it was like the whole world turned to chalk and ash."

Arcove's tail lashed. "You couldn't reason with him very well on either end."

Roup wanted to argue, to defend a dead friend. *No,* he thought, *if you're going to tell it, tell it straight. Tell it all.* "You're right, but he was usually somewhere in the middle."

"Usually, he was on the way to one end or the other," muttered Arcove. He raised his head and looked at Roup with a fierce, desperate focus. "Do you want me to say he was charming? Of course he was. Coden could convince you the sky was green as long as he was talking…when he was up." Arcove's eyes flicked to Storm. "He was also the sort of person who would decide, out of nowhere, that he must have a dip in the sea this very instant. Somehow, it would all turn into a grand adventure."

Roup smiled.

"So, yes," continued Arcove, "Coden was charming and likeable." He looked at Keesha, and his voice hardened. "He was also completely intractable when it came to everything I cared about. Coden would have had us agree to stop fighting, simply on the guarantee of his goodwill. Even if he had been able to enforce his decisions on all the herds—which I doubt—anyone who knew him knew that he would not lead the ferryshaft for the rest of his life. Coden would have won their war for them, secured that victory, then gotten bored and gone off to ghosts-know-where with you! But not before he put the creasia at an immense disadvantage."

Don't fight, thought Roup. *Just tell it.* "This is my story," he began, but Arcove interrupted, his eyes locked on Keesha.

"Coden would *not* agree to any terms that limited ferryshaft breeding or numbers, nor would he agree to anything that limited their range. If I had capitulated to his terms, I would have been right back where I started in ten years or less—outnumbered and surrounded." Arcove's voice rose in a snarl. "I was *not* going to be outnumbered and surrounded again. Ever. Also, I doubted what worked for me the first time would work again. The ferryshaft would have been more wary and certainly under a less friendly leader, as Coden would have gone off to chase butterflies by then!

"So I did what I do best: I fought. And after I killed a few of his friends, Coden wasn't interested in talking anymore. I would have offered him the same terms right up until the end, but he wouldn't listen."

Arcove stopped talking. The silence in the cave felt oppressive. "Are you finished?" asked Roup.

Arcove sank back down and put his head on his paws. "I don't know. You tell me."

Keesha spoke. His voice had an uncertainty that Roup had never heard there before. "When you said…that I got Coden killed…"

"Once you entered the war, Coden didn't think he could lose," whispered Arcove. "On Kuwee…he would have surrendered. I know he would have. He wasn't *that* crazy. If you had stayed out of it, we could have come to some agreement. But he wouldn't budge. He wouldn't compromise, because he thought—"

"I heard you," said Keesha. "Why didn't I hear any of this at the time?"

"That's what I wanted to tell you," said Roup. "You thought you came to the parlay where we tried to come to terms on Kuwee. But you didn't. The real parlay happened the night before. Coden met with Arcove and me. We hadn't spoken in two years, but we'd never been anything but friendly face-to-face. Coden and I had never spoken about the war or the antagonism between the ferryshaft and the creasia. I know that seems strange, but we just didn't talk about it. When we were together, we talked of other things. I was certain that, if we just sat down and addressed the issues, we could sort everything out. Arcove didn't think so, but he was willing to let me try.

"So we talked, and I learned something that night. I learned that Coden didn't see other creasia in the same way that he saw me. In his mind, I was an honorary ferryshaft. He wasn't willing to extend to other creasia the same trust or kindness that he extended to me. Arcove was right. Coden would not compromise, and his terms would have put us at the mercy of ferryshaft and telshees for the foreseeable future. He believed that, with Syra-lay on his side, he did not need to make compromises.

"For the first time in our lives, Coden and I quarreled. We almost fought. Arcove didn't say a word, just got between us when we almost leapt at each other. I left that meeting knowing that we had to win or die. There would be no mercy and no compromises. I told myself that my friend had changed, that the other ferryshaft had poisoned his mind. I reminded myself of every terrible thing they had done to me as a cub, and I did not want my cubs to grow up with creatures like that hunting them. When we met to parlay the next day, it was merely a formality. Coden and Arcove snarled threats at each other, and I kept my mouth shut."

Roup hesitated. *Tell it straight. Tell it all.* "Coden and I used to meet sometimes at the first full moon of fall. I didn't go to the meeting. I didn't think he would. The ferryshaft were all-but trapped in caves on the southern plains, fighting for their lives. A few days later, I did go to the meeting place…and his scent was there." Roup swallowed. "I will wonder until the day I die what he wanted to say to me…whether it would have changed things. We never spoke again, though."

Roup looked at Keesha. "If you need to blame someone for what happened on Kuwee, for the death of your friend, for the way the war turned out, blame me." Roup tried to put all of the pain and frustration he felt into his voice. "Coden was our friend, too, Keesha."

Roup stopped talking, and the room was utterly silent. Somewhere below them, in the maze of little rooms, Roup heard cubs calling to each other in play. Stones rattled softly as some part of the ruin settled.

Finally, Keesha said, "The Shable…"

Roup glanced down at Arcove. "No one knows this part. No one."

"I can guess," said Arcove quietly.

Then you haven't held it against me. "After I watched two friends fight to the death in the place where we used to meet and play," said Roup, "I found the Shable in an old food cache behind a waterfall. It was another place where Coden and I had sometimes met. He'd left it there for me."

Keesha looked puzzled. "Why?"

Roup licked his lips. "Perhaps he just considered me the least dangerous option, since he couldn't get it to either the telshees or the ferryshaft. However, he could have thrown it into a river. He could have taken it to Turis and tossed it into the sea. He didn't.

"I think it was his way of…of saying that he still trusted me… of making peace…of saying good-bye. But it felt like the last devastating evidence of my failure—proof that he would have listened if I had just found the right words."

Roup paused, but no one spoke. "I wanted a piece of him to take to the Ghost Wood," he continued. "I searched the beach for days, looking for any scrap of bone or fur, but there was nothing. Finally…I took the Shable."

"Ahhh," murmured Keesha. "Of course."

"It was the closest thing to a piece of him that I had," said Roup. "I took it to the Ghost Wood and flung it as far as I could. I screamed his name into the wind, and then…I went home. I lived as peacefully as I knew how. I did not go on raids or kill ferryshaft, but I understand why Arcove thinks he has to. It is hard for us to trust ferryshaft, and their populations outstrip ours very rapidly."

Charder spoke. His voice sounded tired. "Our females do not quicken if they do not get enough to eat in the fall. That is how our populations are normally limited, but I cannot produce this effect artificially. Bitterleaf just makes us sick. Also, the herd I inherited was not *my* herd. Most of my herd was dead. Arcove put me in charge of the shattered remnants of a dozen herds. They did not choose me. They resented me a great deal at first. I tried, with the sullen assistance of the elders, to regulate our own numbers for two years, but it didn't work. Attempts to enforce breeding rights were tearing the herd apart. We settled on the creasia cull after the elders would not agree to anything else."

Arcove opened his eyes. He tried to say something, but it came out slurred. Roup noticed that a quivering had started in his hindquarters. "It's not you, Charder," Arcove managed. "It's not…can't…"

"What he's trying to say," said Roup to Charder, "is that he's done his best not to make a friend of you, because he always thought he would have to kill you. But somehow, he went and made a friend of you anyway. He was hoping you wouldn't notice."

Arcove glared at him. "That…is not…what I—"

"No, but it's what you meant." Roup's chest felt tight; the blood pounded in his ears. "Arcove?"

Arcove looked like he was having trouble breathing. The quivering had increased to a full-body shudder. Roup looked at Keesha. He wanted to scream. "What's wrong with him? I know it has something to do with you!"

Arcove's back legs kicked in a convulsive, involuntary manner, and he flopped onto his side, breathing in agonized gasps. His eyes were dilated, fixed and staring. Roup crouched beside him, looking back and forth frantically. He couldn't see any wound, nothing to explain Arcove's obvious distress. He felt, more than saw, Keesha's presence, hovering over and behind him.

Roup laid his head down against Arcove's, desperate to offer comfort. Arcove gasped against his ear. "You...were...right," he managed. "This is...better. Better end to the story. Sorry for... Sorry." He let out a long breath and did not take another.

23

Something New

"Listen to us, ferryshaft!" shouted Sauny. "We have something to say to you!"

The herd—what was left of it—had gathered around Sauny, Kelsy, and Valla. Valla had counted over eight hundred animals, approximately six hundred of which were adults or older foals. She did not know how many they'd started with, but nearly everyone she spoke to reported a friend or family member missing. *Did we lose a hundred? Two hundred? More?*

"This is a great day for the herd," Kelsy began. "We are free, ferryshaft! For the first time in *my* life, we are free."

A cheer went up, and several of the younger ferryshaft howled. However, someone called a question immediately, "Where is Storm? He should be here! Where is Vearil? Where is the Doom of Cats?"

"Storm is on Kuwee Island," said Sauny, raising her voice to carry over the babble, "with Arcove's creasia."

Shocked silence followed.

Kelsy spoke quickly. "Friends, I have a confession to make. As some of you know, I have attended creasia conferences this past season. I have listened to Arcove's plans, and I have made compromises. I made compromises to prevent war, to prevent what happened when we attacked the creasia by the lake last year. I lost a beloved mate that day, and I did not ever want to do that again. My friends, I was afraid—afraid of war, of loss, of death. So I made compromises."

"We all did!" shouted someone. "But that's over! No more compromises!"

"No more compromises!" screamed another voice. "Death to cats! Death to curbs!"

"Highland curbs saved your lives last night!" shot Sauny. "Some of them died to set you free."

A confused murmuring broke out in the herd.

"I made compromises to prevent war," continued Kelsy, "but war came anyway. Hiding did not keep me safe, and it will not keep you safe. It will only make you the victor's trophy. You need to take back control of your lives, ferryshaft. You are not a prey species. You are not deer or sheep. You are valuable allies to the other intelligent species of Lidian. You need to show them that."

Silence. *Some of them see where he's going and don't like it,* thought Valla. *The rest are just confused.*

"One of Arcove's officers, a cat named Treace, has started a war among the creasia," continued Kelsy.

"Good!" shouted someone. "The more they fight, the more they'll kill each other!"

"It was Treace's cats who drove you to that island!" called Kelsy, struggling to be heard over the muttering of the crowd. "They want you as food animals or experiments. They do not view you as an intelligent species at all."

A big male pushed his way to the front of the group. Valla saw, with a start, that it was Kelsy's father, Sedaron—a formidable elder, who was at least as old as Charder. "I hope you are not suggesting, Kelsy," he said icily, "that we take sides in a creasia conflict. We have suffered under Arcove's paws for sixteen years. If the death that he so richly deserves is about to overtake him, then we should celebrate, for it is long overdue."

Shaw expected, right up to the last, that Arcove would ask for help. Obviously, Keesha thought so, too. When Arcove stopped moving, Keesha sat staring for a full breath, before he snarled, "Well, of all the...!" And in the same moment, his hum filled the cavern. He pushed Roup out of the way, and his song swelled in all its terrifying intensity. Keesha made a circle around Arcove's body, all the while muttering. "Stubborn, stubborn, stubborn...!"

It's too late, thought Shaw. *You've waited too long. Not even you can bring someone back twice.*

And then Arcove twitched.

The ferryshaft herd was buzzing like a swarm of angry wasps. "We will not fight for creasia!" someone shouted. "Killers! Hunters! Enemies! Predators! They do not deserve our help! They do not deserve our mercy!"

"Listen to me!" bellowed Kelsy. "Three generations ago, *we* hunted *them*—"

"As it should be," cut in an elder.

Kelsy glared at her. "We hunted them, and they hunted us, and so it has gone back and back. The only way this stops is if someone gives mercy to someone who does not deserve it."

"Well, let *them* make the first move," snapped Sedaron. "You are young, Kelsy. You are trying all the things that have been tried before. None of them work. We have our freedom, and the cats are distracted and off balance."

"Really?" growled Kelsy. Valla could see that he was smarting from the dismissive tone. "Has mercy been tried, father? I've never heard about it."

Sedaron did not answer. He trotted up beside Kelsy and Sauny and interposed his larger body between the two youngsters and the rest of the herd. "Charder is dead or lost, friends. He was Arcove's plaything in any case. Follow me over the cliffs to the southern plains, and we will make a new life for ourselves." His voice sank to an ominous growl. "In time, we will hunt creasia again."

"Perhaps you will." Sauny stepped around him with all the contempt that Valla knew she felt for the high-ranking ferryshaft. "Perhaps you will return to your old ways and keep making the same mistakes over and over again, but I won't. Storm fostered a creasia cub last winter. Do you know what he learned?"

The herd had grown silent again. Valla knew that many of them had been curious about Teek.

"He learned that they are a lot like us," said Sauny. "In fact, they're more like us than any of the other intelligent species on the island. Curbs carry their babies in pouches or hanging from their bellies like ticks. Ely-ary hatch them from eggs. Telshees are both male and female. Lishties…you don't even want to hear how they reproduce. But creasia have babies just like we do, and they love them…just like we do."

"You are a *female*…" growled Sedaron.

Sauny rounded on him. "I am Coden's foal," she snarled.

"Perhaps the creasia *are* like us," said a ferryshaft. Valla saw, with a sinking feeling, that this was one of the younger ones who'd fought with them on the edge of the plain. "But I would hate Arcove even if he were a ferryshaft. My mother died under creasia claws, and I will never forgive that."

"Will you not help Storm, then?" asked Sauny. "He risked his life to save many of you—"

"From creasia!" exploded another adult.

"Storm and I are Coden's foals," said Sauny desperately, "three generations back. I know some of you remember him."

The younger ones looked confused, but Valla saw instant wariness on the faces of the older ferryshaft. "Coden was a talented, but eccentric leader who ultimately lost the war," said Sedaron. "I do not doubt what you say, given Storm's appearance. We all knew it. But that's hardly a reason to follow you."

Another ferryshaft was trying to push her way through the crowd. She'd started near the back, so it had taken her some time. "It may not be wise or right, but I will follow you, Sauny."

Sauny's face brightened. "Mother…"

Sedaron rolled his eyes. "One more of Coden's foolish offspring."

"I'm with you, Sauny, Kelsy." Valla blinked. It was Leep. He'd grown into a sleek, black animal with white forelegs. A ferryshaft who must have been his mate was trailing behind him. Leep looked a little uncertain, but he waved his tail bravely. "Let's go find Storm."

"Yes, let's." Another ferryshaft wrenched herself from the crowd. Valla was not surprised to see Tollee, but she was surprised to see her grinning. She didn't think she'd ever seen Tollee smile like that. "Let's go to Kuwee Island and make some new friends. Let's make history."

Sedaron snorted. "The young can do foolish things as they've always done. Anyone who doesn't want to die defending creasia, come with me." He started away towards the cliffs, and the crowd opened for him. Valla saw many of them turn to follow. Others hesitated.

Sauny looked at the sea of faces—uncertain, angry, hopeful, sullen, frightened. "Please," she said softly, "let's not do the same thing again. Let's do something new."

Arcove was falling. Falling, and he knew there was nothing but pain at the bottom. The rat was eating its way up through his guts into his lungs. He was drowning in his own blood. He was falling.

And then he wasn't.

Arcove opened his eyes. The rat was still there, the room was spinning, he could barely breathe, but he was *not* falling. Keesha had one snowy coil under Arcove's chin, and that point of contact stood still in a tossing sea. In desperation, Arcove struggled up against Keesha's body and latched onto Keesha's coil as though it were the only bit of flotsam in a flood. Distantly, he heard Keesha hiss. He expected to be hurt, but he couldn't help himself. His body moved with the unreasoning panic of a drowning animal.

Not until the pain had subsided and the room came back into focus, did Arcove think, *I should be dead.* He opened his eyes and glared at Keesha. "You promised!" he gasped.

Keesha was breathing quickly. Arcove looked down and saw that, in his fear and pain, he'd sunk his front claws deep into the telshee's hide. He retracted them, and ten points of crimson blossomed in the pale fur. *What is he going to do to me for that?*

But Keesha only said, "Well, you're the one who keeps your promises, aren't you?" He looked around at the others. "I want a word alone with him. I'm not going to hurt him. I just brought him back from the edge of death…a little beyond the edge, actually. But let me talk to him for a moment. All of you, out. Yes, Roup, that includes you."

Arcove could hear them leaving. He lay with his eyes closed, trying to get his breath. Finally, Keesha said, "Your friend is a good talker."

"I did not ask him to talk," muttered Arcove.

"I think I could probably work with him," said Keesha thoughtfully. "Perhaps Storm will even get the kind of peace he wants—on good terms with Leeshwood…whatever remains of it."

"You should not have brought me back," whispered Arcove.

"On the contrary," said Keesha, "I think you need to stay alive until the end of this war. I think that would be best for everyone. And then I will finish my song. I worked very hard on it; I want to finish it."

Arcove licked his lips. Keesha sounded reasonable. He was offering more than Arcove had any right to expect. *But...that song... again? How many times?* He opened his mouth and then shut it without saying anything.

"You could just say you're afraid," offered Keesha.

No, I could not. "I didn't mean to scratch you," said Arcove instead.

"I've had worse scratches from you," said Keesha. "Do we have a deal or not?"

"Do I have a choice?"

"Not much of one. Although I suppose you could hide or try to get yourself killed."

"Deal," said Arcove quietly.

24

Regret

Later in the day, when most of the cats were sleeping, Shaw found Keesha on the eastern shore of Kuwee Island, looking out into the lake. She considered a tactful approach. *But we've known each other too long for that.* "You're going to regret it."

"Regret what?"

You know what. They were silent a moment. Shaw knew that Keesha was expecting her to say something, and she took a perverse pleasure in not saying it.

"You think it was irresponsible," said Keesha at last.

Blood music? Yes, I think it was incredibly irresponsible. "If you had gotten even one note wrong," Shaw said softly, "it could have affected everyone who heard you."

"But I didn't," said Keesha.

"No," agreed Shaw, "you did exactly what you meant to do." *And you're going to regret it.*

Keesha said nothing.

"Can you change what happens at the end of the song? Even if you wanted to?"

"I did not make it to be changed," snapped Keesha.

So that's a no, then. "There's an echo, isn't there?" asked Shaw. "When you're touching him, you soak up some of the effects."

Keesha grunted.

"Could you soak up enough to stop it from killing him?"

"It doesn't work that way," said Keesha. "What makes you think I want to?"

Shaw sighed. "Do you want me to go to Syriot and bring other telshees to help? I'm not sure how many will be able or willing on short notice, but I'm sure some would come at your summons."

"No," said Keesha. "Enough telshees have died on Kuwee Island. This is between me and Arcove." His ruff was bristling. Shaw could tell that, if she said the wrong thing, he would order her to go home.

She looked out into the lake where, more than a decade ago, Keesha and Arcove had nearly killed each other in the shallow water. *It may seem like yesterday to you, but everyone else has changed while you were sleeping.* "I was never in favor of our involvement with land animals," said Shaw at last.

Keesha's eyes flicked at her. "And yet here you are."

"Here I am," agreed Shaw. She allowed herself a mischievous grin. "Because I missed you."

Keesha's ruff settled a little. "I am not the villain here," he muttered.

I think that depends on where you're standing. "I was looking at these human paintings," said Shaw. "They seem to have held telshees in high regard. Do you think they worshiped us?"

Keesha considered. "Possibly. They may have consulted us for guidance, at least."

"And now they're all gone," said Shaw thoughtfully. "Doesn't seem like we did a very good job, does it?"

In the pre-dawn light, Treace paced the edge of the lake, watching Kuwee Island. Every now and then, he caught sight of one of Arcove's cats, peering from the underbrush or moving cautiously along the bank. *Yes,* thought Treace, *take a good look. Figure your odds. Then desert today while they're all sleeping.* They'd welcomed a trickle of Arcove's supporters after the battle in the clearing. Treace had no doubt that more would follow from Kuwee.

How sweet it would be, he thought. *If Arcove ended up starving in there with nothing left but his officers and mates. Maybe I should offer them exile instead of killing them. Send them to eke out a living for themselves in the Southern Mountains and then send young cats after them every spring to hone our fighting skills.* Treace could think of all kinds of uses for hostile exiles. *The young cats need something to fight. Arcove never understood that.*

There was no need to force a confrontation on Kuwee in any event. Treace had had a pleasant night of hunting small game, and he planned to have many more. *Of course, they will try to force a confrontation as they get hungrier. Soon they'll be down to nothing but fish. Then the edge of the lake will freeze... Will they eat Storm and Charder before the end? That would be fitting.*

Treace was startled when the dark silhouette of another cat came staggering towards him out of the gloom of the trees. The cat did not call or speak, and he was walking like a wounded animal. His scent, coming to Treace on the breeze, seemed deeply flawed.

Treace wrinkled his nose and hissed. He was about to call to his followers, when he caught the flash of pale nose leather—closer to white, now, than to pink. Treace's mouth went suddenly dry.

The cat stopped in front of him. Its fur was black, but so bedraggled with mud and twigs that he could hardly tell. White bone showed through the fur of one leg. The eyes glowed green. "Hello," croaked a familiar voice. "I have been Moro."

In the early morning, just as the rim of the sky began to glow, Arcove walked the eastern edge of Kuwee Island. Roup, Halvery, Charder, and Storm came behind him. They'd all slept that afternoon and Storm thought that everyone had gotten at least a little something to eat. *That won't be true for long, though. We need to win and win fast.*

Treace, of course, would feel differently. He was showing his strength along the edge of the lake—creasia lounging, fishing, even sleeping along the shore in full view of the island. Storm saw quite a few curbs as well—trotting through the trees of Chelby Wood, resting in the long lake grasses, hunting small water birds. They stretched as far as his eyes could see in either direction along the dawn shore.

Storm shivered. He glanced at Arcove. *We are outnumbered at least three-to-one.*

If Arcove felt despair, he didn't show it. In fact, he seemed much improved in both body and mind since Keesha's intervention. He studied the shore and listened to Roup and Halvery.

"The problem is," Storm heard Halvery say, "they can sit there and watch us swim over. They've got plenty of time to congregate wherever we're coming ashore. Then they can leap on us from the bank and kill our cats before they've gotten their feet under them. We don't have the numbers to overwhelm them. We need a distraction."

Where are you, Sauny?

Charder said what Storm had been thinking all day. "If Sauny and Kelsy manage to bring the ferryshaft herd, you'll get your distraction."

"That will never happen," said Arcove without looking at Charder. He thought for a moment. "If a few of our strongest swimmers struck out north…came ashore beyond Treace's cats…circled around behind them…"

"Treace would see them swimming," objected Halvery.

"Not necessarily," said Storm. "You get fog sometimes here in the mornings. The first time I swam out to Kuwee, I almost got lost in the fog."

The three creasia considered. "That might work," said Roup. "We'd have to wait for fog."

"Or snow or heavy rain," put in Charder. "Lots of things at this time of year might obscure the view from the shore."

"If those things don't kill the swimmers," muttered Halvery. "It's a good idea, though."

Treace stared. His nose was telling him one thing, and his eyes were telling him something else. He took a step back. "Moro? Is…is that really you?"

The cat cocked his head—an odd, bird-like gesture that Treace had never seen Moro make. "Yes, we are Moro. We have remembered his cubhood with you, his interest in the ghost plants, his many killings of cubs, his matings with dying—"

"That's enough," snapped Treace. "Who…who else are you?"

The glowing green eyes watched him with curiosity. It seemed to consider. "We are also Selka, Melae, Pathar, Oslan…" As the creature continued to rattle off names, Treace saw other shapes farther away along the edge of the lake—walking or staggering or dragging in his direction.

"That's enough." Treace felt as though he could not quite get his breath. He wanted this thing away from him—far, far away. He felt a mixture of grief, disgust, fear, and anger. *Moro… Why did you ever have to take an interest in lishties?* Treace tried to put even these feelings away from him.

"What do you want?" he asked. "My cats and I are laying siege to Kuwee Island. Arcove's creasia are trapped there."

Moro peered in the direction of the island. "We desire more hosts," the thing said, "more names, more memories. Also, we have promised to help you. We remember this."

The knot of fear loosened a little in Treace's chest. He was beginning to see the advantages of forcing a swift confrontation on Kuwee. "Well, then, I think we can help each other."

25

Surprise

Arcove was turning to go back up to the cave when Roup said, "Wait." He'd gone rigid, staring at the far shore.

"What is it?" asked Halvery after a moment. Storm couldn't see what Roup was looking at, either.

"There in the reeds," muttered Roup. "I thought I saw…"

And then Storm saw it, too, although he didn't understand why Roup was excited. There appeared to be an oory slinking cautiously through the tall water grasses. The oory was a strange color—almost white. As they watched, it paddled out into the lake towards the island. If Treace's cats saw it, they weren't interested.

Roup was dancing back and forth. "Get under the trees," he hissed, and then he gave that strange bird-like trill that he used with his clutter. The oory perked up its ears and angled towards them. It gave a mew that carried over the water.

"It's Friendly, isn't it?" said Arcove to Roup.

"It's what?" asked Halvery in bewilderment.

"Caraca's tame oory," said Arcove.

Storm was lost. Charder leaned over and said in his ear, "Caraca is Roup's mate. I've heard about this oory, but I've never seen it."

"I think we're all about to get a good look," whispered Storm. "Why is it—?"

But the white oory had splashed out of the water and was sniffing its way up the bank. Roup had backed into the shadow of the trees and underbrush so that the creasia on shore couldn't see him. He called again, and the oory ran to him. It mewed and rubbed around his legs like a young cub, making that throbbing noise that Teek sometimes made when he was extremely pleased.

Halvery took a step back with an expression of confusion and disgust. "It's just Friendly," Roup tried to explain. "That's its name."

"I gathered that," said Halvery. "What is it doing here?"

Arcove had come forward, but Friendly shied away from him.

"It knows me," Roup said. He was sniffing at the little animal, pushing it this way and that. "Oh, Caraca," he muttered. "You came after all."

Halvery was looking out towards the shore. "It's a little late to get to the island," he said.

"She's not coming alone." Roup was practically cackling. "She's trying to tell us to get ready."

"Halvery," said Arcove suddenly, "get back up to the cave and bring everyone who can fight down to the shore. I think we're about to get that distraction."

When Halvery was gone, Arcove glanced at Roup and laughed. "What did she do? Get them all to lick it?"

"I think so, yes," said Roup. "There's scent here from at least a dozen creasia, maybe more."

"That's clever," murmured Charder. "Sending it through Treace's cats because they wouldn't pay attention to it... Very clever."

"Caraca was always that," said Roup. "I hope she doesn't plan on actually fighting, because she's not very big."

"Who do you think she's brought?" asked Storm. "I thought we had all the creasia here."

"A lot of females stayed behind in their dens," said Roup. "A lot of them didn't even know we were at war."

"It would only take a dozen of them to create enough of a distraction to give us a chance," said Arcove.

Charder hoped that Storm would have the good sense to stay out of the fighting. A pitched battle between creasia was no place for a ferryshaft. However, he was pretty sure that saying so would only make Storm more likely to join in, so Charder just turned and made his way back up the hill towards the cave.

He met a wave of creasia coming in the opposite direction—slipping through the forest like shadows, pouring down the hill to Arcove's summons. Charder felt a mixture of apprehension and relief. *Let it be over today,* he thought. *One way or the other. At least we won't starve slowly in these caves.*

All of the wounded who were able had come out of the cave and sat on the top of the hill, straining to get a view of what was happening below. Charder could see a good bit of Chelby Wood and the shore of the lake, but not the shore of the island. He imagined the female creasia out beyond the wood in the long grass of the plain, creeping closer, hoping their message had been received and that their mates were prepared for whatever assistance they could give. *If both groups don't attack together, the group that attacks first will be slaughtered.*

Cubs were pacing around the silent adults, asking questions that no one wanted to answer. Charder saw Sharmel hesitate. *Don't go,* thought Charder. *It'll be your last battle if you do.*

Sharmel had not been steady on his feet since the avalanche. Charder didn't feel entirely steady himself. His left hip sent a deep, aching pain through his hindquarters whenever he moved, and the run to Kuwee Island had pushed him to his limits. *I really am too old for this. Arcove should have replaced me a long time ago.*

Sharmel started down the hill.

Ah, well, thought Charder. *There's no such thing as an alpha creasia who can't fight. What's left for him when this is over? He'll never keep his clutter.* Charder had always assumed that death would be his own fate whenever Arcove decided to replace him. It was the creasia way. *Was I wrong about that?* Things that Roup had said niggled in the back of his mind. *I never asked. Maybe I should have asked.*

Charder wanted, more than anything, to see Arcove proved wrong about the ferryshaft herd. *But he's probably right.*

A disturbance in the trees along the far shore marked the beginning of the battle. Charder heard the wailing cries of fighting cats and then a cacophony of snarls and screams. There was shouting from the far shore, cats running along the bank.

Storm had not appeared. Something brushed Charder's leg, and he looked down to see Storm's cub. Teek's eyes were dilated, and he was breathing quickly. "Charder," he whispered, "there are dead things coming up the back side of the hill."

Charder blinked. "What?"

And then the lishties attacked.

Storm crouched on a thick tree limb a little way up from the western shore of the island. He had a clear view of both Kuwee's bank and lakeshore, and he did not think the cats below were likely to notice him. As soon as the sounds of fighting began to carry from the far side of the wood, Arcove's cats launched themselves into the water.

Storm could see some of Treace's cats pacing the bank in anticipation, but many of them had disappeared to deal with whatever was happening in the wood. The first of Arcove's cats to reach shallow water met determined resistance, but, as more arrived, it became clear that Treace did not have the numbers to focus on the bank that he'd previously possessed. Storm saw a blur of fighting cats shoot out of the trees—undoubtedly some of the females who'd come with Caraca.

Arcove reached the far shore, Roup and Halvery right behind him, and they cut a swath through Treace's cats. Then there was fighting in the water and fighting on the shore and fighting beneath the trees, and Storm could no longer tell who was who or who was winning. It was all very noisy.

It took him several moments to realize that some of the noise was not coming from the far shore. It was coming from the top of the hill.

Arcove moved through the fighting like a fire through dry leaves. He had one clear purpose. *Find Treace.* He did not expect it to be easy. Treace had not dashed down to the water to meet the enemy. *But he can't just hide, either. His cats need to see him. If they think he's dead, they'll falter.*

Arcove fought his way through several knots of combatants. *Treace would prefer to meet me after I'm injured,* thought Arcove. *He's counting on it.*

A little voice in the back of Arcove's head muttered, *If he only knew.*

Arcove spotted his opponent farther along the shore. He was impressed to see that Lyndi had found their enemy first. She was going round and round with Treace and two of his subordinates in the shallows. Arcove lost sight of them as he met a snarling opponent head-on. He lunged with both paws and struggled for a moment on his hind legs while his enemy tried to lock his jaws around Arcove's throat. Then Arcove's greater weight sent the other cat over backwards. Arcove felt the hind-claws graze his belly, but he was too experienced a fighter to be disemboweled that way. He landed cross-wise with his teeth buried in the other cat's throat.

There was a crunch and a spray of blood, and then he was up again, shaking red droplets out of his eyes, turning to swat as another cat lunged at him.

He caught a glimpse of Roup barreling into a cat in the water, trying to help Lyndi. Arcove couldn't see Treace. Halvery had disappeared in a snarling tangle of fur on the edge of the trees.

Then, over the noises of fighting cats, Arcove heard the unmistakable, chilling sound of telshee song. It was not the song that Keesha had been singing to Arcove. It was a song that Arcove associated with telshees who were calling for help.

Keesha was still asleep in the cave when Shaw emerged to see what all the screaming was about. She found injured creasia and half-grown cubs desperately trying to defend the entrance to the cave from an ever-increasing swarm of what looked like lishties in creasia and ferryshaft hosts.

Shaw had not been truly surprised in decades. She had swum strange waters and tasted the air of foreign worlds. She had walked in the skins of other beasts and spoken forgotten languages to creatures who were probably long dead. No species of creature had surprised her for as far back as she could remember.

Until now.

Lishties! In four-legged hosts? That cannot be.

Most of the cats had been above ground when the attack started, and many of them had been cut off from the entrance to the cave. Those still inside were obviously unwilling to shut the door and abandon their companions.

Shaw shouted for Keesha and then joined the struggle around the entrance. She added her song to the cacophony, hoping it would have the same effect as it had on lishties in Syriot. It *did* seem to slow the creatures.

Shaw managed to knock a pair of awkward ferryshaft lishties from the ramp and darted out of the cave. She found the hilltop in a bloody uproar. The cats had formed protective circles with the smallest and weakest in the center and were trying to defend themselves from the onslaught of ragged, broken, green-eyed monsters that were coming up the hill from the western shore of the lake.

The sun was spreading its first rays across the sky. *And that will help,* thought Shaw. The four-legged lishties seemed less coordinated than those to which Shaw was accustomed. Some were almost comically awkward, and the creasia were able to knock them down and crunch into the backs of their skulls. Shaw's lightning-fast reflexes were more than adequate to deal with those around her, but she wondered at the numbers. *How many are coming? Has the entire ferryshaft herd been colonized?*

Out of the corner of her eye, Shaw saw Storm's cub, Teek, land on the back of a black-furred cat. It was a brave thing to do, but doomed. The cub could not possibly crunch through the neck of a cat that size. The black cat turned to snap at him, and Shaw reacted. She scooped the cub out of the air and flung him clear.

And then the lishty-creasia sank its fangs into her neck.

Shaw bellowed. She felt pain, but, more than anything, surprise. She heard Keesha's most aggressive battle song throb in the air. She struck out in every direction, trying to kill as many of the lishties as possible before…before…

Shaw felt hot and cold. The world was too bright. She could tell that she was slowing, even as she tried to move faster. She heard Keesha calling her name, and she tried to answer. *I'm here. I have been Shaw. No, no, not that. Not yet. I'm still here.*

And then she wasn't.

26

Howl

Storm got just close enough to the top of the hill to see what appeared to be enemy cats attacking the most helpless members of their party in front of the caves. He was certain that Arcove would want to defend the cubs and wounded, so he raced back down to the shore and began shouting, "We've been flanked! Attack at the caves! The cubs! The wounded! Help!"

He thought he'd gotten the attention of at least a few creasia closest to the island. This done, Storm turned to run back up to the caves to give whatever assistance he could. However, he found himself face-to-face with a pack of curbs, wet from their swim to the island.

His heart sank as he recognized a familiar tan and black female. "Ah, Storm," she murmured. "How fortunate. We assumed you'd be hiding."

I would have been, he thought and cursed his own carelessness. The curbs rushed forward, but Storm gave a mighty leap and clambered into the boughs of the tree nearest the water. He heard their jaws snap in the air behind him.

"Treed like a squirrel," he heard Quinyl say. "But you'll have to come down sometime."

Arcove caught snatches of news trickling through the ranks of fighting cats. There'd been some kind of attack on the cave. Enemy creasia were killing the cubs and wounded. *I should have made them go inside and shut the entrance,* he realized. Arcove was unaccustomed to having such an option, and the chance for a successful strike had come so quickly that no one had thought of it.

The fighting on the riverbank had slowed a little. No one could maintain that furious pace for long, and the sun was strong now above the trees. Arcove could tell that, while the females who'd come with Caraca had fought savagely and bravely, they were not numerous enough to tip the outcome of the battle. Treace's superior numbers were beginning to tell, and his cats were working to isolate Arcove's. *We need to rally and put our backs against a defense.*

In addition, the rumor that their cubs might be dying would sap the morale of any cat. *We have to go back to the cave.*

Over the heads of the fighting creasia, Arcove spotted Treace, still maddeningly out of reach among the trees. Treace caught his look and leered at him.

Arcove swallowed a snarl and bellowed, "Fall back to the cave! Roup, Halvery! With me, creasia!"

Storm was working his way east through the trees towards the top of the hill. It was hard going for him, while the curbs moved along easily below. They called a steady stream of insults and challenges, which Storm tried to ignore.

"Do you think you'll find help up there, stupid ferryshaft? They are all dead! Lishties fight for us. Better to die between our teeth than theirs. Your cub is already dead. Or perhaps a lishty wears his skin."

Storm paused to look down at them. "When the telshees get hold of you, they'll bite you in half," he snarled.

"Telshees!" mocked Quinyl. "Telshees are nothing but hosts for a clever parasite. And now it has found new hosts."

Storm didn't know what they were talking about, but he didn't like it. He tried to move faster, jumping from tree to tree, inching along the branches.

"I hope you're not expecting help from highland curbs," said Quinyl slyly. "Eyal died thrashing in his own blood two nights ago."

Storm stopped moving. *It's a lie. She's trying to make you lose your nerve.* But he looked down anyway.

Quinyl seemed delighted by his reaction. "He died because of you. Strange, isn't it? That a highland curb would die trying to help a runty, outcast ferryshaft? Truly, you are bad luck to all your friends, Vearil."

No, thought Storm. *Eyal... No.* But something about the way Quinyl spoke made the knot in his belly tighten. *She's telling the truth.*

The look on his face only seemed to goad her. "It wasn't quick. I think he was all night about it—dying, I mean."

"I'm only bad luck to hunters," whispered Storm. His heart was hammering wildly. His hooves were shaking.

"I intend to keep your tail," said Quinyl. "I wonder what kind of luck it will bring."

Storm sprang down on her.

Nothing could have prepared Arcove for the sight at the top of the hill. Dead creasia lay everywhere—far more than he thought had been left in the caves. More baffling still, some of the bodies smelled as though they'd been dead for a long time, while others were clearly members of his party. He knew, without understanding why, that some of the creatures lurking around the edges of the hilltop were *wrong.* His mind immediately classified them as *other.* Not creasia, not ferryshaft, not any animal he had ever encountered, but definitely enemies.

Keesha lay in the middle of the carnage, his body laced around Shaw, who looked quite dead. Keesha was looking down at the other telshee, his eyes vacant, singing. The monstrous creatures on the edge of the clearing seemed to be cowed by his song, and a collection of surviving wounded creasia and cubs had taken advantage of the fact to crowd around him. However, Treace's creasia were certainly not cowed.

As Arcove arrived on the scene, he saw one of the enemy cats race in to tear at Keesha's snowy coils. The cat ripped out a mouthful of fur and pink blubber. Keesha didn't even flinch.

"Get in the cave!" Arcove roared at the defenders. "Back! Get back!"

As more of Arcove's creasia arrived to drive off the strange, stinking monsters, the exhausted defenders were able to reach the cave's entrance again. Still, Keesha did not move. His coils lay everywhere, and Arcove saw another enemy cat leap in to tear at them. Blood was running freely in the white fur, and still Keesha did not stir.

Arcove remembered the telshees that his cats had found sleeping in the caves when they'd attacked Kuwee long ago. They'd ripped those telshees to pieces, and the telshees hadn't even woken. *This is torpor,* Arcove realized, *or something like it. He can't pay attention to his surroundings and create a new song at the same time. That's why he was asleep for sixteen years.*

More cats were arriving every moment—both friends and enemies. "Keesha!" Arcove shouted in his face. "Syra-lay! Get in the cave!"

Keesha's stare did not flicker.

Arcove got hold of Shaw's thick pelt behind her head and tried to drag her. Finally, Keesha reacted. The rising and falling notes of his song stuttered, and he blinked. His eyes focused on Arcove, and his black lips peeled back from white teeth and pink gums in a huge, gleaming snarl. Arcove let go of Shaw. In the same moment, Keesha darted forward, and his great jaws snapped shut just over Arcove's head.

Arcove went flat on the ground. "Keesha, please! You want to hear me beg? Please don't die here. We need your help." *We need all the help we can get.*

Keesha blinked again. His snarl dropped away. He looked around as though seeing the clearing for the first time. Then, quick as a summer snake, he snatched up Shaw's body behind her head, whipped away towards the cave's mouth and disappeared, still dragging her.

Arcove tried to put the whole episode out of his mind as he turned towards the western end of the clearing. Roup and Halvery had been keeping the enemy cats at bay as Arcove dealt with Keesha, but more and more were arriving. *And too few of mine.*

Arcove knew that at least some of his supporters were trapped, fighting enemy creasia by the lake. *If we go into the cave and shut the entrance, we'll starve to death. If we make a stand here...we may be finished either way.*

This fight was poor odds from the beginning, he reflected. *You can't be lucky every time.*

Storm knew that tackling an entire pack of curbs was a foolish thing to do, but he was beyond caring about foolishness. He made them respect him; of that he was certain. His flying hooves connected with heads and shoulders and hips, and his teeth ripped through fur and muscle whenever he managed to get hold of skin. The curbs were not easy targets, though. They latched onto his legs and belly and shoulders. Each time, he managed to throw them off, but he was losing ground, slipping back down the slope towards the water.

On the very edge of the lake, they surrounded him. They were all panting. Storm could feel blood trickling down his neck and face, but he felt no pain, only the doomed exhilaration of battle. His attackers were bleeding, too. Some of them might not see the sunset.

"This is for my friend, whom you killed," panted Quinyl.

"This is for mine," snarled Storm.

Quinyl lunged at him and landed on his back. Storm felt her teeth graze his spine. He reared up to shake her off, and a curb hit him in the belly. Storm leapt into the air, twisting, and fell backwards into the water. The spot where he landed was deep.

Charder stood at the mouth of the cave with the exhausted remnants of those who'd stayed behind from the battle. Arcove's creasia made a crescent around the entrance, while Treace's creasia gathered all around the edges of the clearing. Both sides were panting and growling at each other, dripping and muddy, scratched and bitten and bleeding.

Treace came through the center of his clutter. He was scratched and muddy, too, although Charder was certain that Arcove had not gotten hold of him. *He'd be looking a lot worse than that.*

Charder could tell by the way Arcove's shoulders bunched that he was thinking about dashing across the clearing and going for Treace's throat. However, it was obvious that the other cats would attack him together if he did so.

"Hello, *sir*," said Treace in a mocking sing-song. "Your luck seems a bit played out today." He cocked his head. "Perhaps the moon is not right." His followers tittered behind him.

Treace waited for silence. "I would hate to begin my ruler-ship appearing less generous than my predecessor. So, I am offering you a chance to live, Arcove. You may take any cats who wish to follow you and go south. Find some tick-ridden patch of woods along the southern shores of the lake or in the mountains and…" he gave a little chuckle, "*rule* over it. I'm sure you'll find adequate colonies of rats and crayfish to feed your dens."

Arcove did not respond.

"No…?" murmured Treace. "Well, it is puzzling to me why anyone would reject such a magnanimous offer. Did I mention you will be king on your little patch of ticks? Of course, I will require some token of your submission. You are currently hostiles in my territory. Your tails, I think. All of them. My creasia will remove them forthwith, and you may go your way. My cats may be by in the spring to shorten the tails of your new cubs, as well…assuming you survive. I wouldn't want anyone to confuse the cats from our two Leeshwoods."

Now the silence from Arcove's creasia was one of shock. Charder was surprised himself. *Clever, cruel, and humiliating*, he thought.

Treace smiled at their stunned faces. "They say the best leaders provide an example. What will it be Arcove? A long life, and a short tail? Or a long tail, and a short life?" Treace's voice lowered in a snarl. "Because if you don't come forward and bend your neck to me right now, I swear we'll kill every creasia at your back and give your bodies to the lishties."

Storm struggled beneath the surface of the lake. He'd gotten a few lungfuls of air at the beginning, but then his jaws closed around Quinyl's throat, and he was determined not to let go. His hold wasn't ideal. He couldn't get any leverage. She had managed to end up on top, and her head kept breaking the surface despite his best efforts. He wasn't sure how much air she was getting, but more than he was. Her sharp claws flailed, trying to open his belly whenever he fought to bring more of his body to the surface. The place where he'd fallen was very deep, so he just hung there with his eyes screwed shut as she thrashed and scratched above him.

Storm realized, gradually, that he was drowning. He had not planned to drown, but somehow he sucked in a breath of water. He almost let go of Quinyl, but then he thought of Eyal, and he did not let go.

Some part of Storm's mind quieted in spite of his body's desperation. *I have befriended curbs and telshees and even creasia. I have flown through the air in the claws of an ely-ary. I have outwitted the greatest hunters this island has ever known. I have helped to raise two little ones, even if I did not father them. I have loved another ferryshaft, and I think that she loved me. Surely that is enough... enough of a life for anyone.*

Storm was dimly aware that Quinyl's thrashing had slowed. They were sinking together. He tried to remember how to swim. He tried to remember how to unlock his jaws, but he seemed to have forgotten both. He opened his eyes and saw the sunlight on the surface of the lake. It looked beautiful.

Arcove took a step forward. His voice was ice-calm. "I made you a promise last fall, Treace. Do you remember what it was?"

Treace gave a disdainful sniff. The cats around him tensed.

"I said that if you did not stop making a nuisance of yourself, you'd die with my teeth in your throat," continued Arcove. "Do you know how often I've broken my word, Treace?"

He wants to go down fighting, thought Charder. *I can't blame him.* Charder realized that he needed to make a decision. *Retreat into the cave and probably starve…or die fighting beside Arcove?* He was surprised at how easily the choice came to him.

Charder stepped away from the cave's entrance and trotted down the ramp. *I suppose I am one of your officers.* He saw Roup and Halvery gather themselves for the final charge.

And then Charder heard a sound that he'd never expected to hear again—the sound of an entire ferryshaft herd, howling. The noise floated up from the direction of Chelby Wood like a dream from the past. Charder knew with absolute certainty that there were *not* thousands of ferryshaft on Lidian. He knew, but, in that moment, he doubted. Because it *sounded* like thousands.

Arcove's head snapped around. He looked west, towards the lake shore. Charder followed his gaze and saw animals running through the trees, their hooves creating an ominous, distant thunder and leaving a plume of dust farther out across the plain. Charder thought that he'd never enjoyed anything so much as the look on Arcove's face.

Then Charder did what seemed natural. He answered the howl.

Treace's cats, already unnerved, looked around wildly. Treace glanced back as though expecting ferryshaft to come charging out of the bushes. It was in that moment of distraction that Arcove flashed across the clearing like a descending eagle and slammed into Treace.

When Storm opened his eyes, he saw water rippling gently against sand. He remembered the stream and the beautiful meadow where the dead played. He thought that he should rise and greet them, but he felt too tired at the moment. The world seemed very quiet. He couldn't hear the bird song that he remembered from that place.

Then Storm noticed something about the ripples. They were tinged with crimson, and they left a dark scum on the sand in front of his nose. Someone was jostling him. All at once, the water ran out of one of his ears, and he heard a frantic voice calling his name. "Storm! Storm, please don't be dead! Please! We're here! We came! Please!"

Storm gagged up lake water. His head spun, and then he gulped in air. He tried to stand, but fell over and vomited again. Tollee was crouching beside him in the bloody mud. Storm saw two dead curbs and another floating in the water.

"I—" he gasped. "Quinyl—"

"I think she's dead, Storm," said Tollee. "If she's the one you were choking when I dragged you out, she's dead."

"Said...she killed...Eyal," gasped Storm.

"Yes," said Tollee. "I know. I'm sorry. He's part of the reason we're here, though. Listen. Listen, Storm."

Storm heard the howls, then. All over Kuwee Island and through Chelby Wood, ferryshaft were howling. He heard fighting and cats wailing, but above it all rose that strange music. Storm lay still and let Tollee lick the blood from his face and listened.

27

Peace

Roup stumbled back into the caves around noon. Kuwee Island had been completely cleared of both enemy cats and the creatures that the ferryshaft called lishties. Treace's corpse lay in the clearing at the top of the hill for all to see. Roup did not think Treace would awaken as a lishty. Arcove had left him in several pieces.

Many of Treace's cats had surrendered immediately upon his death. A few—mostly his officers and those with little reason to expect mercy—had fled. Halvery had led a group of cats after them across the plain.

Most of the ferryshaft were spread out all over the island—resting or feeding or licking their wounds. Some of them had wandered down into the caves as well. Roup saw them scattered among the exhausted creasia, sleeping in the warmer air. The sight made Roup feel oddly content—as though uneasy ghosts were finally at rest.

Roup had not slept well since Arcove's strange illness. With the battle won and Arcove apparently healthy, Roup felt unbearably exhausted, but he did not want to sleep alone. Arcove was still outside, dealing with the fallout from the battle. Caraca had been searching for Friendly last Roup saw her. Lyndi was helping to track down Treace's remaining supporters. Roup decided he would visit his daughter, Mist, and her mate, Percil.

He found Mist alone in one of the strange, half-tumbled rooms, nursing her cubs. She asked immediately if Roup would watch them while she hunted, and Roup agreed. He curled up with the three small, warm bodies—less than a year old. They burrowed up against him, and Roup fell into dreamless sleep.

"Remy went with Sedaron's herd," said Tollee, "because of Teedo. I don't blame her, Storm. I almost sent Myla with her. I was worried about leaving her behind on the plain. She could have been killed by Treace's cats as they fled."

"I understand," said Storm. They were stretched on the grass of the plain in the warm sun of late afternoon. Teek and Myla were chattering away to each other about the adventures of the last few days. Teek looked like he could hardly keep his eyes open, but the story was too good to stop telling. Storm was not pleased to hear that Teek had fought in the battle, but he was impressed to learn that Shaw had saved Teek's life. *She never liked him. She threatened to kill him.* Storm had tried to thank her, but Keesha wasn't letting anyone near Shaw.

"I still can't believe half of the herd didn't come," grumbled Sauny.

"I can't believe half of them *did!*" said Storm. "And I'm sure that some of those ferryshaft will come back to their mates and friends once the fighting is over."

"And some of them won't," said Valla. "We're going to have two herds at least—perhaps hostile to each other."

"I think it was like that before the creasia conquest," said Storm.

"We'll have *three* herds," said Sauny. "Mine and Kelsy's...and Sedaron's."

Storm grinned. "Are you sure you're old enough to lead a herd, Sauny?"

"I led them into battle, didn't I?"

"I suppose so." Storm hesitated. "Were...were you with Eyal when...?"

"No," said Valla. "I'm sorry, Storm. The curbs said that he gave them a message for you." She thought for a moment. "He said, 'Tell

Storm Ela-curb that this year, borrowed from death, was the best of his years.'"

Storm swallowed. "He called me that? He called me a curb?"

"That's what they said. They were going to howl for him, but we told them to wait for you. We thought you'd want that."

Storm laid his head on his hooves. He felt as though the sun had dimmed a little. "He was my friend…one of the truest friends I've ever had. He came out of nowhere, in a place I never expected to find a friend. And I guess…I guess he left the same way."

Tollee drew a deep breath. "Is it better to have all the bad news at once?"

Storm shut his eyes. "Who else?"

"We should probably tell you how Pathar died."

Roup woke at evening. Someone was standing in the doorway of the little room. Roup thought at first that it was Mist, but then the cat took a few steps inside, and Roup saw that it was Halvery. He felt a trace of apprehension. He'd not been alone with Halvery since he'd told the secret of his past with Arcove dying at his feet. He'd had a sense that Halvery wanted to say something to him, but there hadn't been time. Now… *He wouldn't just attack me, would he?*

Halvery seemed to notice that Roup was awake and came on over. His posture wasn't aggressive, although he didn't look comfortable, either. "I meant to say something to you after Arcove's fight with Treace in the Great Clearing."

Roup sighed. "Are you about to challenge me? I suppose we should get this over with."

Halvery twitched his short tail and looked away. "No."

Roup cocked his head. Halvery was always direct and rarely tongue-tied. "Something else wrong? Not sure you can serve under a creasia raised by ferrysh—?"

"Stop," snapped Halvery. "I am trying to apologize."

Roup was shocked. He waited.

"I would have died," said Halvery. "If I had fought Treace, I would have been lured into that curb trap. No one would have started running in time to save *me*. Your instincts were correct, and I was…not helpful." He took a deep breath. "Last year, when Treace and Moro were testing their traps and you and Lyndi almost died in one…you kept me out of their territory…and that probably kept me alive."

"Halvery…" said Roup gently, but Halvery only shook his ears.

"You have been an exceedingly patient commanding officer. I had no right to behave as I did, and I'm sorry."

There was an awkward silence. Halvery still didn't meet Roup's eyes. "Well…have a good evening," he said at last. "I think Lyndi was looking for you earlier. I'll tell her you're in here." He turned to go.

He's not even going to mention the ferryshaft, thought Roup in wonder. "Halvery, wait."

Halvery paused in the entrance and glanced back at him.

Roup took a deep breath. He started to get up, but one of the cubs mewed, and Roup settled back down with the little animal between his forepaws. "Arcove and I didn't exclude you from our private discussions because we thought you were incompetent or disloyal. But some of the things we talked about… I probably should have told you where I came from a long time ago."

"No," said Halvery, "you should not have."

"That's what Arcove thought."

"I would have denounced you to all of Leeshwood as a ferry-shaft sympathizer," said Halvery. "Arcove was entirely correct not to trust me with that information."

"You thought I was a ferryshaft sympathizer anyway," said Roup. "I was. Sometimes I still have trouble sleeping during the day."

Halvery came back into the room. He lay down on his belly so that they were on eyelevel. "Roup, I was jealous. I admired Arcove, and I wanted him to trust me the same way he trusted you. I see now exactly how foolish and unreasonable that was. You were the only person he could trust for years, his only friend. I don't know why I expected to get the same treatment, just because I won a few fights with council members. I was young. That's my only excuse."

"I knew you admired his fights," said Roup. "I should have talked about the early ones more. I know you thought I snubbed you when you were only trying to be friendly. I was afraid I'd give myself away."

Halvery snorted. "Do not apologize to me. You have overlooked my near-constant antagonism for years. Anyone else in your position would have fought and killed me a long time ago."

"Oh, I don't know about that," said Roup. "Arcove always said you were an excellent officer. In any other clutter, you would have been his beta."

Halvery laughed. "Roup, why do you think I never challenged you?"

Roup was surprised. He didn't say anything.

"Because I didn't really think I'd win," said Halvery. "You were fighting, too, all those years. You learned from Arcove."

Roup smiled. "I did. Didn't get to win very often, though."

They were quiet a moment. Roup found himself casting about for something else to say. He'd never had such a friendly conversation with Halvery. Before he could think of anything, Halvery said, "The two of you make beautiful cubs." His voice held a trace of friendly sarcasm.

Roup looked down at the fluffy creatures between his front paws. "I always thought so." He was a little surprised that Halvery remembered—Mist was Roup's daughter and Percil was Arcove's son. The cubs were black, but one opened its eyes, and they flashed honey gold. The cub trilled and nestled into the curve of Roup's paw.

"I'm surprised you and Arcove don't have more cubs in common," said Halvery, "the way you practically den together."

"Well, I don't have very many," said Roup, "and they spend so much time with Arcove's cubs, they think they're siblings. Except Mist and Percil, apparently."

"How many *do* you have? Living, I mean."

"Four," said Roup immediately. "You?"

Halvery laughed. "I would have to think about it...and ask around."

Roup gave a snort of laughter that woke one of the cubs.

"Why don't you take Lyndi into your den?" asked Halvery abruptly.

Roup frowned. "She's a good officer, a good beta. She has a purpose and a function in my clutter. In a den, she's an anomaly with no purpose. Why would I do that to her?"

Halvery rolled his eyes. "Well, you might do it to make her happy."

Roup started to say something, but Halvery spoke first. "My mates cycle through my hunting clutters when they're available. They can be den members *and* run in your clutter."

Roup felt annoyed. "Yes, but your mates aren't officers. You don't like Lyndi as an officer because she's female."

"Now there you are wrong," said Halvery. "It's not that she's female. It's that she's in season half the time, and it's distracting! I don't know how you keep your mind on your business."

Roup swallowed a laugh. "Oh, it's not really half the time, surely."

"Three or four times a year, anyway," said Halvery. "Female that age, not having litters? Got to be that often at least. I'm surprised you don't have more fights in your clutter because of it."

"They wouldn't be in my clutter if they were prone to fighting each other," said Roup. "They've gotten used to her. She mates with a few of the lower ranking males occasionally, I think. Everyone seems happy enough."

Halvery gave an exasperated rumble. "I realize that she's a good beta, and I'm not suggesting you get rid of her. But what's stopping you from taking her into your den? Don't tell me it's because she can't have cubs; you care less about that than any cat I've ever seen. And don't tell me it's because she doesn't want to, either; I've seen the way she looks at you."

Roup frowned. "Caraca wouldn't like it…"

"Caraca doesn't like not knowing where she ranks in relation to your *female* beta. You've created an unnatural situation. If you take Lyndi into your den, she and Caraca will sort it out, I promise." Halvery hesitated. "You're not a ferryshaft, Roup. You don't have to mate like one."

Oh, I don't, thought Roup, *but you knew that.* He considered a moment. "As her superior officer, it doesn't seem right…"

Halvery snorted. "That's funny, coming from you."

Roup looked at him blankly, and then suddenly he laughed. "You're correct, of course."

Halvery snickered. "I'm *what?* Could you say that again? A little louder perhaps?"

Roup smiled. "But, she's never asked…"

"Roup!" exclaimed Halvery. "She's too proud to ask! Would *you* ask?"

"Probably not."

"Well, assume that she's a little like you. She's got to be, otherwise she'd never put up with you."

Roup chuffed.

"You're grooming her for a place on the council," said Halvery. "I know that."

Roup shifted uneasily.

"I won't argue with you about it," continued Halvery. "I won't challenge her, but things will go more smoothly if she's got a high-ranking mate. Otherwise, I predict a lot of fights. Besides, do you really think she likes lying down for the most low-ranking males in your clutter?"

Roup considered. "I…hadn't really thought about it," he admitted.

"Well, think about it now," said Halvery. "Because we've got some places on the council to fill. Sharmel is alive, and his clutter may allow him to leave command gracefully. They're all about his age, and they've served with him for a long time. But I don't think he'll be back to the council. With Treace and Ariand gone, that leaves you and me. And we both know how well that will turn out...sir."

Roup snickered. "Arcove will just sit around and watch us argue."

Halvery's expression changed. "Is Arcove well? I thought he was better after Keesha did...whatever it was that he did. But Arcove was looking unsteady when I saw him earlier this evening."

Anxiety blossomed again in the back of Roup's mind. "Where is he?"

"I think he went off to talk to Keesha," said Halvery.

Roup settled back down. "That will probably be alright, then."

28

Paint You In

"So, the acriss is awake?" asked Arcove.

Keesha grunted. They were moving along the wilder, eastern edge of the island in the light of the hunter's moon—full and golden as it rose over the trees. This was the spot where the lishties had come ashore. Arcove was scanning the mud for fresh prints. He was also trying to ignore the growing sense of nausea and dizziness. *This is the last time,* he told himself.

"Sauny told me that the lishties offered her what they apparently offered Moro," said Arcove. "Except she declined."

Keesha growled. "She should have told me."

"Well, you're not exactly a disinterested party," said Arcove. "How long have they been colonizing your species? A hundred years? A thousand? Before—?"

"Long before cats learned to talk," snapped Keesha.

"Before *telshees* learned to talk?" asked Arcove. He was enjoying this. The knowledge that he was about to die was strangely freeing.

Keesha stopped moving. He was silent a moment. At last, he said, "We do not know. I personally believe that telshees and acriss woke together—that we developed our songs as a defense against lishties from the beginning. You have no idea how terrible it is to be confronted with an alien intelligence that has the body of your friend and possesses all of her most intimate memories and yet is *not* your friend."

"How do you know that?" asked Arcove. "How do you know that they don't really bring animals back to life?"

"You would know if you ever spoke to one wearing the skin of your loved one," said Keesha. "They read memories like writing on a wall, but it is not the same. They feel nothing. They do not always understand what they are remembering."

"Sauny's beta..." Arcove searched for her name. "Valla. She seemed to think that the earliest writing on your walls came from lishties, not telshees."

"That may be," said Keesha carefully. "They are obsessed with memories and the preservation of memories. Memories are all that they are."

"So this skill that makes you feel so superior was learned from your parasites?"

Keesha turned towards him very slowly. Arcove decided that he might have pushed things too far. "How is Shaw?"

Keesha's blue glare pinned him to the sand for a moment. Finally, he said. "She is weak, but alive."

"She's not going to turn into a lishty?" asked Arcove.

"No," said Keesha. He cocked his head. "This beta of Treace's... Moro. Was he insane?"

Arcove looked at the water. "I don't know. I almost killed him two years ago when he started experimenting with traps. I wish I had."

"He seems to have introduced acriss—lishty larva—into ghost plants. Then he drowned creasia cubs in the bowls and managed to produce four-legged lishties. If acriss is ever introduced into the larger Ghost Wood, lishties might gain control of all those plants. Or they might even wake the wood. This seems like an extremely reckless and foolish thing to do."

"But clever," said Arcove, "for a tiny predator brain."

"Are you *trying* to speed your demise?"

Arcove ignored him. "I also heard a rumor that your eggs don't hatch without acriss, so you can't really get rid of the lishties without getting rid of yourselves."

Keesha yawned—a gesture that showed all his teeth and was certainly meant to be more threatening than calming. "I don't know what makes you think you can ask all the questions. I would like to hear about this trip to the Southern Mountains that you took with Coden and Roup."

Arcove was surprised. "It was a long time ago." He realized a moment later how silly that must sound to a telshee. "A long time ago to me."

"So, yesterday as far as I'm concerned."

Arcove hesitated. "It was early summer. I was eight."

"You did this *after* you were ruling Leeshwood?"

"Well...yes. We were only gone for about fifteen days. Coden wanted to get all the way up into the mountains and find the secret valley where the highland curbs kept their queen. But, we..." Arcove realized that Keesha had been moving out into the water as he talked and Arcove had followed. They were still standing in the shallows, but it was about to get deep.

You and I have stood in this lake before. Arcove swallowed. He tried to take another step, but his paws were shaking.

"Continue," said Keesha.

"I— We went along the cliffs until—" He could not find breath to speak. *Are you going to hold me under the water again?*

Keesha's head was suddenly right beside his. "I am trying to distract you. It doesn't seem to be working."

"You don't h-have to distract me," said Arcove. He hated himself for trembling, but at least he had control of his voice. Mostly. "I'm not going to run. Just t-tell me what you want me to do."

"Come here," said Keesha and settled back into the water.

Arcove had to paddle the last little distance. He was afraid that Keesha would catch him in his coils as he had in the tide pool, but Keesha only brought a coil up under his forepaws. Arcove's teeth started to chatter in the cold water. "You can t-t-tell them I was hurt in the avalanche, and Storm asked you to help me, but then my injuries became too g-g-great—"

"Will you stop trying to control everything?" snapped Keesha. "Even after you're dead, you think you can control what's said? What's believed? Trust that I am not a fool."

Arcove bowed his head in Keesha's pale fur. He felt acutely vulnerable without solid ground under his back legs.

Keesha sighed. "I am trying to make this easier."

"For who?" asked Arcove.

"I have more control in the water."

"You could just break my neck," said Arcove and his voice sounded small in his ears.

And then the humming started. Arcove had heard the song enough by now to have a sense of its shape. He knew that he had heard the beginning and middle, but never the end. Some detached part of his mind also understood that the song was beautiful and that it had been made specifically for him. It would never speak to anyone in the way that it spoke to him.

He understood this, even though the pain was blinding. It had an exquisite edge this time—like a mouthful of honey with something sharp in the center. The sharpness became a claw that sliced all the way through him. The rat chewed and chewed, and every time he thought he'd gotten used to the pain, it changed in pitch or character and became fresh agony again. He realized that he was whimpering and then screaming. He thought, distantly, that Keesha *should* drown him to keep the others from hearing.

And then it was over.

Arcove opened his eyes. He blinked. "I thought," he said and had to clear his raw throat. "I thought you said it would kill me."

He raised his head and saw that Keesha was looking at him with an expression of resigned irritation. "I made a different ending."

"Oh," was all Arcove could think to say.

Keesha huffed. "Do you have any idea how difficult it is to compose a song that ends *that* badly? Sixteen years! And now I don't even get to sing it!"

Arcove thought for a moment. "I am sorry for your loss of time."

"You could show it by taking your claws out of me."

Arcove realized that, once again, he'd latched onto Keesha's coil. He retracted his claws and felt embarrassed. "You could have stopped me from doing that."

Keesha said nothing.

Arcove pushed away from the telshee. He felt immediately disoriented and slipped under the water. Keesha scooped him out before he could start to panic and set him in the shallows. Arcove tried to walk again and collapsed. "You may be a bit sore," said Keesha. He paused. "I wasn't actually sure that would work."

"Are you sure that it *did* work?" complained Arcove.

"Oh, yes," said Keesha, who seemed to be enjoying watching his attempts to stand. "If it hadn't, you'd be dead."

Arcove reached the bank and tried to lie down in a more dignified fashion. "I won't get sick again?"

"No."

Arcove knew that he should feel elated, but instead, he felt deep apprehension. "What do you want?"

"You suspect me of ulterior motives?" asked Keesha with a shark's grin. "If I'd wanted you on a short leash, I would not have sung you the rest of the song."

"I will not live on any kind of a leash," whispered Arcove.

"You say that, but you can barely stand."

Arcove shut his eyes. "Are we under telshee law?"

"That depends." Keesha made a circle around Arcove with his body. He brought his head down so that he could look Arcove in the face. "These are my conditions. You will let me or one of my representatives attend your council. You will teach the creasia to read and write, so that they may record and remember their past and not repeat their mistakes. You will appoint your successor instead of being killed by him...or her. Most cats capable of killing their king are not wise enough to rule. The creasia got very lucky with you. Historically, they have not been so fortunate, and there is no reason to think they will be again."

Arcove stared at him. Emotions collided with each other in his head. He had no idea how to respond.

"You will stop trying to control the ferryshaft," continued Keesha. "You will allow them to return to their natural numbers, which far exceed the natural numbers of creasia."

Arcove *did* find his voice at that, but Keesha talked over him. "However, *I* will stand as mutual ally between your two species. I will send telshees to your aid if they attack you. I will not let them kill your cubs."

Arcove was rendered speechless again.

Keesha's voice softened. "Will you allow that? Will you accept counsel from someone older and wiser than yourself?"

Arcove swallowed. "I—" *Careful. This may be a trap.* But, if so, he couldn't see it. At last, he said, in a voice that was almost steady, "Storm's cub, Teek, was trying to...to draw us into the pictures..."

Keesha cocked his head.

Arcove tried again. "The pictures in the human caves...with the talking animals all together...and the creasia off in a corner by themselves... Teek was going around with a rock, trying to scratch in an image of a creasia." Arcove stopped. He did not look at Keesha.

"I will paint you into the picture," said Keesha softly, "if you will let me."

Arcove did not have words to say what he wanted to say. At last, he dropped his head, rested his chin on the ground, and tucked his nose under the edge of Keesha's coil. It was a submissive gesture—a very creasia thing to do. However, Keesha seemed to understand. Arcove felt Keesha's great tongue brush the top of his head. "Peace, Arcove Ela-creasia. Peace between you and me and, I hope, between the creatures of Lidian."

Keesha drew back and nosed Arcove up onto his forepaws. "Now, let's see if you can walk. You were making some alarming noises earlier. We should go back up to the cave and make sure they're not panicking."

"You should have kept me quiet," muttered Arcove.

"Nonsense," said Keesha. "If I'd clamped down on you, you would have died of pure fright."

Arcove tried getting to his feet again and found that he could manage it. "Do you still want to hear about the trip that Roup and Coden and I made to the Southern Mountains?"

"Yes," said Keesha. He hesitated. "If you want to tell me."

"I do," said Arcove and meant it.

29

Epilogue: Two Years Later

"That's my name?" Arcove sniffed at the scratch marks on the wall of the shallow cave. They were so scuffed that many were illegible, especially in the weak morning sunlight, but Charder could make out a word here and there.

"Yes. I believe it says that a council has been called to elect a ferryshaft king, who will unite the herds in order to repel a vicious new enemy, Arcove Ela-creasia." Charder couldn't actually read all of the scuffed words. He didn't have to. He remembered when they'd been written. "The war scattered the ferryshaft who used to keep these records. They did it for generations, but they're all dead now. You filled in the caves before we could write anything else."

"Roup said the words talked about killing creasia cubs," said Arcove.

"They do," said Charder. "But you can't change the past, only the future."

Arcove was silent a moment. Finally, he said, "What are you going to write now that the caves are open again?"

Charder took a deep breath. "I'm not. You are."

Arcove looked at him in surprise.

"You closed these caves, and you reopened them. The next words on this wall should be yours."

"We all reopened them," objected Arcove. A large group of ferryshaft and creasia had been at work on the project for a season, clearing away rocks and digging through dried mud and shale.

"Only because you permitted it," said Charder.

Arcove snorted. "Keesha would have insisted."

"You didn't have to help," said Charder.

"I can't write on your wall. I can't—"

Charder smiled. "Can't" was not an easy word for Arcove to say, and he stumbled over the rest of the sentence. *Can't read.*

"I could teach you in a day," said Charder softly. He remembered the elders of his old herd arguing over whether creasia were sufficiently intelligent to learn to read. *What idiots we were.*

Arcove still looked uncertain. It was not an expression that Charder was accustomed to seeing on that face.

"When you are ready," continued Charder, "I think you should write that you gave the island fifteen years of peace, that you oppressed the ferryshaft as they had once oppressed creasia, that ferryshaft came to your aid during an uprising of your officers, and that you reopened the caves in gratitude."

Arcove chuffed. "Is that what you think happened?"

"I can write my own version of events in my own time," said Charder serenely.

Arcove was looking more relaxed. *Our writing is not your enemy,* thought Charder. *The past isn't even your enemy. You'll see that, once these caves become less mysterious, once they contain your words, and not just ours.*

"In addition," continued Charder with a hint of mischief, "I think you should say that you appointed a ferryshaft to your council."

Arcove frowned. "I have *not* appointed you to my council."

"And that he was your friend," said Charder, "and respected you a great deal."

Arcove clearly had no idea what to say to that. Just when the silence was about to become awkward, Charder caught sight of So-fet, picking her way through the freshly turned earth of the cave floor. The ferryshaft who'd been working on the project were just waking up, while the creasia had mostly either gone to sleep or were out hunting. They'd worked almost non-stop over the last few days to finish it before the fall weather set in.

"Has he taught you to read yet?" So-fet asked Arcove.

Arcove said nothing. So-fet continued cheerfully. "Well, I hope not, because he hasn't taught me, and I think I deserve first go, since I am carrying his foal."

Arcove smiled at last. "Is that so?"

It was Charder's turn to look uncomfortable. They hadn't announced it yet.

So-fet had sought him out after the war. She was curious about her childhood, about her mother. Charder had been living in self-imposed seclusion then. He told himself that he was done with leadership. The fractured ferryshaft herd seemed to be getting along well enough without him. Charder fully expected to live out his days as a rogue, perhaps actively hunted by some of the ferryshaft who felt he'd contributed to their suffering.

He had spent the winter mostly alone. His hip pained him from an injury sustained in the avalanche. He missed Pathar acutely—the only ferryshaft whom Charder had allowed into his full confidence after the war. Charder felt every one of his forty years and wondered whether he could tolerate ten or twenty more years of loneliness before age or predators or disease claimed him.

Arcove showed up twice during the winter. The first time, Charder figured he was just checking on things, trying to keep track of the various elements of the ferryshaft herd who had scattered after the events by the lake. The second time, the snows were very deep, and Charder wondered at the considerable difficulty Arcove had taken to reach him. He came with Roup. They stayed in his cave for three days and brought down two sheep, which they left uneaten. On the morning of the third day, after Arcove had gone to sleep, Roup followed Charder outside. He said, "You should come back to Leeshwood with us."

Charder was startled. "Why?"

"We could use a ferryshaft on the council."

Charder could not tell whether Roup was joking.

"He's worried about you," persisted Roup.

"Arcove?" Charder was bewildered.

"You wouldn't be out here alone if it weren't for him."

That was true enough, but the idea of Arcove openly allowing a ferryshaft to sit on his council was so ludicrous that Charder dismissed it at once. However, as time passed, he could not quite convince himself that Roup had been joking.

That spring, So-fet showed up. Charder was thunderstruck. However, after they got over some initial shyness, they talked for days. She had so many questions. Charder told her stories that he'd almost forgotten—about his herd before the war, his mates and foals—all dead now—about the plains beyond Leeshwood, about Coden and her mother, Lirsy, about feeding So-fet as a young foal and then distancing himself to protect her.

So-fet said that she could remember the sound of his voice— the only kind voice from her childhood. She spoke of her difficult first summer, the life she'd endured as a ru, how she'd given birth to Storm when she was hardly more than a foal herself. She'd taken a second mate because it seemed like the proper thing to do, only to discover that he was a bully who resented her first foal.

Near the end of that spring, she asked, "Why did you never take a mate after the war, Charder?"

"Because I thought Arcove might use mates and foals against me." *Because it hurt too much to lose them.*

"Do you still think he would have?"

Charder considered. "I don't know. I suppose I thought that I did not deserve a mate. I had to make hard decisions for the herd. I'm still not sure they were the right ones."

"You deserve a mate," said So-fet quietly.

Charder had peered at her—an elegant creature in her prime with deep red fur, flecked with just a bit of Coden's gray around her eyes. Something surged in his chest, but he forced it down. "You could get a high-ranking mate," said Charder quickly. "After what Storm and Sauny have done? Males would line up to sire your foals."

So-fet licked his muzzle. Charder felt something warm in the pit of his stomach—feelings he'd thought were long dead. "I am probably too old to sire foals," he continued weakly. "Furthermore, I am a rogue, despised by half of Lidian. You deserve someone young and strong—"

"I had two young, strong mates," interrupted So-fet. "I had my fill of them. What makes you think I want a foal every spring? You led the ferryshaft herd for fifteen difficult years; you are not weak, and you are not as old as you seem to think." After a moment, she added, "And I will always remember your voice as the kindest that ever spoke to me."

Charder gave up after that. They were very happy for the rest of that summer and fall. It was clear by winter that she had not conceived, just as Charder had expected, but he told himself that she would have plenty of years to grow bored of him and find a mate of her own age. In the meantime, he was blissfully content. They remained on the southern plains, far from any ferryshaft herd.

However, Storm and Tollee found them. They had run all the way around the rim of the island that summer with Tollee's yearling foal, Myla, together with Storm's creasia cub, Teek. The youngsters were bubbling over with stories of what they'd seen and done. The group had proceeded to make their way back around the edge of the lake, where they encountered Charder and So-fet.

Storm did not seem to know what to make of his mother's behavior, but both he and Tollee seemed exceedingly happy and willing to forgive past wrongs. Charder was near-certain that *they* would be having a foal next spring. Soon after their departure, a trickle of other ferryshaft began to appear—mostly older adults who'd known Charder before the war. They'd gone with Sedaron originally, but were dissatisfied. They missed the small herds that they remembered from their youth. And they missed their old herd leader.

Charder was surprised and touched. He ended up with about twenty animals—small enough to be friendly, but large enough to fend off curbs and help each other hunt in winter. It was a good little herd.

His friends brought news from across the island. More ferryshaft were wandering to more places than anyone could remember. The years of confinement in an unnaturally large herd on the northern plains seemed to have made everyone restless. Of the remaining herds, Sedaron still had the largest, but Kelsy was rumored to have the strongest with the largest number of young males. Sedaron had gone all the way to the far side of Groth with his herd and seemed to be trying to isolate them from the rest of the island.

Sauny and Valla had attracted a small, but dynamic herd with more females than males—an unusual situation. They were ranging all over the island and had spent the entire spring in Syriot, learning from telshees. Numerous other small herds had already splintered off—groups of five to thirty animals who had loose affiliations with one of the larger herds.

All of this sounded normal and healthy to Charder. He suspected things would settle down over the next five years and these various herds would choose more permanent territories. He found himself drawn back to his old haunts from before the war—hot springs near the foot of the cliffs south of Leeshwood, not far from the old caves where ferryshaft had kept their writing.

That winter was easier with friends to help with the hunting. Charder found that his hip did not pain him as much, or perhaps he simply did not notice it. Spring brought only two additions to their herd, as they had only two pregnant females. "What a world they will grow up in," murmured So-fet. "No cliques. No rues. No rogans."

Storm came again, alone this time. He'd been in Leeshwood recently. Teek had returned there and was living in Roup's clutter. This did not surprise Charder. He *was* surprised to learn that Storm, Tollee, and their newborn foal were living there as well, at least for the spring.

"You allowed your foal to be born in creasia territory?" asked Charder.

"Why not?" countered Storm. "It's safe from lowland curbs. They take more foals than any other predator. Ely-ary and lishties have attacked ferryshaft this summer as well. We're rogues; we don't have a herd to protect us. Roup's clutter is friendly."

Charder thought for a moment. "What about the highland curbs?"

"Oh, they're well. They had another litter of puppies this spring. I'm sure we'll visit them, but underground is no place to raise a foal."

Charder had to agree. Finally, he asked, "What does Arcove think of your foal in his wood?"

Storm grinned. "It made him a little uncomfortable."

I can imagine.

"He asked about you," continued Storm.

Charder cocked his head.

"Lyndi Ela-creasia has taken a place on the creasia council," continued Storm.

"A female...?" began Charder.

"Shaw also comes sometimes," continued Storm.

Charder blinked. "Shaw...?"

"Yes, I think Keesha insisted. They let me sit in a couple of times, but I don't want a place on the creasia council." Storm grinned. "I can't be bothered to stay in one place all year." He hesitated. "But it's not bad—living in Leeshwood."

What is that supposed to mean?

Charder thought about what Storm had said as he watched Arcove practice making words in beach sand. It was the easiest place to teach someone to read and write. The process had taken a little more than a day, but not much. Roup had watched for a while, but he'd fallen asleep near noon. Arcove had continued stubbornly. Once he grasped the basic concept, he was determined not to stop until he'd finished. By the time the sun was setting, he'd memorized the last of the symbols and was consistently using them correctly.

"I think you've got it," said Charder. He was tired and he wasn't even a night animal.

Arcove grunted. He returned to the rocks and flopped down beside Roup, who didn't even stir. "You were right," he said after a moment. "It's not difficult."

Charder lay down a few paces away and yawned. He thought for a moment that Arcove had fallen asleep.

Then Arcove said, "So...your blood and Coden's."

Charder gave an uneasy laugh. "I didn't think she'd get pregnant."

"Do you have enough of a herd to protect the foal?"

"Yes." Charder peered at him curiously. It was too dark to read his expressions. "Do you want me on your council, Arcove?"

Arcove was silent a moment. "I'm sure you've had enough of me telling you what to do."

"Well, you did also threaten to kill me nearly every time we spoke," observed Charder. *I've certainly had enough of that.*

Arcove shifted uncomfortably. He did not look at Charder.

"You didn't answer my question," said Charder.

Arcove spoke carefully. "Ferryshaft are behaving in ways they have never behaved before. They are having foals in my wood."

Charder could not repress a snort of laughter.

Arcove looked exasperated. "You think it's funny, but my clutters do not know what to make of this. They are on edge. Ferryshaft are wandering through the wood with increasing frequency, and I am afraid there will be an incident. Sauny and Valla have offered to foster another creasia orphan. Should I allow this? There have been rumors that Sedaron's herd plans to raid in the spring and try to kill cubs. I am tempted to cross the island and subdue them. Will this destroy the new peace? Keesha has all kinds of ideas. I am not sure what to make of some of them. I am not sure how to handle his meddling."

Arcove stopped to catch his breath. Charder could tell he was tired.

"Cats are not known to be fond of change," Charder observed.

Arcove scowled at him.

"Do you want me on your council?" Charder repeated patiently.

"I would value your advice," said Arcove. He hesitated. "But you have earned your rest."

Charder smiled. "I meant what I said in the cave."

Arcove studied his face for a moment. Then he seemed to relax. He gave Roup a nudge. "Wake up, my friend."

Roup groaned. "Why do I feel like I've been awake all day?"

"Because you have."

"Why am I awake again?"

Arcove rose, suddenly cheerful. "Because I have to go write telshee words on a ferryshaft wall. We will write the past. And then maybe we will write the future."

Author's Note

Dear Reader,

I hope you enjoyed *Hunters Unlucky*. If you'd like to keep reading about these characters, the next book is *Lullaby*. It's a collection of two short stories and a novella. Those stories build on each other and lead into more books. Details at the end of that collection.

As of this writing, many of the digital versions of my books (audiobooks and ebooks) are available only directly from me at shop.abigailhilton.com. Signed paper versions are also there, along with essays and interviews about this world and its characters.

These things change, and I cannot predict the future. If my store moves, you'll likely find more information at abigailhilton.com.

Yours,
Abigail Hilton
January, 2024